*Th*

First Published 2021 by Compass - Amazon

www.ronramdin.com
ronramdin11@gmail.com



**ISBN**
978-0-9569135-8-6

CONTENTS

## CAST OF CHARACTERS

### PROLOGUE

The Story-Teller, In Hackney, 1970
Professor Nidmar Nora
Michael Malone

### PART ONE: A WRITER TO BE
### (1550 –1575)

Edward de Vere, Seventeenth Earl of Oxford. Great Lord Chamberlain of England; and son of John De Vere.
John de Vere, Sixteenth Earl of Oxford, Edward's father. Also called "Earl John."
Margery Golding, John de Vere's Wife. Countess of Oxford. Edward's mother
Lawrence Nowell, Anglo Saxon Scholar, Map Maker. One of Edward's Tutors.
Sir Thomas Smith, Edward's Tutor; Classical Scholar and Secretary of State.
Mary de Vere, Edward de Vere's sister.
Katherine de Vere, Edward's half-sister.
Francis Vere, Edward's Cousin.
Elizabeth Tudor, Queen Elizabeth I of England, 1533-1603.
Horace ("Horatio") de Vere, Edward's Cousin.
George Gascoigne, Poet, Playwright and author of a Collection

of poems: *The Hundredth Sundry Flowers* to which the young Edward de Vere had contributed.

John Bale, Playwright. Friend and associate of Earl John.

Sir Robert Dudley, Earl of Leicester. A close confidante and advisor of Queen Elizabeth. Leader of the Leicester faction, opposed to the Cecils.

William Cecil (Lord Burghley). Queen Elizabeth's Chief Adviser and Spymaster: Her "Sir Spirit." Edward de Vere's Guardian during his Wardship; and later as Edward's Father-in-law.

Robert Cecil, Son of William Cecil. Brother-in-law of Edward de Vere; Secretary of State.

Anne Cecil, Daughter of William Cecil. Wife of Edward de Vere.

Arthur Golding, Edward de Vere's Uncle and Tutor. Brother of Margaret Golding and Translator of Ovid's *Metamorphoses.*

Richard Edwards, Playwright and Editor of the Poetry Anthology: *Paradise of Dainty Devices* containing early poems by de Vere.

Philip Sidney, Poet, Scholar. Edward de Vere's rival.

Charles Tyrell, an associate of Robert Dudley; and Margaret de Vere's second husband. Edward's step-father.

Thomas Brincknell, The kitchen-Servant at Cecil House who was killed by Edward de Vere.

Henry Hastings, Earl of Huntingdon.

Edward Manners, Earl of Rutland. A fellow pupil and friend of Edward's at Cecil House.

Thomas Radcliffe, Third Earl of Sussex and Lord Chamberlain. Edward de vere's Commander and Mentor. Also engaged in theatrical productions.

Mary Stuart, Queen of Scots. Great grand-daughter of King

Henry VII; and Heir to the English Throne. Tried for Treason, condemned and beheaded.

Thomas Howard, Fourth Duke of Norfolk. Edward's Cousin and the highest-ranked Nobleman in Elizabethan England. Linked to Mary, Queen of Scots Treasonous plans.

Christopher Hatton, Lord Chancellor (1540-1591). One of Queen Elizabeth's Court 'favourites.' Edward's rival.

Sir Francis Walsingham, Spymaster with international espionage connections. Associated with William Cecil.

Rowland Yorke, Edward de Vere's associate and Servant. Suspected of being a double-Agent. Suspected as the person who informed Edward of rumours about his wife Anne's infidelity. A real life model for a few of Edward's dramatic characters.

Thomas Twynne, Author of *A Breviary of Britain.*

Thomas Bedingfield, Scholar and Edward de Vere's friend. He translated Gerolamo Cardano's *Cardanus Comfort* into English.

William Byrd, Musician and Composer.

Mildred Cecil, William Cecil's wife. Edward's mother in-law.

Gabriel Harvey, A much-respected scholar at Cambridge, who praised Edward de Vere at Audley End in the presence of the Queen. He later became one of Edward's critics.

Don John of Austria, The Bastard brother of King Philip II of Spain. Military Commander of Spanish and Catholic Forces at the Battle of Lepanto, and during the Lowlands war.

John Sturmius, Famous Classical scholar. Meets Edward de Vere in Strasbourg.

Virginia Padoana, A Courtesan in Venice.
Titian, Tiziano Vecello, A Master Venetian Classical Painter.
Anthony Munday, Edward de Vere's other Private Secretary. Playwright and translator.
Katherine Willoughby, Duchess of Suffolk.
Peregrine Bertie, Baron Willoughby de Eresby. Marries Edward's sister, Mary. English Ambassador to the Danish Court in Elsinore.
Charles Arundell, Catholic sympathiser with whom Edward is associated; but later, reveals the secret practice.
William Howard, The youngest of the Duke of Norfolk's three sons. Edward attended Howard's wedding.
Martin Frobisher, Navigator and Adventurer. Edward invested in Frobisher's attempts to find the legendary "Northwest Passage" that leads to the Pacific Ocean.
Michel de Castellnau, French Ambassador.
Henry Howard, Earl of Northampton. One of three Catholic co-conspirators. He levelled malicious charges aimed at discrediting Edward's Testimony.
John Lyly, Playwright, Novelist and Edward's Private Secretary and Theatre production manager and Book-keeper. Author of the popular Euphuses novels.
Thomas (Tom) Nashe, Satirist and pamphleteer. In *Strange News* he referred to Edward as "Gentle Master William."
Edmund Spenser, Author of the poem *The Faerie Queene*.
Sir Walter Raleigh, Explorer, author and Commander. He was both Friend and foe to Edward de Vere at Court.
Thomas Churchyard, At various time, soldier, poet and, at various times, Edward's Servant.
Thomas Watson, Author of *The Hekatompathia* (1582) which he dedicated to Edward.

Anne Vavasour, Edward's Mistress.

Edward Veer (Sir Edward), Edward's son with Anne Vavasour. A talented scholar, poet and soldier.

Thomas Knyvet, Anne Vavasour's Uncle. Enraged by Edward's besmirching of Anne's honour. He challenges Edward to a Duel. Both men's Servants fought street battles in London.

## PART TWO: BECOMING "WILLIAM SHAKESPEARE" (1576-1593)

Giordano Bruno, The Italian scholar and philosopher whom Edward had met.

Rocco Bonetti, Italian Fencing Master from Italy who opened school at Blackfriars in London.

Thomas Edwardes, Poet and author of Edward's street fights.

King Frederick II, King of Denmark. He hosted visits of Edward's brother in law, Bertie Peregrine, at Castle Elsinore

Henry Evans, A Scrivener and playwright who, with John Lyly, supervised Edward's Earl of Oxford dramatic troupes.

Philip Howard, The Earl of Arundel. Eldest son of the Duke of Norfolk.

Elizabeth de Vere, Wife of William Stanley, the Earl of Derby, and thus Countess of Derby. Elizabeth (whose paternity, Edward had contested) was, at one time, expected to marry the Earl of Southampton.

Anthony Babington, Leader of a Catholic Plot to overthrow

the, and install Mary, Queen of Scots.

Bridget de Vere, Marries Francis Norris and becomes Lady Norris of Rycote. She is Edward's second daughter

Susan de Vere, Countess of Montgomery. She is Edward's third daughter who marries the Earl of Montgomery.

Francis Drake (Sir Francis), The intrepid Explorer and Naval commander who fought against the Spanish Armada.

Charles Howard, Lord Charles. Played the role of Lord Chamberlain and, as Lord Admiral, he fought alongside Drake in repulsing the Armada attack.

Angel Day, Writer and Secretary, whose book *The English Secretary* was published with a Dedication to Edward de Vere.

Thomas Lodge, Poet, Playwright and Novelist who enjoyed the banter and camaraderie at Fisher's Folly.

Christopher Marlowe, Poet, playwright and under-cover Agent. A hugely successful playwright who was murdered in a London Tavern.

## PART THREE:
## OR NOT TO BE
## (1593 – 1604)

Henri de Lorraine, Duke of Guise. A French Noble in contention for the French Kingship.

"Martin Marprelate," A pseudonymous name for Puritan pamphleteer.

Robert Devereaux, Earl of Essex. Closely allied to Robert Dudley, Earl of Leicester. He was Ring Leader of the Essex Rebellion in 1600. He is joined by the Earl of

Southampton.

Henry Wriothesley, Earl of Southampton. Co-Leader in Essex Rebellion. Was expected to marry Edward's daughter. Condemned to death, but was reprieved. Edward dedicates his Sonnets to Southampton.

Julia Penn, A London Landlady to whom Edward de Vere is indebted for rent owed by the tenant, Thomas Churchyard, a friend.

Elizabeth Trentham, Countess of Oxford. Edward's second wife.

John Giovanni, Florio, Poet and Italian Dictionary Editor: Edward de Vere contributes a Sonnet to Florio's book *Second Fruits.*

William Shakspere (Shacksper), Stratford-upon-Avon born and bred actor, manager and businessman.

Thomas Howard, The Earl of Suffolk and second son of Duke of Norfolk.

Michael Lok, Financier and head of Company raising money for the Expedition to find the North-west Passage leading to the Pacific Ocean.

Don John of Austria, Half-brother of King Philip II of Spain.

Robert Poley, A leading Spy for Robert Cecil. Linked to the murder of Christopher Marlowe.

King James VI of Scotland becomes King James I of England.

Sir Thomas Heneage, High-ranking official who became Mary Browne Wriothesley's second husband.

Mary Browne Wriothesley, Countess of Southampton; and mother of Henry Wriothesley.

The Lord Chamberlain's Men, Will Shakspere associated with this Troupe which performed Edward's plays.

William Stanley, The distinguished Earl of Derby. A Court

playwright, married to Edward de Vere's eldest daughter, Elizabeth.

Pierce Edmonds: English officer with whom the Earl of Southampton was linked during the Irish campaign.

Francis Norris, Baron Norris of Rycote, husband of Bridget de Vere.

Edward Somerset, Earl of Worcester, and ambitious Courtier who takes over Edward's Earl of Oxford's Men Troupe and produced plays of a conservative kind at the Boar's Head Inn in London.

Robert Armin, A respected actor with The Lord Chamberlain's Men.

Nicholas Hill, Author and pioneering advocate of "Atomic philosophy." One of Edward's close associates in the later years.

Mary Sidney Herbert, Countess of Pembroke. Sister of Philip Sidney. A scholar and poet.

Ben Jonson, Satirist, poet and playwright.

Henry de Vere, Edward's son with Elizabeth Trentham, Lord Bolbec, the Eighteenth Earl of Oxford.

Ghosts
Fairies
Witches
Spirits

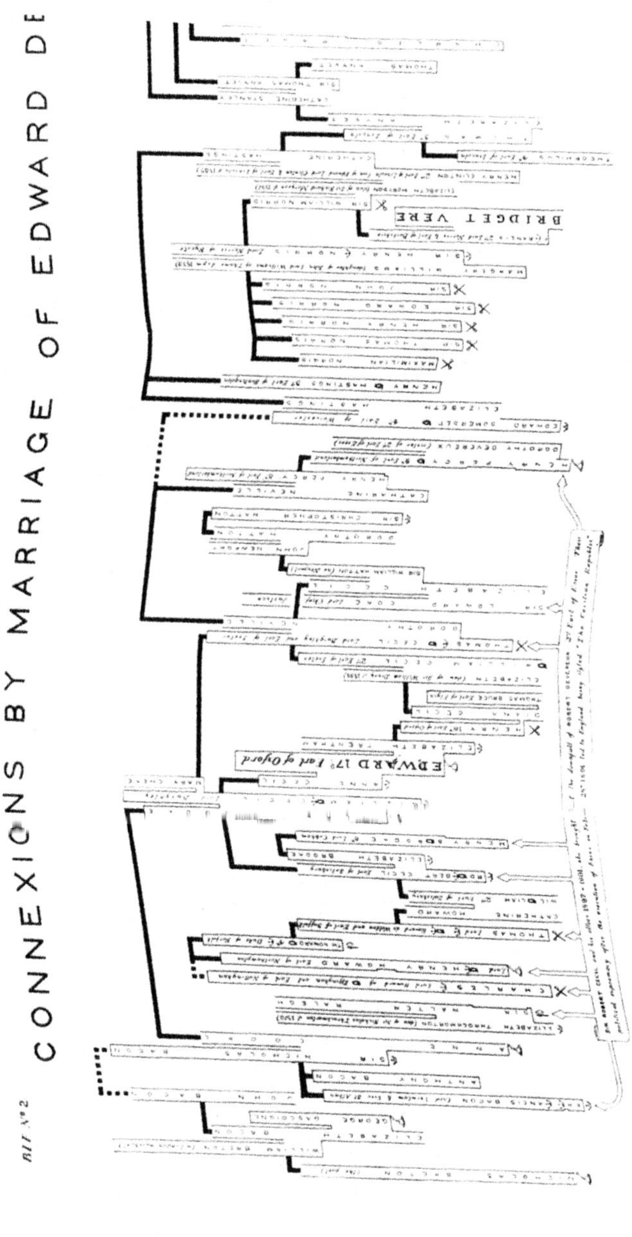


Connexions by Marriage of Edward De Vere
*A Facsimile*

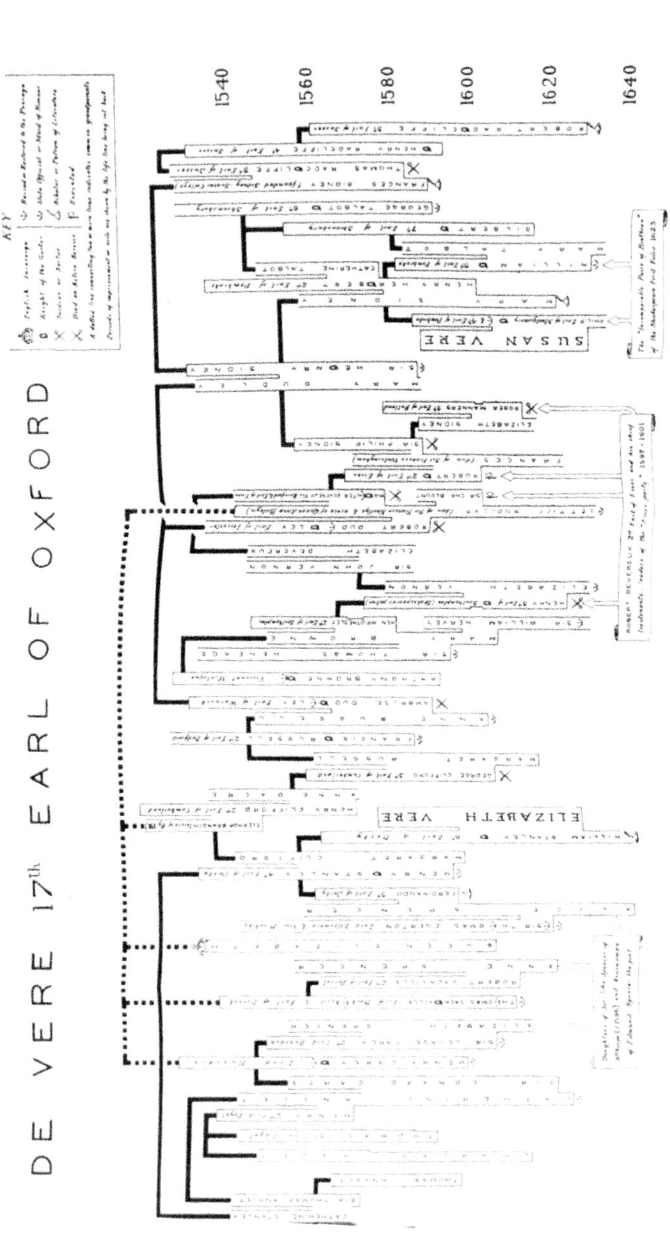


Connexions by Marriage of Edward De Vere
*A Facsimile*

‘For truth is truth, though never so old, and time cannot make that false which once was true.’

*Edward de Vere*

‘You write best about what you know.’

*Professor Nidmar Nora*

# PROLOGUE

**Clapton Square, Hackney, London, Autumn 1970…**

ENTER The Story-Teller. He became a resident in Clapton Square, Hackney in the Autumn of 1970. Here, he began his quest to become a writer. He lived at the northern end of the Square and regularly passed the Church of St John-at-Hackney, formerly known as St Augustine. It was in Hackney where his passion for writing found expression; and, almost two decades later, after publishing his first book, he moved to live elsewhere.

Thirty years on, the Story-Teller's insistent quest was to write his seventh novel about a towering literary figure; a writer *extraordinaire.* But soon after he'd begun work, he realised he needed to know much more to get past the foggy "mystery" that surrounded the man who, to him, seems to be less of an accomplished, working writer and more of a myth. Ever since he was a child, he'd heard different arguments about the iconic writer that had divided opinion for centuries. And so, while researching and writing his novel, the Story-Teller casts his research net wide: He invites a variety of views from those "in the know." One of the persons whom he'd talked to was Michael Malone, a well-respected Bloomsbury Poet and Shakespeare Expert. "It is Shakespeare's immortal works that is of value, dear boy," Malone insists, "not who he was *as a man*. He was a *Genius*. Everyone knows that. Think of his works. Nothing else matters. You're on a wild-goose chase to find the man, I'm afraid." The Story-Teller had heard variations on this mind-deadening, narrow position, time and again. But his belief in the art of Story-telling was paramount; and becomes increasingly so, as over many years, he read voluminously for hundreds of hours and wrote copious notes to bring his novel into being. Time passed quickly: The Story-Teller realised that he's already spent five years researching his novel. But with so little of the text written, he was a long way from achieving his aim of presenting a full portrait of his Hero; of bringing him to life as he'd lived and worked. Though he'd been scratching around, trying to make progress with his story, he regularly turns up at the British Library, where he continues to read, think and write pages of notes. Then one day, while he was ordering some books in the Library, he meets, for a third time, Professor Nidmar Nora, a Scholar at the University of Oxford. Professor Nora teaches English Literature, specialising in poetry of the Elizabethan period. He'd been coming to London each summer over the last three years. "I am doing research for my new book," he'd said when they first met. "Ah! Professor Nora," the Story-Teller says, "How are you getting on with your research?"

"Oh, quite good. In fact, very well!" the Professor says breezily.

"I'm hoping to finish my book this year." A smile lightens his face which makes him look younger. The Story-Teller smiles too. He feels encouraged.

"How is your work? What are you writing?" the Professor asks.

"I'm writing a novel, Professor," the Story-Teller says. There is no point in not telling the truth, he thinks. "But sorry to say," he adds, "I am stuck. I need to get the story moving. At the moment, I am still doing more research than actually writing the text. The story needs a boost. No doubt about that!" There was no smile on his face. Professor Nora listened sympathetically.

"If writing," he says, "is about what you leave out, instead of what you put in, then I recommend that more research into your subject would be a good thing. Greater knowledge would show the way as to what the story could, and should, be. In other words, what the shape of your story should be. Research, as I said, is what I come to this great library to do." That day, the Story-Teller went home with a new resolve. Five years after Professor Nidmar Nora's advice, the Story-Teller has, at last, completed the writing of his novel. Knowing the story as well as he does now, he'd come to more fully appreciate certain places in Hackney: the impressive Church of St John-at-Hackney, to the south of Clapton Square, as well as Kenninghall Road and Brooke Road, to the north, formerly known as King's Place in Tudor Times. He also remembers his first stroll along the footpath on the East side of the Church when he stopped to read the inscriptions on a few tombs and grave-stones. Then, such places and things in Hackney had no more significance to the Story-Teller than the traffic flowing past the nearby Midland Bank towards Mare Street. But what a difference the years of research and writing his novel has made. He'd amassed much material and knew the tale he wished to tell so well that it was easy to leave out what was not germane. Professor Nora was right. "You write best about what you know." What the Story-Teller knows now about his Hero is in his completed novel. It is, above all, an unusual and original literary work. He feels empowered for what had been mysterious, is no longer so. With Manuscript in hand, he feels ready to speak about the Great Man; to tell his Tale which had been long hidden. "Things standing thus unknown," as Hamlet had said, the Story-Teller knows now. More than ever, he knows that a human being is the best plot there is.

And so, Dear Reader, the Story begins:

# PART ONE

# A WRITER TO BE

'Words, words, words'

(1550 - 1575)

# I

## 'At thy birth… Nature and Fortune join'd to make thee great'

"A writer to be," he says. "I want to observe. I want to tell stories." The words are direct: A straight answer to a blunt question from Tutor Lawrence Nowell: "What would you like to be when you grow up?" Nowell's raised eyebrows and silence indicates his surprise at what he'd heard. It is his last day as Tutor to the boy; and before him on the desk at which they both sit is a letter written in French. He glances at it, with interest. The letter is addressed to the boy's guardian, a stern-looking disciplinarian, who thinks the boy is in need of further tuition in the French language.

"I leave Cecil House tomorrow," Nowell says. "My teaching here ends today. And, I must say, for your age, your intellectual ability and potential is greater than any student that I have ever known." Nowell looks, once more, at the letter.

"This is my latest translation," the boy says.

Nowell reads. When he is finished, he says:

"After the first four weeks of lessons with you, I was unusually impressed by your comprehension; your grasp of what I was teaching. Since then, you have continued to improve, so much so, that I have written to your guardian, William Cecil. I was honest with him as to why he'd employed me. I told him I clearly see that my work for the pupil you've charged me with teaching cannot be much longer required. I told him you are far advanced in what you already know, in particular, the rudiments of Latin and French."

Such high commendation from Nowell, a scholar of great distinction, surprises the boy. Nowell stands up. He extends his hand. The boy rises. They shake hands.

"Goodbye, My Lord," Nowell says. "And Good Luck!" As Nowell walks away from the room, he thinks it very odd that bearing in mind the boy's Noble pedigree and illustrious family military background, he should choose the profession of the pen, rather than the sword. Nowell has seen and heard many strange things at Court, but given the boy's undoubted promise, his particular ambition leaves the departing Teacher puzzled. The boy is just past his twelfth birthday; and had only recently come to Cecil House. It is his first visit to London. But who is he? And where does he come from?

After the death of his first wife, John de Vere, the Sixteenth Earl of Oxford, meets and forms a close relationship with a "Mistress Dorothy." Dorothy looks after Earl John's daughter, Katherine. But although John and Dorothy get on well, John's brother-in-law does not favour a marriage between them. And so Earl John looks elsewhere. He meets and marries Margery Golding. Soon, their first child, named Mary, was born. This event, much anticipated by Earl John, was a difficult and painful experience, physically and emotionally for Margery. But as it turned out, the Earl was disappointed too.

"I'd been hoping for an heir," he says to Margery just minutes after Mary's birth. Margery smiles bravely.

"But we can try again," Earl John adds. "I need a boy child to succeed me." He seems happy with the prospect. "Dear Margery, we have something special to look forward to," he says.

Margery remains silent. She thinks of her difficult childbirth. But, as a dutiful wife she submits to the Earl's wishes. A few months later, on the twelfth day of April 1550 the shrill cries of an infant fills the spacious bedroom; a sound that mingles with the general hustle and bustle of Castle Hedingham.

"Now, at last," Earl John says to Margery, "I have a male heir. He will inherit my title, this Castle, my estates and other properties. He will carry the royal name, Edward." Margery smiles. She defers to her husband. She needs no reminding of his mighty position as the Earl of Oxford. The pain of childbirth has subsided. But though Margery is pleased to have given birth to the boy, she is not as excited as Earl John, who seems to be floating on a cloud of elation. From these moments on, he keeps close to, and takes great interest in, his son's princely upbringing, notably his education.

As Edward gets older, he learns about the glorious de Veres; a military family beyond compare in the annals of English history. Though understated, being Margery's second child, he is not free of some rank-pulling by his sister. But soon, he shows he is not prone to accept things as they are. Boyish curiosity leads him to question people and things around him as more and more, he exercises his need and developing power of observation: He realises that Margery is not eager to attend to him. Some months earlier, when his cries were more persistent, he remembers that his need for attention was ignored. Since then, his growing respect for, and closeness to, his father makes him more conscious of his mother. He is perplexed that this should be so. "Does she love me? Is she fond of me? And either way, how much?" he questions himself. Margery knows her place in society as a woman; and, thus far, as wife and mother, she plays her roles as best she could. Before Edward's birth, she recalls the Earl saying to her: "This time, you must deliver a boy child!" These words recur often. They were to all intents and purposes a Command from her warrior-like husband. She was fearful: "What if I give birth to another girl?" she asks herself. Thereafter, each day until Edward was born, she was on tenterhooks. And to compound her fears, her second childbirth was more painful than the first. To all this, Edward is oblivious as the absence of more mothering in these early years, nags him. A doting mother who is partial to coddling, Margery clearly is not. Edward senses Margery's aloofness and measures it against his father's attentiveness; his omnipresence. As he grows up, he warms to his father's caring nature. Now, in his boyhood, he thinks of two outstanding things his father had passed on to him. The first is that five days after he was christened, Earl John had said: "You are now officially the Seventeenth Earl of Oxford. You are also Viscount Bolbec." These titles confirms Edward's pedigree and his father's pride in his nobility. "You are," his father adds, "of ancient stock." The story of your ancestors has deep roots. They go as far back as William the Conqueror." The second thing, Edward remembers, relates to Earl John's pride in introducing him to the de Veres role in English history. "My, our, Royal connections have been (and is) very close; and of long-standing. As you know…," he stops briefly, then continues, "I named you after King Edward VI, who on the occasion of your Christening, had sent you a gilded chalice." Now, at the age of seven, Edward recalls listening to his father's words with wonder; and yet, the way he'd received them shows a degree of his early maturity. Being of noble birth means much is expected of him. Time is of the essence. He must learn fast. And so far, he's done reasonably well: His memory, he feels, is being refreshed in a good way. The personal gift, as well as being named after the King, rouses in him a renewed sense of himself; of life as he knows it within the fortified walls of Castle Hedingham.

***

As Edward's earliest "teacher" Earl John fills his son's head with much more information. He thinks it is a crucial part of what good parenting is. One day when Edward was much older, he says, "After our gracious Queen Elizabeth's Coronation, I came out of retirement; and just a few months ago, Her Majesty appointed me and Lord Robert Dudley, the Earl of Leicester, to welcome the King of Sweden's second son, John, Duke of Friesland. He had come to England to offer Queen Elizabeth a marriage proposal on behalf of his elder brother, Prince Eric. When I had met the Duke I entertained him with great sport in the Valley of the Sour..." He pauses. "But," he adds, "this is just one of my many responsibilities that come with being in service to our Queen and England. My long service continues undiminished. So much so, that I am now popularly nicknamed, 'The Good Earl.'"

Edward delights in what he learns, as well as the additional enjoyment he gets from listening to the dark, rich tone of his father's voice. It has a calming effect upon him. Each time he is told something, he waits for more; and so far, he has not been disappointed. Now Earl John says:

"The Priory of Torington House in Candlewick Street, London, had been granted to my father who was the Fifteenth Earl of Oxford. That great house called London Stone, known today as Oxford House, is a de Vere family heirloom."

Through further conversation, the "Good Earl" reveals another side of his father's character: a tendency towards extravagance. The manner of the Earl's travel from Hedingham on his visits to London, impresses Edward: "The late Earl of Oxford, your grandfather," John says, "hath been known to have ridden from Castle Hedingham into the city, then to his house at London Stone with an entourage. That was quite an assemblage: Some eighty gentlemen, splendidly dressed in Livery, with gold chains around their necks. They were accompanied by as many as one hundred Yeomen who also wore the embroidered Blue Boar, the emblem of the de Vere family."

"What is the Blue Boar?" Edward asks.

"This goes back," Earl John says, "to one of your earliest ancestors, the third Aubrey de Vere. He was a man of ferocious temperament; a fierceness which is linked to, and reflected in, his kinship with the Verres, or Blue Boar, a beast which the de Veres who loved punning chose as a pictorial representation of their name."

As the boy listens to this explanation of the Boar, his imagination takes in his grandfather's extravagant way of travel. This pleases him.

***

England at this time is a Feudal country: social divisions among the people at large are deep. The separation between rich nobles and the mass of people living in poor dwellings is stark. But this is not of much concern to Edward. His home is his castle; and, as curiosity of his habitation grows he learns more about the unusual towering pile: a stone-fortress about sixty feet on each side and over one hundred feet high. Its five stories contain soldiers quarters, munitions storage space and a banquet hall. Surrounding the Castle is a brick wall that encircles the hilltop upon which the Castle stands. Within this enclosure, there is a stable and barnyard, a brew-house, a granary, a chapel, a tennis court, lodgings, kitchens and pantries. This fortified Castle on the hill, dominates the Essex countryside and could be seen from miles away. Wishing he was taller and stronger, amidst a cacophony of discordant noises, the unusually nosy Edward explores as much of the Castle as possible. Soon he finds a favourite vantage point from where he looks outwards.

His alert, dark eyes gives him a piercing gaze; and, overall, a certain seriousness, too. Being close to his father, he never tires of listening to Earl John's stories; and, as he grows older, one story becomes more familiar than others: It relates to the Earl's fondness for sport. In particular, he is told of a hunting incident in which the Earl had killed (fairly, it is said) a wild Boar in France. What gives distinction to this event is that he'd done so at the great risk of losing his life. Before the kill, among the people watching the drama unfold were French nobles and aristocrats who were horrified having witnessed the Earl's near-death experience. It was, they thought, nothing less than an heroic spectacle, which they commended highly. But, for his part, in response to glowing testimonies from his amazed fellow-hunters, the Earl says, quite simply: "What I have done by killing the boar is nothing special. Any fit boy in England would have performed it." For Edward, such level-headedness adds to the respect he already has for his father. But, what he does not know much about at this time is his father's love for women; his magnetic pull, which attracts female attention.

As Lord of the Manor, Earl John has power over all those in his domain. But remarkably, the privileges of nobility, it seems, does not make him either selfish or inward-looking. He is a man of many parts: Added to his sporting successes are his good works for the local community; and generally, in advancing English culture. Being a man of means, which helps enormously, the "Good Earl" is that rare mixture: a man ever-ready for military or sporting action, as well as a keen supporter of drama and learning. His patronage of such things is not lost on Edward, who loves the performances at Castle Hedingham: The mesmerising story-telling by the troupe of actors whom his father fondly calls the Earl of Oxford's Men. Progressive-minded Englishmen of the highest calibre of learning praises Earl John's efforts: "I think no man in England," the scholar Sir Thomas Smith says to James Bradby, a fellow-scholar, "could do so much, and so readily, as my Lord doeth here. He fully deserves the love that the whole country beareth him." Another of Edward's childhood gleanings is realising that he has a half-sister named Katherine, who is nine years older than him. She is the offspring of his father's first marriage. This knowledge comes to him while he was still very young.

*

In Edward's eyes, Margery's distance from him as a mother, makes their relationship awkward. As he moves in and around the Castle, often he feels a tinge of sadness which brings him to an understanding of how sensitive he is, not just about his mother, but also of other people and things. But, he does not withdraw. Instead, he goes about his daily activities, with no other children to play with. Unsurprisingly, he feels alone; and lonely. But, at such times, whenever his father appears, his mood lightens. The Earl is like a beacon in whose welcoming presence Edward is ever-attentive. Such eagerly-awaited moments rescue him from lapsing into temporary moroseness; a creeping inclination to become melancholy. But soon he begins to develop an independence of mind. He realises that the vast place in which he lives is full of surprises. He is struck by stern-looking men dressed in military regalia who come and go; and, by the continuous, often dissonant sounds of feverish activities that resound within, and around, the Castle. In the various rooms, swords and rapiers are commonplace. Earl John wears a belt from which, at different times, hangs either a dagger, rapier or a sword. His martial bearing and noble swagger is in keeping with the times. But Edward appreciates, too, that his father is a stalwart keeper of English culture. He remembers the stories he'd been told; and now more and more, he is excited by his growing love of story-telling through the performances of masques and plays which Earl John spends so much time promoting and staging, especially at Christmas time: Every chance he gets, he uses his Troupe of actors to perform in Castle Hedingham and going on tour around the countryside.

Edward remembers those times when the Troupe of Players stays at the Castle and perform. In the cold winter nights, he warmed to the magical art of theatre performance. He was thrilled by what he was seeing and hearing: He was spellbound by the timbre and pitch of the actors' voices, the lyrical, colourful speech patterns of their story-telling. He paid close attention to the use of certain words; many of them new, foreign, to him. Since then, he has become more self-conscious of the words he uses; everyday words, both in speech and writing. He is mindful of being a student of the English language; and now, more than ever, the English lessons he'd been given by his first teacher makes good sense. Once again, he is powerfully drawn to the actors and their art. He is bright; a precocious boy, who, while using English words is excited, fascinated by their sounds and the vital meanings they convey. Soon, he begins to experiment with words punningly! This playfulness with the language draws him like a magnet to the dialogue and verbal games of the actors: Their call and response, so to speak. He is enchanted by the musicality of the on stage spell cast by the artistry of outstanding performers in these years of heightened boyhood curiosity. For him, Will Somers's comic sense and timing is the embodiment of words, language and play-acting.

*

Each morning after breakfast he makes his way from his bed towards the room in the Castle that has many books and a large desk. On his way to this pleasant place, he passes weapons of war: magnificent, beautifully crafted swords. He thinks with all his youthful enthusiasm that he must follow in his father's footsteps. "Honour and nobility are values worth fighting for," his father had said to him. But now, a few years later, he enters the reading and study room, sits at the desk, picks up his quill and, as he reads more from one of the history books, he pauses often to underline passages and takes notes relating to the writings of men who lived long ago; mostly the poets of classical antiquity. With the familiar feel of the feathery quill he tries his hand at penning letters, verses and poems. Increasingly, he immerses himself in reading the books surrounding him; and, with the process of something new: writing! From here on, as he grows up, he learns fast. Knowing more, he listens more attentively. And as he watches the actors perform, their Patron, his father, continues his running commentary, regaling him with new stories of the de Veres heroic achievements. His receptive mind is a *tabula rasa* that takes in everything he hears. Far from being force-fed, now, Earl John thinks his son is old enough and ready to know a great deal more about the part his forebears had played in the history of England. As in art, history is absolutely vital, Earl John thinks. So, one morning in his study, he relates the following to Edward:

"The de Veres family lineage and my present Earldom," he says, "has its roots deep in the past. It goes back to a man named Alberic, or Aubrey de Vere. It was he who had come to, and settled in, England. He was the offspring of a de Vere of Veer in Zeeland and a daughter of the Count of Flanders, whose family, it is said, could be traced directly to Charlemagne." The name Charlemagne means nothing to Edward; and Earl John is aware of this. But, he presses on:

"Be that as it may, in origin, the de Veres have descended from the Vikings or 'Danes,' as they were called. Alberic had been a top Commander when the Normans invaded England.

And for his bravery, fierce fighting spirit and the victories he gained, he was richly rewarded with the ownership of vast tracts of lands. Among his estates were Cheneston (Kensington, London) and lands in Essex. When Alberic died as a Monk, he was buried in the Priory that he'd built at Colne. Alberic was succeeded by a second Aubrey de Vere who was appointed by the King to perform the largely Ceremonial role of Lord Great Chamberlain of England." Earl John stops speaking to adjust the rapier attached to his belt. Then he says: "It was the second Aubrey who had built this place: our cherished Castle Hedingham. Later, when a third Aubrey de Vere appeared, he was created an Earl. Such an accolade was a first: The grandest and noblest of titles for our family. This Aubrey de Vere chose the Earldom of Oxford. When he died, he too, was interred in the Priory at Colne." After occasional glances, Earl John is pleased and encouraged by Edward's attentiveness. "And so," he continues, "I now move quickly on to more recent times. When the renowned Thirteenth Earl had passed away, he was succeeded by another of the same name, called 'Little John of Camps.' At the age of twenty one, this Earl had accompanied King Henry VIII to the Field of the Cloth of gold, near Calais, where there were extraordinary scenes of pomp and medieval chivalry that had impressed Rulers and aristocrats across Europe. Grand gestures were made. Henry VIII and Francis I of France pledged Friendship and mutual help. The Fourteenth Earl of Oxford's prestige was such that on one occasion he was attended to by three Chaplains, six Gentlemen, thirty three Servants and thirty horses. And later, he'd served in King Henry VIII's Army. When he died, the Fifteenth Earl emerged: He too, was named John de Vere. He had the honour of carrying the Crown during the Coronation of Anne Boleyn, mother of our Queen Elizabeth!" Hearing the Queen's name brings a smile to Edward boyish face. History is not just about things in the past. It bears heavily upon the present moment, too, he thinks. "After this ancestor had died," Earl John adds, "I became the Sixteenth Earl of Oxford. Not long after, my reputation as a Good Landlord and Sportsman began and grew. Some years later, I retired here to Castle Hedingham." While he spoke, he was hugely encouraged that Edward's attention had hardly deviated. This cued him to say more:

"Now, I will bring our story closer to the present time," he says. "After the reign and death of King Henry VIII, during a bitterly cold winter, King Edward VI fell ill. Within a few months he died. Religion, as I'd said before, is central to everything; and after a failed attempt to crown Lady Jane Grey, the next in line to the Throne was Edward's half sister Mary, a staunch Catholic. Mary was pitted against her half-sister, Princess Elizabeth, whom she dislikes. Unsurprisingly, the relationship between the two women was fraught; and, had remained so ever since. History-wise, my dear Edward, that will be all for today," says Earl John. "You have been remarkably patient." Earl John rises from his chair. And while Edward looks up respectfully, in military-fashion, the Earl marches out of the room as if he was doing so to the accompaniment of fyfes and drums.

***

Within the walls of Castle Hedingham, while Edward takes things in his stride. Earl John's careful attention to his son's welfare helps him to make and maintain the desired progress. He notes, with satisfaction, how intelligent Edward has become, as each day he grows physically stronger. But he knows too that as a parent, there is only so much he can say and do: What the boy needs is professional educational guidance. Accordingly, Earl John employs Sir Thomas Smith;

a man well-versed not only in the affairs of state, but also as a Teacher at Cambridge University and rated as one of the foremost Scholar-teachers of his time. On his first visit to the Castle, Smith is greeted at the gateway by Earl John."Sir Thomas, welcome to Castle Hedingham," Earl John says. They both climb the stone steps leading to the room where Edward sits and waits. As they enter the room, Earl John says:

"This is my son, Edward." Smith moves closer.

"My Lord, Edward," he says, "I am most pleased to meet you." The boy's dancing eyes light up. He's sure he has never seen this man before. "This is Sir Thomas Smith," Earl John says in a fatherly tone.

"He will be your Teacher."

As Edward continues to appraise the man before him, Earl John says,"He will take charge of you. This means, you will be leaving here to begin your formal education. The sooner you start to learn at the highest level of tutoring, the better." And so, Edward was taken away from Castle Hedingham. Smith's first response when the idea of being Tutor to Edward was put to him by Earl John, was one of surprise. But, that very day, before he and his pupil to be leaves Castle Hedingham, he is pleased to face whatever challenges this new student was likely to present. For his part, Sir Thomas sees this tutorship as an important opportunity; one that is beyond the call of mere duty. He feels his instructions to Edward de Vere would yield good results. But here and now, he thinks there is nothing further to add. Thus his meeting with Earl John ends.

*

Edward arrives at Ankerwycke, the home of Sir Thomas Smith. It is a manor located near the river Thames in Windsor. He enters an unusually large multi-bedroom house. He'd never been in such a place before: How different is this, he thinks: It is a "house," not a castle. He is sure of that. Soon, as he becomes familiar with his new surroundings, he better understands and appreciates Smith as a man of great learning and distinction. He remembers what Smith had said on their first day together: "You are on the way to becoming my Scholar." The words "my Scholar" have a proprietorial echo which does not put Edward off. Instead, he warms to the prospect. And so Edward begins his Tutor-Pupil relationship in the house at Ankerwycke. At this time, the forty-two year old Thomas Smith has behind him the invaluable teaching experience as Provost of Eton College. He'd only recently come to Ankerwycke; and having recently remarried, he wholeheartedly embraces the additional responsibility of tutoring Edward who is no ordinary child, but a young nobleman with excellent life chances.

Being in Ankerwycke provokes thoughts of displacement in Edward; and much reflection, too. Having spent a good deal of time *on his own* at Castle Hedingham, he now asks himself: Why was this so? Largely, he thinks, because his mother Margery was not given to spending enough time caring for him. Now time brings clarity; and he sees, more clearly that Margery really was not as close to him as was his father. He admits to himself his disappointment that relations with his mother were not better. In sharp contrast, respect for his father continues to grow: This closeness encourages the regular flow of knowledge from father to son, particularly on the harsh blood and gore realities of deadly combat in wars. Having already heard so much, Edward had found his father's military bearing reassuring in the Castle Hedingham environment; and he'd come to terms with the swords and rapiers. He also remembers the quill pens and ink on the large desk of his father's study. On the wall next to shelves of dusty books, a sword in its finely designed and decorated scabbard on which was printed the de Vere Crest and its Motto on Truth. Though the sword is there for display Edward knew that at any moment it could be used as a weapon of war. This is its true purpose. It is integral to the manner in which men dressed for they were always ready for war: Thus the sword was not simply an accessory or adornment for whoever wears or carries it.

*

Another thought that comes to Edward, as a student, is of him sitting at his father's desk, where he'd felt more at ease with the quill in his hand than he was with the ubiquitous rapiers and swords. Twinned with these implements of war is the ability not just to ride a horse, but being able to master horses, while wearing heavy armour in preparedness for battle. He'd heard the stories of chivalry and valour. The romance of such thoughts fills his mind with wonder. Being away from his father and Castle Hedingham, he is conscious of the difference between "home" and where he is. He faces the reality of the smaller enclosed spaces of the rooms at Ankerwycke. Each day here brings him closer to more fully becoming Smith's "scholar." How quickly things change, he thinks. Education starts early, Smith reaffirms: "It is the custom and practice," he says, "for boys like you. Education is absolutely essential for the children of nobles. It is your birthright; and therefore, a very serious matter. Why? Because England's leaders and government officials are, and would be, drawn from members of your class."

So, his presence in Smith's house is in line with educational thinking in Elizabethan England which is primarily to raise the bar of expectation to advanced learning at an early age. Earl John is aggressive in his ambition for Edward, whom he pushes forward. The man he selects to instruct his son is clearly the best he could find. Nothing less. He is at the top of his game, so to speak. He is renowned for his understanding of, as well as delivering brilliant lectures on, law. Some compare him with the philosopher Plato: And, it is said that he dazzles his students by the scope and depth of his learning. Students and fellow tutors are at one in lauding his scholarship at Cambridge University. His knowledge covers an impressive range of subjects: rhetoric, languages, arithmetic, mathematics, law and philosophy. As Edward learns, Smith's Literary Collection is the central store of information. It is absolutely essential to all that he does. Then, the day came when Edward first walks into the library.

As Smith takes him along the book shelves and comments on the large number of books, Edward's excitement is palpable; his darting eyes scan the rows of book spines. Multiple questions come to his lively mind. But before he could ask any questions, Smith says: "My Lord, this library has over four hundred titles." He guides Edward further. "The subjects are," he adds, "as you can see, of a wide range..." While Edward reads the labelled sections, Smith says: "Civil law, grammar, history, literature, mathematics, medicine, philosophy, theology, and so on."

That night, Edward re-runs what he'd seen and heard. He is stunned by the range and size of the Collection. He's never seen more books in one place. He is agog: He wonders about the knowledge the volumes contain. His estimation and respect for Smith rises. He is glad, at least for now, to be where he is. Each day, he is gently, but firmly pressed and expertly cajoled by Smith. Gradually, he comes to terms with language lessons, familiarising himself with written and printed words. Smith is careful, always tactful; unobtrusive, but always on hand, ready to lead. "My Lord, most of my books are not in

English," he says. "They are written in Latin, Italian, Greek, French, Spanish and Hebrew; languages you'll come to know. Hopefully, sooner rather than later."

Smith's masterful guidance is rewarding: This becomes evident as Edward's receptive mind, like blotting paper, absorbs his lessons relating to new words and Smith's accompanying comments. Though he has breaks, through intense periods of concentration, slowly Edward learns about himself: Importantly, that he has a capacity for engaging in prolonged writing sessions. He has never used the quill as much as he does now. He is reminded of how much he likes the feel of the white feather-topped object between his fingers as he makes copious notes from books and manuscripts. Soon, a rising pile, pages of notes, marks his efforts. After several months of step by step, graded tutoring, he becomes familiar with the most distinguished authors featured in the library collection whose names, both as he writes them and how they sound as pronounced, are made more memorable by their foreignness. What tongue-twisters they were to begin with, he thinks. This combination of words, sounds and meanings reflects the enormity of Smith's interests; his overall learning. For Edward, even at this stage, the authors who stand out are Plato, Halle, Pliny, Livy, Tacitus, Virgil, Plutarch, Saxo, Grammaticus, Homer, Ovid, Pindar, Aristophanes, Sophocles, Plautus, Petrarch, Boccacio and Dante. The list takes some getting used to. In the evenings, these names come to mind; and Edward memorises them. As time passes, his introduction to these names become more than just "memory." And so, though he feels a sense of displacement, amidst his Ankerwycke surroundings under Smith guidance, he immerses himself in a rigorous process of Classical and Renaissance learning. Six weeks later, he is in no doubt that his experience has been a baptism of fire: He is reminded that he is a long way from

Castle Hedingham now, both physically and intellectually. For the first time, he reads about far-off lands; and he is delighted to hear Smith talk about his personal experiences of Italy and Greece. Thereafter, Edward visits and revisits these places in his imagination. He wonders about the extraordinary, thrilling stories he reads: "How strange must these people and their lands look?" he asks himself.

*

Another thing which Edward's regular use of the quill leads him to appreciate is the organic link between his hand and brain: Like any well-fitted pair, they go together, he thinks. Scribbling for long stretches each day becomes an acceptable, essential part of the process of writing. The forming of letters, words and sentences on a page. As trust develops, Smith shows Edward copies of books he'd written.

"My Lord, this is the manuscript copy of my latest book," he says. "It is on economics." Smith holds the bundle of loose papers before Edward. As Edward admires the achievement, Smith adds: "My Lord, Edward, I am writing on other subjects too: geography, mathematics and astronomy, to name a few." Smith points to another manuscript: "And this, here," he says, "is my textbook on government and politics. It is called *De Republica Anglorum.*"

Edward likes the title and what he is told about the book. That night, he reflects on Smith's accomplishments: "Oh! To have so much learning as to produce such works," he thinks. Smith's books encourages his growing interest in the lessons he is given; in particular, on history and story-telling.

Edward's sense of his teacher's attainments makes him even more respectful; more mindful of how little he knows! Was this Smith's intention? he wonders. Regardless of his shortfall of learning, he is struck by the importance, the centrality of the law and legal studies in Smith's intellectual universe. For his part, Smith does not hold back. He explains to Edward: "I am opposed to those who practice the law as if it is a subject on its own." During one teaching session, he says: "My Lord, I believe first and foremost that legal training requires a mastery of subjects, namely philosophy, rhetoric, language and history, among other themes." Edward listens, as usual, attentively and increasingly more critically, but he gladly defers to his tutor. He is enthralled by Smith who, so far, has made a deep impression upon him. In turn, Smith is quite struck by Edward's capacity for learning: by his intelligent responses to instructions; by the marked overall progress he's made. This encourages the Master Teacher to press his student harder. Intermingled with lessons in the remaining months of his tutorship, occasionally, Smith fires the boy's imagination by telling him about his own student days in France and Italy. So much so, that this period of learning imprints itself profoundly upon Edward's mind. Alas, much too soon, he thinks, this early phase of formal education has come to an end. But, as he prepares to return to Castle Hedingham, he and Smith had formed good relations; a respectful intellectual bond.

*

Another Tutor responsible for Edward's education is Arthur Golding, his mother's half-brother. Golding is an eminent Translator of works from Latin and French into English, especially of religious texts. His family, and he himself, espouses Puritanism. Nonetheless, his temperamental affinity with young Edward and their coming together, augurs well for literature. Even in these early days, Edward's love of stories and things literary is clear. But where has this interest come from? His family's literary pedigree is rich; and Castle

Hedingham forms the ancestral centre to which many leading scholars and poets of the day were linked. Earl John's sister, Frances Vere, herself a writer of verse was married to Edward's Uncle, the Earl of Surrey, an accomplished poet. Of great importance is the fact that Surrey's literary style attracts, and influences, Edward increasingly as he gets older. Another family member, Anne Vere, was married to Lord Sheffield, the musician and sonneteer, and, of course, there was Smith and Uncle Arthur Golding, Translator of Ovid's *Metamorphoses*. There is also Edward's connection with his father, who runs and maintains a highly-rated Troupe of actors, who perform at Castle Hedingham, at Court and in the public theatres.

***

Edward is eight years old now and after his rigorous scholarship under Thomas Smith, he feels more confident. He is ready to study, albeit briefly, at university level. Smith's high rank and influence in the country, again brings him into Edward's educational life: He (Smith) is instrumental in Edward's attendance at Queen's College, Cambridge University. But interestingly, even with his connections, Edward's enrolment is not straightforward.

He is below the age (usually, the early teens) of entrants to the College. But, he gets in. A few months later, he moves: He enrols at St John's College. For someone so young, the challenges are huge, but they must be faced. Remembering Smith's inspirational Tutorship, he thinks he has a head for it all. Meanwhile, religious life in England is all-encompassing and contentious: Catholics and Protestants are deeply divided: distrust keeps them vigilant.

At Cambridge University, Edward notes, there is no escape from religious bigotry. He hears disturbing stories; one of them is that during Mary Tudor's reign, the university was not free of religious intolerance and autocratic management. Another story pertains to Queen Mary's opposition to the heresies of Martin Luther's evil writings and preachings, as well as the burning alive of a King's College scholar. The thought of such horrific things causes Edward's body to shake. University is no place of refuge, or safety, he thinks. Surrounded by aspirants to higher learning, he is wary. But overall, for one so young, he is delighted that he has reached this stage of his education at Cambridge. He works hard. But once again, his mind is disturbed when he learns of the fate of a brilliant scholar named Dr John Caius, who was regarded as a beacon of hope for better times ahead. Thinking of Caius, Edward is reminded of Smith, and the good fortune of having had the benefit of the intellectual freedom of such a teacher. Edward is told more: That Caius was an even-tempered man; a Catholic Professor of Medicine who had studied at the University of Padua in Italy. Influenced by Italian progressive thoughts and learning, Caius was an English Renaissance Man of a certain kind.

*

While studying at Cambridge, Edward hears of Queen Mary's death. Her passing prepares the way for a new Ruler. On the lips of those in positions of power (or aspiring to achieve some) is the question: Who should succeed Mary? The first in line is Princess Elizabeth, the daughter of King Henry VIII. Eventually, as Edward knows, she was crowned Queen Elizabeth I. As Monarch, from the outset, she stamps her authority as a person who is outward-looking and interactive. And very quickly, she shows herself to be, among other things, a Ruler who is also an astute politician. She is not the sort to just sit around in a resplendent room and, in splendid isolation, Rule from there. Soon, she announces her intention to go to the people; to meet and speak with them. She is an intellectual type, proud of her learning; of her love and appreciation of literature and the arts.

Against this background, her Coronation heralds a Renaissance age in terms of dress and presentation. Before she is crowned, Edward returns to Castle Hedingham; and soon after, Earl John travels to London for the Coronation. In the course of that crowning day, Elizabeth wore four different styles of regalia. Clearly she signals that her dress sense is another strong point. And though she is no Orator, as a speaker, she commands attention. After all, she is the Queen of England; and as such she milks her position for all its worth. Before the crowd at Cheapside in London, she gives her inaugural speech: "I will be as good unto you," she says, "as ever queen was to her people. I do not lack will or power. Persuade yourselves that for the safety and quaintness of you all, I will not spare, if need be, to spend my blood." Earl John listens with great admiration. He hangs on her Queenly rhetoric as she delivers her message. Her voice and nuanced words carry weight: The expectations of a Nation. Her speech is imbued with learning and some style. On his return to Castle Hedingham, Earl John tells Edward about that historic day. As a student and young noble, Edward is duly impressed: He is won over by the Queen's commitment as his father repeats her words that she will not spare, if need be, "to spend my blood." While Earl John speaks about the grandeur and colour of the Coronation: The heady mix of pomp and ceremony of the highest order, conscious of his noble lineage, Edward feels surges of patriotism course through him. He is stirred by feelings of high-mindedness which reminds him of his father's protection and guidance. Thus, he renews his sense of belonging to Her Majesty's Realm.

*

After the Coronation, Queen Elizabeth had turned her mind to finding a husband. Such a man, she'd thought then, as now, may add a sort of completeness to her Supreme status. Not lacking in social sensitivity, she craves company; togetherness. She needs to be admired and praised. Throughout the Royal Court, there is talk of Elizabeth having an heir; and rumours of marriage. But, her enthronement makes clearer her natural feminine desires for she is young, intelligent, beautiful and surrounded by dashing, admiring men at her Court. Robert Dudley, the Earl of Leicester, is her preferred man, at this time. But among others in line as possible marriage partners are interested Royals from overseas.

Two firm supporters of the Queen getting married are Sir Thomas Smith and Earl John of Oxford. The Earl thinks of the King of Sweden as one possible husband. Interestingly, in spite of the Queen's closeness to Dudley, she appoints him and Earl John to meet the King of Sweden's second son John, who had come with the offer of marriage between Queen Elizabeth and his elder brother, Prince Eric. Alas, the Swedish proposition comes to nothing. Meanwhile, Dudley remains the closest man to the Queen.

He is in an enviable position; a real contender for the Queen's hand. But, his nuptial ambition is thwarted. Why? Because he already has a wife. An intriguing situation develops: As the Elizabethan Court and Parliament works to ensure that Elizabeth would marry soon, Dudley is seen by many as less of a contender. But while a suitable marriage partner is being sought, the Queen has to cope with other more pressing and serious matters of State. One of her difficulties is her gender: just being herself; a woman. The unsuccessful reign of Mary

Tudor does not help as the voices of powerful, leading men, are raised against her. "To promote and encourage a woman to bear rule, superiority, dominion or empire above any realm, nation or city," John Knox says, "is unacceptable; repugnant to nature, contumely to God, a thing most contrary to His revealed will and approved Ordinance." Finally, and, for good measure, Knox adds, "it is the subversion of good order, of all equity and justice." The subversion of whose "good order"? And, equity and justice for whom? For Knox and his followers, it means "Good order" as ordained by God. Knox has the strong backing of many religious leaders. But, as Edward and everyone else learns, Elizabeth is no ordinary woman. As time passes, her Queenliness leaves its experiential marks, for whatever early shyness or timidity she may have had as a younger Princess, now she confounds the Queen-watchers: The experts, hangers-on and critics, who see in her refusal to marry the Swedish King, an unhurried attitude towards marriage. They see a woman of grand ambition. Didn't she already say: "I am wedded to England."

***

At the age of eleven, Edward hears of plans for the Queen's visit to Castle Hedingham. He is overwhelmed by the news. Excitement gets the better of him as he imagines what it would be like when she comes. He knows his father is a trusted ally of the Monarch; that very soon she would be in the Castle, his home. For days he thinks of nothing else but the Queen: He asks Earl John many questions.At one point during questioning, the Earl interjects: "My son, soon she will be here. Be patient! I have a surprise for you..." He pauses. Then he says: "Before she comes here, you and I will meet her."

"Where?" Edward asks, his face aglow with anticipation.

"In Ipswich," Earl John says. "My Players are preparing to perform a play there. Just for her. After that performance, you and I will leave Ipswich and return here, to more formally greet Her Majesty when she eventually arrives."

For a while, Edward is speechless. But his face has not lost its colour. "That is the plan," the Earl says. Edward is now about to speak, but he remains silent as his father explains: "The Queen's visit to Essex is a part of her Royal Progress to various country seats. This is not unusual. Another thing that makes Her Majesty move away from London is the spread of disease: The dreaded Plague! The summer months can be deadly in London."

*

At last, on a sunny day, the Queen leaves London on her Progress. She moves through Havering and Chelmsford on the way to her final destination, Colchester. Her Progress is, as expected, not without incident: When she arrives in the city of Ipswich, she is not pleased. She is shocked, unhappy by what she sees as unacceptable behaviour in Colleges and the Cathedral where there are women and children. She is against Clergy marrying. Nor does she like women lodging in universities. On these matters, she is quite clear. When Edward hears of the Queen's attitude, he thinks: How odd a position it is for her, a "learned" woman to take. It makes little or no sense. It is a Royal attitude which he commits to memory, for future use. A few hours later, when Queen Elizabeth arrives and enters the theatre in Ipswich, Earl John's Players are busy preparing to perform *King Johan.* This play, written by John Bale, was chosen by Earl John especially for the occasion. Like her father, King Henry VIII, who had seen a performance of the play, now, Elizabeth is about to see it too. That night in Ipswich is very special for Edward. It is a first for him: Sitting in the presence of the Queen and so many distinguished people had been beyond his wildest dreams.

He looks left and right, then ahead at the candles that lit the stage. In these final moments before the play begins, he brims with expectation. He listens to the hum of voices, then the fading chatter and silent pauses during which he senses a rising collective murmur of anticipation. The Queen is seated on a raised platform, just a few yards away. Edward glances in her direction.

Then, at last, the actors appear on stage. The play begins. As it unfolds, and comes to an end, Edward is fascinated by the power of the story; by the way in which it was presented on stage. The play is a revelation: He'd followed the story-line very closely: and by the end he understood that the Protestant propaganda in Bale's *King Johan* is unmissable. Bale declares his anti-Popist message on behalf of the King who must be defended against attacks from Catholics. The Hero is a noble figure who upholds the Good Name of the House of Tudor and presses on with the anti-Catholic campaign. "He that condemneth a King condemneth God without doubt," says the Hero Verity. "I charge you therefore as God hath charged me, to give to your King his due superiority – and exile the Pope from his realm for evermore."

Edward knows enough now to understand and appreciate this message. He is touched; and is able to relate the story of his own noble ancient family as being intertwined with England's King John, whose signature to Magna Carta, he is now keen to learn more about.

After the performance, there is a movement of people towards Earl John. He is surrounded by his Troupe of Actors and John Bale.

"Congratulations Bale!" Earl John says to the playwright. "You and the Players have put on a splendid show. You have delighted us all. I am sure Her Majesty will agree!"

"My Lord, thank you," Bale says, respectfully.

As the actors mill around, Edward stands a few feet away.

"Edward," Earl John calls: "Come!" Edward moves closer. "This is the writer of *King Johan*," Earl John says to Edward. Then he says: "Bale, this is my son and heir, Edward."

"My Lord Edward, I hope you liked my play," Bale says. Edward smiles shyly. But he looks relaxed.

"I like it," he says, "I enjoyed it very much."

Bale is the first playwright that Edward has spoken to; a writer whose creation he'd actually seen performed. "Edward is keen on masques and plays," Earl John says to Bale, as he gently ushers Edward forward to an area where there was much commotion: It is the place where the Queen's entourage has assembled. They are getting ready to leave the playhouse. Earl John guides Edward toward the Queen.

"Your Majesty," he says, "May I present my son, Edward to you?"

"Yes, you may," the Queen responds. Edward bows. The Queen nods and smiles imperiously.

After the performance of *King Johan*, all things considered, Edward feels unusually uplifted; heady with good feelings. But his thoughts are focused: For him, the hero of the night, the central figure is, in spite of Her Majesty's presence, John Bale and his dramatic work. He was spell-bound by Bale's art of story-telling as a *playwright.* Unlike the masques and plays he'd seen before, he is mesmerised by Bale's particular use of words and actions: their interplay; their meanings and the combined explosive effect upon the audience. Bale's writing has great power. Of this, he is not in doubt. As he and his father leaves Ipswich, he reflects upon his juvenile attempts at writing Verse. Now, the precocious Edward dares to hope that he would one day write a play! For such thoughts as he entertains, given the relationship between his father, the playwright and the actors, he feels he could not be better-placed to learn the art of story-telling through plot, characters, language and history, as the play *King Johan* had shown.

On his return to Castle Hedingham, he delves into his father's Drama Archives. Among the stash of de Vere family papers are some of Bale's writings: A few manuscripts, including his history of a Knight from King Henry the Fifth's day. Such early reading is grist for Edward's mill as a future playwright. He is taken aback by Bale's writings which exhorts English authors to retell English history from a Protestant viewpoint, especially now that England has cast off the burdensome Popish edicts from Rome. He considers the fact and the message that England is a Protestant country; and that this cannot be too often stated. "Set forth the English chronicles in their right shape," Bale urges. To this clarion call, Edward, the young patriot, takes heed.

As he gets older, his firm aim is to promote England's past. Having met Bale, and knowing a little more about him, Edward thinks of the playwright as a man who is in the right place and at the right time to present the history play *King Johan*. History plays! The thought strikes a chord in him. He is respectful of, and receptive to, Bale's message. Being of an impressionable age, he is magnetically drawn to the celebrity status Bale has gained through the rare achievement of having had his literary creation performed before the greatest celebrity in all of England: The iconic Queen Elizabeth herself. Altogether, Edward takes what he'd seen of masques at Castle Hedingham and the Ipswich performance to heart.

While Earl John and the entire household at Castle Hedingham are busy preparing and waiting for the Queen's arrival, Edward spends more time on writing. The daily feel of the quill between his fingers is familiar and comfortable.

Arising from this physical prerequisite, he hopes to emulate Bale by recreating epic *history plays* that had distorted English history, and so discard what Bale says are old "Romish lies" and other "Italian beggaries." In this sense, he is conscious of being a budding propagandist. But, he thinks, it is for the noble cause of his Queen and country.

***

As Queen Elizabeth's Progress wends its way to Castle Hedingham, among the officials is William Cecil. Though not a born nobleman, he is a rare Commoner who rose to become the Chief Minister. At the highest levels of the Elizabethan hierarchy, competition for new posts is fierce as tension grows among ambitious nobles, aristocrats, courtiers and others. Cecil's rise through the ranks of Government has been exceptionally rapid. But his elevation has been the cause of irritation for at least one of his associates, Sir Thomas Smith. This raises the question: How friendly are relations among the highest officials? Not very friendly is the simple answer. Everyone knows that Cecil has unrivalled power; and it is clear that his help in the survival and eventual rise to the enthronement of Princess Elizabeth, was the deciding factor upon which trust was built and thus the good relations between Cecil and the Queen. Cecil plays another important role: He is the Master orchestrator of a Spy network. So prior to Elizabeth's accession to the throne, Cecil was there, at her side, providing her with secret information as well as "good" Counsel. One day within earshot, Edward hears part of a conversation between Earl John and Bale. They were talking about Cecil.

"Yes, he is so well informed," the Earl says, "that he is as savvy and sly as a fox. But, he could also be a frustrating plodder; a man lacking in original thoughts. He sticks to basics. He is fearful of making mistakes, because he is so close to Her Majesty who trusts him more than any other person in her Realm. His understanding of the State is second to none. To his credit, I think, he is the Queen's Code of laws." Earl John speaks of Cecil with more than a touch of concern. With envy? Perhaps not. But, he has no doubt about Cecil being crafty; a wily, charmingly astute statesman. "His ambition knows no bounds," the Earl continues. "At the age of forty, he'd climbed to the top to become the Queen's most trusted Administrator; England's most powerful man. To show her appreciation, and make known her high regard for Cecil, Elizabeth elevates him to Master of The Court of Wards. Cecil is delighted to be so appointed. Why is this so important? Because at this time the Court of Wards has come into being to oversee the lands and wealth of the under-age sons and heirs of noblemen, as well as arranging their marriages. So the real estate of nobles and aristocrats are, as you may know, among the most prized assets in England." Earl John realises he has spoken at length, and is aware that Bale is listening with more than mere interest. So too, does his eavesdropper son Edward. Judging by the fact that the job of Master of Wards was highly profitable to Cecil's predecessor Sir Thomas Parry, Earl John knows that Cecil's appointment was a master-stroke on the part of Queen Elizabeth. Before his appointment, she was able to match Cecil's character with the job description; the combination is the perfect fit, Earl John thinks. So now, Cecil is granted unlimited power to manage and manipulate England's wealthiest estates. To celebrate landing this post, Cecil throws a big, but *understated* party, as befits his personality. From that day, as he learns on the job, he exploits the great Inheritances of his Wards of Court. And so he gains even greater power: He is in charge of large sums of money. He knows that economic clout reinforces political domination. As the man who controls the Elizabethan purse strings, he could not be happier. Would all this wealth change Cecil? Earl John questions. Very quickly, he answers himself: "No, it won't." Why? Because Cecil is dull, dour, even grave. But, Earl John recalls that during the Party to celebrate his becoming "Master," Cecil had allowed himself the briefest of facial relaxation, something resembling a faint cheesy smile. Earl John is just one, of only two Party Guests who can say that they had this rare glimpse of levity from Cecil.

So how convenient is it now that soon after his appointment as Master of the Court of Wards, Cecil should join the Queen on her visit to Earl John's Castle Hedingham home. Being an integral part of the Queen's Progress, Cecil could not be better placed to observe and report, at first-hand, on all that he sees and hears about Earl John's family and, crucially, his highly prized Essex estates. After his talk with Bale, Earl John, whose health of late has been troublesome, remembers the Inheritance Edward is entitled to. He is very pleased, but somewhat uneasy about the Queen's presence in his Castle. The inquisitive, prying eyes of Cecil will, he thinks, peer into every nook and cranny of his domain. But though the Earl is wary, his expansive nature allows him to credit Cecil's tenacity for having risen from the ranks of Commoners, and incredibly to be invited to his noble Manor as an honoured Guest. Though he tries not to dwell on it, Earl John finds one thing of particular concern. As one of the Royal Court's inner circle, he knows of Cecil's penchant for Intelligence gathering; even on his own son, while he was living in Paris. And, God forbid that Edward, his only beloved son and heir, should ever come under Cecil's charge. These are among the Earl's uppermost thoughts just before Queen Elizabeth arrives.

***

After the Queen leaves Hedingham, on the eve of his teens, Edward is the centre of attention: At the age of twelve, he is thinking ahead; and, as Nobles often do, his father is keen to find a suitable marriage partner for him. For this purpose, Earl John and Henry Hastings, the Earl of Huntingdon, meet. They draw up a marriage Agreement to ensure that Edward would choose one of Hastings sisters: either Mary or Elizabeth, to be his wife.

After the meeting, the prospects look good for a high-profile wedding, featuring the Earl of Huntingdon who is of Royal lineage, having descended from a brother of Richard III. Huntingdon was seen, at one time, as the one most likely to be enthroned if Queen Elizabeth had died without an heir. So, the Earl John-Hastings-Huntingdon marriage contract, is drawn up: a done deal that ensures Edward would be marrying into a family with a possible Royal future. But being just a year short of his teens, Edward could not get married. He has to wait another two years. Meanwhile, Mary, slim, tall and fair-haired, the girl he prefers, holds a fixed place in his thoughts. Unsettling feelings and soaring hopes of young love energises Edward's fast-changing, pre-pubescent body. And, as match-makers hover, he imagines the prospects of matrimony. But four weeks after the marriage Contract between Earl John and Hastings was agreed, Edward receives shocking news: His beloved father had died at Castle Hedingham. He was just forty-two years old. Ever-thoughtful of his son's welfare, instead of being caught unawares, the Warrior-Earl was forward-looking: He'd made a Will. But this, and all else, for now, matters little or not at all, as Edward thinks long and hard about his grievous loss: For days he walks around in a stupor of continuous questioning.

He seems, at times, to step out of himself, especially when he thinks of his father's apparent good health. How well he looked before he died. Vivid images come to him now of their visit to Ipswich; his pride in witnessing how well he'd managed the dramatic Troupe, and his overall attention to day-to-day business. Like a drowning man catching at straws, Edward tries hard doing his best to remember as much as he can; to pinpoint any particular thing that may have foretold his father's death. But for now, little or nothing comes to mind.

If anything, there is every reason for him to think that his father was looking ahead to a long life. As he'd said to Edward after his marriage talks with Hastings: "My dear son, I am hoping for nothing less than grand-fatherhood!" So, for a few months, the mingling of his studies and the hammer blow of death robs him of the dearest, closest person to him. He is sad, but there is little time for grieving. Among the nobility, things happen fast; relentlessly, like clock-work.

As Earl John's heir, Edward becomes the Seventeenth Earl of Oxford. He is still a minor, but with his weighty title, as Lord Edward de Vere, he is immediately placed in the care of the Royal Court of Wards, an institution overseen by the Queen herself. Edward is told that as a Ward of Court, his marriage would be arranged; and, anything that he possesses would be traded, treated as property to be bought and sold by the Master of the Royal Wards, none other than William Cecil. For now, at least, Earl John's death ends Edward's thoughts of marriage. The Hastings-de Vere Contract is no longer valid. The chance of Edward marrying into the English Royal family is no longer an option.

So Earl John's passing overwhelms Edward; and the many hitherto boyish pleasant thoughts of Mary that he'd entertained comes to a sudden stop as he tries to adjust to the harrowing grief that envelops him. At times, he could barely think: His mind is a blur; more confused than clear. The suddenness and finality of death leads him to ask even more questions. His loss nudges him to step back: To rethink his father and consider life at Castle Hedingham, hereafter. Bearing in mind his father's insistence on "Truth;" the word so boldly imprinted on the de Vere family Crest, he considers how close he really was to the respected Earl. His questionings prises open spaces he'd not thought of before. He admits he hardly knew his father; a realisation that makes him feel alone, which, in turn, makes his loss more profound. So much so that the memory of the dashing Earl sears itself into his consciousness as he seeks to understand more about Earl John in death than when he was alive. But that quest does not reveal a great deal. So, much as he'd loved and revered his father, in truth, he hardly knew him!

As he continues to absorb the shock of death, his father's body is laid out at Castle Hedingham, where, for twenty two days, it remains until final funeral arrangements are made. Edward feels numb, suspended in stupor, somewhere between what seems like a dream and mournful reality. On these strangely surreal days, there is no shortage of activity around him: There are comings and goings, as preparations are made for a grand send-off. At every turn, Edward is reminded of his father's lineage. Then, at last, the moment comes for the funeral service which is held in the Parish Church. He is surprised by the pomp and ceremony which he could not have imagined; a grand display that makes him more aware of his melancholy mood. Through this slate-grey vise, he witnesses the consequences of his father's death in the forms of heralds at Arms, a Standard, a great banner of arms, a crest, sword and coat of armour, a hearse with a pall of velvet and heraldic shields followed by mourners in black; a colour befitting the sombre occasion. Then, he hears, ever-rising, like the sound of onrushing waves, a great moan for the dead Earl.

*

Three days after his father was buried, Edward bids farewell to Hedingham and makes his way to become a Ward at the Royal Court in London. So, after days of sadness and sorrow, through a veil of tears, he leaves the beloved Castle Hedingham, sitting at the head of a solemn Procession of scores of horses, all in black; a combination of pageantry and mourning. As he rides out, he surveys the lush Essex countryside: The summer flowers are in bloom, specially the red roses that pleases him. But such fleeting feelings are soon overlaid by the reality of the Procession and his fragile nerves. He passes tracks where he'd ridden his first pony alongside his father. Then he rides through lush green forested places that evoke many childhood memories. As he moves further away from the Castle, he wonders what awaits him at his destination.

So far, he has had a cloistered life. All that is now at an end. But, as his journey continues, he considers what his companion George Gascoigne had said: "It is not what you are leaving behind, it is the place that you are going to that really matters." So much is unclear in his mind that he could hardly speak. He knows only what he's been told: "You will be a Royal Ward. Your next place of residence would be in London." What awaits him is unknown. Only time will tell, he thinks. Later, the Procession takes a sharp turn as it moves away from the countryside on the last leg of the journey. Entering London, Edward is struck by noise and congestion. He is blasted by the warm air carrying a sickening stink.

As he moves further into the great city, he has the reassuring presence of George Gascoigne; a man of letters and a poet.

Gascoigne knows the ways of the world, but Edward is, of course, blissfully innocent of London's pleasures and its dangers as the Procession of clattering hooves passes Paternoster Row and St Paul's Cathedral with its busy Yard, where Book-dealers sell their literary labours. Here too, God-inspired Preachers speak with self-righteous passion to passers-by. Criminals stalk the area, where executions are carried out. As Edward reaches Fleet Street, and passes Temple Bar, being close to the water's edge of the River Thames, he hears the voices of boatmen as they ferry passengers back and forth between the North and South banks.

Then, at the Strand, he and the black-clad Procession halts. He has reached his destination: Cecil House. He dismounts his horse, stands for a while, looks around him, then at the House. Just a glance is enough to mark the difference between the old Castle he has left behind and the new pile before him; a sprawling brick house. He is sore and tired; and, as he enters Cecil House, he feels more than a little anxious about what is to come.

***

The death of Nobles has serious consequences, especially in these years of Queen Elizabeth's reign. Earl John's survivors picks over his Will. His widow, Countess Margery, unbeknownst to Edward, oversees the apportioning of household items: livestock, manors and money to friends, family and charities. It is said that Earl John had granted the use of certain properties wherein he conveyed them in trust to a young nephew, the Duke of Norfolk, and, to the Queen's favourite, Sir Robert Dudley. But this apportionment, as it turns out, is a legalistic trick sometimes used to avoid the possibility of a Ward of Court losing his Inheritance. Against a background of bureaucratic under-handedness, how effective is this? Edward questions himself. In the world of grown-ups, he quickly realises his boyish perspective is limited. There is so much that he needs to know about the murky world of inheritance. He could not tell who are the swindlers, the real crooks; and who are the good men. For now, at least, Dudley is rewarded with lands in the counties of Essex, Suffolk and Cambridgeshire, the very estates that forms part of the Inheritance of Earl John of Oxford. On these matters, trust and integrity are fragile things, for within a few months of the Earl's passing, his widow, Margery, flags up the dirty dealings of Dudley, who uses income from Earls Colne for his own benefits.Though Edward knows little or nothing about Dudley, many people question his character and alleged murderous acts. Edward learns that in claiming other people's estates, Dudley is active here, there and everywhere. He has a finger in every pie; and his part in Edward's life now is very worrying. As the Seventeenth Earl of Oxford, Edward begins to have doubts.

Before he'd left the Castle, Edward remembers being told it was the Queen's wish that he would live in the Royal Court. Here, he soon learns that there are factions; that the intrigues and tensions between the various cliques are the very essence of Court life and power. Amidst this maelstrom, his challenge and immediate goal, is survival. To achieve this, brilliant young linguistic student and maverick boy poet that he is, he realises that he must now urgently learn the language of Courtly politics.

***

# II

## 'I am now in Ward'

*'The art o' the Court'*

*'This 'Riotous Inn'*

In these early days, Edward tries to come to terms with the noise and pungent smells of the city. He appreciates Cecil House's immediate surroundings: A beautiful well-kept garden. He is drawn to the flowers; the aroma arising therefrom, contrasts sharply with the unpleasant smell carried by the wind rising up from the riverside. Being in the garden calms him. He misses the very different sights and sounds of the place he'd come from: its spaciousness and fresh country air. Time passes; and Edward comes to know more about life in Cecil House which is unlike anything he could have imagined. By nature, he is curious, a quality that drives him. Often he finds himself in the garden, pleased to be among the flowers. He enjoys their fragrance and is in awe of their brilliant colours. The red roses are strongly scented and gorgeous. Here, there are a few plants he'd never seen before; and, as he walks in the garden, he feels a new sensation of freedom. Slowly, distance from Hedingham feels tolerable. Nonetheless, his sense of place and a new beginning, highlights the stuffy, cloistered existence of life in Cecil House. But here too, there are things he must necessarily know and get used to: There is no shortage of people of all ages. And significantly, most are young; many are his own age, some younger. The House is a hive of activity. Very soon, he learns more about Cecil who, as Master of the Wards, has a healthy respect for learning. This matters a great deal to Edward. To foster educational excellence, Cecil has the largest collection of books he has ever seen. Known as the Cecil House Library, it has a magnetic pull upon him. It is like manna from heaven; the place where he feeds his growing curiosity. It is an airy, liberating space. As the need to write and learn takes hold, amidst the hustle and bustle of the "Riotous Inn" that is the Court and Cecil House, increasingly, Edward feels the need for the meditational space that the library offers.

The range and number of books kept within Cecil House is such that Edward is, at once, deeply impressed and sees its value which is greater and very different from the other unique collections he'd seen: For example, the library of Sir Thomas Smith. He is glad to have used both. One is not better than the other; they complement each other, he thinks.

But now just two weeks after his arrival as a Ward of Court, a potential crisis develops: Queen Elizabeth is struck down with small pox; a disease that has already killed many people. The fear of her dying childless, spreads. Factions declare themselves; and three individual claimants to the Throne come forward. An early and high-powered contender is Robert Dudley. His closeness to the Queen is well known. It is, at least, one reason why, after the death of Earl John, he was favoured as the usurper of a large amount of the de Vere family lands. But now, as other aspirants to the Throne emerge, members of the Royal Court look on anxiously. Should the Queen die now, they worry about Dudley becoming the Lord Protector of England. Amidst all that is going on around him, Edward is, as yet, still too young to become a major player in high politics. But the possibility of the Queen dying, and the chance of Dudley taking over just eight weeks after Earl John's death, is cause for concern.

***

At the heart of Court politics is William Cecil. It is clear to everyone that he has the ear of the Queen. Edward is, for better or worse, under his charge; and, from now on, no aspect of his life would go unnoticed. His Inheritance of numerous estates is a golden prize. Already, the Edward-Cecil relationship is, Edward thinks, at an odd tilt: He is of noble lineage, Cecil is not. This distinction is a source of jealousy on Cecil's part. He had known Edward's father well enough, and in such company, he'd harboured ambitions to lift himself higher. So from the outset of their relationship, Cecil exploits his father-figure persona and role (albeit a "foster father") to the boy in mourning for his beloved father. To his credit, Cecil is canny. To have become Master of Wards of Court, he had what it takes: toughness; deviousness and steely resolve. He is of a certain temperament and personality; possessor of a brilliantly scheming mind that tended, at times, to seemingly go over the top. He thinks he is all things to all men (and women) and so does the Queen. They are both at one as controlling personalities. So naturally, aided and abetted by his Supreme Commander, Cecil takes charge of everything that Edward does, and tries to do. Edward is just one of the Wards of Court: There are at least a score more. For Cecil, there is absolutely no doubt that there is something very special about young Edward de Vere. Nonetheless, his desire to dominate and maintain full control becomes clear to Edward. Based on what he was told, Edward thinks he is right to be careful of Cecil's well-informed network of Spies and Informers. No one is exempt from Cecil's suspicions, not even his own family or closest associates.

So, almost at once, Edward's presence in Cecil House

becomes a very strange experience: the start of a period of being in subjection; the end of which he could not know. Thus, he finds himself at the centre of Elizabethan politics and intrigue. Being fatherless, his instinct to survive kicks in. But though the pangs of bereavement stops him in his tracks at odd times, he is hopeful. As a Ward, he is exposed to, and mixes with, a greater variety and number of people than ever before. Many of them are among the brightest and best young minds in England. This sense of being with his peers has pluses and minuses, but he takes things in his stride. He rises to the challenges that come now in quick succession. Observing that a certain social distance in relations with a few people arises from stiff formality, he hopes for some flexibility. A little more camaraderie, he feels, would lessen the palpable tension. But boyish hopes quickly gives way to Court reality. Strict competition is the name of the game; and the young-bloods are keen to pit their wits. But, as at Castle Hedingham, here too, cliques and factions keep up their oppositions. Edward could do nothing but go along with Court discipline; an essential part of which is the process of learning. Grasping the nettle, he explores and exploits whatever lee-way he is allowed at Cecil House.

His lessons begin early each morning with Dancing from seven to seven-thirty and the day ends with "Exercises with the pen" between four and four-thirty in the afternoon. After Dancing, breakfast is taken and sessions during the course of the day includes French, Latin, Writing, Drawing, Cosmography and French. Religious observance, which is of high importance, follows. On Holy days, Edward is expected to read from the Gospels in both English and Greek. And routinely, he engages in riding, shooting, dancing, walking and other exercises. Then, there is time for prayer.

Overall, the intellectual environment of Cecil House is

among the finest in England. It is a sort of hub for the sons of Nobles; the statesmen to be. It is the best school. Unequalled in its pedigree, the House boasts fine scholars and Tutors. After Thomas Smith, Edward meets another teacher who would supervise his curriculum. That man is Laurence Nowell who is chosen by Cecil to guide Edward through richly textured exercises in English culture and languages, as well as history. As a Cartographer and a scholar of pre-Norman England, Nowell is at the cutting edge of imparting new knowledge on Map-Making and Map-Reading. When he presents Cecil with a copy of his Map of the British Isles, Cecil is hardly able to contain his appreciation. Thereafter, he is often seen carrying around the Map with him.

Edward, still not yet a teenager, warms to the Pupil-Teacher relationship which broadens his horizons. The intricacies of Map-making and Map-reading heightens Edward's imagination as he scans the grid-like lines that gives precise locality, thus adding groundedness to places.

Soon after he'd met Nowell, Edward learns about the connectedness of various subjects. He appreciates, in particular, the breadth of knowledge of Cosmography which is, in essence, a descriptive listing of all the world's cultures as well as the history of Human Civilisation. In other words, Cosmography is presented as an amalgam of history, sociology, geology, astronomy, linguistics, comparative Literature, geography, classics and political science. Thus Cosmography's scope and depth opens Edward's mind like nothing else has before. But although it is an omnibus field of learning, much depends on Nowell's specialism. From his broad knowledge base, Nowell branches off further: He extends his work to include path-breaking Anglo-Saxon Studies: His breath-taking industry leads him to collect and edit ye olde English Ballads and Chronicles. Eventually, he compiles the first Anglo-Saxon

Dictionary *The Vocabularum Saxonicum.*

Edward is pleased to have had the tutorship of Sir Thomas Smith. But now, he sees that Nowell is no less knowledgeable and impressive as a teacher. He is fascinated by Nowell's energy; his urgent quest of making connections between culture, language and history. Edward buckles down to Nowell's instructions; his gentle way of passing on invaluable information. Significantly, Nowell mentions, among other things, a collection of precious manuscripts containing a rare copy of *Beowulf.* Later, he introduces Edward to the "Nowell Codex," containing manuscript accounts of myths and oracles. Edward listens very carefully: he is spellbound by this mix; a combination of the natural world with the supernatural which, altogether, further enlivens his mind. He gains new perspectives; thrilled by the example Nowell sets and the knowledge he imparts. Higher education has come to him much sooner than any other pupil. Earl John had ensured that! And given that *Beowulf* – an "ancient poem" – is among the rarest of literary gems: Not available to most students at Cecil House, its impact upon Edward's memory is extraordinary.

Alas, Nowell's days, as a Tutor, are numbered. His term of employment ends. But though the Pupil-Teacher relationship is relatively short, Edward does not forget Nowell and those things he calls maps! Ideas come and go in his questing mind; but some do not recede or disappear. A few, like the *Beowulf* Poem, ferments. They await germination with other thoughts and ideas. For one thing, the special story of the *Beowulf* saga fascinates him: He is powerfully drawn to this Scandinavian folklore. So much so that after he'd read the original "Amlet" myth, for days, he thinks about little else but *Beowulf:* Beowulf! Beowulf! The story is lodged deep in his consciousness.

Just before Nowell departs, in the face of Cecil's doubts about Edward's progress in the French language (or, his lack of progress, as Cecil sees it!) young Edward drafts a letter in French which he addresses to Master Cecil. He shows this letter to his esteemed Teacher, Nowell. Translated in English it reads:

"MY VERY HONOURABLE SIR: Sir, I have received your letters, full of humanity and courtesy, and strongly resembling your great love of singular affection towards me, and like true children duly procreated of such a mother for whom I find myself from day to day more bound to Your Lordship. Your good admonishments for the observance of good order according to your appointed rules, I am resolved to keep with all diligence, as a thing that may know and consider to tend especially to my own good and profit, using therein the advice and authority and those who are near me, whose discretion I esteem so great… that not only will they comport themselves according as a given time requires it, but will as well do what is more, as long as I govern myself as you have ordered and commanded. As to my curriculum, because it requires a long discourse to explain it in detail, and the time is short, at the moment, I pray you affectionately to excuse me therefore for the present assuring you that by the first passer by, I shall make it known to you at full length. In the meantime, I pray to God to give you health.

EDWARD OXINFORD"

Edward had just turned thirteen; and the letter confirms what Nowell already knows about Edward's linguistic ability. And so, as his Tutorship ends, Nowell writes to his employer Cecil to say: "I clearly see that my work for the Earl of Oxford cannot be much longer required." On this understanding of Edward as an unusually bright pupil, Nowell also recognises Edward's interdisciplinary interests; his innate and acquired ability to make connections and thus transform meaning. After he reads Edward's composition in French, recalling earlier translation exercises from Latin to English, he asks: "My Lord, what profession would you like to follow?" Edward replies:

"A Writer to be. I want to observe. I want to tell stories." These were Edward's last words to Nowell before they parted company.

***

In blazing June sunlight, a son named Robert was born to Cecil's second wife. It was a joyous event for the couple. By now, Edward's reputation is growing; he'd become something of a rising star in the Cecil's household. But with the new-born child, Edward sees a shift in Cecil's attention away from him. He already knows about his occasional feelings of jealousy; his proneness to be envious, too. Human emotions. These are weaknesses that is in us all, he thinks. But not long after Robert's birth, he suffers a terrible misfortune: His nurse accidentally drops him. The fall leads to permanent injury; a lasting deformity.

That same month of Robert's birth, Edward's elder half-sister, Katherine and her husband, threatens to bring a legal case against him and his sister Mary: Katherine accuses him, her half-brother, of being a bastard. She protests that he is not a legitimate inheritor of Earl John's estates. She believes that the Earl, her father, was already married when he took Edward and Mary's mother, Margery, to be his wife. So just into his teenage-hood, Edward is upset by the charge of being born out of wedlock. His Uncle, Arthur Golding, Margery's brother, comes to Edward's aid. In defence of Edward and Mary as plaintiffs, he lodges a petition to the Archbishop of Canterbury to justify that Edward and Mary are legitimate claimants as heirs to Earl John's estates. Golding's stout defence succeeds. But, already this lawsuit about legitimacy has cut deep into

Edward's sensibilities. For the first time in his life, the proud young Earl is touched by the loss of Good Name; by the taint of being called illegitimate, and, the shame arising there from. So much is he affected that he feels compelled to use it in these early days of writing. Feeling helpless in his boyish lyrics on the loss of Good Name, he pens these lines:

"Help Gods, help Saints, help Sprites and powers in heaven do dwell,
Help ye that aye wont to wail, ye howling hounds of hell;
Help man, help beasts, help birds and worms that on earth do toil,
Help fish, help fowl, that flick and feed upon the salt sea soil,
Help echo that in the air doth flee, shrill voices to resound,
To wail this loss of my Good Name,
as of these griefs the ground."

As he re-reads these lines for compositional merit, reflecting metre and alliterative excess, once again, he bewails the loss of his Good Name. And God forbid, the shadow of Shame cast upon himself as a Nobleman and his de Vere family should the practice of his secret art of playwriting become publicly known! Thus the smear of being called a bastard, lingers.

***

On a golden summer's morning, Arthur Golding sits in the library. "Good morning, My Lord, Edward," he says when Edward appears. "I am appointed to be your new Tutor." He smiles broadly, leaving no doubt in Edward's mind how he feels.

"I am very pleased you are," Edward says. "I look forward to working with you. I am honoured to collaborate with you."

Golding motions to Edward to take a seat. He sits at the desk facing Golding. Unlike his previous Tutors, Golding is much younger. He is in his late twenties. But, he is already established as a brilliant Translator of Classical texts. Edward is impressed, but not overawed. He is duly respectful and pleased to see Golding again after his successful defence of the legitimacy lawsuit. They'd worked well enough then as Nephew and Uncle. But now Golding is charged to give instructions to Edward, to the best of his ability. As a Translator, he has a high reputation; and, as a Latin Scholar, one of the exercises he puts before Edward is Ovid's *Metamorphoses.* Golding's teaching is excellent; and as Edward acquaints himself with the texts of this famous literary work, Golding's explanation of the more intricate passages, is engaging.

They maintain a high regard for each other; and work well as collaborators. Edward, so early exposed to the Latin texts, falls in love with Ovid's poetry. As his scholarly work progresses, and mutual respect grows, Golding dedicates to the fourteen year old Edward, the English Translation of an *Abridgement of the Histories of Pompeius.* "It is not unknown to others," Golding writes, and he ends this special Dedication by stating "how earnest a desire Your Honour hath naturally grafted in you to read, peruse and communicate with others as well the histories of ancient times, and things done long ago, as also of the present estate of things in our days – and that not without a certain pregnancy of wit and ripeness of understanding."

Ripeness! That word attributed to one so young. This is heady praise for Edward. Time and again, he thinks of the Dedication. So far, it ranks as the most thrilling literary experience of his life. He considers Golding's observations of qualities that he possesses; especially his liking of history: a sense and appreciation of the importance of things past which give perspective and adds clarity to his cross-fertilizing thoughts on language and meaning. Almost at once, he recognises the lessons that Golding translates.

The Dedication strengthens Edward's respect and admiration for Golding's learning and achievements. It augurs well for the work they've set themselves to do. But, there is a marked difference of views between Edward and Golding. On studies of the past, Golding says to Edward: "There is only one purpose of history which is the upholding of virtue and the banishment of vice."

As a respected student of the *Holy Bible*, he takes every chance to promote its teachings. Virtue and Vice! These opposites come together, like twins. Edward listens attentively. And soon, it emerges that Teacher and Pupil are not entirely at one because Golding's view of History and Contemporary Affairs is strict and Puritanical, while Edward's is not hard and fast: it is more flexible. A source fuelling the difference is Edward's regular penning of boyish Verses and Poems, which he hopes to publish one day.

To these early writings, he puts the signatures: "Earle of Oxenforde" and his initials "E.O." Already, he is unlike many English writers of this time: His poetic pieces are not chest-thumping or special pleadings for religious advantage. So while Arthur Golding devotes a career to moralistic prose, Edward the teenager is already interested in such grand themes as honour and revenge. In his "Loss of Good Name," moral concern is absent as well as in other lines he'd written, one of which is: "I rest revenged of whom I am abused."

So, the Puritan, Arthur Golding, fears that Edward would eventually become a troubled man. But though he sees their paths as heading in different directions, their Pupil-Teacher engagement keeps them in a close and fruitful working relationship. Like Smith and Nowell, Uncle Golding is especially impressed by Edward's desire to learn and pass on knowledge to others. He too, could become a Teacher! The high hopes and expectation that Golding expresses, now propels him to further test Edward's translating skills.

"My Lord, Edward," Golding says one morning, "Today, we will move on to a different exercise in translations from Latin to English. As you know, I am known for my translation of various Latin texts. The one that concerns me, and us now, is Ovid's *Metamorphoses.* This is the work of translation that we will do."

"We?"

"Yes, My Lord," Golding says. "We will *collaborate.* A collaboration, if you would like to call it that."

They get to work. Days pass. The more Edward learns about Ovid's life and the deeper he gets into translating more of the *Metamorphoses,* he sees a disjuncture between Golding's moralistic Puritan Christian attitude and what Ovid and *The Metamorphoses* represent. He says nothing about this disparity as he gets deeper into the work. He finds translating from the Latin text into English words hugely interesting and exciting. He is fond of experimenting with words and their sounds; of playing games with them. Already he is well into his juvenile punning! The excitement he feels about English and other languages opens a new way of thinking! And he wonders not only about Golding's motive for the translation, but importantly about Ovid and Golding: He begins to see that they are of *strongly differing* views of life. So why was Golding, a respectable, God-fearing, conservative Puritan, who espouses the Sermons and preachings of John Calvin, so interested in translating the work of the poet Ovid, a champion of immoral practices and seduction? If this is odd, Edward thinks, it is hardly less so considering that *The Metamorphoses,* far from being a religious and virtuous text, engages in the transformation of human beings into animals and things like plants, rocks and planetary objects. Odder still is that Golding should devote so much of his time and labour translating from Latin into English, the work of the lustful, sexually charged poet Ovid, who was exiled in Rome. No one doubts Golding's commitment to the moral upliftment of Mankind, but why is he so drawn to the discredited Ovid?

As a Translator, Golding is known for being faithful to the original texts from which he translates. But, in this work of collaborating with Edward on *The Metamorphoses,* there are clear deviations in translation. Much of this veering off are suggestions made by Edward; and so the English version of *The Metamorphoses* contains less fidelity to the original Latin text. Put simply, Golding and Edward Englishes and modernises many aspects of Ovid's work. But Golding is not known to be liberal in his translations. So the question arises: Whose hand is behind the *new English words* and the racy style of the translation? Golding had never written anything remotely like this Elizabethan version of *The Metamorphoses.* The Dedication of his recent book to Edward is a clear vote of confidence in Edward's ability as a Translator. So this new style, the inclusion of many new words, is largely Edward's work. But, raises another question: Why is Edward de Vere's name not attached? The answer for this is simple: As the Earl of Oxford, a highly ranked Nobleman, publishing the work in his name is out of the question!

"Your name, Uncle Arthur," Edward says respectfully, "should be the one that appears as the sole author on this English version of *The Metamorphoses.*"

Golding is silent for quite a while after Edward had

spoken. He understands the problem of having Edward's name on the published work as a collaborator.

"Yes, My Lord," Golding says. "You are right. I accept that my name should appear on the publication."

Thus Golding agrees with the maverick boy-poet that Arthur Golding, should be the name printed as author of the English version of *The Metamorphoses.*

*

After their collaboration, whatever doubts Golding may have had about the translation, his concern for the young Edward's soul is evident. Wearing his Tutor's hat, he cautions Edward in true Evangelical Christian style:"Only in true Religion, true Godliness, true Virtue," he warns, "that your Lordship may do God, your Prince, and your Country best Service." After this, he goes further: "The greater gifts of Nature, the more graces of mind, the more worldly benefits that god hath bestowed upon you," he reminds Edward, "the more you must be thankful unto God for without the true knowledge of him, the way is open for the Devil who hath more shapes than Proteus." Golding remains hopeful that his nephew would seek God's word where he himself had found it. But that hope could not be guaranteed.

*

In his thirteenth year, Edward had published his first Poem called *The Tragicall History of Romeus and Juliet.* The Pen-name he uses is Arthur Brooke. The story it tells is based on an Italian romance. It shows that a boy writer borrowing from others is nothing new. It is the way forward, Edward feels, in making progress as a Poet. This is a new exercise for him. Indeed there is something childish about the narrator of this

*Romeus and Juliet* story. Why? Because the author, Edward, is himself still not far off childhood. But clearly he thinks as a boy-Poet and writes as Arthur Brooke:

> "...For sure his virtues were
> As many as his years in number few
> The Muses him in learned lap did bear
> And Pallas dug his dainty babe did chew."

The name Arthur Brooke is an ingenious double pun on Ox-ford; the second part of the name, ford, relates to a brook. But the Boy Poet is keen to improve upon the work he is doing. He practices to improve his juvenile "lumbering fourteeners" for example:

> "The proverb saith unmended off are they that are
> unseen.
> And as out of a plant a nail doth drive,
> So novel love out of mind the ancient love doth rive."

These lines show the pre-teen Poet's addiction to "fourteeners." So "Arthur Brooke" appears just around the time when Edward is working with another Arthur: Arthur Golding, on *The Metamorphoses.* Already, the boy Edward de Vere is inspired as he aspires in his early teens. He is aware of, and fully embraces, his propulsive writer's urge to get his writings into print! And he does so by dodging the authorship problem with his debut use of the Pen-name Arthur Brooke. He continues to show what a remarkably precocious boy he is. To many learned men with whom he'd been in contact, it was quite clear that he possessed a rare talent. As one of them had said to him: "Your infancy from the beginning is sacred to the

Muses."

*

So from his early to late teen years, Edward had continued with his Studies. He knows well the centrality of education to noble families in the Court of Queen Elizabeth. It's chief enforcer is Cecil, the man who, apart from the job-description of being Master, is naturally fond of upholding strict adherence to the Rules. He drums into the minds of his young Wards what he sees as their duty: "As Nobles and landed gentry," he insists, "you owe it to your Queen and country to study; to do things diligently. You are the ones who will be chosen to lead as England's official representatives; as Generals and Ambassadors, both in peace and war." Not surprisingly, he oversees his Wards like a military Commander; and being a Commoner, he draws great pride from fostering the ideal of strict discipline. A motivating factor in his approach, even if he overdoes it sometimes, is his belief that what is good for the high-born is also good for himself and his own children: Anne, Robert and Thomas.

***

While Edward is at Cecil House, the dreaded, deadly plague is rife. At such times, heavily populated London is a place to be shunned. But amidst the scare stories, now at the age of fourteen, he receives the good news that he will be leaving London to attend St John's College at Cambridge University. He is delighted to have this chance; all the more, because he will be joined there by the Earl of Rutland and his Cousin, the Duke of Norfolk.

Towards the end of his studies, the Queen makes a special

visit to Cambridge, where a troupe of undergraduate players request that they perform a masque. The Queen gives her consent; and, imbued with the spirit of performing, the students enact a play caricaturing a few religious leaders; in particular, a few Catholic Bishops who were in jail. Many in the audience are unhappy that the play is allowed to be performed. Among them is the Spanish Ambassador who notes that students in the drama are dressed like the imprisoned Bishops; and disturbingly, one of the actors portrays the Bishop of London carrying a lamb which he appears to be eating! Shocked by this disrespectful behaviour, the Queen leaves the auditorium. Edward takes his leave too. With the sudden change in mood, the men holding the torches that lit the auditorium and stage, left in haste. So ended the students' thoughtless and scandalous representations.

On the way back to his rooms, as he was by the Ipswich performance of *King Johan*, Edward is struck, once more, by the power of staged dramas; by the direct, undiluted effects they produce. For him, a writer of Poems and Verses, playwrighting is a new medium of communication. He finds it most revealing and appealing: Dramatic power is *real power*, he thinks, as he re-runs the scandalous display he'd witnessed in Cambridge. So transforming was the effect of the skit that he would never forget it.

***

While the Queen is still in Cambridge, she faces an awkward problem: A few years earlier, she had proclaimed at Ipswich that no woman would ever be permitted to stay overnight at an English University or Abbey. Yet, here she is now, Edward thinks, lodging at Cambridge University for several nights! Officials turn a blind eye. But Edward notes this Royal hypocrisy of double-standards for future reference. This is the thirty-year old Queen's first visit to Cambridge University, where, for the five days of her stay, she is lavishly entertained. As the University's Chancellor, William Cecil is omnipresent: He has a hand in everything.

As Edward observes, education is paramount. He notes that the Queen's visit is marked by scholarly presentation, sermons, discourses in English and Latin, as well as the staging of dramas: comedies and tragedies. Before Elizabeth leaves Cambridge, she attends a public Debate at St Mary's Church on various themes, including art. The next day, after more debates and a speech of her own in Latin, The Queen bestows a degree upon Edward de Vere. He is now fourteen years old; and within the walls of this place of learning, reflecting upon the diversity of educational themes he's encountered, he thinks about what he'd heard the debaters say and considers, more generally, the interplay between art and life.

*

A year later, he attends the wedding of Ambrose Dudley, the Earl of Warwick and Anne Russell, daughter of the Earl of Bedford. Robert Dudley, the Earl of Leicester, also takes part in the wedding celebrations. It is a special high society occasion, and Edward is pleased to be present. All the more because the matrimonial celebration features plays and revels overseen by someone who is connected to the theatre. His name is Richard Evans, the respected Director of the Children of the Chapel Royal. Evans is also a collector of Courtly poems and song lyrics.

"This is My Lord Edward de Vere," Ambrose says, as he introduces Edward to Evans.

"My Lord, I am very glad to meet you," Evans says. "I have heard that you write poems and songs."

"Yes, I do," Edward says to Evans. They talk for awhile; and soon they realised that they have much in common: mainly in literature and dramatic performance.

"My Lord," Evans says, "I am compiling a collection of poems and songs for publication. A sort of Anthology. Would you be interested in making a contribution?"

"Yes, I would," Edward says. Evans beams with pleasure at Edward's ready acceptance.

They part company with high hopes of literary collaboration. Evans eventually publishes *The Paradise of Dainty Devices*; a compilation that contains a few of Edward's early poems which he signs "E.O," his initials for Edward of Oxenford.

*

After the Dudley-Russell wedding, Edward travels to Oxford University to receive his Master of Arts degree, which complements the Cambridge qualification he'd received two years before. This Oxford qualification carries more academic weight; and is further enhanced not only by the Queen's arrival at Oxford for a Royal visit (which closes with a Cap and Gown Ceremony) but also by a wonderful event of drama and discourses. Of the plays staged, excerpts from one of them has echoes of Edward de Vere's poetry!

Following publication of *The Paradise of Dainty Devices*, Edward's studies take a new turn. It shifts from Cosmography, Language, Philosophy and Physic to Common Law. Though under Smith's tutelage, Edward had learned about Civil and Ecclesiastical Law, now his foster-father and guardian Cecil thinks a grasp of the Common Law in England is necessary. As a former law student at Gray's Inn in London, Cecil advises Edward:

"My Lord, you must further your law studies," he says. "I propose that you enrol at Gray's Inn. I have spoken to the

Master and Tutors there. They are expecting you."

Edward is seventeen years old; sturdy of body and flexible in his thinking. He accepts Cecil's direction and enrols. At Gray's Inn he meets, and gets to know, another student: Philip Sidney, who becomes a regular visitor at Cecil House. Both young men have fine minds.They are now recipients of the best legal training at Gray's Inn and the benefits of Courtly theatrical training, as part of their education. To be so educated, it is no wonder that Edward and Sidney are two of the foremost practitioners of an evolving literati of English poets and playwrights of their time. The art of Poesie is ever-rising within Edward, who is already so outstanding as to be seen by some at Court as a sort of maverick poet!

Among other well-educated aspirants and practitioners of writing are Frances Beaumont, Thomas Campion, John Davies, John Ford, John Marston and John Donne. As Edward absorbs legal principles and cases at Gray's Inn, he is spellbound by the dramas portrayed there. And there too, he reacquaints himself with the highly-praised dramatist George Gascoigne, who stages two plays for students: *Jocasta* and *The Supposes*. Gascoigne is Edward's relative by marriage which is why, after Earl John's death, they'd ridden together in the post-funeral Procession from Hedingham to London. Edward sees performances of Gascoigne's plays, and reads manuscripts of the two plays. In student-mode, he dissects and appraises Gascoigne's plots, character, dialogue and staging. He considers *Jocasta* as a tragic tale, and *The Supposes* as showing a new way. Of the various views expressed, one critic describes *The Supposes* as an Elizabethan Comedy, the first to be performed with multiple costumes and borrows from modern Italian comedy which uses a female leading player in a far from predictable plot. Altogether, this Gray's Inn production of *The Supposes* appeals to Edward. It inspires thought and action *through playwrighting*. So, for the teenager, the art of staged story-telling through the plays *Jocasta* and *The Supposes* pushes him to use his pen more; to continue to write of things that are more poetic than prosaic. Increasingly between his law readings, as he writes verses and poems, he also attempts dramas. In playwrighting, Gascoigne guides him: He shows the smart and willing youth examples of how his plays are put together. Edward is smitten. He rises to the challenges of dramatic construction that are essential to this early phase of his playwrighting vocabulary and training. This Gray's Inn experience is a turning point. It leaves a lasting impression upon him, especially as he reads the case of Hales versus Petit. He has full access to papers and documents relating to this legal dispute, which he finds all the more fascinating for it relates to the usurpation of property from a rightful heir. This matter appeals to him directly also because as the Seventeenth Earl of Oxford, he is a Ward of Court who must wait till he comes of age to claim his rightful Inheritance: his ancestral family lands. So what he learns as a Law student about the compelling case of Hales versus Petit would stay in his mind.

*

It is five years since his father had died. But though the loss feels less raw now, it is ever-present and powerful with the potential to reduce him to tears. Earl John's absence presses him to adopt a re-formulation: a new sense of himself and how he sees others. As he learns more about his father's wealthy estates (soon to be his when he officially turns twenty one), while he is still at Gray's Inn, death, Inheritance and law, like some hard-wired trilogy, commands his attention, not in fiction, as in a play, but in real life as it applies to him personally.

He is in the prime of youth: He is energetic: His mind

is ever-active with a great need for physical recreation. He is not very tall; but to his advantage, he is lithe and athletic. In these fast-paced, growing teen years he reveals a passionate, unhesitant, and, at times, an impulsive side to his personality.

It is summertime; and being a sun-lover, he appreciates the greater sense of freedom he feels now; so much more than was possible in the cooler months. He plays tennis and practices fencing: He does not tire easily, which leaves scope for more activities. There is hardly anything he feels he could not do. One evening while fencing in the yard at Cecil House, Thomas Brincknell, a cook from the Cecil household appears. He is not a practitioner of fencing, nor is he the carrier of either a rapier or a sword. If what happens next is unclear, one thing is very clear: Brincknell is struck with a fencing sword by Edward. The blow punctures an artery in Brincknell's leg. Blood flows freely from the horrific wound; and as Brincknell lay helpless on the ground, a number of people gather around him. But nothing, and no one present, could stop the bleeding. Agnes, Brincknell's wife, sits beside him. She cradles his head on her lap. She cries and bawls in desperation as Brincknell dies.

There is no indication, no evidence of aggressive behaviour on Brincknell's part. Is the weapon used a rapier or a sword? That is now irrelevant for the fact remains that Edward's blow had opened a wound some four inches deep, and one inch wide.

In the aftermath, the Coroner's inquest finds Brincknell guilty of being drunk; of running and *falling upon* Edward's weapon. But, in truth, the incident was an act of extreme violence. It mirrors a disturbing degree of impulsive behaviour on the part of the teenage Earl. If the weapon was not a sword, why was he practising fencing with an unguarded foil? And why no criminal charges are brought against him? As Elizabethan law applies to this case, the final judgement is not for, but against Brincknell. The final verdict blames him. Why? Largely because Edward de Vere is a Nobleman, which is tough luck for the Commoner cook. But, he is human. Agnes feels wretched, having lost her husband whose death is formally ruled as suicide. Is this justice? "No!" Agnes screams. But thanks to Cecil, the most influential Minister and chief fixer in England, the Court decides in favour of the Nobleman. Might is right. And surprise, surprise, for Cecil, the social climber, Edward is more than just another Ward. Cecil hopes Edward would one day marry his daughter Anne. So, while Edward had pleaded *se defendando*, alleging that Brincknell, while attacking him had run upon his sword, he pauses for reflection. And so it was that soon after Edward matriculates at Gray's Inn, he is shaken to the core by the tragic act of killing a man. His brash act, be it his reaction to provocation, namely that he was being spied upon, would not go away. It lingers in his young mind; a murder seared into his memory. This sad incident (or "accident," as Edward likes to think of it) is another part of his nature and personality as the brilliant student and mercurial teenage Poet. It is a portent of things to come.

***

A few months after Thomas Brincknell's murder, Margery, Edward's mother, dies. She is laid to rest next to Earl John at Earls Colne. What are Edward's thoughts on this matter. He leaves no record of his feelings, but her death reminds him of the shocking, indelible memory of her marrying so soon after his father had died. The husband she chooses is well below her social station: That man was Charles Tyrell, an employee of the Dudley family, who are rivals of the Cecil clan. Edward remembers Margery's detachment from him: How after her marriage to Tyrell, she'd remained distant from him. A few times she did get in touch with him, but only through letters sent to William Cecil! Her actions, Edward thinks, were, as usual, hardly motherly; lacking in warmth. In this respect, she was true to form until the end. But for Edward this difficult mother-son relationship does not resolve anything. Certainly not closure. On the contrary, it continues to haunt him.

*

Now, in his late teens, he falls sick. He needs healing hands; and, having not had much caring female attention as a child, Margery's death rankles in his orphan-hood. He is at a low point. Lying helpless in bed, thoughts of his parents and death are never far away. Days pass. And, as he begins to recover, for the first time since he was bethrothed to Mary Hastings he thinks about finding a wife. Closeted in Cecil House, in a feverish delirium, his thoughts wander. One image comes and goes: The face of a girl he'd seen on the day when he'd arrived at the House. That was seven years ago. Now, as he struggles to regain full health, the face of that girl is near to him. Her name is Anne. She is the thirteen year old daughter of William Cecil. "My noble Lord," the girl says, "can I get you anything? Perhaps something to eat. Or maybe, a drink?"

"Thank you," Edward says weakly. "I'm neither hungry nor thirsty."

She seems to understand his loss of appetite for she too had suffered from ill-health the year before. She was struck down by small-pox, so severely, that at one stage, it had brought her close to death. So now Edward's illness draws Anne's attention. Having known each other over the years, as she attends to his needs, she does not hide her interest in him. In spite of the difference in age and social rank, a sense of familiarity had gradually developed between them. For her part, Anne likes, even secretly adores, Edward; and at this time when he feels vulnerable and less than dignified because of illness, she comes close to being a nurse-cum- mother substitute for Edward.

Beneath the outward caring face of the Carer and the submissiveness of the Cared-for, tender feelings stir; and grows. But, as Edward recovers and is back on his feet as a Courtier, he learns that Anne's father had already begun to make marriage plans for his daughter. He is surprised by the news; and more interestingly by his response to it. A stab of jealousy runs through him. Though not his intention, wily-nily, he'd become infatuated with Anne.

"Are you bethrothed?" he asks Anne.

"My Lord," she says, "my father is arranging a marriage-match for me. The man he has chosen for me is Mr Philip Sidney."

Sidney was Edward's rival at Gray's Inn and at Court. Now, the mention of his name triggers in Edward more feelings of jealousy and disappointment. Aiding and abetting the match is Sidney's powerful Uncle, the Earl of Leicester, who sees a marriage between his fifteen year old nephew and Anne Cecil as an astute and strategic political pairing. Leicester presses hard for this coupling to be sanctified in marriage. But he needs to hide the fact that though Sidney has lands, he is short of money. This is not good for Sidney's prospects. Why? Because what matters to Cecil is nothing less than the largest amount of wealth for his daughter's hand.

As the match-making progresses, Edward learns that Leicester is using, as his own property, some of the Inheritance bequeathed by Earl John, which, in effect, means that Leicester is usurping the de Vere estates to advance the marriage of Sidney to Anne. Cecil understands the difficulty with this in relation to the proposed marriage, yet, he persists in thinking:

The more wealth the merrier. But soon, as controller of everything to do with his daughter's marriage, he shows his true intention: He shifts his gaze to an even higher bidder for Anne's hand. And so, the Sidney-Anne Cecil wedding talks falters, then eventually comes to nothing.

***

Fully fit again, as one who has worked hard and has the finest education in England, Edward is eager to prove himself: Strong and fearless, he answers the call for military service. It is a bold decision that chimes nicely with his ancestors heroic exploits on the battlefields. He is proud of the de Vere's legendary achievements and thinks that he too must make his mark. He feels he could do no better than offer himself to defend his Queen and country. The place to do so, he thinks, is in the north of England and across the Scottish border, where Catholic Nobles are in revolt against Queen Elizabeth.

His growing sense of duty mingles with youthful energy, ambition and the great desire to be tested. And, yes, to be noticed! He is just a year short of his majority; and among other Courtiers there is keen competition to become the foremost celebrity. At last, as the autumn days get shorter, Edward tells Cecil of his readiness to Serve England.

"Sir," he writes, "Although my hap hath been so hard that it hath visited me of late with sickness, yet thanks be to God for your care of me, I find my health restored. At this present, if I have done anything amiss that I have merited your offence, impute it to my young years and lack of experience. And having no other means whereby to speak with you myself and am bold to impart my mind in paper, earnestly desiring your honour that at this instant, as heretofore you have given me your good word, since you could not then obtain me license of the Queen's Majesty. But now you will do me so much honour as that by your purchase of my license I may be called to the service of my prince and country at this present troublous time... By your assured friend this twenty-fourth of November."

To this letter, in bold letters, he adds his name: "EDWARD OXINFORD."

So, in his well-chosen words to Cecil, Edward expresses a new-found sense of well-being, of confidence; a commingling of youthful feelings of national pride, and respectful thanks.

***

So far, he reflects, his student days at Gray's Inn had marked a major turning point in his life. Not only did he meet Philip Sidney, his path was again crossed with George Gascoigne. He was encouraged by the fact that *The Supposes* was a rare play which contained less poetry, more prose and, importantly it was presented in the English language. It was then that he began to spend more time practising the art of playwriting! The play's effect upon him was profound. In many ways, it was a continuation of his feelings after he'd seen *King Johan* in Ipswich. So the dramatic portrayals at Gray's Inn were transformative; experiences that had occured at the time of his tragic encounter with Thomas Brincknell.

He is mindful, too, of his passionate and impulsive nature, which pushes him to the edge, but is not always either negative or destructive. On the contrary, it is a combination that pushes him to make connections with the different parts of a play and recognise it as an amalgam represented in production as a plot, language, dialogue, characters and the players' costumes. In short, he marvels at how spell-binding staged stories can be. The writer, he learns, is like a puppeteer who puts words in actors' mouths. This responsibility makes him think harder.

By so doing, he appreciates afresh the true value of plays; the honour and weighty responsibility of being a playwright. He is respectful of, and most attentive to, Gascoigne who, at one of their meetings, says: "My Lord, I suggest, that you should turn your Poetic versifying into plays.Use every device to bring your characters alive. The main aim is to make them believable; as life-like, as possible. Your characters should resemble real people: The true art of the playwright is mirroring life upon the theatre stage. How to do all that is the challenge."

Edward takes Gascoigne words to heart: Such reminiscences of their talks, now brings a smile which both relaxes and fortifies him for he hopes that his interest in English Law and his enjoyment of the Comedies he'd seen at Gray's Inn (the juxtaposition of law and art) would one day come into play as the Elizabethan world faces troublesome and dangerous days.

***

# III

## 'Love hath taught me to rhyme and be melancholy'
## 'Haply to wive and thrive'

*'Love works not with the eyes, but with the mind*
*And therefore is winged Cupid blind.'*

Edward is ready to join English soldiers engaged in crushing the Northern Rebellion. But before he departs to serve his Queen and country, he has other things on his mind. Master Cecil keeps a wary eye on him, in particular, on his expenditures; his taste for things that are costly. His dress sense is not conservative. He likes clothes and is conscious of becoming a dandy. Now, in the seventh year of his Wardship, he continues to spend freely. As his expenditure rises, Cecil takes note. He keeps a list which records that Edward had bought a cape and riding cloth, three doublets, jackets, a black velvet hose, several pairs of Spanish leather shoes, a few pairs of slippers, a handkerchief, velvet and satin for a Spanish cape, a rapier, dagger and belt. And while he'd been recovering from illness, he was also charged for hired lodgings.

Not only is he interested in wearing the finest clothes to look his best, he is determined in his pursuit of gaining knowledge, especially in relation to writing: He is fascinated by the sounds of words; by the use of language as currently used and, excitingly, its possibilities. When he comes back to

Court after his illness, he spends many hours reading in the Cecil House Library. Here, as elsewhere in Elizabeth's England, Cecil and his spies monitor what is going on, particularly in matters to do with money and personal possessions. The acquisition of education and books is not cheap. Over a four-month period, He had bought two books in Italian, as well as a Geneva Bible, a book by Chaucer, Plutarch's works in French and few other books. This selection, from a vast range, reveals his literary interests. He reads his Geneva Bible with much reverence. Often he would pause to meditate upon scriptural words and their meanings. He is no passive believer. He tries to relate what he reads to life; to the events of his day. The questions he pose are no passing thoughts: Often he is so taken aback by the responses his questions provoke in him, that at different places in his Geneva Bible, he underlines certain passages. His wide reading and studiousness even at this relatively young age, incorporating religious metaphors and symbols, gives an emerging, profoundly lyrical flavouring that characterises his writings.

*

With the Queen's permission, Edward is enlisted to fight with his compatriots in the military campaign to quell the Northern Rebellion. His orders are to join Thomas Ratcliffe, the Earl of Sussex, who is appointed to putdown the northern unrest fomented by Catholic rebels. The grand plan of the dissidents is to bring about the marriage of Mary, Queen of Scotland to the Duke of Norfolk, who is Edward's close relative; his first Cousin. Being the great-granddaughter of King Henry VII, puts Mary in the line of Succession to replace Elizabeth on the English Throne. But Mary abdicates, leaving the Scottish Crown to her son James. After two marriages, Mary is not only free to marry again, her claim to the English throne is always a possibility. This "claim" is also a continuing source of deep concern to Queen Elizabeth. Against this background, at last, eager Edward begins his journey on horseback from London to join Sussex and his soldiers in the north of England. He feels confident for he knows the man in whose charge he is entrusted is a soldier of distinction. As Commander of English forces, Sussex had helped to establish English Settlements in Ireland under Queen Elizabeth. He also opposes his rival the Earl of Leicester by promoting potential French marriage partners for Queen Elizabeth. Such support he hopes will weaken Leicester's claim to being Her Majesty's favourite man. It is Sussex's good fortune that his earlier military successes will continue in the battlegrounds of both the Scottish and Northern Rebellions where his ongoing actions are swift and effective. So much so, that much of the fighting during the Uprisings was under full control when Edward arrives at the battle front.

"My Lord Edward," Sussex says, as Edward reaches the Officers' camp. "I hope you had a good journey." These few words are almost drowned-out by gunfire. "Let us go inside," Sussex says in a firm, fatherly tone. They sit at a large table in the Officers tent. "So far, we are winning the battle," Sussex says. "Let us hope we will eventually win the war. These are your orders." He hands a sheet of paper to Edward. "And this," he adds, passing another note, "is a plan of our area of operations."

While Edward reads and takes in the information, sitting in the tent are two battle-hardened officers. The side of the head of one of them is heavily bandaged: The dressing is streaked here and there with dark-red marks; blood seepage from the officer's wounds. The other man has a bandaged leg which he rests on a chair.

"The Queen is much concerned about your safety here,"

Sussex says. His expressive face is serious. "You will accompany me on all our attacks."

Outside the tent, the gunfire is sustained. Deafening. The bangs come in quick succession! Edward coughs as the smell of gun smoke fills the air. He glances at the wounded men. Suddenly, the reality of war becomes appallingly present and dangerous.

Edward spends his twentieth birthday in the company of Sussex. For him, Sussex's military prowess and standing at Elizabeth's Court, makes him a father figure *par excellence*: A man of words, as well as deeds; a reassuring presence, especially now! Five days after reaching the battlefront, hundreds of villages had been destroyed and many castles are looted. Of these acts of violence, Edward bears witness. His youthful, rose-tinted view of life and the world is shattered. Scores of dead bodies lie strewn across the battlefield. But his sense of duty is unshaken. He is truly committed to Queen and country and stands shoulder to shoulder with Commander Sussex, who leads another charge of English troops in their campaign north of the border. Soon, the victorious campaign is over and Edward sets out on his return journey.

***

Hail! The conquering hero. Such a sentiment sits well with him, but being back in England, his baptism of warfare alongside Sussex in the act of "retribution" in Scotland is not well received by everyone. What is seen as Queen Elizabeth's harsh treatment of Catholics; her putting down of the Catholic rebellion, angers Catholic officials in Rome: The Pope does not just speak pious words; now he acts. He excommunicates Queen Elizabeth from his Romish fold; and his Papal Bull announces that she should lose her Crown and all privileges pertaining to it. Catholics in England and elsewhere in Europe sees this Edict from God's Emissary in Rome, as giving the green light to get rid of the Queen.

So it is official, Edward thinks: This dispensation from on high permits Catholics to use all means to depose the Protestant Queen! There is shock and horror across the land. But the English response to the Pope is also prompt. A propaganda Campaign ensues. Two main mediums are used for propagandising the British people: Through the transmission of messages delivered mainly in Churches, and by using dramatic performances in public theatres.

As a lover of plays and poetry, the Queen fully supports her ministers in their use both of pulpit and stage, in getting the message through. So with due haste and passion, Preachers and Actors get the word out to the Common man and woman; words, spoken and written in the English language receives a boost. They are the means used to transform the thinking of the seemingly un-thinking masses. And so, the religious Protestant-Catholic conflict opens a window of opportunity to rally the nation as Church leaders read State-sanctioned Sermons every Sunday to their congregations. In earlier times, Churchmen had used "Homilies" to reach the people; but now one homily in particular is published as a result of the Uprising in the north of England and Scotland. It is titled *A Homily Against Disobedience and Wilful Rebellion* by an "Anonymous" Scribe.

This unique piece, is an early version of Edward's prose. In it, there are elements of rhetoric and poetry that point to the contribution of the budding Poet. More than most Courtiers, Edward steadily hones his Penmanship and compositions. He is fully aware of the vital importance of effective communication through the written word. He thinks of his religious upbringing and the Biblical phrase: "In the beginning was the word." Now in the wake of the Rebellion, the people are receptive, and, he is ready to address what is a captive audience. In tandem, he knows that Church attendance is mandatory, which enhances the Preachers' message.What a moment it is for him as a writer, he thinks, to have this great opportunity to reach, not only the limited audience of nobles, aristocrats and fellow Courtiers, but also his biggest audience: the English people. He is proud of the honour and privilege, as well as, the weight of responsibility it carries! Having been to the battlefield, now he is poised to wield the pen, as a weapon, far mightier than the sword! His patriotic sense before and during the war in the north, was strong but now, it grows stronger as he puts pen to paper: "Is not rebellion the greatest of all mischief?" he writes, "How horrible a sin against God and man rebellion is cannot possibly be expressed." Then he goes on to say:

"For he that nameth rebellion nameth not a singular or one only sin as is theft, robbery, murder and such like; but he nameth the whole puddle and sink of all sins against God and man, against his prince, his country, his countrymen, his parents, his children, his kinfolks, his friends and against all men universally; all sins, I say, against God and all men heaped together, nameth he that nameth rebellion."

These are his carefully chosen words. His new-found confidence reflects his coming of age: He is twenty one.

***

Queen Elizabeth holds William Cecil, her Secretary of State and Chief Administrator, in the highest esteem. He is a man of outstanding ability in whom she sees only the best qualities. She needs him; and, he needs her.

Just before Edward's twenty-first birthday, at last, Cecil gets his much desired Royal reward. Elizabeth announces that he is to become a Baron. And so, the Commoner William Cecil becomes Lord Burghley. He is elevated and elated. But in spite of his grand title and higher status, nothing about him has changed: There is no glossing over the dark side of this man who does not come from the Aristocracy. The canny Queen recognises Cecil's unsurpassed sly traits. She fully understands that as Spymaster he is determined and brutal; not even his son, daughter or other family members, could escape his all-seeing, far-reaching surveillance.Thus the "Virgin" Queen keeps her exalted Burghley as her closest Advisor and confidante. But though she trusts Burghley utterly in all matters, there is one other thing about him that is plain to her in this age when writing is the essential form of communication in all official State business. That "thing" is Burghley's writing style. It is a style which Edward thinks he may one day be able to use in his developing art. For now, the power of the ever-ambitious Burghley grows. There is no one who could hinder or stop him. His keenness to become rich; to acquire property: lands and palatial houses is relentless. "And why not?" he thinks. "After all, I am the Master of Wards. I am in control of the key matters of State. I deserve big rewards," he says to himself.

He is close to being untouchable! Edward remembers well the day at Westminster when Cecil received the title of Baron Lord Burghley. During the investiture Ceremony, Edward had thought that this upgrading of a non-Noble by birth could spell the beginning of the end for the Nobility. But witnessing this ennoblement makes him even more conscious of his own high-caste lineage, so thoroughly steeped in tradition. And not for the first time, he feels a deep and growing sense of responsibility for the talent he's been honing: It is indeed the 'weapon' which he uses (and which he must continue to use) not his sword, but his pen! And so, as his writings about aristocratic status and background gains added urgency, he feels his historical writings (which makes the past ever-present) must be upheld. He continues to experiment with poetic language. It is the best way, he thinks, through which he could express the feudal way of life as it evolves; and thus, explore and present an emerging new kind of English literature.

***

Months after Cecil becomes Lord Burghley, Edward is also promoted: He sits as a Member of the House of Lords. On his first day as a Parliamentarian, as is customary, to perform his duties, he dresses in official regalia and mingles among men who are much older than himself. He feels odd; self-conscious. But, as the morning wears on, he accepts that he has truly come of age and must do his duty. As if this is not enough, another title is bestowed upon him: He becomes the Lord Great Chamberlain of England. In this largely ceremonial role he is expected to partake in the Opening of Parliament and at Royal Processions. Being the holder of such a high office as Lord Great Chamberlain of England, Edward not only rides in the Queen's Royal Coach he also carries her train as she is led into Parliament. Her last two Parliamentary appearances have been contentious. Why? Because Ministers and Members of Parliament were urging her either to marry or, at least, to name a Successor. Such an act of self-demotion, she refuses to perform. But now, as he leads a Parliamentary Parade he is glad that Parliament shows a united front in the face of the Catholic threat posed by the northern rebels. He is proud to have served his Queen in the Rebellion, and feels very pleased to be sitting next to her now. In this dramatic setting, he sees the splendidly dressed Queen Elizabeth as England's rising phoenix; a powerful image that should continue for as long as she reigns.

***

Energetic Edward resumes his fondness for sport. He plays tennis; and takes part in the Knight's tilt tournament at Whitehall. This prestigious event is a big step up for him. When he arrives at the tiltyard, he savours the occasion: The Queen is present; the crowd is buzzing. The scene is set as the first combatants take their places. During the two day tourney, after all the competitors had done their best, the top honour goes to Edward de Vere. He proves to himself that he is a sporting hero; an accolade much prized in the feudal Elizabethan world. Within a few months, his achievements had risen spectacularly. As the young Earl of Oxford, Edward de Vere becomes a marriageable prize among many other attractive single men in Queen Elizabeth's Court. And significantly, to any observer: the Queen leaves no doubt that Edward is her favourite. Unsurprisingly there is much speculation about match-making between Courtiers and Maids of Honour. Burghley, the opportunist, is well-attuned to Court gossip. He is the father of the pretty, much sought-after, Anne. And now, after the failed marriage negotiations between Anne and Philip Sidney, he is seriously interested in Edward de Vere. Anne is four years younger than Edward; and by nature, she is quiet and obedient, just the opposite of Edward who is energetic, sociable and outward-looking. He is high-born; she is from lower social rank. But, as a Maid of Honour, Anne's qualities are highly respected: Edward knows this for she has won the Queen's favour for her inclination towards learning, domestic accomplishments and her general pleasing good looks and personality.

In her own quiet way, Anne stands apart from others

at Court, who are more prone to flirt with young nobles and partake in song. So with Anne, what you see is largely what you get. Edward had seen and known her for almost nine years. They often speak with each other; and since his illness, she has become even more attentive. Edward's youth, Anne's child-like nature and undoubted attractiveness leads to wooing and Courtship.Their deepening youthful feelings marks the beginning of a love, or infatuation, that continues to develop. Burghley is delighted. It is a relationship, a marriage match which he wants very much; perhaps even more than either Edward or Anne. For the status-conscious Burghley this closeness between Anne and Edward is timely, because he is no longer officially a "Commoner," but a Lord of the Realm! This time of love and Courtship is also of great value to Edward: It is a disturbing, but new and exciting emotional experience that is, of course deeply felt. It sears itself into his memory.

Months pass. And as good relations between Anne and Edward gets better: friendlier and warmer, the idea and prospect of marriage looms. But Edward is less keen to marry than is Anne. What's the hurry? Edward wonders. Predictably, Anne's persistence does not wane. Marriage is her goal. In this match-making dance, Burghley is privy to every move that Anne makes as he nudges her forward. He uses every trick he knows, including his fatherly boast that Anne is seen as a "prize in marriage" by many distinguished Courtiers. So while Edward is reluctant, Burghley is stubbornly aggressive in pressing for an Anne-Edward match. As the Courtship proceeds, Burghley, with all his advantages, continues his relentless pursuit to get his way. Soon, the word gets out that Edward has agreed, though no date has yet been set, to marry Anne Cecil.

Meanwhile, the Earl of Rutland, who is in Paris receives a letter from London informing him that Edward hath gotten himself a wife – or, at least, a wife hath caught him! That "wife" is Anne Cecil. The letter-writer goes on to say the coupling has caused disappointment: weeping, wailing and sorrowful cheer among Courtiers who had not been chosen to be Anne's husband. So, the determined, scheming Burghley, fixer and social climber, succeeds in bringing together his prized sixteen year old daughter and the young Earl of Oxford. By now, as Edward's bright and breezy familiarity with, and feelings for, Anne grows, he does not know that marrying into the Burghley clan means entry into a world of political intrigue, serpentine schemes and dark doings.

Then, at last, the day and venue are set for the wedding of Edward de Vere and Anne Cecil. With this announcement comes the news that Edward's Cousin, Thomas Howard, Duke of Norfolk, had got himself into trouble; no mere scrape, but trouble that is treasonable. It is alleged that he is part of a plot. What could such a thing be about? Edward asks himself before he approaches Norfolk's sons. He needs to know more. Soon, he realises that his Cousin is linked with others: the plotters. So while plans are being made for his marriage, Edward hears more about the Ridolphi Plot.

"Norfolk's secretary," he is told, carrying a bag of gold and a certain letter had been intercepted and the bag's contents were passed on to Burghley. The letter contains details of a conspiracy that involves a banker; an Italian named Ridolphi. He is the financier and leader of a campaign to launch a Spanish attack on England from the Netherlands. At the same time, the plotters hopes to depose Queen Elizabeth and install Norfolk and Mary, Queen of Scotland, to be England's King and Queen. Edward is stunned by the audacious, treasonous intent of the plotters. A graver charge against Queen and country he'd never heard of. So while nuptial preparations are under way, Edward's father-in-law to be, Lord Burghley, is busy carrying out secret surveillance designed to result in the Duke of Norfolk's Trial and death. How odd, he thinks, that his wedding celebration should coincide with the worry of the impending funeral of his favourite Cousin.

***

Edward de Vere and Anne Cecil get married in Westminster Abbey on Sunday 16 December 1571. Queen Elizabeth is present. As she looks on, she thinks of the possibility of her own marriage one day. At last, Anne speaks her vows under the watchful gaze of her father. As she says the words, Burghley stares at Edward who, for better or worse, is now formally becoming his son-in-law. After the exchange of vows and rings, Burghley thinks about entrusting his lovely daughter's future into the hands of the young Earl. If any man knows everything about his daughter, Burghley does. He manipulates everything and everyone under his control. But unsurprisingly, he worries now. Why? Because he still sees Anne as a child; and wonders: How would she cope with married life? He tries, for example, to imagine her performing wifely duties under a new Master! The answer to his question is far from reassuring. But, his doubts are irrelevant now, for he'd gotten what he hoped for! Social status and upward mobility through Anne's marriage to Edward de Vere.

After the solemn formalities of the Ceremony, a sumptuous wedding feast is held at Cecil House. Among the great and good who had gathered, is Monseigneur La Mothe Fenelon, the French Ambassador. Anne looks radiant; happy and relaxed. Edward stands beside her. He too, looks pleased as a line of guests forms to congratulate him. Scanning the banqueting room, he sees the Queen and an array of nobles and aristocrats milling around. He is glad to see most of them. This is easily the wedding of the year; and the Royal Court has come out in all their finery to celebrate it. Laughter punctuates the general hubbub and titter. Imperceptibly at first, then distinctly, the sound of the plucked strings of a lute rises, floats and fills the space from floor to ceiling. As more guests enter the room a general light-heartedness spreads among the gathering. Like sparks igniting, conversations start here and there and meld into the general hum. The Lutist plays in a variety of musical styles that enhances the mood and merriment. While guests partake of meat and drink, many begin to dance. To Edward's delight, the Queen seems pleased. She smiles often; and laughs easily. He knows how much she loves dancing. He remembers well her merry footwork which is something to behold. Would she take to the floor? he wonders. And, at that moment, being as close as he is to her (being her favourite Courtier) he imagines what her true feelings are for him right now, *as a married man*. After all, without her official consent, there would be no marriage today!

As expected, with no higher authority in England, bar the Queen, Burghley takes every opportunity to make Anne's big wedding day as memorable a celebration as Cecil House and Westminster has ever seen. For their part Edward and Anne are pleased that their wedding is a worthy and successful society event, as well as an occasion for family, friends and well-wishers to come together. But, Edward cannot ignore the fact that it is also an opportunity for political manoeuvring.

Soon after the marriage vows were exchanged, Burghley was the first to congratulate Anne and Edward. As he moves around, he seems at ease, if not happy. But looks can be deceiving for Burghley is ready to press the Treason charge against Norfolk: His case must not end with him receiving a light sentence. Such disturbing thoughts commingle in Edward's mind as he surveys the wedding scene: The colour and gaiety; the music, dancing, dining, the verses addressed to himself and Anne. But, far from being all sweetness and light, beneath the surface of this "happy" gathering there is real worry among those on Edward's side of the new extended family. They believe that Cousin Norfolk is not guilty of the charge against him; while on Anne's side of the family, Burghley is determined that no mercy must be shown. Any expression of leniency, he thinks, would send the wrong signal to the enemies of Protestant England: namely Catholics, and the Pope in Rome! So among the celebrants at this seemingly joyous high society gathering, there are boundaries; hidden, divisive fissures that separate groups and relationships which, in turn, are profoundly affected by the fractious uncertainties of politics and religion in Elizabethan England.

Burghley, naturally and quite rightly, continues to wonder what might be in store for his teenage daughter. There and then, he makes his own vow: That he would redouble his efforts of keeping a wary eye on the married couple. For their part, Edward and Anne feel as uplifted as they could be. They could not have imagined the wedding scene before them. While Anne is taken away by her mother, for a short time, Edward sits alone at his table. Just then, the French Ambassador Fenelon comes forward. "Congratulations, My Lord," he says. His first words to Edward are in English. He then continues in French. He speaks in this linguistic order out of pride for his own native tongue, but also because he knows of Edward's interest and respect for the French language: indeed his ability to speak and write fluently in French. On the table before Ambassador Fenelon is a glass of Rhenish. It is his second helping of this fine wine. He is in good spirits; and, in playful mood, he shows off his diplomatic skill of conversing in both English and French. Switching to English, he says:

"My Lord, the English food is…mmm... how you say…

very Excellent!" He lifts his glass of wine and sips. "Ah, My Lord," he adds, "but the wine is French." As he drains his glass in one flourish, his generous smile lights up his round, now rosy face, which seems broader. He places his glass on the table. "My Lord," he says, "together, the food and the Rhenish complement each other. A perfect combination I should say, for this very Grand occasion. My Lord, I offer my warm Congratulations to you and Your Countess!"

Having sipped some wine earlier, Edward is at one with the general mood of the guests. He is pleased to share these moments with the Ambassador.

"Merci, Monsieur Ambassador," he says, "Thank you!" He stands up and moves to greet a queue of people who have come forward.

Later, he sees Fenelon talking to the Earl of Leicester. He is curious, but he could only observe from afar: As Fenelon speaks, he gestures with his hands. The conversation between the Ambassador and Leicester is lively; they are fully engaged. What could they be discussing? Edward asks himself. He is mindful that before his closeness to the Queen, Leicester had been her number one Courtier.

Later, Fenelon returns to Edward's table, not to report on his talk with Leicester, but to re-engage with Edward, as Bridegroom; the man of the moment. Ever the wily diplomat, using his finest political language, Fenelon rises to the occasion to speak about another marriage, namely, the proposed alliance between the Queen of England, Elizabeth, and the Frenchman, the Duke of Anjou. So Edward's wedding and the Queen's proposed, potential marriage to a Frenchman and thus an alliance with France, taken together, are of such import that both Edward and Fenelon, buoyed by good spirits, warms to the peaceful, English-French relations of this time.

***

January 1562. A tense atmosphere pervades the Royal Court as Norfolk's Trial is finally set to begin. Rumours abound; and Burghley's ears burns. He is a central character in this real life drama. He hears not only that Edward sides with Norfolk, but also that his persistence in bringing Norfolk to Trial has affected Anne's marriage: in particular that Edward forsakes the marital bed.

While rumours of one sort or another, persist, Edward maintains his support for Cousin Norfolk who is charged with plotting to marry Mary, Queen of Scots; and, with supporting the Northern Rebellion. Before the charges were brought, Burghley had already branded Norfolk as an untrustworthy Catholic Noble.

After weeks of waiting before Norfolk's Trial, Edward has become more aware of his own status and that of Nobles in Elizabethan England. He sees the foundations of his illustrious ancestry and his way of life as being under threat. The time is now, he feels, to remind the Queen, the Court and Englishmen across the country, how valuable the Nobility is to the governance and well-being of England. He thinks of all that he's been taught so far: especially, certain essential values, like Court etiquette. He feels no less Princely now than he'd ever done; and is reminded of the strong impression that a book, *The Courtier* by the Italian philosopher Baldassare Castiglione, had made upon him.

Ten years before *The Courtier* had been translated into English, and since then, it has been held in high regard among many English gentlemen, who had heaped praise upon European Courtly life and living. Now, many more Courtiers adhere to Courtly ideals. Arising from wide reading, Edward's imagination is fully attuned: Having worked closely with

Arthur Golding, he is drawn to communication, meaning and languages; to translations and other cultures, too. But, reading is incomplete, he thinks, without writing. He seeks balance; and, as a budding, head-strong young writer, he looks beyond the shores of England. He aims for a larger audience. Now, he sponsors a Latin translation of *The Courtier* which he hopes would reach many European readers.

As a fan of such a book, he appreciates the great importance of publishing Bartholomew Clerke's translated Latin Edition of Castiglione's work. By so doing, he hopes it would have the knock-on effect of supporting Norfolk's case in two main ways: First, that the book would flatter Her Majesty's intellect, which is useful in gaining her support; and secondly, that it would do so in the language of the learned people who understands the work of nobles and the landed gentry in Elizabethan society. Queen Elizabeth, he hopes, would like his way of thinking.

Given that Edward's noble ideals are largely contained in *The Courtier,* when his former Tutor, Bartholomew Clerke, had completed his translation of the book from the original Italian into Latin, knowing of Edward's close collaboration with Golding on *Metamorphoses,* nearly a decade earlier, he (Clerke) remembers how delighted Edward was when he'd said: "My Lord, as a Courtier of your distinguished rank and learning, you would do me great honour by contributing a Preface to my book?" These words had an immediate impact as once again, a former Tutor had shown respect for him and his work; to the extent that his contribution is wholly acceptable. "Thank you, Clerke," Edward now says. "You know how much I appreciate Castiglione's book and your translation. I *will* write a Preface as you suggest."

True to his word, a few days later, Edward hands a copy of his Preface to Clerke, who visits his office. "Ah! My Lord," Clerke says joyfully. "Your Preface. Thank you!" At once he begins to read it. When he finishes, he says: "My Lord Edward, I am thrilled. I could never have envisaged such a Preface. It is perfect for the publication of my book." The two men shake hands; and Clerke leaves the room. On his way home, he reads the Preface all over again. Though he is respectful of Edward's capability, nonetheless, he is astonished that, at the age of just twenty two, Edward is able to produce literature of this fine quality. And so Clerke's book, with Edward's Preface was ready for publication.

In terms of Edward's writings so far, this piece is very significant: It marks his debut into serious literature; a work expressive of literary ideals that seems destined for further development. He begins:

"...For what more difficult, more noble or more magnificent task has anyone ever undertaken than our author Castiglione, who has drawn for us the figure and model of a Courtier; a work to which nothing can be added in which there is no redundant word, a portrait which we shall recognize as that of the highest and most perfect type of man."

The astute Edward sees the merits of *The Courtier* in a wider context. His words are both cleverly self-advantageous and wise; profound. His Prefatory prose shows that his respect and love of nature is already taking shape as a basic element in his thinking. "And so although nature herself has made nothing perfect, in every detail," he continues, yet "the manners of men exceed in dignity that with which nature has endorsed them; and he who surpasses others hap here surpassed himself, and has even outdone nature which, by no one, has ever been surpassed..." He cites the new glory of language in relation to the Translation. And, of the translator himself, he writes: "All this my good friend Clerke has done, combining exceptional genius with wonderful eloquence."

Then, with his ever-maturing, extraordinary authority, as if it is he who is his former Tutor's tutor, Edward adds:

"For he (Clerke) has resuscitated that dormant quality of fluent discourse. For this reason he deserves all the more honour, because to great subjects... he has applied to greatest lights and ornaments; use of words... richer in the dignity of his sentences. Or who can conform to variety of circumstances with greater art? If weighty matters are under consideration, he unfolds his theme in a solemn and majestic rhythm; if the subject is familiar and facetious, he makes use of words that are witty and amusing. When, therefore, he writes with precise and well chosen words, with skilfully constructed and crystal clear sentences, and with every art of dignified rhetoric, it cannot be but some noble quality should be felt to proceed from the work."

Finally, Edward addresses Queen Elizabeth. He knows without her support, nothing is possible in this Age. Of the "noblest attributes of the wisest Princes," he writes, "the safest protection of a flourishing commonwealth...in the opinion of all who continually encompass her (Queen Elizabeth) around; surely to obtain the protection of that authority to strengthen it with gifts and to mark it with the superscription of her name, is a work which, while worthy of all Monarchs, is most worthy of our own Queen to whom all alone is due all the praise of all the Muses and all that glory of Literature."

The "glory of literature." Already, he sees himself as a passionate proponent of such "glory."

After Clerke had left his office, for his part, Edward feels uplifted. He knows that soon the book will be published. For a while, he reflects upon the pride he felt while he was writing the Preface, which makes him feel even more like a Prince and Patriot in Elizabeth's Courtly Realm. He hopes the Queen would like his Preface: His first serious venture into literature. In essence, what he had written evokes a naturalness, but also a certain loftiness of forms of expression.

On receiving a copy of Clerke's publication, he is filled with good feelings as the book passes on from the Court to the wider reading public. Being a writer, he cherishes Courtly ideals as crucial, even for those who cannot be Courtiers!

*

After his well-received entry into the world of literature, Edward is bombarded by the pace of economic and social change in England. As feelings for his kinfolk deepen, he questions himself. How would his writing evolve? Should he engage with more prose, as in his Preface, or should he continue to write verse and develop a new phase of poetic output? As these matters preoccupy him, he is reminded of his place and the central importance of Courtiers generally. Of the ways in which he tries to support his Cousin Norfolk (and nobility, as a whole) the first and foremost is his confirmation of the value of the text of *The Courtier*. He considers the power of literature and Courtiers and thinks that no other philosophical writing catches the essence of life in the Elizabethan Court like Castiglione's ideals. And now, the empowerment he'd felt after writing the Preface, shades into rising ambition. He reflects upon the many books he'd read on history and Classical antiquity and the stories he'd heard from people of his Courtly class who had returned from European Grand Tours. He hears the Courtiers' excited talk about Italy; and as he gains more knowledge, he admits his lack of experience. One thing, in particular, looms large: He has never been overseas. And the passing of time accentuates his relative immaturity.

Though he is twenty two years old, he senses the direction of his destiny: Not only as a Courtier, but primarily as a Writer. He sees his roles as Courtier and Writer as inter-dependent. They are crucial in Queen Elizabeth's Court. But if publishing his philosophical case for a thriving aristocracy is very important, he wonders how would this protect Norfolk from the might, power and dictates of the State? The answer is clear enough: neither he nor Norfolk could change anything. Nobles passing judgement on their peers is no foregone conclusion. Indeed such a thing is highly unpredictable and brutal. As tense days pass, he sees the forces ranged against each other more clearly: The emerging modern state is pitted against the old feudal order. Leading the new modern men emerging through the ranks is Burghley and his loyal Agents: tough spies and informers, who guard the Queen, and therefore, they claim, England from all threats.

Sometimes perceived threats do not carry real force; and some men are wrongfully tried and convicted. But the outcome of certain Trials have been known well before they were heard. This unsettles Edward who feels a rising tension and worry about Norfolk's Trial as it begins. After the jury is named, he does not sit as one of the Peers in judgement of Norfolk. But, like most, if not all those present in Westminster Hall, he knows that the *result* of the Trial has already been decided. The witnesses who will be called to testify amounts to a form of window-dressing. Thus even for a high standing Peer of the Realm, like Norfolk, who is accused of the charge of High Treason, there is nothing he could do but wait until a Guilty verdict is pronounced.

Alas, after the judgement against Norfolk is passed, Edward does his best to get the Queen to overturn Norfolk's death Sentence. But this is to no avail. Norfolk is told of the date of his execution and Her Majesty orders a scaffold to be built on Tower Hill. Soon after this announcement, she visits the Tower of London, where all preparations have been made to her satisfaction. Did she have any last words to say to Norfolk?

she asks: "Is she more fluent? Does she speak more beautifully than me? Can she dance more energetically, more gracefully, than me? Is she more talented than me? Is she taller than me?" To these sharp questions, after the Messenger tells Queen Elizabeth that Mary is really taller than her, she would hear no more of this. She thinks of herself as "neither too high nor too low." This, Edward thinks, is another self-flattering assessment of Elizabeth which helps to fill out her personality profile. He would not forget this Elizabeth-Mary, rivalry which excites his historical sense, and increasingly, his literary imagination.

***

As Edward writes more verses and drafts of plays, he lets off steam in the pressure-cooker that is the Royal Court. He and fellow-Courtiers get involved in a fireworks display. Among those enjoying the sparkling, colourful explosions of summer light is the Queen whose pleasure is halted when she receives news from Paris. Suddenly the expression on her face changes from happy and celebratory to serious; then grave. Why?

The news she receives is that a horrific Massacre had taken place on the feast day of St Bartholomew. It happened while the French Royal family, the Catholic House of Valois, were celebrating a marriage to the King of Navarre, who is of the Protestant faith. As more information about the Massacre gets through, Edward learns that about forty eight hours before the killing spree, a few Catholics had tried to kill Gaspard de Coligny, an outspoken Protestant. Catholics, fearing a Protestant backlash; a revenge attack, acted. This led to the Catholic Massacre of Protestants.

The bloodbath claims the lives of four thousand Protestants in Paris; roughly six thousand across France. But not everyone sees the carnage as a tragedy. While Catholics in Europe celebrates the slaughter, King Philip II of Spain, in particular, applauds news of the St Bartholomew Day Massacre as one of the greatest days of his life. For one Englishman, a Protestant, it is all too much. That man is Francis Walsingham, a close associate of Burghley.

Walsingham had witnessed the Massacre. It is an atrocity that must never be repeated, he thinks. He expresses disgust; and vows to prevent such a thing from ever happening in England. To enforce this, he becomes an exemplar: He dedicates his life to ridding the country of Popists. And so, the Catholic-Protestant divide and distrust in England takes a new and dangerous turn: It deepens. And, the already murky water between the two sides gets darker. Protestants in England are shocked, frightened, by the bloodshed. In France, fear leads many people to flee: While refugees (among them, Huguenots) arrive in England, three days after the Massacre, in spite of rising tension between Edward and Burghley, they both remain loyal to their Protestant Monarch, Queen Elizabeth. And, while the St Bartholomew Day's Massacre stops the Warwickshire fireworks, it also provokes an extraordinary response from Edward's pen.

He feels that the effect of the mass murder of Protestants extends beyond France. "I would to God," he writes to Burghley, "Your Lordship would let me understand some of the news which here doth ring dolefully in the ears of every man of the murder of Admiral Coligny of France, a number of noblemen and worthy gentlemen and such as greatly have in their lifetime honoured the Queen's Majesty, our Mistress." He goes on to show some respect to Burghley: "And since the world is so full of tiresome and vile instruments daily to attempt new and unlooked for things, good My Lord, I shall affectionately and heartily desire Your Lordship to be careful both of yourself and of Her Majesty… And blame me not, though I am bolder with Your Lordship than any custom is, for I am one that count myself a follower of yours now in all fortunes; and what shall hap to you I count it hap to myself." To these heartfelt words in a rare expression of deferment, Edward adds even more goodwill to his father-in-law: "Thus, My Lord, I humbly desire Your Lordship to broaden my youth, but to take in good part my zeal and affection toward you, as one of whom I have builded my foundation either to stand or fall. And good my Lord, think not that I do this presumptuously, but that I take Your Lordship's advice as one for whom I would spend my blood and life, so much you have made me yours."

For now, at least, it seems marriage has pulled him well into the Burghley family fold.

The St Bartholomew Day Massacre shakes him into a new awareness which gives urgency to all that he does. After his letters to Burghley, thoughts of the Massacre bothers him. Gradually he works it into his broader vision to include the massacre of the Northern Rebellion. Together, these horrific tragedies, nudges him to face up to the harshness and hard realities of life and living in these Elizabethan times. But to the minuses, there are some pluses, he thinks. As the Queen's Joust Champion, having earlier assisted Arthur Golding in his important work on the *Metamorphoses* and gracing Clerke's translated version of *The Courtier*, Edward becomes a vibrant, blossoming young Courtier. He is the one they all look at. He is aware of his popularity and the noble feelings of Patriotism that surge through him; feelings that are enough for him to pause and take stock of his tendency to be impatient and impulsive. After due consideration, though he errs on the side of caution, he sees these traits not simply as faults, but as helpful.

He feels ready to do big things: but, as he knows, nothing can really happen without the Queen's permission. He petitions Burghley to press her to let him join the foreign Service! "If there were any service," he writes, "to be done abroad, I'd rather serve there than at home. If there be any setting forth to sea, to which service I bear most affection, I shall desire Your Lordship to give me, and get me that favour and credit. But if there be no such intention then I shall be most willing to be employed on sea-coasts, to be in readiness with my countrymen against any invasion."

***

In the wake of the St Bartholomew's Day Massacre, the appearance of more Refugees makes Edward think harder that England is not an island entire unto itself. Though newly-married, he is restless and ready to serve Queen and country. And while he practices self-control, he is not a man who nurses false modesty. He considers freedom of expression, as being of primary importance; and in this, he is more at one with a company of artists and intellectuals than persons who are of a different persuasion. He is also self-conscious; and not one who surrenders but someone who fights for what he believes in. He's been weaned on his father's battlefield stories that form the glorious legacy of the fighting de Veres. He is proud of his Military Service during the Northern Rebellion. Now he asks himself: "How best can I bring my literary art and life together?" Going forward, this question, he thinks, is his greatest challenge: Nothing, he feels, could (or should) restrain him. Enthused by the stories and adventures he'd heard or had read about, like those of the explorer Francis Drake, he looks outward: He yearns to set out to sea, to see foreign lands. He brims with desire, which he thinks are neither sleep-induced, nor idle day dreams. Now, he is no longer a pupil closeted in a classroom: He actively seeks to travel to the land of Ovid's *Metamorphoses* and Castiglione's *The Courtier*, the writers and texts that have moved and guided him thus far, practically and intellectually.

The land he dreams of is Italy: where, more than anywhere else in his imagination, art and life commingles; the country of art and culture that his teachers Golding and Smith had spoken so much about. Golding is a most competent teacher of Latin texts of the great tales of antiquity; but Smith actually lived, studied and worked in Italy. Smith's stories and his experiences resonate in Edward's mind, and now increasingly so: at times they come close to being an obsession. Alas, such thoughts are disrupted by the more immediate demands of married life. Having never lived so intimately with anyone before, this partnership, expected to last for the rest of their lives, proves to be odd; often too much for Edward to cope with. In a word, he finds it tough, as he tries to maintain a stable, well-run household, away from London at his Wivenhoe estate in Essex, one of his father's bequests.

The house he lives in is large and attractive. Of that, there is no doubt. But what was life like in it for Edward and Anne as a couple? Since their wedding, relations between Edward and Burghley have become increasingly tense. In Burghley's view, Edward lives in Wivenhoe like a wild man for whom money is easy to come by. And, by his reckoning, apart from Edward's wanton spending of hundreds of pounds, a matter of much concern is that Rowland Yorke, one of the Edward's Servants, is having a bad effect on the marriage. Burghley alleges that Yorke bars Anne from certain parts of the house like Edward's private rooms, apparently with Edward's consent. This charge further inflames Burghley's mind: He is suspicious of Edward being unfaithful to Anne. He is convinced of the truth of this as now, and in the months to come, the relationship between

Yorke and Edward would become even closer.

Rumours are rife: It is said that Servants are running the de Vere family home like a whore-house. For the Puritan Burghley, such reports about his daughter's marriage is loaded and predictable; akin to holding a red rag to a bull, especially when Burghley hears of women becoming pregnant by male Servants employed by Edward.

In this matter, the strong bond between father and daughter prevails: Burghley naturally sides with Anne whom he notes, dare not object to her husband's outrageous behaviour because the Servants are on very good terms with their Master. But, for his part, Edward denies being an irresponsible employer. He readily reassures his father in-law: "Sith I have been so little beholding to sinister reports," he says, once more reflecting his inexperience, "please know that I have behaved carefully to please you. So, whatever hitherto I have done, or that you suspect me of doing, I *did not* do it."

But though he does what he feels is right, his enemies do their damnedest to put him in the worst light to further blacken his reputation in Burghley's eyes. The difference of opinion, as well as personality, between Burghley, the manipulative Spymaster *extraordinaire,* and Edward, seen as an unruly princely character, is now starker than ever. Already the outlines of a battle of wills has emerged and is becoming more pronounced. Edward is determined not to let the rumours and distortions by his detractors pass without some defence."Though perhaps by reason of my youth, your graver and severer years will not judge the same," he adds, in his letter to Burghley, that he is "hoping for the best in Your Lordship and fearing the worst in myself." In these last words of deference to the older man, Edward behaves with maturity beyond his twenty-two years!

***

He yearns to be free of the familiar activities of Royal Court life. But why is this so when there is so much in his favour? He is handsome, excels in sports and is a nimble-footed dancer, who is well-known at Court. So popular has he become that one Courtier, Gilbert Talbot, informs his father that "The Queen's Majesty delighteth more in Edward de Vere's personage, his dancing and his valiantness than any other. If it were not for his fickle head, he would pass any of them shortly."

So Edward's attractiveness to the opposite sex is cause for admiration. But it is also of concern among his protectors. Burghley's wife brings to bear a woman's intuition to Edward's relationship with the Queen. For Lady Burghley, there is much more than meets the eye of a mere onlooker. She does not hold back; she speaks her mind. As Edward's mother-in-law, she dares to declare that she is not pleased with the Queen's attentions to him. Her displeasure reaches the Queen who, in turn, is offended by the audacious charge of Burghley's wife. To her credit, the Queen is able to deal well enough with the delicate situation; and soon, good relations between the Monarch and Lady Burghley are restored.

But this love-matter, between Edward and the Queen does not go away. After Lady Burghley's response, what does her all-knowing, all-seeing husband think? He knows perhaps far more about the supposed Edward-Elizabeth love affair than anyone else at Court. As the rumours swirl, he turns a blind eye. He keeps away, at least in public, from meddling. But what does his wife know that he doesn't? She is clearly jealous of the Queen's attentions to her son-in-law. And, perhaps this is so because of a love affair between the Queen and Edward, her Lord Great Chamberlain. Their passions rise; and for both of them, such closeness stubbornly remains and looks set to continue for the rest of their lives. Time will tell, as the pen of Edward de Vere moves to test, and attest, to this!

Meanwhile, as Edward's youthful impulses grow wilder, one thing remains steady: His desire to travel to new places. As he continues to imagine traversing over land and sea, the long-held idea becomes an urgent need, dramatized each day by Court boundaries and the strictures of life therein. Though his repeated attempts have been thwarted, he remains hopeful.

But his hope does not mean he is in a state of suspension during which he is idle: His attention is fixed on literature. He'd come to know that the two most talked about books among aristocratic readers are *The Courtier* and *The Prince.* Both are written byItalians: The first by Baldassare Castiglione, the second by Niccolo Machiavelli. Of the two books, *The Prince* has less appeal to Edward. This is not surprising because he is steeped in ideas relating to Mediaeval chivalry and the aesthetic essence of the Renaissance. He sees in *The Courtier* an excellent expression of his own day-to-day life: His own personal ideals of princely behaviour. Not surprisingly, he refers to the book often. Months after Clerke's translation of *The Courtier* is published, Edward learns that his Preface has been well-received by readers. His skill as a writer is steadily improving and boosted by the fact that his Preface is reprinted in later editions of the book. Further confirmation of his excellent work comes from a leading writer, Gabriel Harvey, who pays homage to Edward's Preface: "How greatly thou dost excel in letters," he says. To Edward and all those close to him, there is no doubt that Castiglione is his Muse as he creates characters for his literary compositions.

As time passes, the idea of creating characters based on real life; on an amalgam of experiences, are imputed in the plays.

He remembers his early tutor and uncle, Arthur Golding, who was particularly pleased with the interest that he'd shown in history. Now, he reflects upon his growing sense of things past and finds that it helps greatly, because, in essence, story is driven by time. This way of thinking opens a window for him: Through history he gains perspective, clarity of structure and composition. Another thing that catches his attention is this: He makes a connection between Castiglione and the "Prince of Denmark;" a budding character for a new play he hopes to write. So, Princes and Courtiers are much on his mind, as he re-reads Castiglione's work with even greater interest. He is fascinated by, and fully recognises the basic link between the Princely Courtier, the scholar, the soldier and literature.

So, just over a year after Edward comes of age, he thinks of himself even more seriously as an author. While he writes, he feels these moments of learning; of gaining new insights, are significant turning points. He sees himself as nothing less than a Prince, certainly not a minor or insignificant Courtier in Queen Elizabeth's Realm. From here on, he strengthens his commitment to upholding the Renaissance ideals of beauty and goodness. He looks deep into himself. He makes notes and composes aspects of a character he names HAMLET. From notes he'd taken so far, more and more he sees resemblances between himself and the character, as a rough draft of the play takes shape.

He aspires toward gaining physical strength, courage and Courtliness, as well as acquiring the skill of fencing. But becoming a "sweet Prince" does not mean he is incapable of violent acts: And, in line with progressive Italian thinking, he adopts the appropriate dress style, and other essential Courtier attributes that includes the aspiration of becoming a Musician; and even a Painter. He recalls what Castiglione says about a painter's appreciation of line, form and mass of the external world that are essential in order to achieve greatness. Thus, art and reason, come together. This appeals to Edward greatly, as he considers the beauty of the earth and the people who dwell in it. And so, seeing art and life from another angle, the idealistic Italian author of Courtly life opens Edward's eyes to new ways of seeing himself, art, beauty and literature.

***

A few months after his Preface was published, he spends more time at the large oak desk in his study. His new resolve is to publish, at all cost, an English translation of *Cardanus Comfort* by his friend Thomas Bedingfield. After he'd read the manuscript, he saw a fine opportunity, even against Bedingfield's reservations, to bring to an English audience Gerolamo Cardano's original book *Cardanus Comfort.* He writes a Prefatory letter which is neither verse nor poetry, but Elizabethan prose. In this committed way, the young Earl of Oxford adds his seal of approval to the publication of another literary work. As they collaborate, Bedingfield is not quite as confident as Edward who, from his Essex home, writes to Bedingfield:

"I do confess the affections that I have always borne toward you could move me not a little bit but when I had thoroughly considered in my mind of sundry and diverse arguments whether it were best to obey mine affections or the merit of your studies; at the length, I determined it were better to deny your unlawful request than to grant, or to condescend to, the concealment of so worthy a work. Whereas you have been profited in the translating, so many may reap knowledge by the reading of the same that shall comfort the afflicted, confirm the doubtful, encourage the coward, and lift-up the base-minded man to adhere to any true sum or grade of virtue, whereto ought only the Noble thoughts of men to be inclined. And because next to the sacred letter of Divinity, nothing doth persuade the same more than philosophy, of which your book is plentifully stored, I thought myself to commit an unpardonable error to have murdered the same in the waste bottom of my chests, and better I thought to displease one than to displease many: further considering so little a trifle cannot procure so great a breach of your amity as may not with a little persuasion of reason can be repaired again…What doth avail the tree unless it yield fruit unto another? What doth avail the vine unless another delighteth in the grape? What doth avail a rose unless another took pleasure in the smell?...So you being sick of so much doubt in your proceedings…are desirous to bury and insevill your works in the grave of oblivion…Yet, I as one that is willing to salve so great an inconvenience, am nothing dainty to deny your request."

He closes with these words:

"For in your lifetime, I shall erect you such a monument that as I say…you shall see how noble a shadow your virtuous life shall after remain. Thus earnestly desiring you in this request of mine as I would yield to you in a great manner

Your Loving and Assured Friend,
E. Oxenford."

Edward is honest; his friendship and integrity ennobles the letter. It gives authority to, and shows respect for, Bedingfield's Translation. So interested is he in publishing this work that he overlooks his status as a nobleman and adds his name as "E. Oxenford" which is close enough to: Earl of Oxford! This signature sparks interest from some, and deep concern from those nearest to him. It is as close as he would ever get to revealing himself.

None the less his Prefatory letter is highly praised. It is more than just a gesture from him to Bedingfield. It never condescends: It is intimate, but never familiar; its logic is persuasive, its rhythms harmonious. Overall, it has a gentle and compelling charm; and thus far, all these qualities make the Bedingfield letter a most outstanding, memorable and beautiful piece of writing.The character and qualities of Edward's writings at this time, foretells what was to come! But already, his style is verbal, as well as direct. He commits to memory the words "comfort," "chests," "trifle," and "jewels," for future use. And so, amidst the glowing reception to his "letter," Edward has to pause and seriously think about publishing anonymously, or under a pseudonymn or, as he put it to Bedingfield: "bury and insevill" his literary works in "the grave of oblivion."

So, conscious of the harsh reality for Noblemen writers, he comes to terms with the need for disguise: It is crucial that such writers should not print or publish their names as author. The disguise of the word "Anonymous" or adopting a Pen-name or pseudonym is the more dignified and preferable thing to do.

But for now, in the business of writing and publishing, he urges upon Bedingfield that a printed literary work is the best way "to erect a monument to posterity." His advice to Bedingfield is one more indication that literature and literary ambition have sunk deep into his mind. It is something that he must now face; and make a decision. He has a Plan. It is this: "Whatever I write," he says to himself, "from now on, I would not print or publish under my own name. I would write anonymously. I would use a Pen- name or, pen-names. This, is the only way to ensure that my writings are read. They should certainly not be buried in 'bottom drawers' and thus consigned to oblivion."

From the moment his "Plan" was conceived, he follows it strictly. But even in these early days, he is irritated, even haunted, by the fact that he could not claim his literary work as indisputably his: Edward de Vere's! This is against his nature. It is very hard to accept. To soften the blow of the prospect of either losing or burying his steadily mounting well-honed literary compositions to anonymity, he vows to *insert clues* in his plays and poetry about who he really is: his true identity. And so he wears a mask which shades nicely into this age of spies, spying and codifying things. So while he uses disguise, he inserts a number s of clues that becomes an integral part of the literary tapestry he weaves. What's in a Pen-name? Everything, he thinks: Needs, must!

Having made his decision on authorship and the way forward, he feels freer. Literature is his beacon that lights the way. It challenges him to translate his myriad thoughts onto paper. He rises early; and works at a steady pace all day. The scratchings of quill on paper is a familiar sound-track while his brain directs the formation of words and compositions that fill each page. As blank spaces are covered with inky lines, and the pages stack up, they reaffirm, he feels, the wisdom of making sense of the world through language. His poetic way of doing things, allows a freedom of expression that is natural in him. He experiments with words: sounds and meanings in rhyme, in puns, in rhythm. He edits and writes succinctly, incorporating six-line stanzas lyrically and, each time, more masterfully. Many are gems; others he lay aside to be reworked. But, no matter how well he writes verses, and drafts of plays, mindfulness of the deliberate concealment of his personal identity, never flags. At every turn, he is reminded that disguise is paramount.

***

While Edward dazzles the Court with his intellect,

sportsmanship and dancing, he is ever-ready to fulfil a long held dream. He continues to praise *The Courtier*, and singles out Italy as the best example of European culture; and, once more, he expresses the desire for foreign travel. The fact that he'd never been overseas is not for the want of trying. His attempts, so far, have been blocked. He cannot go anywhere without the Queen's permission."I am twenty three years old," he says to himself. "Surely I am old enough! How long must I wait? Even my best dance moves cannot win the Queen's permission." He stews in disappointment that at times, boils over in frustration. On one such occasion, with utter resolve, he whispers in Lord Seymour's ear: "By heaven, one day, I will steal away!"

***

As Edward's popularity rises, he feels the need for more space. He surveys the London scene and chooses to rent apartments not far from Cecil House. Why this move? He needs to accommodate two people: his employees (or "servants") to whom he is Patron; a patronage that befits his rank and growing literary interests. The occupants of the rented rooms are men of learning and certified literary worth: They are Thomas Twyne and Thomas Bedingfield. Twyne is thirty years old; and to his credit are two works translated from Latin into English; one of which *A Breviary of Britain*, concerns the history and geography of England; the other relates to *The Aenaed*. In his "Dedicatory letter" relating to *A Breviary of Britain*, Twyne acknowledges the "Earle of Oxenforde's" interest in Cosmography, too; and hopes that after reading his book, Edward would be pleased enough to judge his time as being well applied.

In *The Aenaed* Twyne dedicates the Preface to Sir Nicholas Bacon, Anne de Vere's Uncle. Conscious of how much authors owe to each other, especially those who write about classical times, Twyne gives biographical information on Virgil, author of *The Aenaed*. Twyne tells a fascinating story: That after Virgil had made public a few lines of his poetic composition, they had come to the notice of the Roman Emperor, Augustus Caesar, who, moved by what he'd read, enquires about the author. A man named Batillus says the Verses are his! When Virgil hears of this usurpation of his work, he pens the following lines:

"These verses I did make, thereof another took praise.
So you not for yourselves, poor birds, your nests do build in trees,
So you not for yourselves, ye sheep, do bear your tender fleece,
So you not for yourselves, your honey gather, little bees."

Ah, Batillus! What a scoundrel, Edward thinks. How unfortunate: What a misfortune that Virgil should suffer the fate of a bee like Batillus!

Edward could not be more conscious of the restraints he was under as a Nobleman and writer. He is struck by Virgil's thoughts on the honeybee which "gathers its nectar for others to enjoy." Having read what Twyne had written about Virgil's hard luck story, Edward puts pen to paper. Under the heading

"THE EARL OF OXENFORD: To the Reader," he writes:

"The labouring man tills the fertile soil
And reaps the harvest fruit, hath not indeed
The gain, but pain, and if for all his toil
He gets the straw, the lord will have the seed...

The Mason poor that builds the lordly halls

Dwells not in them, they are for high degree.
His cottage is compact in paper walls
And not with brick and stone as others be
The idle drone that labours not at all,
Sucks by the sweet honey from the bee
Who worketh most to their share least doth fall,
With due desert, reward will never be.

The swiftest hare, into the mastiff slow
Oft times doth fall to him as for a prey.
The greyhound thereby, both miss his game we know,
For which he made such speedy haste away.

So he that takes pain to pen a book
Reaps not the gift of golden goodly muse
But those gain that, who on the work shall look
And from the sour, the sweet of skill doth choose
For he that beats the bush, the bird not gets,
But who sits still – and holdeth fast the nets."

As a writer of his own time, the thoughts of Virgil are much like his, Edward thinks. Writing, "the pain to pen a book," he says, is a huge undertaking. After penning the Poem, he had no doubts about the dangers and enormous responsibility of his calling. He knows that being a writer of the kind that he is, and envisages himself to be, would not, cannot be easy. So guided by his unique Elizabethan experience, more and more, he sees himself as both a writer and philosopher.

***

The Duke of Norfolk's Trial and death takes its toll upon

Edward. He is surprised how much the tragedy still unsteadies him. And his proneness to melancholy feelings threatens to, and sometimes overtakes him. The combined effect leads to a period of dithering. Then, he snaps out of the dark place and returns to the light, just before getting Bedingfield's text into print. But naggingly, he is nudged by more melancholy thoughts as he reconsiders his publishing and writing predicament. "That is the dilemma," he says to Bedingfield. "A stark choice: publish under your real name and be damned. Manuscripts and printed texts should be shown to, and read by, only a few of our friends."

There is little more that he can say or do about this core problem for he is at a critical stage in his literary development: "What should I do?" he asks himself knowing he must pursue the course he's set. So, in the wake of Norfolk's death, he writes as much as he could. This helps to calm him; to channel and release pent up feelings. Writing in the gossipy environment of the Royal Court is dear to him. It is a practice that goes way back; that has evolved from his first, tentative grasp of the quill in early childhood. Since then, he'd perfected the use of the pen; and, increasingly, his early love of words and languages that has brought him to this stage of reading Translations from one tongue to another which, in turn, deepens his understanding of both the sounds and meaning of words.

***

Now, as Edward retrieves a bundle of papers from the bottom drawer of his desk, he considers the challenge and practice: The "pain" of penning a book that had brought these manuscripts to fruition. He is impressed by the large bundle of poetry and prose; and vows that they must not be hidden away in the desk drawers and cabinet. He purses his lips and thinks the manuscripts are intended for the public regardless of the prevailing custom and practice of noble writers remaining anonymous. So, already for him, the die is cast: Come what might, he is determined to pursue the art of poetic expression which spurs his intellectual growth. Time and again he urges himself not to hide his poetry, verse and prose, but try to get them read and become known. "There must be a way of getting my writings to the public," he thinks. This is paramount! In this quest, he disagrees with Castiglione who urges Courtiers to hide their prose and poetry from the public eye. As an English poet, Edward is unhappy that English literature is now in such a state that verses are kept in the bottom drawers of desks.

He is so troubled by his literary dilemma that he seeks a way forward. He thinks long and hard: Then he decides to break the unwritten rule and publish Bedingfield's manuscript amounting to many neatly written pages which is before him. It is the final copy of the English Translation of the Italian book *Cardanus Comfort*. Now he waits for his meeting with Thomas Bedingfield. A knock on his office door gets him to his feet. He does not go to the door. "Come in!" he says. The door opens. It is Bedingfield. "Good morning, My Lord," he says.

"Good morning,Thomas," Edward says. "It is good to see you…" Pointing at the manuscript, he adds: "and, to go forward and publish this! Please take a seat." Thomas sits in the nearby chair; and they face each other

"Now Thomas," Edward says, his tone is business-like, "I am going ahead with publication of your manuscript." Bedingfield rises from his chair.

"Thank you, My Lord," he says. He beams with satisfaction.

"Both of our names will appear on the title page," Edward says. And so, after all his pre-meeting thoughts about publishing, he goes against Castiglione's advice to Courtiers not to show around their writings. He separates a few pages from the bundle in his hand. "Here," he says. "This is my Preface to your Translation of *Cardanus Comfort*." Bedingfield smiles. "Ah!" he says. He scans the first line; then he sits and reads. After a few minutes, he rises."My Lord, I am delighted with what I have read," Bedingfield says respectfully. The smile that had appeared earlier, reappears and lingers. "And why not," Bedingfield thinks. His Translated book is confirmed as being good by the best man around! Now, all his earlier doubts about publication begins to disappear.

"As you see, Thomas," Edward says, "I've confirmed what I'd said to you before about the merits of your book. It pertains to that part of the Preface which I hope you like. I refer to the two paragraphs beginning 'Whereby…and so on…' "

"My Lord, it is most worthy," Bedingfield says. He remains standing as he speaks: "A better composition, I cannot imagine. Thank you, My Lord." Bedingfield reads after the word "Whereby" a few more of Edward's lines.

In his "Dedication" of the English Translation of the book, Bedingfield says he'd published the book at Edward's suggestion and insistence. In their relationship, Bedingfield's respect for the young Earl of Oxford is clear. But though Edward's aristocratic bearing as literary Patron, gives to Bedingfield's Translation high status, it is obvious too, how much the book is valued by Edward. Few readers admire *Cardanus Comfort* as much as he does. It is a book that touches the inner recesses of his soul. So Edward's reading of *Cardanus Comfort* is no less impactful than *The Courtier*, that other Italian work. Reading between the lines, Edward is curious about *Comfort's* author Gerolamo Cardano's enterprising, melancholy mind. More broadly, he thinks of ideas arising from the Italian Renaissance and philosophical soliloquies relating to death, sleep and travel. Time and again, he re-reads excerpts from Cardano's book;

and not surprisingly, while he considers death, he continues to think and dream of foreign places. He feels the need, more urgently now, to travel. All the more, as he reflects upon the use of his overall power, influence and aristocratic patronage to get Bedingfield's version of *Cardanus Comfort* published. In his Preface, Edward lays the case for publishing, persuasively. Thus far, he's guided not just one, but two Italian books toward publication in England: *The Courtier* and *Cardanus Comfort.* Now his involvement in these publications are less overt than covert. So while he embraces his commitment to writing: To the public stage and audiences, he knows he must be very wary of the publishing pitfalls.

***

As writing boosts his creative imagination, no less than before, his desire to travel overseas is markedly heightened. He recalls with regret how often he'd been prevented from going abroad by the Queen and, in particular, by Lord Burghley. But soon rumours at Court spread: The talk on the lips of many is that Edward has left London  and is heading to Brussels. Francis Walsingham, Burghley's close associate, is told that Edward and his friend Lord Seymour has gone abroad. Walsingham relays the news to Burghley, who, in turn, writes to Edward's friend, the Earl of Sussex. Naturally as the Lord Treasurer, uppermost in Burghley's mind, is money. How has Edward funded his travels? Burghley speaks plainly to Seymour. He says "Howsoever, My Lord of Oxford be for his own part in matters of thrift inconsiderate, I dare him to be." He reminds Edward of this: "My Lord Edward, always be resolute in your duty to Her Majesty and England." His concern, as Edward's father-in-law, is to be expected. But there is still the core problem: That Edward's absence from England is *unauthorised.*

The Queen, who loves his many talents, not least his dancing, is much closer to him. But now, she is displeased that he has run away! The question both she and Burghley asks is: How do we get Edward back? The man chosen to go and find Edward and bring him home to England is Thomas Bedingfield.

Following the Queen's orders, Bedingfield crosses the English Channel in haste. Two weeks later, Bedingfield and Edward are back in London. After explaining himself fully before the Queen, Edward regains her favour: She pardons him for fleeing overseas without a licence. But he is still seen by Elizabeth and others at Court, as a wayward young nobleman who, having evolved from being a maverick Boy-Poet-Translator to this point, shows he has lost none of his essential nature.

*

At the age of twenty four, Edward passes on to William Byrd, one of his family estates: Battails Hall in Essex. Byrd is a highly accomplished musician: a Composer and organist to whom Edward is drawn because of his love for music. Meanwhile, his and Anne's life together in their Essex house is not happy. Married life is problematic. They must learn how to adapt. Like her father, Anne is less tolerant of many things than Edward. Reckless behaviour is one charge which she holds against a few of Edward's servants whose behaviour is grist for Edward's playwrighting mill. One of them is alleged to have taken money from Byrd; while another had committed murder. These experiences with dodgy Servants and employees Edward keeps in mind for inclusion in future stories.

*

Throughout all the misdemeanours and allegations made about his Servants, Edward strives to reclaim and keep his

Good Name. It seems he inclined towards being a liberal employer. In this, his sense of other people helps. His outgoingness, his social mingling at masques and plays are where he excels. Already, a luminary, he stands out among all others. But, though his misdemeanours are adding up, yet he rises above the ordinary: Overall he cuts a most attractive figure. But, Burghley wonders: Does Her Majesty not see Edward for his fickleness? This is the question he discusses with Walsingham, who has no doubt: He sees Edward as an outlaw poet. Both Spymasters are positively at one, in seeing Edward de Vere as a man to be watched!

But in spite of Burghley's lack of sympathy for Edward's behaviour, he cannot understand the Queen's tolerance. Like many others at Court, she is fascinated, intrigued by the talented Edward. Many at Court are aware of his charm. Edward's growing closeness and alleged intimacies with Elizabeth remains an intriguing question for Court observers. Are they lovers? Or, just friends?

If Edward is mercurial and flighty, there are signs of fickleness in his Queen, too. Their mutually warm relations excites the artistic Edward who recalls that day at Castle Hedingham when, as a boy, he was agog seeing Her Majesty close up. He was dazzled. But now, while he guards their relationship, Elizabeth surprises him: She flirts with another man. His name is Christopher Hatton. He is at least a decade older, and physically, he is taller than Edward. Hatton is also a good dancer; an ability that is a big bonus for him in the eyes of the Queen. But it galls Edward that Elizabeth has nicknames for Hatton. She calls him "lids," "mutton" and "sheep," terms of endearment that fuels jealousy in Edward who does his best to step back and appraise the situation.

He does so with much difficulty. Hatton keeps his distance. And, from hereon, he and Edward becomes rivals for the affections of Queen Elizabeth. As the rivalry smoulders, by the summer of 1573 when Hatton falls ill and travels abroad to seek a cure, he sends letters to Her Majesty. In one of them, he writes "Forget not your Lids that are so often bathed with tears for your sake." Sentimental, but strong stuff! Adding fuel to fire, Court gossip about Hatton's letters makes Edward even more jealous. The best way of responding to "lids's" musings, he thinks, would be through his own pen, which, more assuredly now, is his most lethal weapon. Alas, more writings means once again, considering anonymous publication, and its negative effect on him as a Nobleman-author. Compositions of work done earlier, are now submitted for publication in a new book: *A Hundred Sundry Flowers,* to which he contributes a few verses. This anthology of poems contains contributions by authors who use Latinized pen-names or pseudonyms. "Fortunatus Infroelix," for example, is one of the pseudonyms. Expectation is high, but the publication is short-lived: Ever-vigilant Court officials ends its existence and appearance in bookshops and on book-stands. This has always been the danger, Edward thinks. But he keeps his vow to remain true to himself. He is convinced, the pen is mightier than the sword; and that his desire to write overrides the all-encompassing dragnet of Burghley's network of Spies and Informers.

*

As a married man, running his large household is an ongoing worry, which raises the question of Edward's promised dowry. Almost a year and a half after his wedding, following various leads, he has still not received this overdue payment from his father-in-law. Was this the reason for him running away to Flanders? Who knows? There is no record of him having received a dowry payment. So, while he waits, the matter rankles. And for the avid researcher or seeker of truth, the paper trail ends.

***

Since Edward and Bedingfield had returned to England, Edward has not been free of the humiliation he'd felt, and still feels. What did this journey achieve? His dowry is still outstanding. When will he be paid? he wonders. He's married and in need of money: in particular, his due dowry. Was this the reason why he'd gone to Flanders? And did he come back with, or without, the money that is owed to him? He does not say. Neither does his father-in-law, Lord Burghley, the ultimate keeper of the official archives who places nothing about the dowry on record.

For Edward's detractors, his "fickle head" is not far from the minds of a few Court observers. The French Ambassador Fenelon, reports back to Paris that the Summer Progress continues on its way toward Bristol and the Queen is quite happy that the Earl of Oxford has obeyed her command and has returned to England. That same day, Burghley sends one of his typically long-winded letters to Spymaster Sir Francis Walsingham. In it, he explains and apologises for Edward's actions. "But, overall," he writes, "I am pleased with My Lord, Edward's return to Court." His son-in-law, he says, is a "mixture of contrary affections, although both reasonable and commendable. The one, fearful and doubtful in what sort he shall recover Her Majesty's favour because of his offense in departure as he did without license; the other glad and resolute to look for a speedy good end because he had in his abode so notoriously rejected the attempts of Her Majesty's evil subjects and in his return set apart all his own particular desires of foreign travel and come to present himself before Her Majesty, of whose goodness towards him he saith he cannot commit." What Burghley really, truly feels about Edward is held in check.

For her part, though the Queen is, at least, outwardly reconciled with her unruly Earl, she is not fooled into thinking that he is free of the ambition for foreign adventures. At Court, feelings come to the fore and often, find expression in print. One unsigned letter, penned just over a week after Edward had come back, states that his desire for travel is undimmed, but he dare not seek Her Majesty's favour to satisfy that desire! He must stay put, at least for a while yet. Meanwhile, his attractiveness and popularity in the eyes of the Queen and the Court, draws even more attention to him. For good or ill, he knows he's being watched. And not surprisingly, after years of close surveillance, he feels uneasy about the overbearing closeness of the Cecil family.

***

It is late summer: Lord Burghley holds a Garden Party at Theobald's, his big house in the country. Relations between Edward and Anne are strained, but as a couple they present a united front. On the Party's distinguished Guest List is Margaret, Countess of Lennox, an elderly woman who is fond of telling stories. She is the mother of Lord Darnley, the last of Mary, Queen of Scots two husbands, who was murdered. Edward mills around near the Countess; and soon he is joined by Burghley. "Countess," Burghley says, "Please allow me to introduce you. This is My Lord Edward, the Earl of Oxford. He is now my son-in-law. He is married to my daughter Anne."

"Thank you, My Lord Burghley," the Countess says brightly. Her remarkably strong voice is as clear as a bell. She looks directly into Edward's eyes. Her gaze lingers as she talks. Edward strikes the Countess as a youth who may be receptive to some words of advice. Her wisdom is legendary; unquestioned by many who know her. But, with it comes a tendency to interrogate; to be short with people; even those of high rank. Edward is not forewarned of any of Countess Lennox's habits or characteristics. But, like her, he too is perceptive. He is not put off, at least, so far. If anything, he warms to her. "My Lord Edward," she says, her voice now a shade shaky and high pitched. "And what is your prres-ant ok-you-payshun at Court?" Edward is careful not to say too much. But feeling at ease in the Countess's company, he admits his love for, and practice of, writing Verses, Poems, and recently, two prefaces to translated books.

"Good!" the Countess says cheerily. "Verry good! I hear you ahrre a Poh-it. I hear you write plays too. Young man, is this all really true?"

"Yes, My Lady," Edward says. "It is all true."

"Before I came here, I was told a great deal about you," she says. "I've been told, educating people is important to you."

"Yes, it is Countess."

"That, is verry good!" Countess Lennox says. "We must *edyou-kate*. We must tell our stories. We must record our his-ter-rees and pass them on. Young man, I am pleased with what you say you do." She pauses. Then, she glances to her left side to look at no one in particular. "What else have you written? Are you interested in his-ter-ree?" Countess Lennox's questions are direct. But Edward, unused to such aggressive talk and condescension in conversation, soon comes to terms with it.

"As a writer of Verse and, as you now say, of plays for the stage," the Countess says, "you must come to see me. You may find my family Archives of in-terr-est…" As her voice trails off, Edward is aware of someone standing close by. It is Chief

Treasurer Burghley himself. As the Party's host, he is ready to introduce the Countess to another distinguished noble Guest.

When Burghley leaves, Edward considers the Countess's attitude towards him: "Am I so obviously in need of advice?" he asks himself. Being older and bold, the thing that strikes him is that she had absolutely no doubt as to the potential she saw in him. He considers those few words of talk with the wise, if abrasive Countess, as worthwhile. Following their meeting, Edward thinks about the Countess's invitation, which he'd accepted. He is surprised how much he looks forward to visiting the Countess's family home.

***

The Dos and Don'ts coming from Burghley's office, mainly because of his personality as a Puritan, creates tension between Edward and Anne. For a while they had not been seeing much of each other; and therefore not sleeping on the same bed! Burghley knows this because Anne tells him everything. It is in hope of reconciliation that he throws this big Garden Party, to which comes the cream of English society: England's Nobles and members of the Court. Most importantly, it is the occasion for Anne to meet and reacquaint herself with her husband. For Anne, her father's insistent meddling in her marriage does her no favours. His interference is intertwined with her marital unhappiness. She is anxious to see Edward; to express how she feels about him, to make good the vows they'd exchanged. But Edward is stubborn. He keeps his distance. Anne, in turn, tries to catch his eye. She is desperate to be with him; to be together again! After all, they are still married, she thinks. But Burghley's Party ends with no meeting of minds; no reconciliation, and certainly no meeting of bodies.

Days pass, nothing happens. Anne becomes anxious and

edgy; her sad face dulled and marked by tension. Months of stress has taken its toll: She feels unwell. She makes an appointment to see the Queen's private doctor, Richard Master. Assured by utter confidentiality, Anne tells the doctor what Edward had said to her: "If you become pregnant, it is not by me." Master listens in silence. He wonders about Edward's way of thinking. If indeed, as Edward had said to him, he had not slept with Anne since their wedding day, there was a problem. Did he? Or did he not sleep with his wife?

Meanwhile from far away, Mary, Queen of Scots writes to Queen Elizabeth. She is reported to have written to the Queen saying she'd heard that Edward had not had sex with his wife because he wanted to preserve his association with her as Queen. If this is so, why should Edward be in danger of losing favour with the Queen? The Scottish Queen thinks, like Lady Burghley, that Elizabeth is perhaps too close to Edward. Are they hoping to, or have they already become lovers? Is this just another rumour? Who knows? But there is no smoke without fire. The marital discord and the couple's physical distance and sexual separation is better known at Court than Edward thinks. And, for her part, the Queen (whose closeness to Edward had been a source of jealousy from members of the Cecil family) herself now seems to be aloof from, and unhappy with, Edward's treatment of his wife. After he'd run away to Flanders, and knowing about his earlier violent and bad behaviour, though the Queen has good and warm relations with Anne and Burghley, she is now more wary of Edward. She knows not what she will do next. But for his part, Edward is still itching to travel to the Continent. Anne knows this; and her unhappiness deepens.

***

A few weeks after Burghley's Party, Edward goes to see Countess Lennox. In her spacious home, he is shown several boxes containing letters; and, a large collection of jewels. He is in awe of what he sees. While perusing the collections, he finds in this family archive, a manuscript of the Kings of Scotland. At once, he is stunned.

"Countess Lennox," he says, "this manuscript interests me. May I borrow it?"

"Young man," she says, "of course you can. Why do you think I have invited you here? You ahrre a writer, aren't you?"

"It is what I have been working hard to become, Countess. A writer! It is what I am," he says.

In the silence that follows, he could hear an echo of what he'd said. Now, he thinks, one day I will use this manuscript. I will use it as part of one of my plays.

"And a great writer, I have no doubt, you will become!" Countess Lennox says. For the first time since their encounter, she smiles. "It is good of you to come, young man," she adds. Somehow, she seems livelier now. "I hope the family manuscript will enlighten you. You must come again!"

On his return home, Edward studies the manuscript; and, in his Special Secret Notebook, he sets down a rough structure and notes for a play he hopes to write.

***

After months of worry, Anne's physical and mental health takes a turn for the worse: She gets sick. Her body deteriorates; and for a tense while, it is feared she would die. She becomes so ill that she could neither ingest, nor digest, medicines. On hand to help, is the learned Thomas Smith, who prescribes a potion for Anne. She follows Smith's prescription and regains full health. But how did this come about? The learned Smith is also a practitioner of Paracelsian medicine. He believes in a new way of healing: one based on the teachings of a German doctor named Paracelsus. Smith is no doctor, but Anne believes in him. Ever curious and interested in new knowledge, Edward lends his name as a Patron of the current alternative medicines.

***

Edward's strayings beyond the boundaries of certain Court practices: its conventions and rules, are now seen more sympathetically. He is forgiven; and soon he is back at Elizabeth's Court. So much is he reconciled, it is to his credit that he is able to present Her Majesty with a gift of jewellery containing precious stones. Her Majesty is pleased; and, as if nothing had been amiss before, Edward is again in her good books, so to speak. Then, at last, Elizabeth grants him leave to travel. But why now? Edward thinks. Soon, his assignment abroad is revealed: It is not to be a mere Grand Tour jaunt. The Coronation of the French King Henri III is due within a few days; and what luck Edward has: The timing of his travels is near perfect. Elizabeth needs an English representative to attend the Coronation; an Englishman of intelligence and sensitivity who would tread a fine line, someone who will be careful not to offend French Catholic sensibilities. So, he knows why he is now allowed to go overseas. His Queen needs a competent Courtier-diplomat to undertake the delicate and hugely significant tasks she has outlined.

On the eve of Edward's crossing of the English Channel,

from London, Ambassador La Mothe Fenelon reports to Paris: "I have heard Edward de Vere is about to lead a regiment of soldiers to the Low Countries," he says. "But that has changed: Now he is getting ready to go to Paris. I think Edward, the Earl of Oxford, is a good choice to meet our Monarch. Though he is untried as a Diplomat, I think he would be loyal to both his Queen and the King." Fenelon goes further: "So, all things considered, I would advise that King Henri should treat Edward de Vere with due courtesy, for he is, no less than a staunch upholder of England's Nobility."

***

# IV

## "You have sold your own lands to see other men's"

Before he leaves England, Edward spares a thought for the challenge of the vast distances of travels he is about to undertake. He considers his stake in England; his cherished values and beliefs arising therefrom; the properties of his Inheritance, which leads him to put out a statement ensuring family continuity, namely, that should he die while he is out of the country, his sister Mary and her heirs would possess the bulk of his estates. And though he and Anne are childless, he provides for her too. These matters remind him of his large debts. But that is something which, for now, he puts aside.

Early in February, he finally crosses over to France. As a nobleman, his travelling entourage includes a groom and horses, as well two men to oversee the day-to-day management and security of the expedition. Overall, everyone in the travelling party has a sense of adventure, but also that a huge task awaits them. And so, Nathaniel Baxter leaves London with Edward and the travelling group. They are later joined by two other servants: Ralph Hopton and William Lewyn. Are they men of good character? Perhaps not entirely, for it seems Edward is somewhat inclined towards dodgy persons.

The open sea is a forbidding prospect: choppy waters and cold winds blasts Edward and his fellow-travellers as they sail towards Calais. Then, the moment comes when he lands, and takes his first steps on French soil. He savours these moments before proceeding to the French Royal Court at the Louvre.

"Paris, at last!" he exclaims to Baxter, who regards him closely. Baxter has not seen Edward as excited as this. As Edward strolls around, he likes the city. He breathes deeply, taking in the Parisian air. Later, the big moment comes when he attends the Coronation of King Henri III. Admist the grand Ceremony of French pomp and glory his thoughts are stirred. Having come through the ceremonial rites of his own marriage, he is mindful that Alencon, Henri's younger brother, is being pressed, in a word, groomed, by his mother Catherine de Medici, as a potential marriage partner for Queen Elizabeth.

During the celebrations, Edward mingles. He meets Pierre de Ronsard, as well as Jacques Amyot, Henri III's former Tutor. Edward's interest in literature is now richly rewarded for Amyot is the translator of the French version of *Plutarch's Lives,* which features noble Greeks as well as Romans. It is significant, too, that this is one of the books that Edward had bought earlier in his teens. Amyot had served as French Ambassador to Venice; and now Edward's meeting with the sixty-two year old Scholar, is most interesting.

"Monsieur Amyot," Edward says, "Paris is beautiful. Enchanting. But, from what I've heard and read, Italian cities are also of great renown." Edward feels he could not have been more fortunate than to have met Amyot there and then on his way to Italy. For a while, Amyot remembers the Ambassadorial role that he'd played in Venice. "Ah!" he says. Then, he regales Edward with vivid stories. He suggests a few things that Edward might like to do while he is in Venice.

But for now Coronation-fever spreads as the celebrations proceed. A troupe of Venetian actors perform: Edward's attention is fixed. He watches spell-bound as the troupe enacts something new for him; a sophisticated form of Italian Comedy. "They call it, the Commedia dell'arte," Amyot says.

Altogether, the show is spectacular and fantastical. It whets Edward's appetite for more. He delights in what he sees of this new theatrical and literary means of expression. The audience response to the characters, and their portrayals, in the Commedia dell'arte thrills Edward; all the more so, because it is a dramatic format that melds Comedy with Tragedy. Marvellous! Between the two genres, there is much scope, he thinks. He is especially struck by the character "Magnifico," whom they also call "Pantalone." As the old stingy head of the household, Pantalone is unable to fully control his disunited family, whose behaviour unsettles him. Often mocked, even by his own Servants, Pantalone tries and fails to keep his daughter calm as he attempts to make sense of his money. And interestingly, this Pantalone character is seen as a Venetian Merchant who carries a knife. "Merchant" and "knife" provokes further thought, as many ideas fill Edward's mind: Material, he thinks, for later use.

*

After seeing the Italian Comedy, Edward stays in Paris for a few weeks. He diligently performs his official duties as Queen Elizabeth's representative at the Court of King Henri III. Valentine Dale, the English Ambassador is present when Edward speaks with King Henri and his Queen. "Lord Oxford," Dale writes to Francis Walsingham, Secretary of State, "has spoken with the King and taken his leave with many great words of compliment. He uses himself very moderately and comely. He is well liked as a goodly gentleman." This commendation by Dale is encouraging. Later that day, he goes further: "My Lord speaks well," he says, "his wit and good grace are proper and significant."

So far, it seems all diplomatic doubts are allayed. The

King asks Dale: "Is the Earl married?"

Dale replies: "Yes, Your Majesty. He has a fair lady." Thereafter, Edward meets members of the sinister Medici Valois group, whose members fascinate him. Their presence in the French Court is rich material to be worked into his dramas.

So Edward, the English Courtier in the French Court, cuts a dashing figure. His confidence grows, though outwardly little has changed. He dresses elegantly; and walks briskly: His piercing eyes gives him a look of thoughtfulness and maturity, even at this age. He is now twenty five; and overall, he is not ordinary looking. Being a Nobleman, people of many kinds are attracted to him. He carries himself with the princely dignity of an Earl, and his outlook on life is broad. Having been more or less closeted in Castle and Court, he likes being in Paris where a thriving Bohemian community of artists inspire a sense of openness that gives the city added allure. Any chance for freedom of expression and action, he takes. Dale ensures that Edward not only visit certain places, but also that he meets and speaks with a selected, distinguished few.

"My Lord, Oxford," Dale says, "while you are here, perhaps you should be the subject of a painting."

"A portrait?" Edward asks. Before now, he'd not seriously considered himself to be so portrayed. "Paris, I hear," Edward adds, "has many fine artists, especially painters. Do you have someone in mind?"

"Yes, my Lord," Dale says, "I have in mind an artist from the Lowlands. He is Flemish." After these words, Edward reflects on what Castiglione had said about painting; about form, line, mass and chiaroscuro. And knowing his diplomatic time in Paris is short, Edward says, "Let's do it. Can you make the arrangements?"

"I would be happy to do so, my Lord," Dale replies. He

is pleased his suggestion is so well received by Edward. In turn, the prospect of a painted likeness of the Earl while he is in Paris, excites him. He wastes no time in getting things to move on. He writes to Burghley to let him know of his part in getting a Portrait done.

In his search for an artist, Dale aims high. Having set his sight abroad, his choice is a painter from Flanders. The serious-looking Fleming comes to Paris, and though his meeting with Edward is friendly and respectful, he gets down to work immediately. A few sittings later, the portrait is finished. Edward and Dale appraise the likeness. They are pleased; Edward surprisingly so. King Henri is the next person to see the painting. He likes it. But, what does the painting reveal? What does the Flemish artist see and capture in oils on canvass? How much of Edward, the inner man, is revealed in his outward bearing? His face is sensitive, with few or no lines; his complexion luminous, even feminine. Edward knows of his softer, vulnerable side. To many, including the Flemish artist, the picture is a fair representation. In his absence, Edward thinks of it as an appropriate gift. He sends the painting and two horses to his wife Anne in England.

As it turns out, this is not the only portrait of Edward, as a young man! Just over a year earlier, a painting of him was done! In this portrait, though both the collar and doublet he was wearing are elegant and of the finest quality, the overall composition of his dress sense is out of the ordinary, which matches perfectly the complex personality that he'd already become. This new Paris painting and the earlier portrait bear strong resemblance in that they are a true likeness of the man Edward de Vere (and not someone else!) there is no getting away from the truth for "truth is truth," as his family Motto proclaims. Whatever else may have been in Dale's mind, when he broached the idea of a painting, these portraits of Edward in his twenties are already forming part of the story of the man he is likely to become.

So while he is in Paris, he is immortalized in paint. It is a grand gesture as now he moves on from France to honour his Ambassadorial duties to his Queen and country. Dale's complimentary view of Edward's diplomatic performance as reported to Walsingham is to his credit. Though he could not know of Dale's good feelings about his performance, from the moment that he'd landed in France, his heightened sense of himself as an Emissary of the Queen had added to his desire to excel. After his meeting with King Henri and attending his Coronation, Edward had felt uplifted. Now empowered and hopeful he leaves France to continue his journey.

***

Meanwhile, in England, Anne, realises she is pregnant. When the Queen hears the news, she says: "This is a matter that concerneth my Lord Edward's joy first and foremost. But let me say that apart from my Lord and Countess, there is no one that is, or can be, more happy of it than I am." Bearing in mind their increasing closeness, though the relationship between the Queen and Edward is warm, it is complex; and now it involves Anne! At this moment of realisation, only Dr Richard Master, Anne and the Queen know about Anne's pregnancy. But, as gossip spreads, soon everyone at Court knows.

While Edward was in England, relations between Anne and himself seemed good. What did he know of the possibility of Anne's pregnancy? Of one thing he was sure; and determined to make it known to Richard Master. It is simply this: Should his wife become pregnant, he would not be the father of the child. It was a positive statement that cleared the deck, so to speak, before he had boarded the ship. But why did he make the statement?

Dr Master was surprised by Edward's forthrightness. And now that Anne is pregnant, he recalls the conversation that he'd had with Edward about his potential fatherhood. Silence intervenes between Edward and Dr Master: "If not you being the father of Anne's child," Dr Master said, "who could it be?" Edward's answer was clear: "It would have to be somebody else." That conversation had taken place three weeks before. But, while he was in Paris, on the eve of his departure to Germany, he'd received news that Anne was pregnant. Outwardly, he looked calm; in full control as he digested the message from London. But having declared that Anne's pregnancy would not be because of him, Edward had written from Paris to his father-in-law, Lord Burghley:

"My Lord your letters have made me a glad man... I thank God... that it hath pleased him to make me a father, where Your Lordship is a grandfather. And if it be a boy I shall likewise be a partaker with you,... But thereby to take an occasion to return I am far off from that opinion; for now, it hath pleased God to give me a son of mine own, methink I have the better occasion to travel, since whatsoever becometh of me, I leave behind me one to supply my duty and some service either to my prince or else my country."

Bravely, Edward prides himself in the prospect of fatherhood and is pleased that God hath given him a child. He even hoped it would be a boy: "a son of mine own." Against this family backdrop, Edward's thoughts during his last moments in Paris, relates to what he'd said to Burghley about his French experience and prospects of his travel:

"The King hath given me his letters of recommendation to his ambassador in the Turk's Court," he'd written, "likewise the Venetian ambassador that is here knowing of my desire to see these parties hath given me his letters to the Duke and his kinsmen in Venice, to procure me their furtherances to my journey which I am not yet assured hold; for if the Turks come, as they be looked for upon the coasts of Italy or elsewhere, if I may I will see the military service; if he cometh not, then perhaps I will bestow two or three months to see Constantinople and some part of Greece."

His travel plan is quite an ambitious one, he thinks. But, as he nears Strasbourg, he is excited all over again that he is really, truly overseas; and on his way!

*

Edward and his fellow-travellers journey over flat, as well as hilly, land. Then, at last, they arrive in Strasbourg. Here, at the University, Edward meets a man he'd read much about: Johan Sturmius, a sixty eight year old Humanist and Scholar. As Edward listens to this man, the leading European intellectual of his day, he is mindful of his English tutors. Sturmius is impressive; and Edward appreciates his learning. Being in his presence so soon after meeting the French King, Edward feels privileged; and enjoys a raised sense of self-esteem. Undoubtedly meeting Sturmius is a major milestone on his intellectual odyssey as a seeker of new ways of thinking.

What were fragments of knowledge makes more sense now: understanding deepens, while Sturmius talks. He learns that Sturmius had been influenced by Cicero and Plato. And it is no wonder, he thinks, that Sturmius is nick-named the "German Cicero."

In Strasbourg, Edward makes another important connection: He learns that it was from Sturmius that Roger Ascham had developed his own Platonic philosophy of drama. This relates to an understanding of the belief that Comedies and Tragedies are an imitation; a painted picture of life reflective of all aspects of man. Sturmius's wisdom struck many intellectual chords in Edward. His head brims with new ideas, as he leaves

Strasbourg. In just a few weeks of being away from London, so much has happened: Having had an oil portrait of him, and heading for Italy now, given his new experience, how has it all impacted upon him physically. What might he look like at this time as he travels towards Italy. One of his contemporaries, George Chapman offers this pen-portrait:

> "I overtook coming to Italy
> In Germany a great famous Earl
> Of England, the most goodly fashion'd man
> I ever saw, from head to foot in form
> Rare and most absolute; he had a face
> Like one of the most honoured Romans
> From whence his noblest family had derived
> He was besides of spirit passing great,
> Valiant and learned and liberal as the Sun
> Spoke and writ sweetly of learned subjects,
> Or of the discipline of Public Weals,
> And 'twas the Earl of Oxford."

***

The summer sun warms Edward's back as he makes his way to Italy, the land he'd long imagined while closeted in stuffy rooms, under the tutorships of Thomas Smith, Thomas Nowell and Arthur Golding. Through these men, he'd learned about the great minds and works of Classical literature; of writers among whom are Ovid, Virgil, Cicero, Petrarch, Dante, Castiglione and Cardano. Now, in his mid-Twenties, Edward knows of these writers only as names, authors who had described people, places and scenes in antiquity and more recently, all of which, up to this point, still only exist in books. He thinks particularly of Dante and Machiavelli, Castiglione and Virgil, who have respectively made Florence, Urbino and Sicily famous; and, of the mass of references to the eternal city of Rome, the marvellous descriptions of Venice and the fabled University of Padua (where Smith had studied and lectured), places that he looks forward to seeing!

As he reaches the Alps, high above, he sees the mist-shrouded mountains, near and far, disappear into the clouds. Moving along with his entourage, he gets glimpses of the icy peaks, ridges and spectacular landscapes as he feels the relief of descending to flatter ground. Then, at last, he sets foot on the land called Italy! He knows of it as a country and region that, at this time, is politically, a collection of independent states. But such thoughts are, for now, of little interest to him and his weary fellow-travellers who stop to rest. The place where he stays for a while is called St Gregory's Well; a Churchyard hostel which is beyond Milan's northwestern gate.

Edward follows local custom and continues the final phase of his journey by boat. Going on to Verona from Milan means travelling by canal and interconnecting rivers. The journey between these two cities last several days. But all is not smooth sailing. As he gets closer to Verona, the boat he is in is tossed about by surges of turbulent waters that ebb and flow because of the Adige River.

In Verona, he strolls, allowing himself some leisure through the city; and, as he prepares to leave, he could hardly believe how close he is to the fabled Venice; the city of his imagination. And, from all that he'd read, he learned that Venice is an Emporium of world finance and trade; that it is the birthplace, the generator of a Renaissance of learning, literature, theatre, music and art. The excitement he feels rises as he anticipates entry into the famed city. Soon enough, an Italian accent, proclaims it as: La Serenissima. At last, he makes his final approach to the shore of the Venetian lagoon. As the Italian navigator guides the boat, Edward looks expectantly ahead. Still some distance out, he gets a snapshot of the city; rows of buildings, an amalgam of houses, palaces, piazzas, canals and bridges. It is an island that is home to some one hundred and fifty thousand people, his guidebook informs him. As dusk descends and night falls, the lamplighters had almost completed their work of giving an overall glow to the floating city. How enchanting! he thinks as he travels along the Grand Canal towards his last stop.

After he off-loads his luggage, he goes to the French Ambassador's residence where he presents his papers; his letters of Introduction from the Venetian Ambassador in Paris to the Duke and his Court at the Palazzio Ducale. He is struck at once by the grandeur and splendour of the Palace's rooms and artistic décor. Everywhere he sees statues, murals and paintings by Italian Masters, including Tintoretto and Veronese. Later, he strolls beside the canals: The glittering waterways shimmer and the buildings look magical. It is a wonderful spectacle of glitter and glow; and instead of getting carried away, he knows that all this is no longer an imagined place: What he sees is real. He is in Venice!

*

Early the next morning, and in the following days, he explores the city that is alive with excited chatter and gossip. But the gossip here is unlike that of the gossip at Elizabeth's Court. He hears about the yearly Theatrical Season. And having seen the Commedia dell arte performances in Paris, he learns more about two recently established theatres and Players troupes that form a vibrant theatre community. He attends plays and becomes a student of the Italian theatre. Many ideas, he admits, are new to him. After he'd seen a few plays, he reconsiders their plots and characters. As a playwright, he thinks of new ways of presenting his characters and stagings. He feels he is at a great watershed in his life: That he is at the centre of the creative universe. Amidst this Venetian scene, the very air he breathes inspires him. Art is everywhere. And, theatre-wise, he is determined to learn. Walking on the streets, he is drawn to everything he sees and hears; mostly, the gaiety and artfulness of Venice and Venetian dramatic productions. Combinations of things are foregrounded; and he often stops to make copious notes in his ever-present Notebook. He observes how the Italians mix plots and characters from high and low, rich and poor backgrounds, and juxtaposes the comic and tragic on the dramatic stage; presentations of philosophical musings through artful reason.

Knowing more, now he is able to consider Pantalone more fully in his true theatrical home! He casts his mind back to the great libraries of Sir Thomas Smith and Cecil House, where he'd often imagined these places, scenes and characters as he observes, studies and appreciates the wonderful productions of the Commedia dell arte in Venice. On his way to attend performances at the Public theatres, instead of using the gondolas, he walks. And often, he stops to admire artworks. Not far away from his apartment are two buildings, landmarks to which he is drawn: The Church of Santa Marya Formosa and the Church of the Greeks. These are places of worship, adorned with religious images: paintings and sculpture; art which he thinks, is second to none. Further on, he passes the piazza, St Mark's Square, the Rialto Bridge and the newly-opened theatres. Three weeks have passed; and these places have become familiar.

The time he spends with people in the theatre community brings him in contact with many characters. One of them is a woman called Porsina Padoana. She is a Courtesan. As the curious, ever-questing Earl gets to know Porsina better, he learns that a Courtessina is not an ordinary "Lady of the Night" as is known in England. She is a member of a long and special tradition. As she speaks, her feminineness and foreignness fascinates Edward. He finds her to be a well-spoken and highly intelligent debater. This surprises him; and he says so. "But it shouldn't," Porsina says, "because Courtessinas are often trained: They are schooled as poets, scholars and musicians. It is part of Italy tradition." Edward nods appreciatively, because his hunch is right. He finds that between himself and the Courtessina, there is, at least, a meeting of minds, if nothing else!

*

Not far from Porsina's house is the Jewish Ghetto; a commercial area of great interest to Edward. He hears that sixty years before, the Venetian Senate had set aside an old foundry ("Geto" is the Venetian word for foundry) as a residential district for Venetian Jews. He'd never been so close to so many Jewish people. He knows a little about their story of persecution; and wonders why Venice is so welcoming of their settlement. He remembers what he'd learned from the histories he'd read. After the Spanish Inquisition and expulsion of the Jews, the new thinking of the Renaissance in Europe had led to a cultural reawakening and Venetians were keen to show how liberal they were by welcoming Jews to come to Venice to live and work. This was thought of as the most Christian thing that Christians could do. But, he is told that Venetian Jews were not entirely free to move around: At night they had to wear Special badges which further sets them apart. Because the law had forbidden Jews from joining trade unions (and given that the *Torah*, unlike the Christian *Holy Bible*, favours

Guide on the galley. "How does it become known?"

"The Oracle," the Guide says, "mostly, it takes the form of either a riddle, or an unclear utterance that could have different meanings for different individuals."

Since he'd received the news of Anne's pregnancy, Edward's feelings of fatherhood had changed. He believes the child she carries is not his! And what would she think when she learns of his charge of infidelity against her. With so much doubt and conflicting feeling within, what in his heart of hearts is he expecting on this Greek journey? Some kind of reassurance would help, he thinks. Having come so far, his anticipation rises. Then, at last, he receives a message: It is from the Delphic Oracle of Divine Prophecy. It is not what he expects. His hope for clarity is dashed: The Oracle's verdict is neither one thing, nor the other. In a word, it is inconclusive. He is without the Oracle's reassurance in support of his suspicions of Anne's guilt. His demons gather. And so, as self-doubt festers, his journey continues.

***

From the land of the Oracle, Edward goes to Palermo, the capital city of Sicily. He visits the Duke of Sessa, Spain's official Viceroy to Sicily. He gets on well with the Duke who loves Masques and tilt Tournaments. And, to Edward's delight, he learns that the Duke is also a respected Poet whose friends and associates are accomplished scholars and actors. Edward sees in this man of high military bearing, a fine example of Castiglione's ideal Courtier.

In Palermo, Edward enjoys himself. He attends equestrian sports; and takes part in a joust to honour Queen Elizabeth. After all, he is Her Majesty's Ambassador, her Diplomat abroad. Though his participation in the Tournament is daring, the young Earl, full of ancestral and patriotic pride, feels it is worth any risk. During the Tournament, there is much curiosity among those in the expectant audience. An Englishman in the crowd is moved by what he sees: "One thing did greatly comfort me which I saw a long time ago in the city of Palermo," he writes. "It is a thing worthy of memory. It is where the Right Honourable the Earl of Oxford, a famous man of Chivalry, being then personally present made a challenge against all manner of persons, and with all manner of weapons... and with horse and armour to fight a combat with any Challenger in defence of his Queen Elizabeth and his country. And yet, no man is so brave and hardy to face him, so that in all Italy, he is acknowledged as the only chevalier and noble man of England. This title they give him as worthily defended."

This memory sums up Edward's own sense of Chivalry. His confidence continues to grow, as he proves himself to be truly ambassadorial. After this Tournament challenge, of tilting with lances, the Duke stands and applauds Edward's valour; his bravery and sportsmanship. His respect for the Earl is heightened. That night, he hosts a Special Banquet to celebrate Edward's challenge and spectacular victory. After a toast of congratulation, the Duke says :

"My Lord Edward, I have just come back from Napoli which is part of my jurisdiction. I think you would like it there."

Edward had read many books about the "city in the South" in Italian histories. "I look forward to visiting Naples," he says, "But, of course, it has been a great pleasure being here!"

Before they part company, knowing of Edward's interest in drama and poetry, the Duke says "My Lord Edward, there is an interesting and talented young Spanish poet and writer whom I had met in Naples. He is outstanding. He is coming to Palermo tomorrow. I would like you to meet him."

"Duke," Edward says, "yes, I would like to meet the poet you speak of."

"So far, as a writer, the Poet has gained some prominence," the Duke says. "His name is Miguel de Cervantes. I am so glad that a meeting is possible between the both of you. *I very mach hope so.*" The stress on the last five words, Edward thinks, expresses more than mere hope. And so, Edward's mild expectation of a meeting with the Spanish writer, rises to interested curiosity. Already a talented novelist, Cervantes had served under Spanish Commander, Don John, in the Battle of Lepanto. That bloody conflict had left him nursing an injury: For a while, he'd been unable to use his left hand. But now, four years later, it is summer, the season when Cervantes ends his military service with honour. His immediate plan is to go to Palermo and visit the Duke, then return to Spain to continue his interrupted, and most promising, literary career. Edward is two years younger than Cervantes. As an astute judge of character, the Duke's hunch is an inspired one. He thinks the time is right to bring these interesting young men together.

The next day, Cervantes arrives. After the Duke introduces him to Edward, Cervantes speaks for a while about his poetry. He does so in an open unselfconscious way with characteristic energy and the expressive use of his hands and arms, Spanish style. Then, he discusses, at length, his ambitious new book.

"My Lord," he says to Edward, "It is a work of fiction. I have been thinking about it for quite some time. Even in the heat of the Battle of Lepanto! I'd wondered often if I'd live to write such a book."

Such sustained thoughts, Edward thinks, says much for the strength of the *idea* behind the book!

"One of the characters in my new work," Cervantes continues, "dreams of being a Knight of sorts. But," he pauses and takes a fresh look at Edward. "You are a real Knight of the

Realm from Queen Elizabeth's Court. I have heard of your victorious performances at
the tilt Tournaments in England, and, your appearance and challenge to all-comers here in Palermo. Bravo Senor! Congratulations, My Lord."

"Thank you, Senor Cervantes," Edward says. He is pleasantly surprised by Cervantes ability to speak English so well. But to avoid being misunderstood, he speaks slowly and uses the best Spanish pronunciation he is capable of.

"I am interested to hear more about your new work," Edward says. And he listens intently as the Spaniard speaks with passion about his writings; in particular, about his new story. Then, as curiosity gets the better of Edward, he intervenes: "And what might that 'ambitious new book' be?"

"It is at an early stage of development. It is in my mind, much more than on paper. But soon, I will begin to write the story," Cervantes says. "I've been told about your outstanding horsemanship; about your great success at tilt Tournaments. Those who have seen you on a horse are amazed by your ability. No one was able to unseat you from your horse. Your challenge to all comers in Palermo was brave and courageous. You are truly a man of Chivalry, My Lord. As a Knight on horseback you faced many opponents whom you combatted with your lance. I am curious to know more about this sport of Chivalry and honour. My Lord, you are the Champion tiltsman of England and now of Palermo, too, I'd say."

Edward glances at the Duke who gives him the nod. He explains the English tradition of Noblemen, Knights, tilts Tournament and gallant displays before the Queen and Fair Ladies: A tradition of Chivalry and Honour. He is proud of his heritage and pleased to explain this way of English life now to Cervantes, a man of high class and good breeding himself, who takes note.

"Thank you, My Lord," Cervantes says finally. "I am thinking of writing as the main character of my Spanish story about a man, sitting on a horse who approaches and is ever tilting at things, real or imagined, on his travels as he journeys through life."

While Edward the essential Courtly Traveller is in Palermo, he feels fortunate to have gained the experience he has from which he could draw upon later. "This is a good time," he thinks for both himself and Cervantes as young writers. They are on the brink of their writing careers. As Cervantes talks about his novel, Edward thinks about writing more plays.

And so, by the end of that summer in Palermo, Edward de Vere, the Seventeenth Earl of Oxford, is seen, certainly by Cervantes, as a chivalrous visionary who fears no one: He is always ready in the name and honour of Queen and country to tilt against any Challenger. Cervantes's power of observation, on the other hand, is such that after leaving Palermo, he begins to transform his own adventures into fictionalised works: novels and plays.

***

Edward leaves Palermo and travels to Genoa, via Messina. Genoa is a City-State that is engulfed by feuding between its nobility (supported by Spain and the Pope) and the ambitious lower classes who resents their hold on power. As a Nobleman, Edward sides with the Genoese elites and their Spanish defenders, led by King Philip II's bastard brother, Don John, who commands the Spanish military presence in the city.

Alas, the travails of travel in Italy takes its toll on Edward. He is exhausted as he moves from place to place on his costly Grand Tour. Soon, he realises how quickly the money he'd brought with him had been spent. While he is in need of financial help, he'd written and sent letters to his wife and father-in-law, Lord Burghley. But, on his return to Venice, he learns that the letters are still in Italy. Delivery could not be made because of the out-break of Plague.

To lessen his disappointment, Edward receives two letters from Burghley. In one of these, Burghley announces that Anne has given birth to a daughter named Elizabeth. So, whatever thoughts and doubts he had had about his paternity, the hard reality is that a baby was born to him and Anne. Parenthood has come! This news unsettles him as a wave of doubt overtakes him, all over again. He wonders about Anne's child; and the pregnancy of which he is now in denial. After reading the letters, he writes again to Burghley. He explains why his letters could not reach England; and makes an urgent request for money to pay a debt of five hundred crowns that he'd borrowed.

He suggests to Burghley that he would repay him with money received from the sale of some of his estates. In other words, he is selling his lands to see other men's! This matter relates to a letter that he'd posted in Venice, which was addressed to Burghley: "My Good Lord," he writes, "I have been grieved with a fever; yet with the help of God now I have recovered the same and I am past the danger thereof, though I had been very weak and hindered from travel which grieves me most. I fear my time is not sufficient for my desire. For although I have seen so much as sufficeth me, there is more that I feel I must do! Your lordship is desirous to know how I like Italy, what is mine intention in travel, and, when I mean to return. For my liking of Italy My Lord, I am glad to have seen it, and I care not, ever to see it anymore, unless it be to serve my prince and country. Thanking Your Lordship for your good news of my wife's delivery, I recommend myself unto your favour…"

So far, Italy has not disappointed Edward: He has seen a

number of unusual, magnificent and picturesque places; and, had met a number of extraordinary people. But although his sickness has stopped him from seeing more, to appease Burghley, who is inclined to think that being away so long in the homeland of the Pope is a temptation for him to become a Catholic, Edward does not declare his *genuine love* for Italy. Instead, he decides to keep his feelings, his desire to see more of the country, to himself. He tells Burghley not to expect any more letters. And though he refers to the birth of Anne's child by "thanking Your Lordship for your good news of my wife's delivery," he does not really believe the child Elizabeth is his. Her conception is a mystery to him.

***

## V

## "You look so strange upon your wife"

*"God hath given you one face, and you make yourself another."*

Edward returns to Venice. Cold swirling winds blasts the buildings and disturbs the glistening surface of the canals. He feels nauseous. Bubonic plague spreads; people are quarantined. The death toll rises; and there is great alarm as a growing number of "Lanterns of the dead" appear. But rising above the doleful cries, there is an abundance of creative energy and creators, who are hopeful as they give expression to life through their calling. Titian, a painter and artistic celebrity of his time, lives and works near the Grand Canal. Fresh from having sat for his portrait in Paris, Edward visits Titian. He learns fast about art and the artistic life from this Master practitioner. Not just drawing and perspective, but the mixing of paints, the melding of colours and the different ways of applying paint (brush strokes) on canvass. Titian is a celebrated man. He moves easily among the people at the highest echelons of Venetian society. Everyone, who is anyone, either know him or has heard about him. He has painted Popes, Cardinals, artists, philosophers, Dukes, Kings and so on. Edward's interest in history: In the people and places of times past, adds immensely to his growing understanding and appreciation of the world of Titian, and Venice.

In Titian's painting of Ovid's *Metamorphoses,* he portrays the Classical lovers Venus and Adonis, not as a love affair of equal intensity on both sides, but as one in which Venus is more interested and passionate than Adonis. By so doing, Titian had unknowingly planted the germ of an idea in the mind of Edward who on seeing the picture, hopes to use poetically.

Another artist from whom Edward learns is Titian's friend, Julio Romano, whose work inspires ideas for Edward's poems and plays.

***

On the rest of his travels to other Italian cities, Edward experiences unforgettable moments and records what he sees and feels. Throughout the fourteen months in Italy, he has had much on his mind, but he leaves the country in relatively good spirits. When he reaches Paris, he is told of spreading rumours at Court that he is a cuckold. This adds to his doubts about Anne's pregnancy. He feels the blood rising to his head. He is unhappy; and would have been even more so, if he knew what only Dr Master, the Queen and Burghley knows about Anne's pregnancy: What do they know? For one thing, soon after Dr Master had seen Anne, he'd hastened to contact Burghley. "Her Majesty has asked me how the young Lady did bear the matter," Dr Master had written. "I answered that she kept it secret four or five days from all persons and that her face was much fallen and thin with little colour. That when she was comforted and counselled to be gladsome and so rejoice, she would cry. She would say: 'Alas, alas, how should I rejoice seeing that he that should rejoice with me is not here.' And, bemoaning her case, would lament that after so long a sickness of the body she should enter a new grief and sorrow of mind."

Dr Master adds: "At this, Her Majesty shewed great compassion. In turn, I repeated my Lord of Oxford's answer to me which he made openly in the Chamber of Her Majesty namely that if she (Anne) were with child it would not be his!"

Summing up the matter, now Dr Master says that "the Queen showed herself openly to rejoice. And in great offence with My Lord of Oxford, she repeats the same to My Lord of Leicester when he came to see her." If Edward had known all of this, his rage would have been greater. Nonetheless, now as he crosses the Channel on his way back to England, a fusion of rising anger, doubt and suspicion befogs his mind.

***

Back at Court, Edward's sensitive side is unusually disturbed. He is touchy about any loss of Good Name. Doubts, as rumour spreads, prompts him to ransack his memory while thoughts of Anne's unfaithfulness grows. On landing in England, he has no intention of seeing Anne. He distances himself from her. And for those who see him as a jesting Courtier, this is no laughing matter. So, with France, Germany and Italy behind him, as he tries to fit-in with Court life, once more, he finds any attribution that Anne's child is his, questionable.

Already, one Courtier, Lord Henry Howard, is especially keen to discredit him; and thereby, turn the Queen against him. This is hurtful for a man as proud as Edward is. So, while he is being laughed at all over London as a cuckolded husband, like an automatic switch, the impulse to write becomes urgent. He thinks of the many Italian productions he'd seen, as he drafts plays, using plots and characters based upon people that he'd met and places he'd seen in Italy and elsewhere on the Continent. But, his emotionally unsettled state is no bar to his literary creativity which thankfully is not confined: Like breathing, he feels free to explore; to compose from experience the essential ingredients that forms the foundation of his dramas. No one should escape his pen, he believes. And so through hard work and the bonus of the calming, therapeutic effect of writing, aspects of his life becomes clearer: For example, the cold fact that his father-in-law, Lord Burghley, is a man who stands for almost everything his father Earl John was not.

As time passes, the triangular relationship between Edward, Anne and Burghley breeds unmistakeable uneasiness. Anne, Edward feels, is less of a wife and more a dutiful, obedient daughter overwhelmed by her father. Edward does not like Burghley's meddling in his marriage. He'd been feeling strongly about this for some time, even before he'd left for Italy; and now it festers. But as tensions persist, he feels glad; enriched and refreshed that he'd gone overseas: And interestingly with the tensions comes new energy: He admits that the months in France and Italy have transformed his way of seeing himself and England. Whatever else is going on in his life, as Queen Elizabeth's diplomat, his mission abroad had been successful. Now he is full of new thoughts and ideas. But human frailties and how he is seen by others gets in the way: His charm and outstanding sporting and intellectual abilities, the source of envy and jealousy among his peers, are abundantly clear. This leads to contention; and observing from the side-lines, Burghley is not pleased. He notes how exposed Edward is to the unforgiving Courtiers' gaze, because he is seen for what he really is: hugely talented. But alas, in him the elements are mixed; and therefore, his critics use it like a whip to beat him. "He is also unstable, fickle, wayward, passionate, financially extravagant and proud," they say.

He reflects that months after the child was born, Burghley, as chief Official Recorder of events and gossip in England, had written that Edward had confessed to Lord Howard that he did not sleep with his wife Anne; and that her child, born in July, could not be his because it was less than the duration of a full twelve month period of pregnancy. So timing, the fire of anger and a sense of betrayal by Anne burns fiercely within Edward. This propels him to make up his mind: "I cannot, I must not, live with Anne," he says to himself. "She is an object of derision, of jokes, of tittle- tattle." The shame of it, is barely bearable. He is further disturbed by the attentions of the Queen, who regards him highly as her Lord Great Chamberlain of England. So far, he feels he'd served her well: To the best of his ability: at home and abroad.

The appointment, he thinks, is a fitting and just reward. Since boyhood, when he first saw Her Majesty at Ipswich and more closely at Castle Hedingham, she has always been around; a towering figure, the omnipresent, omnipotent Queen. Such is her power! But interestingly, though he would never admit it to anyone, secretly, at no time has he felt "lesser" than her. He remembers his father Earl John telling him about his family's pedigree and contributions as staunch defenders of the Realm. They were one-off brave fighters: Unique, true heroes: English King-makers. Of this, no one knows more than Queen Elizabeth.

So the coming together of the young Earl and the Queen has been positive. She likes him; and he is dazzled by her beauty, learning and charm; by her love of fashion, literature, masques and staged plays. Elizabeth, at this time, sees Edward as a rising star; the one most deserving to be at the top of the pecking order of eligible men around her. He is her handsome Courtier; her Emissary who had gone to foreign lands and, had brought back with him a fine present for her from Italy. The learned Queen is deeply touched. How thoughtful of him, she thinks. His seeking, finding and returning with the rarest of exquisite gifts: a pair of perfumed gloves trimmed with four tufts, or roses of coloured silk. The presentation of this gift to Queen Elizabeth is a major moment for Edward.

Fashion conscious Nobles look on as she takes great pleasure in showing off those gloves in public.

Soon the gift becomes known as "the Earl of Oxford's perfume." In fashion, like Edward, Elizabeth inclines to the exotic. She cherishes Edward's gifts which draws them closer. Togetherness breeds rumours. And the chemistry between the young Earl and the Queen is evident. An observant Courtier went as far as to confide in one of his colleagues: "Elizabeth, I feel positively sure," he says, "is as much in love with Oxford as she is capable of being with anyone. And if he does not openly reciprocate, it is because he can't. Protocols dictate. So, he pretends, just like a few other besotted hot-headed Courtiers."

It is morning. He sits at the desk in his study. Before he begins work, he leans back in his chair, closes his eyes and thinks of his experiences with women. His relations with the Queen are close, but his wife Anne, still has a strong hold upon him. He knows how much more she loves him than he loves her. She has angered him; and he has put distance between himself and her. Now he thinks of how deep her love is. He thinks of such feelings as the raw, real stuff he imputes into his art of writing plays. As time passes, he considers the Queen as a possible real life parallel for one of his characters. Now with quill in hand, he is about to begin his compositions. He stares at the ceiling as his inquisitive mind formulates thoughts into print. He writes not just lyrical poems (six stanza lines!) but drafts a new play about love as an ongoing, problematic theme that runs through the story. And more and more, he experiments, combining elements of the real with the imagined: life with art.

*

Edward's Italian adventures are vivid. They speak powerfully to him: All that has happened and ideas arising therefrom, jostle for attention. How could they be used to form the basis of a new play that he had been thinking about to the exclusion of everything else.It is a story which he had read titled: *The Tragicall Story of Amleth.* He thinks: "How can I use it?" he asks himself. "How can I write my version of a play from the story of Amleth?" Good questions, he thinks. And as the idea takes greater hold, he writes copious notes and drafts for different compositions which generates further thoughts as his working day ends on an artistic high: He rises from his chair, opens the door of his study, steps out and closes it.

***

Since his return from Italy, as rumour of his marriage problems circulates at Court, Burghley pays much attention to one of Edward's Servants; a man named Roland Yorke. He thinks Yorke is whispering things in Edward's ears: The cuckoldry idea that is aimed at turning him against his wife, Anne. For his part, Edward does what he can to play down the divisive rumour. He tells Burghley not to worry. But already things have gotten out of hand; the matter has become a scandal that engulfs him and Anne. Once rumours take hold at Court, as Edward knows, they do not just disappear or go away easily.

Amidst all the ensuing unpleasantness, Burghley invites Edward to come and stay at Cecil House. But after the freedom of travelling far and wide; and having experienced extraordinary things over the past seventeen months, being under the wary eye and close surveillance of his father-in-law is not an option for Edward. He decides against Burghley's offer. Instead, he lodges at Rowland Yorke's house. Burghley feels let down as the question of paternity gets out of his control. He dislikes nothing more; and turns to confiding his thoughts to the Queen in a typical, long-winded letter; a Burghley trade mark. He feels he and his daughter are wrongly accused and abused: And he hopes, as he says to the Queen, that "in anything that may follow, I may have Your Majesty's princely favour to seek my just defence for me and mine."

In the midst of the accusations that go back and forth, Burghley invites Sir Thomas Smith to visit him in his office. On the day that he is due to meet Smith, he sits at his desk working on various documents: Slowly, deliberately, he weeds out some and keeps a few; vastly more "out" to be destroyed than those he keeps! This is his approach to Official Record keeping. Thus he regards documents that would see him in a favourable light by generations to come as being of paramount importance!

As he riffles through the papers, he scans a document which deals with his expenses. A knock interrupts his concentration. He rises and opens the door.

"Sir Thomas," he says, "It is good to see you." His voice is even and pleasant. He is on the brink, but stops short of adding his thoughts on how well the scholar looks. "Please take a seat, Sir Thomas."

As Smith settles in his chair on the opposite side of the desk, Burghley returns to his place. Now he observes Smith more closely: His eyes express alarm. "You have lost much weight, sir!"

"I have my Lord, as you see," Smith says. "I've been coughing much too much of late. My medical knowledge, good as it is, leads me to try many remedies…" He pauses.

Burghley thinks Smith looks quite disappointed with himself. Is he irritated because he coughs repeatedly? he wonders. Then, Smith break the silence. "Eventually," he says,

"I went to see my doctor…"

"What did your doctor say?" Burghley asks.

"My health is much impaired, my Lord," Smith says. His

voice as he speaks the last two words, quickly fades into a hoarse whisper.

"My condition is getting worse." He coughs. "I have throat cancer, my Lord. My doctor says I'm in the final stages of the disease."

Both men are silent. Then, to Burghley's surprise, Smith says, "My Lord, I have heard the rumours. My physical pain is heightened by the emotional anguish I feel for your family: For your good self, for the Earl of Oxford and for his dear wife, Countess Anne. I very much grieveth for the love I bear your son-in-law Edward, because he was, as you know, for a time as a student, brought up in my house." Smith pauses. Then, with a pained expression, he says: "What counsellors and persuaders he hath around him to so behave, alas, I cannot tell." Smith is not the only observer who feels that Edward is being persuaded.

After Smith leaves, Burghley notes in his Diary: "Lord Edward is not able to resist the enticements of certain lewd persons which makes him a stranger to my dear daughter, his wife. Rowland Yorke, the same unruly Servant who had upset Anne when he'd prevented her from entering Edward's private rooms, is the lewdest person that is likely person to lure Edward away. He is the dishonest poisoner. The one who deceives Edward."

Yorke is not lacking in self-aggrandisement: He is fearless, audacious and sexually aggressive in the company of women. Slowly but surely, he's worked his way into Edward's affection. So now Edward chooses to stay at Yorke's house after returning from his travels in Europe.

***

After his experiences abroad, Edward's understanding of the factions in Elizabethan England is much deeper. Two of the most powerful are the Leicester and Cecil clans, who compete for Royal favours; and so doing their plans include dishonouring and destroying each other. They are power-hungry, dodgy people; and the questions that Edward face now are: Whose side is Yorke on? Is he a faithful Servant? Or, is he an Agent working for the Earl of Leicester's faction?

Whilst Yorke stirs up things, Edward turns to his father-in-law. He addresses what he calls his "mislikes." He writes: "By your letters to satisfy you the sooner, I must let Your Lordship understand this much." And hereafter, he takes a principled stand, adding: "That I am not touching my wife nor do I accompany her. Some things that otherwise discontent me, I will not blaze or publish until it pleases me. And last of all, I mean not to weary my life anymore with such troubles and molestations as I have endured nor will I, to please Your Lordship, discontent myself. This might have been done through private Conference before and had not needed to have been the Fable of the World if you would have had the patience to have understood me. But I do not know by what or whose advice it was to run that course so contrary to my will or meaning – which made me disgraced, the world raised suspicions openly that with private conference might have been more silently handled, and hath given me more greater cause to mislike." This letter exposes the rift: Edward's voice is firm, eloquent and expressive of a man shaken and offended. It is one thing to feel a private and personal sense of embarrassment at the Countess of Oxford giving birth to, for all Edward knows, a bastard. But such an allegation sits badly with him. It renews the accusation of bastardy levelled against him. The shame of it, he feels sharply. It is an awful blemish on his character. And while illegitimacy among aristocrats is not unheard of, as Edward puts it, Burghley, rather than keeping things quiet and private, hath made of this crisis of

estrangement from his wife, something far more:
"*the Fable of the World!*" By so doing, he makes matters worse.

The ever-present tension between Edward and Burghley rises. And from here on, Edward tries to reclaim his family's name. Who is right? Who is wrong about the marital breakdown? Edward or Burghley? To be fair, both are alarmed by it. For his part, the interfering Burghley is keen to defend the honour of his beloved daughter's fidelity: her devotion to her husband. On the other hand, Edward keeps his silence. While the uneasiness between Edward and Burghley becomes palpable, neither man is at his best: Burghley is anxious and unwell; Edward is weary, still exhausted from his incredible adventures and narrow escape from death. But the more deep-seated issue between Edward and Burghley is that they represent opposites: like chalk and cheese. Would they? Could they, respect each other's differences? That is the basic question. Time will tell. But, for now, there is a glimmer of hope that they would address the divisive matters that would bring a shift; maybe even some positive change.

Soon after he'd sent his letter, Edward meets Burghley face to face. He is defensive about charges made against him. Thus he is very careful to preserve for posterity his side of the story. But Edward is stubborn, even bullish. He accuses Burghley of meddling in his affairs; of communicating directly with his servants, for instance, while he was away in Italy. Why the interference? And, are Edward's claims true? He contends that at times, Burghley had left him without enough money; and had shown a letter written by him to Queen Elizabeth with the aim of setting her against him. But that is not all: He sees Burghley as a stirrer; a man who not only makes trouble for him as at Wivenhoe; and someone who thinks badly of him. But Burghley denies that he is mean with money. In his defence, as Chief Treasurer, he says he'd been generous, having given over two and half thousand pounds of credit to Edward, when money was scarce. "So, is this 'credit' a special dispensation from Burghley?" Edward asks himself. "Or, is it my rightful due?"

***

Edward uses experience as the basis of each line of lyrical poetry; and increasingly, the characters and plots of the plays he writes are combinations of people and events in real life. He is twenty six years old, and following his birthday, he looks forward to the year to come, which promises to be eventful. But though he is hopeful, as he moves around, he is beset by doubts: He is unable to forgive Anne; and being suspicious of her meddlesome father the trauma and shame he feels continues.

But imbued with a new post-Italy awareness, he spends his days writing like a man possessed. His immediate concern relates to the dramatic and traumatic events of the year past. He is infected with a sense of well-being and optimism which is the start of an intense and interesting period of playwriting. He accepts that doubts about his wife's unfaithfulness and his reactions are distressingly real. They are not founded on idle thoughts and suspicions. The fact that the Queen's Physician, Dr Richard Master, had written to Burghley, saying that a distraught Anne had tried unsuccessfully to get him to perform an abortion just a week after Edward had left for Italy gives credence to Edward's feelings. It is just as well that he knows nothing of the Physician's letter. "My lady of Oxford being with her at Shrovetide," Master had written, "had dealt with me to prepare some medicines and menses promotions to cause the menses to resume. I counselled her to stay awhile." Of this, Dr Master informs the Queen. He then tells Burghley that "Her Majesty asked me how the young lady did bear the matter. I answered that she kept it secret four or five days from all persons; that her face was much fallen and thin with little colour, and that when she was confronted and counselled to be gladsome and rejoice, she would cry: 'Alas, alas! How should I rejoice, seeing that he that should rejoice with me is not here,' and to say truth, I stood in doubt whether I should pass judgement upon myself and, the pregnancy." How much more hurtful and doubtful would Edward have been had he read Anne's and Dr Master's words.

So four months after conception, as her slim body swells, once more Anne had sought the help of Dr Master. Being with child reveals the truth of the closeness between Edward and Anne. And a few things are clearer now, after his return from Italy: Either, he is father of Elizabeth, Anne's daughter or, the possibility that his suspicion then (as now) is the truth. But Dr Master's letter raises other questions: How little known is Anne's meeting with her doctor? And why the medical query? Because someone, other than the Queen, must have known, news of Anne's pregnancy, and doubt about Edward's paternity were carried across the English Channel to Paris where a whisper into Edward's ear had grown louder each day; so much so, that he'd returned home agitated: in a state of rage and unhappiness.

***

Troubled and distrustful, moving around London, he is more wary of people; particularly those at Court. As he settles in the home of Rowland Yorke, the man who becomes his confidante, nonetheless Edward feels an aloneness akin to being abandoned, not unlike the time when his mother had remarried soon after his father had died. In recent months, thoughts of Earl John had been resurfacing often. With so few people to turn to, he trusts the boastful Yorke, more than anyone else now. He listens to what Yorke says. Yorke, in turn, likes being a clever chappie and is keen to impress Edward. He casts himself as a source of rumour and gossip arising from the Court. He remains the prime suspect and instigator of the defining crisis in Edward de Vere's life. Is Edward naïve? And did Yorke know Edward so well that he sees him as a jealous man who could be swayed?

As Edward's marriage goes from bad to worse, the person at his side is Yorke. Anne continues to complain to Edward about Yorke as she'd done before. But as Edward and Yorke's friendship- relationship thrives, Anne becomes more distant from Edward. So is Yorke, in part, at least, really the instigator of the Edward-Anne marriage crisis? This is not a question that Edward asks himself right now. But one thing is clear: In these tricky months of marital discord, Yorke is always in close attendance. As the Edward-Yorke's relationship develops, Anne becomes even more absent and distant from Edward.

Living apart from his wife, Edward's feud with Burghley gets worse. Ever-suspicious, as befits his character, Burghley records almost everything to do with his son-in-law. He unfairly highlights Edward's unkindnesses; charges that are grievous for Edward. Such untruths persist in secret letters and reports passed to those of the highest ranks. Being privy to everything about the nobles in her Realm, the Queen calls time: She pleads with Edward to go back to his wife. But this is a forlorn hope. Edward has no intention of seeing Anne; and now he vents his anger to Burghley: "I understand that your Lordship means this day to bring Anne to the Court," he writes, "and that you mean to prosecute the cause with further hope. Now if Your Lordship shall do so, then shall you take more in hand than I have or can promise you. For always, I have and will still prefer mine own content before others, and observing that wherein I may temper or moderate for your sake, I will do most willingly. Whereof I shall desire

Your lordship not to take advantage of my promise till you have given me some honourable assurance by letter, or word of your performance of the condition – which being observed, I could yield, as it is my duty to Her Majesty's request and bear with your fatherly desire towards her. Otherwise, all that is done can stand to none effect."

***

As time passes, Edward commits himself to do what he must. He decides and insists that "Always I have, and will still, prefer mine own content before others." But then, he admits to a compromise, on one condition: Only if the Queen orders him to do so. So far, he thinks, she wishes a reconciliation. But, she has neither expressed nor ordered it. And though Burghley's power over State affairs leaves him free to do almost whatever he likes, even he could not command his son-in-law to do his bidding. Nonetheless Edward feels under attack. The barriers are many. He feels hemmed-in on all sides. And, once more, he recognises that his travels abroad have been instructive. He'd been in sticky situations before, but nothing quite like this. He responds positively by exercising his freedom of mind through the art of writing.

Following his Italian adventures, he continues to write with more purpose, urgency and passion. He is bolder; more creative. Many things are clearer now. He sees a bigger picture. He sees where he is: even through the fog of unforgiving anger; and he sees the huge importance of the Court where the power of stories is paramount in enabling the Queen to rule as an enlightened and enlightening Monarch. Story-telling through plays and masques delights her, especially during the Revels Season around Christmas each year. *The play is the thing*. And,

Edward is mindful that the Queen is in Command. So given that dramatic stories commands the Queen's attention and the Queen is the person with ultimate power in England, his blossoming talent as a lyrical poet and dramatist, he thinks, could enable him to release and realise his poetic potential! Such thoughts insistently nudges him forward. But, admitting that he is more unsettled now than ever, he takes a broader view. He thinks more deeply about relationships and the meaning of things: of life and death. Feelings of melancholy encroaches; they come and go, but now they are suddenly overlaid by his great hope of playwrighting success.

***

Often he thinks of his boyhood and his early liking and practice of the art of writing, which he now thinks is fundamental to Civilisation. "What would civilised life in Elizabethan England be without it," he asks himself. He attends plays and studies performances. He sees the theatre stage as mirroring reality; and he appreciates his privileged background as a youth from a Noble family who having gained the best education through hard work from an early age, had been trained and groomed for the top positions, either as a leader or spokesman for Queen and country.

"It is my birthright," he says to himself, "to hold high office. And, to enjoy its benefits." So writing, as a form of self-expression, serves him well, especially now. "It demands and holds my concentration like nothing else," he says to Rowland Yorke. "I would say it is absolutely essential for Civilisation." In this, he is right, for as lamentations continue to trouble him, he finds that writing helps him to deal with the inner turmoil. It allows him to have a dialogue with himself; a soliloquy, so to speak. It is just this kind of self-examination scenario and mental state that helps him to develop a soliloquy! This form of writing he practices, hones and use in his work. So, like characters in a play, he gives voice to aspects of his many selves; and to many real life issues.

But writing is not a panacea for all ills. He is too grounded to think otherwise. He knows, only too well, how much effort is demanded. Instead of mystifying art, he demystifies it. He admits to "the pain to pen a book." This admission to himself is no idle comment. What he does with his quill is difficult. Translating thoughts into words, takes him to places within himself like nothing else can. He thinks his literary engagement helps as self-therapy. But, as a Nobleman writing for a sophisticated public in Elizabethan England, he knows that he would be going against the established, prevailing practice should his name appear as the author. Being anonymous as a writer of poetry and plays, is imperative. His options are few: He could either adopt a "Pen-name" or use "Anonymous." It would, for the most part, ensure that his writings are read, but he himself would be hidden. It is a necessary form of willed self-exclusion. In other words, he thinks it is akin to putting away his work in a secure place like the bottom drawers of his desk. For quite some time, he'd been keeping secret Notebooks containing notes and sketches of working drafts of verses, poems and plays. So while pitfalls appear, he deals with them as passion and great ambition propels him. He is disciplined and works hard. Then, a remarkable thing happens: Some of his writings appear in print, published in *The Paradise of Dainty Devices,* an anthology of verse. These writings catches the public imagination; and many editions follow. Edward is very pleased with his contribution of verses and song lyrics. In particular a few of the verses adopts the "Complaint" style through which he vents his teenage angst. In '*Not Attaining to*

*His Desire, He Complaineth"* he writes:

"I am not as I seem to be,
Nor when I smile, I am not glad.
A thrall, although you count me free,
I most in mirth, most pensive sad.
I smile to shade my better spite
As Hannibal that saw in sight
His country soil with Carthage town
By Roman force, defaced down. ..

Aye Hannibal, that smiles for grief
And let you Caesar's tears suffice.
The one that laughs at his mischief,
The other all for joy that cries.
I smile to see me scorned so;
You weep for joy to see me woe.
And I a heart by love slain dead
Present in place of Pompey's head

O cruel hap and hard estate
That forceth me to love my foe.
Accursed be so foul a fate,
My choice for to profix it so.
So long to fight with secret sore
And find no secret salve therefore.
Some purge their pain by plaint I find
But I in vain do breathe my wind.
E.O."

He is so proud and pleased to see his work in print that he forgets the protocol of Noblemen writers and signs it: "E.O." But these initials are not cryptic enough. They are dangerously close to revealing his name: Edward Oxenford. Or Edward, Earl of Oxford. The problem is that as author, he could have been easily identified. But he feels, it is worth the risk. Richard Evans had spotted something rare and published the budding talent evident in the young Earl's deeply-felt words.

Overall, Edward's "Complaint," his early form of "soliloquy" expresses juvenile frustration. Thus, the teenager had set down the first inklings of character sketches for plays that he hopes to write.

One day after passing St Paul's Cathedral, his heart leaps as he stares at a shop window. He sees, for the first time, the best-selling *The Paradise of Dainty Devices* on display and casts his mind back to his teens when he had written what is published. He remembers what he'd thought were bad times, as opposed to all that he'd experienced since. He has moved on most certainly, and now he needs a form of literary address that is more accommodating than "song lyrics." His Italian experience has opened new vistas: he considers new ideas for transforming the "Complaints'" verses as a stage presentation for English audiences. He seizes the opportunity because he thinks the time and place are right. Like him, people and things are moving on: The actor James Burbage and a relative, John Brayne, had erected a building in Shoreditch which they call: *The Theatre.*

***

Edward keeps a wary eye on developments. His movements in London are focused around writers. He is totally engaged; immersed in dramatic activities. He writes masques and plays to be performed by his Troupe of players. And between plays and performances, troubled by his real life experiences, he considers certain stories and new forms of presentation: How, for example, to bring art and life together, to greater effect. His memory bank is brimming as he thinks of a fund of ideas arising from the Commedia dell'arte productions: The dramatic portrayals of real people in the enchanting, almost other worldly environment of the stage.

For a while, he thinks about the most popular theatrical venues and the best actors who attracts the crowds. He knows that play Productions mean much planning and collaborative activities that has transformed his life to the extent that he is able to peer into the depths of the human mind and the world they inhabit. All this demands a certain bohemian way of life which appeals to him. Slowly he becomes the unconventional Nobleman that befits his roles. But, he is conscious too of the competition that exists between the dramatic troupes or Companies. He is, at this time, associated with the Children's Company of Choirboys from St Paul's Cathedral known as "Paul's Boys," or the Earl of Oxford Boys. Sebastian Westcote, is the Supervisor and Director of the Company. It is a prestigious and highly responsible post which entails Westcote also staging plays for the Royal Court with which the Queen is familiar. To his credit, thus far, most of what the Queen has seen, she likes. Westcote's track record speaks for itself: It is better than good; and now during the Court Revels, he presents multiple entertainments for the Queen.

So towards the end of an incredibly memorable year for Edward, Westcote leads his troupe the Paul's Boys as they prepare to perform a play by Edward titled: *A History of Error* which is to be performed before the Queen at Hampton Court. The day before the performance, Edward sits in at rehearsals. His deep-set eagle eyes takes in every detail of what he sees. He is fascinated by the children's ability to act well. He hopes they would do well before Her Majesty, the respected Nobles and others. As a playwright he is heartened because he understands the paradoxical nature of the talented Choir Boys. Far from being problematic in terms of conveying his intended message, Edward notes that the children are allowed more freedom of interpretation.

Conscious of protecting his anonymity, Edward uses child-actors to speak lines that lampoon well-known people. In this way, he disguises his authorship and thus deflects criticism. So child actors serves his purpose well. But, by so doing, he has to be very careful because there are pitfalls. Therefore, he treads a fine line. Nonetheless, as an Elizabethan writer, he presses on using the Paul's Boys as his preferred way of presenting contentious matters in his plays. What a child on stage can say and get away with, an adult can't. So, following the saying that "Children and fools speak *truth*," the intention of his play *A History of Error* is to tell the *truth!*

This experience with the Paul's Boys heralds a new phase for Edward as a writer. He is energized by the process; the steps that must be taken to get a play-script into production. It means mingling with the actors, the directors (often he directs himself) and co-producers. Just being in the theatre, especially since he'd come back from Italy, generates a new momentum to his playwriting and stage presentations.

*

While Edward is troubled by inner demons relating to his marriage, he gets more tense and his need for creative expression grows. One of the changes he makes to *A History of Error* pertains to coming to grips with his attitude and behaviour toward his wife and family. The question he poses is simply this: Why am I making these moves now?" He answers: "Because *A History of Error* is controversial. It dramatizes my own difficult relations with Anne and her father." Furthermore it is a play which shows a man who is incensed, and, as a playwright he creatively commits his experience to drama. Simply put, the story is about marriage into a distinguished and well-connected family; the odd coupling of an offended husband (Edward) and a headstrong wife, Anne Cecil.

So given that the play's plot about mistaken identity is largely drawn (from the Commedia dell arte) the mechanics or inner workings of the play is entirely Edward's invention. He continuously and boldly experiments, imputing experience into his characters. He creates new personas; and portrays himself and his wife Anne as dual characters. This is reflected in the characters LUCIANA and ADRIANA represents two shades: one light, the other dark. He goes further: He portrays Anne both as the person he'd first met and what she later became. As he gets deeper into writing the story, he feels the need to control the gnawing jealousy within himself. To deal with his emotions, his own private turmoil is one thing, but using the art of playwriting to publicly dramatize human frailties, is quite another: Ever inventive; he pushes the boundaries, creating characters based upon real people at Court; most controversially (and worryingly for some) the Queen!

So understandably, now he is somewhat nervous during rehearsals. He wonders how the Court and the Public would receive the play. Then comes the day of performance: It is an auspicious occasion. Why? Because it is the first time that the Queen will see, and seriously appraise, Edward's work as a Court playwright. In the hushed atmosphere, the audience witnesses Edward's daring: he presents history in a comic way. Although the play is a Comedy, he takes satire to a new level. He portrays the Queen as NELL, the wench. This is an insanely radical thing to do! No other playwright has gone as far as he has. Normally, they all toed the line as Courtly writers who presents the Queen as the embodiment of all that's good and virtuous. But more than portraying her as the character

NELL, jokingly, Edward uses a map to characterise NELL'S physical self. Enriched and enlightened by his Continental travels, he relates geography to anatomy. Boldly, he gets the character ANTIPHOLUS OF SYRACUSE to ask: "What's her name?"

To this DROMIO answers: "Nell, sir, but her name and three questions - that's an ell and three quarter - will not measure her from hip to hip...

ANTIPHOLUS: Then she bears some breadth?

DROMIO: She is spherical, like a globe. I could find out countries in her.

ANTIPHOLUS: In what part of her body stands Ireland?

DROMIO: Marry, sir, in her buttocks, I found it out by the bogs.

ANTIPHOLUS: Where Scotland?

DROMIO: I found it by the barrenness, hard in the palm of her hand.

ANTIPHOLUS: Where France?

DROMIO: In her forehead, arm'd and reverted, making war against her heir...

ANTIPHOLUS: Where England?

DROMIO: I look for the chalky cliffs, but I could find no whiteness in them...

ANTIPHOLUS: Where stood Belgia, the Netherlands?

DROMIO: O, sir, I did not look so low."

Knowing of Edward's other talents, what the Queen sees is Edward's extraordinary talent, his ability as a storyteller in *A History of Errors* of which she fully approves. In Edward, she sees a highly-prized man. The gift of his perfumed gloves (which she continues to show off publicly) symbolises something deeply personal between them: something secret; something that no one else in the Realm must know. And, of course, she is good at hiding; cloaking, her true intentions. But she is even better at showing how she feels. Her attentions now are fully directed at Edward. He, in turn, blushes with delight, and loves her even more.

At the age of twenty six, he is a playwright of unusual magnetism. The freshness of his Italian adventurers resonates in his receptive mind, broadening his vision and colouring all before him. He sees England now as never before. And slowly he is being transformed: From youthful cockiness to becoming a man to watch! Fellow-Courtiers eye him suspiciously, jealously, especially after they'd seen his mind at work through his Court Comedy with the apt name: *A History of Errors*! After this dramatic showing, as a lover of plays, Queen Elizabeth takes note of her unpredictable Courtier who, with greater purpose moves his pen quicker as he creates more fine theatrical treats. He'd become the English theatre's bright star, casting a glow beyond the Court.

A few weeks after A *History of Error* was performed on Shrove Tuesday, the Paul's Boys end the Revels Season with a performance at Whitehall Palace. The Masque they perform relates to *The History of Titus and Gisippus* in which Edward experiments, using more creative ways of presenting people and life as diverse. This, he sees as the key concept of his art going forward: He feels he is right about showing two sides instead of one of the human self.

***

Early one morning, after much thought about his portrayals of love and friendship and their portrayals in the Courtly theatres, he sits for a while at his desk with his head in the palms of his hands. Then, he begins to write an outline: The draft of a new play which he titles *The Two Gentlemen of Verona*. In this drama he brings love and friendship at Court in opposition. He names the male characters as PROTEUS and VALENTINE; gentlemen who are good friends whose love interests are closely linked. And he composes the love stories of PROTEUS and VALENTINE around themselves, *as writers*. It is their work, as writers, that touches their manhood. When VALENTINE'S lover SILVIA requests that he compose Verses, he becomes acutely conscious that his writings are, fundamentally, for no one else but himself. The exchange between VALENTINE and SILVIA makes this point.

> "SILVIA: You writ them sir, at my request.
> I would have had them writ more movingly.
> VALENTINE says to SILVIA: "Please you, I'll write Your Ladyship another."
> SILVIA says: "And when it's writ, for my sake read it over."
> VALENTINE: And if it please you, so: If not, why, so.
> VALENTINE: If it pleases me madam? What then?
> SILVIA: Why, if it please you, take it for your labour; And so good-morrow, servant."

The character SPEED, VALENTINE'S Page, listens to the lovers' conversation: "My master…her Suitor," he says, "He being her pupil, to become her tutor. O excellent device. Was there ever heard a better? That my master being scribe to himself should write the better." This self-consciousness, reflected in the character VALENTINE, guides and drives Edward through the writing process.

***

So Edward is fully aware that he writes best about what he knows, as he was taught by a teacher and fellow writer. Thus he expresses more about himself. But, as desire for identity gains momentum, he finds he is not alone in wanting more self-knowledge and self -expression. His sister, Mary, is keen to make her own mark; to establish her independence, especially now as she tries to decide who her husband should be. Edward is the one to whom Mary turns to discuss marriage partners. The man she favours is Peregrine Bertie, Lord Willoughby. He is in his early Twenties; and carries himself in a soldierly way with a swash-buckling style. He has a reputation for being bullish, with little or no respect for Elizabeth's Courtiers. In her pursuit of love and happiness, Mary's strength of character, prevails, for in spite of opposition from her own family and the Queen, she prepares to marry Bertie. To further complicate the situation, some months earlier, it was clear that Edward did not like the pugnacious Bertie. Added to this mix, is the behaviour of Bertie's mother, the Duchess of Suffolk, who has no good feelings for either Mary or Edward. The lovers look forward, but the marriage-to-be between Mary and Bertie is delayed.

Why so? Because it needs the consent of both Edward and the Queen. Meanwhile, Bertie's mother, having heard of the Edward-Anne marital, paternity problem, hatches a plot of her own to deal with it. Alas, her devious plan does nothing to bring Edward and Anne closer. If anything, the Duchess's interference hardens Edward's already strong doubts: his belief that Anne's daughter, Elizabeth, is not his own. But, the Duchess of Suffolk's view of the matter and her strength of character are much on Edward's mind. Why? Because she strikes him as unusually obstinate, like her son. She stands up to him. This rare behaviour touches upon his unchallenged self importance. No woman has done so in quite the same way before.

So with talk of marriage in the air, later, Edward attends the wedding of one of Norfolk's three sons, William Howard, who is the youngest. Thereafter, Edward's relations with the brothers get closer and better. As heirs to their father's estates, Edward understands well the boys' Inheritance predicament. Their overall welfare and betterment, in particular, their education, is of concern to Edward. One day, he says to himself, "I would write about them."

After the William Howard marriage, closer to home, the last thing that Edward wants is a troublesome wedding for Mary. Both parties needs to calm down a bit. Thus he and the Queen withholds their decision on the Mary-Bertie Peregrine marriage. While he considers the whys and wherefores of his sister's pending matrimony, thoughts of the Duchess of Suffolk, Katherine Willoughby, reverberates in his head. Her strength of character impresses him.

***

Elizabethan society is keen on Astrology. As Edward writes, he is aware of magic, and the part it plays in social life. A few learned men in his circle of friends and associates study and explore the subject. A Comet shooting across the sky, is witnessed by many people; and is seen by some as a bad sign. After he'd consulted the Delphic Oracle, now he thinks about the Comet: It's spectacular, fiery blaze. How ominous could it be? he questions. He speaks about this celestial event to two respected men: His Cousin, Francis Bacon and Dr John Dee, whom he'd met a few times.

On Astronomy and Astrology, Dee explains what he thinks about superstitious, dark forebodings, as well as enlightened Scientific explanations. "But," Dee says, "there are many learned men who see the Comet as a portent of bloody and bad things to befall the people of the earth." To the backdrop of knowing that the heavens and the earth are twinned, Edward listens with unusual interest to Dee. What he hears, is another way of seeing things in these times of Codes and the decipherings of texts, as the world is being opened up. He thinks about the latest ongoing explorations and discoveries; the persuasive words of Drake and Frobisher; of Oceanic voyages to far-flung unknown lands; and, he gives due respect to Dee's learning.

The Comet is a powerful symbol too for people who are thinking of getting married. But such superstitions are ignored by the young unconventional couple: Mary and Bertie who, after all the talk and tension, are, at last, married. So finally the unlikely duo becomes part of Edward's family: his kith and kin. He remembers, even fondly now, the couple's far from calm and peaceful pre-nuptial wooing and their wonderful wedding. What a pairing, Mary and Bertie are. "They could become characters in one of my plays," he says to himself.

***

On the eve of his twenty-eighth year, Edward is aware of his distance from the Court. He feels estranged. Increasingly, he criticises aspects of the Court; and he takes a hard look at his own life. He questions and considers a combination of things: in particular, marital discord and money matters. True to his passion for writing, his pen's black ink covers many more blank pages: He is challenged and glad to express himself creatively. But, he still does not feel at ease, or fully free, as money matters nag him. With the potential Inheritance he has, this should not be the case. So why this money problem? After his expensive Italian travels, he sees his predicament as arising largely from his natural tendency, as well as the necessity, to spend, spend, spend! His generosity, at times, is a well-known feature of his popularity. He gives money to rogues. But, he also gives to the needy; an admirable trait. Such acts of compassion, he performs with little restraint. But, is such largesse a strength or a weakness? "I am what I am," he says to himself, with some frustration. "This is my natural way. It is how I behave. But it does not mean I do not care about money. That would be a mistaken view." This opinion of himself is correct for there is perhaps no one else in Elizabeth's Court who is so vigilant and hawk-eyed a money-lover as Edward de Vere. Money is akin to being one of his greatest weaknesses: His Achilles heel. The lack of his full Inheritance is the background mood music which he hears each hopeful day.

So, simply put, his predicament is this: The money he gets he spends; and soon he needs more. Now, he's on the look-out for gainful opportunity.

His search leads to him becoming an investor in an overseas venture, as profitable speculation excites members of the business community. England's explorers are not idle. They continuously step-up their search for a route through Northwest Canada to reach the Pacific Ocean. Queen Elizabeth's conquering ambitions knows no bounds: The world's her oyster, so to speak, as her sea-dogs scours the immense seas. Extending England's reach to foreign lands is central to her vision. "We must invest more in the North-west Passage," she says. "It has unlimited potential."

"I agree, Your Majesty," Burghley says. "I know you have been thinking along these lines. It is worth saying, indeed considering, that the overseas expansion advantage for England is all the more important because our competitors, the Spaniards and Portuguese, are right now seeking a Southern passage to the Orient. They must not beat us to it. We need investors. The more the better. Count me in as one of the first investors in the Northwest Passage venture."

Such talk is music to the Queen's ears. The golden prize;

the potential pay-off is trade with India and China. Elizabeth's imperial ambition is given the filip it needs. It enlarges her autocratic vision. "An English Empire?" is a question which he is fond of raising with her Ministers, especially Burghley.

"That, my dear Sir Spirit," she says confidingly to Burghley, "is my goal. Empire. An English Empire! I imagine it often. Not just in my dreams, but each waking day. It is among my greatest ambitions to draw the riches from every corner of the earth. We must look outward: We must get ahead of the Spaniards and Portuguese. We must colonize and exploit. All for the glory of God and survival of the people of England!"

Burghley is roused by the energy behind the rise in her voice.

"Nothing less, Your Majesty," he says. "Our language and learning must be transported there to teach the natives; and thus ensure the continued flow of the riches to come." She pauses and rearranges herself. She sits bolt upright in a more formal, regal pose.

"Remember, Sir Spirit," she adds, "language is the instrument of Empire! And, I need not remind you, we in England have the finest Poets and Playwrights in the world. Literature..." She pauses again. "I mean the English language is essential in trade relations. Never forget, language is the key instrument; our most potent weapon in gaining an Empire! And in this quest our "Men of the Pen" have a great duty to perform for England. They must continue to create and add new words to our expanding English language. This form of communication, Sir Spirit, we must export to enlighten the dark, heathen races of other countries."

"Yes, Your Majesty," Burghley says. As ever, he speaks softly, his voice a colourless monotone. "I agree, Your Majesty. What a great victory this would be for England if we could find that

Passage to the Orient *before* the Spaniards and the Portuguese."

Soon after Burghley speaks with the Queen, Edward performs his Courtly role as an Investor in expeditions. He brims with optimism. He sees such investments as, more or less, win-win situations that could enrich him, strengthen England's economic growth and advance its colonial ambitions. To fund the Northwest Passage Expedition, the Cathay Company is formed with Michael Lok as head of the Company. Lok hires Martin Frobisher to lead the expedition with three ships to find the Passage to the Pacific. Edward is mindful that seventy five years before, another European Admiral, Cristobal Colon (Christopher Columbus) had also set out Westwards with three caravels. Each day, after his Investment is made, Edward's hopes rise. Then, he learns of Frobisher's failure. But ever-hopeful, he makes a second Expedition Investment, which also fails to achieve its goal of Frobisher returning with gold and silver. Instead, Frobisher brings to England three Eskimos: two adults and a child whom he shows to the Queen. Forcibly taken away from their environment and paraded around like "trophies," the three Eskimos die. But even in death, their bodies are put on display; a source of curiosity for the English public. The death of these exotic people, plays on Edward's mind. So much so, he scribbles these words in his Notebook for future reference:

"That England that was won't to conquer others,
Hath made a shameful conquest of itself."

He makes one more Investment, totalling three, like the number of ships. "Having lost money twice," he says to himself, "perhaps I will be third time lucky." He waits anxiously: Nothing ventured, nothing gained, he thinks. Then, at last, Admiral Frobisher returns to England: not with gold, but with iron ore! "What on earth was I thinking," Edward reflects, "when I trusted Lok and Frobisher?" And so all his hopes of making some money are cruelly dashed.

"Fool's gold!" he exclaims. He is barely able to contain his disappointment. His losses now tally three thousand pounds; money he thinks he could hardly afford. He is not pleased at all with Lok. Unsurprisingly Michael Lok is a name which he finds hard to forget!

***

# PART TWO

## BECOMING "WILLIAM SHAKESPEARE"

"The Italianate Englishman" Playwright

(1576 - 1593)

# VI

## "Those brambles and frays."

*"So learn to read what*
*Silent love hath writ."*

Edward's travels to other countries has broadened his vision and deepened his sense of self and the world; in particular, international affairs. He understands that England's place among nations is ever-changing. And, not always for the better. Now, into the last third of the sixteenth century, three countries: Spain, France and England vie to become the leading nation. Nothing less than superiority in trade and commerce matters. Relations between the three are tense; almost always volatile. Each try, but often fail to form political alliances. Agreements between them are, more often than not, of short duration. This is the evolving scenario within which England must operate to best protect and maintain the well-being of its people. Overall, like the set-design for one of his plays, this is the backdrop against which Edward tries to summon up new hope of finding the money he needs.

*

He lives, loves and wields his quill each day in the most meaningful way possible. As he drafts plays combining the general with the particular, in other words, relating the big picture with the details of a character's life, he reviews and considers new ways of reflecting the human condition. For every text, there is a context: And, each has its own dynamics of progression. England, as he knows, is not just an island unto itself.

At the heart of each of the contending European countries is religion. Christianity, preaching its essential message of the one God, instead of uniting its believers, divides them largely in two main groups: Catholics and Protestants. One, or other of these groups is dominant in Spain, France and England. In England, Queen Elizabeth and her Ministers, should they dare on religious matters, to be idle, does so at their peril. No one could be less than vigilant. Key roles of trust in government are granted by the Queen to advisers and preferred admirers. Her proneness to be dazzling and vain could not be separated from a cold capacity to Rule. It is a contradiction of Queen Elizabeth's personality; a double-sidedness that fascinates Edward. Since her father's anti-Catholic Reformation process, the Queen's defence of Protestant England has depended upon a few Noblemen - the aristocrats, their families and servants; as well as the masses, who reside on their fiefdoms. But, as personal religious positions shift, a divide appears: Protestants, like Leicester, Walsingham and Sidney are not as open to change as were the Earls of Sussex, Worcester and the Duke of Norfolk. In terms of national movements, everyone moves either one way or the other, to gain advantage.

For his part, Edward keeps a wary eye on events. But he keeps an open mind. According to the French Ambassador, Michel de Castelnau, Edward, the Earl of Oxford, has become a "Secret Catholic." Later, the Ambassador recalls that on his return from Italy, Edward had moved close to the Catholic faith; and together with a few of his relatives among the Nobility, and his best friends, he had sworn and signed with them a dedication that they would do all they could for the advancement of the Catholic religion. One of Edward's pro-

Catholic sympathisers is Henry Howard. Edward respects Henry, as a learned man who had taught Law at the University of Cambridge. But shifting allegiances leads to Howard's belief that Queen Elizabeth should be replaced by Mary, Queen of Scots; a treasonous belief that had led to his brother's beheading. Henry's opposition to Queen Elizabeth shows undoubted, but foolhardy courage; and, as an admirer of his boldness and brilliance, intellectually, Edward thinks of him as a commanding figure, not unlike Thomas Smith. Charles Arundell, Edward's Cousin, is another Catholic associate. But, he asks himself: "Why did I change my religious allegiance?" With spies and informers aplenty in the country, surely he knows the risks. The stakes are high. Arundell gives two reasons (or versions) as to why Edward has moved closer to Romish belief. The first, is to favour a former Teacher; the second, is to atone and clear his conscience of an act of murder. This reference to committing such a crime is due not to the "accidental" death of Thomas Brincknell ten years ago, but to another killing.

Edward thinks the leading practitioners of Protestantism and Catholicism, both reveal their hypocrisy. Disenchanted, he is drawn into the company and, to some extent, to the persuasion of a few Catholics. But, this is a dangerous path to tread in Protestant England. So allegedly, he flirts with the wrong side; and, having strayed from his marital bed, a Priest, Father Boniface says to Edward: "I will not give you Communion until you go back to live with your wife." So, siding with Catholics, he thinks, offers no way of resolving the religious sectarian divide. What next can he do? The temptation to escape to Catholic France is not an option for he knows his enemies are already on alert. The Earl of Leicester, Robert Dudley, contacts Burghley:

"I am sorry," he writes, "my Lord of Oxford should for any

respect think any more of going overseas, I can but wish and advise him to take such advice in all things as were best and most honourable for him - and especially in his consideration toward Her Majesty and his country."

Edward is one of the closest men to the Queen; and interestingly, at this time, he dislikes the Cecil faction and others. But he, like any transgressor at Court, is targeted and advised against his perceived wrong-headed Evangelical zeal. This charge arises, in no small part, from his frustration with the hypocritical ministrations of Protestants, particularly as practised by Lord Burghley and the Earl of Leicester. And so, for now, at least, the Howard-Arundell accusations must run its course.

***

Edward thinks of the request made by the Priest, Father Boniface, that he should return to cohabiting with his wife Anne. But this is not of urgent interest to Edward. With his first published poems and songs behind him, foremost among his day-to-day concerns are insistent literary matters which grow, and snow-balls into a bigger business, demanding larger accommodation and more staff. To achieve his ambitious ends, he looks for assistance: His literary goals are high; and the secretarial help he seeks has to be of a certain calibre: he needs a bright, educated person; someone well-acquainted with researching essential source material, whose knowledge spans the range of Classical literature: from Boccaccio to Ovid. That someone should also be well versed in the Romance languages. So now Edward thinks of some sort of an Assistant or Secretary to help as he plots the way forward.

Though he is not a poor man, relatively speaking, he has financial problems. Therefore, the cost of hiring a Private Secretary has to be within his means. At just this time, as if to endorse his line of thinking, he receives news from the Queen, who recognises his growing diligence and literary output. She cites the "true and faithful Service you have done and given to Us," and grants him the highly valued Castle Rising property. Edward is relieved; delighted. How timely, he thinks. But when the Queen agrees to grant the property to him, did she know anything about his Catholic dealings; his intrigues and conspiracies with Arundell and Howard? Or, did she already know and presents the gift of the property as a broad hint to him to reconsider his new religious alignment and shady associates?

***

Castle Rising manor earns Edward an income of two hundred and fifty pounds a year. It is timely; just what he needs as a writer and producer of plays! But given his ever-rising expenses, the income from Castle Rising stretches only so far. It is being swallowed up fast. And soon, he feels he would not be able to deal with any looming shortfall. So while he is thankful, whatever "Service" he has yet to perform for the Queen, his search for a Private Secretary continues. This need for secretarial assistance points clearly to the direction and scope of his literary and theatrical ambition.

*

While he composes poetry and plays, he feels uneasy about a widening rift: He is becoming more unhappy with life at Court. Why? Because of a combination of things. One in particular is central: His marital discord that persists. But, he is thankful for, and uplifted by, good feelings about his extraordinary Italian experiences that move him nearer to creating new dimensions of art and culture for his Court theatre audiences. Among the Courtiers who attend his plays, many dislike the productions because they see it as coming from an "*Italianate Englishman*." Of all the names he'd been called, this is the strangest. The nickname irks him somewhat. But it confirms too that he is on the inventive path he has chosen. He is ready and works artistically to cross boundaries; to transcend Court constraints. He sees very clearly the need to promote an English Renaissance by moving away from Royal flattery. The narrowness of certain "acceptable" literary works, the standard to which he is expected to conform, cramps his style. They are too limited, and limiting: Theatre presentations, he thinks, needs to shift to new thinking. So boldly, he envisages and works towards a larger vision: He aims to provide an artistic theatrical space that would embrace humankind. And so his experience of the Italian Renaissance pushes him to write poems and plays that are neither of a conservative or inhibiting temper. He feels the Royal Court must no longer get in the way. Thus liberating himself, like a torrent, new ideas jostle for attention and take shape in his mind.

*

His less than comfortable abode at Rowland Yorke's house has, it seems, run its temporary course. But, his direction is not to go back to Court or reside at Cecil House. Independence of mind and body is paramount. Propelled by fresh thoughts and ideas, he decides to buy his own residence. The place he chooses is Watling Street, a thriving area of commerce and trade in the heart of London. This," he says to himself, "is where I would live and create my new works as a writer." Nearby are the printers and publishers, who conveniently adjoins St. Paul's

Churchyard. Here, the largest booksellers in London are to be found. Just a short distance away is the "long shop" in the vicinity of the Church of St Mildred. Edward enters the shop; and while browsing along the bookshelves, he is approached by a young man.

"Good morning, sir," the man says. "Can I be of help to you?"

"Yes, you can," Edward says. "I see you have a good selection of printed books. Not only the original works in Latin, but also these translations here." He points at two books on a nearby shelf. "I see you have English translations of Ovid's *Metamorphoses* and *The Courtier*, for example." He thinks of his contribution to, and collaboration with, Arthur Golding on the English translation of Ovid's book and smiles broadly.

"Yes, sir, translated books are one of our specialities," the young man says. "Our choice of Latin and English books attract more and more buyers and readers." He shuffles along the bookshelves. "The two books you mentioned are among our best-sellers." On hearing this, Edward feels proud and contented. As a consequence, the man seems more at ease. Edward likes the young man's helpfulness, in particular, his knowledge. And, his general bearing is pleasing too.

"Do you work all day in the shop?" Edward asks.

"No, sir, just the mornings," the man says.

"What do you do for the rest of the day?"

"Sir, I spend the time at the back of the shop learning about the printing trade. I am employed here as an Apprentice Printer-Assistant." Having said this, he feels emboldened and adds: "My name is Anthony Munday, sir. When I am not learning my trade as an Apprentice Printer, I write poetry."

Given this extra information, Edward is even more impressed by the young man. He sees potential in him as a Secretarial Assistant.

"How soon will your Apprenticeship end?" Edward asks.

"My Apprenticeship Course as Printer's Assistant here ends in two months time," Munday says. "In June, to be exact."

"What will you do next?"

"I have no job to go to after this," Munday says. "But, I will continue to *write*."

His stress on the last word prompts Edward.

"I have a vacancy for the post of Private Secretary," Edward says. "I'd like you to consider working for me. Come for an Interview. This is my address." He hands a piece of paper to Munday on which is written: "Edward De Vere, Earl of Oxford." They shake hands and Edward leaves the shop.

Soon after their meeting, Edward appoints Munday to do certain Secretarial tasks. Munday's presence frees Edward to devote more time to his increasing, many-sided literary interests. But even with the help he has, his large drama-oriented enterprise expands. He has no choice but to seek more Secretarial help. Accordingly, he approaches the translator and novelist John Lyly whom he employs. Unlike himself, Lyly is a conservative type of person; not a bad thing, Edward thinks for their working relationship. For their parts, Lyly and Munday are pleased with their posts as Secretaries. On their first day together, Edward says: "You are my team. My trusted collaborators. We have much work to do. Let us go forward!" And so he launches himself into a new exciting, career defining phase of literary and theatrical ventures.

***

He joins the Queen's Progress of 1578 as it heads out to the Essex countryside. It stops at Audley End in Essex on the way to Cambridge. Edward knows there will also be a stop at Theobald's, the Cecil family estate. He intends to avoid that part of the journey so that he would not be close to his wife

Anne, from whom he is still estranged.

Edward is glad to be at Audley end where a few of England's most promising writers and scholars from the University of Cambridge have gathered. Among these worthies is Gabriel Harvey, who, like Edward, was one of Sir Thomas Smith's students. Smith had died of throat cancer some months before; and now for a few moments, Edward remembers him fondly. Harvey had gone further: He'd written a Eulogy to Smith in Latin. Now, Edward and Harvey are glad to meet again: They shake hands; and greet each other warmly. They'd known each other since their late teens; and like an older brother, the young Earl had given money and granted favours to Harvey when they were students at Cambridge's Christ's College. Since then, Harvey's academic and intellectual star had been rising; and, it continues to grow. Now, he is titled Professor of Rhetoric at Cambridge; a status befitting his academic achievements. But, affected by success, he does not wear his knowledge lightly. He has a reputation for being too learned and argumentative. So here they are once more in Cambridge. Given that their paths have diverged, Edward is not surprised to learn that Harvey had once written: "Gallant audacity is never out of countenance, but hath ever a tongue and a hand at will." But exactly how audacious has he become? Edward wonders.

During this pause of the Progress at Audley End, the stage is set as Presentations are about to be made. The opportunity and setting for Harvey to impart his learning could not be grander. He could hardly believe his luck! With barely contained excitement, he steps up to the lectern to make his address. He glances down at the distinguished gathering, graced by the Queen. He'd prepared a Series of lectures aimed at influential people at Court, many of whom are in the audience. He believes, and says, that men of rank and stature should perform actions that are worthy of the most glorious and immortal fame. He is conscious too of imminent threats to England's security; and during his lecture, his voice rises: slowly at first, then it gets louder with the cadence of well-articulated words. He targets war as the traditional occupation of the Nobleman. Then, he turns to writing, which, in his high-handed, audacious view is a matter of secondary importance for men of education and their Secretaries. Hearing this, Edward feels self-conscious. The mention of "Secretaries" is a plant, he thinks. And why, here and now? In no uncertain terms, the star Speaker Harvey singles out Edward de Vere, the Earl of Oxford, for special praise. Boldly, he speaks out as Her Majesty listens:

"You, a Nobleman and Lord," he says looking directly at Edward, "are following a literary career path, namely to do with Poetry and Court dramas." This is true, and Edward is pleased to hear it. But, he wonders if Harvey may have heard of his search for a Secretary and is now auditioning to fill the vacancy! Then Harvey says:

"Thy splendid fame, great Earl, demands even more than in the case of others – the services of a poet possessing lofty eloquence. Thy merit doth not creep along the ground, nor can it be confined within the limits of a song. It is a wonder that reaches as far as the heavenly orbs. For a long time past Phoebus Apollo cultured thy mind in the arts. English poetical measures have been sung by thee long enough! Let that Courtly epistle – more polished than even the writings of Castiglione himself witness how greatly thou dost excel in letters. I have seen many Latin Verses of thine, yea, even more English verses are extant. Thou hast drunk deep drafts not only of the Muses of France and Italy, but hast learned the manners of many men and arts of foreign countries. It is not for nothing that Sturmius himself was visited by thee. Neither in France, Italy nor Germany are there any such cultivated and polished men."

At this point, Edward is deeply moved, but quite uneasy too, by Harvey's praise. But this is not all. "O thou hero worthy of renown," Harvey adds: "*throw away* the *insignificant pen*, throw away *bloodless books and writings* that serve no useful purpose. Now must the sword be brought into play.

Now is the time for thee to sharpen the spear and handle the great engines of war!...What if suddenly a most powerful enemy should invade our borders? If the Turk should be arming his savage hosts against us? What though the terrible war trumpet is even now sounding its blast? Thou will see it all. Even at this very moment through art fiercely longing for the fray. I feel it. Our whole country knows it. In thy breast is Noble blood. Courage animates thy brow. Mars lives in thy tongue. Minerva strengthens thy right hand. Bellona reigns in thy body, within thee burns the fire of Mars. Thine eyes flash fire, thy *Will Shakes Spears*. Who would not swear that Achilles had come to life again."

Shakes Spears! Edward is taken aback by this expression. He had listened with wrapt attention. At the end of Harvey's address, many thoughts flash across his mind. Of all the things Harvey had spoken about, for more than a passing moment, Edward thinks of these words: "Thine eyes flash fire, thy Will Shakes Spears. Who will not swear that Achilles had not come to life again." Having forsaken the Sword for the "insignificant pen," the words "Will Shakes-spears" is firmly lodged in Edward's brain for quite rightly he is the Scribe at the very top of the ratings, even while Harvey was trying to turn him away from literary achievements! They have a certain ring, especially being placed among names like Mars, Minerva and Achilles. Hereafter, for Edward, the punner and wordsmith extraordinaire, the thought and these words: *"Thy will Shakes Spears"* recurs.

*

While Harvey praises the twenty eight year old Edward before the Queen at Audley End, *an unknown fourteen year old lad* named William Shakspere, lives with and works for his father in Stratford-upon-Avon. This country boy is still a very long way from London; and even further away from the class-structured sophisticated London theatrical Society, which is most exclusive. Significantly, the Society's members are long settled Noblemen, not only with the best education, but also large sums of money, which counts! The distance, intellectually and socially, between the man Edward de Vere, the Earl of Oxford, and the country boy Shakspere, could not be greater. So Harvey's presentation points to an extraordinary coincidence in that Edward would one day find his words useful in disguising himself and his work.

But for now, Edward is well known among his peers. And though concealment of his name is absolutely necessary, in spite of Harvey's mighty sword argument, Edward's commitment to the pen as being far mightier, is reinforced. He feels very good about his writings: His reputation as a poet and writer of published song lyrics. But while Harvey's praise is in keeping with Edward's growing stature, his hope of rousing Edward to throw away the pen and take up a military career is a gross miscalculation of the intellectual range and direction of the man Edward de Vere is. His course is set. To fulfil his literary ambition, he has already had the help he needs. So Harvey's high-profile, public flattery in the hope of working for Edward, falls on deaf ears. But this quiet response from Edward has deadly consequences in the snake-pit that is the fraternity of writers. Harvey's failure leads to him venting his spleen. What a turn-around of opinion, Edward thinks, that Harvey's astonishing admiration for him should so soon turn to disappointment. He decries Edward as a "foppish Italianate Englishman," a Nobleman of stirring words, but "frivolous deeds;" a man of "womanish works." These are damning words from Harvey. As the war-monger berates the Earl for his pen-pushing, effeminate appearance, unable to accept matters as they stand between himself and Edward, his sarcasm knows no bounds.

***

Meanwhile Father Boniface's words to Edward about getting back together with his wife Anne, is not a matter of urgent interest. To assist with his day-to-day concerns at this exciting time of rising literary ambition and challenges, Edward is confident he is on the right track. His clued-up Secretaries, men well-versed in Classical literature and languages, who are adept with a quill show-case their abilities by finding the suitable source material he needs for his dramas; as well as carrying out the duties associated with play productions. It's all about story-telling! On the face of it, there are not many such helpers around. Edward appreciates this fact; and nurtures good relations.

Of the two Secretaries, he is closer to John Lyly. And having writers as Secretaries does not threaten, or usurp, Edward's authority or authorship of the stories he pens. He is confident and open enough to show and even discuss aspects of drafts, but he alone is the writer of his plays. That much is abundantly clear to both Lyly and Munday, as well as other associates. Nonetheless, he is pleased with the research assistance which saves him precious time. So while he appreciates his Secretaries' camaraderie, he needs no advice as to how he should either write or present his dramas.

Months into his literary enterprise, given his financial

problems, the cost of hiring Secretaries is foregrounded as he tries to keep within his budget, which is running low. Frustration creeps in, as once more, he broods over his Inheritance which is locked up in Burghley's iron grip. This galls him.

Thanks to the recent Castle Rising income, he manages to keep his staff and make progress with writing and the production of dramas for the theatre. Whatever official service he has yet to do for his Queen and country, he stands ready. So for now, at least, it is not the sword or the national war cries of Harvey that excites him: It is the insistent need to write more plays. But though he is uplifted by feelings about his Italian experiences and the new dimensions of art that he creates, many Courtiers dislike his work: 'I am an Englishman, a proper Englishman,' Peregrine Bertie says: 'I have no love for people and things foreign.' He speaks to his wife Mary who knows about her brother's reputation as an 'Italianate Englishman.' Peregrine goes further, but stops short of using this nickname against Edward, who is always ready to artistically cross the boundaries of the Royal Court's dos and don'ts. The shock of the new is central: It stirs his creativity. He acts with urgency and hopes to engender an English Renaissance by moving away from the strictures of Royal flattery. He writes with greater freedom, exploring a range of experience encompassing Comedy, as well as Tragedy. Literary genres do not hinder him. The freedom he feels, like his noble-minded playfulness of punning words (often turning the language on its head, so to speak) allows him to engage with larger scenarios that embraces humankind. But even so, such a vision is seen as foreign and therefore problematic.

"I know of your husband's preferment as an Englishman," Edward says to his sister Mary. "Peregrine believes strongly in tradition, in English values. There is nothing wrong with that.

And so daringly, before the Queen, Edward dramatizes his tense relations with the Cecil family on stage. What would Burghley and his wife think? Would they feel offended? Any nervousness, on his part is kept in check with seemingly no visible signs. He is more drawn into the unfolding spectacle of performance; into seeing how well the players perform. Above all, he hopes for the Queen's enjoyment of his story and staging. She acknowledges his outstanding artistry; and he feels a new-found sense of personal upliftment. Like an addictive drug, the Queen's approval is the thing he needs and craves. Soon, he is at work again on the drafts of two other plays.

Over Christmas and the New Year holidays and festivities, Edward and the Queen exchange gifts. He presents Her Majesty with jewellery studded with gold and diamonds. The Queen's acceptance of his offering is a filip: It seals their good relations. A few days later, a Company of players, the Lord Chamberlain's Men, enacts the play *The History of the Rape of the Second Helen*. He is drawn to the name Helen which he uses in the drafts of two other plays: *Troilus and Cressida* and *All's Well That Ends Well*. After the performances of his plays at Richmond Palace, as never before, he is overwhelmed, taken aback by the inextricable links he makes between the real and the imagined, as he experiments with the interplay between art and life.

And so, using his brain and hand, the act of writing has the added benefit of being a balm that brings an inner calm and strength as he incorporates troubling truths of his life. It opens a new window of personal-artistic perception. Having done the first draft of *All's Well That Ends Well,* he shows it to John Lyly who takes the script to his desk, where he reads it. Lyly is intrigued; surprised by the resemblances between the Helen character and the real-life Countess Anne de Vere. He says to himself: "For an Earl, being a writer is dangerous enough. But, portraying his wife in a play for public entertainment is brave, as well as risky for his reputation."

Later that day, Edward approaches Lyly: "What do you think of the draft?" he asks.

"It is the best of its kind that I have ever read," Lyly says. "The rhythm, the variety of words. I especially like the metering of lines.They add lyrical power to the story. It is a true drama."

"Thank you, John,"

Lyly hands over the script and says:

"Such a drama will touch the audience. *Any* audience, I think. The characters are vivid and revealing. Life-like, but better still, they are larger than life! I would say you have caught the essence of human nature."

"Thank you, John," Edward says.

As Lyly moves back to his desk, he reflects on *All's Well That Ends Well.* He has no doubt it is his boss's dramatic marital tour de force. Parts of the play gave him dramatic, startling new insights into Edward's intimate relationship with the Cecils. As a fellow-writer, he is taken aback by Edward's bold theatrical experiments of art portraying life on the stage. So Lyly, the novelist, appreciates more than anyone else around, the intricate interplay between art and life: He marvels at how beautifully and powerfully they come together in *All's Well That Ends Well.* The characters BERTRAM and HELENA, Lyly thinks, are clearly drawn from the lives and marriage of Edward and Anne. The play, in part, shows the social difference between the high-ranked Edward and lower-ranked Anne. Their marriage was made possible by the Queen's action: Her promotion of William Cecil to becoming Lord Burghley. In the play, the reference between life and art could not be clearer. The character BERTRAM (Edward) loses his father, then he is sent to London to become a Ward of the Elizabethan Court. So, in reality, Elizabeth's generosity of ennobling William Cecil was crucial before Anne and Edward could be married. Furthermore, in the play, BERTRAM forsakes his wife's bed and goes to Italy! This is also true in Edward's life. Then, HELENA wins back BERTRAM by using a "bed-trick" on BEATRICE that Anne is said to have played on Edward. Marriage, for better or worse, besets Edward, and finds its way in his playwriting. Art is about truth, he believes; and marriage and faithfulness are expected to go together: It is an arrangement of Holy wedlock, and being true to oneself, is important. But, as a Christian, however far he deviates, he always readjust himself by following certain guidelines as contained in his beloved Geneva Bible; a close companion of his since he'd bought it as a teenager. In the Book of *Ecclesiasticus,* he reads:

"A man that breaketh wedlock and thinketh thus in his heart: 'Who seeth me? I am compassed about with darkness. The walls cover me. Nobody seeth me: Whom need I fear? The Most High will not remember my sins.' "

After this passage, comes the following line:

"Such a man feareth the eyes of men and knoweth not that the eyes of the Lord are ten thousand times brighter than the sun, beholding all the ways of men.

So marriage and estrangement from his wife is much on his mind.

***

While he is uncertain about the paternity of Anne's child Elizabeth, Burghley's interference in his marriage troubles Edward, who turns inward. He goes further than ever as he explores his feelings, using his pen poetically and dramatically to deal with the matter. It is the most satisfactory and best way forward, he thinks. After weeks of mulling over it, his jealous nature keeps in mind what he imagines as a real betrayal - a bed trick by Anne. Then, after finalising *All's Well That Ends Well*, he begins another play: *Measure for Measure,* which deals with sexual unfaithfulness. He dares to consider Anne's deviousness; her alleged infidelity. It cuts deep into him. He seems to be almost paralysed by it. He is unable either to forgive or forget his separation from Anne; and, the reason for it. Such deception brings forth its exposure in his plays, namely, *All's Well That Ends Well, Measure for Measure* and *Titus Andronicus.*

Does he have doubts about his accusations? Does it ever cross his mind that Anne may well be innocent of the charges? This last question, at this time, is certainly not to be entertained. It is a preference that serves him well. How? In the sense that he transmutes his obvious self-inflicted pain into powerful art; into plays. But, for how long would this theme of his marriage be part of the wonderful dramatic stories he tells? Another question he asks himself now is: Could Anne have been raped? But what he doesn't question is his treatment of, and actions towards Anne. He asks himself: "Have I been cruel to Anne?" Time and again, he tries to review any possibility of cruelty or heartlessness on his part, and like the verdict of the Delphic Oracle, alas, the Jury is still out on his behaviour. But, as time passes and doubts begin to creep in, he derives satisfaction as he translates life into art. In rough notes for a play, yet to be named, he writes dialogue in which he shows a developing double-sidedness in his attitude towards Anne. He puts these words in the mouths of the characters of *The Merry Wives of Windsor*: In the draft he is finalising, he confronts his obsessive jealousy as he begins to have serious doubts about Anne's unfaithfulness. In the interaction between himself as FORD and three other characters: PAGE, EVANS and CAIUS, he writes:

"PAGE: Good Master Ford, be contented. You wrong

yourself too much.
FORD: True Master Page. -
Up, gentlemen! You shall see sport anon. Follow me gentlemen.
EVANS: This is fery fantastical humors and jealousies.
CAIUS: By Gar; 'tis no the fashion of France. It is not jealous in France...
MISTRESS PAGE Listens and intervenes: "You do yourself Mighty wrong, Master
FORD: Ay, ay, I must bear it…
EVANS: If there be any body in the house, and in the chambers, and in the coffers, and the presses, heaven forgive my sins at the day of judgement!
CAIUS: Be Gar, nor I too. There is nobodies.
PAGE: Fie, fie Master Ford. Are you not ashamed? What spirit, what devil suggests this imagination? I would not ha' your distemper in this kind for the wealth of Windsor Castle.
FORD: 'Tis my fault Master Page. I suffer it."

***

Money matters. Having lost his investment of three thousand pounds with financier Michael Lok and his Northwest Passage Expedition, Edward is disappointed and angry, but far too engaged with other aspects of life to dwell on that triple disaster. For one thing, he is busy making notes and sketching a new play: *The Merchant of Venice.* In the notes he mentions Michael Lok. The name Lok in connection with money matters: financial and business dealings, has a certain ring to it. In the sketch of his story, across the page in capital letters, Edward writes the name: "S-H-Y-L-O-C-K." The play he envisages, he notes, will deal with money and debts that, alas, are never far from his mind. Would he ever again invest in foreign ventures? Who knows? he asks himself. Unsurprisingly, no clear answer is forthcoming, because he is, at heart, a risk-taker; an adventurer. After all, what is life without taking chances, he thinks. Gains and losses: Money in, money out. More out, than in! These tabulations preoccupy him now.

***

While the suffering playwright moves among his fellow-Courtiers, he holds his head high. His relations with the Queen continues to be good; and by Tuesday March 3, 1579, he, and his Cousins present a Masque and a play performed for the Court at Whitehall. The Queen is in the audience as the Lord Chamberlain's Men performs a history play and a Masque. The link between the two reflects Edward's basic outlook. In terms of content, these presentations see the twenty eight year old Edward at the margins from where he pushes the boundaries and flirts with danger. But having gone public with a private matter, he gets some satisfaction. He is at ease and empowered by the overall reception for his recent plays. And being a stubborn man, who could blame him for interweaving his wife's supposed infidelity into his work.

His commitment to theatrical productions at this time, is clear. And his story lines are interesting enough to hold the audiences' attention. While the history play performed, based on fact, tells the story of a woman who tries to kill her husband with the help of her servant, the Masque hints at a more fully realised tragic play to come; a play about obsessive jealousy and featuring another Servant character. Obsession is one thing; but Edward is a suspicious fellow, too! He has to be. Why? Because Spies and Informers are never far away. He thinks of his many escapes from being ambushed. Now, at the end of a performance, he pauses a while to keep safe after he'd lampooned the powerful Lord Burghley and his family. Perhaps his life, so far, has been spared, because he thinks he is married to Burghley's daughter.

*

Meanwhile, as marriage negotiations between the Queen and Alencon continues, before the Frenchman's visit, Elizabeth needs a suitable Nobleman to go to France and serve as guarantor of Alencon's safe return. The Queen chooses Edward to undertake the task, which he graciously accepts. He performs what is asked of him very well. But, he is very touchy about what else might be asked of him. Pride matters; and now, in his new diplomatic role, he feels he must not be taken for granted. "I am what I am," he firmly believes. Much depends on his self-belief; his huge sense of pride. All the big events at Court are grist for his artistic mill. On his return from diplomatic duty in France, he begins to draft and write *Twelfth Night*. In it, he portrays himself as the jester FESTE; and Queen Elizabeth as OLIVIA, who, in the play, listens to the two MESSENGERS who put forward the suitors marriage proposals. OLIVIA turns down the first Messenger, but listens to the other.

This is how it was when the French Ambassador on behalf of Alencon had come to make the case for marriage to the Queen. Edward uses another parallel of his time: He casts his sister, Mary, as MARIA, her husband Peregrine as TOBY BELCH and Peregrine's friend Philip Sidney as SIR ANDREW AGUECHEEK. As in the play, the closeness of BELCH and AGUECHEEK reflects reality. And yet, in *Twelfth Night* the personality of AGUECHEEK that emerges is not straightforward. In Edward's art, personalities never are! Nonetheless, BELCH has warm feelings for AGUECHEEK.

This empathy is reflected in the friendship between Peregrine and Sidney. On the other hand, the Edward-Sidney relationship is interesting too: After their tennis court "quarrel," they seem to meet often as their writing careers converge. And, the once contentious matter of Sidney's proposition for Anne Cecil's hand in marriage, that had come to nothing, also seemed, more or less, to have been resolved when Edward became her husband. Nonetheless, Edward continues to be wary of Sidney; as Sidney is of him. They compete; and both have their supporters. One of Sidney's loyal allies, a man named Stephen Glosson, dedicates a pamphlet of his to Sidney. In this work, Glosson, a Puritan, sees Literature as evil! While Sidney opposes this aspect of Glosson's thinking, he goes on to defend poetry. It is not "an art of lies," he says. On the contrary, it is an art of "true doctrine; not of effeminateness, but of notable stirring of courage; not of abusing man's wit, but of strengthening man's wit, not banished but honoured by Plato." A stout defence.

But, though Sidney agrees with Glosson on a few of the new English plays, harsh criticism of other writers is never far from his mind. Though he does not single out any author, his critiques are aimed at just one man: Edward de Vere.

Sidney is not happy about the techniques of story-telling on stage. He rails against the theatrical way of using time and space. In particular, the tendency to fore-shorten whole life-spans into a play of two hours duration, or assuming too much about moods and settings without explanation which confuses audiences. He presses his argument further by citing ladies walking on stage to gather flowers, "and then we must believe," he says, that "the stage is a garden!" Further, "we hear news of shipwreck in the same place; and then we are to blame if we accept it not for a rock…while in the meantime two armies fly in, represented with four swords and bucklers, and then, what hard heart will not receive it for a pitched battle field?" So staging is a problem for the fastidious Sidney. Inventiveness and imaginative presentations on stage distorts reality; a neater approach is much preferable, he thinks, than the messiness of life imputed into the current displays of dramatic art. But instead of avoiding his disagreements with Sidney, Edward confronts him by using a draft of his play *Henry V,* which refers to, and apologises for its shifts in time, mood and settings. On glossing over of the Battle of Agincourt, for instance, with delightful sarcasm, the CHORUS responds to Sidney's concerns as follows:

> "And so our scene must to the battle fly;
> Where – o for pity! – we shall much disgrace
> With four or five most vile and ragged foils
> Right ill dispos'd in brawl ridiculous
> The name of Agincourt."

Thus, on the eve of Edward's thirtieth birthday, personal feelings between himself and his *bete noir* Sidney, two brilliant literary Courtiers, who differ on at least two levels: First, on what is written in scripts, and second, on what is real life.

*

A few weeks after the completion of Alencon's seemingly successful mission to win Queen Elizabeth's hand, Edward and Sidney's rivalry takes a sinister turn. They decide to fight a duel. When the Queen hears about this proposed fight to death, she demands that it must not happen. But this could not and does not, stop the rumours from being spread by Edward's enemies: namely, that he plans to kill Sidney. Time passes. There is no duel. For his part, Edward explains: "The confrontation," he says to Lyly, "did not happen because Sidney is not brave enough to face me." By integrating real events into his dramatic compositions, Edward uses his quill to meld art and life. So in his draft of the play *Twelfth Night,* Sidney is portrayed as the character SIR ANDREW AGUECHEEK, who, challenged to a duel, shies away from it. But, this is not all. Edward also suggests that Burghley is the person responsible for stoking the fires. Through his wife, Lady Burghley, who had wanted Sidney to be her son-in-law. Burghley is the ever present thorn in Edward's side, who would again come into Edward's mind as he creates stories in play format for growing English audiences. So more and more, as he writes, he recognises the power of the pen: It is far mightier than the sword!

***

Hopes are raised that the Alencon-Queen Elizabeth marriage talks would come to an agreement, one way or the other. At the same time, Burghley tries to temper the strained relationship between Edward and Sidney, so that it would not interfere with the marriage negotiations. These are delicate diplomatic discussions; and fearing that it may get out of control, the Queen takes no chances: She issues an order to Burghley to keep the young bloods Edward and Sidney under close watch; and mandates that, for a while at least, Edward must not leave his lodgings at Greenwich. On Sidney's side, his friends feel great pain for him after his quarrel with Edward. In turn, Edward sees his house arrest as another manifestation of punishment as he considers the Queen's clever hand-in-glove technique.

But while both Edward and Sidney are highly thought of by the Queen, they have a competitor at Court for her affections: He is the older man named Christopher Hatton. Though

Hatton is fond of writing letters, in the "war" of words and intellect, he is no match for either Edward or Sidney. Hatton knows this; and though he is charming and a good team-player, he also knows that Edward, the gifted Earl of Oxford, is unpredictable; a force of nature. So throughout the Elizabeth-Alencon negotiations, while the badly smitten Hatton continues to send intimate, sweet words to the Queen, for her part as the one who presides over Court passions, making a decision on her own marriage to the Frenchman Alencon is, alas, still far from clear-cut, or close to being a done deal.

While Edward works on the draft of his comedic tale *Twelfth Night,* he shows his discontentment with the mean-minded Christopher Hatton. Edward follows Hatton's rise; and within a few weeks he finishes a second draft of *Twelfth Night*. Now, he reflects upon his manuscript titled: "*A Pleasant Conceit of De Vere, Earl of Oxford, discontented at the rising of a mean gentleman in the English court, circa 1580.*" In it, he gives reasons for discontentment. The first relates to his notes for the draft of *Twelfth Night* in which he and Hatton are hardly friends. He underlines the words "We do not like each other." So not surprisingly, in *Twelfth Night,* he casts Hatton as MALVOLIO, a man full of his own self-importance. Who is just as the character SIR TOBY BELCH calls him, a "rascally sheep biter." Then, Edward does an interesting thing: Perhaps for only the second time in his career: He places the MALVOLIO character in the play as receiving a letter that makes him look silly; a document that significantly is signed as "The future Unhappy."

This is a coded Pen-name which, in Latin is *Felix Infortunatus*: or, in English - the happy unfortunate, the very pseudonym that Hatton had adopted.

The second reason, is that *Twelfth Night* relates to the Mission work in England of Edward Campion, a Jesuit Priest. This is close to home for Edward remembers Campion who was one of his Commencement Speakers at Oxford University when he was sixteen. In the following years, Campion preached overseas, mainly in Prague. When he returned to England religious intolerance had reached worrying new heights; a topic that was on everyone's lips because the Pope had passed judgement on Queen Elizabeth: She must, he says, be assassinated. This call from Rome encourages anti-Catholic feeling in England. And, importantly, it is bad news for Campion. The Queen is urged by her Chief Advisors, Burghley, Walsingham, Leicester and Hatton to take more anti-Rome measures. These men feel that Campion must not be allowed to continue preaching. They arrest him; and after brutal torture, he is told to prepare his case for the Trial to come.

Campion faces the dilemma of preparing his case without the wherewithal to do so: For example, paper, pen and ink. This, and other Courtroom information is passed on to Edward by his Secretary Anthony Munday who attends the Campion Trial. Though the facts are true, Edward as playwright puts words in the mouths of characters who are not always the original, real person. And so, the information he receives about the Trial, is used in his play *Twelfth Night*. In Act 4, Scene 2, he writes that MALVOLIO is imprisoned without pen, ink and paper; and, he casts himself as FESTE who questions MALVOLIO about a man who never saw pen and ink. FESTE questions what Campion was denied! In the scene MALVOLIO says:

> "As I am a gentleman, I will live to be thankful to thee for't.
> FESTE: Alas, sir, how fell you besides your five wits?
> MALVOLIO: "Good fool, as ever thou wilt deserve well at my hand, help me to a candle and pen, ink and paper. Fool, there was never man so notoriously abused.

I am as well in my wits, fool, as thou art.
FESTE: But as well, then you are mad indeed if you be no better in your wits than a fool."

Through this scene Edward reflects his view of the harsh treatment Campion received because of his religion. Then comes the last of the reasons Edward gives for relating *Twelfth Night* to the "*pleasant conceit of De Vere, Earl of Oxford...*" manuscript. It has to do with the scenario of foreign affairs at this time. *Twelfth Night* holds within it a certain *international mood.* Edward is well attuned to the real life actors and political situation between Spain and Portugal where a man named Antonio had high hopes of becoming Ruler of Portugal. So not surprisingly in *Twelfth Night* Edward casts Antonio as one of the two friends in the play: ANTONIO and SEBASTIAN, as well as the Englishmen Sidney and Hatton as the characters: SIR ANDREW AGUECHEEK and MALVOLIO, respectively. As the friendship between ANTONIO and SEBASTIAN evolves in the play Edward shows off his skill in using misunderstandings as a dramatic device to tell his stories.

So the manuscript "*A pleasant conceit of de Vere, Earl of Oxford...,*" plays its part in Edward de Vere's story as the unusual and brilliant writer he is fast becoming!

***

Edward senses the good and growing reception he gets for his writing and theatre productions that take him hither and thither. His days are long and tiring. Life moves quicker now; often at a dizzying pace. He needs a place where he could relax, recharge and make more things happen. He needs a home. He buys Fisher's Folly; a large, attractive house that has a private Chapel and is surrounded by gardens and trees. It's central Bishopsgate Street location is very interesting; befitting of a man as curious as Edward. Here he is within earshot of the notorious Bedlam, the Insane Asylum, which houses mentally afflicted men and women. He often hears the inmates cries; their chattering, their sharp screams; their disturbed, disturbing voices, so to speak. From these troubled human beings, he learns about madness.

A short distance away from Fisher's Folly stands *The Theatre* and *The Curtain*. These are new structures; among the first commercial public theatres in London. With every performance, they spread the magic of staged story-telling to tried and tested audiences, as well as new spectators. Edward observes how the theatres are transforming the lives of Londoners. It is in these places that he feels he could explore and push further the production of the plays he is busy composing. Like the raised pulpit in a great church, he sees these theatres as mediums through which he could get across certain messages. Such thoughts underscore and propel him to write with greater purpose; and now crucially anchored in Fisher's Folly with his two Secretaries, he attends to business and, as a priority, he goes more often to the theatres.

*The Theatre* and *The Curtain* are magnets for theatre-goers, especially now in summer. People throng to see what are on offer. And as if for the first time, he marvels at the power of a staged play; at how ordinary men and women are taking to it. "The play is the thing!" he thinks, as it gains popularity. Although London Puritans detests drama, Edward is thankful for the theatres' progress. He knows the Queen is on his side. Pleased with how well aspected things are, he is astonished that there has never been a drama-loving Queen like Elizabeth! She loves poetry, and enjoys masques and plays. In short, she revels in dramatic entertainments. He knows that she is flexible; a reflection of her capricious, chameleon-like nature. He knows that she could, to some degree, turn a blind eye to certain vices, including some gambling, thieving and even some prostitution that takes place within the noisy theatres; and that one can pay to see a show, but see nothing of it! He knows too, that vagabonds and criminals who play cards and dice, use ill-gotten gains to buy the services of a Lady of the Night. But, it is the upside of the theatres that interests Edward. He and the Queen know that overall the theatre business is worth every penny spent on it because the stories they tell are able to reach the common people through the *spoken word*, as articulated by actors in live performances, in real time. For these lay Common folk, the ability to read and write is not a prerequisite for dramatic enjoyment. As he knows only too well such education and knowledge that he possesses is largely limited to the toffs; those at the top. It is the privileged preserve of the upper classes. He also knows that reaching out and inter-dependence are at the heart of the stories he tells.

*

So living in Fisher's Folly, he finds himself in the midst of an ongoing and extraordinary phenomenon: He sees Londoners passing through the doors of *The Theatre* and *The Curtain*. But, before their entry into these public spaces, he notes with utter satisfaction that a large number walk along along Bishopsgate Street, through the park, then make their way past the Bedlam, the tradesmen and street vendors, to the theatres. And, at the end of the performances, from his gallery, he sees the people returning to their homes as they pass Fisher's Folly. Whereas before, dramas were only performed mostly at Court and in Royal Palaces, now they can be seen in the public theatres. Londoners love what they see. And, as a golden rule for him as a playwright, he takes note of his audiences!

One evening while standing at the entrance to *The Curtain*, he recalls the excitement he'd felt on seeing the Commedia dell'arte performances in Paris, then in Venice, and he warms to the possibilities of this new format for the masses, as people file past and enter the theatre. The theatregoers' excited chatter and anticipation touches him as a playwright, all the more, as he aspires to become the best for Comedies! But, he thinks, there is the other side of the theatrical experience, too: The Christian Puritans. The self-proclaimed defenders of English morality, who hates, with a passion, the theatres which they see as evil, sinful places that should be avoided. On the contrary, Edward does not hide his love for, and association with, the theatres. But being upfront, brings him dangerously close to disrepute. Although he gets a bad press, a reputation for being notorious because of his love for the theatre, while his enemies demonise him, nothing can deter his resolve.

He moves quickly, decisively: He takes charge of a Company of Players who performs at *The Theatre.* Public interest moves apace: The groundswell of interest in the theatres rise; Edward and his Secretaries Lyly and Munday are excited.

"My Lord," Lyly says, "the prospects are better than encouraging."

"That is indeed so, Lyly," Edward says. "From here in the Gallery, each day, I watch. It is thrilling to see the people going past the Bedlam and the Ale wives to the theatres. They love what they see and hear! While this growing interest in our dramatic work continues..." He pauses. Then he says; "It will keep the Puritans, and Moralists at bay. But, for how long? That is the question."

Lyly nods in agreement. They both know that they must be ever watchful, as does Munday, who sits at his desk, just a few feet away in the large open-plan office. Their detractors are zealous in prosecuting anything to do with the dramatic stage. The very success of large and growing theatre attendance is seen by those in authority, as a blight; an unwelcome development and a threat that is likely to cause mob violence.

Soon, Edward learns of the Privy Councillors intention: They lobby London's Lord Mayor to send an urgent letter to the Queen's Lord Chancellor, begging him to shut down the theatres. The Mayor identifies both the players and plays as the culprits. "They are," he says of the players, "very odd and superficial men whose thinking and actions fall outside the law and, therefore, performing their plays is not in the interest of Serving God!" Not content with this demeaning accusation, the Mayor presses the Committee to act against the evil, heathen players and their plays. Tarring the Common-folk as unGodly troublemakers is, Edward thinks, to be expected. But, he is very pleased that eventually the Lord Chancellor bowed to the theatre-loving Queen's inclination and does nothing.

And so, Edward breathes somewhat easily; relieved that the first Elizabethan public theatres in London can continue to enjoy this first boom. So as he faces his enemies, he is at the heart of the London theatre world. Sitting at his desk, next to the spacious gallery, he drafts and, at times, discusses certain sections of plays and stories with his secretaries and visiting fellow-writers. Many weeks pass and Edward feels more settled and content at Fishers Folly. He likes the ambience. It is never a dull place. It hums and crackles as ideas are floated and debated at the highest intellectual-artistic levels, with studious ease and witty asides. This whole comradely experience is the closest he comes to something he'd longed for, since he'd separated from his wife Anne.

***

Like their boss, John Lyly and Anthony Munday feel at home at Fisher's Folly. They serve importantly as researchers, often copying passages from original manuscripts taking dictation from Edward. They also sort out correspondence and, when necessary, respond to Edward's queries. Taken together, they are fully employed; and, as scribes in their own right, they are stimulated by Edward's ideas and compositions. They discuss poetry, prose and plays written by Edward who, in turn, examines their work and comments. Their talks are often lively; and Edward masterfully guides both Secretaries whom he trusts with various projects. As the word gets around, a few more writers visit Fisher's Folly. Soon Edward's new home becomes not only his workplace, but also a venue for interested visitors who enjoy being in that literary environment. Creative energy abounds!

And so Fisher's Folly, close to the booming Shoreditch theatreland, becomes a bohemian literary retreat where Edward produces literary works of the highest quality. Here, he conceives and writes the final drafts of his plays. Fisher's Folly is the nearest thing to an Elizabethan writers workshop, with Lyly and Munday as supportive figures in an unusually ambitious literary enterprise, master-minded, at all times, by Edward de Vere.

Munday is energetic and determined-looking. He uses his literary "Apprenticeship" to good effect; and from what he learns, he creates his own high quality literature. One example is his Poem *Mirrour of Mutability* in which he experiments with verse and meter; and a few months later, he publishes *Celauto.* With time, a remarkable degree of openness develops between Edward and his Secretaries. Such intellectual closeness leads to more trust; and, after Munday returns from his travels in Europe, not surprisingly, he dedicates *Mirrour of Mutability* and *Celauto* to Edward. Munday also collaborates with his

"Master" on a poem titled the "Pain of Pleasure" that laments and celebrates the life of the true Renaissance Man.

So, what does their co-authorship offer? Whatever intellectual sparring there had been, now their Poem speaks of the joys and vanities of a Courtier's life! The "Pain of Pleasure"' upholds all that goes with being a nobleman: sportsmanship, honour and learning. And significantly, the poem reveals the kind and quality of writing Edward is doing in his Thirties. The themes he grapples with mirrors a capacious mind. But, interestingly he shows a tendency towards either being too wordy, or too brief. For sometime, he'd been maturing, but he is still a long way from what has yet to be realised. Nonetheless, the poem marks a major juncture in Edward's development as a Poet and Playwright.

"Thank you, Munday," Edward says, "for your *Mirrour* and *Celauto* Dedications to me. It is kind and generous of you. After these fine works, more publications will, I'm sure, flow from your pen. Well done."

This one instance of co-authorship with his titled Master, the Earl of Oxford, Munday, the hired employee, feels, is ample reward; profound social and professional recognition that is invaluable. It augurs well for his future, especially now with a new book in the making.

***

Of the two Secretaries, though Edward collaborates well with Munday, he is more drawn to John Lyly. Their personalities are mutable. Their many after working hours social meetings are in effect, ongoing literary discussions; sessions that often lasts late into the night. Intellectually, Lyly is bold, enterprising, learned and importantly, he has good judgement. Once again they meet.

"What are you writing now?" Edward asks Lyly:

"My Lord, right now," Lyly says,"my time is largely spent on something new. It is demanding. It overtakes me fully."

"What might that project be, Lyly?" Edward asks.

"It is a big challenge. There are not many books of its kind. My Lord, I am writing a *novel.* It is, as you know, something that is still a new form, a new genre of writing in England."

Edward knows that, as an art-form, the novel is relatively new. This is enough to drive his curiosity.

"Very interesting, I must say, Lyly," Edward says encouragingly, his curiosity raised. "From what you've told me, it is certainly new. But what is it called?"

"I call it *Euphues: The Anatomy of Wit,*" Lyly says. "It has been my working title for many months. I think I shall keep it. As a novel, put simply, it tells the story of an Italianate Courtier. It deals with themes like travel and death. And, there is love in it too. It is a work-in-progress which I hope to complete soon."

"How far in are you?"

"I'm reading over the final draft of the manuscript," Lyly says.

After that meeting, and later conversations, Lyly had finished the novel. Edward recognises it as an important work of English literature. After *Euphues* is published it sells well. And, as their Master-Secretary relationship evolves, Lyly says to Edward: "My Lord, I intend to Dedicate what I'm working on now, the sequel to my *Euphues,* to you." Edward is surprised. But, he cannot deny the importance of their many discussions and Lyly's respect which is revealed in his Dedicatory words. In the Dedication Lyly admits that while composing the novel, he'd regularly consulted Edward; a Homer-like figure whose literary advice he gratefully received. "For a whole year," Lyly says, "My *Euphues* was nursed by a Nobleman with great love, so that wheresoever Euphues wander, he hath his *nurse's name* in his forehead, where sucking his first milk he cannot forget his master."

Lyly's "Homer" is Edward de Vere; a man whose respect for Courtly matters and Castiglione's *The Courtier* has been a major influence upon Lyly's novel. Time and again, Edward had pushed Lyly to infuse his work with more playful linguistic creativity. Lyly remembers that while the novel was in the making, how much Edward had pushed him. "Experiment more with the language," Edward had urged. "Be more playful with words. Be more inventive." Coming from Edward, the English punner *extraordinaire*, the advice to be playful is understandable.

Lyly likes Edward's suggestions; and, after his second novel was published, both books enjoy popularity. In the wake of these publications, other euphuistic writers like Thomas Watson for example, are drawn to Fisher's Folly.

The collaboration between Edward and Lyly leaves its mark on both men's writings. Edward experiments with Euphuism, as he takes notes and writes drafts of plays that reflects his life at Fisher's Folly: Of these drafts of four plays, three of them are set in Italy: *Romeo and Juliet, Much Ado About Nothing,* and *Love's Labour Lost.* The fourth is *Twelfth Night.* So stylistically, at least in Comedy, Edward and Lyly shares much. But, this is not all. Lyly's innovative novels undoubtedly points to a new way forward. It introduces more diversity than hitherto to Elizabethan writing. It mixes wit and romance, using female characters and interweaving them into the stories of Common folk and Nobility.

Soon after he'd employed Lyly, Edward recognised that his relationship with Lyly would be beneficial. They bounce important ideas off each other. Theirs is a win-win relationship for Elizabethan literature. That they influence each other at Fisher's Folly is not in doubt. But, as Lyly knows, his day-today work, and literary development takes place, fundamentally, and only because he is Edward's employee at Fisher's Folly.

***

So Edward's residence at Fisher's Folly teaches him new things. He's in a fertile environment where he and those with whom he engages gains invaluable knowledge and learns new lessons. It is a liberating experience; a haven for all who are desirous of intellectual flights of fancy. As his interaction with his Secretaries and others sparks novel ways of composing literature, now Edward's life takes a new turn. While matters of the mind preoccupy him, he is susceptible to physical needs. Passionate desire wells up when he sees and meets a beautiful young woman at Court.

"What is your name?" he asks.

"My Lord," she says, "My name is Anne Vavasour." She smiles broadly; if a touch shyly. And, if he is not mistaken, he thinks she is green; almost entirely innocent, a novice in the ways of the "Riotous Inn" that is the Court. He likes her at once. She is a slim, dark-haired, teenage Maid of Honour. Her family is of good pedigree in the feudal social pecking order, ranking somewhere between a Baron and a Knight. He learns that Vavasour's Uncle is Thomas Knyvet, who is employed in the Queen's Private household; and that it is he who got her the job as a gentle-woman who serves in the Queen's private quarters.

Edward and Vavasour recognise each other at once as hot-bloods; and, interestingly, Edward is pleased to know that Vavasour is fond of writing Verses. The relationship between Edward and Vavasour develops quickly. And soon the two lovers' feelings finds expression in words. Together, Vavasour and Edward pens a poem about a girl who thinks about love.

himself, he asks many questions. He knows that the "cause" would disappoint the Queen, his wife Anne Cecil-de Vere, as well as Lord and Lady Burghley. Meanwhile as Vavasour gets bigger carrying his child, Edward's thoughts on how to leave England, intensifies. But, he pauses to ask: "What would I do in Spain? Or, even in France?" Life, as he'd known it, has been far from neat and tidy; or as he would have liked it to be. But, the literary work he had done these past four years, takes him aback. He has made great progress as a playwright, he thinks; and just as he's employed Secretaries to get on with the current productions and works to come, this Vavasour affair, intervenes. He broods; but he must cope with the situation. For the time being, he stays in England. He worries and waits. As a counterweight to his anxiety, he feels strongly that he is on the brink; the verge of entering a new, mature phase of an unknown journey with his ever-handy quill.

"Miscarriage! Miscarriage!" He repeats the word after being told that Vavasour's pregnancy has ended. At first, he reacts with disbelief. Then he feels some relief and acceptance: It is true, he thinks, she has miscarried. For a long while, a mixture of emotions overtakes him. "There's no need now," he says to himself "for me to run off to Spain, or anywhere else. And I do not have to admit anything about this to Cousin Henry Howard."

At this juncture, he sees new dramatic possibilities and begins work on another play: *Much Ado About Nothing*. In this draft, the "miscarriage" is interwoven as the stuff not just of life, but of the stage, too!

***

Though nothing could stem the whispers and some tittle-tattle at Court about the Vavasour miscarriage, Edward enjoys a feeling of unspeakable relief. But, alas, carnal desire gets the better of him: He and Vavasour continue to meet in secret. Then, some weeks later, she says: "My Lord, you have done it to me again! I am with child!" Edward is speechless. Suddenly, he is plunged again into a dark place. Anger with himself and helplessness coalesce as all his earlier fears of Vavasour being with child and the shame he'd felt, comes back. "I am pregnant again, My Lord!" she says. And this time, all attempts at hiding her growing belly is futile. He thinks of concealing his paternity, perhaps in the short term, but he knows that soon he must tell the Queen, then his wife and father-in-law. And what would he tell his Cousin Henry Howard this time? Momentarily, he considers, once more, a trip to Spain. But as months of enormous personal and social pressures on himself pass, at last, Vavasour's labour pains come.

The rumours are true; and soon all at Court anticipates the real-life drama of the playwright and the Maid of Honour's personal creation that has yet to see the light of day, a new-born child. Though it should be a matter worthy of celebration, such a thing does not reflect his mood just now. He is deeply unhappy about Vavasour's second pregnancy. It is Edward's doing, another example of his impulsive behaviour! And, for prolonged periods, he stews in self-pity and shame. He thinks of the pain his action would cause to others. "Consequences, young man," one of his early tutors had once cautioned: "Think of the consequences of your actions."

Alas Edward's troubles are not concerned only with Vavasour. He chooses this time to tell the Queen of another error of judgement: His treasonous pro-Catholic meetings. A more damning revelation by a stalwart defender of the Queen and Protestant England, is hard to comprehend. This places him as a high-ranking nobleman, the Earl of Oxford, in a very awkward position: For the last four years, he'd been in close contact with two Catholics: His cousin Henry Howard and Charles Arundell. Together, with another man named Francis Southwell, they'd been planning ways and means to convert England to the Church of Rome. In these times of heightened religious tension and secret plots in England, the schemes he'd been devising with his associates are highly unusual. Nothing, he thinks, could be more dangerous. In a word, it is explosive. And for a few moments, he considers the imminent birth of his child with Vavasour in the larger scheme of things: the contentious politics and religion of Elizabethan England which is highly-charged. Is he befogged by his usual tipple of Rhenish of which he had had a few glasses the evening before? Or, amidst all his troubles, is he becoming a man of deranged mind? The charge of treasonous Catholic plotting against him is grave. He is to be tried. And how would he defend himself at his Trial? He has never felt so conflicted and lacking in confidence, as now. Time is of the essence.

Then the day of his Trial comes. It is on a Friday just before Christmas in 1580. The scene is set: Tension fills the air as Edward walks into the Courtroom and faces those sitting in judgement of him. He has no prepared plan of defence. In the stillness and quiet of the room, having been, for so long a Star Courtier, Edward drops to his knees before the Queen. He confesses that with Howard, Arundell and Southwell, he had joined with Roman Catholics under the guidance of a Jesuit Priest. His humiliating prostration before the Queen gives much satisfaction to his enemies. Even the normally severe-looking face of Christopher Hatton breaks into a smile.

Later, after he confesses Edward had turned to Mauvissiere, the French Ambassador, for support of his account. But Mauvissiere knows that the danger of supporting any plot or conspiracy against the State would end his political career. So he does not corroborate Edward's story. Overall it is not a dignified sight before the Queen. But, if Edward feels humiliated, Mauvissiere is, to some degree, tainted too.

Having decided to end his treasonous pro-Catholic meetings with Arundell and Howard, Edward had tried to persuade Arundell to become a witness for the Crown. But later, when he meets both men in a local tavern, they mount a strong attack upon him. He is accused of many terrible things: The list includes telling lies, being a murderer, an atheist, an alcoholic and engaging in dark practices such as bestiality and necromancy. And believing Edward to be monstrous, Arundell also accuses him of going as far as preferring to drink blood, rather than wine! The allegations made are very serious.

"These are libellous charges," Edward says. "But how true are they?" The air is thick with contentious arguments as the three men remember times past when allegedly Edward regaled them with many tall tales. But this last meeting ends quickly. Edward protests against the charges his opponents make against him, because these men are no lovers of poetry and drama their "libels" shows bad feelings towards him and a downright negative attitude towards the English theatre. So, from being fellow-believers (as Catholics) and colleagues, Edward, Arundell and Howard are now far apart: More serious charges, Edward has never faced. Who is telling the truth in this unpleasant, heady confrontation. The acrimony and bitterness continue, but neither Edward's "crazy criminal acts," nor the Arundell Libels can be proved. There is stalemate; and though no one is prosecuted, the sulphurous fall-out of the malicious accusations depresses the Queen. It is, by association, she thinks, a scandal that affects the Court and, as such, it has to be dealt with firmly.

A few months after the meeting and heated exchanges between Edward, Arundell and Howard, Vavasour, nearing the end of her second pregnancy, gives birth. Once again, Edward becomes a father. The child is named Edward. And this time he does not deny paternity. But after his dramatic confession before the Queen, now amidst the rancorous, loud echo of the Arundell-Howard libels, and a "bastard" child with Vavasour, Edward desperately strives for some peace of mind. But, he is surrounded; never far away are adversaries, past and present, who line up to defame him now after the bastard child's birth. Though much time has passed since his tennis court quarrel with Philip Sidney, relations between them has not mellowed: It is still edgy. Another Howard, Philip Howard (not to be confused with Henry Howard and his libellous partner Charles Arundell) inherits the Earldom of Arundel.

To celebrate his new title, a tilt Tournament is announced to take place at Whitehall. Earl Arundel chooses to joust as a Knight named Callophisus, meaning "lover of beauty;" and having sent out the call for combatants to participate in the tourney, Edward and Philip Sidney respond positively. Sidney appears as the "White Knight" and his opponent, the Earl of Arundel, are set to compete.

On the day of the Tournament, before the Royal stand and a large audience, Sidney tries hard to overcome the Earl of Arundel. The large crowd and all in the Royal reviewing area, follow each move as Sidney's valiant efforts fails to defeat his young opponent. Soon after, Edward follows Sidney. He picks up the fallen Standard. This act is both symbolic and real. In these years of Elizabeth's reign, the Sun Tree is a symbol of her Queenly power. While Sidney had played the role of the White Knight, Edward favours participating as the Knight of the Sun Tree. This gesture is not lost on the Queen who recognises that Edward is going all out to win the battle against his opponents; and thereby show contrition and his need of her forgiveness after his recent treacherous religious transgressions. For his challengers who had tried to unseat and defeat him, it was not their day. Edward proves to be a steadfast and strong Knight. The Queen applauds him. Is this a clear signal that she would not punish him? Perhaps. Now sitting astride his victorious horse, thoughts of the Queen's forgiveness fills his head, while loud applause ring out for him as winner of the top honour of the day. "I've done my best," he says to himself, as he approaches the Royal stand. "I could do no more." His expectations are high. But soon he is a little crest-fallen. Why? Because he senses that the Queen's presentation of his prize is tempered with restraint. Her almost sombre regal mood mirrors this: All is not forgiven, she seems to be saying.

It is a fine Spring day and, at last, the Queen is told that Anne Vavasour, her young Royal Maid of Honour, has given birth. And, to rub salt into her well-hidden, but still open wound of disappointment with Edward's misdemeanours, she learns that the child is named Edward, after his father. Thus Edward's questionable behaviour adds more distance between himself and the Queen, in whose eyes, the situation is dire. "How can I escape from this sorry predicament?" Edward asks himself.

***

Forty-eight hours after Vavasour gives birth, Sir Francis Walsingham notes that she has a son in the Maiden's chamber; and that the Earl of Oxford, the father of the child, "hath withdrawn himself." Why is Walsingham so concerned? Because it is thought Edward intends to flee across the Channel. But the ports are being closely watched to prevent any chance of escape. He knows that running away would not be helpful. And, unbeknownst to him, Walsingham records that the gentle-woman, Vavasour, on the self-same night her child was delivered, was taken away from the birthplace. She was committed to the Tower! Others, who have been found in any way to be parties to the cause, have been interrogated. Then, he says "Her Majesty is greatly grieved by what has happened." Finally, Walsingham expresses the hope that there will be no need for anyone else associated to be put in jail. But how much worse would Edward feel if he'd seen what Walsingham had written. As the chief culprit, the central character in this real life drama, Edward is arrested. He is taken to the Tower, where melancholy feelings overwhelm him. He hits a new low. His mind is in turmoil. Childbirth and father-hood outside wedlock, are stunning news. Members of the Royal Court, even the gossipy gossipers are pleasantly shocked: Some rejoice; and not for the first time, because of Edward's actions. The scandal has mileage; it transcends national boundaries. It reaches Germany where it is reported in a Newsletter with utter candour: "The Earl of Oxford," it proclaims, "is in the Tower for forgetting himself with one of the Queen's Maids of Honour. She too, is in the Tower. This is the situation, although the Earl has a pretty wife, who is the daughter of England's Lord Treasurer. It is said the Earl will not live with her."

Another keen observer, Master of the Revels, Sir George Buc, commits his thoughts to paper. He writes that for impregnating Vavasour, by fathering this "base son," Edward is sent to the Tower. This imprisonment reflects the Queen's disappointment and unhappiness in her relations with the Earl of Oxford.

So altogether, Edward's life takes a turn for the worse. He is in the wilderness; in deep trouble. There is more than one reason for this: It hurts to think of the Queen's displeasure which he'd brought upon himself for stubbornly separating himself from his wife; for scandalous and traitorous pro-Catholic behaviour with Arundell and Howard, and for dishonouring a Royal Maid of Honour. He tries to be as hopeful as he can; and daring to peer into the future, he considers the days ahead: "What can I expect?" he asks himself. Most certainly, a lengthy exile, he thinks. His fall from grace is spectacular: No longer is he one of Her Majesty's favourite Courtiers. Her action: the order to imprison him shows a side of her which he'd not seen before. No doubt, she feels very strongly about him! And sending him into exile, to the Tower, is a warning to him for future reference as to how far she will go to discipline and keep him in check.

His long days in jail jolts him into a new awareness. He thinks of the sad tales of great men and women of England who, for long stretches, had "lived" in the cells of the Tower before brutally losing their lives. It is the first time that he's been denied his freedom. He wonders about other offending Courtiers and thinks his punishment is too severe. But whatever else he may have been denied, he is allowed visitors. Among them are his trusted Secretaries, Munday and Lyly. They visit him separately. As their employer and literary Master, they discuss current and new plays. When Munday first comes, Edward speaks to him about a new idea inspired by his imprisonment. He explains to Munday the idea he has in mind:

"It is a play about another man who had been imprisoned here,"

he says: "Sir Thomas More."

"Ah, yes, My Lord, a great man of his times," says Munday.

"Quite so," Edward says. "As I envisage it, the play will tell the story of a loyal Servant to Henry VIII. A man who quells an insurrection and is later thrown in the Tower and executed."

More, as Edward envisages portraying him, at least at this early stage of thinking about the story, is a full spirited principled, genial man whose downfall comes not due to his own failings, but rather to the fickle whims of the fates: "I see Sir Thomas More as a cosmic tragedy," he says to himself. Munday is most attentive: And as if he was taking dictation, his face lights up as Edward speaks. He scribbles fast, getting down each word of what Edward says in his notebook before he leaves the Tower.

Writing in the cell is quite an experience as Edward sketches a structure of the play he has in mind. Every day brings new meaning to his presence in the cell. He sees things in a different light: He is sympathetic to More; and is at one with him in his contempt for rebels and rebellion. He imagines himself in conversation with More. Like tolling church bells, their voices chime in unison. With nothing to distract him in solitary confinement, unlike Campion, he is granted paper, pen and ink; and within days he finishes a rough draft of the play. He titles it: "Sir Thomas More." He admits, that he'd been keen to flee the country when Vavasour had first become pregnant. He'd thought of going to Spain or France. But such an action would have cast him amongst those whom More detests: So now in his play sketch, he puts these words in More's mouth:

"Who will obey a traitor?
Or how can well that proclamation sound
When there is no addition but a rebel
To qualify a rebel?...
What country by the nature of your error
Should give you harbour? Go you to France or Flanders;
To any German province, Spain or Portugal,
Nay anywhere that not adheres to England,
Why, you must needs be strangers...
Give up yourself to form obey the magistrate,
And there's no doubt but mercy may be found if you so
seek it."

But this Tower-inspired idea of a play is one more draft of dramas that interests Edward; a consequence of his punishment for which, humiliatingly, he seeks mercy. This shameful stretch in jail is cause for pause. He will not write about his misadventures in a play, if he does not feel strongly about it. How strange, he thinks, sitting for hours without the convenience and comfort of his books and papers to hand. Unnerving silence pervades the seemingly interminable long hours in his cell. Soon, he lapses into a melancholy state which provokes a stream of thoughts. He recalls Munday's visit; and how much he'd appreciated their conversation: How intently he'd listened, hanging on to every inflection of the words that Munday had spoken. And vice-versa. After that meeting with Edward, as Munday walks away from the Tower, he feels liberated by the idea that Edward had raised; and before he gets home, a storyline had begun to form in his head.

The next morning, from the notes he'd taken, Munday begins to sketch his own version of a play about Sir Thomas More. "There is more that I'd like to talk to Lord Edward about," he says to himself. But he knows that has to wait until the next time that he meets his boss. So, he expects a future meeting with Edward to develop the idea of a play.

*

Edward learns that he is not the only one who is put in jail at this time. He is told that after giving birth, Vavasour was also taken to the Tower. They are kept in different places. And soon Vavasour's relations with Edward takes a new twist. Her white-hot sexual passion and feelings for Edward, it seems, begins to cool. The birth of her child and the sudden interruption of their affair takes its toll.

Not seeing each other, as Vavasour spends more lonely days

in jail, her thoughts shift: They are directed at another man, someone who is one of her jail visitors. He is Sir Henry Lee, a former tiltyard champion. Being much older than her, Lee is flattered, and deeply attracted. But, he wonders: Are Vavasour's attentions, another of her brief, youthful fancies? Only time could answer that question. For now, things with Sir Henry move fast. It marks the beginning of a passionate love affair between her and Sir Henry. As Edward knows, Vavasour is of a mercurial nature; prone to act on her impulse. But, in spite of her shifting attentions, to Vavasour's credit, though Edward is out of sight, he is not entirely out of mind, for now, at the end of their tempestuous romance, she writes a parting poem. On receiving her correspondence, he recognises the handwriting. Hurriedly he opens the envelope and reads:

> "Thus farewell, friend, I will continue strange.
> Thou shalt not hear by word or writing ought.
> Let it suffice my vows shall never change;
> As for the rest, I leave it to thy thought."

Edward re-reads the lines of this parting poem, not once, but twice. Then, three times. Their remarkable affair has taken them from passionate embrace to the cold Tower. Still holding the letter, Edward's feelings for Vavasour are stirred. But, he realises that things have run their course. It is the end for them. He must now come to terms with himself, Vavasour and the world *outside* the Tower.

***

At last, Edward is released. His long boring days in "idle cell" are over. He walks away from the Tower and basks in a new sensation: The feeling of being free in a different way; freedom blessed by the gorgeous shimmer of light on a summer's day in June 1581. He breathes slowly, deeply of the fresh gentle breeze. But, as he moves further away from the Tower, he knows he is not entirely free of surveillance: For a few weeks yet, he would still be under house arrest. Then, he receives the Queen's acknowledgement of his freedom. Now, officially free, but knowing he is in the midst of Spies and Informers who lurk in the shadows, gradually he regains his stride and lives again as a Courtier. He is delighted to be back at Fisher's Folly. Munday greets him and says:

"My Lord, I have added to your notes and outline of Sir Thomas More." He hands the playscript to Edward who takes it to his desk. Later, he passes the script back to Munday. "You've done an excellent job," he says to Munday. Then, he calls Lyly to join him and Munday to discuss outstanding issues: They dwell for quite some time, on certain plays and productions.

***

Edward is mindful of Burghley's mediating role on his behalf while he was imprisoned. Just being out of the Tower, gives him a renewed sense and appreciation of what being free is. But being out of prison, doesn't mean he is out of the woods, so to speak. He fears the scandalous bad-mouthing he gets from Lords Arundell and Howard who are bent on turning the Queen against him! As the rank, peculiar smell of the Tower lingers in his memory, he accepts that his all powerful father-in-law Burghley is the man best placed to turn for help. So, "Unless your Lordship shall make some move to put Her Majesty in mind thereof," he writes, "I fear, in these other causes of the two Lords (Arundell and Howard), she will forget me. For she is nothing of her own disposition, as I found, so ready to deliver or speedy to commit – and every trifle gives her matter for long delay."

As if haunted by a spectre, time and again, Edward is touchy about his loss of Good Name. He tries his best to retrieve it. But how could he, when he is surrounded by enemies. He does not underestimate the under-handedness; the treachery of Arundell and Howard. And while he admits to a smidgen of truth to the slanders, he cannot forget his enemies' exaggerations. He likens the world to a cunning place; and notes that his accusers make of a shadow, something of substance that is akin to a truth. Of these fellows, he adds, "I do not doubt but so to decipher them to the world as easily Your Lordship shall look into their lewdness and unfaithfulness."

Burghley reads the words "lewdness and unfaithfulness" used by his wayward son-in-law with some amusement and smiles as if freed from his own severe critical thoughts that he'd expressed earlier about Edward's "lewd friends."

For weeks after his release from the Tower, Edward, a popular and good socialiser is, as always, surrounded by people, but now, he feels the sharp prod of being less popular at Court. Sometimes he feels like an outsider. He is the lone Earl, who is without his wife or a Mistress. And while lingering thoughts of Vavasour comes and goes, he keeps his distance from her. Feeling isolated, he becomes increasingly reflective: He thinks about his wife, Anne, and weighs the pluses and minuses of his marriage. Then, at last, before Christmas, after their long separation, he decides that he and Anne should meet. He writes to her: Not once, but twice. She responds in writing. This is a rare experience for Edward, who reads Anne's correspondence with interest, as well as some trepidation. Why so? Because he is confident that Anne's response is not entirely her own. She is doing so under the firm advice and guidance of her father, Burghley, who is in on the act. Edward reads Anne's first letter: "My good Lord, I beseech you in the name of that God which knoweth all my thoughts and love towards you, let me know you are moved to continue me in this misery, and which you would have me do in my power to recover your constant favour – so as Your Lordship may not be led still to detain me in calamity without some probable cause, whereof, I appeal to God; I am *utterly innocent*."

"Utterly innocent." The words play on Edward's mind. He thinks of the lost years of marriage: in particular, his original charge of Anne's unfaithfulness which has upset her deeply. Less than a week later, she writes once more: "Most sorry to perceive how you are? Unquieted with the uncertainty of the world," of which she too, she adds, is "familiar with." And, as if to underline her honesty and collaboration with her powerful all-knowing, all-seeing father, she assures Edward of his best wishes. So, for better or worse, Anne admits that Edward is right about her father's interference, and of him being privy to her letters!

So before the end of the year, with Yuletide greetings in the chilly air, Edward and Anne re-engages practically as man and wife, as partners. And how odd, indeed symbolic, it is that while the Alencon-Queen Elizabeth marriage proposal is still unresolved, Edward and Anne ends their long separation and recommits themselves to the bond matrimony.

***

Back in harness as a husband, Edward's melancholy feelings of the last years had already left its indelible marks; notably propelling him as a playwright to use the themes of exile and abandonment in an early draft of his play *Timon of Athens* which follows the decline and fall of a man who is unable to deal with money, power and responsibility. That man is

TIMON. His reduced state is a painful experience with which he tried to come to terms. His devoted Servant FLAVIUS (a portrayal of Edward's Secretary John Lyly) informs his spendthrift Master of the hard reality: That his dwindling estates and income is not enough to pay his mounting debts. It is a gloomy fate that Edward in real life recognises as becoming all too likely. He reflects this in the play.

> "FLAVIUS: O my good Lord
> At many times I brought in my accounts,
> Laid them before you; you would throw them off,
> And say you found them in mine honesty...
> My loved lord,
> Though you hear now, too late! – yet now's a time -
> The greatest of your having lacks a half
> To pay your present debts.
> TIMON: Let all my land be sold!
> FLAVIUS: 'Tis all engaged some forfeited and gone,
> And what remains will hardly stop the month
> Of present dues."

FLAVIUS speaks up. He shows himself to be an honest man: "If you suspect my husbandry or falsehood," he says to TIMON, "Call me before the exactest auditors. And set me on the proof." As Edward's Secretary, Lyly plays an omnibus role. For a while he has been serving as Edward's Book-keeper. So not surprisingly, Edward casts him as the trustworthy FLAVIUS.

***

# VII

## "Thus I made lame by fortune's dearest spite"

*"No legacy so rich as honesty"*

Being together again, Edward and Anne develops a new mutual respectfulness. And while they are reunited, the Alencon-Elizabeth marriage talks are still alive; but only just. Burghley favours the marriage for political reasons. But the Queen herself, having basked in the Frenchman's whole-hearted attentions for quite some time, is less keen. As her feelings get cooler, she assumes a diplomatic, Queenly persona for as long as she could. Then suddenly, all talk of marriage breaks down. And with this, a veil is lifted. As Elizabeth feels relieved, for now, at least, hopes for an heir to the English Throne ends. Not having a Successor is of lesser importance to Queen Elizabeth than her right to Rule; to wield, at will, the power of seeming omnipotence. She is a superb self-publicist. Being a childless Queen, she thinks, could be used to symbolize purity: She feels the need to be a "Virgin Queen." As Ruler, she thinks of her daily preoccupation of exercising unchallenged authority, bolstered by the power of myth and Virginity. And so, the long anticipated Royal marriage talks that had so divided Protestants and Catholics in England, die. But, from its ashes rises a new Phoenix: The Virgin Queen. Instead of seeing Elizabeth as growing older, Court poets, playwrights and painters portray her as desirable and still marriageable; an earth-like Venus with metaphysical allure and power. Thus as Venus, she lives in hope of meeting her match, an Adonis. The nearest person to the Queen who resembles an Adonis at Court, is Edward. But he is now back with his wife. Nonetheless, the power of myth building; of upholding the idea of a "Virgin Queen" persists. Soon, she becomes a cult figure who rises to become a Moon Goddess. But Edward does not accept the Elizabethan propaganda. In his imagination, as playwright and poet, the Queen has more of an earthly feel; she remains young and marriageable, as she herself wants to be.

Knowing the Queen as well as he does, Edward reflects upon their intimacies which, set against his misdemeanours, helps him to ward-off any seriously hard feelings towards her. But, overriding all his reasonable thoughts, things have changed. He finds himself estranged: There is, he admits, much distance between himself and the Queen, even though he is still her Lord Great Chamberlain of England. He remembers her stubbornness in keeping him out, and asks himself: "How long would she do so? How can I get back in favour?" But, as he poses these questions, he is embroiled in a fray; a fight that relates directly to his affair with Vavasour.

Aggrieved members of the Vavasour family feels the need to restore what they see as their honour and pride; their tarnished reputation. Hard words are exchanged, and the adversaries are ready and willing to go further. They draw their swords and clashes in brabbles and frays follow between members of the de Vere and Vavasour families and their loyal servants. The chief instigator in all of this is Thomas Knyvet, Anne Vavasour's Uncle. News of the personal fight between Edward and Knyvet spread quickly: Word reaches Nicholas Faint, Francis Walsingham's Secretary, who reports that both men are hurt. But it is very clear that Edward is the more dangerously injured! This "duel" nearly ends his life. It leaves an indelible mark upon him; both in body and in mind. And, not without effect upon his writings.

The wound from Knyvet's sword is horrific; a deep cut in Edward's leg. The injury is painful; a daily reminder that the damage to his leg will not heal quickly. The horror and starkness of this hits home; and once again, he is reminded of how close he'd come to death. He'd escaped being hurt many times as the sportsman *par excellence*, but now he can no longer stride freely. He walks with a limp. Slowly as weeks and months pass, the memory of the clash with Knyvet recedes, but it does not fade. The mental and physical scar and pain remains a profoundly disturbing part of his life. This, he thinks, will continue to be so. "I am, at least, alive!" he consoles himself, for in the fierce clash, one of his Servants was killed. As he mourns the death of this man, he feels incredibly lucky that he is not totally disabled. He feels a new sense of commitment to his work, knowing that he is able-bodied enough to get around: Most importantly, that he could walk and ride his horse.

But, the fight does not end with that deadly confrontation. Bad feelings and hostile behaviour between the two families continue. It merges into a "war;" a war that arises ironically from an act of love and its dire consequences. A dramatic love story suggests itself. He thinks about a story that concerns warring families; in particular, the family that has left him lame. He broods over the street clashes in London for some time. Then, he mulls over a story surrounding the fights. He writes copious notes and makes rough sketches as he drafts a play. He is specially interested in the family quarrels and now, he remembers his Italian travels; in particular, his memorable visit to the city of Verona. He scribbles more notes and writes the names of two families: The CAPULETS and the MONTAGUES. Having done so, he thinks of his passionate, but brief love affair with Vavasour.

As he writes, more of a draft, more fights between his men

and Knyvet's servants follow. One of the casualties of these clashes is an Italian Fencing Master named Rocco Bonetti, a teacher *extraordinaire*. Bonetti's tutorship of students in London is seen as a threat to the monopoly of English Fencing Schools. Edward's men are unhappy about Bonetti and a campaign is waged against him. Bonetti takes no chances. He flees to Scotland for a while. But when he returns to London, to fend-off attacks, instead of using his skills as a Master of Fencing, he seeks the help of the French Ambassador, Mauvissiere, who complains to Spymaster Walsingham that the threats by Edward's men leaves Bonetti unprotected and insecure in England.

The street fights continue; and Bonetti is faced with the dilemma of defending himself. But this, he knows, is not easy or straightforward because he is up against unreasonable and violent men. So while Bonetti's return to London keeps him in employment as a teacher of Fencing, as if giving the lie to any charge of timidity on his part, Bonetti opens a school in Blackfriars, the notorious area where ruffians loiter. Here, he finds it difficult to avoid the ongoing street fights. "You do know, don't you?" Bonetti says to the French Ambassador, "that these rogues use the so-called 'Blackfriars Liberties' to rob and cause mayhem."

Bonetti's complaint and fear is justified because surprise attacks between Edward's servants and Knyvet's men continue on the streets. Soon after Midsummer's day 1582, two of Edward's servants, one named Gastrell, attacks Knyvet's men at Blackfriars. Later, more fights follow. Then, for a while, there is a lull before fights between the quarrelling families stop. Alas, in the fragile peace that follows lasting damage had already been done. On his last visit to Blackfriars, mindful of his first fight with Knyvet, Edward limps away, seething with anger.

In the days that follow, he nurses his wound: Moving slowly and carefully, he tries to disguise his pain. With every step he takes, he thinks of how he might use that near death street fighting experience in his art as a playwright. When he gets back to the safety of his home, he opens his Notebook and reads the scribblings he'd already made. He considers the rough sketch for a play. After more thought and note-taking, a few days later, on a new page, he writes fresh words to which he later adds new lines on the composition of characters and dialogue. He consults the notes that he'd taken while he was in Verona. And, instead of duels in London streets, he shifts the location of the tale to Verona. Now he is totally immersed in the evolving story: A few days later, it becomes the rounded draft of a new play. He titles the manuscript "Romeo and Juliet." For a while he reflects upon what he'd written, so far: Then he decides to open the play at the point of truce between the combatants, setting a scene in which the PRINCE OF VERONA tries to prevent another MONTAGE-CAPULET street fight. Of this PRINCE, bearing in mind his and his Servants three Blackfriars street fights, Edward writes:

"PRINCE OF VERONA: Three civil brawls bred of an
airy word By thee, old Capulet and Montague
Have thrice disturbed the quiet of our streets
And made Verona's ancient citizens
Cast by their grave beseeming ornaments
To wield old partisans in hands as old,
Cankered with peace to part your cankered hate.
If ever you disturb our streets again
Your lives shall pay the forfeit of the peace.
For this time all the rest depart away.
You Capulet shall go along with me;

And Montague, come you this afternoon
To know our father's pleasure in this case
To old Freetown, our common judgement place."

He is excited as he polishes what he writes. Here and there, he adds words to the draft. He likes the way the story has been evolving. Apart from the original duel, he wonders how much Burghley knows about the Knyvet quarrels and street brawls. But, Edward knows better: In his play, he puts these words in ROMEO'S mouth:

"Doth not JULIET think me an old murderer
Now I have stained the childhood of our joy
With blood removed but little from her own?"

And so the young lovers ROMEO and JULIET, whom Edward creates, engages in struggles during which a MONTAGUE is killed. A few months later, before a truce is called, one more CAPULET is killed. While Edward writes of this last CAPULET, he has in mind another death: that of one of Knyvet's men.

Against this background, he feels the full impact of the Queen's aloofness from him. A disgraced Courtier he agrees he is. But this admission does not detract from the well-spring of creative energy that surges through him. Uplifted, he is moved to even greater efforts to distinguish himself as a writer. But, as a Nobleman, especially at this juncture, he vows, and is absolutely clear about one thing: That he will not use his name as the author of any of his literary works. The only way forward is to use either "Anonymous" or a Pen-name. The shame of revealing himself as an author has to be avoided. So, the distinguished Nobleman-poet maintains his daily output as the mysterious playwright, but, for better or worse, the name of the game is disguise. Another way of ensuring his anonymity, is through puns on words; as well as combining aspects of real people and experience with artistic portrayals of character; a mask which he places between himself and authorship. Necessity, is the mother of invention, he thinks.

***

After the street brawls, the pain of Edward's injury is compounded, not only by his exclusion from Court, but also because he needs money. His options are reduced and his isolation disturbs him. But he feels renewed satisfaction that, so far, an unusual number of books have been Dedicated to him. This shows enormous respect for him; even though, outwardly, many fellow-Courtiers see him as an outsider. To his credit, he is very pleased that Fisher's Folly, his literary workshop, is running smoothly. It is, as Lyly puts it, a "hive of activity, where honeyed words flow with ease." While Edward encourages the flow of "honeyed words," Munday and Lyly, necessarily see a lot of each other. All together the Folly's camaraderie keeps Edward remarkably even-tempered.

"Here, Munday," Edward says, "take a look at this." He walks over to Munday's desk with a script in hand. "I have acted upon what I'd said to you when you visited me in the Tower. In my darkest moments of those shameful days, from my lower depths, I'd vowed to write a story; a play. But being locked up in jail, as I'd said, I was reminded of another man who'd sat alone in a Tower cell. How must he have felt? I thought. How must it have been for him?" Edward pauses. Then he says: "Here's an outline of the play." He hands Munday a manuscript.

Munday scans the title on the first page. He looks serious: "I like the title, My Lord," he says. Then, he adds in a stronger voice: "Sir Thomas More!"

Among scholars and writers like Lyly and Munday, Edward is held in high esteem: His title, the Earl of Oxford, commands respect among his fellow Scribes; and he is always relaxed and willing enough to be a Patron of good causes. He is proud and happy to promote English literature of which, poetry and drama are essential parts. He strives to enrich the world of the Elizabethan theatre; to make for his band of players, a playground, so to speak, where playfulness and invention – his beloved puns - would characterise what they do. He feels a sense of mission; and of purpose, recognising that it is not by accident, but by design that he lives close to the London theatres and the booksellers. And though he is delighted to have had a book Dedication to him just the previous year, now in 1582, he welcomes another.

Thomas Watson dedicates his highly-rated book of Sonnets *The Hekatompathia* to Edward. It is a courageous, well-timed act on the part of Watson, particularly now that Edward feels the full force of being disgraced. But, by dedicating his Sonnets to Edward, there is no doubt that Watson is a beneficiary, too. Humbly, he writes to the Earl: "For since the world hath understood that Your honour has willingly vouchsafed the acceptance of this work and, at convenient leisure favourably perused it, being as yet, but in written hand, many have often times, and earnestly, called upon me to put it to the press, that for their money they might but see what Your Lordship with some liking had already perused."

So Watson's Dedication of his book to the Earl is a master stroke. As an author, Watson is overwhelmed by the attention his Sonnet gets. He is very pleased that Edward had done more than just skim the manuscript: That his reading has been with an expert's eye: each Sonnet gets the attention it deserves. Overall, Edward displays a breadth and depth of learning that justifies Watson's Dedication. He had learned well from his wide readings thus far. After presenting his commentary on *Hekatompathia*, Edward had invited Watson to meet him in his office. "My dear Lord," Watson says, "a more thorough reading and commentary of my work would be impossible. Thank you!"

"Your work is of the highest quality," Edward says. "It must be acknowledged as such. Students and general readers will welcome it. Well done."

Watson is grateful for these remarks. He recognises Edward's thoroughness about his mastery of the subject. Edward is bold and honest: praiseful when he needs to be, but also uncompromising in his critique of Watson's work, citing the great Classical writers. Sir Thomas Smith and other tutors at Cecil House would have been proud to claim Edward, the anonymous Commentator as their former student! But, the benefit of the *Hekatompathia* is not a one-way street, so to speak. The two-way effect is reflected in one of Watson's Sonnets in which he addresses an unnamed "ancient friend" whom he calls "Titus." He writes:

> "Alas, dear Titus mine, my ancient friend,
> What makes thee muse at this my present plight,
> To see my wonted joys enjoy their end
> And how my muse hath lost her old delight?"

With these lines in mind, Edward says to Watson "*All* your Sonnets are delightful and insightful. They are playful and thought-provoking. And, I am mindful too of the mention of your friend 'Titus' in one of your Sonnets."

"Ah, yes, my Lord," Watson says, "it is my disguised name for you!"

"I understand your method very well Watson," Edward

says.

"I fully appreciate your approach. As you know, in the literary business, disguise is the only way forward for me."

After that meeting with Watson, Edward's Pen had never been still. Now he composes a draft of the play *Titus Andronicus*.

"Why this play? And why at this time?" he questions himself. "Because, I admit that I need to address my exile from Court; and the shame of it that I feel." The distance between himself and the Queen and Court irks him like an unbearable itch. And so expulsion looms large in the play. He writes of the character LUCIUS who returns from exile:

"LUCIUS: Myself unkindly banished,
The gates shut on me and turned weeping out
To beg relief among Rome's enemies;
Who drowned their enmity in my true tears
An oped their arms to embrace me as a friend...
Alas, you know I am no vaunter, I.
My scars can witness, dumb although they are,
That my report is just and full of truth.
But soft, methinks I do digress too much,
Citing my worthless praise. O, pardon me,
*For when no friends are by, men praise themselves.*"

Estranged from Court, Edward reveals his inner loneliness! Often, at this time, embarrassment and shame takes him by surprise. At such times, writing is a way of putting feelings in perspective. To some extent, it is his way of coping. No wonder, he re-engages with work.

Soon after *Titus Andronicus*, he writes a new play: *Timon of Athens*. In this story of exile and banishment; and the failure of a man to deal with the life of power, money and responsibility into which he was born. TIMON journeys from patronage and means to being in a state of want; to being an outsider, which is where relatively speaking, in reality, Edward is: The properties he owns, for the most part, falls far short of his present and rising debts. It is no surprise therefore that he portrays himself as TIMON in the play, and writes: "Let all my land be sold," TIMON says. But his trusted servant and steward FLAVIUS replies:

> "'Tis all engaged some forfeited and gone,
> And what remains will hardly stop the mouth
> Of present dues."

As he works on *Romeo and Juliet* and *Timon of Athens*, Edward has many discussions with his Secretaries. While John Lyly acts as Book-keeper, he also oversees some of Edward's dramatic and literary matters. Like TIMON, Edward casts himself as being out of London. He makes his way to Castle Hedingham. It is a rare trip to his ancestral family home; the first with his wife Anne and a few servants.

With clear physical and social distance between himself and the Royal Court for now at least, there is little in London to tempt him back. Perspectives are clearer now. He has never really been one for fudging issues: and being inside his Lordly Manor as the Seventeenth Earl of Oxford, he feels his exile from Elizabeth's Court, more sharply. Memories crowd in. He is overwhelmed as he thinks of his childhood here: His mother Margery's aloofness, the shock of his father's death, the unforgettable and grandest of all funerals for his father; and his tearful departure from Castle Hedingham. Now, exactly twenty years on, he could hardly believe he is back. And after all his overseas travels and experience, here he is, incredibly, with a family of his own! The boy who had left, he reflects, returns as a man. He shows Anne around Hedingham. The pace of life is slower than in London. It is peaceful; conducive to thought. He thinks of Sir Thomas Smith, who had inculcated in him what is expected of a Noble country Lord, whose duties devolve around learning, exploring, questioning, reading and writing. So being away from the distractions of the Elizabethan Court; and from Burghley's interference, almost eleven years after saying "I do," Edward finally begins to lead some semblance of a "married life" with Anne. And for the first time, they both feel a falling away; an absence of accusatory tension. They are at ease with each other. Edward is pleased with the degree of marital commitment he feels. So much so, that as Christmas time comes and the Countess of Oxford sleeps contentedly with Edward in their castle, once again, she becomes pregnant. Their new-found mutual trust and joy overlays Edward's earlier paternity doubts and the bitterness that had arisen therefrom.

***

Over the months of their countryside solitude and wedded understanding, Edward's quill has never been still. Looking back, he thinks of his comic play *Much Ado About Nothing*, a story about wrong-doing that had made the Queen unhappy and led to his exile. The story the play tells is that his misdemeanours amounts to much ado about little or nothing. There is no apology or apologising. In other words, expressing contrition or regret is not his style or in his nature. So, he makes light of his errors now when he is below par; not really feeling at his best or committed to the latest political trend.

As he writes, he re-runs and dramatizes aspects of his past life. He thinks of his extra-marital affair with Vavasour and uses it in the story of a proud soldier named BENEDICK, who woos BEATRICE, a Maid who thinks highly of herself. So while there is no admission of regret, by staging this drama, Edward is hopeful that his presentation of BEATRICE would absolve him from blame for his extra-marital coupling with Vavasour. But his presentation of BEATRICE does not bring the success he hopes for.

Another element which he weaves into the play is the shameful matter of the Arundell Howard charges. On this, again, there is no convincing apology. Overall, he thinks the message of *Much Ado About Nothing* comes dangerously close to insulting the intelligence and integrity of the Queen, and frankly, all those who are unhappy about him cheating on his wife. But he accepts that his streak of stubbornness is a part of his natural self; and that Knyvet's challenge to him reflects BEATRICE'S uncle's feeling of being wronged: "Win me and wear me, let him answer me! Sir boy, I'll whip you from your foining fence, nay, as I am a gentleman, I will!" So apart from providing an entertaining reflection of Courtly romance and sexual relations, Edward thinks, that the play *Much Ado About Nothing* does not suggest his regret over the Vavasour affair. His dignified sense of self, as a Nobleman, would not allow him to do otherwise, but also because he is stubborn. More of this personality trait will become evident as he continues to disguise his name; and thus himself as the author of his plays.

***

Shrove Tuesday night – the 12th February 1583.

One of the Queen's dramatic troupes appear on stage at Richmond Palace in *A History of Ariodante and Genevora*. The Italian legend of this play forms the basis of *Much Ado About Nothing*. But what Edward presents on stage is now timely for given the apology which his story *The Comedy of Errors* makes for his marital mistakes, he feels the need to make another artistic presentation: one that would win the Queen's favour so that he can come back to Court. He works harder to present something different: He creates a character of dual personality to symbolize his sadness that he, as a husband, had only related to his wife with just *half of himself*. Which part of himself is the natural man, and which part the Spirit? In the play *The Comedy of Errors,* he creates the characters ANTIPHOLUS OF EPHESUS and ANTIPHOLUS OF SYRACUSE who are twins. His message to the Queen is clear: He must not be blamed for the wrongful accusations that have led to his exile: namely, the preposterous slanders upon his wife and the love affair with Vavasour, mirroring his unruly behaviour, and thus the two sides of his personality. Brilliant though his theatrical metaphors are, his sincere appeal to the Queen falls on deaf ears. She refuses to accept his explanations. So, in dignified stubbornness, he remains an outsider from the Court. Feeling his life is on hold, he takes a step back and reappraises the situation: "So far," he says to himself, "in spite of all my attempts to repent, I have been incapable, or unwilling to admit my flaws." This admission he thinks, is a big step for him to take. And, being more self-aware, he questions himself: "What would have been the outcome if I'd admitted to wrong doing? Would the Queen have reacted differently?" But merely confessing that he has made mistakes may not be enough. Only an apology, he thinks, would suffice.

***

While his dramatic enterprise expands, after the Revels Season, as Secretary Lyly continues with his managerial and book-keeping duties, Edward rents the theatre at Blackfriars for the staging of more productions. This is the area of London where Thomas Knyvet and his men had attacked Edward and his supporters. Inside the theatre, Lyly and Evans conduct rehearsals, putting the Boy Players through their parts, as here and there, Edward tweaks the lines of the story to be performed.

Standing near Fisher's Folly, unlike *The Curtain* and *The Theatre* in Shoreditch, the theatre at Blackfriars is a private stage which serves a more elitist audience. The price of admission is higher and the plays performed are largely attended by young Courtiers. Unsurprisingly, the stories presented are aimed mainly at impressing the Queen; just the platform that Edward needs.

Two days before the Opening Night at Blackfriars Theatre, Evans says:

"My Lord, we have sold out. The Queen and top-ranked Courtiers will be attending."

Edward is delighted.

"Evans," Edward says, "before Opening Night, more publicity should be given to the play. Someone, perhaps a gossipy Courtier should, in advance, get the *message* of my play to Her Majesty."

"My Lord," Evans says, "I'll make sure of that."

Prior knowledge of what the Queen should expect, Edward hopes, will have the desired effect.

So, in addition to the Courtly venues, Edward sees the Blackfriars Theatre as a magnetic attraction; another stage from which his dramatic message could reach the ears of the Monarch, as well as England's policy-makers.

*

Lyly's reputation grows. He is an integral part of the Literary-dramatic team. Excellent and well-known novelist that he has become, Lyly is an eagle-eyed commentator and publicist. He is adept, too, at tampering, even poisoning poems! Fellow-writers are wary of his protection of Edward's interests. But Edward knows more intimately than perhaps any other Nobleman that the Blackfriars stage is the one place in high society, where he does not want to hear his name. Why? Because he fears the shame and disgrace that would come upon him.

After the Winter gloom, the Spring weather is gorgeous: It is brighter, warmer; and a feeling of renewal is in the air. Edward and Lyly are ready with two plays to be performed at Blackfriars: One of them is a production written by Lyly, titled *Campaspe*. It is a risky venture; a story about the scandalous Edward-Vavasour affair. More particularly, Edward is cast as Alexander the Great who, generously allows his lover to form a relationship with someone else. Such a dramatic presentation is aimed at pleasing the Queen. Edward's hope is that she would forgive him if he is portrayed as a magnanimous lover, who in giving up Vavasour, frees her to engage with someone else. This is exactly what Edward had done in reality. Why? And was this staged presentation just a clever move on Edward's part? Or did he have knowledge of Vavasour's doings while she was in jail? She is a quick mover, as the whole Court knows: She'd wasted no time forming a liaison, then a full blown love-affair, with Sir Henry Lee.

*

Increasingly, theatre audiences warmed to the Edward-Lyly productions. *Campaspe* is a hit. It finds its intended mark: Court observers recognises Edward's plea for the Queen's forgiveness. And so the Lyly-led production *Campaspe,* makes it clear that the Vavasour scandal is now in the past. But, while the public is happy with the play, how will the Queen respond? Would Edward's message get through? He endures a suspenseful wait.

Meanwhile, following the joyous news of Anne's pregnancy, she gives birth to a son: An unquestionably *legitimate* child in the eyes of Edward, his heir to the Earldom of Oxford. But alas, the couple's joy is short-lived: Two days later, the child dies. Edward and Anne are deeply saddened. So too, is Burghley, who loses his grand-child. Now Edward poses this question to himself: Does this family tragedy do more to soften the Queen's heart than his recently staged plays had tried to do? Perhaps. Already he is told that on hearing of the child's death, Her Majesty had wept profusely. He wonders why this should be so. But, he is not complaining now either to himself or anyone else. On the other hand, he understands Anne's sadness, only too well. As the grief-stricken mother, she writes of her loss to family and friends. And in a moving Epitaph, she pours her heart out. Her scribal talent is revealing: But at this moment, Edward does not question her ability, either as a writer of Verse or Poetry. For him, it matters not. What is abundantly clear though is that her grief has drawn from all who know her, empathy and much sympathy for the passing of her son.

Alas, the solace she gains at this sad time is fleeting: Her sorrow is compounded when the Grim-Reaper visits once more: In April, Elizabeth Burghley, Anne's sister, passes away. Her powerful father, the seemingly rock-like, indestructible Burghley, is so seriously affected that he leaves the Court and London. "I need to allow myself time and space to come to terms with myself," he says. A few days later, Edward's close friend, mentor and father-figure, the Earl of Sussex, dies. So quickly, so much has changed: Death casts a pall of gloom over the de Vere-Burghley-Sussex families. Altogether, it is a heavy toll, Edward thinks.

United in grief, Edward and Anne, travel with their young daughter Elizabeth to Castle Hedingham to bury the body of their son. After the funeral service, the child's body is interred in St Nicholas Church. It is not a showy affair. Afterwards, Edward goes back to his Castle retreat. He sits at Earl John's old oak desk. Childhood memories engulf him; and his son's death prompts him to reconsider and fully appreciate his Noble position and responsibilities as the Seventeenth Earl of Oxford. The pedigree of his title is without peer: Ensconced in his Castle, he feels, further ennobled knowing that his is perhaps the oldest Earldom in England. His nimble mind makes connections: While thoughts of childhood come to him as he surveys the Castle and its long, illustrious line of de Veres, history, in particular, English history and historical plays, he thinks, are foundational.

"I own this pile," he says to himself, marveling at the Castle's fortifications. He takes a closer look at things, some of which he'd either not seen before or perhaps had overlooked. A few days later, he revisits the Church. He lingers in the Chancel where an imposing monument marks the resting place of his grandfather, the Fifteenth Earl of Oxford. In the tomb beneath the floor, his son's remains lie among the bones of his forebears.

Being in St Nicholas's Church as the Earl of Oxford, Edward has a brand new experience: He is surrounded by ancestral artefacts. He feels the presence of family ghosts. His meditations, at this time of exile from the Court, once again throws up deeply enriching thoughts of the de Veres' intertwined histories with England: From William the Conqueror to Magna Carta and now with Queen Elizabeth.

Anne is more pleased now than she'd been since her wedding day. Having seen the pastoral contours and colours of the Essex countryside, now inhabiting Castle Hedingham, Anne is delighted: She is a Countess in her own Castle. How far has she, through her father's machinations, come, Edward thinks. The wheeling and dealing; and status seeking. She is low-born; he is high-born. And in spite of everything, now, she and Edward are close together as one, ready to face the future. But this particular year, Fifteen Eighty-Three has so far, been unpromising. With dismal prospects for advancement at Court, and the death of his son, his mind is full of memories and things to do. Having been "brought low by fortune's spite," as he puts it, he walks upon the same cold stone floors where once his father's dramatic Troupe had performed, when he was just a boy. Little did he know when he'd left after his father's funeral that one day he would come back here, as a married man, to claim the Castle and lay his own child and heir to rest.

***

Edward is thirty three years old. Time's winged arrow moves swiftly on. Since he'd read the story of Amleth and had composed drafts of story lines, he has not stopped thinking of writing a play titled "Hamlet." Unlike other plays, he feels a more personal connection to the story which preoccupies him. It is of importance too, for this is the first time that he feels more hatred for Leicester, than he feels for Burghley. The alleged poisoning of his mentor, the Earl of Sussex, and bitter feelings about usurped family properties provoked by this visit to Castle Hedingham (as well as thoughts of his reworking of the Hamlet story) are made worse by what to him is Leicester's negative influence upon Queen Elizabeth and her Court. But while he is at Hedingham, interestingly the shape-shifting Burghley proves himself to be one of his sturdiest allies. It is a very surprising, rare showing, to say the least, he thinks. And, as if to confirm this, Edward sets his thoughts down in a letter that shows genuine, if grudging, respect for Burghley.

"I am in a number of things more than I can reckon bound into your Lordship," he informs Burghley, "I hope you doth account me now – on whom you have so much bound – whereby I count my greatest stay – and by Your Lordship's friendly usage and sticking by me in this time wherein I am hedged by so many enemies."

To meet his need, he feels no one else can help. But, more than anyone else, he knows that Burghley's character is inflexible. He cannot be accommodating because he is determined to be himself: The Fixer and Spymaster, the most powerful man in England, as he rightly thinks of himself. But even as Edward turns to this man (who as his father-in-law could hardly be closer) to postpone a few of his debts to the Crown, he learns that Burghley is keeping him under surveillance by questioning his Servants without informing him. "I think it very strange that your Lordship should enter into that course towards me," Edward writes, "whereby I must learn what I know not before both of your opinion and good will towards me. But I pray, my Lord, leave that course. For I mean not to be your Ward or your child." Edward then makes it abundantly clear: "I serve Her Majesty, and *I am that I am*, and by alliance near Your Lordship, but free. I scorn to be offered that injury to think I am so weak of government as to be ruled by Servants, or not able to govern myself."

It is an honest, direct declaration to Burghley. It sets the record straight, once and for all as to where they stand in future relations. But even while Edward is being watched and spied upon, he is thinking and making more notes, adding scenarios, subplots and composing characters for the story to be worked into his play: *Hamlet*. As he frames characters drawn from real life persons, he scribbles down ideas and phrases which he incorporates in poetic form. He consults his Geneva Bible from which he reads in the Book of Exodus: "I am that I am," God's words to Moses. Now, he uses these very words that he'd already quoted in his letter to Burghley, in the draft of a poem.

"'Tis better to be vile than vile esteemed,
When not to be receives reproach of being;
And the just pleasure lost, which is so deemed
Not by our feeling, but by others' seeing:
For why should others' false adulterate eyes
Give salvation to my sportive blood?
Or on my frailties why are frailer spies,
Which their will count bad what I think good?
No, *I am that I am*, and they that level
At my abuses reckon up their own:
I may be straight though they themselves be bevel;
By their rank thoughts my deeds must not be shown
All men are bad and in their badness reign."

So Edward takes a stand, even though he needs help. His independence matters. He knows Burghley's power is founded upon the information he receives from his Spies and Informers, even from his own Servants. For Burghley, the job he does for the State must be conducted upon the strictest lines, especially in relation to Courtiers, all of whom must be spied upon. He is, after all, the Queen's Master puppeteer; the multiple string-puller of a magnitude far greater than the Queen knows. How could she know, Edward thinks, what exactly Burghley is doing at any given time? As a man who rose through the social ranks, Burghley has England's Nobles, more or less, where he wants them: Always within his sights. "I am the *one* who is in control," he strongly believes,"not the privileged aristocrats."

He is correct in that Her Majesty neither could, nor would, ever know. This unbridled freedom he delights in. Rightly, he feels a sense of omnipotence: A Lord "in command" of all he surveys. And to a large extent, England is entirely Burghley's fiefdom, which he administers and governs with the support of his loyal Protestant devotees. "He isn't just the power behind the throne," Edward believes, "he's the power in front of it!" What makes Burghley's power even more scary, Edward thinks, is this: In the eyes of the Queen, Burghley can do no wrong: He is unblemished, above criticism. So he feels justified in thinking that whether or not one was a Lord of the Realm, there must be *no* special treatment for anyone: All should be subjected to his personal, political scrutiny. He wallows in his power; and takes pleasure in making the high-born uneasy. He is fond of saying that "Gentility is nothing but ancient riches." This statement, much like waving a red rag to a bull, enrages Edward. "Such a remark is disrespectful," Edward says to Lyly, who is himself a Gentleman. "It devalues the willingness and bravery of countless Noble Englishmen, who have given their lives for the honour and glory of England."

So now that Edward is away from the Court and London, while in Essex, as Lord of the Castle that he, his father and mother had once called home, he thinks of long lapsed questions that comes back to him: What was his much revered father Earl John really like? What was the cause of his death? Why was his mother so aloof in his childhood? Why did she remarry so soon? Why is Burghley such a controlling figure? Why had marriage to Anne Cecil been so troubled? What had really happened with her first pregnancy? And why does she continue to say nothing about her father's spying on their marriage? Sitting at his desk, the questions pile up; they come in quick succession. No satisfactory answers are forthcoming: only the surrounding silence of the Castle which dramatises his thoughts; and, in the process of creativity, he reaches for his pen and scribbles pages of notes. Having done so, new ideas for the story and structure of the play *Hamlet* emerges.

***

The next day, soon after rising from bed, he remembers the dark days of his life that had brought new awareness; new creativity. After the pleasant experience of breakfast in his Castle, he goes to his desk. On this particular morning, for quite a while he sits meditatively; in deep thought. Then, he lifts his head and begins to write with a new-found sense of playwriting. Bent on doing his best, his upper body is slightly arched over the desk as he scribbles continuously, translating thoughts and ideas into compositions of plot, characters, Acts and Scenes. Rhythmically, at intervals, he dips his quill in ink, threads the letters and words with a jet black liquid trail on white paper. The story evolves, the pages add up and, as he writes more, that morning feels like a new beginning: It dawns on him that the lines he scribbles, comes from experience: From learning and perception. Now he sees more clearly how two or more things, how life and art come together on the page; a cross-fertilization that becomes the bud of a flower that bursts open and blossoms, at first in two parts: one mirroring the other. Together, they reveal colour and light that casts a glow upon other things. He rests his pen, once more. He considers the day's work; and thinks about the creative process. He is in a zone of consciousness as if floating. He sighs. Then, he re-reads what he'd written.

A few days later, he gets closer to completing the first draft of the emerging play *Hamlet.* Now, he writes the grave-diggers scene. He is thrilled by this section of the story, for it is these characters who explain that HAMLET knew YORICK, the grave digger, as a boy. This link mirrors his own boyhood experience in Castle Hedingham, where plays performed had featured the famous actor and Jester, Will Somers, whom he knew and liked.

After the first draft, Edward revises *Hamlet.* At certain dramatic points, he pauses as he feels the transcendental power of his rhythmic, lyrical words; his poetic art, arising from hard experience: the emotion infused words of each line of the story as it comes alive in real time.

Though Edward is Lord of all he surveys here at Hedingham, he considers the thick impregnable walls of the Castle which, alas, offers him no protection from the shame of his exile from the Royal Court. This adds to his feelings about the hero of his play, HAMLET, the character whom he portrays as also being *out of Royal favour!* Now, more than ever before, he sees his pen as his greatest asset. He thinks, and hopes, if and when he was again accepted at the Royal Court, that he'd have access to a Troupe of players who would enact his new play! So now energized by the play's content and parallels, he writes at pace, but in a more conscious, disciplined way.

The next day soon after day break, he is back at his desk. It is unusually quiet. Against the sound-track of his scratchy quill moving across and down the page, he is utterly absorbed as he creates more of the story of *Hamlet.* In the days that follow, as his creative juices flow, he hits new highs as a writer. And after completing his latest revision of the first draft of *Hamlet,* he leaves Castle Hedingham.

On his return to London, he finds that he is still an exile from Elizabeth's Court. He is disappointed; and he says so to Lyly. But estrangement and the uneasiness he feels does not deter him. The challenge and excitement of bubbling creativity that he'd experienced in his castle, spurs him on.

So after his son's funeral and the bracing fresh air of the

Essex countryside, Edward works feverishly on his story: He structures and restructures; fills gaps, adds speeches and interestingly more soliloquies which breathes greater tension and dramatic life into *Hamlet*. Soliloquies: an inner form of self-revelation, is perfect for him, he thinks. The idea of making this form of dramatic literary expression an integral part of his story, first arose when he read a French writer named Montaigne, who had written that the greatest thing in the world is to know "how to belong to oneself." Whatever that means, Edward's invention of soliloquy, he thinks, suits the persona of HAMLET perfectly.

While he creates more of the play's storyline, he feels the need to contact Burghley: Not only because he feels the time is right for him to once again be in the Queen's favour, but also because the profound thoughts he expresses takes him back to the superb and unrivalled book collections that is Burghley's library. He is glad to be back sitting in that studious space and atmosphere. He'd spent most of his life in such settings, usually taking lessons. He thinks of his tutors: Smith, Nowell and Golding; his years of wide reading and getting to know more about the great Classical literary works housed in Cecil House. Here, in the familiar library he re-reads two primary sources for use in *Hamlet*: The Chronicle histories of Belleforest and Saxo Grammaticas. Afterward he sits in meditation, once more, with his upper body leaning over a draft of *Hamlet*. At this moment, he remembers Burghley's rude intervention one day while he was reading in the library. And he adds aspects of a Burghley-like character into the play. He writes the name POLONIUS, the character who accosts HAMLET while he is reading a book! Thus, real life becomes art as the expanding, unfinished play within a play, evolves.

***

Lyly is curious and excited too about Edward's work on *Hamlet*.

"My Lord," he says, "Why write about Denmark as a setting for your play? It is a country you have never visited."

"That's true, Lyly," Edward says."But, I do have a family connection with Denmark. My brother-in-law, Bertie Peregrine, Lord Willoughby, whom you know, has been to Elsinore. He'd been to Denmark on behalf of our Queen Elizabeth to invest King Frederick II as a Knight of the Garter. Trade and Shipping, as you know, are vital for England's prosperity. Our ships plying the seas while trading with Russia needs to be protected from our rivals. We see the Danes as allies. So, as the Queen's Ambassador, Lord Willoughby, through inducting the King into the Order of the Garter, had hoped to get a favourable shipping agreement. But though King Frederick and Willoughby had got on well on a personal level, Willoughby had failed to persuade Frederick to agree on any of the outstanding aims and objectives of his mission. But, during a later visit to Denmark,Willoughby had spent a few months in the Danish Castle about which he'd spoken to me on his return to England."

Since then, Edward had been considering that place as the possible setting for a drama. A play? Yes. On this matter, he is further encouraged, when one day, Willoughby tells him more about his visits to Denmark: The lavish Royal feasts, hunting expeditions and fireworks, followed by volleys of celebratory cannon shot. A stickler for detail, Willoughby had chronicled his time in Denmark. He shows Edward a copy of notes he'd taken. This largely illegible manuscript becomes a cherished document for Edward, the Playwright, whose imagination at this time, is attuned to Willoughby's Scandinavian exploits.

"The Danish King," Willoughby says, "was pleased to be honoured with Elizabeth's Knighthood. And, in recompense, I was warmly welcomed. I enjoyed many nights of revelry. Grand speeches were made about our Queen Elizabeth and, of course, the Order of the Garter."

Thereafter, Willoughby's words had resonated in Edward's mind. He thinks creatively of the grand speeches, the mention of key figures like the King, a Queen and a Castle. A grandiose setting for his play, to say the least, Edward thinks. He turns now to Willoughby's "Notes" which jogs his memory of a visit to Castle Hedingham that was made by a Danish Prince, who had come to see his father, Earl John, when he was a boy. And in the days and weeks that follow, Edward fixes his attention on his story that brings together elements of Willoughby's Danish experience. Soon the "Notes" and compositional sketches that he'd made earlier, becomes a fuller, more detailed draft play-script of *Hamlet.* Now he includes in the play a peculiar Danish drinking ritual and puts the following words in the mouth of the character KING CLAUDIUS:

"There's no health the King shall drink today, but the great canon to the clouds shall tell."

In his composition of *Hamlet,* Edward adds other aspects of Willoughby's time in Denmark. As a diplomat, he'd met high ranking Danish officials among whom were Courtiers whose family names are Rosenkrantz and Guildenstern. Edward is mindful too, of his meeting with the famous Astronomer Tycho Brahe. "Ten years before," Brahe had said to Edward, "I saw a Super Nova in the Constellation Cassiopeia." Now, Edward inserts into his play, a luminous "star that's westward from the pole," which the Elsinore battlements Guards see. Edward shows a keen interest in astronomy and astrology; and, he recalls his meetings with Dr John Dee, who speaks highly of Brahe. "My Lord," Dee says to Edward, "Brahe is ahead of his time. To date, he makes the most accurate observations on planetary conjunctions, oppositions and retrograde motions..." Dee stops to clear his throat. Edward considers the technical language Dee uses. His mind is unusually enlivened, not quite in the clouds, but reaching higher and ever-outwards as he creates *Hamlet's* characters, plot, language and relationships.

He reads more of his play's notes: and, almost moment by moment, looming ever-larger is his character KING CLAUDIUS whom he thinks of portraying as denying PRINCE HAMLET'S request to go back to school. He revises other aspects of the play that includes KING HAMLET and GERTRUDE. After this, he stops for a while. He thinks some more about Bertie Willoughby. Then, as he resumes writing, he gives his brother-in-law a nod as the English Ambassador who speaks the words: "ROSENKRANTZ and GUILDENSTERN are dead."

***

As Edward builds up the draft, *Hamlet* becomes more complex: Its shape changes, dramatically, so to speak. He pauses writing often.Now, he leans back on his chair and re-reads certain sections. In this relaxed position, he hears the words; Their sounds. Their meanings. This is how he reads what he writes. Here and there, he adds words, phrases and, sometimes, new lines. It is the way he polishes his composition for voices on stage. Apart from his dancing prowess, he has also been adept at performing in masques and plays, but as an actor too! This is an all-important talent which underscores where he should place the dramatic points to achieve the greatest effect as he writes. He is increasingly fascinated by the story of *Hamlet*. And, as time passes, it becomes more difficult for him to accept that he is still kept away from Her Majesty. To break the stalemate of exile, he thinks, would need some quite extraordinary intercession. This comes from someone whose prospects at Court are bright. That man is Walter Raleigh who argues for Edward's return to Court. That another Courtier should intercede for Edward, fills him with more than a hint of self-disgust. But this is how far he has fallen from grace; and the Queen's favour. But who is this man Raleigh? Edward had heard much, but knows little, about him.

"My Lord, he is an explorer," Lyly says. "An adventurer; and yes, a writer too!"

Elizabeth would like all those qualities that Raleigh possess, Edward thinks. He concludes that this stranger is perhaps his best ally; a man of striking presence, whose standing at Court, at this time, at least, is unquestioned; the very opposite to his. He hears the gossip that Raleigh has greater influence with the Queen than Lord Burghley! He does not believe this: That is impossible. He considers the Raleigh comparison with Burghley as mere talk, below gossip. But, he is glad to have Raleigh's support.

On balance, Raleigh's interventions on his behalf of getting him re-admitted to the Courtly fold, stands a good chance. But he also knows that Elizabeth is not easily swayed. He hears that she is thinking of reopening legal proceedings *against* him. Why? Because of his lack of respect and loyalty to the Crown. She tells Raleigh she means to be tough, which should serve as a warning to him. More rumours circulate about his alleged treacherous behaviour; charges that open old wounds relating to the "traitor" Henry Howard, who is about to publish a certain pamphlet that accuses Edward of owning books concerning a Successor of Queen Elizabeth to the English throne! Such a thing is treasonous. Seething with anger, he tries to keep calm in the face of these wrongful charges. He feels it is more beneficial to direct his energy to other matters. He returns to his re-worked draft of *Hamlet*. At once, he is surprised and pleased by how much bulkier the script is. But he feels more needs to be said: He makes more jottings; and mockingly, he adds elements of the Arundell-Howard libels therein.

*

So far, all seems well with Raleigh as his foremost mediator. But he knows nothing of what Raleigh thinks of him: what his doubts are about playing this role. But why the doubts? Because Raleigh knows well how lethally brilliant Edward is with his quill; how searingly lyrical and poetic his use of words can be to the detriment of fellow-Courtiers whom he belittles; portraying them on the dramatic stage as characters to be laughed at. Raleigh had seen the Court dramas in which satire is used to cut deep and thus damage the reputations of the likes of Sir Christopher Hatton, whom Edward had cast as MALVOLIO in *Twelfth Night* and, Sir Philip Sidney, not only as *Twelfth Night's* SIR ANDREW AGUECHEEK, but also as SLENDER in *The Merry Wives of Windsor.*

So Raleigh thinks long and hard. How could he stop the literary Earl from the real possibility, if not now, at some future date, of using his poison pen to undermine him. This worries Raleigh enough for him to get in touch with Edward's father-in-law. He writes to Burghley; and draws a powerful analogy that relates to the Greek legend of a man who cared for a snake that turned against him. Raleigh says he is happy for Burghley's sake "to lay the serpent before the fire, as much as in me lieth, that having recovered strength myself may be most in danger of his poison and sting." What Raleigh fears is certainly not out of the bounds of possibility for Edward the artist and playwright.

In the very play Edward is now writing, *Hamlet*, he is creating characters, one of whom is OSRIC, the historical parallel of Raleigh, a rich and florid landowner! So while Raleigh fears being lampooned, his words on Edward's behalf has a good effect on the Queen. At last, Edward's separation from Court comes to a head on a Saturday; the first day of June 1583, when he is brought before the Queen at the Royal Palace in Greenwich. During this meeting of reconciliation, though their gaze are fixed on each other, they had grown apart; and the distance shows. After some strong, confrontational words and speeches that lay bare their feelings for each other, the Queen and Edward reconciles their differences. Once again, he is allowed to engage as a member of the Royal Court, as and when he chooses. But, alas, there is some fall-out following this good outcome. Rightly, Raleigh is lauded as a great man even by Burghley himself who, for all his influence over the Queen, could not broker the matter of Edward's return to Court!

To say Burghley is not pleased, is putting it mildly. He is hopping mad; very angry. But, after Raleigh's timely and successful intervention on Edward's behalf, though Edward is grateful, he does not spare Raleigh from the thing he fears most: Raleigh does not escape from the withering gaze of Edward, who uses the writer's creative impulse that so entirely inhabits him, body and soul, as the Master artist. And, for his part, neither does Burghley, whom Edward had already decided to characterise as POLONIUS in *Hamlet.*

And so for all the good feelings, Edward's return from exile is not without its challenges. He is back in the familiar hurly-burly of Court intrigue and politics. Since the death of his long standing, respected Mentor, the Earl of Sussex, he feels the loss which leaves a void because he was a dependable father-figure. The Earl's widow laments his passing: She speaks about the "Sea of Sorrows" she faces, and the urge to take her own life. Edward recalls Sussex's advice on the rivalry and factions at Court; his warning about "the Gypsy," as he'd called the Earl of Leicester. Now that the comforting voice and good advice of the trusted man is gone, Edward appreciates even more his extraordinary qualities. He reflects on the fleetingness of life and does not tarry: he scribbles with utter concentration, transforming reality and experience into art; filling blank pages with metered lines of moving, poetic words. Occasionally, he stops writing to reconsider how the story is unfolding and now he considers the hard reality of Leicester snatching his lands after Earl John's death. In his play, he writes of CLAUDIUS'S taking over of HAMLET'S Inheritance after his father's death. It is a powerful connection; and using it in his drama, Edward's playwrighting perfectly mirrors life mimicking art!

Leicester's link with poison and poisonings, is well-known. An "artist in poison" is how Arundell describes him. Suspicion of murder by poison, like a dark cloud, hangs over Leicester. Some even say that Sussex's death was caused by poison administered by Leicester's hands! Edward finds it hard to dispel the possibility of Sussex being poisoned by "the Gypsy."

As he expands the draft of his play, he aligns his characters to more real people. He casts Leicester as the poisoner CLAUDIUS; and, composes two visionary connections for the poisoned character KING HAMLET to certain people: The first is Earl John; the second is the Earl of Sussex, which clears the way for the usurpation of power and lands. These infusions into characters in *Hamlet* release pent-up feelings within Edward about historical and current affairs. The play pushes him to extend his range; to cross boundaries that concern him personally, as well as relating to the wider human condition. As he works on the play-script, he adds new scenarios; and thus, he continues to build up the story.

Being back at Court, like a sharp prod, he immediately realises that Leicester is still very much in the thick of things. He is ubiquitous. "I must not be hasty. I must feel my way back in," Edward says to himself. "Go with the flow, for now, at least."

Each day, he makes use of the Cecil House Library. While researching and writing, he is presented with an opportunity when the Earl of Leicester is appointed to lead a group of Courtiers on a visit to Oxford University. Burghley says to him, "My Lord, you would be a member of the select group to welcome the Polish Prince, General Albert Laski." Edward accepts the invitation to attend as a member of the greeting Party for the four-day planned programme in honour of Laski.

At Oxford University, once again, he is in the midst of a distinguished gathering of learned people. He is pleased to get back into the literary and intellectual swing of things which he understands and had enjoyed at Court. Now, as he moves among the Invitees, he engages with scholars in debate; and attends dramas, one of which is directed and produced by his fellow-playwright, George Peele.

Edward is delighted to be in the company of Courtiers who, with the visiting Prince, are treated to a new play titled *Dido.* It is a tragedy about the destruction of Troy; a drama specially staged for the military-minded Laski. During the performance, Edward is reminded of his own play *Hamlet* in which a father's Ghost appears.

Seeing *Dido* has further benefits: It generates new ideas for characters in *Hamlet* in which Edward portrays Leicester as CLAUDIUS.

Among those at the Oxford University assembly is Giordano Bruno, the Italian philosopher, who is the Guest of Mauvissiere, the French Ambassador. Bruno is a Star attraction: one of the featured Speakers. Born in Naples, he is an ebullient Free Thinker. Though he is brilliant, he is loud; the possessor of one of the biggest egos. In this age of fine intellects, Bruno wallows in the challenges posed by all-comers: Edward de Vere included! On the day of Bruno's talk, Edward walks into the hushed, cavernous auditorium and takes his place on a Front Row seat. He looks to his left, then to his right, and like everyone, he waits to hear what the Italian intellectual has to say. He is conscious of the distinguished men who have assembled, no doubt to test their minds and learning.

The setting could not be more appropriate or finer, Edward thinks, as the bullish-looking Bruno enters the Lecture Hall. At once, Edward is surprised; even shocked to see that Bruno is short and stocky. But, intellectually, he stands tall! Certainly in terms of his reputation as a Speaker, many in the Hall wait eagerly. Amidst the hush, Bruno looks directly ahead and around as he scans the assembly. Then, he begins to do what he obviously delights in: He lectures to his audience. On this occasion, he speaks on two subjects: The Immortality of the Soul and the Five-Fold Sphere. In his preachy, animated accent, the self conscious Italian first explains the ancient knowledge and wisdom of the geocentric theories of Aristotle and Ptolemy which argues that every object in the heavens orbits the earth; that the earth occupies the centre of the Universe; and that *all* matter is composed of five elements: earth, water, air, fire and the heavenly Fifth element: "quintessence." While the University of Oxford's students are "forbidden to defy these teachings," Bruno would have nothing to do with an unscientific, backward-looking approach to Scholarship. Instead, he energetically promotes the *new thinking* of Nicholas Copernicus, who argues that the Earth orbits the Sun.

After the lecture, Bruno is introduced to Edward.

"My Lord of Oxford," Bruno says, bowing slightly. "I am very pleased to meet you. Before coming to England, I'd heard a great deal about you. Your work as a playwright goes before you."

"I enjoyed listening to your lecture" Edward says.

"Thank you, My Lord," Bruno says. "I am glad you liked my

presentation. I am very pleased to come to Oxford, your great University. But I will be returning to Wittenburg to teach; mostly to give lectures. My main subject would be philosophy. And, of course, I will lecture on science, too."

"I was in Wittenburg a few years ago," Edward says. "I met Sturmius..."

"Oh! Ah! Have you my Lord?" Bruno responds before Edward is finished speaking. "You met the revered man himself. Sturrm-ee-yuss! Alas, I have not met him. I wish I had. Being in his presence, they say, is special. His knowledge is unique. Is he really the personality they say he is?"

"I can vouch for that," Edward says. "If knowledge is power, Sturmius has much power. But, he has something more than knowledge, I'd say."

"What is that something?" Bruno asks.

"He has wisdom!" Edward says.

"Ah!" Bruno exclaims. "Meeting him alas, was not my luck. But, I have now met you, My Lord of Oxford. Your wisdom is, of course, in your fascinating, poetic work: Your plays. Your dramatic, ingenious stagings. The stories you tell, speak truth: They relate to a larger picture: To the human condition."

"Thank you, Signor Bruno," Edward says, a touch embarrassed, even though he is no stranger to being complimented by learned men. "I have travelled to your wonderful country," Edward continues. "And I've seen great art works: paintings, sculpture and dramas, too. Your Italian Renaissance theatrical works are the best I've ever seen. Your Commedia dell arte says a lot about drama and creativity in your country. Your learning is highly respected."

"My Lord," Bruno says, "you are very generous to the people of my country. I appreciate. Thank you!"

"To you, personally," Edward says, "the connections you make between science, art and philosophy stimulates the mind. You are unusual among European Thinkers, Signor Bruno. From old ideas to new thinking, your lecture has been enthralling: To me, at least. Your Wittenburg students will have the good fortune of your teachings. They will, I'm sure, have great respect for your knowledge. I wish you continued success."

"Thank you, My Lord of Oxford," Bruno says. "I look forward to seeing a lot more of your dramas."

As Edward leaves the Hall, like bees to honey, Bruno is immediately surrounded by Courtiers. Uppermost in Edward's mind now, are ideas about the Universe, the stars, the Earth and Man. He is mindful of dust, of animate and inanimate objects. As if he'd found something worth holding on to, something really precious, he gives voice to what he is thinking: "Knowledge comes, but wisdom lingers," he says to himself, soliloquy-wise. He considers many ideas that are at the root of life itself. He thinks that even the dust from which we are made contains the divine spark. What is quintessence? he wonders. Such thoughts, he realises, verges on overturning the Medieval Order of a fixed universe. So, overall, he is impressed by Bruno's knowledge and intellectual insights. In particular, he thinks about the Theory of an Infinite Universe, of which, he has had reservations. But, now as he returns to writing *Hamlet*, he reconsiders each of Bruno's tenets. He makes more changes: He thinks that HAMLET himself should recite the theory of an infinite universe; although he admits that the idea is disturbing: "I could be bounded in a nutshell and count myself king of infinite space were it not that I have bad dreams." Wondering what the stuff stars are made of, and their movements in the sky, after further musings, he in relation to love adds, in the form of a poem from HAMLET to OPHELIA, these words:

"Doubt thou the stars are fire
Doubt that the Sun doth move
Doubt truth to be a liar
But never doubt I love."

Then, he enlarges the character of HAMLET whom he portrays as reflecting on the loss of comforting thoughts about the celestial framework of five elements: "This, goodly frame the Earth seems to me a sterile promontory," he writes. "This most excellent canopy the air, look you this brave o'erhanging firmament, this majestical roof fretted with golden fire – why, it appears no other thing to me than a foul and pestilent congregation of vapours."

Having set these lines down, Edward places HAMLET in a frame of mind in which he thinks about the essence of human life and divinity; and asks: Could inanimate matter contain the divine spark? This section of the play pushes the boundaries of his thinking. Edward is clear in his mind what he wants to say as he muses over the particular and the general; the detail and the big picture. At this juncture, he adds these words to his evolving play *Hamlet:* "What a piece of work is a man! How noble in reason, how infinite in faculty, in form and moving, how express and admirable, in action how like an angel in apprehension, how like a god - the beauty of the world; the paragon of animals! And yet to me, what is this quintessence of dust?"

At the end of this intense session of thinking and writing, after the question mark to the word "dust?" he rests his pen. Slowly, gently he rubs his eyelids. He feels drained, but not tired. A sense of satisfaction courses through his body. After a while, he re-reads the lines he'd just written. He thinks the rest of the story needs to be fleshed out some more. But, he is too tired now. That must wait, he thinks. "I would do that later," he says to himself. "I'll do it tomorrow!"

***

As Edward works on his play about the Prince of Denmark, all around him, he sees evidence of England's changing social system. His feudal heritage and Prince-like Court upbringing have not prepared him for life among the new men: The rising ambitious newcomers at Court. Among Edward's beloved sporting pursuits is horse-riding or horsemanship and participating in tilt Tournaments. After the recent Accession Day Tournament honouring the Queen's Enthronement, Edward takes part in yet another joust in the tiltyard fields at Whitehall. He performs brilliantly; and at the end of the Tournament, amidst the sound of trumpets, he rides toward the Royal enclosure and receives the Queen's highest award.

He is elated. This grand public acceptance of him as Her Majesty's Champion gives him added confidence. It helps him to move on from his earlier battered pride and wounded reputation. And as if to underline her acceptance of him, the Queen addresses him before her Nobles and the crowd. How quickly things change, he thinks, as he reflects on his high-profile roles as a Member of the House of Lords, as Lord Great Chamberlain of England and as a Member of the Parliamentary Committee that considers Petitions from sea-faring explorers of the New World. In this position, he is privy to debates on helping to foster grand plans to colonize lands overseas. He is excited by Raleigh's voyages to the New World; and realises that England is on the brink of a new dawn.

It is the time of seeking wealth and glory for England, whose Imperial ambition is boundless as it expands its trading relations and lays claim to lands abroad as colonial possessions. And now that Queen Elizabeth's marriage talks had come to nothing, being older, she considers how best to maintain her power. She harks back to her Virginity, the trait that gave her an aura of Purity akin to the Virgin Mary, Blessed Mother of Christ which, she hopes would forever remain the focus of her public image. This self-projection is political gold. And when the latest Colony in the New World is discovered, Elizabeth names it Virginia. Her declaration of purity is inextricably linked with the quest for ill-gotten wealth and the possession of foreign lands. And so, another Royal Elizabethan myth is born.

***

Amidst the winter chill Edward is warmed by a fire within him as he bids for higher office; for an official position that is not just ceremonial, but one of national importance. This move is unlike any other that he'd made, so far. It is a test about looming threats and defence; about keeping England safe from foreign invasion. He is vigilant.

*

Religion and international affairs, the backdrop to social and political relations continues to preoccupy leaders. Protestant England faces Catholic France, Spain and Portugal. Spain has become wealthy from plundering ships carrying gold and silver from the New World. Emboldened by their conquests, Spaniards see England as a target. Why? Because they are angered by the interception of Spanish ships on the high seas by English pirates. So politics and religion creates tension and, thus the real possibility of aggressive acts between Spain and England. Some months earlier, across Europe, there had been talk of a "Spanish Armada," an assembly of ships ready to attack. But now, prospects of a Spanish invasion casts a black shadow over fair England as Edward takes his seat and listens to the debates in Parliament. He learns about formal national security and fears not only for Elizabeth's political survival, but also for Protestants in England. If the rumours are true, war with Spain is inevitable. Or, so it seems now. A War, he thinks, could provide an opportunity to take advantage of Spain's weaknesses.

All things considered, this year, 1584, brings the chance of conflict with Spain closer. On England's side is the Netherlands which is Protestant. Under the leadership of Prince William of Orange, Dutch rebels have the potential of keeping the Spaniards at bay. Meanwhile, in England, support for the rebels grow and patriotic Protestants like the Earl of Leicester comes to the aid of Prince William's struggle to crush Spanish forces in the Low Countries. Edward asks the Queen to give military and economic help to the Netherlanders. But, in spite of Leicester's requests, the Queen is cautious. She refuses to take immediate action. The lapse of time brings no action. It is a waiting game. More time passes, and still the Queen takes no action. But when, on July 10, 1584, Prince William is killed, at last, the regretful Elizabeth moves: She gives the Lowlands soldiers and the military Commander the support they had asked for. Events move fast; and, in the unfolding scenario, Edward asks himself: "Who would lead the ground forces against Spain in the Lowlands? Who would assume the Governorship of this possible English colony?" As a Nobleman, he is groomed to be, and sees himself as being in the front line for such leadership jobs. Although he faces stiff competition from other Courtiers, he takes his candidacy for a leading post in the Netherlands with utter seriousness. He is ready, if need be, to use his greatest weapon, his pen, to achieve this goal. He is determined to take centre stage; and does so during the Elizabethan Christmas Revels of 1584 when he gives voice to his aspirations as Henry Evans leads the Oxford Boys in his play titled *A History of Agamemnon and Ulysses* which is performed before the Queen and her Court at Windsor Castle.

While writing *Agamemnon and Ulysses*, Edward considered the Lowlands campaign and connects the historical with the contemporary. He uses the names of legendary Greek Commanders AGAMEMNON and ULYSSES in his grand presentation. And importantly he is keen to convince the Queen of his candidacy as a Commander! So through the performance of *Agamemnon and Ulysses*, he makes the case for both English support and military leadership in the Lowlands. As an upholder of English Courtly values, simply put, his play's message is: Patriotism, writ large. Not surprisingly, he casts his rival Leicester as a bad choice to lead Englishmen in battle. Thus, through the guise of his play's character ULYSSES, he presents himself as Her Majesty's best choice to lead English soldiers in the Lowlands. So, on that cold December day, the Queen and members of Court watch Edward's play.

As the story unfolds on the Windsor Castle stage, Edward's dramatic message to the Queen is his worthiness as a Military Commander; a General, no less. With characteristic brilliance, he expresses the need for discipline, and uses ULYSSES to get across his passionate promotion of the Elizabethan regime. In the guise of ULYSSES, as he sees it, a clear vision is necessary to deal with disunity and confusion arising from too much respect for equality among military officials. Order and hierarchy in the Army must be upheld: They are paramount for at this time of his ULYSSES presentation, Edward is still stuck in the English feudalist mould. But, there is another side of him that is emerging fast and strong. As the student and admirer of Italian Renaissance ideas, Edward, as set down in his draft of *Hamlet*, is already outward-looking and open to new ideas which fits the developing story of *Hamlet*. He knows his thinking has shifted, once and for all, from Greek

Military leaders to Italian thinkers like Gerolamo Cardanus and Giordano Bruno, who are forward looking; a far cry from his play *Ulysses*, which is backward-looking.

So while the drama is well-performed, its message is not progressive. It is representative of Feudalists and Royalists, who strongly oppose ideas of equality: Nonetheless, for now, at least, the play *Ulysses* is Edward's stated position; and, for all the Queen's learning, her love for the arts and interest in science, she is a firm believer in the Medieval view of Royalty, no less so than Edward is for Prince and country. Unsurprisingly, the Queen is powerfully drawn to Edward's forthright defence of rank and deference in *Ulysses*. The reality she faces is whether or not to appoint him; her most gifted and foremost playwright as a military Commander and Governor in the Lowlands.

After the play's performance, Edward waits expectantly for the Queen's decision. But true to her character, she is in no hurry to either confirm or deny Edward the job he hopes for. He knows of her desire for personal adoration and praise. The need to be liked, keeps all her Courtly admirers on her side. The longer the attention she receives from those who wants her favour, the better. He must play a waiting game. During this state of limbo, he adds to his case by giving the Queen a portrait of himself: an oil painting, which in itself, is a magnificent vote of confidence for his status. In this depiction, he looks confident, proudly holding his ceremonial sword. He is richly dressed and altogether the commanding image is a positive boost to his candidacy for the post he aspires to. He hopes the Queen will see him as a no-nonsense dutiful General, who will, above all, follow in the line of his distinguished father Earl John, and the de Veres who, are among England's greatest military warriors. But the Queen's decision on the top Lowlands appointment is delayed. Edward must wait longer.

Soon after the performance of his play and presentation

of his portrait to the Queen, Sir John Norris is appointed, not to the Governorship, but as Commander of Troops in the Lowlands. He is sent to liberate Antwerp; and after the Queen had signed the Treaty of Nonsuch, she eventually commits thousands of English soldiers to join Dutch fighters. This alliance is a clear signal to the Spaniards about England's position: England is fully committed to participate in the Lowlands-Spanish conflict. So, at last, the Queen gives her assent to go to war with Spain. And the Treaty killed any last ditch hope of averting a Spanish naval attack on England. Now Edward sees more clearly that international politics has real meaning in London and elsewhere in the country. The work of shipwrights and shipyards grows as building and repairing becomes urgent. Everywhere there is an increasing level of activity. These are unusual times, he thinks. And now he writes about them. He puts them into his draft of *Hamlet*. In his composition he writes these words for the character MARCELLUS to speak:

"So nightly toils the subject of the land
And why such daily cast of brazen canon,
And foreign mart for implements of war,
Why such impress of shipwrights, whose sore task
Does not divide the Sunday from the week.
What might be toward that this sweaty haste
Doth make the night joint-labourer with the day?"

So now in the middle of a hot summer, Norris and his troops leave England. After landing, they battle with Spanish soldiers at Arnheim. Though Norris enjoys some success, he feels the most urgent need for more troops. But he has to wait. The Queen does not act. She remains maddeningly silent and indecisive or deliberately stubborn, as ever! For his seeming impatience, Elizabeth would later rebuke him for disobeying orders, reminding him to "defend, not to offend." But this is easier said than done, Norris thinks. Amidst such frustrations and mixed messages sent to the battlefront, at home, Edward is informed that he'd been appointed to one of the most important posts in the English Army: Commander of the Horse. But still, the overall General Commander's post had not been decided.

After he'd been told of his appointment to serve in the War, in the days that follow, a sense of foreboding is felt among a few people around him. Then on the eve of his departure from London to join English forces in the Lowlands, Lyly enters his office.

"My Lord," Lyly says, "I hope you will have a safe crossing of the Channel tomorrow."

"Thank you, John," Edward says. "One can never be sure, but I hope the weather will be good in the Netherlands. At least better than it has been here!" Rain falls heavily as they speak.

"What time do you embark?"

"Early tomorrow morning," Edward says. "We leave from Harwich at six o'clock sharp."

"We?" Lyly asks.

"Yes," Edward says. "I will travel with a large consignment of soldiers heading for the battlefront. We need more men on the ground. Such a shortfall is long overdue! As I understand it, Commander Norris had sometime ago asked for…" He pauses. Then he adds: "He's been asking again and again, for more men. Thank goodness he is now getting the support he so desperately needs. And I'm glad to be among the party going across."

Hearing this, suddenly Lyly feels the war has come closer

to him. It has become real! He tries to imagine Edward, who is always so elegantly dressed and far from being the beefy, robust soldierly type on the noisy, dangerous battlefield.

"My Lord, I wish you well," Lyly says finally. "Have a safe crossing. I am sure, with Commander Norris at your side, all will turn out well. I shall await your victorious return!"

Lyly closes the door of Edward's office. Then gathering his things: some papers and a brief-case, he leaves Fisher's Folly. On his way home, that sense of foreboding he'd felt before he spoke to Edward, still lingers. He fears for his Boss's safety. In this, he is not alone. Earlier that day, when they had spoken to each other, Munday had voiced his own thoughts: "I do worry for Lord Edward's safety, too!"

***

So Edward's dramatic message in his *Agamemnon and Ulysses* play has had some effect: He gets a top position among English war personnel in the Lowlands. After arriving there, he is followed by a fact-finding team in Flushing. Meanwhile, in London, having been less than hasty in making up her mind about sending Edward to war, Queen Elizabeth's advisers, ensures, as best they could, Edward's protection: Her loud and clear message is that he must be kept out of harm's way. But, in the circumstances, this is easier said than done.

Just a few hours before Edward arrives, the Spanish Ambassador, Mendoza, had reported to his King that Edward was on his way to join English troops in the Lowlands. When he steps on land, he and the English soldiers are warmly greeted by crowds of people who stand along the roads leading to the Hague. "God Save Queen Elizabeth," they chant. The sense of Mission he feels is enhanced by the reception of the people, which swells his breast with pride as a servant of his Queen and country. So now in his mid-Thirties, at last,

Edward de Vere, as the Seventeenth Earl of Oxford, fulfils the generations-long, glorious tradition of doing Military Service for the English Crown. This war-time processional pomp and ceremony chimes harmoniously. It fits perfectly with Edward's other role as the Lord Great Chamberlain of England. Being in the Lowlands, he feels uplifted; ambassadorial, with a sense of belonging and responsibility greater than ever before.

As Commander of the Horse and a Nobleman, he is not free of a financial contribution towards the Lowlands campaign; a cost relating to his support of soldiers, as well as paying for a "musical logo" that is used to distinguish between his group and other Noblemen's soldiers. Fighting men needs Patriotic arousal to rally them on; and music played on trumpets, he agrees, stirs the soul. To this end, he'd commission's his friend and music Composer, William Byrd to write a piece titled "The Earl of Oxford's March." In the Hague, Edward meets and dines with Lord Norris and other Commanders. Later, he surveys the environment: in particular, the lines of assembled soldiers.

"My Lord, Edward," Norris says, "I understand that you are lobbying for the Governorship of the Army operations here."

"That is true, Sir John," Edward says.

"No announcement as to who will get the job has yet been made," Norris says. This is welcome news for Edward, who thinks no news, is good news. It keeps his hopes alive!

"At least, not as far as I know," Norris adds. "Do you know of someone who might get it?"

"The top names," Edward says, "the favourites, are few..." He pauses. "But, I have one or two people in mind. Their names, I'm afraid, I cannot say."

"In the circumstances, it is perhaps best not to speculate: At least, not too much, My Lord," Norris says. "Let's wait and see." Distracted by commotion and loud gunfire, Edward agrees: "Yes. Let's wait and see," he says.

And so Edward's wait for a decision continues. As Commander of the Horse, he is hopeful. But while he is here and the top Generalship post is still vacant, he faces the problem of having left behind no prominent person to lobby the Queen in his absence. With the Earl of Sussex now dead, his potential supporter at Court and, a powerful one at that, is Burghley, whose relations with him now is, at best, fractious. So all things considered, this situation does not inspire any great desire on Burghley's part to promote Edward. While nothing at Court is as it seems, behind the scenes, secret machinations, eventually come to light. After Edward had left for Flushing, Spymaster Francis Walsingham wasted no time. He'd contacted the Lowlands Commander Norris and informed him that the Queen was thinking of appointing a Nobleman to fill the top post. Once again, Edward speculates: Who might that man be? Soon, he learns, his secret prediction is right. Norris approaches him and says:

"My Lord, Edward, I hear that the Earl of Leicester is involved as a candidate for the appointment of the Generalship here. It is not official, but he is a Contender."

"Thanks for letting me know, Commander Norris..." Edward says. His voice trails off in disappointment. He says to himself: "Even though I am here on the battlefield, and very proud to be serving, I feel that opinion at home is not on my side, no matter how dramatic, powerful and persuasive ULYSSES'S speech had been." And soon, his hopes of remaining as a "Commander," vanishes.

The Queen recalls him to England; and, gallingly, he hears that his replacement in the Lowlands is his rival Philip Sidney, as Master of the Horse. The Supreme Commander's post goes to Leicester. These new appointments cut deep into him. He is rattled. On his return to London the memory of his disappointment finds its way into his writings, as now he continues to work on *Hamlet* and a new play titled: *Othello.* Like himself, OTHELLO is disappointed in wars. And now with Leicester and Sidney winning the key roles in the Lowlands, of HAMLET, he says, he "lacked advancement."

So he takes the sharp prod of his recall to England very badly. And, as if to add insult to injury while, on his way back to England, Spanish sailors plunders the ship carrying his possessions: money, clothes, letters and notebooks, wine and meat. The ship's capture just off Dunkirk reminds Edward of a earlier stroke of bad luck when he was attacked and robbed while crossing the Channel. Now, he adds this new, unfortunate attack by thieves to his Notes, and includes it in the draft of *Hamlet* in which he refers to pirates and "suborned letters at sea."

*

The Lowlands war drags on. Thousands of soldiers confront each other. Sadly, the numbers on either side diminishes. Flesh and bone are torn and broken; much blood is spilt. Instead of using his sword, now Edward is armed with experience; with new thoughts and ideas. He wields his pen with even more poetic brilliance; and to greater effect. Through his range of styles, he has been increasingly adventurous: daringly innovative. He continues his long standing love of experimenting with words, creating and adding many new ones to the English language. He puns more and more: Turning words on their heads, so to speak, he enlarges and refines the sounds and meanings of words. He compares word structures which he underpins with the philosophical relationship of difference; juxtaposing the part with the whole. With more determination now, he works on the metering of his six-lined stanzas; and transforms the rhymed or metered lines. He writes more lyrical Verses and subtler dialogue into his stories. Altogether, as his understanding of human strengths and frailties evolve and change, in scope and depth, his stories lifts the dramatic experience of the spoken word to new heights.

Meanwhile, alarming news comes from the Netherlands. The death toll rises. He thinks again of the real possibility that he could have died there. This was, in part, at least, the Queen's thinking when she recalled him home! On this, as in so much else, she was her usual stubborn (or perhaps, diplomatic) self: She'd insisted that he should not remain in harm's way. And now with equal stubbornness, Edward asks himself: "Why is she being so protective of me?"

So more than anyone else at Court, Queen Elizabeth has the true measure of Edward. Or so she thinks. He remembers when he'd arrived at Cecil House at the age of twelve, how he'd felt in Elizabeth's presence. Since then, she'd not only overseen his Wardship, she had also put a protective arm around him. She watched over him as his special talents developed; amazed by inklings of his early, startling genius with the pen; his penetration and portrayal of essential aspects of human life through a variety of larger than life, but deeply insightful, believable characters. From the moment she'd agreed with Burghley to send him to the war, she knew it was the wrong decision. She admits to herself how worrying a time it had been, while he was on the battlefield. As bulletins of the ever rising war death toll come in, she reassures herself now, months after his return, that she'd made the right call. And so, after one wrong decision and one right call, she thinks Edward, her maverick Earl, is still some distance away from the full flowering of his maturing literary talent; and, had he died in the Lowlands War, England would have suffered the grievous loss of the man who enriches it with a profoundly meaningful vocabulary and language. Already, he is a very precious asset! But for her as Monarch, the great lover of drama and literature, Edward de Vere as playwright, promises a lot more. As the shrewd Ruler who understands the great merits of Propaganda in international affairs, instead of commanding troops, Elizabeth thinks Edward could be far, far more useful to her at home in England. And so from here, he creates and sends out essential stories of people as he sees them through the power and glory of intricate, exquisite compositions of both written and spoken words to an expanding English world!

***

# VIII

## "A Tongue tied Poet"

Having got Edward back, the Queen marvels anew at his ability to write like no one else of his generation. She lauds how he shapes his stories that give fresh insights and draw out new meaning as time and again, she sits spellbound enjoying the skill and generative power of Edward's staged presentations. How does he do it? she wonders. Every play is different, but so far, with few exceptions, his plays are winners. Like a ventriloquist, he has the rare ability of inhabiting another persona. He knows well the selves within. The Queen reflects upon his most recent play: She is very pleased by his use of lyrical eloquence to uphold the finest Courtly values. She waits expectantly to see what next his unique way with words; his wizardry as a story-teller might produce. But now she shudders to think that it was his mesmeric power with the pen, as portrayed through the character of ULYSSES that had led to her letting him go to the battlefield. So from art to politics: That is the progression which he now sees, and intends to use, at this dangerous and threatening time in international affairs.

Thus far, Queen Elizabeth has guided the country through very difficult times. But now, she questions her judgement and treads more carefully. She takes stock of the economy: and as tension grows in the conflict between England and Spain, tax rates that had been stable since the Queen's Succession, now looks set to rise. An increase in money is necessary to fund the war. Government officials know well the state of affairs, and how their departments are run. One leading official, Spymaster Francis Walsingham dabbles in the theatrical business. He manages the Queen's Men troupe of actors. But, it seems, he is not fully committed to making a success of his company. Knowing about such artistic endeavours is, for him, of less concern than the darker arts, or side, of humanity. Having witnessed the St Bartholomew's Day Massacre, as an experienced Spy, and, for the sake of his fellow countrymen, he takes it upon himself to protect the people of England from such horrible killings. To this end, as a devout Protestant, he vows to question and even torture those suspected of fomenting trouble. He is so well placed that he is able to keep track of Catholics in England. This, he feels is his duty; his way of living for the glory of God, as well as for Queen and country.

"So help me God," he says to Burghley. "My mission from here is to ferret out Catholic trouble-makers."

"Your service to Her Majesty and England, Sir Francis," Burghley says, "echoes my own commitment."

***

Although the Queen loves the Revels and various dramatisations enacted on Court stages specially by the Troupe of players carrying her name, the messages of such displays amount to much more than just entertainment: They are, in essence, political. So the true purpose of the dramas on stage and the messages they deliver are political propaganda for, and on behalf of, the Crown. And, in this sense, Walsingham is a Master political propagandist. No wonder, he is, for now, at least, spear-heading a Troupe of players or actors; and perhaps more dangerously, he understands the value of English history which makes him an effective propagandist: He uses, for example, actors to dramatize the message of the play *King Johan* to reach the widest audience. He revisits the tale of the *King* to support the Queen, and thus engender solidarity among the British people in the face of any Catholic plot or aggression. These are lessons that he presents to play-goers. And in this way, Walsingham uses the theatre essentially to spread propaganda. Thus, his Secret Service interest in drama is but a side-show compared to the outstanding Englishman who pens the extraordinary plays. No one in these Elizabethan times sees more clearly the value of harnessing the Glories of England's past than Edward de Vere. No one, so far, has written more "history plays" than Edward; and, he plans more. For him, England's history and now its defence against threats and rumours of war, other than the Lowlands conflict, is of the highest importance.

So unsurprisingly, the Queen's Men's plays like *The True Tragedy of Richard III* promotes historical "truth."

"But what is historical truth?" Lyly asks Edward.

"It is a particularly Elizabethan view of 'historical truth,' " Edward explains: "Of such a view, the facts of history mean little in themselves. History, to the forward-looking English mind, and to the Queen's Men's players in particular, is never just a study of what happened in the past, for history is really the means of understanding the present, thus providing new interpretations of current affairs. So past events are never simply gone and forgotten. They have consequences. They live on. History is as much past, as it is present."

So not surprisingly, history is the main theme in many of the Queen's Men's presentations. To write plays like *The True Tragedy of Richard III*, historical research is needed; and to this end a few of Edward's first drafts rely upon information gathered by his researchers, John Lyly and Anthony Munday.

Edward often talks to Lyly about a more adventurous and freer use of language, especially in the new form of writing known as: the novel. Lyly has gained popularity as author of two Euphuist novels. As Edward gets to know Lyly better, they sometimes meet after work for a glass of Rhenish or perhaps some ale. Their socials at Fisher's Folly have been known to continue late into the night as they engage in lively debate-discussions on novel ideas, particularly when Lyly was bringing his novels to fruition. And of late, their socials at Fisher's Folly have gradually become well-known among a group of writers.

"History," Edward elaborates, "is not just about facts: dates, events and numbers. "As I see it, it is an act of *creation.* It has to be; all the more so now, as we, and our beloved England, face hostile forces: Possible attacks from our enemies cannot be ruled out."

Lyly agrees with his boss. He is happy as he enjoys his new status as a best-selling author. He feels grateful to have the attention of adoring readers. As an added bonus, he warms to the work and artistic relationship he has as Edward's Secretary.

Lyly respects and accepts Edward's ideas, as well as his pet practice of being inventive and, at times, a re-creator of English history on public stages to make more popular Queen Elizabeth's Protestant Church and the English State. By so doing, Edward fosters Elizabeth's Policy of Plays, as his fellow-writer Tom Nashe calls it. Thus Edward enjoins Evangelism and politics.

"My plays," he says to Lyly, "are of higher value, paticularly now as foreigners threaten us, and the chance of war, looms. So far, a few of my plays have made political statements; or, as you may say, they call more directly for political action. Or, put another way, they promote Tudor Evangelism. In the war of words with Spain, I will use the English stage as a propaganda platform."

Before and while writing the historical plays, time and again, while reading historical documents, Edward is confronted with his noble background and his aloofness from the poor masses. He is surrounded by bedraggled people in London. And though he is the exalted, privileged Earl of Oxford, occasionally, with fellow-writers, he goes to Taverns where people of the lower classes often meet. So, as a man of the theatre, he is not averse to being among Commoners in certain London Taverns. Keen observer that he is, nonetheless he accepts that he could never fully understand the predicament of the poor: their grinding poverty and desperation. But, as a passionate, at times impulsive human being, he senses their plight. Thus his depictions of Common-folk are revealing. He is, above all, a playwright, guided by the truth of what he sees and experiences. He is a pragmatic poet.

On the likelihood of war with Spain, he considers the views of other writers on the Common-folk. A flavouring of what they feel generally concurs with what he feels and thinks: That there is indeed a waste of the people, especially rowdy Londoners, for whom there is seemingly no use but as canon-fodder in war!

"Shouldn't they have some form of employment to occupy them? Should they remain idle and free?" Edward asks. "No," he answers himself. He goes on to say: "But they must not become a leisured class; and, certainly 'Higher matters' must not be among their concerns." So he accepts the status quo. He has no doubt that they must occupy their place in the

"Order of things." *Order!* That word again. It hints at a divine influence to natural order. And, to this effect, the Policy of Plays is necessary: central to state protection; to maintaining order regardless of the crackpots who peddle shallow thinking.

So in opposition to them, Edward welcomes other pamphlet writers like Nashe, who rails against all forms of supine behaviour.

"The theatre," Nashe says, "is not a form of sloth as Puritan censors are claiming, but rather an expression of Patriotism."

Because the Policy of Plays is so central to the Church and State, Edward steps back: He begins to take serious notice of the "Puritans" in his midst. He considers what Nashe has to say in his Pamphlet and he gives examples of the Policy. He notes that according to the Puritans, all arts are vanity. Edward, at this time, is writing a play about *Henry The Fifth.* When he sees Lyly, he says, "I had another look at the Pamphlet and I'm pleased with Nashe's interest in Kingship and historical plays as represented on stage." He adds: "No one can accuse me of being unpatriotic."

A few months later, Edward finds a new job. The role he is expected to play remains a "secret," at least, for a while. Then he is finally told what it is. But since nothing "secret" in the State could be kept from the two leading Spy masters, Burghley and Walsingham, Burghley says to Walsingham: "My concern for my son-in-law's problems is reaching its limits." Why? Burghley does not tell Walsingham that Edward's problems are about his finances. Naturally, he is irked that his daughter is not fully provided for by Edward. Anne loves Edward, but she continues to be troubled by his lack of money. For neglect of his husbandly provision, not only Burghley, but also his son, Robert Cecil, grows to dislike Edward for his treatment of his sister Anne. The situation is fraught: So much so that now, after Edward's many misdeeds, his brother-in-law Robert's respect for him steadily lessens.

***

Given the circumstances, Edward needs no reminder as money troubles beset him. It plays on his mind for a reason that is fundamental and different from how Burghley sees his plight. Burghley is the man who controls Edward's Inheritance which pertains to his ownership of lands and properties as the Seventeenth Earl of Oxford. More than that, Burghley, as Chief Minister and Treasurer, is overall and firmly in charge of the national purse strings. It is to him that Edward now writes about a case that had been raised before. But now, he makes it clear that the Master of the Queen's Men had first-hand knowledge of this "Suit." What the Suit relates to is some money he expects to receive from the Royal Treasury. And, as it was with his dowry when he married Anne, he is impatient.

"The matter is being finalised," Burghley says cajolingly. "It is not yet settled. You must wait." These words add to Edward's curiosity about the "Suit" to come. But it does nothing to temper his urgent need which prompts him to ask Burghley for a cash advance on the money owed to him.

"My Very Good Lord," he implores Burghley, "as I have been beholding unto you divers times, and of late by my brother-in-law, Robert Cecil, whereby I have been the better able to follow my suit; and wherein I have some comfort at this time from Master Secretary Walsingham – so I am now bold to crave Your Lordship's help at this present. For being now almost at a point to taste that good which Her Majesty shall determine, yet am I, as one that hath long besieged a fort and not been able to compass the end or reap the fruit of his travail, being forced to levy his siege for want of munition."

It is clear Edward's need for money is becoming worse. He feels desperate. But what he says is not all. "Being therefore disfurnished and unprovided to follow Her Majesty," he continues, "as I perceive she will look for, I most earnestly desire Your Lordship that you will lend me 200 pounds till Her Majesty performs her promise."

So he is reduced to borrowing. But what could that "promise" be? is the question he asks himself. Then, he adds:

"I would be loathe to trouble Your Lordship with so much, if I were not kept here back with this tedious suit from London...I dare not having been here so long and the matter growing to some conclusion be absent. I pray Your Lordship bear with me that at this time wherein I am to get myself in order I do become so troublesome. From the Court this morning. Your Lordship's ever bounden."

A few days after he writes this letter, the Queen delivers her "*promise.*"

It is the twenty sixth of June 1586, an ordinary Sunday morning. A Messenger arrives at Edward's house and hands Edward an Official Document. Edward opens it immediately. It is from Queen Elizabeth. She has put the Special Seal of the Privy Council to a Royal Warrant on a document that grants to him: Edward de Vere the salary of one thousand pounds each year, for the rest of his life! He re-reads the document: For a while, he dwells on the wording of the grant: "An Annuity!" he exclaims as he reads, pausing here and there. Hoaxes are prevalent at this time. But he realises this is not one of them! It is *official.* It is almost unbelievable, he thinks! But here it is, in print, with the Queen's stamp, her Royal approval. The full gravity of what it means slowly sinks in: He would get the payments in regular quarterly instalments. And, still wary of a possible catch, as if to reassure himself of the veracity of the salary, once more, he checks the wording of the document. He realises that what is given to him is free and above board; and at once, he considers his neediness in relation to the grant.

He is stunned all over again when he re-reads the official line that neither he "nor his assigns nor his or their executors... shall by way of account, imprest or any other way whatsoever be charged towards us." So, with no restraint as to how he could or should spend the money, for the first time since he'd come of age, he feels a little more secure knowing that he'd be getting this handsome Annuity each year until he dies. He holds the Royal Warrant firmly for some time and asks himself: "Why this money from on high? Why now?" His questions does not bring enlightened answers; and neither the Queen's Seal nor the wording of the Grant give clues as to Elizabeth's motives. On his third reading of the document, he is compelled to pause and again consider the timing, the huge sum and the duration of the Grant. He is overwhelmed by the Queen's generosity: by her unconditional beneficence and confidence in him.

So that Summer Sunday ended with Queen Elizabeth's bestowal of the most magnanimous gift ever upon a citizen of England. And because it is *for the rest of his life,* the Grant *is* all the more extraordinary! In the days that follow, Edward is reflective: "Benevolence," he says to himself, "comes in different guises: For one thing, this large amount of money for work not yet clearly specified, or done, is unheard of in all of English history. And by a very long way, no Senior Government Minister or Civil Servant's income in Elizabeth's

Administration comes close to my Grant."

That she should bestow this largesse upon him, specially at this time (when Government finances are relatively low, and Administrators are worried about funding a potentially prolonged war with Spain) is truly astonishing. Edward knows the Queen well enough: She is not a giver of money, especially large sums to members of Noble families. So not being an easy touch, he wonders what is really behind her generous payment? And, as more questions are posed, and, old ones recur, the one with which he feels comfortable is this: "Could it be," he asks himself, "that Her Majesty is funding me so that I would have the time I need to develop my literary work, and thus realise my full potential as a playwright?"

He knows how dearly she loves the arts: music, poetry, plays, language and history. And now he remembers her saying to him after the performance of *A History of Error*:

"So far, your history plays are among your most compelling works. Court audiences think highly of them, I've been told. That is very important for me and England. You show how important education is. And, apart from Court performances, I hear that crowds gather at the public theatres too. The people are eager to see your plays. Being Patron, as you know, I have added my name to the Troupe of players known as the Queen's Men. The nation needs to understand its history. And no one tells it like you."

But, Edward thinks, this is not the whole truth about the annual grant, though he admits that it lessens the financial burden of keeping theatre arts alive; importantly the expense of supervising his group of playwrights, including Lyly and Munday, who do a number of jobs mainly some editing and making minor changes to a few of the Queen's Men's play-scripts. On these matters, the financial pressure on his personal funds is eased. But yet again, he asks himself: "why has the Queen singled me out for such generosity?" To get to the bottom of this, he admits, would be time-consuming and nearly impossible for the truth about Queen Elizabeth's relationship with him is intricately involved and very complicated. So is there more than just money involved? For now, he thinks the question is best left hanging in the air. In the days that follow, Edward smiles at the thought of being on the Public Payroll. He thinks the Queen is astute; a brilliant political strategist and manipulator. She surpasses everyone who is now in her pay and benevolence. But what, he still wonders often, is the catch? Knowing that nothing in life is free, what, if any, are the strings attached?

And how much of a puppet is he willing to be from here on? Time will tell, he thinks. But for now, the payments are handy while he writes and prepares to stage *The Comedy of Errors* in which the character ANTIPHOLUS OF EPHESUS, is partly based upon himself. In the play ANTIPHOLUS makes a particular request. He tells his Servant to go and make a purchase: "buy some rope." The servant replies: "I buy a thousand pounds a year. I buy a rope." There are no cut and dried answers. But now it becomes very clear to Edward that in large part the official Grant is for Propaganda, through the production of plays aimed at educating the masses about England's glorious history, thus rallying them in England's defence.

And so, consecutive performances of Chronicle plays performed by the Queen's Men, follow. As expected, history is at the heart of Queen Elizabeth's public relations policy and campaign. Through his dramas, Edward incorporates his experience and presents certain characters based on real people among whom are a few of his enemies or those who think ill of him: For instance, the character *Richard III* whose similarity Robert Cecil bears. And stories that rouses English people to feel good about themselves. So given his relentless work-rate and unsurpassed brilliance, he measures up, delivering dramas that uphold national pride. And often in the audience, in the side-lines and, it seems everywhere, he has a sense of the closeness of a watchful Queen who feels her investment in him is thoroughly worth it!

*

Just four weeks after the Queen's breath-takingly generous Grant to Edward, according to the Venetian Ambassador to Spain, King Philip is deeply unhappy: He feels he is being made fun of by actors who portray him in a bad light in English theatres. "What enrages the King," the Ambassador writes, "causes him to show a resentment such as he has never displayed in all his life because of the Masquerade and Comedies which the Queen of England orders to be acted at his expense." At this time, Edward's plays are becoming more popular with English audiences. He feels that as a playwright he and his audiences have formed a strong bond. Why? And how? Because, he thinks, he reads their moods and understands the issues that affect them. Often, he plays to their prejudices. They feel the theatre recognises them! And, for one person close to Edward, reference is made to his good fortune in book form: In his allegorical novel *Endymion,* Lyly thanks the Queen for her generous grant, and places at the heart of the book, a secret love affair which upsets the Moon Goddess, Queen Elizabeth.

As the story unfolds, the Moon puts Endymion to "sleep:"

This slumber refers to Edward being kept distant from the Queen and the Court for many years. But eventually, he is awakened from his sleep with a kiss, which represents the grant that Edward is given. Lyly's respect for his boss goes further in his book: "Your Highness hath blessed me," ENDYMION exclaims. "Your words have again restored my youth. Methinks I feel my joints strong."

***

As Edward's history plays thrill audiences, he is careful to sign his play-scripts as "Anonymous" to avoid detection as the Nobleman author, Edward de Vere. But, he persists, in giving clues about himself. He inserts passages into his texts with words such as "ever" and "never;" and puns upon his name E. Ver. He refers to who he really is, and writes in the following passage from *The Two Gentlemen of Verona*:

> "SPEED: You, never saw her since she was deformed.
> VALENTINE: How long hath she been deformed?
> SPEED: Ever since you, loved her.
> VALENTINE: I have loved her ever since I saw her, and still I see her beautiful."

Edward's puns on connecting the E. Ver, points to the name de Vere. Another link to who he really is, his identity, relates to the essential word "Truth" that is part of the de Vere family Crest Motto: VERO NIHIL VERIUS!

Sometime after his wife had given birth to his daughter Elizabeth, Edward was moved to write in the fly leaf of a Bible, a Latin Poem of ten lines. Translated in English, it reads:

"Words of *truth* are fitting to a Vere; lies are foreign to the truth, and only true things stand fast, all else are fluctuating and comes to an end. Therefore since thou, a Vere art wife and mother of a daughter, and seeing that thou mayest with good hope look forward to being mother of an heir of the Veres, may thy mind always glow with love of the truth. And that thou mayest better attain to this, pray to the Author of all truth that his word may teach thee; that his spirit may nourish thy inner life. So that thus alleviating the absent longings of thy dear husband, thou, a Vere, mayest be called the *true glory* of thy husband."

By his own admission, now he tells the truth. But if all along he knew Elizabeth to be his child, why did he go through all those years of denial and questioning of his fatherhood? The Poem he'd written in the Bible, tantamount to having taken an oath to tell the truth, had found its way into his wife's possession! It is the truth; and Edward had, it seems, intended that it should one day be found out! By now, he'd mastered the art of punning; of leaving clues in his writings as to who he really is. Like an addiction, but thankfully his stock in trade as a Creator, Edward does not stop his wordplay: puns and punning upon the words Vere, Veritas, Verite, and so forth. And so, "anonymity" and clues of his authorship, continue.

***

Of seemingly little or no importance at this time is that a man from Stratford-upon-Avon, named William Shakspere, at the age of twenty two, with no prior experience as either a poet, playwright or a writer of any other kind, arrives in London. At first, he seeks work in the city: But his main interest is to become an actor. How would he go about achieving his goal?

Where does he begin? These are big questions for the young countryman in the poverty-stricken areas around the London theatre venues. Details of his progress in the Acting profession is sparse, to say the least, never mind him seeking and gaining further education in the great works of Classical literature and languages that are so intricately bound up with philosophy and drama.

*

Edward, is now thirty-six years old, he bears witness to fast moving events in the making of England's history. The year 1586 marks a major juncture for Mary, Queen of Scots, who had been a prisoner as decreed by the Elizabethan State. The Scottish Queen had left Scotland following a murder in which, some believe, Burghley's henchmen had played a part. Mary feels her claim to the English throne is legitimate and just. But, as a Catholic, her chances of being crowned as Protestant England's Monarch is strongly resisted. She is seen as a threat; and so the protection of Queen Elizabeth is a real and pressing matter. Walsingham and Burghley have long been hoping for the day when Mary could be charged, tried and executed for planning to overthrow Queen Elizabeth. To protect Queen Elizabeth and ensure the security of England, vigilant Spies and Informers abound. They are on the look out, hoping to uncover any plot or potential rebellion against the Elizabethan State. As events evolve, the Spymasters step-up surveillance for potential trouble and trouble-makers. They shine a light on every shadowy nook and cranny. But in spite of this, a Plot is hatched in which secret letters are passed to Mary by a brewer. In a cryptic way, Mary engages in correspondence with Catholic conspirators, who intends to kill

Queen Elizabeth. With others, the Plot includes a young man named Anthony Babington. What Mary does not know is that her co-conspirators are Agents of the Elizabethan State and their activity is known to Walsingham! The Plot thickens as Babington writes to Mary about his assassination plans. Mary responds: She writes back to Babington. But unbeknownst to Mary, in the exchange of letters, one of Walsingham's Agents realising the great importance of this written evidence, feels confident that Mary's fate is sealed. He draws a gallows on Mary's letter. Soon after, Mary is caught. So is Babington, who is arrested and tortured. He cracks under the pressure and confesses to his part in the Plot. But in spite of such seeming sentimentalities as "the truth" of the charges that have been brought against Mary, Trial proceedings are immediately set in motion.

*

It is the day of reckoning for Mary. She appears before the Jury in the Star Chamber to be tried for Treason. The Jurors sit before her. They listen to every word Mary utters. Those who are ready to pass judgement on her comes from the highest ranks in English society. Among them is Edward who just before the Trial had learned that he is to be a member of the Jury. Another development is that, Queen Elizabeth had come to an agreement with Mary's young son James V1, who had been wearing the Scottish Crown in the absence of his mother. James's finances are low, and there are things that need to be done. His sights are set on raising his profile; on becoming a successful Monarch. To his rescue, comes a four thousand pound pension from Queen Elizabeth to secure his loyalty to her and England. Among members of the Jury at his mother's trial, only two are of the Catholic faith.

It is September: And after the charges against Mary are made, she feels helpless; like a lamb to slaughter. It is very clear, her entrapment allows little or no leeway for manoeuvre. Why? Because just before her Trial, a law was passed which implicates, by act of association, anyone who has been party to a plot against the Queen, as Treason. But, as Edward knows, the Act is applied to English subjects as well as to non-subjects. It is a key provision that includes not only the Queen of Scots, but also others like the Duke of Norfolk and Edward Campion. So Mary, as a defendant, is the victim of a tragedy choreographed by the Elizabethan State. Now, she is fully aware of what she is up against. She tries hard to hide the shudder that runs through her body. Then, as the sense of helplessness comes again, she makes a stalwart, spirited, defence. The Jurors are silent: they listen with grave expressions to Mary's every word.

"I do not deny that I have earnestly wished for liberty – and done my utmost to procure it for myself," she says. "In this I have acted from a very natural wish. But can I be responsible for the criminal projects of a few desperate men which they planned without my knowledge or participation?" She pauses; then summoning strength from her inner depths, she says "I prayed that God might grant forgiveness to the Commission for treating me somewhat rudely." Instead of combatting anger with anger, she uses politeness as the way of conveying her deepest regret and venting her spleen, too.

At the end of the Trial, as she leaves the Courtroom, she stops near Walsingham. She whispers a few words as if confiding in him. Then, she turns around to face her accusers – the Grand Jury. "May God keep me from having to do with you again," she says. But when the Commissioners' meet again and announces their pre-arranged Guilty decision, Queen Elizabeth's response is predictable: She is slow to respond. Everyone waits as she delays making the official pronouncement of the date for Mary's Execution.

Elizabeth's strategy of getting Mary's son, King James, on her side, works. During his mother's Trial, his protests were more mild and gestural than serious and determined. But, he is canny. He knows that if he goes along with Elizabeth's wishes, it could be a move that would, in the future, place him in an advantageous position: It would bring him nearer to his ultimate goal of being crowned King of England! This is no idle, self-aggrandizing, dream. It is the hard, cold logic of real-politics: It is about gaining power.

***

While a date for Mary's execution is still pending, Edward learns that fellow-poet and rival, Sir Philip Sidney, after suffering injury in the Netherlands war, has died. The response to his passing takes many people by surprise. Deep mourning follows. The Earl of Leicester and other distinguished figures, who were close associates of Sidney, are determined to honour him. They decide that his body should lay in state for over three months in the Church of the Holy Trinity Minories. This extraordinary public showing is, however, not without wider significance: it serves as a Royal and public distraction from the enthralling, even disturbing, Mary, Queen of Scots Trial and her condemnation.

But while one thing cannot neatly be separated from another and Sidney's death adds to Queen Elizabeth's unsettled, deeply disturbed mind. Did all the "evidence" against Mary really stack up? In the eyes of the Jurors, of course the evidence was clear. Before and during Mary's Trial, the Spymasters' evidence was seen as being strong enough to persuade Elizabeth to sign the Execution order. But now, she remembers her resistance to previous appeals for her to authorise Mary's death warrant, as when the Duke of Norfolk had planned to marry Mary and replace her as Queen of England. Elizabeth's unwillingness to take action too quickly is, in part, a mark of her sense of Judicial patience. She is respectful that Mary is, after all, an annointed Queen. Is she not? she asks herself. And, as such, is Mary not also God's messenger of the Divine Order here and now? So executing the Queen of Scotland, Elizabeth thinks, would be going against God's design. It would set a new and dangerous precedent; a standard that could well apply to herself as Queen of England. It is not a risk it seems, she is willing to take lightly. Weeks pass: The mounting pressure takes its toll; and now Elizabeth weeps. She thinks about the date, time and place for Mary's Execution. Then finally, she announces the day: The first of February 1587. She speaks to William Davison, her Secretary. She commands him to bring to her Mary's death Warrant. Davison does so. And she signs the order.

Daybreak: Mary's final day has come: It is a slate-grey, wintry morning as the Executioner walks with his axe to the place of execution. With her head close to the ground, every sound is amplified. She hears each heavy step as the Executioner's footfalls get louder. Then silence. He must be very close now, she thinks. He is. He stops for a moment. Then he moves nearer to where Mary kneels. With axe raised, he stands over Mary. The wait seems to go on and on. She trembles. Her last moments are neither pleasant nor straightforward. The

Executioner's axe comes down: the action is swift. But he fails to land a decisive blow with his first stroke; the result is messy. Mary is in unspeakable agony as the Executioner strikes once more. Her head falls from her body. And, as if the chops to her neck were not horrific enough, the sad spectacle has one final twist. Mary had worn a wig that morning; and when the axe-man lifts up her severed head, the wig came off and Mary's head fell heavily to the floor. In this two-stroke Execution, many people saw a Divine condemnation. One Balladeer is moved to write:

> "To quit a queen of noblesse so renowned;
> There was remorse in hangman and in steel
> When peers and judges no remorse could feel!"

These words capture the mood and feelings of witnesses to the Queen of Scots last moments.

***

News of Mary's Execution reaches the Queen while she is at Greenwich. Mary is no more: The finality of death now hits Elizabeth hard. Her witch-hunt to ensnare her prey, Mary, then dispatch her, has finally been achieved. But as more news of the Execution reaches Elizabeth, it adds to her remorse. Later that day, she is in a tearful state; deeply upset and not just about the Executioner's ineptness. Known for her vanity, she is keen to distance herself from having authorised Mary's Execution.

For his part, Edward, as a member of the Jury that had delivered the Guilty verdict which Elizabeth had ordered, is aghast! Why? Because of the odd behaviour the Queen displays. He feels there are hidden depths within her even though he thinks he knows her well. He needs no reminders about her hardness of heart; and now he wonders, seriously, about the Queen's state of mind; the person who has for years ennobled her top ministers and spies to do, more or less, as they pleased.

Having set the tone and standards for a decent and good life in England, now she writes to both the French King and the Venetian Ambassador expressing her sorrow and deep regret over Mary's death. Edward, keen observer that he is, especially at this time, sees in Elizabeth a deeply disturbed woman: One prone to disown her actions. She behaves as if she did not sign Mary's death warrant. And so, the trauma of weeks and months from the entrapment charge through the Trial and Execution of Mary, Queen of Scots had taken its toll on all concerned. Edward, a Juryman and expert witness feels he must speak truth beyond politics and religious dogma. Thus after Mary's Execution, he puts pen to paper. He drafts a play with due conviction for The Queen's Men's Players to perform. In the play titled *The Troublesome Reign of King John,* the character PRINCE ARTHUR who was targeted to be blinded, in the process of so doing, he was accidently killed. The KING is enraged that this had happened, even though his Servant was obeying orders. Now Edward dramatizes the Queen's predicament thus:

"KING JOHN: Art thou there, villain?
Furies haunt thee still,
For killing him, whom all the world laments.
HUBERT: Why here's my lord Your Highness's hand

and seal, Charging on life's regard to do the deed.
JOHN: Ah, dull conceited peasant – knows thou not
It was a damned execrable deed?
Showest me a seal. Oh, villain, both our souls
Have sold their freedom to the thrall of hell
Under the warrant of that cursed seal
Hence villain, hang thyself and say in hell
That I am coming for a kingdom there."

So Edward sees parallels between the historical and the contemporary. He casts KING JOHN, (as a substitute for Queen Elizabeth) and PRINCE ARTHUR, as Mary, Queen of Scots. In his play, Edward attributes authorship to the by line: "Anonymous" to conceal his true identity. He shows that KING JOHN'S avoidance of responsibility, not only reveals the inner workings of Elizabeth's Court, it also allows her as the Queen an easy way out. Thus, in *King John*, Edward deflects attack upon Elizabeth for the Execution of Mary Queen of Scots. So, in one of his most influential plays, he absolves his Queen from blame. But, he is himself part of the stark, dark display of power politics.

After he'd written the play, there were, and are now, times when he feels deeply ill-at ease. His unusual gift of seeing and portraying in his dramatic stories, not just one side, but many to present a more rounded portrait of the human condition. His characters could be either good or bad; and various shades between. The beheading of Mary plays on his mind as he remembers her heartfelt last words in the Star Chamber before she was led away. He is haunted by her voice, which since the day of her Trial, comes and goes. Her words, appealingly free of malice, echo in his head: so direct, so personal as if she is addressing him alone. Over the weeks, at times, he wakes up in the night; and in the morning he'd read his cherished Geneva Bible, a much-treasured companion which he keeps on his beside table. For him, the lives of anointed Kings and Queens are sacred. Now he sees a Monarch like Mary as being, above all, anointed by God. He turns to his Geneva Bible and reads from the Book of Samuel. He stops to underline several words that pertain to Samuel's anointment of David as the one to succeed King Saul. Jealousy, which he understands so well, rears its ugly head; and though Saul has many chances to murder his King, he thinks like Queen Elizabeth, of the sanctity of Divine Kingship.

As he reads more of the Bible story of David and Saul, he pauses to make more markings: He thinks of his student days and note-taking from what he'd read. The purchase of his Geneva Bible while he was in his teens, says a great deal about his appreciation for Biblical lessons and knowledge; his respect for God's anointed as he sees the Queen. And why not? Is he not a Nobleman, well-schooled in the Christian faith? At times like these, which implicates him as a participant who has sent a Queen to her execution, he often reads and reverentially turns the pages of his Bible. So doing, he delves deep into himself: into the whys and wherefores of human behaviour and the human predicament. Mary's death troubles him greatly while he tries to come to terms with himself and what has happened. It is a Scots tragedy that reminds him, once more, of his play, *King John.*

*

Days pass: And each morning, religiously he attends to work.

Sitting at his desk he thinks long and hard about relations between Scotland and England. Then, he begins to sketch another play. Its working title is "Macbeth;" a story with characters carrying Scottish names. He begins the first draft in his usual way: writing fast and continuously. A few days after setting down the rough outlines of the play, he revises and reworks the draft. But, as he goes through this old habit, he finds he is not free of the tragic fate of Mary. That real life drama, haunts him. As he fills out the sketch of *Macbeth,* he refers to a severed head and checks his memory for possible people and places that would fit the historical events and issues of his time, and thus hold in thrall the attention of theatre-goers and thus the nation.

Once more, Edward draws upon his Royal Court experience as he invents the main characters upon whom he hangs his tale. He thinks of the possibility, then he uses Queen Elizabeth as one of the best models for LADY MACBETH, whom he casts as the murderous woman who has the blood of a deceased Queen on her hands. As he works through the play, Edward is forced to re-think his part in the Trial and Execution of Mary, Queen of Scots. That he, as a member of the Jury, is not free of blame, he accepts. But guilt must also be placed upon Burghley, the chief plotter of Mary's Execution. He, and Elizabeth, have acted in concert as violators of Mary's rights, for she, as a Monarch and a guest in England, should have been protected from persecution. She wasn't! She should have been in legal terms under what Edward understands as "double trust." Therefore, he uses MACBETH, particularly in Act 1, Scene 4 of this early draft of the play to explain this Scottish legal understanding:

"MACBETH: But in these cases
We still have judgement here that we but teach
Bloody instructions which being taught return
To plague th'Inventor. This even-handed justice
Commends the ingredience of our poisoned chalice -
To our on lips
He's here in double trust:
First, as I am his kinsman and his subject,
Strong both against the dead; then his host,
Who should against his murderer shut the door,
Nor bear the knife myself."

At this point in the story he is composing, he stops work abruptly. After a fitful night's sleep, dawn breaks; alas, but too soon. Later that morning, he is back at his desk. The quill between his fingers feel good; even comforting. It is something to hold on to. "What would I be without it?" he asks himself. The familiar movement of his hand across, then down the page, has a somewhat calming effect upon his troubled mind. He writes for a few hours, but there is still much more to do. He presses on with daily routine, which steadies and brings him closer to finishing the first draft of the work in hand. The story has taken a firm hold of him, but each working day his personal demons are never far away. They hover, suspended over and around him, but they never prevent him from writing.They spur him on; and being disciplined; a true professional, he sticks to his task.

Now as he thinks of what happens after a Sovereign is deliberately murdered, he puts words in MACBETH'S mouth: "What gives anyone or anything else a greater right to life?" And how much of his conscience is he addressing when in Act 2, Scene 3, MACBETH says:

> "Had I but died an hour before this chance,
> I had lived a blessed time; for from this instant
> There's nothing serious in mortality.
> All is but toys; Renown and grace is dead,
> The wine of life is drawn, and the mere lees
> Is left this vault to brag of."

***

Now past his mid-Thirties, though he has a slight limp when he walks, he is still quite sprightly. Some Courtiers, who take him seriously see him as a man of dignified bearing; and for the select few who know, his literary work is of the highest kind. But, all things considered, since Mary's beheading, he becomes more grounded. Life has taken its toll. It has stamped its mark. In some ways, he is lonely, and inclined to feel bitterness. At such times, he often steps back and reflects upon his wild behaviour in the years before he'd come back to his wife, Anne: Those times when he'd not been supportive or responsible as her husband. But, in spite of uneasy relations with his meddling father-in-law, perhaps now is the time for him to make amends, he thinks. What Anne is like as a lover and partner, only he knows. But one private matter becomes known to the public in this hot summer month of August 1586: Anne is pregnant again. She and Edward already have three daughters: Elizabeth, Bridget and Frances. Now, they are expecting a fifth child.

Months later, after the initial joyous news, as Anne experiences the final weeks of her pregnancy, once more,

Edward points to her perceived misdeeds: Her supposed infidelity! His ability to unsettle and make Anne very unhappy has always been, and still is, abundantly clear. His insults to her face are such that, as Burghley says, perhaps with some exaggeration, "She cries in the night and asks: What can I do to please my lord?" Her deference to Edward's noble caste and class is an unspoken factor in their marital relations. And, like so much in real life, this Class division finds expression through Edward's pen.

But why this new phase of bad behaviour from the principled, high-minded Earl, towards his wife? One reason is Edward's belief that Burghley is excluding him from his share of certain properties – his Inheritance. As the man who knows most about England's estates, Burghley, who was keen on his daughter marrying into a higher social class, now expresses his concern to Walsingham:

"No enemy I have can envy this match for thereby neither honour, nor lands nor goods come to their children for whom, being three already, to be kept and another likely to follow, I am only at charge…for their sustenation."

Clearly unhappy, he goes on to say: "if their father were of that good nature as to be thoughtful for the same, I would be less grieved with the burden."

So, instead of continued joyous expectation of a new child to come, Burghley complains about Edward, whom he thinks is bad-natured and thoughtless; a good-for-nothing son-in-law.

***

Being mature, Edward's and Anne's much-improved good

feelings towards each other becomes stronger after their fourth daughter is born. She is named Susan. Alas, the joy that Susan's birth brings is followed, a few months later, by Frances's death. Having now lost two children, Edward and Anne are thankful to have Elizabeth, Bridget and Susan. Altogether they are now a family of five; large enough to demand greater attention, thus focusing the minds of the parents upon their upkeep. If Burghley is to be believed, Edward gives no financial support to his children. Burghley claims that it is left to him to support and protect Edward's daughters.

Meanwhile as, Anne tries her best to cope with Edward's regular absences, she looks after the family's well-being. It is an onerous, tiring task; and after five pregnancies, the demands of motherhood and insistent worries brought on by her wayward husband, weighs heavily upon her. Often she feels mentally and physically exhausted. Always near to Anne, Burghley knows all aspects of her life. He knows for now, at least, that some things have changed for the better. Anne is very happy with her new-born child, Susan. And, she takes more of an interest in Edward's work. She notices that he is devoting even more time to his playwriting and interestingly sometimes he would stop and gaze upon little Susan in a fatherly way. This pleases her very much. Always in close attendance to Susan, Anne is so unlike his mother Margery was to him. At such moments, the Earl and his Countess seems happier than ever. To an onlooker, there is no visible trace of bad temper or thoughtlessness on Edward's part, as Burghley charges. Now, Edward is genuinely in some harmony with Anne. Everyone at Court are pleasantly surprised. And even Burghley acknowledges this phase as a good sign that things are improving. Then, quite unexpectedly, on a Summer's day in June 1588, Anne dies at Greenwich

Palace. She was thirty three years old.

At this time, Edward is not in London. He is on the South Coast, where Naval exercises are ongoing as the English Navy prepares to seek and confront the imminent threat of invasion by the Spanish Armada. When Edward gets the news of Anne's death, he is utterly stunned. Outwardly, he shows no sign of sadness. But the suddenness of her passing stirs and compounds his feelings. Soon a veil of sadness overlays his thoughts. An urgent need to speak with her, one last time, wells-up within him. It is a need that surprises him as once again, the suddenness and finality of death that he'd felt before, comes. He is reminded of Castle Hedingham; of being told that his father is dead. He was just a boy then and remembers weeping for days. Now, as a man, he is tearless. Nonetheless he is numbed by a deep, indescribable sorrow. And to compound his loss, he is overwhelmed by guilt that he was not in London when Anne had died; and that, he will miss attending her funeral. The reason for his absence from London is nothing less than his call to duty. He reassures himself that he is where he should, and must, be: With Sir Francis Drake, Admiral Charles Howard and other Commanders as they prepare for war. England expects! The call is for every able-bodied person to come forward and stop the invasion of England by the devout Catholics who are spear-heading the Spanish Armada. The life and death seriousness of approaching war fixes Edward's mind almost totally on what Commanders Drake and Howard are saying about the weather off the South Coast; and the expected mass of Spanish ships yet to be sighted.

*

Meanwhile in London, Burghley attends to Anne's funeral arrangements. Conscious of her social status, he ensures that her body is buried in Westminster Abbey. The tensions and fractious relations between Edward and Burghley had, over the years, been a matter of often vexatious concern for Edward. In these Elizabethan times of great handwriting and voluminous correspondence, especially among people and officials at the top levels of society, Edward worries about record-keeping. He takes great care to write as honestly as he can, his formal letters; and he worries increasingly that as the Chief Official Records Keeper of the Realm, Burghley will select only those documents which he thinks should be kept. Edward is loathe to think that any correspondence will be destroyed. Yet even such thoughts at this dark time, does not stop him from writing.

Apart from his absence at Anne's funeral, no records survive to suggest what Edward had been doing earlier during the Spring months and early Summer of 1588. His scribal silence and physical distance from his wife's funeral is all the more remarkable when contrasted with the effusion of Memorial Verse that Anne's death generates. In Memorium Tributes are written in English, Latin, Greek and Hebrew. On these days of mourning, Burghley is distraught by the loss of Countess Anne, his favourite daughter. Several letters from peers and colleagues are sent to Burghley, expressing condolences. But there are no words on Anne's death from Edward. Burghley, it seems, is careful that this must be so. Of significance though are the thoughts of a little known writer who praises Anne's gentle nature and goodness; her modesty, patience, Christian zeal, humility, reverence for her father, respect for her Noble Lord Edward and closes by saying she lived like "an Angel who doth sit on high." Such praise catches the essence of the Anne-

Edward marriage. The writer speaks of Anne being married to a man of Noble birth, who treats her badly, but she does not complain. More broadly her stoic fortitude is lauded by Elizabethans who uphold her as a good example for young girls and women to follow.

Months before Anne had died, she'd noted that Edward was writing with greater discipline and purpose. This means he was spending more time in his study; absence from her which interestingly, did not make her unhappy. On the contrary, being a diligent reader and, in her own way, a lover of learning, she too, was writing Verses and often wished for conversation with Edward about his literary work. Her intellectual reach was not as low, or wanting, as Edward thinks. But this was, indeed, part of their unequal relationship. So never having spoken out against her Lord, now she is gone, while Edward is at his Plymouth naval post. He thinks of her impending funeral. He knows not the date of her interment. He could only hazard a useless guess. But putting such thoughts aside, in the face of war, he questions himself: "How would I now cope with my motherless daughters: Elizabeth, Bridget and Susan?"

***

In his Plymouth office, Edward sits at his desk: As usual, he is thoughtful, his expression serious. Like a powerful spectre hanging over him, the memory of Anne, like the ebb and flow of the surrounding sea waves, haunts his imagination. He thinks of writing new plays (and reworking others) as he comes to grips with his marriage to Anne. Days pass. Knowing he'll never see Anne again, Edward misses her: His thoughts are of London and Cecil House. She is ever-present now, lodged in his mind as he composes various lines. In these moments, he remembers and uses his marriage, creatively: The words come easily; and driven by the dangers of impending war, he scribbles down ideas for plays which, in one form or another, features aspects of his relationship with Anne. He thinks of the writing he has done so far, the projects he thinks of doing and those in various stages of development. Altogether, he lists *Hamlet, Othello, The Two Gentlemen of Verona, Cymbeline, Measure for Measure, Much Ado About Nothing, The Comedy of Errors, The Winter's Tale* and *All's Well That Ends Well.*

From his South Coast environment, with everyone on tenterhooks, awaiting the appearance of the dreaded Spanish Armada, he considers and sees very clearly how his marriage comes into his plays. In the different scenarios, he allows a few characters like OTHELLO, HAMLET and heroines like GRISELDA (Anne) to die; while others live. In his relationship with Anne, he recalls the thinking behind his creation of certain characters: As HELENA, for example, he portrays Anne as forward-looking and bold. Then, as OPHELIA, she is presented as a malleable girl used and controlled by her father; and, as DESDEMONA, Anne appears as the character upon whom he vents his misplaced, extreme feelings of jealousy.

As he remembers every creative detail of HELENA, OPHELIA and DESDEMONA, Edward thinks of three other leading characters: HERO, IMOGEN and HERMIONE, the female characters he creates confirm his original plot and character intentions: namely that they deal with suspicions of the heroines' unfaithfulness, their presumed death and ends with their resurrection. This is, as he'd intended and composed the stories of HERO in *Much Ado About Nothing*, IMOGEN in *Cymbeline* and HERMIONE in

*The Winter's Tale*. Through them, now in Plymouth, he re-lives aspects of his vile accusations of Anne's unfaithfulness which, it seems, he could only deal with in his art. If he did not love the real Anne, he comes much closer to loving her in his plays, where he gives free rein to his selfish, tyrannical behaviour and innermost feelings. The three plays reveal an evolving transformation from life into art; works through which he feels more able to confront himself as a jealous husband. In *A Winter's Tale*, the character LEONTES is a fair representation of himself. Following death, real or presumed, the suspected lovers are transformed into literary creations. After LEONTES "kills" his beloved HERMIONE, she becomes a painted statue! Here Edward imbues his plays with current thinking: statues are popular in England. And, after Anne had been laid to rest in Westminster Abbey, her tomb, he knows, will become a painted monument: cold stone. But, supreme artist that he is, he remembers now the words he'd given LEONTES to speak as he looks at HERMIONE'S statue:

> "The fixture of her eye has motion in't
> As we are mocked with art."

***

A few days before Edward had left London for Plymouth, talk at all levels of society were no less urgent than they are now. Among Nobles, Aristocrats and Courtiers, speculation was rife: What if the Spanish attack is successful? And what if the Queen is replaced by a Spanish Catholic Ruler? Just posing such questions strikes terror in the hearts and minds of Englishmen; in particular, among members of the commercial elites: not only traders and business speculators, but those of other professions too!

"What would become of our literature: Our plays and thriving theatres?" Edward asks John Lyly.

"My role is clear: It is to defend England, the English language, literature and the arts. How do you see things, John?"

"My Lord, I will do all I can," Lyly says, "to defend our shores. And, of course, our literature and theatres."

"I will be seeing my father-in-law, Lord Burghley this evening," Edward says. "He is meeting with Her Majesty this afternoon. Soon, I'll be leaving Fisher's Folly to attend an Emergency Debate in Parliament. The fear of invasion is spreading fast now: across all sections of the nation. Having served in the Lowlands, I am ready to let my feelings be known: That first and foremost, I am a Patriot. This is something that once and for all, Burghley must get into his head." Edward rises from his seat and walks toward the door. "Goodbye, John" he says. "And good luck with the work in hand."

From a folder on his lap, Lyly takes out a piece of paper and hands it to Edward. Edward stops at the office door. He scans the page he is given. Lyly knows the power of propaganda; and now such a thing is more timely than ever. Edward reads Lyly's draft propaganda Poem in which he is given prominence:

"When from the Hesperian bounds,
With war like bands.
The vowed foemen of his happy isle
With martial men drawn forth from many lands...
The rumours ran of conquest, war and spoil
And hapless sack of this renowned soil....

De Vere whose fame and loyalty hath pierced,
The Tuscan clime...
By winged fame for valour is rehearsed,
Like warlike Mars upon the hatches stands.
His tusked boar 'gan foam for inward ire,
While Pallas filled his breast with warlike fire."

*

Now at Plymouth, Edward reflects upon these rousing, personalised lines. Poetic words for the Dramatist-Poet at the ready for War! He is where he belongs: At the forefront with highly-respected, honourable persons who are ready to defend England against Spain. He is very pleased to see his name in Lyly's timely Poem. This adds to his desire to serve, as well as increasing his respect for Lyly.

After he'd read the poem, he hands back the Poem to Lyly; and as they part company, he says: "Good work, John. It is most timely! Goodbye and Good luck." He is fired-up to follow in the footsteps of his ancestors, the illustrious military de Veres. Determined to serve his Queen and country, he knows that Sir Francis Drake's voyages to distant lands quickens the English pulse and swells people's pride as tensions rise. The fearless Drake is on the look-out for the Spanish enemy. With Edward in attendance, a break in the bad weather allows the English Fleet to conduct more surveillance of the Southern Coast. As yet, there is still no sighting of the feared Armada. But the search intensifies."We endured great storms with the wind southerly and at Southwest for seven days," Drake informs Burghley.

For days, gale force tempests, gets in the way of preparations to fight the Armada. As tension rises and extraordinary scenes unfold before Edward now, the nautical expressions he hears, the language of seamen and sailors, impresses him. He makes more notes which he hopes to use later.

***

So during May and June of 1588, while the Spanish ships are still out of sight, Edward is with Drake and Admiral Howard. As they wait for the weather to clear, Edward thinks of his wife's funeral. He is unsure when that would take place. For a while, his thoughts alternate between death and the war to come. A few days later, at last, the Armada is sighted just off the southernmost tip of Cornwall.

Then soon after the battle begins, as if a switch is flicked in his head, Edward thinks the South Coast is not the place where he should be! So he hastens inland to reach the English troops camped at Tilbury. When he arrives, he finds that his rival, the Earl of Leicester, is already there. At this time of emergency, surely as two Earls of the Realm, Edward hopes and expects, at least some fellow patriotic gestures would be expressed. Could they ever work with each other? he wonders. A chance for some solidarity, perhaps? And, if so, there is no better time than now, he thinks.

Meanwhile the Armada is somewhere near Calais; and from Tilbury Leicester contacts Walsingham. As tense days pass, the two men have many things on their minds, one of which is the unpredictable movements of Edward. In particular, they ask: What role should he play? And where might he be posted? The matter needs urgent attention, Leicester thinks. In haste, he writes to Walsingham: "Your other letter concerned my

Lord of Oxford, who was with me... went and returned again yesterday with Captain Huntley in his company. He seemed... to have gone to my Lord Admiral Howard and at his return he (Oxford) seemed also to return again hither to me this day from London, whither he went yesternight for his armour and furniture. If he comes, I would know from you what I shall do. I trust he will be free to go to the enemy to participate in close combat for he seems most willing to hazard his life in this quarrel."

And so, after long and hard self-examination, as Edward says he would, he decides to risk his life for England. He is not a timid or conservative man. He is bold: a true Patriot. He seeks no one's advice. After reaching Tilbury, he dispatches himself and heads back to London to fetch his armour and furniture. By so doing, as Leicester admits, being "free to go to the enemy," Edward de Vere is evidently totally committed to lay down his life for Queen and country. Soon after the battle starts, the Armada is in disarray as the English ships chase and bombards the Spanish fleet. At this critical time, fearing that Spanish ships might land along the Essex coast, Edward acts decisively. And the Queen does not hesitate to give her wayward Earl, a top post in the Armed Forces: He is assigned to Command some two thousand men at Tilbury. Thus, at last, he gets a Commander's assignment at a critical time in England's history. But he is far from satisfied; and soon he tires of his land-based role.

He itches to be somewhere else: To be nearer the action, as he sees it. He is keen to be on an English warship in hot pursuit of the enemy. But instead of heading back to Plymouth, he leaves his Harwich post and returns to London. Leicester's anger to this toing and froing reaches new heights. "Deliver to my Lord of Oxford, Her Majesty's gracious consent of his willingness to serve her," he writes to Walsingham. "She was pleased that he should have the government of Harwich and all those that are appointed to attend that place, which should be 2,000 men. He has a place of trust and of great danger. My Lord seemed at the first to like well of it. Afterward he came to me and told me he thought the place of no service, nor credit and therefore he would go to the Court await Her Majesty's further pleasure."

Leicester feels Walsingham must make it known to Edward that as the Noble Earl of Oxford "it was of good grace to appoint that place to him, having no more military experience than he hath." Then he stresses: "for my own part being of gladder to be rid of him, but only to have him contented – which now I find will be harder than I took it. And he denieth all his former offers he made to serve…" In justification of his anger, Leicester adds for good measure: "I am glad I am rid of my Lord Oxford, seeing he refuseth this. I pray you let me not be pressed any more for him, what suit so ever he make."

Leicester's displeasure could not be more pronounced. And so Edward's serious rival, Leicester, makes abundantly clear his true feelings towards Edward not just in peace time, but now in war-time too as England faces its greatest threat! "Good riddance!" Leicester says. "Me first, you second," he seems to be saying. He likes the limelight, but his rival Edward needs to be centre stage, too! The two men: The great writer and the not so Literary-inclined Leicester, never had and never could or would see eye to eye. Something has to give! And thus far, few men have had the eye that Edward de Vere has.

He sees people and things as they are; and in the round. He feels he has too as a Poet-Dramatist. Meanwhile the battle against the Spanish Armada rages on until England's naval forces defeats the enemy. It is a victory that has great significance for Queen Elizabeth and England. It has deep personal meaning and resonance for Edward de Vere, too. The patriotic Earl is overjoyed. And so the story of the Armada invasion of England which begins around the time of Anne's death, then sees Edward leave his military posts to best serve his country, ends with Leicester distancing himself even further away from Edward.

Weeks later, heavy winds blow across the land. Gone is the caress of light breezes and the warm glow of summer's golden sun-rays. But, the changing weather does not dampen English spirits. For Edward, the coolness stiffens his resolve.

Autumn comes again. The English nation breathes a deep sigh of relief. Edward joins a Grand Parade of Nobles, Courtiers and leaders of the Armed Forces. With military precision, they march through London in celebration of a great victorious day. Victory over an enemy: The dreaded Spanish Armada. This grand show sees Edward performing his Civic Duty: He holds the golden Canopy over Queen Elizabeth's head; a symbolic and real reflection of their closeness. It is overall a glorious spectacle; a Victory Parade unlike any other. It warms the hearts of all Englishmen. Poets and artists come forward: One proud, anonymous Balladeer is moved to write about lovely London and his Noble Queen thus:

"To lovely London fair, our noble Queen would go
And in Paul's Cross before her God her thankful heart would show;
Where Prince and people did consent with joyful minds to meet

To glorify the God of heaven with psalms and voices sweet...
The Lord Marques of Winchester bareheaded there was seen
Who bare the Sword in comedy sort before our Noble queen;
The noble Earl of Oxford then High Chamberlain of England,
Rode right before Her Majesty his *bonnet* in his hand...

And after by two noblemen along the Church was led,
With a golden canopy carried o'er her head.
The clergy with procession brought Her Grace into the choir,
Whereas Her Majesty was set the service for to hear.
And afterwards unto Paul's Cross she did directly pass,
There by the Bishop of Salisbury a sermon preached was,
The Earl of Oxford opening then the windows for Her Grace
The children of the hospital she saw before her face. "

Once more, Edward, the Noble Earl of Oxford is named, this time in a Commemorative Ballad. Thus he receives recognition for his contribution at the highest level; and, at this auspicious time of the greatest of England's victories.

***

A few weeks after the Paul's Cross Parade, a momentous year in England's history ends. It also brings to a close eight years of Edward's bohemian life-style and residence at Fisher's Folly.

Being so near to the theatres, this beloved home had been Edward's literary sanctuary where he sleeps, eats, meditates and continues to practice the art of playwriting. Doing his multifaceted job for so many years, does not make it any easier: "Oh, the pain to pen a book," he never tires of saying to himself.

But Fisher's Folly is not seen in a good light by some; and increasingly so, by none other than Edward's father-in-law, Lord Burghley. Only a few months before the Armada battle, he'd complained about Edward's "lewd friends" whom he believes rule the forty-eight year old Earl by "flatteries." Such condescension does nothing to endear Burghley to Edward. Why? Because these "friends" are regular visitors to Fisher's Folly; an essential social and intellectual presence in Edward's life and work. Knowing the relentless pressures of writing and producing plays at Court and in the London theatres, he asks himself: "How lewd are trusted friends like his Secretaries Lyly and Munday?" It is a fleeting question, not one he cares to dwell upon for he was never a follower of anyone. It is not in his nature to be so, as Burghley could readily confirm. Edward is a leader, who behaves like one, though not in the strict military sense. He is a sociable man, who genuinely likes most people; and works well, with some. He has to, as a playwright. And, in the normal course of living, a few collaborators become friends. His work with Lyly is a creative partnership that is productive and energizing. How "lewd" is that? he thinks.

Since publication, Lyly's Euphues novels have become best-sellers. Other writers take note: They imitate this style of writing. "Oh, to be Euphuistic!" Edward says. Book-lovers enjoy these novels which symbolizes artists pushing the boundaries of social convention thus exercising the freedom of expression enjoyed by the vibrant community of like-minded people at Fisher's Folly. Edward's own literary vision and enterprise does not take long to achieve success for it is soon after he'd moved to Fisher's Folly that the Euphuists' genre-publications became popular. Thereafter Fisher's Folly had gained a reputation for excellence: a sort of In-crowd, multi-purpose venue for serious discussion and is aptly named: Mount Fisher. Writers looking in from outside Euphuist circles, sees the Folly as much more than a palatial pile or just a liberal house. Overall, it is a magnetic place for lovers of literature. It offers to ambitious writers heights to aspire to: Mount Fisher indeed!

"It is my retreat," Edward had said to Lyly and others at various times. One writer who visits Fisher's Folly often is William Gray. More of a polemicist than a scholar, Gray dedicates one of his books to Edward. In it, he lauds Edward as a worthy Patron; "a favourer and fosterer who favours and fosters… at the shrine of your Lordship's courtesy." A shrine? It is how Gray sees it. Another author at the Folly is, of course, Edward's Secretary and translator, Anthony Munday, who writes chivalrous and mythical stories. Like Gray, Munday does the extra bit: He pays more than just lip service to his literary Master. He dedicates one of his translations to Edward. "If Palmerin hath sustained any wrong by my bad translation," he writes, "being so worthily set down in other languages, your honour having such special knowledge in them I hope will let slip any faults escaped." Edward's reputation as a well-versed forensic literary expert, foreruns him. Munday's respect for his patron, mentor and employer is warming. The lively intellectual environment of Fisher's Folly is most encouraging of new literary works as writers discuss and share ideas. Munday, for example, translates *Amadis de Gaulle,* the story of a loved one who is replaced by a statue; a work of art so convincing that it is mistaken for the dead person. This device of deception becomes clear later in the story. From tales like the *Amadis,* and other romances and legends, Edward makes his usual melding and mixing of various elements for his plays such as *The Winter's Tale* in which the character HERMIONE is supposed to be dead, but is later revealed as being alive! Edward is attracted to Munday's romance which he hopes to use in future plays.

The writer, Angel Day, so appreciates Fisher's Folly that he decides to immortalize it. In his book *The English Secretary,* a "Guide" to letter writing, he writes a Dedication to Edward de Vere, describes the first days of the Fisher's Folly tenancy and praises Edward who is "ever sacred to the Muses." In this age of great writing, in particular, letter-writing, *The English Secretary* is a timely contribution to the smooth and efficient communication networks that links the State, the rich and powerful and ordinary individuals. But given the flow of highy sensitive information, a "Secretary," as Edward knows, could and should be a trusted keeper of private and confidential matters.

***

On Thursday each week, in his spacious office, Edward meets, discusses and dictates letters to Lyly and Munday. While doing so, habitually, he paces to and fro: Sometimes, he stands still, as he thinks: Checking and rechecking what he is communicating. Careful letter-writing and meticulous research are the hallmarks of Edward's literary enterprise. He has an unusually keen eye for detail and composition. From these regular exercises, he and his Secretaries learn a great deal about each other. The earlier, wary, strict and tight formalities of their relationships had gradually been transformed. It is now a relaxed camaraderie.They know each other so much better now. And Fisher's Folly has become, more or less, like another home for Lyly and Munday. But after eight years, Edward rethinks his residency. He mulls over the good and bad times; Of the good times, there have been many. He remembers the five years before he came to Fisher's Folly and the years of residence there as his most intense, prolific period of playwriting thus far: It was right here that he'd conceived, drafted and had written most of his plays, especially those set in, or relating to his Italian travels. All those great dreams that demanded so much from him came to fruition in various drafts of play scripts. "Ah! The pain to pen a book!" he says to himself. But, there has been great pleasure too! He recalls the afternoons and evenings of lively, even heated discussions on literary styles.

He feels lucky to have able men like Lyly and Munday as Secretaries. They appreciate that over the years, they have learned from each other; and are better men for it. And now sharing easy and warm relations, once more after work, socialize; they listen and speak. Such sessions are something they all look forward to. And, adding to their respect and good feelings, is the liberal flow of Rhenish and ale. As artists, these Fisher's Folly folks needs no lessons on how they, as bohemians, should behave. But, the days of wild parties at Fisher's Folly are numbered. Alas, Edward had reached a cross-roads: This rare retreat (so closely linked to many of his plays and theatre productions, as well as the Euphues novels and Euphusists) Edward announces to his Secretaries and close associates, would no longer be their meeting place.

"Fisher's folly is in the last stages of being sold!" he says, betraying not a hint of emotion, even though he feels deeply about having to part from it. "But, before the Folly closes," he says turning to Lyly and Munday, "all who are regular attendees or even occasional visitors, will be invited to attend a final get together!"

On the day of the Leaving Party, soon after breakfast, Edward gives his Servants all the instructions they should have. Well before midday, Guests begin to arrive: Soon almost every part of the building is occupied. It is turning out to be the biggest gathering of writers and Socialites ever. Edward is not surprised. Fortunately, the large house accommodates all the Guests and the buzz of excited chatter gets louder. At intervals, Edward shuffles around surveying the scene: He scans the familiar faces and feels a mixture of emotions: excitement and nostalgia. These moments mark the evolution of eight years of hatching ideas, drafting and writing plays, planning productions and performances; intense years of continuous expectation, some disappointment and the astonishing wine of fulfilment. Overall, the scene before him is bitter-sweet.

It is late afternoon now: The large rooms and the Gallery resound with the agreeable noise of people talking, and interspersed, here and there, with bursts of laughter. In his roles as the distinguished host and as the Seventeenth Earl of Oxford, Edward is now ready to say a few words. He claps his hands: But the sound is not loud enough. He has to do so again, before he wins attention. He is flanked by Lyly and Munday. And before him are his intimate friends, fellow writers and aristocratic guests. The "Speech" he gives is unlike anything anyone present has ever heard a man of his standing give.

"My Lords, Ladies, Gentlemen, fellow-writers and staff," Edward says, "it is good to see you all! Thank you for coming, not just today, but over the years that Fisher's Folly has been my home. The years I've spent here, have been of great importance: They mark a relentless and intense phase of enterprising work. Many ideas that became published books have been conceived here. Fisher's Folly is both symbolic and real. It has served me well. It is not just a house. Not just *my* residence. It has served many purposes, as most of you know. Over the last eight years, I have written and produced many plays, masques and other dramatic presentations. And being here, I have witnessed a rather wonderful thing that has been happening in England: A theatrical revolution has been taking place. It is twelve years since I came back from my travels in Italy; years during which I have incorporated some of the Commedia dell arte dramatic devices that I'd seen in Italy, into my plays. Yes, My Lords, Ladies, Gentlemen and fellow writers, we have in London a theatrical revolution..." He pauses; and looks in the direction of the Gallery.

"From my Gallery," he continues, "I can see the theatre-goers. They pass along the street, going to, and coming from, Shoreditch. From the excited talk I hear, they are deeply interested in the plays they see at *The Curtain* and *The Theatre*. Playwrights' write, and these are the people, the spectators who sustain them. Yes, we have our Court plays and audiences, but we also have public theatres and knowledgeable audiences: They are two different audiences: I understand that very well. But, why can't we have both? For some years I have been trying to bring the two kinds of presentations closer together: Why can't they, to some extent, become more interchangeable? I ask myself. Such a combination is better: I do believe it would be more enriching and rewarding for both playwrights and spectators. Don't you think so?"

Loud applause fills the room.

"So, Fisher's Folly is linked to this new and exciting theatre revolution. We are witnessing the emergence of an *English* Renaissance, I'd say." He stresses the word: English."English literature, poetry and plays are increasingly finding their way into the lives of the people of our nation. Writing plays and maintaining our theatres and theatre-going are essential expressions of this.

My enterprise here at Fisher's Folly has contributed, I think, to this growth in English cultural awareness and achievement. Finally, My Lords, Ladies and Gentlemen and special guests, we who create the dramatic arts, the Comedies and Tragedies that uplift our people, our nation, the human spirit and human soul, let us drink a toast to this dear pile that has served me and many of us so well. It is, without doubt, a place that has been an inspirational haven to us all! "To Fisher's Folly!" he says as he raises a glass. "And to all who have come to celebrate."

Everyone repeats Edward's parting words in unison: And, admidst the comradely echo of the many voices, he thinks, the words were well meant!

***

Edward sells and leaves Fisher's Folly just before Christmas 1588. And so the curtain falls on a unique intellectual home. He transfers the deed of the property to William Cornwallis, a friend. Later, what seems likely becomes a reality: A book by Thomas Lodge is published. It is well-received by many writers who believes that Fisher's Folly is a gem of historical value.

One positive benefit of selling Fisher's Folly, Edward hopes, is that it would take him one more step away from Burghley's control. But this is easier said than done, because the ever-watchful watchman knows everything about his outstanding payments for the support of his children. Alas, Anne is no longer a thorn in his side; someone whom he would also have been expected to provide for. Undoubtedly, she was reason enough for Burghley to keep on friendly terms with him. But now that restraining link is removed. As Lord Treasurer of England, Burghley has no qualms and is ready to sue Edward for his outstanding back debts; the payment of which could be made good through the loss of more of his inherited properties. This is no simple problem. It has been ongoing. And so, Edward confronts his indebtedness, and tries to resolve his highly-charged, strained relations with Burghley. He weighs up his options: Given that there is little room for manoeuvre, he takes the action that best suits him. He smiles knowing that his sale of Fisher's Folly is one asset that is beyond Burghley's reach. Sad though it is for Follyites, for the new owner it is anything but a straightforward transfer of ownership. When Burghley hears of the sale, his anger rises. In turn, Edward is no less upset because of what he sees as Burghley's interference in his business. He regrets the sorry situation in which William Cornwallis, Fisher's Folly's new owner is placed. But knowing the literary value of Fisher's Folly, Cornwallis and his wife are happy enough with the house. They place great value on its literary legacy as they inhabit and convert it into their new home.

So, from a bustling intellectual hub, the Folly becomes a private dwelling. Edward is relieved; very pleased that the property is secured by the Cornwallis' family. But memories of the place are so strong that Edward's friend, Thomas Watson, is drawn back to Fisher's Folly as a Teacher to Anne, the daughter of Cornwallis. This coming together is fortuitous and most fruitful. Arising from her relations with Teacher Watson, Anne's love of literature grows so positively that she puts pen to paper in the hope that one day she would realise her ambition of publishing her verses and poetry.

***

A few months short of his fortieth birthday, Edward leaves Fisher's Folly and sets his sights on a new home: While he builds a new house near Earls Colne in Essex; he hires men to work on a house in Plaistow, a new property in East London. Money is still scarce, but he fixes up Plaistow House as a place that would accommodate himself, his servants and Secretaries. So he is still thinking of, and working with, his Secretaries. Like LEONTES in *The Winter's Tale* and CLAUDIO in *Much Ado About Nothing*, Edward needs space and time to think; to reflect. But even now, he is unable to banish thoughts about his marriage, his jealous rages and his irrational attitude towards his deceased wife. But what is he experiencing now? Is he in another relationship? If so, with whom? At this time, Thomas Lodge publishes a Poem and accompanying it are a few verses, one of which is by Edward whose words reveal his state of mind at this time:

> "I will become a hermit now
> And do my penance straight
> For all the errors of mine eyes
> With foolish rashness filled

My heritage shall placed be
Where melancholy's weight
And none but love alone shall know

The bower I mean to build…
Of faithful hope shall be my staff
And daily when I pray
My Mistress's picture placed by love
Shall witness what I say."

Loss, loss, loss. The melancholy he feels is clear: The loss of Anne and the sale of Fisher's Folly compounds his feelings. He confides in himself, as he writes:

"But plainly say thou lovs't her well,
And set thy person forth to sell."

While he is on his estate on the Avon River Valley in Warwickshire, as a widower, he realises how much he needs the distance of being away from Burghley's surveillance. He occupies his Bilton country house; a property with spacious grounds. This is a different kind of retreat from Fisher's Folly; one that is pastoral, a quiet village surrounded by hills. He likes this lush greenness of the countryside, which provides a contemplative space. But soon, his official duties as the Earl of Oxford and Lord Great Chamberlain of England brings him back to London; to Westminster. The Queen calls her politicians together; and opens a new Session of Parliament. Edward attends as a Member of the House of Lords, but he could only be present for five of the thirty five days of sittings. He is struck by how time has moved on. Being among his peers, not all of whom have been close to him, he thinks now of those who are absent. One of them is his rival the Earl of Leicester, who has died.

***

Soon after Parliament adjourns, Edward becomes a good friend and confidante of the sons of his cousin, the late Duke of Norfolk. The eldest son, Philip Howard, had been held for several years in the Tower of London charged with being a Catholic sympathiser and of trying to leave England without Royal permission. Earlier, in the heat of the Armada battle in the English Channel, Philip, the Earl of Arundel had been caught holding Mass and charged with treasonous behaviour. A date for his Trial is announced; and, for this purpose, Edward is inducted to join twenty-two Peers in Westminster Hall to witness and pass judgement on another of the Queen's Nobles. Like the Trials of Mary, Queen of Scots and the Duke of Norfolk, the verdict on Philip was almost pre-ordained; designed to lead to one conclusion: Conviction. After the evidence given, the Attorney General presents the Jury with a curious thing called a "painted prophecy." This is an allegory in picture-form that is presented as added proof of the Earl of Arundel's guilt: his pro-Catholic treasonous activities.

As expected, the Treason verdict is followed by a death Sentence! But given her perceived procrastination and past behaviour, the Queen does not act quickly. She delays giving the order of Execution. Then, at last, she grants Philip Howard clemency. But, she keeps him in the Tower. For his part, Edward does not forget Philip's brother, William. In the draft of his latest play, *As You Like It*, he deals with the difficult process of

William's Inheritance. In the play, Edward creates characters who are brothers: OLIVER and ORLANDO De BOYS. As the story unfolds, OLIVER comes close to being killed. But unlike the reality of the Howard brothers, in Edward's artistic presentation, the younger ORLANDO saves his brothers life. And so, Edward writes his Norfolk cousins into *As You Like It* which he sets in the forest of Arden, close to his house and land at Bilton. As a disciplined writer, with much of the play conceived and written while he is in Warwickshire, he takes time out to visit his grandmother, Elizabeth Trussell, at her estate in Billesley near Stratford-upon-Avon. The Trussell family's library at Billesley Manor is an impressive collection. Here, Edward spends a good deal of his time. At times, he finds the silence unnerving; and this affects his mood. He becomes reflective as he reads and adds to his knowledge by taking notes from documents and books that ennobles his sense and respectful appreciation of the past; his beloved histories.

***

He keeps busy in his country retreat, but he feels unusually alone; an aloneness which makes him think harder about his work and his place in the world of Elizabethan literature. His outlook is all the more interesting because of the publication of a book titled: *The Art of English Poesie.* It is a guide to Courtly writing and Courtly writers that sets the bar. It is regarded as the standard by which literary criticism is judged. In this age of Penmanship, as well as much talk and debate on good writing and Court life, *The Art of Poesie* cites authors from Noble backgrounds; some of whom are publishing their works, but not under their own names. They prefer the word: Anonymous. On this matter, though *The Art of English Poesie* is a closed book, so to speak, its author explains:

"I know very many notable gentlemen in the Court that have written commendably and suppressed it again, or else had suffered it to be published without their own names to it, as if it were a discredit for a gentleman to seem learned." This is the central concern of Edward de Vere, who is close to being the highest ranked Nobleman. In these times of magic, codes and ciphers, who these "very many notable gentlemen" are, is largely left to guesswork. But, as expected, many are ready to critique, even belittle the book for not naming the anonymous (or pseudonymous) Courtly authors. So naturally, the serious engagement with anonymity arises. For his part, getting into print for the first time, Thomas Nashe is pleased, but concerned too!

He writes about sundry other gentlemen whom he knows have "vaunted their pens in private devices and tricked up a company of taffeta fools with their feathers." Who are these "Tafetta fools?" Nashe, the fearless satirist, does not hold back. He pokes fun at his fellow-writers, the brilliant dramatist and star playwright, Christopher Marlowe, who is not a constrained Nobleman. He basks freely in the limelight as he makes a name for himself. His popularity grows. And Nashe names him: the "English Seneca." Then, he makes a reference to *Hamlet*, a play of which Edward had already written extensive notes and a second draft. "Marlowe," Nashe writes, "reads by candle light. He yields many good sentences; and if you entreat him fair on a frosty morning, he will afford you whole Hamlets and handfuls of tragical speeches." Here Nashe warns Marlowe that borrowing from Seneca might allow him to create more than one Hamlet. He also refers to the tragic drama by Marlowe: *Tamburlaine.* So, at this time in the late

1580s, Nashe, like other writers in London, already knows about *Hamlet,* if not about Edward specifically as the author.

For his part Edward is very careful to give his plays the by-line "Anonymous." But so far, his steadily accumulating output of brilliant writings is not going unnoticed by many at Court and in literary circles. The unknown author of the publication *The Art of English Poesie*, already admits to knowing Noblemen and Gentlemen in Her Majesty's Service, who have written commendably well. Of these Nobles, Edward, Earl of Oxford, is singled out as being the "best for Comedy." This is no mere passing comment. It confirms what was said of Edward just three years earlier, when he was praised by another critic. "I may not omit the deserved commendations of many honourable and noble lords and gentlemen of Her Majesty's Court," William Webbe had written, "which in the rare devices of Poetry have been and yet are most excellent skilful." He cites the Right Honourable Earl of Oxford who he says may challenge to himself the title of most excellent among the rest."

So, with *Hamlet* already in hand, Edward's mercurial mind accepts the good comments of *The Art of English Poesie*, but he never gloats or harps on the praise his writings receive. He moves quickly on to the next poem or play! As he works, he is more conscious of his standing and responsibility: For example, that his writings are much appreciated and have a public following. But he knows that as a Noble Courtier this is not what any self-respecting Gentleman should aspire to, as his much-admired philosophical guide Castiglione had taught. So, for a while, he steps back. He thinks very seriously that the time has come for him to be not just *discreet*, but *Courtly* too. This becomes his guiding philosophy. Why? Because at this juncture in his career, his essential thoughts are mirrored in his life and work. Several of his plays have been performed both at Court and to public theatre audiences.

He is encouraged by the positive feedback that his unique dramatisations, both Comedies and Tragedies, receive. And from this vantage point, as he adds to his works, he carefully maintains his anonymity.

***

Meanwhile, his daughter Elizabeth - the cause of so much trouble between him and his wife Anne - enters her teenagehood. The time has come, her grandfather Burghley thinks, to find her a suitable husband. Now Edward is faced with responding to his daughter's marriage proposals. Thus far, on family matters, the best form of expressing himself on a range of personal, private issues has been through his pen. Already, in spite of disguise, a few characters in his plays bear striking resemblance to family members: namely Anne - specially at the time of her pregnancy with Elizabeth - and Burghley himself. Now he thinks he must be kind to his daughter. He must neither ruin, nor spoil, her prospects as she enters the arena of tough Courtly match-makers and match-making. These marriage brokers are not just interested in Elizabeth's good looks.Being in the spotlight, more questions are asked of her: Would she, for example, be exposed as the daughter of an Earl, who wears a masque, but in truth is a disreputable Dramatist whose plays frankly discuss her mother and father's unhappy marriage? To his credit, whatever his reputation, Edward is brutally frank in portraying the drama of his personal life. So whether or not he is labelled as a "vulgar playwright," for better or worse, it is the occupation he follows and is never forgetful of his steely ambition: A writer to be!

That enthusiastic boyhood quest has since formed the core of his being. *Writing!* Certainly writing the plays is a complex process. He considers the basics: pen, paper, ink and the power of his capacious brain. After a hard look at himself, he thinks of his critics who have said, more or less, that he is not just a good practitioner of playwriting: he's very impressive. Certainly, the *best* for Comedy.

***

Many Courtiers and others at Court, who know young Elizabeth de Vere, have great respect for her father. He is after all, the Honourable Seventeenth Earl of Oxford, one of the most admired men of the Realm. Having lived through tempestuous years with Anne, he feels the time has come to make amends. How? The least he thinks he could do now for his first-born is not to allow anything to do with himself to get in the way of a good life for Elizabeth.

And so although he'd been practising anonymous authorship, now he makes a profound decision about his writing and publishing. "From here on," he says to himself, "I will be even more strict with myself so nothing that I write, will either appear, or be published, under my own name: Edward de Vere." So, though the pace at which his pen moves quickens, on the delicate matter of using his real name as author of his writings, he feels he must *forever be silent!* "But," he says to himself, "I will continue, come what may, to insert clues in my plays as to who I really am. I will use only pen-names."

***

Amidst the political flux in Europe, in the last year of the decade of the 1580s, with the Armada defeated and King Philip of Spain's expansionist ambitions weakened, England could breathe a sigh of relief. When the Queen's Men stages his play *The Tragedy of Richard the Third* as an Insider, Edward's intimate knowledge of the Queen and the Royal Court serves him well. He knows his way around, which empowered him to write the play; a draft of which he shows to Lyly and Munday. Conscious of having infused some bias in favour of an ancestor, a former Earl of Oxford, he wrote:

"Oxford…will not wink at murders secretly put up, not suffer upstarts to enjoy our nights…content thee good Oxford and tho I confess myself bound for thy especial care, yet at this time I pray thee hold me excused." He chooses his words carefully. Given his strong historical sense and his father's contribution and allegiance to King Henry VIII, as well as his love for dear Queen Elizabeth, his main aim in the play is to glorify and celebrate Queen Elizabeth's right to Rule, but also to remember Henry Tudor's resounding defeat of Richard III.

Ever conscious of his Queen, in the play's closing speech, Edward lauds "Worthy Elizabeth" as "…the lamp that keeps fair England's light," and through her faith, England lives in peace, having put Catholic Spain to flight, and thus "Civil Wars did cease." In turn, Elizabeth acknowledges Edward. She literally embraces him; and once more, he is back in the fold as her chief propagandist. The power of Edward's pen fills Elizabeth with unbounded admiration, but thoughts of her more passionate feelings for him are held in check, just beneath the surface.

***

Edward's keen sense of the international scene leads to regular reviews of the situation. In the interlude after England's defeat of the Spanish Armada, the Catholic threat of deposing Queen Elizabeth is much reduced. But trouble from other quarters is not far away. In France, another drama is being played out. After the death of Alencon - Queen Elizabeth's former long time suitor - two men vie to become the French Monarch. As time passes, impatience gives way to the aristocratic-inspired assassination of the Duke of Guise. This collective act of murder is much like the assassination of Julius Caesar; an act for which no individual could be identified. It is a crime that rankles. And as retribution for the French King's death remains outstanding, revenge is taken: A monk stabs the King and soon a dagger finds its mark upon the murderer. For his new play, *Julius Caesar*, Edward writes these lines for CAESAR'S assassin to speak:

"BRUTUS: O, JULIUS CAESAR, thou art mighty yet!
Thy spirit walks abroad, and turns our swords
In our own proper entrails."

Edward is aware of the high esteem in which Guise was held by Catholics in France. After much thought, he makes a connection between Guise and CAESAR. He knows of Catholic supporters of the Duke of Guise who refer to him as "Caesar," and he explores the comparison infusing dramatic power by playing on the similarities and differences of CAESAR and Guise. One similarity is the assassins timing. As with the murder of the French King, the party of assassins enact their plans early in the day.

"...Sham'st thou to show thy dangerous brow by night
When evils are most free."

Edward's creativity extends to his plotters pun on Guise's rank:

"BRUTUS: It must be by his death. And for my part I
know no personal cause to spurn at him,
but for the general. He would be crowned."

Faithful to the historical record, Edward writes of the encircling plotters who are ready to fulfil their own prophesies of Royal death foretold. So Edward's exploration of his art in *Julius Caesar* leads him to combine allegory and imaginative story telling. His hold on his quill is assured, as it moves rhythmically, at a steady pace along the page. Now he experiments: Like his metered six-stanza lines of verse writing, he adds to an early draft which is now close to completion. Habitually, as he works and re-works drafts, he matures as a playwright. His work gains depth and reaches new heights of lyricism and craftsmanship. He delves deeper, exploring the quirks and oddities, as well as the nobility of the characters he creates; and by combining different human traits, he gains new insights from the Italian tragedy. Sometimes, he is taken aback by his close resemblance to CAESAR. Like the Roman Ruler, he is prone to be arrogant and is reluctant to form political partnerships. Overriding all, as he creates, is his understanding and use of *English history* with which he deals, time and again, in the conflict of Kings like the Henries.

***

Edward rises early; and after he'd been at work for most of the morning, he stops. He stands on the spot a while; then paces around in his study. He thinks not of the lines he has penned that day, but of all the plays he'd so far written. He hears the sound of rain. He moves closer to the window that overlooks the neat flower beds and the paths between them. As the light rain gets heavier, he lifts his gaze to view the dense green canopy of tree tops at eye level that surrounds the house. The leaves of plants and petals of flowers in the drenched garden glistens. He breathes deeply and feels liberated from the regimes of Cecil House, the Cecil family and the Court. But, his mood is unsettled, much like the weather. The sky is overcast; slate grey clouds hovers, but he thinks of times past: Of Italy, a brighter, sunnier clime that had unlocked his creativity in relation to the theatre and thus of life generally.

Those foreign places that had wonderfully triggered in him spectacular, unexpected ways of thinking that now seem as if the dark clouds had rolled away. Since he'd come back, he had not stopped writing plays! Now he slowly walks back to his desk on which he'd earlier placed a bundle of his plays. He'd retrieved them from storage in the bottom drawers of his desk where they were locked away for safe keeping. Looking at the pile of scripts, he remembers the explosion in his brain when he'd first seen a Commedia dell arte performance in Paris, as well as the plays that he'd set in Italy, which he thinks justifies the nick-name: The "Italianate Englishman." A logical extension of this, he thinks, is to be called by the fuller description "The Italianate English Playwright."

So now for the first time, since returning from his travels

and the years of playwriting thereafter, knowing of their importance, he prepares to read and review the bundle of his "Italian plays," as he calls them. With his reputation high and rising, he feels strongly that plays should reach beyond performance on the stage. They should be prepared and presented as integral to the wider corpus of English literature. "This is the body of writings," he says to himself, "that has made me the playwright and poet that I have become."

He no longer feels the need to put off for some other time, but to now urgently prepare the long hidden texts, by very carefully reading and revising every one of his "*Italian plays.*"

***

# IX

## "The Italianate Englishman:" The Playwright

*"A traveller!"*
*"I'll teach you differences."*

### ONE

### *ROMEO AND JULIET*

Differences? For Edward, the quintessential English Nobleman, travelling through Italy could not be more different from anything else that he'd ever experienced! Now in his Study, he is eager to begin work. But before he does so, he is mindful that the plays stacked on one side of his desk share one thing: They are all set, either in part, or wholly, in Italy; importantly in places that he had visited.

The first play script he removes from the bundle is *Romeo and Juliet.* He turns the title page; and, as he reads thoughts of a passionate teenage experience of infatuation and love envelops him. He recalls the loved person as his "Little Western Flower," who was forced to marry an older man. In these opening lines of the play, he vividly recalls his time in Verona where, for the first time, he sees the grove of sycamore trees, just outside the city's western wall. In the first Scene of the First Act, he reads that this is the place where ROMEO'S mother, LADY

MONTAGUE, meets her nephew BENVOLIO on the street. BENVOLIO is ROMEO'S best friend. LADY MONTAGUE asks where ROMEO might be. BENVOLIO says:

"Madam, an hour before the worshipped sun
Peered forth the golden window of the East,
A troubled mind drove me to walk abroad,
Where underneath the grove of sycamore
That westward rooteth from the city's side
So early walking did I see your son.
Towards him, I made, but he was ware of me,
And stole into the covert of the wood."

Edward had written the lines of this play as his own version of an old Italian tale. He remembers that while he was in Verona, his love for literature and history had guided him to the source of a story about which he'd learned all he could. But now, as he reads more of his play, no story or account that he'd previously read had said anything about "sycamore trees." He pauses; and thinks about those trees. "Yes, I had seen them in Verona," he says to himself. "They are not an invention. They must grow and thrive there now!"

Then, he thinks about Freetown, which he'd also written into the play. He knows that a "free town" is a place where everyday commerce and trade transactions are, to some extent, conducted free of taxation. But, in his version of *Romeo and Juliet*, he injects something significant – his own version of the Freetown in the first Scene of Act I. And, he does so, much before he mentions the sycamore grove. But, as with the sycamore trees, this Freetown, has nothing to do with an imaginary Capulet Castle or a Noble country retreat. It is about things far more serious and germane to the play. He pauses; and, once more, considers the first Scene which deals with dangerous youths out on the Verona streets in an agitated state: They are intent on a fight; on drawing blood! They belong to families who are seen as enemies. Namely: The MONTAGUES and the CAPULETS. When these angry young men meet, they draw swords. Older members, the heads of the families enter the fray. They appear not to stop the brawl, but make it worse. Then, comes the angry overlord, the Prince of Verona, ESCALUS. He is unusually bad-tempered and stops the actions of the combatants. In his composition, Edward gets ESCALUS to speak these words:

"You, Capulet, shall go alone with me;
And Montague, come you this afternoon,
To know our farther pleasure in this case,
*To old freetown, our common judgement place…*"

ESCALUS exits as suddenly as he appears. Attention is turned to BENVOLIO who tells his Aunt about the sycamore trees. So, as Edward reads, he is reminded of "Freetown" and the sycamore. He calls Freetown "old." But, in what way is it old? He knows that no writer has called it old or had said anything about public judgements. In this, he'd taken a new approach: Having written about Freetown both as "old" and as the place of Princely "public judgements," he asks himself two questions: "Why have I included these elements into the story? and What am I getting at?" He knows that those particular elements are in the play, simply because he had been there. Hence the expression "old Freetown" which is that "common judgement place." So, Edward uses a real place to symbolize Prince Bartolomeo della Scala's power base in Feudal Italy. Furthermore, he remembers that as an English Nobleman his favourite books include *The Courtier* and *Cardanus Comfort*, both by Italian authors. "It is no wonder," he thinks, "that I was powerfully drawn to this place within the walls of Verona."

His love of history and his finely attuned historical sense enriches his play's composition. He understands the feudal power wielded by the della Scala Scaligers' conquest of Verona; that over time, the family and the town had become synonymous and that the Castle at Villafanca di Verona was the site of the Princely Court of Scaliger Rulers and the forum for their public judgements. So, Edward knows the story of the town and the family to be old; that power and medieval protocol were strictly observed; something he is well acquainted with in the Elizabethan Court. As he reads more of the *Romeo and Juliet* script, he is happy about the place where MONTAGUE appears on that afternoon as arranged. So both MONTAGUE and ESCALUS know of Freetown as "old." And, as indicated in ESCALUS'S command, Edward reveals more of himself in his play. It is something, he thinks, that should interest every Englishman. So while he was mulling over his characters, he thought that a Feudal code should be honoured by ESCALUS, when he separated the CAPULETS and MONTAGUES.

But, at the time of writing, Edward had added ESCALUS'S violation of that Code; and what is worse, he does so in public: on the street. Therefore, ESCALUS doesn't allow parity of dignity to both Noble families. Instead his commands to them are very different. So, Edward portrays his character ESCALUS, as a ruling Prince who behaves as one who is about to violate the ancient rights and obligations between Ruler and Nobles, who were assumed to be of equal dignity. Edward feels this injustice as he reads more of the play which favours the CAPULETS, and relegates ROMEO and the MONTAGUES.

At this juncture, Edward is, once again, immersed in

the dramatic effect of his play. The images are vivid. He feels transported back to Verona. In his mind's eye, he is conscious not only of the sycamore trees and Freetown, but other landmarks as well, like Verona's Saint Peter's Church. He thinks of his habit of naming, or describing a person, place or thing that may seem like an invention or perhaps a mistake. On the contrary, he is satisfied that such elements are actual and not imagined! He remembers strolling past the building which he named as Juliet's house, then continued along the route that Juliet had taken on her way to Friar Laurence's Monastery, which both Juliet and Romeo had visited. It was in the Monastery Church where they had been secretly married. And just a short distance away, was the Capulet Parish Church, which Edward had named at least three times in *Romeo and Juliet.* In his mind's eye, he is transported by the story's places and people in relation to the city of Verona. At the end of his reading of this tragic tale of star-crossed lovers, as if to confirm his memory, he notes in the margin of the script that Saint Peter's Church is located in Juliet's Parish; and that Juliet's house is where he'd placed it: along the way to Friar's Laurence's monastery.

***

# TWO

## *THE TWO GENTLEMEN OF VERONA*

The next play Edward attends to is *The Two Gentlemen of Verona*. He was so struck by Verona that he'd decided to set another play there. His leading characters are VALENTINE and PROTEUS; the sons of Noblemen. "You write best about what you know," he thinks. In this sense, everything he knows is about Nobles. He is pleased with the two young characters he'd created. As he reads, he stops to make minor adjustments, here and there. He reappraises the context of the story as he reconsiders the experience he'd had in Verona which he'd imputed in the adventures of VALENTINE and PROTEUS. Though the story is light-hearted and highly imaginative, it is based on places that Edward had enjoyed being in; an enjoyment deepened by his understanding of the history of that city and region in Italy. Having alluded to specific sites in Verona in *Romeo and Juliet*, he does not do so in *The Two Gentlemen of Verona*. In this play, he sees the city as an important centre of Italian trade and progress. But now he turns his attention to people, places and things in Milan; a very different Italian city. While he was composing the play, he remembers asking himself how best to deal with these different cities in relation to his story. Eventually, he'd decided to send his two fearless young men of Verona to Milan. Through them, he felt the audience would learn about Milan.

So the play opens with the two gentlemen: VALENTINE and PROTEUS on stage. As VALENTINE prepares to leave for Milan, his friend PROTEUS tries to detain him; to get him to stay at home. Edward is conscious of his own eagerness, his thwarted attempts, to go abroad, in particular, to Italy! Now, he reads the lines he'd written for VALENTINE to speak:

"Cease to persuade, my loving Proteus;
Home-fleeing youth have ever-homely wits…
I rather would entreat thy company
To see wonders abroad
Than (living dully sluggardiz'd at home)
Wear out thy youth with shapeless idleness."

Ever restless, Edward knows only too well the value of these lines: He's at one with his character VALENTINE who says to PROTEUS:

"Once more adieu; my father at the road
Expects my coming,
There to see me shipp'd."

Later he adds: "At Milan, let me hear from thee by letter." So now Edward has VALENTINE sailing from inland Verona to inland Milan "in a ship." Sailing inland? How is this possible? Edward knows how: He's been there! VALENTINE is using a nautical expression, which he had used in other plays. But now, he pauses his reading. He reflects upon his usage of words in the play; on his knowledge of the city before continuing with his reading and revision. His fondness for, and remembrance of, things past, enriches the moment: For a short while, he re-runs his understanding of Verona's backstory: Over centuries, Verona had been an important city for shipping. By means of the Adige River travellers and traffic can reach the city. It is so placed that a traveller could sail from Verona and arrive at the Adriatic part of the Mediterranean Sea. Edward pauses at the word "shipped" as spoken by VALENTINE. He does not think of "shipped" as being odd or out of place, for in those days "Shipped" meant going by vessel not by land! So, he is aware that there might be misunderstanding among some readers of the play; and, of course, among theatre-goers too, about the oddness of VALENTINE going to Milan "by vessel" when there is no sea. The closest sea water to Verona is the Adriatic, and the nearest sea to Milan is the Tyrrhenian Sea. But during the play's composition, and now, Edward feels it is right: Not only to have sent VALENTINE to Milan by water in Act II, but also to have dispatched PROTEUS on the same sail-borne voyage. He muses over any potential confusion about Verona as a seaport? And now he questions himself: "Did I really put Verona on a highly imaginative false sea?" "No," he answers himself. For one thing, he mentions the word "tide" in Act II of the play. But by "tide" he does not mean "salt water." He'd first used the word when PROTEUS'S father orders him to go to Milan. And when PROTEUS goes to JULIA, the woman he loves, to bid her goodbye, he says:

> "My father stays my coming. Answer not.
> The tide is now – Nay, not thy rush of tears!
> That flood will stay me longer than I should.
> Julia, farewell!"

In this touching Scene, PROTEUS'S last words to JULIA are heartfelt. But, as Edward now reads further, it is, as he'd intended: That his audience should also have a moment of light-heartedness. So he uses puns on the word "tide." Thus he shows his fondness for puns; and his creative use of them continues in the play. In Scenes 2 and 3 of Act II, he repeatedly puns on the word tide. He gives it different meanings. Later in the story, he revisits Scene 3 which opens with one person on stage. It is LAUNCE, PROTEUS'S simple-minded young servant. Edward is conscious of having chosen the name LAUNCE. Why? Because he wanted to keep the audience alert; to get them thinking about the sea, because a "sand launce" is a small fish to be found in sandy beaches.

So he positions LAUNCE as having been ordered to go with PROTEUS to Milan. He is wary and unhappy about leaving home; something he's never done before. What would become of my dog "Crab," he thinks. The name crab is another seaside link. And so, on the Verona quayside, the character PANTHINO urges LAUNCE on. The problem with taking the Adige River to Milan is that not long into the journey, it wends its way Eastwards and flows into the Adriatic Sea. This is not good for the travellers because Milan is far to the West. Edward knew that overland travel was possible, but such a route is not free of its difficulties: Bandits robbing travellers was well-known and feared. By contrast, water transport was safer. So, Edward sets the course for his young travellers. Thus "sailing" from Verona to Milan was the way to go, in Edward's way of thinking. And so travel by river and canal, was preferred.

But why this trip? Because these young men are going to Milan for an event of the utmost importance for their future. They aim high. They hope to meet the Emperor and offer their services to him. Each of them is leaving his hometown with excitement and hope to find his place in the world. They look forward to meeting their Emperor; the ultimate enabler of their particular goal. But before this point on their life's journey, they had been well-versed in the ways of Courtly life: They'd read (as Edward had done) the ultimate guidebook: *Il Libro de Cortegiano*: The Book of the Courtier, written by

Castiglione, Edward's hero!

So by making the journey to Milan, the Veronese Gentlemen cross boundaries between the two states that have always quarrelled. But, divisions apart, PROTEUS and VALENTINE have to do what they were brought up to believe. Their fathers expect much of them! Their training have fitted them to choose careers relating to going to wars, discovering distant lands and studying at a university. In some respects, Edward's experience had served him well. Not only in this play, but in others too. He remembers casting Courtly characters like BERTRAM going to war in Tuscany in *All's Well That Ends Well*; and LUCENTIO, the wealthy youth who attends Padua's University in *The Taming of the Shrew*. *The Courtier*, as he knows is invaluable for the privileged in many countries.

Having channeled Castiglione's teachings into his two main characters in *The Two Gentlemen of Verona*, now Edward pauses his reading to reflect on what he'd said to his Secretary while he was creating the characters PROTEUS and VALENTINE: "As you know, Lyly," Edward says, "Castiglione's teachings are highly regarded among Gentlemen in Europe, especially in his homeland Italy. Noblemen speak of him with reverence. Castiglione's ideals have seeped deep into his fellow-countrymen's conscience and their way of thinking."

And so, the young Gentlemen leave Verona for Milan, eager for personal success. At the Emperor's Court, they expect a great deal: an abundance of opportunities. No less. They'd read all they could about The Holy Roman Emperor Charles V, King of Spain. News of his arrival in Milan, and plans for it were set in motion. He understood that before the Emperor had arrived in Milan, excitement in the city – and the whole Duchy - rose to fever pitch: it was an extraordinary time. The preparations were of a different order. Not only did Italy's Nobles and common-folk begin to gather, but so too were artists and artisans who came from far and wide to help; to embellish the city. The Duke of Mantua, Federico Gonzaga had sent his famous Court artist Guilio (Julio) ROMANO. Edward had seen exhibits of Romano's work; and is not surprised that this artist was called in to enhance Milan's appearance for the Emperor's coming. For a while, Edward stops his reading. He recalls how impressed he was with Romano's art; and how, later on, while writing *A Winter's Tale*, Act V, Scene 2, he'd written Romano into the story. After this pause for reflection, he resumes reading. He is now at the point in the play where he refers to a Church outside the walls of Milan. Its name is Saint Gregory's Well. When in Act IV, Scene 2, THURIO asks PROTEUS: "Where meet we?" PROTEUS says: "At Saint Gregory's Well."

In Milan, as in other Italian cities there was a Lazzaretto; a place named after Lazarus, the man who, according to the *Holy Bible,* rose from the dead. The Lazzaretto was therefore to keep within its bounds lepers, diseased travellers and victims of Plague. People in, and around, the city were frightened of that hellish place that was outside the city walls, where the afflicted were administered to, before they died. "How could I ever forget that terrifying place," Edward asks himself. He shudders just thinking of what he'd heard about Milan's Lazzaretto. He remembers the Plague of 1575 that had affected many parts of Italy; and a few months later, it had reached Milan! The rising number of sick and dying people were brought to the Lazzaretto where, at its height, some sixteen thousand people had died. The Church named San Gregorio was near to the Lazzaretto.

But where was Saint Gregory's Well? The answer is as he'd written it in Act IV, Scene 2 when THURIO had asked PROTEUS: "Where we meet?" But now, as Edward reads in Act V, Scene 4, he'd shown how well he understood the meanings and difference between the "wilderness" and the "woods" or forest, where his characters meet to speak their last words.

He shudders now at the thought that the large quarantine compound of the Lazzaretto is where thousands had died. Their bodies were taken, he was told, to Saint Gregory's Well, an ever-expanding Churchyard and burial ground. Unlike the implication of its name, Saint Gregory's Well was neither a fountain, nor a source of water. It was just a Churchyard containing mass graves. This, as Edward remembers it, is Saint Gregory's Well! It was here, in this terrifying place, where he had placed the play's characters.

After he reads the final Scene, he reflects, with nostalgia (and some wonder) how deeply inspired he'd been on his travels between Verona and Milan; and the sense of satisfaction he feels now in London about portrayals of the characters he has immortalised in his art: namely his proud presentation of *The Two Gentlemen of Verona.* He is pleased with the casting of PROTEUS and VALENTINE, Noble men like himself, as he turns the last page and puts the manuscript on top of the revised copy of *Romeo and Juliet.* Beside these two scripts is the bundle of plays to be read and, if need be, amended or corrected. He rises wearily from his chair and walks out of his Study. So ends that working day.

***

# THREE

## *THE TAMING OF THE SHREW*

The next day, Edward is eager to get on: He is back at his desk and in his disciplined way he begins to read *The Taming of the Shrew.* He'd set this drama in Padua and immediately recalls his visit there and the journey he'd made to Pisa. But soon, other images of the travels he'd made to Venice and Verona, just the day before, crowd in. Nonetheless, cocooned in that imaginative bubble, as he revises, he focuses on Padua, where the play opens. Once more, he'd placed two young men onstage: LUCENTIO and TRANIO. LUCENTIO speaks to his companion TRANIO and from what he says, as playwright, Edward reveals details about his specific knowledge of Italy. Not surprisingly, he feels a comforting familiarity as he reads the story.

While speaking to TRANIO, LUCENTIO gives much information. In this way, Edward had cleverly set the scene in which LUCENTIO tells the audience a great deal about himself: The place of his birth and youth, the journey and why he came, where he received his education and who his father is. As the drama unfolds, Edward describes the play's wider setting through LUCENTIO, who refers to the region known as Lombardy, which he mentions in the first few lines of LUCENTIO'S speech:

"Tranio, since for the great desire I had
To see fair Padua, nursery of the arts,

I am arriv'd for fruitful Lombardy,
The pleasant garden of great Italy."

So here LUCENTIO was: in Padua. He comes in search of higher learning at Padua's famous university. While reading this, for a moment, Edward thinks of his former tutor, Thomas Smith, who had studied and taught in Padua. Soon after he'd arrived, LUCENTIO sees a young woman named BIANCA, who is the sister of KATE. The sight of BIANCA unsettles LUCENTIO. His infatuation transforms him; and he has a very different reason for being in Padua. He says: "I have Pisa left / And am to Padua come…"

Edward reads more of what he'd written about LUCENTIO and his companion taking the same route backward, and using the same connecting canals, they sail from Ostiglia to Padua. Here Edward replicates his own experience for LUCENTIO'S. So what LUCENTIO knows, does and says, is really what Edward knows, had done and said

Edward thinks now about the significance of Revere and Ostiglia to his play. Both places are in the Duchy of Mantua; a part of Lombardy. So when LUCENTIO says to TRANIO "I am arriv'd from fruitful Lombardy" he is speaking the truth. At this point in *The Taming of the Shrew*, Edward makes the important point that LUCENTIO had "journeyed from Ostiglia to Padua *in a boat,*" A journey the first part of which was undertaken overland from Pisa to Revere. As Edward saw it then, and sees it now, such a difference is of much importance in Italy. Rivers and canals were crucial to Edward's Italian travels. So now, at the end of TRANIO'S opening lines, these are his last few words:

"No profits grows where there is no pleasure ta'en

In brief, sir, study what you most affect."

In turn, LUCENTIO says:

"Grammercies Tranio, well dost thou advise
If, Biondello, thou wert come ashore,
We could at once put us in readiness,
And take a lodging fit to entertain
Such friends as time in Padua shall beget."

As before, LUCENTIO'S words reveal the truth about Edward's own visit. So before leaving for Pisa, like Edward himself, LUCENTIO knew about both the land and water routes to Padua. As LUCENTIO says, his father, a merchant engaged with the traffic of the world, had given him the best advice as to the most practical route to follow from Pisa to Padua. At this point in the play, he reads what he'd written about a place in Padua where travellers could moor their boats. Where could this be? On his Italian travels, Edward had been true to what he'd observed and recorded.Meanwhile, as the play evolves, KATE'S suitor PETRUCHIO arrives from Verona hoping to marry her. Then, in Act III, Scene 2, KATE'S hastily arranged wedding is witnessed by GRUMIO in a local Parish Church.

As Edward reads further into *The Taming of the Shrew*, he is reminded of his original intention of composing the story so that it is only at the end of Act IV, Scene 4 that play-goers learns the name of the Parish Church in Padua. In this Scene, BIONDELLO says to LUCENTIO: "The old Priest at Saint Luke's Church is at your command at all hours." Edward remembers Saint Luke's Church very well! But this is not the only time that the Church appears in the play. Once more, at the end of the Scene, the Church is named when BIONDELLO says: "My master hath appointed me to go to Saint Luke's to bid the Priest be ready t'attend against you come with your appendix." The character BAPTISTA MINOLA and his daughter live in the Parish of Saint Luke; and now Edward recalls seeing the small Saint Luke's Church which was within Padua's Medieval wall, near to an arched opening. Through that Arch was the setting that Edward had chosen for Act I, Scene 1 of *The Taming of the Shrew*. Here, there were various elements that fits the dialogues in the opening Scene: A waterway; a landing place, quay or road, where a boat could be tied-up; a bridge across the waterway connecting the street on which Saint Luke's Church stands, and a nearby cluster of buildings. Here, Edward locates LUCENTIO, BIONDELLO, BAPTISTA and his daughter. Here, the man taken on by BIONDELLO as a PEDANT, converses with TRANIO towards the end of Act IV, Scene 2:

"PEDANT: God save you, Sir!
TRANIO: And you, Sir! You are welcome. Travel you far on, or are you at the farthest?
PEDANT: Sir, at the farthest for a week or two,
But then up farther, and as far as Rome;
And so to Tripoli, if God lend me his life.
TRANIO: What countryman I pray?
PEDANT: Of Mantua.
TRANIO: Of Mantua sir? Marry, God forbid!
And come to Padua, careless of your life.
PEDANT: My life, Sir? How I pray? For that goes hard.
TRANIO: 'Tis death for anyone in Mantua,
To come to Padua, know you not the cause?
Your ships are stayed at Venice, and the Duke,
For private quarrel 'twixt your Duke and him,

Hath published and proclaimed it openly.
'Tis marvel but that you are but newly come,
You might have heard it else proclaimed about.
PEDANT: Alas, Sir it was worse for me than so,
For I have bills for money by exchange
From Florence, and must here deliver them.
TRANIO: Well, sir, to do you courtesy
This I will do, and this I will advise.
First, tell me you have been to Pisa?"

Looking back, Edward is pleased to have had the precise knowledge of an essential Italian banking practice. Some distance away from Padua is Pisa. He recalls his visit there too, and in the play, he mentions Pisa more than a dozen times, but not only because it is LUCENTIO'S home-town. As part of his playwriting skill and inventiveness, he delights in using words creatively: Thus he lapses into punning; his old habit which he enjoys. No wonder he uses Pisa for one of his word-play exercises. The Pisa pun has a nice ring to it. And word-play artist that he is, he'd worked it into his dialogues. For a while, he stops his reading and revising of *The Taming of the Shrew*, to reflect upon the pun that he'd used in *Romeo and Juliet's* Scene I, Act III in which MERCUTIO, stabbed by TYBALT, dies in ROMEO'S arms:

"ROMEO: Courage man. The hurt cannot be much
MERCUTIO: No, 'tis not *so deep* as a well,
*Nor so wide* as a church door;
but 'tis enough 'twill serve.
Ask for me tomorrow,
and you will find me a grave man."

Now, in Act I Scene 1 of *The Taming of the Shrew*, telling where he was born, LUCENTIO says: "Pisa, renowned for grave citizens." And again, in Act IV Scene 2, when the PEDANT is asked if he has ever been to Pisa, he says: "Ay, Sir, in Pisa I have often been, Pisa renowned for grave citizens."

So like MERCUTIO of *Romeo and Juliet,* who is about to become a "grave man" and the PEDANT and LUCENTIO'S "grave citizens" – meaning those who are not its living residents - the Pisan "grave citizens" of which Edward has written in this Scene are not ordinary folk. They are descendants of honourable Pisans, whose last resting place is the "Campo Santo," Pisa's most distinguished Cemetery. To such detailed knowledge as he brings to bear on his play, he also refers to Italian sail-making. He mentions a "sail-maker" in Act V, Scene 1 when VICENTIO (LUCENTIO'S blood father) comes to Padua to see his son. TRANIO'S insulting behaviour shocks VICENTIO. TRANIO pretends to be a rich man's son: "Why sir, what 'cerns you if I wear pearl and gold, I thank my good father, I am able to maintain it." To this, VICENTIO says: "Thy father! O villain! He is a sail-maker in Bergamo."

Edward knows of Bergamo as an important medieval city that specialises in the manufacture of textiles: velvet, silk, wools, broadcloth and, of course, sail-cloth, the much demanded material made from hemp. His references to Lombardy gives essential meaning to his story. At the time of his visit to Italy, the quality of the hemp that came from Piedmont, next to Lombardy, was the finest. He also knows that Bergamo is located in Lombardy, and, that the cloth made from this hemp is known in Italian and Greek as canovaccio and Kannibis, respectively. It's name in English is canvass. It is the vital product in sail-making. So for both sails and sail-making, the place of production is a key factor. To make sails, as Edward knows, the canvass had to be seamed together. Sailmakers were the essential workers in canvass production; and they were to be found where canvass was produced.

With just a few more lines of the play to read, Edward's head is full of images of Italians and Italy. And once more, his knowledge underscores his drama; a tale in which he interweaves the real with the imagined that comes together beautifully in *The Taming of the Shrew*. By the end of his reading and revising of the play, he takes pleasure in thinking that his invention VICENTIO, the character who is TRANIO'S father, could have been a real sail-maker in Bergamo.

***

# FOUR

## *THE MERCHANT OF VENICE*

Edward turns now to the text of *The Merchant of Venice*. He'd spent much time exploring Venice: Its harbours, canals, streets and squares. He was delighted to witness and learn about the city's Courtly pageants, parties and celebrations, as well as investigating its laws, banking  and commerce. As an art and culture-lover, he'd observed what was symbolic, what was real, and he had looked deep into the Venetian soul. The play begins with three characters onstage: ANTONIO, the Merchant; SOLARIO, his Servant, and SOLANIO, his Merchant friend. ANTONIO says:

"Forsooth I know not why I am so sad
It wearies me, you say it wearies you
But how I caught it, found it, come by it,
What stuff, 'tis made of, whereof it is born,
I am to learn;
And such a want-wit sadness makes of me
That I have much to do to know myself."

SALERIO responds:

"Your mind is tossing on the ocean,
There were *your Argosies with portly sail*
Like signors and rich burghers on the flood,

Or as it were the pageants of the Sea.
Do overpeer the petty traffickers,
That curtsey to them, do them reverence,
As they fly by them with their woven wings."

While he was in the Venetian Lagoon, he wanted to know about Argosies. What are they? A particular kind of vessel manufactured, owned and operated by merchants of the Illyrian city of Ragusa, he was told. With his knowledge and understanding of Argosies, in the play he has ANTONIO deviating from the norm; from an old Venetian custom and practice which is: that merchandise, such as ANTONIO'S should not be carried by a foreign vessel: in this case, a Ragusan ship. Should ANTONIO be worried about this? SALERIO thinks he should. He says:

"What harm a wind too great might do at sea
I should not see the sandy hour-glass run
But I should think of shallows and of flats
And see my *wealthy Andrew* docked in sand...

Should I go to church
And see the holy edifice of stone
And not bethink me straight of dangerous rocks,
Which, touching but my gentle vessel's side
Would scatter all her spices on the stream,
Enrobe the roaring waters with my silks,
And, in a word, but even now worth this,
And now worth nothing?
Shall I the thought
To think on this, and shall I lack the thought
That such a thing bechanced would make me sad.

But tell not me; I know Antonio
Is sad to think upon his merchandise."

ANTONIO says:

"Believe me, no. I thank my fortune for it.
My ventures are not in one bottom trusted,
Nor to one place. Nor is my whole estate
Upon the future of this year.
Therefore my merchandise makes me not sad."

So through the words of SALERIO, Edward speaks to his audience and Elizabethans, especially those engaged in shipping. He informs mariners and traders to be wary of running aground on entering Venetian waters. Reading further, he remembers what he'd written about ANTONIO: Not only that he is using Ragusan Argosies for his business, but also another type of ship which SALERIO calls "My wealthy Andrew."

Clearly, ANTONIO breaks the rules: He uses different ships; and, as he says in his conversation with SALERIO "My ventures not in one bottom trusted." So, instead of using Venetian ships only, ANTONIO'S merchandise is carried by both Argosies and Andrews. Ships and shipping matters greatly to Edward. He is aware, as were many people in England, of the Venetian custom and law that forbids Venetian Merchants from owning and hiring foreign ships. Through the words of his characters, he tells his audiences that there is change in Venice. This is all the more original and surprising because the stories that had inspired his *Merchant of Venice* says nothing of such things. What were these stories?

Edward stops reading; and for a while, he reflects upon two stories and links them to the time when he'd first learned about them. The first one was *The Blockhead,* also known as "The Pound of flesh Story." It was written in the fourteenth century by Giovanni Fiorentino. The other tale is the "The Casket Story" which is about winning the hand of a fair maiden. To do so, meant choosing the right Casket. The story is not set in one place in Europe, but many. It is also one of a collection of stories. After he'd read these tales, while writing *The Merchant of Venice*, he had decided to add new elements in creating his own version of "The Casket Story." He thought of ships and existing shipping relations; and realised that while Venetian ships carry merchandise in "The Pound of Flesh Story," in "The Casket Story," there is none! Knowing this, he took the opportunity of exploring the possibilities. Thus, he created the play before him, in which he now reads of his references to Argosies and Andrews that marks a shift away from "The Pound of Flesh Story" and traditional Venetian Rule. "Why introduce these different nationalities?" he asks himself. Already he knows the answer: That because of his love for Italy, he would be faithful, never careless, about the Italian details in his play. Trade and shipping news in England are crucial, and while writing the play, he felt it was timely. It is no less so now as he revises *The Merchant of Venice.* He feels that some sense of history is always helpful and reconsiders what had happened less than two decades before when Venetian ships had stopped coming to England. Among the reasons given for this were: That young Venetian men were against going to sea because of piracy, the ever-growing dangers of lawlessness and buccaneering.

From an English point of view, and given his historical sense, Edward knows of other contributory factors like Francis Drake's exploits on the high seas as well as the timber scarcity in Italy and failure to meet the demands of Venetian shipyards. With fewer ships available, it made good business sense to hire Merchant vessels from outside Venice, in particular, from Ragusa and Genoa. In all this, one year stood out: 1573, a time when English ships and explorers roamed far and wide. They increasingly plied Mediterranean waters, and were welcomed in certain Italian ports, where English intelligence-gathering was twinned with trading relationships. Significantly, it was a time, too, when the English Upper Classes visited Italy to learn the Italian language, history, painting and sculpture, as well as creativity in theatre and dramatic arts. As more trade led to a greater English presence abroad. Financial success followed; and three years after Edward had returned to England from Italy, Queen Elizabeth issued the Royal Patent for the Levant Company to trade in the Eastern Mediterranean.

Against this scenario, Edward reaffirms his understanding of the context of *The Merchant of Venice* as he reads more of it. His powers of recall serves him well as he considers the destinations of ANTONIO'S Argosies. In Act I, Scene 3, SHYLOCK, the money lender, speaks of ANTONIO'S credit-worthiness; of his being a "good man." SHYLOCK says to BASSANIO: "My meaning in saying he is a good man, is to have you understand me that he is sufficient, Yet, his means are in supposition. He hath an Argosy bound to Tripoli, another to the Indies. I understand moreover upon the Rialto he hath a third to Mexico, a fourth for England, and other ventures he hath squandered abroad." Later, in Act III Scene 2, BASSANIO receives a letter from ANTONIO and speaks to SALERIO: "But, is it true, SALERIO?" he asks while reading the letter:

"Hath all his ventures fail'd? What not one hit?
From Tripolis, from Mexico and England,

From Lisbon, Barbary and India,
And not one vessel scape the dreadful touch
Of merchant-marring rocks?"

The destinations named by SHYLOCK and BASSANIO corresponds fairly well. In addition to SHYLOCK'S five named destinations, BASSANIO lists at least six others and, almost all are in harmony with those of SHYLOCK'S. Here, once more, as playwright, Edward de Vere is the Master Ventriloquist, speaking truth through his characters. He was careful to convey the message that overall, vessels flying the Ragusan flag were not banned, but welcomed. Nonetheless at an earlier date circumstances were different. And Edward, like the Merchants in sixteenth century Venice, knew this. So he'd moved his play forward in time.

Of all the many delightful and interesting places that he'd visited in Venice, he'd decided to cite just one in the play: The Rialto. This relatively small public square is the financial district of the city. Though he mentions The Rialto five different times in the drama; and while it is not a setting for the story, it is a place of particular importance to *The Merchant of Venice*. Edward had been to the Rialto many times; the place where the city nobles, merchants and financiers gathered and did business, each working day. There, he'd heard the bargaining urgency and preferment in the lilt of Italian voices: Merchants transacting business, gossiping, reporting vital shipping news, making trade agreements, forming joint ventures, buying and selling cargo; as well as borrowing and lending money.

Money-lending, like a lubricant, kept a certain fluidity in the Rialto's transactions: it kept the wheels of business and commerce in motion. Here, the Bankers' Benches were set up: Opened Ledgers inviting commitment in the form of agreements. Edward recalls being entranced by the Rialto's commotion; its energetic hustle and bustle; its high born, rich participants. He felt the pulse of the place and people; and the more he learned, the more he felt justified in thinking of the Rialto as the centre of the business world. Money! Money! Money! It makes the world go round. How true the saying was then, as it is now, he thinks. Within the Italian States, the Rialto attracted Merchants from various places: among them were Mantuans who came with Bills of Exchange. In relation to his drama, apart from SHYLOCK, he had included two other Jews in his play: JESSICA, SHYLOCK'S daughter, who elopes; and TUBAL.

At this point in Edward's reading and revision, again, he remembers the Italian setting which is central to *The Merchant of Venice*. But he knows, for instance, that no Jewish person living in Venice in the sixteenth century would have been regarded as a Venetian. He, or she, would be a foreigner, even though residency is permitted. He knows, too, about the banishment of Jews from England in the late thirteenth century; how they were harassed out of Spain and Portugal and bullied in Germany. He thought if there is one place in Europe where Jews could live in some safety, that was Venice. The evidence for this, he's seen himself. But, he also understood that though they were welcomed in Venice from the fifteenth century, it was only grudgingly so!

How then did Jews live? What jobs did they do? One thing of which Edward was especially intrigued and observant, was that of all the world's people, money and Jews were synonymous. And while most professions were closed to them, Banking was open: So, with capital, lots of money to hand, Jews combined Banking and Money-lending (Usury) at certain interest rates. This was one of the ways of earning a living! From this brief backstory, and knowledge gained in Venice, the character SHYLOCK had emerged. Edward remembers giving him personality, perspective and voice. As a financier, SHYLOCK makes large loans at the prevailing rate of Interest which many Christian Merchants argue is a sin. Nonetheless, as borrowers, they are willing participants in the sinful business of Jewish Money-lending! But having closely observed the lending and interest gathering, Edward sees clearly how this alleged sinfulness can, and does, lead to growing distrust and animosity between Jews and Gentiles.

And so, he is mindful of first introducing SHYLOCK in Act I, Scene 3, at which point, he engages in conversation with BASSANIO. They talk about a large sum of money: three thousand ducats. BASSANIO, a Nobleman, is alas down on his luck. He needs money fast; and he needs it not just to pay off debts, but importantly, to show he has the means to impress the wealthy PORTIA, who resides in a Grand Villa in the Venetian Veneto.

While SHYLOCK and BASSANIO converse, the professional lender and the prospective borrower does not discuss the loan itself. SHYLOCK says: "that I may be assured... May I speak with ANTONIO?" BASSANIO replies, making the request conditional: "If it please you to dine with us." The remark begs the question: Does BASSANIO not know that as a rule Jews do not eat non-kosher food? And therefore they do not dine with Gentiles? Maybe not. But, thinking that BASSANIO is not as ignorant as he seems to be, nonetheless SHYLOCK informs him of Jewish practice. He points out some fundamental observances of Jews in Mercantile Venice and draws a sharp religious distinction between himself and BASSANIO. So in response to the invitation to dine, he says:

> "Yes, to smell pork, to eat of the habitation of your Prophet the Nazarite conjured the devil into! I will buy with you, sell with you, talk with you, walk with you,

> and so following: but I will not eat with you,
> drink with you, nor pray with you."

These words carry a steel-like sternness of razor-sharp differences that are unbridgeable. Then, ANTONIO arrives on the Scene. Instead of greeting him, SHYLOCK speaks of his hatred for ANTONIO. And when BASSANIO calls for his attention, SHYLOCK says:

> "I am debating my present store,
> And by the near guess of my memory
> I cannot instantly raise up the gross
> Of full three thousand ducats: what of that?
> Tubal, a wealthy Hebrew of my Tribe,
> Will furnish me… how many months
> Do you desire."

After he'd written this section of the play, Edward shows how familiar he was with the Jews of Venice. He is aware that Hebrews are not all from the same Tribe: He understands the differences among them. SHYLOCK refers to the different "nations" of Venetian Jews in many things: dress, language and other particularities. As Edward considers these details of what he'd written, he realises that though the Jewish population in Venice is small, it is diverse. For a while, he pauses his reading of the play and reflects on what he knows about the "nations" of the Venetian ghetto, which is hardly everyday knowledge gained on the spot by a traveller just passing through! What he knows about the Rialto in Venice is little known to most Englishmen, never mind a nineteen year old teenager named Will Shakspere, who was living in Stratford-upon-Avon. Was he planning a trip abroad? What, and how much does he know about Jews? Does he know anything about Jewish dress? Who knows the answers to questions that are the furthest thing from Will Shakspere's mind.

At this juncture in his reading, Edward shows how much he knew about Jewish clothing in Venice. In Act I, Scene 3, recounting past insults, SHYLOCK says:

"Signor Antonio, many a time and oft
In the Rialto you have rated me
About my moneys and usances.
Still have I borne it with a patient shrug…
You call me misbeliever cut-throat dog,
And spit upon my garberdine.
And all for use of that which is mine own."

Garberdine? It is a garment which in Italian is called Gabbano. Edward, a smart and unconventional dresser himself, is interested in this form of dress. So what is Jewish garberdine? He learns that it is a distinctive cloak worn by Venetian Jews. And further into his story, another aspect of Jewish life in Venice comes into play. For the first time, in Act II, Scene 2, Edward mentions "Ghetto." It follows words spoken by SHYLOCK'S Servant, the light-hearted, happy-go-lucky youth LAUNCELOT whose father old GOBBO enters the Scene. His bad eyesight prevents him from recognising his son. "Master young man," he says, "you I pray you, which is the way to Master Jew's?" The old GOBBO hopes to find a way to the Ghetto, specifically to find SHYLOCK'S house. And why this errand? Because he has a gift to deliver. But there are no address numbers on Venetian buildings, so how would GOBBO find the house?

This search follows the instruction SHYLOCK gives to

TUBAL at the end of Act III, Scene 1 in which TUBAL is told to find SHYLOCK'S house in the ghetto: It is a dramatic and significant turning point. Here, Edward portrays SHYLOCK as receiving repeated criticism and insults: He is told about his daughter JESSICA, stealing from him; and that his precious early courtship gift from his beloved wife LEAH was exchanged for a monkey! A monkey? He is aghast! He thinks he is made to look a fool by his own flesh and blood. But how much of what TUBAL tells SHYLOCK is true or false? Either way, it is burdensome for SHYLOCK. This far into his drama, Edward feels the emotional impact: He pauses for breath, before he reads more of his ingenious plot with which he is quite pleased.

Now he turns to Act III, Scene 1: While JESSICA is shown to be a thief and had not gone to Genoa, as alleged, but only as far as PORTIA'S Villa, having delivered that painful message to SHYLOCK, TUBAL suddenly changes the subject. He says, "But ANTONIO is surely undone." The outstanding debt due to SHYLOCK, is to get nothing more and nothing less than a pound of human flesh. Was SHYLOCK using this dramatic demand as baiting tactics?

Just a few months before, unusually, SHYLOCK was short of funds. He did not have the available money to lend those three thousand ducats upon the bond of ANTONIO, who is the debtor; the one who had borrowed it. This loan to ANTONIO, SHYLOCK reminds himself, is borrowed from TUBAL! So, everything depends upon ANTONIO paying his debt. But now that JESSICA had disgraced SHYLOCK, soon he must return to TUBAL his own tender, that same number of (three thousand) ducats! Now SHYLOCK says to TUBAL:

> "Go, Tubal, fee (hire) me an officer: bespeak him a fortnight before. I will have the heart of him if he forfeit, for were

> he out of Venice I can make what merchandise I will.
> Go, Tubal, and meet me at our synagogue; go, good
> Tubal at our synagogue, Tubal…"

Here, once more, Edward pauses his reading of the play and repeats to himself "our synagogue"; the words he'd given SHYLOCK to speak. Why? Because for every Jewish nationality, or "nation" in the Ghetto, there is a synagogue. By making SHYLOCK and TUBAL meet there, in their particular synagogue, Edward indicates and thus confirms a diverse community of Jews; an aspect of life which few foreigners or visitors to the Venetian Ghetto would have known.

Another telling detail is Edward's inclusion of a "Penthouse" in the play. It is knowledge of this kind that he understands and masters, so that he was able to interweave into the play twists and turns that now leave him pleased and still emotional! It is late in the day: Dusk has begun to fall now. There is more of *The Merchant of Venice's* script to be read. "I'll do that tomorrow," he thinks, as he stops work and leaves his Study.

Early the next morning, he resumes reading where he'd left off. He has reached that part of the play which deals with trouble and trial. Both for the purpose of the story he tells, and for England and Englishmen, he saw Venice as a most fascinating place; a combination of "trouble and trial." Already, he'd introduced the heroine PORTIA, as well as the medieval Castle named Belmont. But the Nobleman Edward, presents Belmont not as a Castle, but as a Villa in keeping with the story and its setting. He reflects upon the early scenes; and as he'd intended in the opening of Act I, Scene 2, the audience is presented with one of the large, elegant rooms in which two women are talking: One is a blonde, PORTIA, the other is a younger woman with black hair. Who is she? Edward had named her NERISSA, PORTIA'S companion. Both women discuss men: In particular, those who have already presented themselves as possible husbands for PORTIA. Of these hopefuls, who will be the lucky one to solve a puzzle set by her father, the Lord of Belmont, before he had died. The solver's prize is PORTIA'S hand in marriage. So far, no man that PORTIA had met was acceptable. On this matter, she is merciless: She mocks them. Being highly cultured she is especially tough on FALCONBRIDGE, a young Englishman, whose dress-sense she decries; and, for good measure, she adds:

> "You know I say nothing to him for he understands not me, nor I him: he hath neither Latin, French, nor Italian, and you will come into court and swear that I have a poor pennyworth in the English: he is a proper man's picture, but alas! who can converse with a dumb-show?"

"A dumb show?" Edward had carefully inserted this expression into his play. As at highly-educated Nobleman, he knows, to be accepted in the Palazzio and villas of Venice, one had to be fluent in Latin, French and Italian, especially among sophisticated Venetians. So wealthy, beautiful PORTIA, hard-nosed and practical in her approach to life, lives in a splendid Villa. Now he remembers being inside one of these noble villas and had noted that many were to be found along the Brenta Canal. If he knows of such villas, where is the place called Belmont? He knows well where it is; and importantly, his familiarity with the travel route had informed him *how* to get there. At the end of Act III, Scene 4, PORTIA is with her companion NERISSA. She turns to the trusted BALTHAZAR and says:

"Now Balthazar.
As I have ever found thee honest-true,
So let me find thee still: take this same letter
And use thou all th'endeavour a man
In speed *to Padua*, see thou render this
Into my cousin's hand,
And look what notes of garments he doth give thee,-
Bring them ( I pray thee) with imagined speed
Unto the *tranect, the common ferry,*
*Which trades to Venice;* waste no time in words
But get thee gone - I shall be there before thee."

The two women hurry to wait for BALTHAZAR'S arrival. As they board the ferry to cross the lagoon to the landing place next to the Ducal Palace, PORTIA calculates the duration of the trip. She says to NERISSA: "We must measure twenty miles today." So, on reflection, Edward's memory had served him well. He'd used the real life Belmont as the Noble Villa and the combined distance of PORTIA's trip there which covers exactly twenty miles! After PORTIA'S spirited defence of ANTONIO, she decides to return to Belmont. On these facts about places, people and practices in relation to his drama, Edward is on solid ground. But, before he completes his reading of the rest of the play, he pauses to confirm what he'd felt at the time of the play's composition and writing: That it will be performed before English audiences and not Venetian ones. It's educational value is therefore important to him. He's especially pleased that language, plotlines and characters are, as he'd intended. And though he does not follow the practices and protocols of Mercantile Law too strictly in relation to the Trial, as usual, he uses much creative licence.

Would PORTIA'S plea for mercy in her defence of ANTONIO be permitted under Mercantile Law? Perhaps not. But, he is quite happy with the original composition and thinks PORTIA should be allowed to do her lawyering in his play: Let her speak her eloquent words on behalf of the defendant ANTONIO. He re-reads the Trial Scene and sees it, apart from everything else, as a farce of Mercantile Law.

Finally, he completes his reading of the play. He'd absorbed the twists, turns and tightening tension of the drama, so he is not surprised how disturbed his thoughts have become. There will be many interpretations of his story, he thinks. But, for now, all that he'd originally intended is therein. He closes the script, but his thoughts linger on the Trial Scene: On the one hand, the speech
he'd written for PORTIA about the Mercy she claims for ANTONIO; and, on the other hand, the fines and forfeiture she demands of SHYLOCK. High drama? Or Farce? Whichever it is, he feels even more strongly now, what he'd felt when he'd first written the play: That it had the potential of becoming an enduring play; a satire on injustice and the law. That feeling, he now thinks, has - with the passage of time - unquestionably been achieved.

He sits upright in his chair. Then he leans back, and, in meditative mood he thinks of his enthralling creation *The Merchant of Venice*. But fundamentally, he knows his authorship of such a play could never have been possible without his presence in Venice! And so after a well earned break, he removes the next script to be read from his bundle of plays set in Italy.

***

# FIVE

## *OTHELLO*

Edward's separation from his wife Anne immediately after he'd returned from his continental travels, had irritated and worried him. The thought that she'd cuckolded him, still has the potential to drive him into jealous rages. Over the years, he'd tried to contain his feelings; to better manage his behaviour. So much so that he'd decided to write the play *Othello,* which he is now about to read and revise. It is the tragic tale of a Moor; a swarthy-looking man. The first Act is set in Venice. The rest of the play, Acts II to V, are set largely on the island of Cyprus.

The idea for the plot of *Othello* had come to Edward from one of a collection of stories titled *Cinthio,* written by an Italian named Giovanni Battista Geraldi. Edward is, as usual, thorough in his research. A characteristic of his Italian dramas, is that he alters and enriches the source with brilliant dialogues to make his own version of the story on which his play is based.

It is night: And *Othello* opens with two characters on stage: IAGO and RODERIGO. IAGO is OTHELLO'S trusted friend, and RODERIGO is a kind of romantic fool whom IAGO makes fun of. Except for these two actors, the other participants in the play are from Venice.

RODERIGO, like IAGO and OTHELLO, is also in the

Military Service. While he is in Venice he got to know DESDEMONA'S father, who, in Act I, Scene 1, tells him: "I have charged thee, not to haunt about my doors. In honest plainness thou hast heard me say: My daughter is not for thee..."

With this clear rebuff to RODERIGO, Edward had written about jealousy and tension between the two characters. In the same Scene, during the conversation between IAGO and RODERIGO, IAGO complains about OTHELLO who has been granted Command of the Venetian military forces in Cyprus. IAGO says he does not like OTHELLO because he (OTHELLO), refused to appoint him as a Lieutenant in Cyprus. But why if he hates OTHELLO does he want to be so close to him?

The rank of "Lieutenant" in the sixteenth century Army is akin to being second in command. But IAGO'S appointment as OTHELLO'S "ancient" was of a lower order.

Now IAGO and RODERIGO stand on the street outside the house of a Venetian Senator named BRABANZIO. He is no ordinary nobleman. What he does not know is that DESDEMONA has eloped with OTHELLO. At this point in the story, Edward had seen an opportunity for the sensitive, jealous character IAGO to exploit. With no love lost between him and OTHELLO, IAGO is ready to cause maximum trouble for OTHELLO. But he is very careful not to be found out. So IAGO tells RODERIGO to face BRABANZIO'S upstairs window and shout about the elopement. The loud voice attracts BRABANZIO'S attention. Though he is not fully dressed, he hurries to the window and opens it. From below, on the street, IAGO says: "Swounds, sir, you're robbed, for shame put on your gown!" Here, IAGO is referring to a particular black gown, worn in public by Venetian Senators.

And so, as Edward reads more of the play, he re-lives his first encounter in Venice with a new political practice. He pauses a moment; and smiles at the thought that from the notes he'd taken, he could, in such detail, describe the Senator's gown. Moving on, he reads that in the still night outside DESDEMONA'S home, IAGO intends to make more noise and scandal. He uses coarse language, shouting crude vulgarities about DESDEMONA that are aimed at BRABANZIO.

"Because we come to do you Service and you think we are ruffians, you'll have your daughter covered by a Barbary horse," IAGO says: "Your daughter and the Moor are now making the beast with two backs, you'll have nephews neigh to you..." Such utterances receives RODERIGO'S full support. At this juncture Edward had introduced another specific Venetian place name into his play. Given that IAGO feels sure that BRABANZIO will do all he can to find DESDEMONA, he leaves the scene. But, as he does so, he instructs RODERIGO to "lead to the Sagittary, the raised search." What, or where is the Sagittary? Edward knows of such a place for it is there that he'd placed both characters. And so, through IAGO'S call to RODERIGO, he reveals the meeting place of OTHELLO and DESDEMONA. The direction that IAGO gives to RODERIGO, is simple enough: "lead to the Sagittary" which is obeyed immediately because RODERIGO knows where it is.

As he reads more, Edward makes a couple of spelling corrections to his script. During BRABANZIO'S conversation with RODERIGO, BRABANZIO says: "At every house I'll call." Here, Edward is specific: He identifies houses, not Inns or any other kind of building. In Act I Scene 2, on a street at the Sagittary IAGO warns OTHELLO that BRABANZIO is angry and bent on finding him. Very soon CASSIO arrives from the Ducal Palace with a message for OTHELLO from the Duke and Senators, summoning him to meet with them. Why? Because they have just been told that Turkish troops have begun the invasion of Cyprus. CASSIO tells OTHELLO of an urgent search that is on to find him "Being not at your lodging to be found." In turn, OTHELLO says to CASSIO:

> "'Tis well I am found by you:
> I will but spend a word here *in the house*
> And go with you."

By this, Edward means that OTHELLO is going inside the house to bid farewell to DESDMONA. In OTHELLO'S absence, CASSIO says to IAGO: "Ancient, what makes he here?" IAGO makes snide comments and says: "He's married." So once again, Edward specifically sets the scene at the Sagittary, where OTHELLO is found in a house.

At this point in the story, as Edward had intended it to be, he reflects upon his choice of the specific place he knew in Venice with the unusual name: "Sagittary." Here was a suitable place for DESDEMONA to arrive in her Gondola. Edward had thought long and hard about his leading character OTHELLO; and soon he introduces him to the audience. In Act I Scene 2, while he and CASSIO converse in front of that great house in the Frezzaria-Sagittary area, RODERIGO arrives with BRABANZIO, his Servants and some Officers.

RODERIGO says to BRABANZIO: "Signor, it is the Moor." Just then, OTHELLO, sees them: "Holla, stand, there!" he commands. BRABANZIO is in a state of fury: "Down with him thief!" he shouts. At this point in the script, Edward notes that he did not give any stage direction but shows his awareness of another Venetian practice: a Rule against the carrying of swords. He knows that only the privileged and those in positions of authority are allowed to do so. OTHELLO, as Edward portrays him, is not a swash-buckling, Sword-drawing type of character. He is the opposite: a man of dignity and composure.

Thus in a respectful manner, OTHELLO turns to BRABANZIO:

"Good Signor, you shall command more with years
Than with your weapons."

As a believer in tradition, Edward also has a great love and passion for freedom: The freedom to say and do things. He remembers the glow he'd felt for Venice's libertine ways while he was composing the play. But Libertine ways for whom? Italian girls and young women are kept very much at bay: indoors. When, at the beginning of Act I Scene 1, BRABANZIO is told that DESDEMONA has eloped, his immediate response is:

"O heaven, How got she out? O treason of the blood!
Fathers from hence trust not your daughters, minds
By what you see them at..."

The treatment of young Italian women had intrigued Edward while he was in Venice; and it does so now. He reappraises DESDEMONA, the only daughter of BRABANZIO the nobleman, who was locked away in the house at night. This was the accepted practice, especially in noble households.

For Upper Class Venetian women there was much physical confinement and boredom; their social contacts were limited to family and friends. Their outings extended no further than the church, and they were often chaperoned by governesses. Fathers tended to think this was enough to keep their daughters quiet and content. But Edward felt this practice was wrong. His character DESDEMONA thought differently. For some time, she'd been thinking of escape. In Act I, Scene 3 of *Othello*, after OTHELLO and DESDEMONA had given a full explanation to the DUKE, BRABANZIO and the Councillors in the hope that their marriage would be recognised, BRABANZIO'S anger subsides, but the hurt he feels is hard to assuage.

"God be with you..." he says. Then, he turns to DESDEMONA and says:

"For your sake, jewel,
I am glad at soul I have no other child.
For thy escape would teach me tyranny
To hang clogs on 'em. I have done…"

Clogs! What are they? Edward's Venetian curiosity had led him on; and now, he knows them well. He knows too, that clogs have different meanings, one of which is that it refers to a wooden or a built up shoe. While they tended to slow down movement, a wealthy woman like DESDEMONA wore higher clogs: So high, that she could not walk in them without the support of her Servants' shoulders. Not quite like walking on stilts, but clearly clogs were, or could be, cumbersome footwear for a woman like DESDEMONA.

As he reads and reviews more of the play, Edward is

reminded of how he combines current with historical events. Beside him are some notes he'd taken while he was in Italy. Over the years occasionally, he'd consulted them. Now he recalls how by separating the chaff from the wheat, he gets to the heart of the matter which gives credibility to his "fictions." It is a device that he'd used in *Othello* which arises from events relating to Cyprus in 1570.

Having had some ambassadorial experience at the highest levels in France and Italy, Edward is keen on international affairs. Given his historical understanding, the story of the Moor in Cinthio's writings had fed nicely into his creative imagination. As Venetians were, Edward is aware of reasons for the Duke and Signoria to send a Military Commander, troops and galleys to the Colony of Cyprus. This build-up of force is in response to the continuous encroachments of Turkish forces in Europe, North Africa and the Mediterranean that had begun when Suleyman the Magnificent became Sultan of the Ottoman Empire. To prevent Turkish advancement on Cyprus, Venetians felt the need to reinforce their garrison in Cyprus.

After Suleyman's death, his Succeessor Selim II, had sent an Ambassador to Venice. On arrival, the Ambassador had requested a meeting with the Duke and delivered a stern message from the Sultan of the Ottoman Empire: "We demand of you Cyprus," he said, "which you shall give us willingly or perforce." He warned "about awakening our horrible sword, for we shall wage most cruel war against you everywhere." And, as for "your trust in treasure, we shall cause it suddenly to flow away from you like a torrent."

Beware of arousing our wrath, he adds. This is more than just a threat: It is incendiary; a call to war.

News of this confrontation and impending crisis between Venice and Turkey had reached England where accountability to Venice and Cyprus was important. Edward had, at the time, heard talk at Court about English trading ships that were plying the waters of the Straits of Gibraltar after an absence of twenty five years! And being the international-minded Nobleman, he had woven this historical backstory into his dramatic composition: Thus, the character of OTHELLO took shape at this time of the Turkish fleet's appearance off the coast of Cyprus and the start of the attack. By then Venice had assigned to its Ruler of Cyprus the title of a Lieutenant; and so Edward portrays IAGO as being bitterly disappointed that CASSIO, a foreigner, is appointed as Lieutenant on Cyprus; the man who, in OTHELLO'S absence, would take command. But CASSIO, as Edward creates him, is flexible. He is able to play two roles: one military, the other, economic. As it was for the Merchant Princes of Venice, the economic role mattered more!

And so, IAGO'S bitterness grows. He devalues and damns CASSIO as being unfit to make war. In Scene I, Act 1, he complains:

> "And what was he?
> Forsooth a great Arithmetician,
> One Michael Cassio, a Florentine,
> A fellow almost damned in a fair wife,
> That never set a squadron in the field
> Nor the division in a battle knows
> More than a spinster – unless the bookish theoric,
> Wherein the toged Consuls can propose
> As masterly as he. Mere prattle without practice
> Is all his soldiership; but he, sir, had th'election..."

But though CASSIO gained the Lieutenanship of Cyprus, he lacked guile and a steady direction. Time and again, he is deceived by IAGO, who is hopelessly caught up in his adoration of DESDEMONA. As Edward understands his play now, CASSIO was based on the real life Lieutenant of Cyprus at the time of the Turkish Invasion, a man named Niccolo Dandolo who was described as weak and directionless, just as Edward had cast him. Now he raises his arched body and sits upright in his chair. He breathes a deep sigh as another long day draws to a close, and reflects fondly on his Venetian experience after he'd read the last lines of his tragic play *Othello*. As a playwright, he is conscious of the complexity of international affairs that affects English ambitions for trade and power. And, as ever, his first allegiance is to his beloved Queen Elizabeth and England.

***

# SIX

## *A MIDSUMMER NIGHT'S DREAM*

Two days after his last play-script revision, he is back at his desk. After reading the last few plays, and in some senses, re-living his Italian travels, he'd been thinking, in particular, about his journey from Verona to Florence and the few days of his stay in Mantua. His main interest was to see the great works of Julio Romano. For him, the art-lover, this visit was something of a pilgrimage. Why? Because he reveres Romano. So much so that he gives the artist an exceptional place in his own work.

Now as he reads *A Midsummer's Night's Dream*, he remembers the sunny days he'd spent in Sabbionetta, the small city near Mantua. He was drawn there by the breath-taking architectural style. One thing of particular significance which he mentions in his play, is the place called the "Duke's Oak." Again Edward is up to his compositional tricks: In part, the play is set in Athens; and the sense of place, such as it is, relates to the story that he had created. He'd wanted his "Dream" to take place only there in Athens. But, as the story evolves, it becomes increasingly clear that that place is actually Sabbionetta La Piccola Athena – "Little Athens." It is not in Greece, but right there in Italy! And what about the Duke's Oak? Early in *A Midsummer Night's Dream*, in Act I. Scene 2, with due respect to Duke Theseus and his bride HIPPOLYTA, six characters: QUINCE (the Carpenter); BOTTOM, (the

Weaver); FLUTE (the Bellow-Minder); SNOUT (the Tinker) and STARVELING, (the Tailor) come together on stage to present their version of an old love story, *Tyramus and Frisbe*. The characters are hopeful, and forward-looking. BOTTOM says:

"We will meet, and there we may rehearse
Most obscenely, and courageously.
Take Pains, be perfit: adieu."

QUINCE responds:

"At the Duke's Oak we meet."

Edward had included this, not just because it is a tree. It is a landmark in Sabbionetta which he uses for his story in another place. Further into *A Midsummer Night's Dream,* as part of its setting, Edward refers to the word "Temple," which appears in Act IV, Scene 1. Towards the end of this Scene, he had used "temple" in the following lines spoken by THESEUS:

"Fair lovers you are fortunately met.
Of this discourse of more we will hear anon.
Egues, I will overbear your will.
For in the temple, by and by, with us
These couples shall eternally be knit..."

Then temple reappears in the following dialogue:

"DEMETRIUS: It seems to me
That yet we sleep, we dream.
Do not you think

> The Duke was here, and bid us follow him ?
> HERMIA: Yea, and my father.
> HELENA: And Hippolyta.
> LYSANDER: And bid us follow to the temple."

So, in his play, Edward carefully places references to the "Duke's Oak" and the "temple." The Duke's Oak, as he remembers it, was a place of entry or a passage-way, to Sabbionetta; so known because it led to an oak forest that is the Duke's hunting ground. The "temple" too, is a word of importance. It relates to the real place that is "Athens." In Sabbionetta, "little Athens," there is a "Temple;" a place of worship, known as the Church of the Crowned Virgin. With remarkable story telling artistry, Edward uses a real reference point to which he'd grounded his dream sequence with a title that describes what he had seen. As he reads the play now, though he'd taken his education for granted, he realises the importance of his broad early education in Greek and history. He remembers how those lessons had led him to knowledge of the ancient Greek love story to attempt writing epic poems about the Greek King who had married HIPPOLYTA. But, Edward makes it clear now in this revision that the romance of his play is a coupling of two people who are very different from the Greek heroes. And so, through three references in *A Midsummer Night's Dream*: Little Athens, the Duke's Oak and the Temple, Edward had revealed other aspects of his Italian travels, his visit to Sabbionetta.

***

## SEVEN

## *ALL'S WELL THAT ENDS WELL*

After reading *A Midsummer Night's Dream*, Edward, the Italianate English playwright, picks up the next script from the dwindling bundle on his desk. It is: *All's Well That Ends Well;* a story that has at least eight Scenes set in or near Florence. To write so dramatically and meaningfully about the city, he had shown off his knowledge and experience. And so doing, he has rewarded playgoers. He is bold in his use of artistic licence, as well as being devious, and ingenious too, with double-meanings. He makes odd allusions to specific places which reflects his presence there.

Turning the pages of the script of *All's Well That Ends Well*, he follows the play from France to Florence. The story begins and ends in France; and through his characters, he makes many references to people in his personal life; one of whom, was his wife, Anne. There are a few Scenes in France; and, at the beginning of the drama, he brings forward a character named BERTRAM who is the young Count of Roussillion. He is a vassal of the King of France because his father, the old Count of Roussillion had died. But BERTRAM, heir to the title, hasn't yet reached his majority. This dramatic situation of death and Inheritance is exactly what had happened in Edward's life. Thus, life mirrors art! HELEN, the heroine, is low-born; a Commoner. When her father died, she came under the guardianship of BERTRAM'S mother, the Dowager Countess. HELEN falls in love with BERTRAM and the King commands that they get married. BERTRAM objects. He is angry. "I'll to the Tuscan Wars and never bed her," he says. These events are, in large part, another reflection of the reality of Edward's own life!

The Tuscan Wars? What are they? Through a conversation at the beginning of Act I, Scene 2, between the King and his Nobles, Edward informs his potential audience about these Wars; and so,while they are being entertained, they get a lesson in history!

"KING: The Florentines and Sienese are by th'ears;
Have fought with equal fortune, and continue
A braving war.
FIRST LORD DUMAINE: So 'tis reported, Sir
KING: Nay, 'tis most incredible; we here receive it
A certainty, vouched from our cousin Austria,
With caution that the Florentine will move us
For speedy aid - wherein our dearest friend
Prejudicates the business, and would seem
To have us make denial.
FIRST LORD DUMAINE: His love and wisdom,
Approved so to your Majesty, may plead
For amplest credence.
KING: He hath armed our answer,
And Florence is denied before he comes.
Yet for our gentlemen that mean to see
The Tuscan service, freely have they leave
To stand on either part.
SECOND LORD DUMAINE: It well may serve
A nursery to our gentry, who are sick
For breathing and exploit."

In other words, the King's message is that the Florentines and Sienese are in a fierce war that continues. By Act III, Scene 2, BERTRAM has departed from France and arrives in Florence from where he'd sent two letters to Roussillion: one for his mother, the other to HELEN.

He is still furious and writes to HELEN:

"When thou canst get the ring upon my finger, which
Never shall come off, and show me a child begotten of
Thy body that I am father to, then call me husband; but
In such a 'then' I write a 'never.' "

Here, Edward makes clear BERTRAM'S challenge to HELEN. This is the foundation, the central plank, upon which the play stands. So now HELEN can have no doubts. She knows what she must do to call BERTRAM her husband. She, sees BERTRAM'S letter as her "passport" to get started on her journey. The following Scene III, Act III is set in Florence, where the DUKE knew BERTRAM sufficiently to grant him the distinguished appointment as "The General of the Horse."

So BERTRAM and his men, enters the DUKE'S Service. Meanwhile back in France, HELEN has left a message for the Countess, part of which says: "I am Saint Jacques' Pilgrim, thither gone…" Tantalisingly, it ends:

"He is too good and fair for death and me,
Whom I myself embrace to set him free."

And so, HELEN begins her Pilgrimage. But Edward's authorial voice has given no evidence in *All's Well That Ends Well* that she did so. But revising it now, he reads that soon after BERTRAM had left for Italy, HELEN goes there too. She does so in disguise through which she hopes to learn more, at least enough to save her marriage. Very soon, she learns all she needs to know; and reappears!

At this juncture in his reading, Edward is re-acquainted with the many devices he'd used in relation to Florence in Scene 5 Act III. As another of his Italian plays, he leaves no doubt about his familiarity with the city. He'd walked the streets and had come to know a particular building near a square, which itself, once had a local name. What is that local building? For now, in the play, he had left the question in abeyance. Instead, he'd shifted attention to another question: Where are BERTRAM and the other men going? He and the proud warriors are heading back to Florence. They enter the city through the Monumental Porta Romana and the place where BERTRAM and his soldiers will march past is the Piazza Goldoni. It is also where WIDOW and the crowd of onlookers stand. WIDOW knows, from experience, that Military Parades in Florence pass this way. And to be sure that she does not miss it, she stands on a certain spot! Why? Because it has to do with a pre-arrangement: An arrangement with whom? Soon, the disguised Pilgrim arrives at the very place where WIDOW is standing. It is HELEN, dressed as a Pilgrim. She is not dead as reported. Here, Edward's dramatic timing is perfect. HELEN'S presence in Florence had enabled her to monitor Edward's movements and activities. So what was he up to? The Pilgrim HELEN was determined to find out. And, arising from her machinations, the play-goer and reader of *All's Well That Ends Well* learns now more about Edward's knowledge of the city he'd visited. HELEN eventually meets WIDOW before the Parade is due; and on seeing WIDOW, HELEN says:

"Look, here comes a Pilgrim. I know she will lie at my

house; thither they send one another. I'll question her: god save you pilgrim! Whither are you bound?"

HELEN replies:

"To Saint Jacques le Grand. Where do the…Pilgrim's lodge?"

WIDOW'S answer is very important: "At the Saint Francis here beside the Port." The Port? A port in Florence? What does WIDOW mean? Edward was abundantly clear about Florence being the setting of this Italian part of *All's Well That Ends Well.* "At the Saint Francis here beside the port" in Act III, Scene 5, confirms Edward's sound knowledge and understanding of Florence. Not only its physical layout, but also its history.

He knows that "Port" with a capital P is the ancient name given to a specific area between the southern wall of what was Roman Florentia and the Arno River. In Italian Porta means "gate" or "door," and porto means "port" or "harbour." Furthermore, and significantly, a "port" does not need to be along a sea coast. A river was often the location; and the Port of Florence was vital and well known. It had lived in the memory for generations, and was called the Port. But then a new name came into use: The area came to be known as the Church Ognissanti. Later, the "Port" official name became the "Piazza Ognissanti." Nonetheless, for centuries, the area continued to be called "the Port." Near the Piazza Ognissanti, linked by a street is the Piazza Goldoni. Edward had placed BERTRAM and his military men as passing through the Piazza Goldoni on their way to the Fortezza da Basso, and placed WIDOW standing at the corner of the Piazza Goldoni and the Borgo Ognissanti, which affords her a clear view of the Parade. Here is where she meets HELEN, and directs her to the Pilgrim's lodging that is next to the Port.

Another element in the play is a sign. Why a sign? Because Edward knows that in Florence a sign is used to identify a place. When WIDOW says at the Saint Francis, it means *at the sign of.* So now, as Edward reads more of the play, he is reminded that the Saint Francis of WIDOW'S lines does not say "here within the Port." Instead, she says: "here beside the Port."

Given that "beside" also means next to, Edward smiles as he thinks that a few steps beyond at one end of the Piazza Ognissanti, just past the Franciscan Monastery's wall, there was the sign of Saint Francis: an impressive carving of a cross at the top, and just below, two crossed arms. At this point, Edward stops reading the play. He vividly remembers that carving; and immersed in the story and the characters he'd placed in Florence, he realises that he is nearing the end of his revision of *All's Well That Ends Well.* He continues to read: After WIDOW tells HELEN where the Saint Francis is, the sound of a trumpet is heard. And as the military Parade gets nearer, WIDOW says to those around her: "Hark you! They come this way." In military fashion BERTRAM leads his men in the direction of Fortezza da Basso through the Piazza Goldoni. Once more, Edward stops reading to make a correction to his original stage direction for the play: He writes: "Drums and colours. Enter Bertram, Parolles and the whole army." After he'd read the last page, in his mind's eye, he could see and hear stirring drumbeats. He pictures the image of his creation: BERTRAM, as he marches proudly and salutes the cheering crowds; a glorious sight. Then, as he closes the script, a warm glow about the play overtakes him: All is well that ends well, he thinks.

***

# EIGHT

## *MUCH ADO ABOUT NOTHING*

Having spent the last two weeks reading and correcting the first seven of his Italian plays, once again, Edward considers their value. They are more than mere performed stories, he thinks. Therein are many of life's lessons; and as such, they should reach a wider audience. If he was either reticent or too busy before, no longer is he so: Now he is convinced of their merits as rounded works of English literature.

Day-breaks: It is a cold winter's morning. After breakfast, with warm thoughts of his Italian travels, he enters his Study to revise and make any necessary corrections to the few remaining play-scripts on his desk. As if his passion for writing, of appreciating the Italian Renaissance, knows no bounds, he turns his attention now to one of the first plays that he'd written on his return from Italy. It is *Much Ado About Nothing* which he'd set in Messina. He remembers how keen he was to write this play. Why? Because it had much bearing on the vital trading relations between England and the Mediterranean world.

Detailed knowledge is essential to his story-telling. Messina, a city in north-eastern Sicily, had a harbour that was one of the deepest and safest in the region. As a port city, its location was attractive to foreign invaders, who figure largely in the Island's chequered history. While Sicily and its capital Palermo had been largely engaged in agriculture and fishery, the economy of Messina in particular was centred on

Maritime Commerce and naval activities. As he understood it, these circumstances required a different kind of overlord as Governor; someone with experience in both administration and general affairs. Against this backdrop, he sets the opening Scene of the play at the Governor's Palace in Messina. For the Elizabethan theatre audiences of which Edward is an integral part, and is fully attuned to as a writer, the events behind *Much Ado About Nothing* (and their potential consequences) are of much concern: He recalls that 1573 was an important year for England, and its people. It was then that English trade with the Mediterranean, had resumed. But how would these mercantile ventures work out? This question was uppermost in his mind at the time of writing the play, and now as he engages with his script. English interests, he always foregrounds, never forgetting and hoping that his audiences will also be alive and alert to national well-being. In Act I, Scene 1, the characters on stage are Governor LEONATO, his daughter HERO, his niece BEATRICE and a man named MESSENGER. In LEONATO'S hand is a piece of paper. He says:

> "I learn in this letter that Don Pedro of Aragon comes this night to Messina.
> MESSENGER: He is very near by this, he was not three leagues off when I left him.
> LEONATO: How many gentlemen have you lost in this action?
> MESSENGER: But few of any sort, and none of name."

Edward wrote these lines with great confidence for he is a strong believer in holding the attention of theatregoers. So, to some degree, the audience will, he hopes, know and understand that while a battle is raging, LEONATO and MESSENGER will keep cool heads while many lives are lost. What Governer

LEONATO says about DON PEDRO'S imminent arrival as well as enquiries about the dead and injured, form the background and context of *Much Ado About Nothing.* The action that follows, in large part, makes clear the behaviour of DON PEDRO, who is much-maligned as the character "John the Bastard." In this opening Scene, another dialogue takes place; and we learn more about a few men of distinction who are about to arrive as part of DON PEDRO'S entourage. One of them is CLAUDIO, a young Count from Florence upon whom DON PEDRO has given much honour; a man who will come to know the heroine, HERO. Among the men due to arrive with DON PEDRO'S party is CLAUDIO. He is highly thought of by DON PEDRO. There is also BENEDICK, a young Nobleman from Padua. So Edward had created two Nobles and sets them on their way to do what he and other young Nobles are expected to do: seek glory in a foreign war. Also on stage is BALTHAZAR, a Commoner and professional singer who entertains DON PEDRO. As the drama unfolds, Edward weaves into it his first-hand knowledge of people, places, expressions, things and behaviour that are uniquely Italian. For instance, "pleached alley." What is this? Edward raises the question in the audience's mind. A "pleached alley" relates to gardens; a feature that had caught his attention in Messina. Now, he uses "pleached alley" in Act I, Scene 2, when LEONATO'S brother ANTONIO tells LEONATO about CLAUDIO'S love for HERO. ANTONIO describes, a "thick-pleached alley in mine orchard" where, out of sight, he'd overheard DON PEDRO and CLAUDIO (who were inside the "alley") discussing a private love matter. Later, in Act II, Scene 3, Edward again mentions this dense foliage. Here is where he overhears the well-planned conversation between DON PEDRO, LEONATO and CLAUDIO, which BENEDICK, who was standing outside the "pleached alley" is supposed to have heard about BEATRICE'S love for him. Then, once more in Act II, Scene 1, BEATRICE finds herself in a pleached alley, listening to another and different invented conversation: A dialogue between HERO, MARGARET and URSULA. HERO says to MARGARET:

> "...And bid her (Beatrice) steal into the pleached bower
> Where honeysuckles ripen'd by the sun, forbid the sun to enter..."

As the two women talk in raised voices outside the pleached alley or arbour, BEATRICE is inside. She hears what they say about BENEDICK'S love for her. Edward had made good use of what he'd come to know, and to variously use, as "thick pleached alley," the "arbour," the "pleached bower" and the "alley." He loves gardens and flowers; and was naturally drawn to the beauty and fragrance of climbing vines. So in Messina, He learned that vines, as HERO says, were so tightly woven as to "forbid the sun to enter." Thus pleached alleys provided much needed shade on hot days!

In Italy, Edward was often reminded of his aristocratic bearing. He was conscious of the social classes; and in a few conversations in *Much Ado About Nothing*, notably those between HERO, MARGARET and URSULA, he spotlights Master-Servant relations Italian-style. He depicts their talk as easy-going; a far cry from the less relaxed Class interaction in Feudal England. But, as the story develops, he displays his range and depth of human understanding. Who are MARGARET and URSULA? They are certainly not of the same Social class as their Mistress HERO. In Act II, Scene 1, MARGARET'S conversation with BALTHAZAR, the singer, gives a sense of social levelling. By contrast, later, URSULA has a short, but quite insolent chat with HERO'S Uncle ANTONIO, an important, highly respected Nobleman. URSULA'S conduct and behaviour also hints at social equality, which Edward highlights, posing the question: who is equal to whom? In Act III, Scene 1, MARGARET, URSULA and HERO are in LEONATO'S garden. MARGARET leaves, but URSULA stays. She chats for a while with HERO, the Governor's daughter, near the "pleached bower." The conversation is open and honest between URSULA and HERO, who sees nothing wrong in it. Later, Edward gives more details of the women's relations. In Act III, Scene 4, he shifts the action to a dialogue which takes place in HERO'S private residence. HERO is getting dressed for her wedding with the help of MARGARET and URSULA. This is what they say:

"HERO: Good Ursula, wake my cousin Beatrice
And desire her to rise.
URSULA: I will, lady.
HERO: And bid her come hither.
URSULA: Well (She exits)
MARGARET: Troth, I think your other rebato were better.
HERO: No, pray thee good Meg, I'll wear this.
MARGARET: By my troth, 's not so good;
and I warrant your Cousin will say so.
HERO: My Cousin's a fool, and thou art another: I'll wear none but this.
MARGARET: I like the new tire within excellently, if the hair were a thought browner; and your gown's a most rare fashion,
i'faith. I saw the Duchess of Milan's gown that they praise so.
HERO: O, that exceeds, they say..."

This social juxtaposition is revolutionary for Edward's English audience. And he is aware of the waves it would create. But, he had pursued his design of social tolerance (so well-suited to Renaissance Italy) through MARGARET'S and HERO'S talk. Though his English class-consciousness is jolted, he sees it as an opportunity for him to introduce an element of surprise, of forward thinking, into his story through the interplay of the three women.

Now, he remembers something else that he'd done on his Italian travels. Something that was close to his heart: The purchase of a special present for Queen Elizabeth. The pair of perfumed gloves that he'd brought back for her, was much appreciated by Her Majesty: At the time it was a focus of high fashion in England. The thought of those heady days with the Queen brings a smile to his lips now, as he reads what he'd written in the play before him: "These gloves the Count sent me," HERO says, "They are an excellent perfume."

When Edward had returned from Italy, it was well-known, and much noted, that one of his gifts to Queen Elizabeth was a pair of perfumed gloves. It was a greatly valued present for the fashion-conscious Monarch, who enjoyed being the then most powerful and elegant Lady in all of England. Perfumed gloves were a novelty among the wealthy classes and much sought after. Through her public display of Edward's private gift, the younger Elizabeth had set a trend. While Edward was writing *Much Ado About Nothing,* perfumed gloves were still received as a highly appreciated, luxurious present worthy of the Noble HERO in the play. Later, toward the end of Act III, Scene 3, the inebriated BORACHIO says HERO's wedding would take place "next morning at the temple." Edward's spelling of places and things is very important. It requires a specific knowledge of Italian cities to appreciate this. He knows too that when "temple" is used as a synonym for "Church" or "chapel," the first letter of the word is not capitalized. But when used to identify a particular building such as a Temple in Messina, it is spelt with a capital T. This difference between "t" and "T" is clearly of importance to Edward in *Much Ado About Nothing*.

In Messina he recalls, there was an ancient and significant place of worship called the Temple of Hercules Manticles. When the Roman writer Marcus Tullius had written about it, visitors from far and wide flocked to see it. They came from Britain, Flanders, France and Germany. Over the centuries, the building's renown grew. When the first Christians took possession of the Temple of Hercules Manticles in Messina, they dedicated it to Saint Michael, and established it as a Parish church. Later, it was renamed the Church of John the Baptist. By 1572, a new Viceroy of Sicily was appointed. He was Prince Marco Antonio Colonna, distinguished Commander of Papal Forces during the Battle of Lepanto, who was very proud of the Temple of St John the Baptist's beauty to the extant that he compared it to the Pantheon in Rome.

For the intended marriage between HERO and CLAUDIO, Edward had chosen the right church in Messina for the ceremony. Once again, he displays his depth of understanding of the history and location of the building. It was the only Church in Messina that had Temple as part of its name. And not surprisingly, Act IV, Scene 1 begins in that very Temple.

The principals of the play come together for the marriage of CLAUDIO and HERO. The officiating Priest is Friar Francis. When he asks the time-worn question: Whether either of the couple knows of any reason why they should not be married, CLAUDIO responds with an attack on HERO'S good name. The source of CLAUDIO'S behaviour is what he'd heard of the false tryst planned by DON JOHN, earlier in Act III, Scene 2, on the night before this wedding. Sadly, even LEONATO believes CLAUDIO's outrageous accusations. Shocked by what she'd heard, HERO collapses and seems dead. CLAUDIO, DON PEDRO and DON JOHN, perpetrators of the stunt, walks away. In their absence, HERO is revived. Friar Francis, who believes in HERO'S innocence, hatches a plan. In his reverential way, he says to LEONATO:

"Pause awhile,
And let my counsel sway you in this case.
Your daughter here the princes left for dead,
Let her awhile be secretly kept in,
And publish it that she is dead indeed;
Maintain a mourning ostentation
*And on your family's monument*
*Hang mournful epitaphs*, and do all rites
That appertains into a burial."

The Friar's next move is to change CLAUDIO'S anger toward HERO into remorse. And, in keeping with the pretense of HERO'S "death," the good Friar thinks that this "tragedy" should become widely known. He is even ready to go as far as posting a notice of the Funeral Mass at the Church, thence to the burial place and the ceremony of interment at "*your family's old monument.*" What could this be? The Friar may even have seen this "old monument" himself, so it must be somewhere in Messina. But what is he talking about? He is referring not to a single grave, but to being interred Italian-fashion in the family tomb or monument. In this sense, Messina is unlike other places. Here, graves and tombs were to be found in one single place: the Cimiterio Monumentale, a large cemetery filled with rows of impressive old family monuments.
"The Cimiterio," one local official tells him, "is where Messinans

post on family tombs, Epitaphs, tributes and poems to the deceased. It is the place where most Messinans are able to see messages of loved ones. So, in line with ancient custom and practice, Edward puts words in Friar Francis's mouth as he advises LEONATO: "And on your family's old monument / Hang mournful epitaphs."

So the "plan" is that all Messinans will know of HERO'S death! At the close of Scene I of Act IV, after Friar Francis and the wedding guests have left the Temple, BENEDICK and a distraught BEATRICE are alone on stage. They speak with haste as BENEDICK tries to calm his tearful lover. He says to her: "Come, bid me do anything for thee." BEATRICE responds at once: "Kill Claudio!" Edward understand well the tradition of "blood vengeance" in Messina. Later, when BENEDICK responds: "Ha! Not for the wide world." BEATRICE could hardly contain herself. Enraged, she spews the words:

> "…O that I were a man!…
> O God, that I were a man!
> I would eat his heart in the market place."

Thus far, the combined effect of the play's emotional power touches Edward. He is surprised that he has still not come to terms with the raw passion of native Messinans. He re-reads the words he'd written: "I will eat your heart," which is not a fiction of his creation, but an expression of Messinan culture. That he should have written this section in all its stark barbarity, takes Edward back a bit. But, he is pleased and perseveres now with his review of the play: He recalls that at the beginning of Act I, Scene1, the order of entry of the warriors are as follows: DON PEDRO, CLAUDIO, BENEDICK, BALTHASAR and last JOHN THE BASTARD. Interestingly in the *Dramatis Personae* "JOHN THE BASTARD" is listed *after* the Commoner BALTHASAR. So who is he – JOHN THE BASTARD?

At this stage in the story, the information Edward gives is that JOHN THE BASTARD was born out of wedlock; a character based on the historical DON JOHN of Austria. But why this devaluation of a man of Royal blood? Calling him a Bastard is an insult.

As creator of the story, Edward does not add, but limits the insults to DON JOHN to two scenes in *Much Ado About Nothing*. They are: When BENEDICK, furious with DON JOHN for the harm he has caused HERO in Act IV Scene 1, refers to him as "John the Bastard" and, in Act IV Scene 1, when BENEDICK again speaks to DON PEDRO about JOHN as "Your brother the bastard." Though not direct, as the play evolves, more slights to DON JOHN follow.

Elizabethan theatre-goers, Edward had thought at the time of writing, would readily know who this DON PEDRO represents. In reality, his historical parallel is the half-brother of Philip II, King of Spain, Don John of Austria. Later in the play, Edward pauses his reading. He thinks about the real DON JOHN'S backstory that is so crucial to his construction of the play. He knows that he was the illegitimate son of the Holy Roman Emperor, Charles V, who was also the King of Spain from 1519 until 1556. As Emperor, Charles was a kind of model; setting the tone of good behaviour: He believed in, and practised, temperance and moderation, and treated his wife with kindness. After she died, he fathered DON JOHN who, though born out of wedlock, was recognised by Charles. Before he died, the Spanish Crown had passed to his legitimate son, Philip II. At the same time, Charles had recognised DON JOHN as a member of the Royal Family and ordered that JOHN be titled: John of Austria. Later, in the Court of his half-brother Philip II, DON JOHN became increasingly popular for his distinguished Military and naval victories on behalf of Philip II. These successes mark a new beginning. DON JOHN is catapulted to world fame: At the age of twenty four, he becomes Supreme Commander of the Fleet known as The Holy Roman League and is heralded as the Victor of the Battle of Lepanto; and Saviour of Christendom from the threats posed by the Turks. Now DON JOHN commands the combined Squadrons of Spain, the Papacy, Venice and Genoa. He is a Hero; lionised by the people and the Pope.

No one else of his time has achieved such glory from both secular and sacred leaders. But long before Lepanto, DON JOHN'S mind was elsewhere. His ambition was to have a throne of his own: A dream? Perhaps. But this "dream" became an obsession. Before the "Battle," Pope Pius V, had been considering the prospects of an invasion of England. Audacious, it seems, but not impossible for it was expected to be led by DON JOHN with his half-brother, Philip II's support. The grand Plan was nothing less than to rescue Mary, Queen of Scots, Elizabeth's prisoner, install DON JOHN as King of England and Mary as the Queen of England. Earlier, Pope Pius had ex-communicated Queen Elizabeth I and had sought ways of deposing her. A very good idea in DON JOHN'S mind. But not for Philip II. He spurns the grand design. DON JOHN is disappointed. Nonetheless, he presses ahead with a new plan to gain a Kingdom of his own. Alas, this, and other ideas (including the Rulership of Tunis) comes to nothing.

In his relations with half-brother Philip II, each time DON JOHN is promised a Kingdom, Philip dashes his hopes. In *Much ado About Nothing*, as Edward reads more of it, he describes, and portrays, DON JOHN as profoundly bitter. Why? Because he understands the repeated thwarting of DON JOHN'S ambition: In truth DON JOHN feels his efforts not only in Tunis, but at Lepanto, too, had turned out, shockingly, to be really much ado about nothing! He feels constrained, betrayed by Philip. Edward, the Master Dramatist, recognises the importance of DON JOHN'S personal story, and in the play, CONRAD asks JOHN: "What the Goodyear, my lord, why are you thus out of measure sad?" John's reply emphasizes his sadness."There is no measure in the occasion that breeds it," he says, "therefore the sadness is without limit."

Philip's jealousy prevents him from helping DON JOHN in achieving his dream; his dearest ambition. In this situation, JOHN is at the mercy of his kingly half-brother, whom he continues to trust. As his disenchantment deepens, in Act I, Scene 3, Edward puts these words in DON JOHN'S mouth:

> "I cannot hide what I am. I must be sad when I have cause,
> and smile at no man's jests, eat when I have stomach and
> wait for no man's leisure; sleep when I am drowsy, and
> tend on no man's business; laugh when I am merry, and
> claw no man in his humour…
> I had rather be a canker in a hedge than a rose in his grace
> and it better fits my blood to be disdained of all than to
> fashion a carriage to rob love from any…
> I am a plain-dealing villain. I am trusted with a muzzle
> and enfranchised with a clog; therefore I have dared not
> to sing in my cage. If I had my mouth I would bite;
> if had my liberty I would do my liking."

Since DON JOHN, the Bastard, had become a man, joined the Military and had gained glorious achievements, he was, in effect, fully under Philip's domination and control. Promises made to him were held in abeyance. He was so engaged in winning battles for Spain that he tended to over look Philip's tight grip on him. The sad realization of being controlled comes only very gradually. He questions himself: "Was all my victories and glory really much ado about nothing?" he asks himself. As the character JOHN THE BASTARD'S emotion spills out, Edward does not misunderstand the historical sources of DON JOHN'S anger and sadness. To do so would be wrong. DON JOHN'S aggressive behaviour is not because he is an illegitimate Bastard, it has to do with him being repeatedly denied his cherished ambition. And yet, even now, at this late stage, he hopes!

Later, following the Spanish Governor General of the Low Countries' death, Philip appointed DON JOHN as his substitute. Why? Why? Why? JOHN questions himself. He protests, but once again, he undertook the dangerous responsibility of leading men in battle. Why does he still not see Philip's deviousness? In this real historical development, Edward follows the fact that with DON JOHN in command, it is possible, as he warns his English audience, for Spanish forces in the Low Countries to assemble, cross the English Channel and occupy England! Really? Another Invasion attempt. Yes! In this way, rebellious Protestants in the Lowlands would be unable to get Queen Elizabeth's vital help.

Thinking that he has King Philip's honest agreement, DON JOHN arrives in Brussels. In this particular scenario of the play, Edward had hoped to sound alarm bells in England. He knows England's Naval Fleet is small and Spain's is large. Rumours of an attack is rife at Court: everyone knows the risks are real and growing. And, through the play, Englishmen should know this. He feels he'd presented and warned of the dangers! He'd often chatted with Lyly and Munday about the threat. But, as the story enters its closing stages, Edward's attention is drawn back to DON JOHN, who, while doing his duty of faithfully serving Philip in the Lowlands campaign, was badly injured. He suffered terribly before he died. He was just thirty one years old.

Now as Edward ends his reading and revision of *Much Ado About Nothing*, it is late evening. He feels emotionally beaten up by his own creation. A good thing, he thinks. It is how any good story; indeed any good play, should make you feel. With the benefit of hindsight he is quite pleased to have made a few corrections; in particular, he puts more stress on the historical importance of DON JOHN's roles and the very real, ongoing Spanish threat of another attempt at invading England! He gazes at the window. The evening light is fading. He remembers well the Spanish Armada days of tension and peril. War, and talk of war preoccupies him. Dusk falls swiftly. He rises from his chair and calls it a day!

***

# NINE

## *THE WINTER'S TALE*

So far he feels good about the work of revising the plays. He begins a new day with the reading of *The Winter's Tale.* This story reminds him of many things: of love and hate; of journeys to distant places, as well as of pride and redemption. It verges on the tragic, but it is not quite a tragedy. Of all his "Italian plays," this one is set in various places, covering a diverse area. Among the locations are two Kingdoms: Sicily and Bohemia. In keeping with his tale, he interweaves events that had occurred at different times into the drama as if they were happening in a particular medieval period. In like manner, he uses historical figures of the past as if they were of the time of the play. The first Scene is set in Sicily at King LEONTES'S Palace. On stage, there are two Noblemen: ARCHIDAMUS and CAMILLO, the kind of people most familiar to himself, and thus he is enabled to write best about what he knows! ARCHIDAMUS is a Bohemian Royal attendant, while CAMILLO is similarly employed in Sicily. ARCHIDAMUS says:

> "If you shall chance Camillo to visit Bohemia on the like occasion where on my services are now on foot, you shall see, as I have said, great difference betwixt our Bohemia and your Sicilla."

The differences between the Kingdoms are clear. Of the

many islands in the Mediterranean Sea, Sicily is the largest. It's a Civilisation that stretches back to Greek Colonization about 750 B.C. While most of it is easy to travel across, Bohemia's terrain is more difficult: It is largely steep with snow covered mountains and rivers. In response to ARCHIDAMUS, CAMILLO says:

> "I think, this coming summer, the King of Sicilia means to pay Bohemia a visitation which he justly owes him."

In these few words, Edward refers to "Bohemia" as the kingdom of POLIXENES, the King of Bohemia, who is on a visit to Sicily to see his dear friend KING LEONTES. ARCHIDAMUS speaks to CAMILLO about a particular worry he has about the visit:

> "ARCHIDAMUS: Verily, I speak it in freedom of my knowledge.
> We cannot with such magnificence–in so rare-I know not what to do say,
> We will give you sleepy drinks, that your senses, unintelligent of our insufficience, may, though they cannot praise us, as little accuse us.
> CAMILLO: You pay a good deal too dear for what's given freely.
> ARCHIDAMUS: Believe me, I speak as my understanding instructs me, and as mine honesty puts it to utterance."

This dialogue takes place at the Royal Palace in Sicily known as the Palazzio Normani. Among the rich European Rulers, Sicily's Medieval Kings were the wealthiest, and

Palermo was one of the largest and most important cities. It has a mixture of cultures; and adorned with parks, fountains, palaces and religious buildings, Edward uses this setting. In Act I, Scene 1, CAMILLO speaks about POLIXENE'S visit to see LEONTES; and how warm, respectful and gracious their relations have been. But, in the following Scene 2 of the first Act, LEONTES'S suspicions grow. He speaks his thoughts out loud. He says POLIXENES "hath touch'd his Queen, forbiddenly." True? Or false? CAMILLO is stunned. But, while he reels in surprise, he is ordered to poison POLIXENES. It is too much for CAMILLO to bear. He decides to disobey LEONTES'S order. He tells the accused POLIXENES about the shocking charge. POLIXENES is alarmed and says:

> "My ships are ready and
> My people did expect my hence departure
> Two days ago. This jealousy
> Is for a precious creature… "

CAMILLO tells POLIXENES of LEONTES'S plan to kill him, and to escape from LEONTES'S rage, CAMILLO is ready to flee with POLIXENES. So, having been on his Sicilian visit for several weeks, POLIXENES'S ships are ready to take him away from Palermo and sail back to Bohemia.

Sail? To inland Bohemia? Is a Bohemian coastline on the Adriatic Sea, a fantasy? What is Edward playing at here? Once more, as with his other Italian plays, he has a nose for the extraordinary: The creative! He knows there is something unusual and significant about Palermo. At the time of writing the play, he knew that the Palazzo Normani was inside the city walls; and that the city's official port was at the northern end.

Crucially, he knew that the port was continuously guarded; that its traffic and use was, in the main, limited to day-to-day mercantile business and naval functions. King POLIXENES had arrived in Palermo with an entourage of soldiers and naval officers, who were staying at different locations in the city. Escape is tricky. To break away at midnight, or soon after, POLIXENES'S men would need certain gates in Palermo to be unlocked. As it happens, CAMILLO was in charge of the keys; and soon, the Fleet was on its way down the Adriatic coastline. This stretch of water would provide ample space for the King of Bohemia's ships. In his imagination, Edward uses time wisely to serve his story's needs. In Act II, Scene 1 LEONTES'S anger reaches new heights. He puts his Queen HERMIONE in prison! And though he is certain of the truth of HERMIONE'S alleged infidelity, Edward is mindful of his own experience with Anne Cecil. So not surprisingly, LEONTES wants sacred affirmation; acknowledgement from a "higher authority," so that the entire Court will agree with him. Thus LEONTES announces:

> "...I have dispatch'd in post
> To sacred Delphos, to Apollo's temple,
> Cleomenes and Dion, whom you know
> Of stuff'd sufficiency. Now from the oracle
> They will bring all, whose Spiritual counsel had,
> Shall stop or spur me. Have I done well?"

It is evident in other plays that Edward is prone to using anachronisms: In this play, he inserts the ancient stories and belief in the Oracle of Classical Greece. Is this inclusion of the Oracle of a faraway place, to verify Truth, just another side-show; an oddity of Edward's playwriting approach? Perhaps. Or, is it a central pillar of his plot. In Act II, Scene 2, HERMIONE, who is in prison, gives birth to "…A daughter and a goodly babe," says EMILIA. This is another historical parallel with his wife, Anne. PAULINA, HERMIONE'S good friend brings in the child to LEONTES in the hope that seeing the baby would lessen his anger and lead to acceptance of his fatherhood. Yet again, this has been Edward's and Anne's hard experience, too! PAULINA'S attempt fails; and LEONTES rages against the alleged bastard of HERMIONE and POLIXENES. He orders Lord ANTONIO (PAULINA'S husband) saying:

> "…We enjoin thee
> As thou art liege-man to us, that thou carry
> This *female bastard* hence and that thou bear it
> To some remote and distant place, quite out
> Of our dominions; and that there thou leave it
> Without more mercy to its own protection
> And favour of the climate…"

At this point, Edward stops reading the play. On reflection, he is taken aback by the amount of emotion and self-doubt that he had had about Anne's pregnancy! And most surprising, how, while writing this play he got rid of much pent-up emotion! When he resumes reading and revising the script, he skips a few pages and restarts at Act III, Scene 3. Here, on a beach is the mild-mannered ANTIGONUS, who holds a baby: and next to him is the ship's Master who had brought him there. ANTIGONUS questions whether, "our ship hatch touch'd upon the deserts of bohemia?" The Mariner says it has.

So the Bohemian Coastline is factual, real; and Edward uses it. Now, as a storm threatens, the Mariner goes back to the ship. Beset by sadness and guilt, and recalling his dream in which HERMIONE had told him the babies names is PERDITA, ANTIGONUS places the name and a box of gold coins beside the baby. The weather turns bad: Loud cracks of thunder fills the air and, as a storm breaks, ANTIGONUS leaves the scene. Soon after, a Shepherd appears. While searching for a lost sheep, he finds the child and the gold which he thinks is most unusual. He hurries home, and takes care of the babe.

In Act II, Scene 3, the action shifts back to Sicily's Royal Palace. LEONTES is arguing with HERMIONE'S friend and supporter, PAULINA. A while later, a Servant enters. The news he brings is happy:

> "SERVANT: Please your highness posts
> From those you sent to the Oracle, are come
> An hour since: Cleomenes and Dion,
> Being well arriv'd from Delphos, are both landed,
> Hasting to th'court.
> LORD: So please you, sir, their speed
> Hath been beyond account.
> LEONTES: *Twenty three days.*
> They have been absent: 'tis good speed..."

By numbering the days of the Messenger's trip so exactly, LEONTES'S words of specifying twenty three days, shows that Edward knew about this route for he'd made the journey himself! He is precise, too, in how long it took: ten days of sailing; three days at Delphi, then ten days back to Sicily and the Royal Palace: A total of *exactly twenty three days!*

Of the route that he'd taken, Edward remembers both the out bound and the return voyages of his characters CLEOMENES and DION. Sailing through the Strait of Messina, then down the southern tip of Italy, they go East, pass Lepanto and dock in Itea. They then disembark and made their way up Mount Parnassus. Here, CLEOMENES and DION take their final steps to Delphos and the Temple of Apollo. After putting the vexed question of HERMIONE'S unfaithfulness to the Oracle, CLEOMENES and DION make their return voyage.

In Scene I of Act III, on stage are two Noblemen hurrying to see the King with the much-anticipated sacred message in hand. Moving along at a good pace, CLEOMENES and DION talk about where they are, where they had been and about the hoped for result of their Mission. CLEOMENES gives their location which he describes thus:

"The climate's delicate, the air most sweet,
Fertile the isle, the temple much surpassing
The common promise it bears."

They are back in fertile Sicily. Further on their way, as CLEOMENES and DION pass the Temple of Segesta, they remember their visit to the Oracle:

"DION: I shall report
For most it caught me, the celestial habits
Methinks I so should term them and the reverence
Of the grave wearers. O, the sacrifice -
How ceremonious, solemn, and unearthly

It was i'th'offering!
CLEOMENES: But of all, the burst
And the ear-deaf'ning voice of the Oracle,
Kin to love's thunder, so surpris'd my sense,
That I was nothing."

At this point of his close reading, Edward is creatively, dramatically absorbed by the final pages of *The Winter's Tale.* In Act II Scene 2, LEONTES calls into being a Court of Justice before which he could present a guilty verdict against HERMIONE, his queen. But HERMIONE defends herself saying that having lost her three greatest blessings (LEONTES'S love, her son's company and her child), she has lost the will to live! At this moment, CLEOMENES and DION arrive. Officers escort them into the Courtroom. LEONTES looks anxious as CLEOMENES and DION is about to reveal their message:

"OFFICER: You hear shall swear upon the sword of justice,
That you, Cleomenes and Dion, have
Been both to Delphos, and from thence have brought
This seal'd-up oracle, by the hand delivered
Of great Apollo's priest; and that since then
You have not dared to break the holy seal
Nor read the secrets in't.
CLEOMENES and DION: All this we swear.
LEONTES: Break up the seals and read.
OFFICER (Reads): Hermione is chaste: Polixenes blameless;
Camillo, a true subject; Leontes a jealous tyrant, his innocent babe truly begotten

And the King shall live without an heir, of that which is lost be not found."

LEONTES is shocked. He is at a loss to understand the message delivered. He refuses to accept the Oracle's pronouncement. It is "mere falsehood," he says. Just then a Servant arrives:

"SERVANT: My lord, the King, the King!
LEONTES: What is the business?
SERVANT: O Sir, I shall be hated to report it!
The Prince, your son, with mere conceit and fear
Of the Queen's speed is gone.
LEONTES: How 'gone'?
SERVANT: Is dead."

LEONTES soon comes to his senses about the horrific and distressing decisions he had taken and is deeply regretful. He says:

"Apollo's angry, and heavens themselves
Do strike at my injustice."

HERMIONE collapses and is declared dead. She isn't dead, but many years pass before this truth comes to light. Act IV begins with the action back in Bohemia. After the passage of time, POLIXENES, who has a son named FLORIZEL, is now being matched with PERDITA who is now a graceful girl, supposedly the daughter of a Shepherd. The character AUTOLYCUS arranges for FLORIZEL, PERDITA and the Shepherd to go to LEONTES'S Palace in

Palermo. POLIXENES learns of this plan; and is determined to stop a marriage between his son and the girl of lowly birth. When they had all assembled, the truth about PERDITA'S identity becomes known. There is much joy. Edward leaves the audience to imagine what follows the disclosure. But there is one more twist in the tale: In the final dramatic Scene, PERDITA enters and presents HERMIONE, who is still alive! And so, through his reading of *The Winter's Tale,* Edward re-experiences a number of extraordinary things; and, as for his characters, their joy is limitless.

***

# TEN

## *THE TEMPEST*

Now he looks at the last script from the bundle of plays. By now, after ten days of reading, he'd reacquainted himself with his Italian adventures: A wonderful sojourn of memorable dramas and characters for posterity. His plays, he's convinced, are much more than stories to be performed. They must also be seen as literature. He is in no doubt that through the plays he'd set in Italy, his horizons as a playwright, and intellectually, have broadened. After he'd come back to England, he recalls how excited he was to fulfill his youthful ambition: A writer to be! Now, as the writer he has become, he begins to read *The Tempest,* one of his latest draft compositions. He considers the storyline, the plot of terror and magic and knows the location of the island of wind and fire upon which his play is set: That place is in the Tyrrhenian Sea, a few miles north of Sicily. ARIEL, one of the play's leading characters refers to a "deep nook," as well as, "Bermoothes." But where exactly is the place referred to?  Of this, Edward has no doubt. He chooses an island not far from the coast of Sicily. In Act I Scene 2, Bermoothes is mentioned once:

> "…in the deep nook, where once
> Thou call'dst me up at midnight to fetch dew
> From the still-vexed Bermoothes."

Where was ARIEL when PROSPERO ordered him to go to the Bermoothes. Is the deep nook the same as the Bermoothes? ARIEL clearly believes it isn't. He thinks it is a different place from the deep nook. Some interpreters of the play, to Edward's amusement, still thinks Bermoothes is an island somewhere in the Atlantic Ocean. But why would PROPSERO want ARIEL to travel thousands of miles away just to collect some "dew" and bring it back to Italy? The answer is that he didn't! In *The Tempest*, Edward thinks of places where humour is necessary: Dark places that need some light. He uses ARIEL to say something clever or amusing for as always, he is mindful of his London audiences, who must, above all, be entertained. And, for some light relief, he chooses the lowly, poorest places in London. He refers to them as either the Bermudas or the Bermoothes. One of the most depressed parts of the city is the area within the boundaries of Carey Street, The strand, Chancery Lane and Clements Inn. Within this place there are run-down buildings that accommodate prostitution, gambling and the illegal manufacture of alcohol in distilleries known as Stills. For Edward, this was a key feature in his play: It was there to the London Bermoothes that PROSPERO had ordered ARIEL to go and fetch a different kind of "dew"!

While Bermoothes or Bermudas could mean to a Londoner two very different places, dew also means two very different kinds of liquid. Importantly, Edward was aware of the illegal stigma of distilleries or Stills nonetheless, he includes them in the setting for ARIEL'S words:

"...Thou call'dst me up at midnight
To fetch dew from the still-vexed Bermoothes."

As he reads more of the play script, he reaffirms that he has chosen the right island, namely Vulcano, an unusual place with yellow sands, hot mud pools, springs, sulphur, rank smells, pines, oaks, cliffs, grottoes and caves that he refers to in the play. It is a magical place. So *The Tempest,* as yet unfinished, is one more Italian setting for his later drama. Against this scenario, he pushes the boundaries of inventiveness and tapping his capacious imagination he combines disparate elements: magic with reality; ancient Roman legend with Italian history. Such combinations, are characteristic of his more mature playwriting style. He reflects upon the fact that after his visit to Italy, he had devoted himself to writing with new enthusiasm. "What you put in is what you get out," he says to himself. "Nothing of myself must be spared. My commitment must be greater than hitherto: It must be *total!*" In this mode of thinking, he feels free as he continues to push the boundaries. He dresses in the Italian style, and the foreign with the familiar. To many Courtiers, he appears like an odd hybrid: No wonder, some have dubbed him: "The Italianate English playwright."

After he finishes reading *The Tempest*, as he places it on top of the other play-scripts, he considers the names he'd been called by both friends and critics, including "The Italianate Englishman" which he had said to Lyly: "is apt." After all, over the years in London, Italy had been the "imaginary" setting for at least ten of his plays. His journeys which took him from Italy's Alpine terrain to the Southern tip of its Peninsular, then across the length and breadth of Sicily, as well as sailing trips on both the Adriatic and Tyrrhenian Seas, had profoundly affected him as a Dramatist and Poet.

Now he sits in his chair and glances at the bundle on his desk. All that detailed reading done in just under two weeks, he admits, has drained him both emotionally and physically. He still feels wound-up. And, given the "pain to pen a book," in a moment of frank self-assessment, he reflects upon his life and travels thus far. From boyhood, into his teens and as a young man, he'd dreamed of going to the land of Ovid, Castiglione and Cardano. Such a journey was full of mystery, as well as promise, heightened by repeated disappointments. Then, at last, the long-held dream was fulfilled: It became experience; the reality and essential material upon which the proof of his travels: the places he had been to, the art and architecture he'd seen and the people he had met, have all been transformed by his fertile imagination and boldly, dramatically portrayed in the art of his "Italian plays." He remembers now the heady days of "First Night" performances. There was surprise and questioning among Court audiences, as well as wonder. His presentations of these dramas had broken new ground in the English theatre. The Queen was delighted; and so were his closest associates.

"My Lord, you have taken story-telling in the theatre to new levels," he recalls Lyly's words after a performance of *The Merchant of Venice*. "You show what can be done on the stage. English theatre and drama is alive and well; and your new 'Italian plays' are at the forefront. They set the tone and direction. Your inventions bring life and art into a seamless whole. The messages you convey will live on."

"Thank you, John," he'd said to Lyly. "And your work, particularly your role as my Production Manager has been crucial to the success of my plays."

He looks at the revised play script with a feeling of deep satisfaction. Italy had changed him. He thinks of Messina and Palermo; and his meeting with the young Miguel Cervantes who was so full of excitement and hope of writing his novel about a heroic Knight in Spain. Of his own writings, his thoughts shift to Lyly's prediction of longevity for his plays which is already becoming reality. And given his respect for, and immersion in, Italian learning and Classical culture he has earned himself the nick-name: "The Italianate English Playwright." The "Italian plays" now seem destined for wider presentation. He glances again at the scripts. The whole Italian experience, he thinks, is forever imprinted in these life-affirming dramas. The play is the thing: He knows well that if you give a man a mask, he will tell you the truth: That is the power of his art! "And this," he says to himself, "is the writer that I have become."

***

# PART THREE

# OR NOT TO BE

"Every word doth almost tell my name"

1593 -1604

# X

## "There is no darkness but ignorance."

Edward, the history playwright, follows developments in current affairs closely. As French writers engage in a campaign of propaganda that had partly brought about King Henry III's death, in London too, scribes have been restless. A rising war of words in the form of pamphlets challenges Queen Elizabeth's right to Rule. It is spear-headed by a Puritan; a self-styled zealot named Martin Marprelate. Some months earlier, he'd begun to publish writings attacking high-ranking men in the Anglican Church. He is against the State-appointed Bishops who controls how Church of England's religious service is conducted, because, he thinks, it is too strongly in favour of the Church of Rome.

Nothing less than being rid of the top Anglican Bishops is acceptable to Martin Marprelate and his followers. So, religious battle lines in Elizabeth's England are tightly drawn as licences, notably on all religious matters become absolutely necessary. But, amidst claims and counter-claims of the arguments, somehow a Martin Marprelate Tract had got past the legal barriers. For the Church hierarchy, the question is: How to stop the spread of the Marprelate message? Lord Burghley, Church authorities and State officials are worried about such a publication being stocked and sold in the thriving London bookstalls. But Lo and behold, here and there, the Marprelate Tract appears. The alarmed authorities ask more questions. And in these heady times, they see fighting fire with fire, so to speak, as one way forward. But as matters get more serious, it becomes clear that the Elizabethan State needs an effective writer; someone who could destroy Marprelate and his insidious message. Time is of the essence.

Soon, "Martin Marprelate" faces another writer: "Pasquill Cavaliero," a pen-name used by Edward de Vere. In his reply to Marprelate, Caviliero lands a counter-punch. "It is impossible for thee," he writes, "to cast the religion of this land into a new mold every new moon." After these opening words, Caviliero uses his pen-craft to maximum advantage. He brims with confidence. Then, as if tempting the reader, he insists (as he'd done habitually in songs, poems and plays) that he is not just another hack writer; that he is high-born and sits in Courts of Justice where he acts on behalf of the Queen. He mentions Star Chamber speeches and places abroad that he'd visited, namely Italy and the Netherlands. Caviliero even goes as far as signing his name on a piece of his writings with the words: "from my Castle and colours at London Stone." This "Castle" is very near to Vere House in London. A few weeks later, after heated exchanges, Edward, as Caviliero, publishes another pamphlet in which he sets up a conversation between himself and a character named Maforious. In this article Edward shows his evolving artistry as a playwright: His attention to character, use of language, pace and dramatic colour, are evident: In part, Marforious says:

"I marvel Caviliero that you press not the Martinists with much Scripture. They are great quoters of commonplaces if you mark them."

Pasquill responds:

"Therein they are like a stale Courtesan who finding herself to be worn out of credit, borroweth the gesture of a sober matron which makes her to everyone that knows her the more abominable..."

Edward's use of light, shadow and nuanced words are all present in this dialogue. So using his Pen-name, Edward defends the English established order. Surely, the Queen and her officials know who Pasquill Caviliero is. Thus Edward's unique ability is a strong counterblast to Martprelate's propaganda. He deals a hard blow to his opponents. It is clear that few writers could match him at this highest level of discourse and debate in Elizabethan society. But, there is another side of Edward which shows his distrust of ordinary people. Nonetheless it is not a wariness that he alone has. It is more generally held by members of his Aristocratic Class. This is mirrored in certain mob scenes of his plays *Julius Caesar, Henry VI, Part 2* and *Richard III.* Now, as Caviliero, he writes about the chronicles of England and the daily land enclosures of the commons which "teach us sufficiently how inclinable the simpler sort of the people are to routs, riots, commotions, insurrections and plan rebellions when they grow brain sick, or any new toy taken them in the head! They need no…Martin to increase their giddiness…I would wish the whole realm to judge uprightly who deserves best to be bolstered and upheld in these dangerous times, either they that have religion and constantly preached obedience to Her Majesty's loving people or they that with a mask of religion discharge them of their obedience."

So as he and Marprelate compete for public attention, Edward the Aristocrat does not hide his intolerant views. He knows well the clear and wide divide between those who are served and their Servants; the Haves and the Have-Nots in feudal England. To his credit, he does not duck the issue. He accepts, wholeheartedly, his place among the elite core. So even though he is likely to veer slightly, it is paramount that the status quo in Elizabeth's England should prevail.

But stability is not on everybody's mind. Martin Marprelate

and the Puritans go beyond Church matters. They turn their attention to the thriving but sensitive issue of entertainment through play performances in the theatres. What took them so long? Edward asks himself. For years, they'd been doing their best to drag the reputations of writers, players and playgoers into the dirt. But the people of the theatre who aspire to rise above the muck, are resilient: They strike back at the Puritans and Marprelatists.

A spin-off of the anti-Marprelatist movement are a few play performances, one of which is authored by Anthony Munday. Another writer, the satirist John Nashe, publishes his own Anti-Marprelate pamphlet; and, Edward's other Secretary, John Lyly, also takes a stand: "Will the Marprelatists not be discouraged by the common players?" he writes. "Should those Comedies be allowed to be played that are penned, then I am sure Martin Marprelate would be deciphered, and so perhaps discouraged." He reflects upon the status of the actors: "A stage player," he says, "though he be but a cobbler by occupation, yet his chance may be to play the King's part," whereas whatever his calling Marprelate can play nothing else but the Knave's part.

Later, he says to his boss:

"My Lord, Edward, the Marprelatists have gone too far. You give them a foot, they take a yard. We must get the measure of them alright. We must take stock. They are dangerous men."

Edward notes that Lyly speaks with unusual animation.

"I fully agree with you Lyly," Edward says. "The dangers of stirring-up more violence is clear and present."

"If nothing is done to stop them soon," Lyly adds, "I fear violence!"

Edward follows Lyly's drift to the point where he considers the dramatic impact that mock hangings of Marprelatists on stage could have on theatre audiences. "You are right," he says to Lyly. "The danger is real and present. We *must* be vigilant."

But in spite of this combined and wider anti-Marprelatist onslaught, the Puritan pamphleteers' campaign heats up: It shows no signs of cooling. Edward monitors the support for, and against Puritanism, while Puritans keep an eye upon him. Overseeing all this, the Queen's stance is to avoid excessive or extreme behaviour in dealing with Church and State affairs. But, as Marprelatism to some degree, dies down, Edward is not at ease: He is still edgy; concerned about the future of the theatre and plays. These arts need protection, he thinks; all the more, because Anti Marprelatism has claimed it's first victim: The Paul's Boys Actors are *disbanded*, and the Queen's Men are sent away from London. While they toured the Provinces and performed in Ireland and Scotland, Edward takes a long, hard look at himself as he writes his final words as Pasquill Caviliero in the Marprelate confrontations. And so in the wake of the "war," now the peace: After the pamphlets he'd written as Caviliero, though self-critical, he feels his writing has improved. How and why? He is conscious of being older at the age of forty; and in reflective mood, among his last words as Caviliero, he writes:

"Because by the length of other men's frailties every man may take the measure of himself, I will carry my mouth in my heart and let them pass. And though there be a pad in the straw that must be roused, I have taken out this lesson from the wise: there is a time for speech and a time for silence."

That word *silence* resonates. For now, at least, Edward de Vere has come to the end of the pseudonymous Pasquill Caviliero disguise. And so, having answered the call to deal with the Martin Marprelate threat to Queen and country, he is on the eve of adopting, for better or worse, another Pen-name. "But for how long?" he asks himself. At that moment, he can't be sure.

***

As the Pen-name inclined Nobleman, Edward makes another visit to his Warwickshire retreat: His estate at Bilton, (not far from his grandmother's property at Billesley) which serves as his country home from home. Here, he collects his thoughts: He thinks of matters he must get on with now. He thinks of new possibilities.

He sees with remarkable clarity, the immense value of the literary and theatrical activities that had consumed him since he'd come back from Italy. He'd been writing like a man possessed for over twenty years; and to his credit, now he has an enviable list of plays-dramas well received at Court and; more and more in the public theatres. All very good, he thinks. But with the dawn of new, exciting developments in the London theatre, he feels there is need for a fresh approach. He strolls out of his living room into the garden: a mixture of plants and flowers in bloom. Among this multi-coloured patch are his favourite: red roses. The intoxicating scent adds to the freshness of the country. The setting sun is orange red; and admist the surrounding quietness he breathes deeply of the Warwickshire air. He feels remarkably calm and energized.

The next day, as usual, he wakes up early and writes in the office-Study for most of the morning. Then, he rests his pen; and, for a while, he looks around him. The faint mustiness of the room reminds him of other rooms. The memory of Fisher's Folly and being away from London arouses thoughts of the last few years: essentially of the way in which he'd been living. There is much room for change. He remembers those who are dead: The bodies are piling up. And, he is mindful too, of the final acts of the tragic plays he'd written so far. A strange nausea creeps over him and, as it deepens, his sense of being alone, comes with memories of Anne; in particular, of him not being around during her final hours and days. His feelings about all this have not changed: He is still regretful that he was not at her funeral. He sighs. Then, once more, he lifts his pen. After another spell of writing, his attention shifts to times past at Castle Hedingham, a way of life long gone.

In Billesley, he peruses more of its fine book collection. And while considering his age, a slight shudder runs through him as he thinks of his youth - that fleeting passage of time – and his infirmities arising from his leg injury; a lameness that becomes more pronounced. And not unlike the finale of a revenge tragedy, reflections on his family, Court members and others, reveal a body count of those who have passed on, that is sobering. Parent-like figures and mentors like the Earl of Sussex and Sir Thomas Smith, as well as his rivals and enemies Sir Philip Sidney, the Earl of Leicester and the shadowy Spymaster of the Queen's Men Players, Sir Francis Walsingham, are all dead. Sir Christopher Hatton is still alive; but only just. So, time and middle age brings him to an interesting moment: Burghley is alive, but the power-struggle between him and Edward (and other Courtiers) is shifting. This man who had made Edward's marriage, at times, unbearable is getting on: he is nearing seventy. "Three score and ten!" It is how Burghley would have put it. At this age, he's now England's grand old man, whose most trusted son (and heir) Robert Cecil is just twenty seven. But "old Burghley," as Edward thinks of him now, is no less inquisitive about his son than he is of known criminals.

"You are, and have been," Burghley says to Robert,"the one closest to me. Apart from myself no one else, but you, knows more about State secrets and my Spy network. You are a quick learner, Thank God. So far, you have done a very good job. But don't worry, you will become more knowledgeable, and therefore an even better Servant to your Queen and England when the time comes for you to take over my job. That time, officially, is when I retire."

Robert has had his fair share of being ticked off by his father. He has coped (and is coping) well. But how good would he be at taking charge of the Cecil household? Experience has taught Edward to take nothing for granted, specially on matters to do with the Cecil clan. He has always been aware that Robert is not athletic in his movements. He is slow-moving, largely, the unfortunate effect of an injury to his back after a fall in early life. He is round-shouldered, but his physical disability does not inhibit any display of his strengths: a suspicious, secretive nature and intellectual cunning. In these respects, he is cut from the same cloth as his father. Nonetheless, in his own right, Robert is dangerously brilliant. He is subtle in his ways of working. So faced with Robert, Edward is wary; his distrust of him grows. If Burghley is a problem, Edward thinks, his son could be far more dangerous: Not only is Robert hypersensitive: He holds grudges!

***

Unsurprisingly, in the flux of Court life, old men are being cleared out to make way for a younger generation. Two leading figures among the newer Elizabethan Courtiers are the twenty five year old Robert de Vereux, the Earl of Essex, and a seventeen year old, Henry Wriothesley, Earl of Southampton. Edward had, from time to time, observed these young men (especially Henry Wriothesley, the one closest to him) who were raised from childhood as Royal Wards in Burghley's household. Essex and Southampton know Edward's three daughters: Elizabeth, Bridget and Susan, well; in some ways much better than perhaps Edward does. One of these girls is being spied upon as a potential wife. Once again, Burghley plays Match-Maker. He fixes upon Southampton as a possible husband for Edward's fifteen year old daughter, Elizabeth. With marriage in mind, Burghley meets Southampton's grandfather, Anthony Browne, Lord Montague, at his country seat in Surrey.

No one in the Kingdom tells Burghley what he can, or cannot, do for he has the law fully on his side in deciding whom his Wards of Court could marry. And so, the grandfathers (Burghley and Browne – Lord Montague) talk strategy. The problem for them is: How could they press the stubborn Southampton to get married. Alas, the regular income, the boon of the Queen's one thousand pound Annual Grant, (and considering that Edward had already sold most of the estates inherited from his father) does not free him from mounting debts. So now, during the Burghley-Browne meeting at Oatlands, Burghley is approached by a Messenger who informs him of Edward's pressing money troubles. He owes a large debt which is compounded by another money matter relating to a man named Thomas Churchyard. Edward had agreed to pay Churchyard's rent to a landlady named Julia Penn for rooms near St Paul's Cathedral. As the occupant, when the first quarter's rent payment was due, Churchyard had called on Edward to pay it. But Edward had been unable to do so.

The ongoing debt leads to Churchyard being forced to seek shelter at the nearby Church. Hearing this news, the pious, but unsympathetic Burghley throws up his hands in the air: "God help me!" He thinks the words, but does not say them. It's not a gesture that Lord Montague had seen Burghley make before. Consequently, he looks at Burghley questioningly.

"Lewd friends!" Burghley mutters."Those lewd people; those actors and writers again. Ah, the folly of Fisher's Folly! It follows me even now after it had been sold!"

Burghley is not right about blaming actors. But, in his indebtedness, Edward can add a poor man defaulting on his rent to his list of problems arising from his humanitarian concerns. A dispassionate man, he is not. He feels for those in need. No wonder Burghley throws his hands up. But he dare not breathe a word about this issue of indebtedness to Montague

Edward's careless spending of his money is nothing new. But, this Churchyard rent arrears with landlady, Julia Penn, makes Edward stop to think: And very seriously so! The matter is lodged firmly in his brain; and the chances of him being allowed to forget it are very slim indeed.

His intimate knowledge of the area near the rented apartments is grist for his literary mill: Churchyard's apartment is quite close to the Church of St Benet's of Paul's Wharf. Edward uses this backdrop for his play *Twelfth Night.* The association of coins and bell-ringing with the number three is interesting. In the opening Scene of *Twelfth Night's* Act 5, Edward has the character FESTE begging and soon he gets three gold pieces. As FESTE says: "The old saying is the third pays for all. The triplex, sir, is a good tripping measure, or the bells of St Benet's, sir, may put you in mind – one, two, three."

Edward ends *Twelfth Night* with FESTE ultimately getting his money. But Thomas Churchyard does not get his rent arrears paid. And having written about his troubling money matters, Edward's outstanding Churchyard-Penn rent debt, remains unresolved. For now, his attention is drawn elsewhere.

*

Though his money worries tends in the direction of bringing him low, his literary master-works reach new heights. He receives acclaim from his peers. His fellow-poet Edmund Spenser, who had hoped to become Edward's Secretary, publishes a Sonnet dedicated "To the Right Honourable the Earle of Oxenford." In his allegorical work, *The Faerie Queene*, Spenser refers to the "antique glory" of Edward's ancestry which

Under a shady Veil is therein writ,
And eke thine own long living memory
Succeeding them in true nobility."

The fraternity of poets is fraught with pitfalls: Envy and jealousy are never far away, or absent for very long. But fine poet that he is, Spenser knows how to flatter. It is an art he has honed masterfully. Edward welcomes Spenser's friendship for what it is. It is certainly unlike the attitudes and comments that had come from Sir Philp Sidney and the Earl of Leicester. Edward is convinced that Sidney was "groomed" by Leicester who gave Sidney a false, one-dimensional view of him. But Spenser's praises does not come without criticism of Edward. As Edward reads Spenser's work, he tarries at the lines that recognises him as a fictional hero, and qualifies his heroics as having been written under a cloud of suspicion that is aimed at his liberties which, put bluntly, are inaccuracies in his English historical plays as performed by the Queen's Men. And not for the first time, Spenser takes a dual approach: While he praises Edward's soaring poetic brilliance, he also accuses him of narcissism. In another one of his works, Spenser keeps Edward in his poetic sights and writes of him in *Tears of the Muses* as

"That *same gentle spirit* from whose pen
Large streams of honey and sweet nectar flow,
Scorning the boldness of such base-born men
Which dare their follies forth so rashly show;

Doth rather choose to *sit in idle cell*
Than so himself to mockery sell."

"Sitting in idle cell?" Spenser senses Edward's slow withdrawal from Public exposure and criticism. But now, two years after his fortieth birthday, being more and more in relative seclusion does not protect or relieve him from money troubles. His debtors follow him. The pressure grows. "Who can I turn to?" he asks himself. Burghley gets another letter from him. But Burghley takes little notice of it. He wonders: how could Edward continue to do this? For his part, Edward is keen to get some recompense.

He is determined to get a large estate in keeping with his due and social status. His sights are set on a Welsh Manor. But as time passes he reaches a point of impatience that is close to desperation. Sadly, regretfully, he decides to offer his most prized possession, Castle Hedingham, in exchange for the Welsh property. This is a major move: A big loss. And pressing him to regain his "Good Name:" his sense of Self, is the regret he feels for not having done more for Elizabeth, Bridget and Susan, his three daughters. So with his children in mind, he'd written to the ageing Burghley asking, as a supplicant, more or less begging for help to get Denbigh Manor. To avoid the shameful charge from Burghley that he is not paying his share of the cost for his daughters' upkeep and well-being, his letter is not only longer than usual, it is the last straw: He recalls what he'd requested.

"The effect hereof as I would be glad to have an equal care with your Lordship over my children, and if I may obtain this reasonable suit of Her Majesty who granting me nothing but what she hath done to others and mean persons, then those lands that are in Essex, as Hedingham, and the rest which will come to some five hundred or six hundred a year, upon Your

Lordship's friendly help towards my purchases in Denbigh."

He remembers at this point while writing the letter, having thoughts of Anne. What would she think of what he is proposing? In her absence, his conscience over not supporting his daughters pains him even more. Towards the end of his letter he points to his distress and hopes that once provision has been made for his children and he himself is settled quietly and contentedly, he'd give Burghley no cause, as he puts it, "for you to think me an evil father, nor any doubt in me, but that I may enjoy friendship from your Lordship."

An "evil father!" Edward dares to think this of himself. A bitter grimace overlays his face as he re-reads these words before he'd sent the letter on.

Again shame eats into him. The slippage of loss of respect, he feels intensely. How to cope with this pain? One way is to leave England. But knowing how difficult it is to do so, he thinks of retirement. But where to? His preferred choice is that Manorial estate in Wales. He feels the need to be far away. Never again would he want to be the cause of any fellow Courtier's discomfort or unhappiness. Those who were once close to him are no longer near. And even more sobering, is that his request for understanding leaves Burghley and the Queen unmoved! In terms of money matters, Her Majesty and her Chief Minister had, it seems, lost the confidence they had in him. He is, in two words: inept and reckless. The expression *persona non grata*, plays on his mind. Mired in this mess, he tries to find a way out! A way forward. He is distressed by the loss of what he intimately knew as Her Majesty's favour. What he feels now is akin to a lover's complaint; or something quite close to it. Free thinker and free spirit that he is, he dares to think about the value of Castle Hedingham; his sacrosanct childhood home. For a while, he considers it as a bargaining asset that would bring him money in some kind of trade-off agreement. With this in mind, to complement his letter, he now has a face-to-face meeting with Burghley.

"My Lord," he says, "after my last letter to you, I am forced by circumstances to act. Now, I intend to do something odd; and personally almost unthinkable."

Burghley's ears are pricked; his gaze direct. Already familiar with Edward's unpredictable behaviour and actions, he looks directly at him. He searches for a clue (or clues) as to what Edward's thoughts might be. But, it is a hopeless attempt. Edward's face is impassive. Betraying no emotion, he adds, "To ensure my daughters' upkeep, I am thinking of my family inheritance." He pauses a while and notes that Burghley's eyebrows are raised.

"Yes," Edward says, "I am thinking of Castle Hedingham."

"What of it?" Burghley asks, feigning ignorance as if he'd not read the letter.

"I'm thinking, My Lord...," Edward pauses again. "I'm thinking...I am thinking of using my ancestral home to get the money I now need so badly."

"What do you mean, My Lord Oxford?" Burghley could hardly believe what he'd just heard.

"I mean, My lord," Edward says, "that my financial burden forces me to dispose of Castle Hedingham. It is the only way I could help to provide for Elizabeth, Bridget and Susan."

Burghley's earlier stare is transformed: it is now one of utter surprise. His unshifting gaze upon Edward's supplicant face, lingers. "Do you mean, My Lord Oxford..." he pauses before adding: "that you would like to *sell* Castle Hedingham?" Silence follows the question. Then:

"No, My Lord," Edward says. "I mean it to be a gift." He stops speaking and looks away to his right, to no one in particular. The intervening silence dramatizes the sound of the word *gift.* Edward thinks of Burghley's grand, unchallenged position and guardianship of his children.

"I would give you My Lord," Edward says, "Castle Hedingham as surety, so that Elizabeth, Bridget and Susan can be fully looked after."

Burghley's eyes open wide. It is an expression that Edward had never seen before. Burghley's eyes and the bags under them bulge. For a moment, the Mighty Man looks puzzled. Then, it seems, what Edward had said is fully understood. Slowly, the hues of Burghley's face changes for the better. It brightens. He beams with a lighter expression that resembles pleasure. Edward notes that it is a total transformation from his usual dull, serious, dead-pan countenance. For a while, he is speechless. He appears even modest as he ponders the extraordinary decision that his son-in-law has come to: "Do I understand you correctly, My Lord Oxford," he says, "that you are not bargaining – I mean, exchanging Castle Hedingham for some other property as a trade-off. But that..." He hesitates a moment: "That you are simply passing it on: In other words, that you are signing it over in trust to your daughters?"

"Yes, that is correct, My Lord," Edward says.

And so, the deed is done! Castle Hedingham passes on to Burghley. On the outside, Edward shows no emotion. But while his insides churn, he also feels some relief. He bears no further financial costs for the welfare and well-being of his children. He could live without guilt. But, for many days, the great, sad loss of ownership and control over his cherished family heirloom, plays on his mind. And so the link with his ancient heritage, the Castle, does not come to a simple and neat end: He feels numbed; very odd. As he walks away from Burghley, he realizes the finality of his decision: "Is this as it should be?" he asks himself. "Or, is it another of my reckless turns?" By now, he'd given away almost every precious thing, and is left with no back-up of financial support for himself.

From impulsive youth to rash adult, Edward, Earl of Oxford, takes another, and very hard, fall: He feels more of a landless Lord, without his beloved Castle. Steeped in feelings of regret and loss, he is plunged into a dark place. For a while, in short phases, his mood takes him away from his rational himself, until desperation and rage leads him to destroy some of the Castle grounds. And, as if to repent for his wilful ill-deed, he stops the destruction and saves what he can from the Castle. "After all, the Castle now belongs to my daughters," he mutters to himself, "but alas it is fully under Burghley's control." This realisation renews his angst. At a stroke, so to speak, he'd thrown away his Inheritance and self-sufficiency. The hard reality cuts deep. It resonates while he commits himself to copious note-taking and furiously making sketches for a new play. Into this drama, *The True Chronicle History of King Leir*, he channels his feelings which, among other things, presents a man who fritters away his inheritance. Of the main character, LEIR, Edward writes:

"Oh, what a combat feels my panting heart
'Twixt children's live and care of common weal.
How dear my daughters are unto my soul
None knows but he that knows my thoughts and secret deeds.
Ah little do they know the dear regard
Wherein I hold their future state to come,
When they securely sleep on beds of down."

Once more, Edward brings together life and art beautifully. Like LEIR, he too, is a Widower, coping with his loss of Anne. The losses in his life keeps adding up and he reflects upon the words he writes now:

"Wanting now their mother's good advice
Under whose government they have received
A perfect pattern of a virtuous life."

And, like LEIR (later *King Lear*), Edward notes that as yet, his own three daughters are not all married.

At this time, Edward is approached by the Queen's Men's actors, who are interested in performing his play. But he keeps his options open. He continues making notes; then rewriting and updating his work. So there is no reason to think that *King Leir* will not have new elements added to it later on. It is the way he works. But for now, there is no happy ending to the play. And, in spite of things being as they are, he is still hopeful of better times; of being reconciled with his estranged daughters and, maybe, just maybe, one day reclaim the outstanding portions of his ancestral estate!

As creator and play-master at the head of his Group of writers, after he structures and writes the first drafts, he passes around a copy of the script of *King Leir* to his Secretaries. Having done so with other plays of English Kings, like the authorship of *The Tragedy of Richard III, The Famous Victories of Henry* V and *The Troublesome Reign of King John*, he gets responses to the scripts. He is careful though to keep a firm grip as initiator and creator of the final draft intended for the Queen's Men's players. His approach is crucial; and, in this, he'd learned about certain work methods from others like Titian, the Master Painter, when he was in Italy. To enable him to produce plays, in his unique way, Edward provides the blue-print; the basic, important first draft which guides and dictates his playwriting in relation to his group. But at this low point in his relations with the Queen and the Court, he delegates a little more. As time passes, overall his writers' workshop evolves, as more or less, as intended: essentially, a creative enterprise.

So, in spite of the shame and loss of respect of others, Edward, battles on: The Court and the theatrical world that had been, and is, his life-blood, his career these past two decades, is far from being over. There is still life in the old dog. He smiles at the thought. He is mindful too of the Queen's special encouragement when he'd first started to write plays; and how much he has achieved. Thoughts of escape he decides to hold in abeyance: He would not run away. He would stick around for a while yet, for as he knows his followers and Secretaries are waiting in the wings to rewrite for the Queen's Men to perform, at least a few of his "anonymous" plays for the Court and/or public theatre audiences.

***

Time passes much too quickly, he thinks. At the age of forty-two, he feels older than that number suggests: The pain in his leg is sharper. It comes and goes; more often now. The injury, he thinks with utter horror, did not kill him. But, it has left him lame. How different things are now? Time and tide; and all that! He remembers the elegant nimbleness of his younger dancing, sporting days. Though he thinks he is fully mobile, with a shrug of the shoulder, he tries to disguise his defect. He reluctantly accepts that getting around means a slight drag of his feet. This hard reality fills him with regret. What a fleeting thing youth is: The sweet bird of youth soon flies away! But age, and slight disability, does not stop him from getting to the theatres in Shoreditch.

As he rides his horse to and fro, he recalls his glorious triumphs as the Queen's jousting-tilt Tournament champion. He was her undoubted favourite! But all that is a memory.

Now, his physical prowess and Her Majesty's favour are gone: The effect is palpable and evident: He is less gregarious; more withdrawn. But he salvages some positive elements for though he is less rash than he was in his youth, he does not fall short of intensity of purpose, as once again, he is confronted with his Churchyard-Penn debt: The unpaid rent to Landlady Julia Penn that had lapsed becomes most urgent, the next step being an appearance in Court!

At this point, Ms Penn thinks of an unusual way of dealing with the money owed. Knowing that her debtor is the Earl of Oxford, she gets in touch with a woman who is virtuous, someone whom she thinks might be helpful. That woman is Mistress Elizabeth Trentham, a Maid of Honour at the Royal Court, who has some connection with the Earl. To Mistress Trentham, Edward makes an important admission: "I am in desperate need," he says. He is conscious of the inferences of what he says: That it would surely mean some loss of personal control. So far, he admits, he's been woefully hopeless with managing his money and Inheritance. But, as a High and Mighty Earl; a man of great learning and independence, his business weakness (arising, in part, from his generous nature) he feels can only be justifiably admitted to someone of unusual, if not equal, he dares to think, independence of mind. On the face of it, it seems an impossible ask. But Edward, the Widower, is lonely: He has, at this time, no female partner, and chastened by his losses, financial and otherwise, unlike before, he thinks more now about his children; and importantly, about the future. With three daughters, and no son, he feels a pressing need for an heir to follow him as the Eighteenth Earl of Oxford.

***

So, being a single man, he thinks of closer ties with a woman as the possibility of a new relationship looms. His pending debt of unpaid rent to Julia Penn is the pressing matter in hand. "My Lord," Penn writes to Edward, "deal with me in Courtesy for that you and I shall come at the dreadful day and give account for all your doing." She refers to "that virtuous gentlewoman, mistress Trentham," and the possibility of good relations between he and Mistress Trentham. Discreetly, she closes her communication with Edward by saying: "I would be loath to offend your honour in anything." Julia Penn knew a lot more about Edward and Mistress Trentham than she'd stated. But who is Mistress Trentham really?

If Edward thinks his liaison with a new woman in his life is a well-kept secret, Ms Penn's letter dispels any doubts. The "gentle woman" is Elizabeth Trentham; one of the daughters of a wealthy land-owner from Staffordshire. Beautiful and smart, Edward first knew about her at Court as a Maid of Honour to the Queen. Unlike most Maids, Mistress Trentham is in her Thirties. She is astute; unusually knowledgeable in money matters. A better God send, Edward thinks he could hardly have wished for. He reflects upon the timely connection between Mistress Trentham and landlady, Julia Penn.

The calling-in of Edward's long overdue rent payment by Penn, adds to his vulnerability; and, in a life, thus far, of great highs and lows, amidst the depths of this new low, after the solitude of his Bilton and Billesley retreat, on his return to London, he begins to *see,* so to speak, Mistress Trentham. Considering his past hard lessons, now he feels and recognises the need for restraint. He does not flaunt his new relationship. But whether or not there was open courting, soon enough, Courtiers and others come to know of the pairing. "Is this inevitable?" Edward asks himself. Perhaps, he thinks. But through the grapevine: the network of Court gossipers, Julia

Penn had learned about the courtship. And, no-nonsense business woman that she is, she exploits the romance between Edward and Mistress Trentham to get her money. This is the hard reality of Edward's predicament as he gets deeper into wooing Mistress Trentham. So, the writer of genius in love, is also a writer in debt. Which raises the question: Would he ever have become a writer at all, had he not been an Earl? Question: But how did a rich, princely nobleman become "poor"? The question galls him; always alert, he seeks every chance to get money. But he applies now to the Queen for a monopoly on commodities such as wools, fruits and oils. He fails; and his money troubles rise as he finds himself unable to meet the normal expense of paying his Servants. He broods. Melancholy and dark moods hover. In this depressed state, he learns more about regular misbehaviour among his Servants; a few of them still prone to stealing things. So not being in total command of everything, not even in his own household, at times, he feels helpless. Once again, he writes to Burghley. He thanks the great Lord Treasurer for imposing discipline upon his Servants for their "evil doings;" something which he finds some difficulty in doing!

Meanwhile, as he and Mistress Trentham gets to know each other better, their courting gets warmer and more interesting. To his surprise, albeit a pleasant one, he sees a trend in Mistress Trentham's behaviour. She asserts herself through her financial expertise as she considers Edward's case of indebtedness to Julia Penn. After she sorts out Edward's debt, Mistress Trentham turns to her brother Francis, who, with his business partner, John Woolley, had bought the unsold part of Fisher's Folly. Thus, one business transaction leads to another! By sorting out the payment of Edward's debt, Mistress Trentham enriches her relationship with the hard-working Earl, thereby rescuing him from potential penury; and even more shame. So, the man of unrivalled artistry with the quill, defers to a woman of sound business sense and experience; a woman who sees an opportunity and grabs it with both hands. Elizabeth Trentham feels secure in their relationship; so much so, that even before wedding vows are exchanged, she steals a march on the wily Edward: She, more or less, takes charge, having already pulled a few preliminary strings in their relationship. No one, except Burghley, does that for the Earl of Oxford. But surprisingly, no grumbles come from Edward! He is happy with Mistress Trentham; not at all offended by her bold, but helpful initiatives. "Why?" he asks himself. Keen observer and extraordinary reader that Edward is of human nature, of human frailties and strengths, at this opportune time, he sees in Mistress Trentham, a woman of rare qualities: Her business ability is outstanding, certainly better than his, and her three clued-up brothers.

Edward does not fully understand her independence which is all well and good for her in the eyes of her family. But how would her overall attitude sit with him? Though he is surrounded by women, in essence, he is wary of them. As things are now, close relations with a dominant woman is a brand new experience. How would he cope? He adjusts his old habits: With fresh eyes and warm feelings, he allows good sense to prevail: He is happy for Elizabeth Trentham to take the lead. As his feelings for her grow, he reflects on how, unlike the past, he feels now. At once, Anne Cecil comes to mind: He wonders how different his marriage to her might have been without her meddling father. And, how interfering or not, another Elizabeth, none other than Her Majesty, the Queen herself, had been during his relations with Anne. On the themes of love and marriage, he thinks of the clues he's planted that have so far characterised his writings: Almost two decades before, he had published *A Hundredth Sundrie Flowers,* under the Penname "Meritum petere grave." And in "prayse of a Countesse," his wife Anne, he tells how

"My bashful spirits be full ill afraid
To purchase payne by my presumption
Such malice reigns (sometimes) in heavenly mynds,
To punish him that prayseth as he finds."

Then, bravely ignoring the prayers and entreaties of the loving, though apprehensive maiden "to let go," Edward smothers his own fears and hers, and leads her triumphantly through the "Temple gate," confident in the power of love to shield him:

"But ever more my shield did me defend
Against the storme...
Thus safely with my love I then did wend."

The love which so demands his attention, also leaves him vulnerable; and, as in the case of Anne Cecil, like a tempest it blows him hither and thither as portrayed in compelling dramatic detail in *Romeo and Juliet*, *Hamlet* and *Othello*. As he alludes in Sonnet Eighty Eight:

"...a story has
Of faults concealed wherein I am attainted."

But as he'd already admitted in *A Lover's Complaint*:

"All my offences that abroad you see
Are errors of the blood, none of the mind:
Love made them not; with acture they may be
Where neither party is nor true nor kind;
They sought their shame that so their shame did find.
And so much less of shame in me remains,
By how much of me their reproach contains."

And so from his viewpoint, he writes honestly in Sonnet One Hundred and Nine:

"O never say that I was false of heart
For nothing this wide universe I call.
Save those my Rose; in it thou art my all."

The Poem *A Lover's Complaint* closes with the Lady's admission of her lover's compelling and irresistible charm:

"Ay me, I fell and yet do question make,
What I should do again for such a sake.
O, that infected moisture of his eye!
O thou false fire which in his cheek so glowed!
O, that forced thunder from his heart did fly!
O, that sad breath his spongy lungs bestowed!
O, all that borrowed motion, seeming owed,
Would yet again betray the fire betrayed,
And now perverted and reconciled maid."

Such words reveals Edward's largely unhappy life with his wife Anne, but also his complex relationship and secret feelings for Queen Elizabeth, his Tudor Rose.

***

A few months after the rent debt is paid, Edward and Elizabeth Trentham crosses the threshold: They become man and wife. The Queen, ever-watchful over her Maids of Honour, gives her consent to the marriage. After she'd been seduced by Edward's charms, not least his dancing feet and his poetic nature in years past, the Queen, now older and wiser, may, or may not, have regrets about Edward, once again, tying the knot with another of her Maids. How must she be feeling? he wonders. Would she wear an understanding smile as she reflects on her jealous rages (and all the trouble she had caused, some of which are, so far, immortalized in poems and plays) before and during his marriage to Anne Cecil. But now, it seems, both the Monarch and Edward have moved on: It is the second time that she sees her dear and much loved Edward, take another woman under her charge, as a wife!

Before the wedding, Edward thinks of his former closeness to, and ongoing relations with, the Queen and the many times he'd upset her. But regardless of her feelings for him, conscious of her Supreme role as Monarch, Queen Elizabeth sees the great value of Mistress Trentham's marriage to her "problematic," headstrong Lord Great Chamberlain. More than this, the Queen exceeds her benevolence by giving wedding gifts to Edward and his bride. It is a fitting and happy gesture, just two days after Christmas. And so, at the end of another year, as the Revels Season is about to light up the wintry gloom, on the face of it, it seems all's well that ends well.

After their marriage, Edward dwells upon an interesting fact: That Elizabeth Trentham had, as a Maid of Honour, stayed single for as long as she did - well pass her Thirtieth birthday. Was this sheer stubbornness? Or, strength of character, on her part? In his reworking of a version of *The Merchant of Venice*, his model for PORTIA is, in part, Elizabeth Trentham; a strong character with whom he'd formed a loving bond just three years after Anne's death. In this play of debt and indebtedness, BASSANIO woos PORTIA to free himself from debt.

> "BASSANIO: Gentle lady,
> When I did first impart my love to you,
> I freely told you all the wealth I had
> *Ran in my veins – I am a Gentleman -*
> And then I told you true; and yet, dear lady,
> Rating myself at nothing, you shall see
> How much I was a braggart, when I told you
> My state was nothing, I should then have told you
> That I was worse than nothing."

BASSANIO'S words "My state was nothing," and "I was worse than nothing," mirrors Edward's predicament in reality. As a playwright *extraordinaire* he shows, once more, how deft he is at combining elements of various people and places in his experience and bring them together to form a coherent dramatic play.

***

So from the lonely period after Anne's death, and through the troubled time of his relatively low finances, Elizabeth Trentham, as Countess of Oxford, stands beside Edward as wife and companion. After their marriage he leaves central London. Thus his bohemian days comes to an end. The great Fisher's Folly literary whirligig is over. Now, he shares a house with Elizabeth in Stoke Newington, a quiet, residential area adjoining Clapton and Hackney. Here, he lives at a slower pace. He begins to draft a Poem titled *Willobie His Avisa*, largely a depiction of Elizabeth.

In the Poem, he identifies a nearby public landmark: the Well of St Agnes, as well as two of his favourite places of play productions: *The Theatre* and *The Curtain.* These theatres in Shoreditch stands on land that had been the property of two popular men in the theatre business: the actor James Burbage and John Brayne. Now, through his pen, in the guise of "Avisa," Edward paints a picture of his Countess of Oxford, the woman he now wakes up with and whom he sees each day. Soon, the habit of being married again grows on him. He does not doubt that his new wife is a woman who would stand by him, come what may. His relationship with Elizabeth is something he values very much. As "Willobie" in the poem, Edward adds more details to the portrait of his wife as "Avisa." He notes that when she was single she'd attracted the attentions of a rich gentleman, who was a steady and passionate wooer. But, she shows no interest. Why? Because in the words of Willobie, she says:

"Nay yet welfare the happy life,
That need not blush at every view...
Although I will be a poor man's wife,
Yet then I'll laugh as well as you,
Then laugh so long as you think best
My fact shall frame you no such jests."

Utter seriousness, underlines her character.

In Stoke Newington, Edward and Elizabeth live not as a retired couple, but are still very much in touch with their theatrical connections. Sometimes, they socialize in a well known pub in Shoreditch. Avisa is alluring; and it is noticeable to Edward that though she flirts with handsome bachelors, her eyes are firmly fixed on her husband. She fends off men's unwanted attentions. Further into his Poem, Edward (Willobie) writes frankly that his wife, Avisa, is beautiful and yes desirable. But while he witnesses her flirtatiousness, he knows upon whom her eyes are fixed. Such assurances are absolutely essential, especially for a jealous man like Edward. He lauds his wife's faithfulness when he writes:

"My loving mate hath forc'd away.
No Juno's wrath to wander far
From loving bed can make him stray…
My sweet Ulysses near stays
From his desired home so long…
My heart is fixed since I did give
My wedlock faith to chosen friend."

So, in his Countess Elizabeth, Edward finds a good and steady wife. After their honeymoon, as love and affection matures he thinks, not for the first time, how unlike his life with Anne, with all its upheavals and humiliations, this second marriage is. As a man of strong feelings, for the sake of his well-being, this new life with Elizabeth offers much-needed warmth and security which is like a balm for his exposed, battered sensibilities.

***

Edward's links with literary friends, and other associates, continues. The regular meeting place is the St George's Inn. Here, he meets an Italian named John Florio, a larger than life character; a bookish man who mixes with people in the theatre, including high-born men like the Earl of Southampton. On meeting Edward, whose reputation had forerun him, Florio talks about a Dictionary.

"My Lord, Edward," he says with hardly concealed excitement.

"I am working on an Italian Dictionary. It is very essential for communication between the peoples of England and Italy. I have been preparing it for many years. Now, at last, it is completed. And, I am very happy. It is ready to be published..." He pauses. Then, he says "My Lord, money is my greatest need. It will help to get my Dictionary in print. And yes, therefore, it will help to get my work in the Bookshops. My Good Lord, my Dictionary is a very important contribution to our better understanding of languages; especially of Latin and Italian in which, I know, you are much interested and, of course, well-versed. I am thinking of educated people; and those who wish to become educated. I am thinking of the reading Classes in England, not only those who love Ovid's *Metamorphoses* and the Classics, but also *The Courtier* and *The Prince*, to name just a few..."

Edward listens intently, and is ready to speak, but Florio's continuous flow of Italian-accented English words, keeps him waiting. He thinks Florio knows he's waiting to respond, but emboldened and excited by what he is saying, Florio persists. In his inimitable style and scholarly way, he says:

"My Lord, the Twelve Dialogues of my book *The Second Fruits* are arranged to show as many of the Proverbs, as possible. In the Italian column, every phrase which is proverbial is marked. My Lord, most people in their compositions seek for words to express themselves and their interests, but I have tried to present those Italian words and phrases, that never yet saw Albion's cliffs."

He then compares his work on Italian proverbs with that of Erasmus in Greek and Latin. "Many words that I have in the Dictionary," he says, "relate to popular sayings like the pith, the proprieties, the proofes, the pureties, the elegancies and the commonest in phrases of both the Italian and English languages."

After this speech-like, but learned, interesting few minutes of talk, Florio adds:

"My Lord Edward, whatever help you can give, I shall most gratefully receive."

"I cannot help you with money," Edward says. "But, I agree: Your Dictionary is a valuable help to our mutual understanding of literature and language; and therefore, better communication between the peoples of England and Italy."

"My Lord, Edward," Florio says, "Thank you. Thank you!" He then unwraps a parcel to reveal a copy of the manuscript of his Dictionary. "Here, My Lord," he says. "This is it!" The rising pitch of his voice hits a new high. Edward draws closer to examine the manuscript: As he reads and turns a few pages, he realises that the scholarship and learning the Dictionary contains is impressive; hard to ignore or dismiss.

"My help is not in terms of money," Edward says. "Now that I have seen your manuscript, I will offer something which, I think, is more than money: I will contribute a Preface. Would that suit you?"

"A Preface from you, My dear Lord Oxford," Florio says, "would be marr-velous. Thank you! Thank you, My Lord." He is visibly moved. He bows low in a respectful way. As he leaves the Earl, he feels very pleased and smiles at the thought: Nothing ventured, nothing gained!

Soon after their conversation, he does as he says he would. He keeps his word: Mindful that anonymity of authorship is all important, he writes a Sonnet under the Pen-name "Phaeton" which he addresses to "His Friend Florio"

"Sweet friend whose name agrees with thy increase
How fit a rival art thou of the spring!
For whom each branch hath left his flourishing,
And green-locked summer's shady pleasures cease,...
Thou with thy fruits our barrenness o'erspread
And set thy flowers pleasure to be seen.
Such friends, such flow'rets of mortality,
Were ne'er before brought out of Italy."

Such flattery is gladly received by Florio. But, Edward as "Phaeton" inserts clues, as he'd been doing in his plays of who he really is: Among Elizabethans, for example, Edward de Vere is sometimes referred to as the "Spring" which is Ver in Latin. Hence de Vere! He is especially conscious of this time of writing the Sonnet as "Phaeton." Why? Because it is a watershed; a hugely significant moment in the history of British literature which marks the start of a steady process and progress that brings Edward closer to another Pen-name that would become more and more popular.

***

As he and his Countess enjoy life in their Stoke Newington home, developments in the theatre take a turn for the better. A new spirit and energy make things move faster: Public stages like *The Theatre* and *The Curtain* are no longer the only theatres in London. Across the River Thames, on the South Bank, *The Rose Theatre* begins to pull in large crowds, with performances by two resident Troupes: Lord Strange's Men (also called The Earl of Derby's Men) and, the Lord Admiral's Men. At the forefront of this booming, lively theatrical Scene is the work of young playwright, Christopher Marlowe. Many theatre-goers talk about his literary brilliance. They cite the refreshing inventiveness of his plays. As more literary and theatre-going people flock to see his work, some in the know, say he's brought about much-needed change at the *Rose Theatre* through his exciting blank verse productions of the Tragedies *Tamburlaine, The Tragical History of Dr Faustus* and *The Jew of Malta*. Marlowe's impactful dramatizations has broad appeal. He writes compelling and innovative plays; and notably, he moves away from the old format of rhyming verse. But his threat to the prevailing dramatic "style" is not enough to subvert the Queen's Men's approach for, as so often happens, the young playwright brings in the new which builds upon the foundation laid by those who were writing before him. So, it is a generational thing too! For while Edward and the Euphuist writers, who had come together at Fisher's Folly and created new literary standards; a revolution, no less, they are now in their Thirties: a group that includes Lyly, Munday, George Peale and William Gray. Now, hard on their heels are younger writers who are full of energy and gearing up to implant their own penmanship upon the fertile environment that is the Elizabethan literary Renaissance.

Edward's contributions so far to English theatre and drama have been marked. His plays are powerful and distinctive. His style unrivalled. After he'd left Fisher's Folly in Central London for the greener surroundings of Stoke Newington, Countess Elizabeth's companionship gives him a boost: The hectic pace subsides. He is not rushing about, as once he did. Now imbued with feelings of contentment, at least twice a week he rides to the Shoreditch theatres on his favourite horse.

*

In his off-stage office at *The Curtain* Theatre, he works on preparing new productions and continues his habit of reading and tweaking his old plays. He can no longer fund troupes of players like The Earl of Oxford's Men and The Earl of Oxford's Boys. The financial burden has been heavy; and now he faces competition from new troupes that have been formed. Of the new Companies, or Troupes, that have come into being, two of them, Lord Strange's and the Admiral's Men's boasts having the leading actors: Richard Burbage, Edward Alleyn and Will Kemp. By raising the bar, the reputation and attitude to English drama and theatre reaches new heights. Edward thinks about the nobility of poetry; the power of staged story-telling, and he smiles. He observes with joy day-to-day, how audiences grow and English actors are becoming a new kind of celebrity. Commentators liken this phenomenon to being second only to Royalty and Noble families. He notices something else: Though the stories enacted are important, people are especially eager to see their favourite actors: Edward Alleyn, Will Kemp and Richard Burbage. They have a public, street following too!

So as theatrical performances becomes more popular, writers vie with each other. But competition does not always produce good personal outcomes. One writer, William Gray, a domineering, jealous man, is often irritated when an actor improvises using the lines he'd written in the script. Edward knows Gray well and thinks of him as a man on the make. Edward offers him, as a fellow-writer, sanctuary at Fisher's Folly. In turn, Gray warns Edward of men in the theatre business who are not averse to selling plays to rival companies; often the same play-script is sold to different companies, namely, The Admiral's Men and the Queen's Men. Trying to make ends meet, when Plague hits London in the summer, Gray's mood darkens. Edward is aware of Gray's hardship; and, as he'd done when he was owner of Fisher's Folly, now he tries to help.

Writers meeting for a drink is an acceptable aspect of social, theatrical behaviour. One day when writer Thomas Nashe and Gray meet, another writer "Will Monox" joins them. "Will Monox" is a made-up Pen-name for Edward de Vere, Earl of Oxford: Monox being French slang for "My Ox."

It is a summer's afternoon when the three men Edward, Gray and Nashe meet in The Steelyard; a regular haunt for Medieval traders and businessmen, including many who are engaged with the Hanseatic League. As usual, Gray scribbles enthusiastically to get his next piece of writing done and published. He is never short of a word or two: He is always ready to talk. Nashe, on the other hand, has been working on a play. In it, a leading character is called Ver or The Spring. In this Comic play, Ver says: "I tell you none but assess live within their bounds!" This ten-word statement is an almost perfect fit for Edward de Vere! And Nashe can be relied upon to be exact about his characterisations: In this case, a good caricature.

For their meeting, Gray appears well dressed: He certainly does not look like a struggling poor writer. Edward and Nashe are also in fine, befitting garb; Edward more so that Nashe. The scene is set in The Steelyard. A den of iniquity? Who knows. A den of revelation? Perhaps. The sound of lively talk rises, it hits the low ceiling and spreads across the room. The smell of sea-food is strong.

"The Rhenish is very good," Gray says. Edward and Nashe both agree. In that crowded, close atmosphere, people of many backgrounds mingle. There is an air of tolerance; an unspoken sense of freedom and free speech, which Edward and his companions welcome. In the conversation that follows, what Gray says about a "Country player" he'd read about in a piece of writing titled *Greene's Groatsworth of Wit*, Edward finds most interesting. Gray talks at length about a base-minded "Upstart Crow," who does not write plays, but steals them and puts them on stage. "This man flaunts himself: He parades around dressed in borrowed plumage," Gray says. Edward listens intently. And by the end of the evening a jolly good time was had by all.

A week later, Edward reflects upon his conversation with Gray in The Steelyard. "Who is this man? This 'Upstart Crow,' whom you mention," he'd asked Gray, whose information comes from what he'd read. "He is a man from the Country," he said. "A 'Country player.' A Warwickshire man from Stratford-upon-Avon who has come to London with hopes. Very high hopes of becoming an actor and…" He'd paused. Then he added: "Perhaps he has other ambitions too! His name is Will Shakspere."

"Ah, Shakspere. Very interesting," Edward had said. "It is a name, that is close sounding to one that has been attributed to me some years ago at Audley End before the Queen and Courtiers. Gabriel Harvey, a Professor of Literature, in his grand Address had spoken of me as the one who 'Shakes-spears!'"

On hearing this, Gray had said,

"My Lord, I had no idea you were so-called; and quite so long ago! I can say this man Shakspere does his best to become better known. But, at times, his broad Warwickshire accent takes some getting used to when he is among Londoners, especially those of the Upper Classes, who are the Patrons and regular theatregoers."

"Is he is a playwright?' Edward had asks.

"In truth, My Lord Oxford," Gray had said, "he *pretends* to be a writer of sorts. Never mind being a playwright. Working in the theatre, Shakspere sees the scripts and reads the plays; a number of them gives no hint of the author. The word 'Anonymous' is written on many title pages. Such unnamed playwrights, as you know, wish to remain Anonymous, so they use Pen-names to protect the hand that has written them. How could he be a playwright when the art of such writing is so specialized; so intellectually demanding. Of course, many of your Anonymous plays have already been written and performed at Court, and, in public playhouses. But take heed. This Shakspere is among us. He doubles as Manager-Player. He is learning fast and knows our business increasingly well. From what I hear, he is not gifted as an outstanding actor, and though he may not have the intellectual scope and depth to write plays, he profits from them! He is a man with a talent for business. As I understand it, acting is more of a side-line activity for Shakspere. In essence, he is a businessman. Money; not art, is his thing! Not only that, I hear he is buying plays, which he reworks with helpers; writers whom he pays. He then claims these plays as his own. So I hear."

While Gray spoke, Edward's curiosity had grown: He wondered who this man might be. After a while, he had said: "I may have seen this Shakspere at a performance of one of my plays at *The Curtain*, not so long ago. If he is the person, he is a busy-body, alright. He looks like a Grain-dealer or Manager-Administrator. I had no idea, he interferes with Anonymous play scripts."

"That, My Lord, is what I'm saying," Gray had said. "He is among us. He counts himself as one of the Actors' Company. But, he is certainly not one of us: He is not a writer, as he pretends to be! I'd say he's less of an actor and more of a collector. I mean, a collector of anonymous plays for which he acts as a Broker. He sells play-scripts to different companies and theatres. This man Shakspere is brazen. He is not a playwright; and his acting does not compare well with even moderately competent actors, never mind being an Alleyn, Kemp or Burbage!" Gray's mood was mellow and pleasant. He chuckled. Then he laughed out loud. "Rumour has it that he'd once played the part of the Ghost in a play…" At this point, Edward had interjected:

"You say he'd been cast as the GHOST in a production of my play *Hamlet*."

"Yes but, My Lord," Gray continues, "the reality is that in our *make-believe* world, Shakspere wears the mask of being an actor when, in truth, he is a sort of theatre Impressario; a seller of other writers' plays to the highest bidder."

Since that last meeting and conversation, Edward and Gray meet again in The Steelyard. They are served Rhenish. As Edward sips the wine, he thinks of Shakspere as a salesman who sells plays to the "highest bidder." He feels a rush of blood to his head. He sips some more of his Rhenish which warms his insides and steadies him. "I have been told by Lyly," he says, "that two of my plays have been performed at *The Rose Theatre* on the Southbank."

"That is indeed true, My Lord," Gray says. Suddenly as if he'd rediscovered the taste, once more with relish, he lifts his drink to his lips and takes a gulp. A rosy-redness appears on his cheeks.

"You say *two*, My Lord," Gray adds, "but who knows how many more!"

"So, he, the Stratford man, is less of an actor, and more of a Manager businessman who steals," Edward mutters confirming to himself what he'd heard. "He makes money by selling *my* plays!" The concern in his voice is evident. On the face of it, the theft seems to really trouble him.

"Yes, My Lord, he makes changes to Anonymous plays, then he sells them," Gray says. "He is the Pretender, the "Upstart Crow" from Stratford who makes a good living, buying and selling the fruits of playwrights' labour."

"So *that* is what the man Shakspere does," Edward says. As irritation and anger rises, he tries to keep his feelings under control. He looks out at the sunny weather beyond the nearby glass-paned window. The bright scene jogs his memory: He remembers that glimpse he'd once had of the person he thinks is Shakspere.

"On one occasion," Gray continues, "I had overheard Shakspere speaking to people after a performance. He'd asked one man, then another: 'Did you enjoy *my* play?' I was shocked to hear this. He insinuates himself and acts in a grand, make-believe manner far above his station as the Actors' Company's Impressario. And, of course, he uses some of the money he gets to fund the actors' wardrobe. But more than that, I hear that Shakspere now plays a middleman's role between playwrights and theatre audiences. He is young and puts himself about. He makes himself available. Not surprisingly, he could be seen more often than most people in and around the theatres."

Edward's silence encourages Gray.

"So, My Lord," Gray adds,"Shakspere is becoming better known! His popularity is rising. He is not a shy fellow, I must say. Far from it. I'd say he's thick-skinned. Why? Because he is beginning to take liberties. He comes close to boasting about *his* plays. Thinking about himself as a playwright is becoming too much to bear for me as a practitioner. But his presence in and out of the theatres, and, so clearly involved with the actors, alas his boasts of being a playwright becomes more believable and acceptable. Hence my growing concern for you My Lord; and all playwrights."

Gray lifts his glass to his lips. "My Lord," he says, "I'd been wanting to speak to you about this man Shakspere much before now." After Gray had spoken these words, both men left The Steelyard. The memory of what had been said at his meetings with Gray, provokes what is now very much a live issue for Edward: The usurpation of his hard-won work with the quill; the "pain to pen a book" (as he often thinks of the writing process in general, and, in particular, of creating a play) is not just a rumour: His plays had been, and are being stolen! For a long while, given what he already knows, Edward dwells on Gray's words; on the honesty with which he'd spoken them. Like Nashe, Gray was devoted to being a writer. He craved success; and Edward had respected his commitment by encouraging him to come to Fisher's Folly and pursue his career.

***

By now, Edward had written an impressive list of plays: most are completed, some are drafts, others are in sketchy note-form. He'd seen them performed at Court, as well as in public theatres. And having painstakingly re-read and reviewed most of them (certainly the Italian-oriented plays) he hopes to go through the same exercise with his other dramas. Altogether, the play scripts amount to quite a pile, which he categorises and ties in bundles. A few of the unfinished versions, he shows to his Secretaries, Lyly and Munday. Showing them such scripts and related material does not mean they are co-authors of any of his plays. His stories are his own: from conception to completion. So, he questions once more, who is this impersonator-Impressario? This man from Stratford-upon-Avon, who masquerades in the theatre world; that someone who is in the Lord Chamberlain's Men's Troupe as an actor, but also ambitiously poses as nothing less than a new playwright. The provocation Edward feels is personal: "How should I deal with this?" he asks himself. "As I have done before, he answers positively, I would use my art: The art of story-telling."

*

So as Gray's knowledge of the "Upstart Crow" echoes in Edward's ear, now in one of their regular update-conversations, John Lyly enlightens Edward some more about the Imposter among them. The difference between Will Shakspere and himself could not be clearer: Some years earlier, when Shakspere was just a fourteen year old boy and still in Stratford, Edward de Vere was being highly praised in the presence of Her Majesty Queen Elizabeth and her Courtiers as one of England's leading writers: a poet-dramatist of rare and lofty eloquence. Now, at the age of forty two, Edward's knowledge of Shakspere beyond what he knows and what Gray had told him, is still quite patchy. He learns from sources in the theatre world that when Shakspere was eighteen, he got married; and three years later, his wife gave birth to twins. But soon after, the green country boy, drawn to the glamour and excitement of Show Business, comes to London to seek his fortune; and yes, fame too! Thus far, as Gray had said to Edward, "We know very little about this Shakspere." But now, Lyly confirms what he knows about the sketchy biographical trail of Shakspere. He says to Edward:

"Informed by the historical records, what I know is that a 'Wilhelmus Shakspere' had left Stratford to come to London. His sole aim: To become an actor, a player in the theatre!"

"If there are any further encroachments by Shakspere affecting my authorship," Edward says to Lyly, "I should know about it."

As it was, Edward does know a good deal "about it." Simply because he is the author of *Greene's Groatsworth of Wit* which Gray had read. But unbeknownst to Gray, Edward was unable to say anything about his Pen-name "Robert Greene," because of a libel charge brought against him by Gabriel Harvey. To avoid being sued, Edward ceases to use "Robert Greene." This change marks a moment of huge significance as, he thinks long and hard about the fulsome praises that Harvey had heaped upon him at Audley End when he said "thy will shakes spears." How ironic and timely those words from Harvey are to him now! Time is of the essence; and Edward knows he must act quickly. As the great punner and wordsmith of his time, he considers "will" and "shakes spears." He thinks long and hard: Then he scrawls upon a piece of paper: William Shakespeare. While the ink dries, he comes to terms with the look and sound of the words. For a while longer, he considers the composition: "This," he says to himself, "*will be my last* Pen-name: WILLIAM SHAKESPEARE!"

*

His heightened curiosity leads him to think more and make an association between Shakspere and Anonymous plays. Shakspere's choice of Show Business, beginning with the Acting profession, as a means of making his fortune is very interesting; and bearing witness to the various theatrical events, Edward takes Gray at his word. In large part, he is told that before coming to London, Will Shakspere had been travelling in the Provinces as a Player and puppet master; that he eventually reached London and had worked with the acting troupe: The Earl of Pembroke's Men and other Companies.

As time passes, Edward cannot ignore the presence of Will Shakespere in the theatre business. It is 1592, the year when Philip Henslowe, Manager of the *Rose Theatre* in London records a significant event: The inaugural performances of two of Edward's Anonymous plays about King Henry. Henslowe says that another play *Titus of Andronicus* was performed at the *Rose Theatre.* At the time, one of Edward's first tragedies, was performed not only by Pembroke's Men, but also by Lord Strange's Derby Men as well as Sussex's Men. Edward's labours yield a bountiful harvest: His popularity rises. As one of the leading playwrights and men of the theatre, everyone, who is anyone, works closely with him. But, his popularity comes at a cost: with enormous pressure to maintain a certain distance from his work as author. True to himself, he steadfastly refuses to add his name to his plays. *Anonymous* will suffice; it *must*! Whatever the temptation to do otherwise, he is ever-conscious of the Queen's displeasure; and the great trouble she would cause should he reveal himself as the author of his plays. Maintaining a Pen-name is absolutely necessary. Realising he is riding the horns of a dilemma, he would have it no other way, from here on! To show too much of himself, in whatever way, in his work, would unduly stir the wrath of the Queen with whom, for better or worse, all his life has been so intimately entwined.

He thinks he must be very careful. A slip of the pen now could spell utter disaster. So, as he experiments and expands the English vocabulary and language, he disguises his characters' identities by a clever use of words. Already he is the proven master of puns and punning. But using metaphors and personalities to portray himself and other people, can only be hinted at when he writes. He is very glad to have the Tudor Queen's extraordinary life-line: the largesse of the one thousand pounds annual Grant, but he knows it is the price he has to pay for *his unwilling silence* as author of his literary works. This reality is the Scenario against which he casts himself as characters mirroring himself as a young man in *Measure for Measure* and in *Romeo and Juliet* and, as a mature man in *As You Like It*. Variously, he portrays the Queen metaphorically as a lioness who, though old, at the age of fifty six, she is resolute and ever determined. Above all, she expects him to keep his silence and not claim his rightful self as the real person behind the mask: "William Shakespeare." The symbolism of the following words is central to the life of William Shakespeare:

> "for 'tis,
> The Royal disposition of that beast…"

She will be fair and allow him certain freedoms, and will continue to pay his yearly due, but he must remain quiet; be dormant, "asleep." In the following Scene of *As You Like It,* Edward's disguised self is again evident:

> "I do not shame
> To tell you what I was, since my conversion
> So sweetly tastes, being the thing I am-"

These words offers perspective on life: His wayward early years, his misdemeanours and run-ins with the Queen and Burghley, and the relief of repentance and reform of his older years. In one poem about his newly-wed young Countess Anne, he blames not himself, but the jealousy of the serpent the Queen. On this matter of his wife and the Queen, he believes he was wrongly blamed "without cause why?"

So, as with the poems under Edward's earlier Pen-name "Meritum petere grave" he has had to in such plays as *Troilus and Cressida*, *Twelfth Night* and *As You Like It,* disguise his portrayals of intimate relations between himself, the Queen and his first wife. Interestingly, while his Comedies and Tragedies are widely staged and well received, the problem of the business-minded Shakspere claiming authorship of plays from his pen, does not go away.

***

Edward knows Nashe well enough. He knows how good a Satirist Nashe is. But how much of a joke is the "idea" that the relatively uneducated, little known provincial actor, Shakspere, who never left the shores of England, but claims to be the author of a sophisticated historical tragedy set in Rome, like *Titus Andronicus?* Furthermore, and incredibly, Shakspere positions himself as a fount of knowledge about aristocratic life, so powerfully nuanced that he is able to write *Henry VI.* Nashe's reference to Edward as "Will Monox" is an open admission of the fact that the actor William Shakspere had been playing the role of authorial usurper; that he'd paraded around in Edward de Vere's "feathers" on the stages of public theatres. Now, as a few friends think, there is every reason for Edward to take notice. But his seeming casualness keeps him, outwardly, at least, remarkably untroubled. Little does he know how insidious this creeping usurpation of his work really is. And in truth, it is but just the start; the thin end of a pretentious, but long and ever-hardening wedge. The writing, so to speak, is already on the wall; clear enough for Gray and for Nashe and Lyly to sound their own clear warnings. So what had started as a trickle now moves forward and gains momentum, causing some confusion about the man Shakspere who, worryingly for Edward, is now gaining credence in people's mind. And though few, if any, at the time could have known it, the die was already cast.

Slowly, but surely, the creeping concern that Edward had been feeling, takes greater hold. He becomes more alert to the ever present threat and danger that another hand could lay claim to his anonymous manuscripts. He remembers The Steelyard meeting when Gray had put it to him:

"My Lord, do you know there are eagle-eyed hacks ready to swoop and scoop what is not theirs? They steal and claim authorship of *your* plays?"

Though it has crossed his mind often, Edward still had not seriously asked himself if someone is usurping his literary gems. He has, at least, been made aware that someone in the theatre business is providing props, costumes and masks, for actors, as well helping some who are desperate and in need of money. Distinguished literary man that he is, Edward acknowledges that such services are essential to the smooth-running of the theatre. More than most people, he knows that Team-spirit and collaboration are key factors in theatre operations. In this sense, Shakspere's activities in the production-managerial side of play production is crucial to ensuring and delivering regular performances. So wily-nily, he manages to build a theatrical reputation that is rising.

*

So far there is nothing to indicate that some of Edward's plays would have been snatched, rewritten and sold. Such works are not treated any differently from the Scripts that had already been performed by the Queen's Men and eventually published anonymously. But, the comic side of all this does not escape the Satirist's attention. Concerning jokes, Edward is not one to resist the allure of his Muse. Nashe's next move is significant. In his pamphlet *Strange News*, wherein he mentions "Will. Monox" Nashe dedicates it to a prolific poet nicknamed "Gentle Master William Apis lapis."

His dedication is among the highest accolades he could give. Though he plays the anonymous game, his "Gentle Master William Apis lapis" and "Will. Monox," are in truth, Edward de Vere. So following his fellow-writer Gray, Nashe distinguishes between two men in the theatre world. Edward de Vere, the respected and popular playwright; and the "Upstart Crow, country-player," William Shakspere. To the Elizabethan public: readers and theatre-goers, Nashe's presentation of his pamphlet to "Will. Monox" as an outstanding poet is the *first* time that Edward appears *in print* under the guise of a writer and wit called "William." Will and William are interesting; and now most timely! So what is Nashe's intention? What does "Gentle Master William Apis lapis" really mean? According to one translation of the nick-name, Nashe refers to Edward as "a stubborn old Ox"! But he also praises "Gentle Master William's" literary brilliance. Nashe goes on to say William likes a bit of drinking; and tends to combine dirt with wisdom. He adds that on a few occasions, Edward's enemies points to grammatical inconsistencies in his writings. Though no love is lost between Nashe and Gabriel Harvey, Nashe warns Harvey to avoid drawing anger from Edward: His "Gentle Master William" character does not mean Edward is a push-over. Then Nashe speaks of the "little fellow" (alias "Gentle William") as one of England's best wits, whose jests he enjoys enormously. So the link and fine line between dirt and wisdom, from which Edward's wit derives are not lost on Nashe.

Edward repays his fellow scribbler Thomas Nashe when he revisits his play *Love's Labour's Lost.* Apart from their friendship, Edward reworks the play, a comedy set in France in which he introduces three women: Anne Vavasour (ROSALINE), Mary Hastings (MARIA) and Queen Elizabeth (as the PRINCESS OF FRANCE).

And, as the "Upstart Crow" gains a greater hold in the theatre business, Nashe spotlights the author Edward who is synonymous with the names "Gentle Master William" and "Will Monox." Meanwhile, Edward becomes more wary over the possibility of his work being usurped. He trusts his feelings about the warnings and thinks the moment has come to confront, through his art (there is no other way), the emerging Imposter-Author of a few of his plays. But why now? Because most of his plays (Comedies and Tragedies) have already, in one form or another, been written and are being performed. They amount to quite a collection; and Edward is, as Nashe puts it, already an author with a list of plays that is without peer. So Edward senses the true value of his accomplishment thus far. He feels as if he has been at the heart of a movement of great energy and creativity: Truly, at the dawn of a new literary Age. He is immersed now in a new version of *Love's Labour's Lo*st in which he presents characters who are part of his experience, including Nashe and Harvey, as well as, a less than flattering representation of the Imposter Will Shakspere from Stratford-upon-Avon.

***

As Edward approaches his mid-Forties, he feels he is at a crossroads; a crucial juncture on his extraordinary literary journey. After his first awkward, unconfident grasp of a quill, then making marks on a blank page: initially forming letters and words, later composing lines of verses and songs, as well as seeing his father's Troupe of Players perform at Castle Hedingham (where he'd made friends with the great actor Will Somers) he feels a long apprenticeship had been served. Now, he allows himself to think that he has come a long way since he'd declared to his stunned Tutor, his ambition: "A Writer to be!" Of this he had absolutely no doubt. Neither did Nowell. Now he reflects on the writer he has become!

The Quill or the Sword? That was always the big question for him. All the more so, because no other family in English history has so valiantly, consistently and gloriously wielded the sword like the de Veres? He reconsiders how he got to where he is now: "Which route of Military endeavour should I take?" he says to himself, "is one of the questions, that I'd asked myself as an eight year old. No matter what grand ambitions were plotted for me by Earl John, I felt I knew best. I knew then, as I know now, that I had the visionary awareness, the mind-set of an artist. And having seen the Actors perform each winter, my imagination was fired. I liked the energy and goodwill, the warm feelings and friendliness of the Actors. This gave me a sense of balance during the years of relentless learning that had enabled me to imagine and combine so many disparate elements of life: my own and others into my dramas; stories of reality, mirrored in art as presented on the theatre stage."

Of much importance to Edward now as he approaches the end of a new version of *Love's Labour's Lost* is the timing of its performance. Instead of complaining either to friends or fellow writers about his feelings on the false claims of Will Shakspere, he completes the final copy of the play as it is to be performed. He sets the scene of his present relations with Nashe, Harvey, and, once and for all, he expresses what he feels and knows about Shakspere. On the matter of Pen-names, he reminds himself; that to ignore such disguises is to imperil himself and thus, his envied and enviable literary output. There is no room for complacency, he thinks, as he pushes the boundaries. He feels he is entering a new and critical, creative phase. In particular, he feels, with some urgency, that a clear distinction must be made between his disguised self and Shakspere. And he does so in the most effective and powerful way he could think of: Through the art of dramatic story-telling.

In *Love's Labour's Lost* four characters are on the stage, whose relationships provide a window through which Edward views his literary and public life with that of Will Shakspere. No more glancing blows. It has to be a point-blank confrontation.

This marks the beginning of a new and exciting literary phase; the age of his emerging new Pen-name: William Shakespeare. More self conscious than before, he is deliberate, very careful as he places the historical originals: namely himself, Nashe and Harvey as the characters BIRON, MOTE and HOLOFERNES, respectively in *Love's Labour's Lost*. His Self-characterisation serves as a light-hearted reference to gossip that spreads because he is unhappy with the English Court, and therefore, he is thinking of leaving for Spain. Whether or not this was true, in his play he writes:

"Our Court is haunted
With a refined traveller of Spain,
A man in all the world's new fashion planted
That hath a mint of phrases in his brain.
One who the music and his own vain tongue
Doth ravish like enchanting harmony;
A man of complements, whom right and wrong
Have chose as umpire of their mutiny."

But the character ARMADO declares his love. For whom? The person in question is a woman named JAQUENETTA Though she is a base wench, she is ARMADO'S muse. What follows is talk between ARMADO, MOTE and HOLOFERNES. After the dialogues between the characters, Edward spotlights Shakspere whom no writer in London knows as either a playwright or a Poet. But once and for all, in *Love's Labour's lost,* Edward deals with Shakspere's pretense; his audacity in claiming authorship of his plays in the form of the character COSTARD. Edward's literary art is the most telling means through which he could and does address the serious threat he faces from Shakspere. His heightened awareness of the man from Stratford whose background is far removed from his own, leads him to bring them together on stage, where he unleashes the power of his pen. The characters he creates in the play are certainly not straightforward. But, as he's done, so many times in his work, he combines the characteristics of one person with those of another to create, and recreate, characters for his purposes. In *Love's Labour's Lost*, he does so again: Having cast himself as ARMADO, he presents Will Shakspere as COSTARD who says:"For mine own part, I know not the degree of the worthy. But I am prepared to stand for him."

As time passes, Edward gets more concerned and angry with Shakspere. He wonders if he should confront Shakspere. He is reluctant to do so because a fight with Shakspere would endanger his reputation. As he'd written in the play, he gets MOTE to speak these words of advice: "Master, let me take you a button hole lower. So you not see (COSTARD) is uncasing for the combat? What mean you? You will lose your reputation!" So the make-believe portrayal onstage has indeed become a matter of utter seriousness for Edward de Vere. He feels surrounded: marooned amidst an unfolding, tragic reality. How would he cope?

***

Against the shadowy encroachments, there is real danger that threats to Edward's literary reputation is being usurped by another man in the theatre business. It is, he thinks, too close for comfort! Meanwhile, his wife Elizabeth Trentham gives birth to her first child. Edward is very pleased and names the boy Henry. England is synonymous with Kings named Henry. And, of course, he'd written many plays which he'd titled Henry! He himself is named after a Monarch, King Edward. Now, he names his son after the latest Henry, father of the present Queen. He is overjoyed; for Henry becomes his much desired heir to the Earldom of Oxford. But Henry's birth is a powerful reminder to Edward of his first son's death; and once more, he thinks of his own mortality. Though he is only in his early Forties, he feels remarkably old; a feeling not to his liking. Being active, living to the limit, is what he has been, and is, about. Mentally and physically, he's been in step with all that has been in his gift to do. But the cumulative wear and tear of living at full pelt, at all levels, has taken its toll. He thinks particularly about the dangerous and violent choices that he'd made, and how narrowly he'd escaped death. Overall, he is reminded of the swift and unpredictable passage of time's winged arrow. He takes nothing for granted now in leafy, suburban Stoke Newington. Some days he feels very ill; on other days, past injuries haunt him. Now the shameful thought crosses his mind: That in time Henry would come to know and appreciate the enormous inheritance of money and good name that Earl John had bequeathed; a fine legacy. But what of it? he thinks. What does it really mean in his case; and at this moment? Alas, not very much. He admits his excesses: Being reckless and a squanderer.

From his son Henry, his attention shifts to another family matter. His eldest daughter, Elizabeth, now eighteen years old, and being groomed to be the bride of a boy named Henry Wriothesley, the Earl of Southampton, whom she'd known since she was child. Like Elizabeth, Henry is also a Ward of Court, and will be so until he is twenty one. Thinking of the Wriothesley's proposed marriage to his daughter, Edward is reminded of his own youth; of his vexed, disastrous and painful marriage to Anne Cecil.

The Earl of Southampton is two years older than Elizabeth. Like Edward, he too, lives under the watchful eye of Burghley, who is the arranger of marriages. So far as Edward knows, the handsome, fresh-faced Southampton has a good reputation; no blemishes to disqualify him from being a suitable husband for his daughter. A better suitor, indeed son-in-law, would be hard to find, Edward thinks. He likes Southampton who is well educated and fits in almost all aspects, the requirements of nobility: From hawking and hunting to music and Poetry; refinements that are absolutely necessary. But, as expected, a snag appears: Burghley, as Match-Maker, is bullish. Rather than allow Southampton and Elizabeth the freedom and enough time to get to know each other better, Burghley imposes his own immediate, strict, conservative standard: "Marriage." The sooner the better! This rubs Southampton up the wrong way. And soon mild concern becomes stubbornness. If he'd had good, honourable intentions,Unfortunately Southampton quickly losses interest in getting married to Elizabeth. His refusal displeases Burghley, so much that he wastes no time imposing himself and his usual string-pulling ways. He begins with his fault-finding attacks, one of which is that Southampton fancies *himself* too much. Handsome he is; and, in Edward's opinion he is outstandingly so. Perhaps the handsomest! He is proud of him. But, like Burghley, he too feels that Southampton should move away from self-love. He urges him to marry his daughter and become a parent. These thoughts lodge themselves so deeply in Edward's mind that he begins to write in an unprecedented way: He creates in a new format, and in a sustained way, more than a dozen Sonnets; an intense emotion-charged exercise through which he shows how much he hopes Southampton would get closer to becoming part of his family. Seasoned by age, a mellower Edward writes almost pleadingly:

"When forty winters shall besiege thy brow
And dig deep trenches in thy beauty's field,

Thy youth's proud livery, so gazed on now,
Will be tottered weed of small worth held.
Then being asked where all thy beauty lies -
Where all the treasure of thy lusty days -
To say within thine own deep-sunken eyes
Were an all-eating shame and thriftless praise
How much more praise deserved thy beauty's use,
If thou couldst answer, 'This fair-child of mine
Shall sum my count and make my old excuse'-
Proving his beauty by succession thine,
This were to be new made when thou art old,
And see thy blood warm when thou feel'st it cold."

So with thoughts of his own wild early years, after "forty winters," he reaches out to Southampton. Given that he had wilfully poisoned his married years with jealous rages and bad-tempered behaviour, a son-in-law like Southampton would be the best thing that could happen to him and his daughter. He thinks of them in an advanced way: as having children! "I am old and experienced enough to offer advice," he says to himself. The mellow feeling persists as he commits his thoughts to another Sonnet:

"O! that you were yourself; but love you are
No longer yours than you yourself here live.
Against this coming end you shall prepare,
And your sweat semblance to some other give.
So should that beauty which you had hold in lease
Find no determination – then you were
Yourself again after your self's decease,
When your sweet issue your sweet form should bear...
Against the stormy gusts of winter's day

> And barren rage of death's eternal cold?...
> You had a father, let your son say so."

Since he'd written these Sonnets, Edward's feelings have deepened into fondness for the young Southampton. He remembers being Southampton's age; and how grateful he'd been for the fatherly advice he'd received as a young man, and later on from the Earl of Sussex. Being a father figure is well and good; in deed greatly appreciated. But Edward's feelings for Southampton are neither simple nor straightforward. As his Sonnets reveal, he harbours strange private feelings for Southampton, which surprises and shocks some readers. While relations between Southampton and Edward are good, the sexual undertones expressed by Edward for Southampton is greeted with shock. It is a scandal! Though these Sonnets are his private thoughts committed to paper, they are just one aspect of the mixed emotions Edward feels and expresses poetically as a Sonneteer. So, the relationship between the older man and the youth, encapsulated in the Sonnets, develops beyond a possible marriage of Edward's daughter to Southampton. How could this be? Dark, very dark machinations are at work. The big and present question in all of this is: How would this play out with his enemies?

The potential of these Sonnets to arouse the anger of Puritans who are among Edward's foremost enemies, plays on his mind. In his memory, the Arundell-Howard Libels are still fresh. The charges were of an extreme nature, including his alleged sinful sexual behaviour and necromancy; allegations that were a scandal then; and now promises to be so again.

Meanwhile Edward's prolific pen brings into being more beautiful Sonnets and poems. But, as yet, these writings are, to use his own words, to remain hidden in his "bottom drawers." They are available only for the eyes of a very few. Against this shadowy background, a different picture of Edward emerges. But he is unafraid of his enemies' warped interpretations. Whatever he feels about human relations in all its manifestations, he crafts an epic poem titled: *Venus and Adonis.* So far he has been the recipient of numerous Dedications in books by distinguished authors. But now, he openly Dedicates *Venus and Adonis* to the Earl of Southampton, thus:

"DEDICATION
*To the Right Honourable HENRIE WRIOTHESLEY Earle of Southampton and Baron of Titchfield.*
*RIGHT HONORABLE,*
*I know not how I shall offend in dedicating my unpolisht lines to your Lordship, nor how the worlde will sensure mee for choosing so strong a proppe to support so weake a burthen, onelye if your Honour seeme but pleased, I account my selfe highly praised, a vowe to take advantage of all idle hours' till I haue honoured you with some grauer labour. But if the first heire of my invention proue deformed, I shall be sorry it had so noble a godfather: The neuer after heire so barren a land, for feare it yield me still so bad a harvest leaue it to your Honorable suruey, and your Honor to your hearts content which I wish and the world's hopefull expectation.*
*Your Honors* in *all dutie.*
WILLIAM SHAKESPEARE."

What is that graver labour ("grauer labour") that he hints at? In his Poem, he retells the ancient story of *Venus and Adonis* and recounts the myth of two lovers: A hunter and the Goddess of Love. As in Ovid's original story, the couple meet and fall in love. But, ADONIS disobeys VENUS and goes off to hunt wild boar. Alas, he is killed; and the unhappy VENUS mourns him. In Edward's portrayal of the tale, Queen Elizabeth is portrayed as VENUS and Southampton as ADONIS, who faces the challenge of gaining and keeping Elizabeth's ever-shifting feelings and favour.

As Edward intends, *Venus and Adonis* promotes less active participation and more meditational spectating, poetically stated. In Lyly's view, as well as other writers, though the reader is told little or nothing, he is expected to see and hear most, if not everything. As the story unfolds, VENUS attempts to kiss ADONIS, but he avoids doing so. Her "thousand kisses buys my heart from me," is Edward's reference to his one thousand pounds yearly Grant. Her warm, gentle kisses are beguiling. They are metaphors both of warning and the potential penalties that may arise from Elizabeth's behaviour. So the young Earl of Southampton should be careful about the Queen's attention. From his own experience, Edward warns of her "red lips." Given that VENUS is more active than ADONIS, she tries hard to get ADONIS to kiss her; and not surprisingly in Titian's painting of *Venus and Adonis*, ADONIS couldn't care less about VENUS who assures him that their love secret is safe.

"Art thou ashamed to kiss? then wink again;
And I will wink; so shall the day seem night
Love keeps his revels where they are but twain;
Be bold to play, our sport is not in sight."

ADONIS is overwhelmed with attention: With seductive kisses symbolised by extraordinary financial generosity. He writes:

"To sell myself I can be well contented…
A thousand kisses buys my heart from me,

And pay them at thy leisure, one by one.
What is ten thousand touches unto thee?
Are they not quickly told and quickly gone?"

VENUS'S kisses are sweet, but they are also the Queen's loving form of control. In this way, she keeps ADONIS in a tender trap. Her demanding, all-conquering lips wins his lips obedience. What language these words are. They continue:

"Paying what ransom the insulter willeth;
Whose vulture thought doth pitch the price so high
That she will draw his lips' rich treasure dry."

But all good things must end; and the Wild Boar, the beast that kills ADONIS, snatches him away. This is another reference to himself as the Earl of Oxford on whose Heraldic Crest is imprinted such a beast. Of ADONIS'S death by the boar, VENUS says:

"'Tis he, foul creature, that hath done thee wrong:
I did but act, he's author of thy slander:...
Grief hath two tongues, and never woman yet
Could rule them both without ten women's wit...
But this foul, grim and urchin-snouted boar,
Whose downward eye still looketh for a grave,
Ne'er saw the beauteous livery that he (Adonis) wore,
Witness the entertainment that he gave."

So Edward's poem *Venus and Adonis* follows the Ovidian story, but the secret message of his relations with Queen Elizabeth is embedded therein. He is surprised by the public response to *Venus and Adonis*. "A very large number of copies have been sold," Lyly says. "And more are being bought each day. This public attention looks set to continue." A pleasant smile of satisfaction lights up Edward's face. This increasingly rare expression makes him look more handsome. "You should smile more often," Lyly thinks, but does not speak.

***

This publishing success of *Venus and Adonis* is unusual. The poem spawns many, and predictably, different responses. Suspicions are aroused about the real people who are portrayed through Edward's use of the Ovidian myth. These are tricky, even dangerous times, in terms of Puritanism and censorship. Edward's ears are close to the ground. He listens for rumblings. His eyes are on the look out. A man named Williams Reynolds comes forward. Though he is seen as a public ranter, he takes a step further away from his ordinary street corner position: He writes to Lord Burghley. In his letter, he identifies the Queen as VENUS, who greatly desires to kiss Adonis. She "woos him… telling him that although she is old, yet she is lusty; fresh and moist and full of life…" He ends: "And her footsteps not seen: And much ado with red and white." These colours, as Edward knows, represent the Royal House of Tudor, and in particular the Tudor Rose. But the question arises: Is *Venus and Adonis* a smutty, sexually charged poem as Reynolds declares with Queen Elizabeth at the heart of it. While it is true in the poem that Venus is desperate to kiss Adonis, Edward thinks, this allegation against Elizabeth as aggressive and with sexual overtones, is dangerous. Has Reynolds gone a step too far? And, what does Burghley think of it? Soon, Reynolds fate is sealed: He is charged as being of unsound mind. And so the best-selling *Venus and Adonis* becomes controversial: Just the thing that Edward's enemies are hoping for: Now they engage in a Literary War.

Gabriel Harvey, the highly accomplished man of letters takes up the cudgels after Reynolds. In his literary hostility toward Edward and Thomas Nashe, Harvey lambasts Edward's "Dedication" to Southampton in *Venus and Adonis* and publishes a pamphlet in which he refers to the authors Thomas Nashe and "Pierce Penniless."

But who is "Pierce Penniless"? Harvey exposes him as Edward de Vere! This is a blow well below the belt. Harvey's standing in the literary world is such that he knows who is who? If he is right about Edward being "Pierce Penniless," the signature "WILLIAM SHAKESPEARE at the end of the Dedication to the Earl of Southampton in *Venus and Adonis* points to a misunderstanding of the author as being an entirely different person! But, as Edward alone knows and proudly says of his epic poem, "I leave it to your Honourable survey, and Your Honour to your heart's content which I wish may always answer your own wish and the world's expectation."

The "world's expectation!" indeed. And so, for better or worse, from then onward, the name WILLIAM SHAKESPEARE as a poet, enters the vocabulary of English literature.

***

# XI

## "Good name in man and woman is the immediate jewel of their souls"

"Ah, Lyly! Do come in," Edward says. He ushers his Secretary into his large living room.

"Good of you to make the trip to see me."

"Thank you, My Lord. It is my pleasure," Lyly says as he is guided towards a nearby chair.

He sits opposite Edward at a wooden table.

"It is not a bad journey from the centre, from the hustle and bustle of the city to this suburban area of London," Edward says. "Is it?"

"Not bad at all," Lyly says. "My horse behaved well all the way. He seemed to have enjoyed the outing. And the road, paths and tracks from Aldersgate are in good order, I must say."

From a bag, Lyly retrieves a notebook and a bundle of papers.

"Since you left Fisher's Folly," Lyly says, "I've been meaning to bring these for you."

Almost at once, during this exchange, Lyly and his former regular employer lapses into an easy-going, respectful, but friendly banter. Tea is served; and they talk for a long while about plays and new productions. To a limited degree, the conservative Lyly and the more free-thinking Edward, touch upon the latest political intrigues. It is late afternoon and before dusk falls, Lyly gets ready to leave. Edward sees him to the door. Lyly mounts his horse and says: "How quiet and peaceful it is here. It is a delightful country retreat. So unlike Fisher's Folly where we spent so many wonderful days and years!"

"Yes," Edward says, "You can be sure, the memories linger."

"But, my Lord, I am very pleased to have come here to see you. My spirits are lifted: Thanks for inviting me!

This area is off the beaten track for me, alright. But I know where you are and how to find you!"

As Lyly waves goodbye, Edward stands at the doorway thinking of the journey, both intellectual and physical that he's made from Fisher's Folly to this leafy part of London.

***

In the peaceful retreat that Edward shares with his wife memories crowd in. There are days now when the pain in his leg stops him in his tracks: It checks his movement. The slight limp is becoming more cumbersome and noticeable. He sees this as humbug, as irritating. He hates it as if he is being told how he should think. Body and soul; mind and body are never separate things for him! He realises, afresh, how central physical and mental freedoms are to him. Life has been the stage upon which he's been playing his parts. But, at every turn, it has been a challenge. He acknowledges, his privileges; and yes, he's very proud and honoured to be one of the members of the illustrious de Vere family.

Queen Elizabeth is sixty years old. And as she prepares to celebrate her thirty-fifth year as Monarch, she remembers her early years of being troubled by ill-health, as well as by the fears and uncertainties that had surrounded her as a young Princess. But now as celebrations of the Anniversary of her

Coronation approaches, quite rightly, she sees it as hugely significant: She is hit hard by the laudable fact that she has survived three decades as Monarch. And, for Edward too, as playwright and lover of history, the Queen's survival proves her toughness which deserves to be celebrated. She has outshone the Tudors, and, with the exception of her father, King Henry VIII, she has reigned for longer than any Tudor Monarch. But not content just to sit on her Throne, she pushes forward to ensure that England and herself would enjoy wealth and power. So now, though older, faded and worn, but no less cunning and chameleon-like than she had been in the past, Edward sees his Queen as having reached the pinnacle of her life and career. He acknowledges, and credits, her pedigree as being the greatest of the Tudors; a Dynasty that not only ended the War of the Roses, but also instituted the Anglican Church that had dominated and generated new ways of thinking that is opening up an English Renaissance. This cultural shift, in turn, had laid the basis for steady English overseas encroachments: The formation and expansion of an Empire. It is a time too, when the books and language of Empire takes on new meaning in the reimaging, and thus, reshaping of the British Isles.

But alas, from the peak of pomp and glory, Queen Elizabeth's days are numbered. Edward senses, and witnesses, the gradual slippage of power from her, as well as the nervousness and excitement of her trusted minister Lord Burghley, as he and members of his regime prepare for power. Though the Coronation anniversary matches expectations, much sadness is mingled with the celebrations.

Having lived for most of his life close to Queen Elizabeth, Edward knows the shape and contours of her thin, long face. He reflects on how resplendent and regal she'd looked when he first saw her as a boy. But now, Courtiers and visiting dignitaries still feel it is their duty, to some extent, to pretend that she is the most radiant Star in the firmament. Any young man seeking Royal favour is expected to act as if she is still both supremely powerful, as well as beautiful. For her part, she wears clothes which she hopes would add allure to her body and personality; and, because of her love for sweet treats, the price she pays for over indulgence and neglect is that her teeth turns colour and begins to decay. Being self-conscious, she is embarrassed by the condition of her mouth. But though surrounded by her Ministers, Courtiers and Administrators, she does not let up; she speaks as befits her supreme Majestic role. This is one of her great strengths, which is just as well. But, with the passing of time, many things have changed. Bad breath is symptomatic, and she deals with it: But it does not stop her from seeing herself as she really is now!

Edward knows his Queen intimately. And thus far, in a few plays, he has been able to combine elements of her persona in various characters. As the joyous noise of Coronation celebration rings in his ears; Edward hears another less audible sound heralding a slow, but relentless shift of power. Many Courtiers look ahead and asks questions: Who will inherit Elizabeth's coveted Crown? And more curiously, how did she become Queen in the first place? How had she kept the Crown on her head over these years? Altogether, these questions add up to versions of neither a pleasant nor an uplifting story. Past deeds play on Edward's mind, as he too, dares to think about the candidates who might succeed Elizabeth as Monarch.

He remembers the beheaded Mary, Queen of Scots son, James; and for quite a while, he is again troubled by her Trial; the one-sided brutality of it. If James does become a credible contender for the English Crown, and wins it, Edward asks himself: "How would he fare?" It is a question which sets in train many more: "What would be the position of today's

Nobles and Court favourites? Who, among Elizabeth's favourites, would remain in high standing? Who would be falling from grace? Who are the newcomers upon whom the next King would bestow gifts, as well as elevation, to enviable positions of power? And who would find themselves out in the cold altogether?" These are troublesome questions for hundreds of people of this Elizabethan social class.

In the struggles relating to the Succession - especially in the two years past - two main factions have emerged. They jostle more and more aggressively for power as the ageing Queen's health declines.

On one side, Sir Robert Cecil, at the age of thirty, guided by his father, spear-heads devoted support from Nobles, Gentlemen, Spies and Informers; on the other, there is a Personality-Cult following for the Earl of Essex. While Robert Cecil continues his rise to power on the connections and networks laid down by his father, Lord Burghley, Essex, on the death of his step-father, the Earl of Leicester, has risen to become one of the Queen's favourite Courtiers. He soon realises this relationship is a blessing, as well as a burden. Thus, the Leicester-Cecil power struggles of old, continues. As the rival factions eye-ball each other, Robert Cecil exerts his own authority. He meets a man named Robert Poley, a Spy of some experience. He hires Poley and a number of Agent-hit-men to strenghten his father's established spy operations. Given that Robert Cecil's training has been long and thorough, he could not be better-placed. To his credit, he is a good listener who had learned well from Burghley; and now that fearful Cecil legacy brings Poley back into Service.

*

So who is Robert Poley? He is none other than one of the

team that had earlier planned and carried out the downfall of Mary, Queen of Scots. Before she was entrapped, Poley had held a dinner in a London Tavern to which he'd invited the conspirators. By all accounts, Poley was good at hosting dinners for unsuspecting victims. Of this talent, no one is more impressed than Robert Cecil. He likes the affable, canny Poley, who excitedly relates how he'd caught the Queen of Scots.

"I wined and dined the Conspirators," Poley tells Cecil. "And, during the evening, after dinner, while there was much movement, I was successful in arousing a degree of trust among the diners. When all trace of suspicion was gone, I pounced upon them. Like rats in a trap."

Robert Cecil's eyes lit up. "What a perfect outcome," he says. "You saved Elizabeth's Crown! I congratulate you, as indeed my father has already done."

Robert shakes Poley's hand, firmly, vigorously. "But since that stratagem," Robert says, "some things at Court have got better; some worse." Poley's ears pricked. He's keen to hear every word of what Robert is about to say: "I am, as you know, finally briefed about your excellent work; notably, your most recent whereabouts." From his desk drawer, he lifts a sheet of paper and brings it closer to his face. He scans, then he reads: "Here it is recorded," he says, "that 'between last December and March of this year you had spent several weeks at James's Court. Is that correct?' "

"Yes, Sir Robert," Poley says. "Things, as you know Sir Robert, are tense and getting worse. The factions are stepping-up their opposition and aggression. We must hold our ground by all means. We must defeat our enemies who are never far away. They lurk here, there and, it seems, everywhere."

Poley stands erect, military fashion, like a soldier. The correct, respectful stance, Robert thinks, and smiles appreciably. Poley is ready for war. He waits for Robert, to speak. "I have another job for you," Robert says. Poley waits in silence. "As you are privy," Robert says, "the man who pays you, Sir Thomas Heneage, is on our side – I mean the Cecil Faction. With such a friend and ally like Sir Thomas, your activity of 'rydeing' and 'knowledge-gathering' would provide the intelligence that I think is necessary to keep the Cecil Faction at the heart of power. In this way, we move forward to make possible a new era that would follow the Succession of a new Monarch to the English throne.

Those engaged in the power struggle know that establishing links with Scotland relating to the possibility of King James's Accession to the English throne, is treason. Queen Elizabeth is Monarch. She alone Rules. She dislikes any talk of being replaced. She forbids discussion of her Succession. But each passing day is a reminder that among those holding High positions in her Government, there is increasing tension and readiness as members of one faction tries to gain advantage over the other. For these aspirants, nothing, and no one, is entirely safe or can be trusted. On the contrary, everything is fraught with danger: Who is enemy? Who is friend?" Robert pauses. He and his father know they cannot take anything for granted in the Elizabethan power game. They must fight to keep their places in their threatened rankings. Now Robert looks thoughtful. Then, he says to Poley:

"These are your orders." He lowers his voice, a tone. "Your task is to seek out and destroy a man whose star is rising fast. He is well known but…" Robert stops again. "*This man* is *very dangerous*," he continues. "Why is he dangerous?" Poley wonders, but keeps his silence. As if reading Poley's mind, Robert adds: "This man knows too much. He knows about our Faction and…" Robert's voice trails off. Then, he says, "He knows about you, Poley. He knows about your 'rydeings.' "

Robert is careful not to stray too far away from his strict allegiance to the Crown. Any contact with James of Scotland would be seen as subversive. He knows that for anyone on either side of the power struggle, any communication with Scotland concerning James's potential Succession of Queen Elizabeth to England's throne, the penalty is nothing less than Treason. And woe betide anyone so charged. Poley is in no doubt: He knows what is at stake. Like his employer Robert, he understands that aside from Elizabeth's vanity, the thought of her being replaced as Monarch is unbearable. For his part, Robert is ready to do anything to defend his Queen. He is very careful not to rub salt in her wounds; or, in any way, add to her anxieties and thus further weaken her ageing body. Her safety, and thus the protection of her Realm, specially as Robert Cecil's faction sees it, is paramount.

Finally Robert says to Poley: "Report back to me, as soon as you can."

"Yes, Sir Robert," Poley says, still standing stiffly. He turns on his heels, and dutifully leaves Robert Cecil's presence.

*

Meanwhile, as Edward writes and consults Lyly on business matters, elsewhere in London, at a Tavern in Deptford, Poley hosts a Dinner Party to which he invites two other Agents, who works for Sir Thomas Walsingham. Together, all three men drink wine and dine with their intended target: Their Guest, the "dangerous man" referred to by Sir Robert Cecil. That person Poley now knows is a "part-time Agent," who had himself been accused of communicating with King James of Scotland. From earlier enquiries, Poley learns that this "Agent" had recently testified before the Star Chamber; and, had been released on bail while investigations continue. Poley understands that this Agent's release is timely. Why? "Because," as Robert had said to him, "the Agent had been released to avoid him giving testimony that may have exposed our Agents and the under-cover dealings of the Cecil faction."

So, much like Poley's previous dinner party, on the face of it, this one is also a friendly, sociable meeting. It could even have been seen by an unsuspecting observer as some sort of comradely celebration. Poley bides his time. Towards the end of the evening, when the bill is presented to the diners for payment, strong words are exchanged. A fight breaks out. In the melee, a dagger is drawn and the suspected Agent is stabbed. The injured man falls to the floor and dies. The only witnesses to this act are Poley and his fellow Agents.

The victim of the attack is Christopher Marlowe, the famous playwright, who is at the height of his popularity among theatre-goers in London. He was a brilliant story-teller; a talkative person with liberal, even republican views. As such, he'd become a marked man; and, as an Agent he was seen by some as a risk. A few of his more secretive, less open associates had questioned a few of his unguarded comments, especially about things he might, or might not, be saying about the Cecils? Now, in the wake of his horrific death in the Deptford Tavern, many more questions are being asked. One, in particular, which Edward asks himself, is this: "Is Marlowe's murder really part of the strategy adopted in the bitter factional disputes?" And, in so far as he knows, none of the Agents who were present in the Deptford Tavern has been charged or punished. Why? Because there are those like Robert Cecil, who knows that Poley and his Agents are quite rightly following the dictates of powerful men in the higher echelons of Government and society that could have been exposed if Marlowe had lived to reappear before the Star Chamber.

When Edward had first heard of Marlowe's murder he was

(and still is) stunned. It is a death, close to home, so to speak: A fellow-playwright is brutally killed. He knows why; and he feels no need to be reminded of the fierce power struggle rooted in these tense manoeuverings. He considers moments spent with the ebullient, if a touch boastful, Marlowe. Apart from his role as Secret Agent, he was also the only serious literary competition Elizabethan England could offer to his own work. Marlowe had, over a few brief years, revealed the great potential of dramatic culture in England. Of this, Edward needs no reminders for he'd been raised by his father's Troupe of Players and recognises Courtly performances as the ultimate purpose of the Courtier's upbringing, education and theatrical endeavours. In this, Earl John had taught him well to serve Queen and country. Thus his main aim has been, and now is, to write more innovative plays that would catch the eye and conscience of the Monarch. "The play is the thing," he says to himself. He had long followed this guiding thought and now, more than ever, he sees the play as absolutely essential; his lifeblood! The popularity and acclaim of Marlowe's *Tamburlaine and Doctor Faustus* makes him think harder.

He compares the success of Marlowe's plays with the works of the Euphuist-inspired writers, as well as the Queen's Men's Players' contributions and he finds the latter, to be lacking in movement and substance. But after all is said and done, Marlowe's passing is cause for pause, as he, the English historical playwright *par excellence*, takes stock of himself and surveys the scene.

He considers the English theatre which favours traditional Court Comedies and admits that such conservative, old-fashioned voices like John Lyly's and George Peel's are still around and could be relied upon to produce more of the same. So having taken a broad, futuristic view, he appreciates Marlowe's contribution. He understands the need for taking new directions; for combining the old with the new. "English Renaissance Man," he feels is a worthy expression; a goal that he's been aiming at for years. But, there is more to do. The sad, tragic end of Marlowe's life is a kind of watershed for him. It provokes a reappraisal of his life generally, especially now, as a few fellow-writers spreads a rumour that he is, or has been, ill and retired! But even if it is just a rumour, such talk makes him uncomfortable. The other thing that spreads alarmingly, is the plague. Illness – or God forbid, death - could spell the most untimely disaster for him. For one thing, it will give all the added encouragement that Will Shakspere so badly desires in pursuit of his usurpation of the plays of Edward de Vere, including those penned as "William Shakespeare."

So while the news of Marlowe's death sends shock waves throughout the theatrical community, it is a sharp reminder to Edward of his own mortality. It justifies his view of the stage as a metaphor for life in the round! Of Comedies and Tragedies, he'd written several. But now his imagination soars as he takes a hard look at the quality and potential of his work, which brings him closer to himself as a playwright. He sees afresh the play's possibilities: Its inherent power to touch the human heart and soul. Now, the sharp reminders of more pain in his leg, brings a renewed sense of his fragility and life's end; and thus a greater awareness of the need and urgency to fulfil his literary ambition.

***

Writing, he knows, is synonymous with publication. At this time, his attention is drawn to a London printer, John Danter, who Registers a new "booke" titled *A Noble Roman Historye of Tytus Andronicus.* Why is this significant? Because it is Edward's *first published* play-script. Interestingly, it is described as a violent drama reminiscent of Marlowe's dark outlook. But there is no mention of the author's name in the "booke." Nonetheless among those associated with the plays performance are Edward's associates: The Earls of Derby, Pembroke and Sussex.

Three months later, Theatre Manager, Philip Henslowe places on record a performance by the Queen's Men and Sussex's Men of the play *King Leare*. He also records that two other Troupes (the Admiral's Men and the newly formed Lord Chamberlain's Men) had performed a play called *Hamlet*. This is a significant time which sees not only his *King Leare* performed, but also his *Hamlet*. Productions of both plays, within months of each other, is a huge advancement. How could this be explained? It is likely there is no one factor to account for this positive shift. Edward knows that one of his strengths as a playwright is his imaginative use of combining elements of different personalities into believable, rounded characters, as well as bringing together aspects of different stories, into a coherent composition. And now that various factors coalesce, at last, he enjoys a settled married life. But amidst the stability and tranquillity of having a home and the pleasures of a companion and wife, he feels with some sadness, a greater sense of the fleetingness of life that is, in large part, prompted by Marlowe's death and his own infirmities. Altogether, at times, these thoughts verging on morbidity, stirs his capricious passion for life; and thus a new wave of creativity.

***

Edward uses the bedrock of experience to create new plays. Now, he faces new twists and turns as Burghley engages with matching up his grand-daughter Elizabeth as a marriage partner for the Earl of Southampton. This does not go well. The young Earl pleads that he is not ready for matrimony. He refuses

Burghley's proposition. But his decision has consequences. It risks the displeasure of, and alienation from, the powerful House of Cecil. Edward wonders how much Southampton knows about the Royal Court's factional tensions; and how quickly positions change and continue to shift.

After refusing to join the de Vere and Cecil families through matrimony, Southampton's widowed mother, Mary Browne Wriothesley, makes the opposite move. As Dowager Countess of Southampton, she plans to marry into the Cecil Clan. Her husband to be is Sir Thomas Heneage; the man who pays Robert Poley. Heneage is an ally of the Cecil faction. For Mary Browne Wriothesley, the wedding is a smart move. Why? Because Heneage is also a rich and powerful landowner; and through her marriage, she would secure for her family a close connection with the Cecil Clan. But how would her example be received by her son? So far, nothing has yet been decided.

Meanwhile, as Edward observes the shifting power game with his usual, penetrating gaze and concern, he knows that what Heneage owns would one day change hands; especially the Forest of Waltham and Havering Park that had traditionally been the property of the Earls of Oxford. Edward longs for these lands to be returned to him. He and Heneage had studied law at Gray's Inn and had, over the years, kept good relations. Now, as Heneage gets older, Edward is not without hope: "Who knows?" he says to himself. "Those properties may one day be mine; and rightfully, Earl of Oxford's possessions once again."

He remembers another connection that he has with Heneage: The love of plays which gives Heneage great excitement and enjoyment. So Edward's optimism grows when he realises that Heneage holds the top position of an ambitious new theatrical Troupe of players, which aims at bringing the Best Actors and theatre administrators in the Realm under one organisation.

Edward is encouraged; and is enthusiastic about the new direction that the English theatre is taking: not only in the kind of plays being written, but also the new Companies of Actors that have come into existence. He notes, for example, that The Lord Chamberlain's Men have England's finest actors: Tragedians and Comedians. As news of this Company and the rise of popular entertainment on stage spreads, the star actors and the stories they tell on stage are increasingly warmly welcomed by a wide cross-section of the theatre-going public.

At this time of heightened interest, since Will Shakspere's arrival in London in search of work as an Actor, he'd not shown a high level of competence, never mind outstanding ability. Knowing this, he prefers not to pit his lack of talent with the leading actors of the day, but to chart a career more in keeping with his ability and interest.

Shakspere veers to the less creative side of the theatre world: To business and administration. From the knowledge he gains, and the contacts he makes, wily-nily he eases himself into becoming a kind of Theatrical Player-manager with an eye to rising through the ranks as a broker of plays and even a theatre share-holder! So being deficient as an actor, Shakspere profits as the theatre business expands: He sees and seizes new opportunities. He realises that with few competitors around, he has a richer talent: a canny business acumen. Exploiting this is a timely change of direction as slowly, he combines his minimal acting with certain managerial tasks. Soon the prospect of becoming a theatre stakeholder, beckons. This would give him a toe-hold, at least. But he wants more. He would love to have a foot-hold: and access to meeting the good and the great in the theatrical world. To achieve this, he is willing to be flexible. With an eye on expanding his business ventures, he exploits loop-holes and quickly strengthens his theatre ambitions. There is money to be made; and Shakspere as part of the successful Lord Chamberlain's Men, plays a central co-ordinating role as Theatrical-Player-Manager-cum-shareholder.

He undertakes greater responsibility as his popularity grows. Knowing the importance of finance and funding in the theatre, Shakspere puts his money where his mouth is, so to speak: He continues to talk to theatre-goers about "his plays" before and after performances. With repetition of his idle boast, Shakespere feels empowered as he works himself in: Working cheek by jowl with an active successful Troupe of Players he becomes better known and thus more prominent. From the side-lines, Edward's enemies see this development as a good thing! But for Edward, concern is a key word. "How ironic a story this is?" he questions himself. Then he thinks of what he'd heard about Shakspere's aspirations to be an actor. On that matter, so far, he has failed. He is neither a competent or successful treader of the boards! Edward has never admitted speaking to Shakspere; in the main, perhaps because of his status as a Nobleman. Social class and disparity between Aristocrats and Others in these status-conscious Feudal times, is pronounced. But now, as Shakspere brings another one of Edward's "Anonymously" written plays into production and performance, Edward recalls what Lyly had said to him: "Have you met the Stratford man, yet?"

"No, I haven't," Edward had said, with more than a hint of irritation. He and Lyly had been preparing a production of *Hamlet.* And in it, Lyly tells Edward, he had cast Shakspere to play the part of the GHOST!

Since those earlier, heady days of writing and play production, Edward has withdrawn somewhat from the theatre world to his retreat in Stoke Newington. Meanwhile, Shakspere's star, so to speak, as Theatre-Manager-Stakeholder rises steadily. He becomes more daring; even boastful. And more news about the "Upstart Crow" fills Edward with a nagging worry, and disgust too.

***

Spring approaches. It is Edward's favourite time of year: He loves flowers: It is a time when the sap rises, buds open and roses of many colours blossom. It is a time too, when he feels a little more hopeful, as perhaps he should. Why? Because there is a new-found sense of excitement in the Theatre world as the number of play-goers continue to rise. There is much to celebrate, Edward thinks. For the marriage of Heneage and Mary Browne Wriothesley, appropriately, his play *A Midsummer Night's Dream* is to be performed by the Lord Chamberlain's Men. The performance will take place on the night before the wedding; and its timing becomes more meaningful because it is like so many of Edward's dramas; a story rich in symbolism, as well as message. While *A Midsummer Night's Dream* deals with misunderstanding of identity, its main theme is about the marriage of two people formely from opposing factions. Thus Heneage is depicted as the DUKE OF THESEUS and Mary Browne Wriothesley as HIPPOLYTA. The lesson of the play for the strong-willed Earl of Southampton is as Edward had intended: That Southampton should follow his mother, and through marriage, join the Cecil family. So in the play, THESEUS mirrors what Edward is hoping for from the young Southampton: That he should marry, become a parent and thus preserve his blood line:

> "THESEUS:...Earthlier happy is the rose distill'd
> Than that which, withering on the Virgin thorn
> Grows, loves and dies in single blessedness."

While the play's performance is specifically for the older

couple: Heneage and Mary Browne Wriothesley, who may not have been planning to have children, nonetheless, its symbolism extends beyond Edward's wish for Southampton, to other real people like himself and the Queen. Though the play was drafted and written almost ten years before, when he was writing of real events, it seems like a dream now while Shakspere, the second-rate actor foregrounds himself in the public gaze. Edward is not amused; and words he'd written in *Othello* comes to mind. "He who steals my purse, steals trash…"

So on the night before the marriage of Heneage and Mary Browne Wriothesley, *A Midsummer Night's Dream* is performed. The script is flexible. It allows for a Will Shakspere-like character who manipulates things to suit his own designs. Thus, the Crow-like Impersonator persists in crowing! In this magic-spinning play, Edward uses a sub-plot to reflect the "Upstart Crow's" presence and role in theatrical activities. Shakspere is clearly Edward's target: An ordinary actor-player who wants to be an accomplished actor. Edward transforms the star BOTTOM into an ass with whom queen TITANIA falls in love. And, as with Shakspere, who experiences the pleasures of becoming better known and the high life, BOTTOM too, a man of lower order, has a taste of Royal life. "Mistaken identities" is a catch all!

Edward de Vere the Nobleman-playwright has had a Princely upbringing, and given his closeness to Queen Elizabeth, the Courtiers and Court, as his writings show: "One writes best about what one knows." No wonder, he writes about life at the Royal Court like no other playwright. Such a claim raises the question: Could Will Shakspere of Stratford have written this play? Perhaps not. But in the play, Edward reveals the real experience of his much-rumoured flirtatious, amorous relations with the Queen in his earlier "dancing" years. He was close enough to her; but be that as it may, how strange it is that two decades later, *A Midsummer Night's Dream's* vision of a Faerie Queen playing around with an ass, must seem. Now, Edward reads lines he'd written:

"TITANIA: Come sit thee down upon this flowery bed,
While I thy amiable cheeks do coy,
And stick musk roses in thy sleek smooth head,
And kiss thy fair large ears, my gentle joy."

Soon the magic spell ends. And as BOTTOM, the Clown with the ass's head returns to his human form, and TITANIA to the fairy world, BOTTOM reflects upon a most rare vision.

"I have had a dream, past the wit of man to say what dream it was…Man is but a patched fool if he will offer to say what methought I had. The eye of Man hath not heard, the ear of man hath not seen, man's hand is not able to taste, his tongue to conceive, nor his heart to report what my dream was. I will get Peter Quince to write a ballad of the dream. It shall be called 'Bottom's Dream,' because it has no bottom…"

So this entertaining play of shape-shifting identities engenders equally diverse and profound interpretations from witnesses of its performance. While it celebrates a notable wedding, it sounds an alarm bell for Edward de Vere as the author of this, and his other plays and epic poems as *William Shakespeare.*

Concurrently as Shakspere's business dabblings and dealings expands, more and more, he becomes an integral figure in the Lord Chamberlain's Men Troupe. His social status appreciates; he meets Courtiers and Aristocrats, who are play-lovers. He can hardly believe his luck: No longer does he think of himself as a second-rate actor. He feels emboldened and aggressively promotes himself as a man of the theatre within the Lord Chamberlain's Men Troupe, whose productions increasingly gives his claims on "Anonymous" plays, legitimacy. No one challenges him. Edward is aghast. But there is nothing he could do to stop the theft as Shakspere thrives and wallows in the overall buzz he gets while consolidating his position as part of the Acting Troupe. But though he tinkers with the "Anonymous" plays, for all his exaggerated self worth, he is not known as a Writer. Never mind being a stage-worthy playwright! Nonetheless, he buys and sells play scripts and after hiring writers to alter scripts of plays, he says: "These play-productions are my own!" Thus Edward's Anonymous plays opens the way for Shakspere to claim authorship! But while Shakspere gains a reputation, Court insiders, as well as actors and writers, know that Shakspere is, as Gray had warned, the "Upstart Crow" parading in the feathers of someone else. So, in this make-believe world of the theatre, the whispers growing ever-louder about Shakspere's usurpation and ownership claims, neither pleases nor amuses Edward. As if this is not worrying enough for him, there is another blatantly obvious thing: The similarity of the names Shakspere and Shakespeare: They are too close to differentiate sufficiently, or clearly, who the real author is from the Imposter!

Like the character BOTTOM in *A Midsummer Night's Dream*, Edward seems to be waking-up from a "Dream" of his own. Or, is it a nightmare? For make no mistake about it, Will Shakspere is becoming much too well-known.

***

The Heneage-Mary Browne Wriothesly marriage related performance of *A Midsummer Night's Dream* goes well; and Edward realises that the play is no simple dream. He is reminded of the dramatic power of his pen. Since the death of his father and the Earl of Sussex (a father-figure) Edward had not had a close confidante. Now, in a quiet way, he confides to himself that only he could write such a play. But, as he tries to come to terms with this, he feels constrained by the conventions of his time; by having to use "Anonymous," as well as other Pen-names, to obscure and thus protect himself. It is a door through which Shakspere is now passing in and out, at will and with rising bravado. Edward reconsiders how fundamental history and experience are to his plays and poems. And for this, in large part, his first teacher, Arthur Golding must be thanked.

So if *A Midsummer Night's Dream* was meant, not simply as a wedding celebration, but also to nudge Southampton towards marrying Elizabeth de Vere, its success was partial. But, as father of the potential bride, Edward is not easily fobbed-off. Soon after the wedding, he makes another attempt with his pen: With remarkable determination and skill, as a poet, once more, he writes another epic poem: *Lucrece*. Soon after completion, he sends the work to John Harrison, the bookseller and publisher. Harrison reads the manuscript, then answers the call to meet with the author.

"My Lord Oxford," Harrison says, "I'll be happy to publish your poem, *Lucrece*. I think it will be successful. I am very hopeful. I think it will be like your *Venus and Adonis:* another bestseller!"

Soon after their meeting, *Lucrece* is published; and later Edward visits Harrison's shop.

"Lucrece," Edward says to Harrison, "as you know, is the sequel to *Venus and Adonis.*"

"My Lord, why the title, Lucrece?" Harrison asks.

"Lucrece," Edward says, "because it is Classical. I have set the tale in Classical times. It is an allegory about the fall of

Rome's ruling elite. And, as intended, like *Venus and Adonis*, *Lucrece*, is an epic too. As you see," he speaks now in a low tone and in utter confidence, "I have Dedicated *Venus* to the Earl of Southampton. Putting my poems in print under the Pen-name WILLIAM SHAKESPEARE is a first for me. And, I dare say, for readers too! Please know that the spelling of my Pen-name Shakespeare is different from a similar name that is circulating in the theatre world. Privately, I have been using "Shakespeare" for a while. But never, until now, has it appeared *in print*! But..." he pauses. "The idea behind the printing of *Venus and Adonis* and *Lucrece*," he adds, "is that it should serve as a warning to Southampton, not to reject the chance to become part of the De Vere-Cecil's family."

Dedicating his poem *Venus and Adonis* to someone is a very rare thing for Edward to have done. It means a great deal to him. Until now he had been the recipient of "Dedications" from the most distinguished authors around. Before *Venus and Adonis* was printed to maintain his cover, it was his Secretary Lyly who had taken the manuscript to Harrison. Now, he says to Harrison, "Here is the *original* manuscript of my Dedication."

"My Lord, what I had seen before *Venus and Adonis* was printed was a copy of a copy," Harrison says.

Edward hands him the original document. Respectfully, Harrison slowly reads the DEDICATION. He notes, in particular the capital letters WILLIAM SHAKESPEARE at the bottom of the page. He hands the Dedication back saying: "Thank you, My Lord." Before he and Edward part company, Harrison was in no doubt whatsoever about the first printing of the signature "WILLIAM SHAKESPEARE." It was chosen by Edward to send the clearest possible message to the public that, as it appears in *Venus and Adonis* and *Lucrece*, he wishes to be known hence by his new Pen-name "WILLIAM

SHAKESPEARE." For days he was utterly absorbed by this signature change. It was an historic moment; a disguise that will help Edward to become bolder in following his family's Motto of Truth-telling.

So his use of the name William Shakespeare, arising from a reference to him made by Gabriel Harvey as the man who "Shakes-spears," now offers him the protective shield he needs to say what he feels; especially because the Truth he tells is unsparing and unadorned. So once and for all, he draws a line between himself and the Imposter from Stratford. He makes it clear that "William Shakespeare" is not Will Shakspere. On the contrary, he is a very different person. So much had he hoped for Southampton's acceptance of his daughter as his wife that with grave honesty he'd inscribed his Dedication, which coincides with the change in Pen-name. Thus WILLIAM SHAKESPEARE is printed in large capital letters. Such and unmissable signature is unusual, but absolutely necessary, he thinks. It is the layer of protective cover for his identity, which he hopes will stick. But, in spite of his hopes and beautifully expressed feelings, Southampton stands firm against marriage to his daughter Elizabeth. To the question: Why? Southampton does not say much more than: "I am not ready for marriage."

For honesty and devotion, Edward cannot be faulted. But, as he knows a major weakness in trying to persuade Southampton to marry, is his relative poverty in terms of offering a large dowry, because of his lack of substantial properties. "But what about my full Inheritance?" he asks himself. He'd already sold many of his estates, no longer owns his ancestral home Castle Hedingham and, adding to his predicament, his reputation is tainted. How dramatically things have changed, he thinks. While *Venus and Adonis* paints a world of the past, notably, in the early 1570s when he and Queen Elizabeth had very close and flirtatious relations, almost twenty years on, *Lucrece* portrays England differently. It is now a situation in which female power is losing its grip and the near invincible Tudor reign is fast declining.

Though Edward's dedication of his poems as William Shakespeare is heartfelt, regret that he has failed to persuade the young man to marry, persists. Interestingly, his feelings are complex: he feels no rancour towards Southampton. As a seasoned Courtier, he knows the ways of the Court (that "Riotous Inn" as he once referred to it) perhaps better than any other Courtier. He hears the gossip of Courtly intrigues and notes the changing of the guards, so to speak, as a few new possessors of power, who remain mostly under cover, are installed here and there. All the while, ill-health and old age cast an unpredictable shadow over him.

The Queen waits and watches; as does Burghley, whose son Robert is ready and eager to take the place of his father. Edward sees the relentless shift, now much more clearly as femaleness loses its hold on power while Her Majesty, like himself, gets older and more infirm. For some time, he had been aware of the growing gender move towards maleness, which he depicts in *Lucrece*. The slide is not abrupt. It is deceptively gradual. In *Lucrece,* Edward sees parallels between the birth of Republican Rome and the steady rise to power of the Cecils as Tudor Rule weakens and fades. As either virtual incumbents, or the new men waiting in the wings, the Cecils are within touching distance of becoming outright victors. They are far ahead of their rivals like the Earl of Essex's faction, who seem ignorant of the brutal capacities of the Cecils. Edward's understanding of the Cecils is much too involved for him to be naïve about their use of various ways and means of achieving their ends. Power and politics are the meat and drink of the Cecil faction, especially now as it relates to the Queen's Succession. The power of the pen, in the face of all the oppressive forces of the State, as Edward has proved, and continues to prove, is undeniable. No one knows better than him that playwrighting and being in the public eye are highly dangerous.

He has lived too close to, and for too long, under the Cecil regime not to be aware of Robert Cecil's designs of holding on to power before a new Monarch of England is enthroned. He wonders how much of his knowledge of the Cecils and their ambitions is known by others. He thinks of former fellow playwright Christopher Marlowe: What did he know? And why was he murdered? Now, under the guise of "William Shakespeare," *Lucrece,* an allegorical story, is aimed at his patron Queen Elizabeth, the "Virgin Queen," who symbolically sees herself as a dutiful wife, married to England. In the story, male Courtiers like TARQUIN and BRUTUS dominate.

LUCRECE is powerless. But it is discovered that she alone of all the wives, is faithful. And following the ancient story, the Courtier TARQUIN'S jealousy gets the better of him. He seizes LUCRECE, sexually violates her and runs away.

Thus, *Lucrece* is the opposite of the *Venus and Adonis* story. They pass on different messages about male and female aggression, domination, submission and victim-hood that are reflected in the shift from Queen Elizabeth's autocratic and forceful Rule to a male-controlled power structure.

So Edward, as William Shakespeare, the author of the poems *Venus and Adonis* and *Lucrece* does the best he could to alert Southampton to be wary of causing offence to the Cecil regime. Upsetting them would have consequences, Edward warns. But the young man does not heed the warnings. Soon after he makes it abundantly clear that he will not marry Elizabeth de Vere, having reached his twenty-first birthday, he feels legally free to do whatever he likes. But this is not how Burghley sees it. The mighty Lord Treasurer of England is cut to the quick by the young Southampton's refusal to marry his grand daughter. "Robert," Burghley says to his son,"what do you make of this childish impertinence from Southampton?"

"He is spoilt and stubborn," Robert says. "Another one of that privileged few. Another insolent, jumped-up Courtier. He must be punished..." He pauses. "He must be punished *severely!*" Burghley is pleased to hear Robert's thoughts, which reflect his own. Burghley has taught his son well; and being no respecter of the high and mighty, he wreaks revenge: He demands that Southampton should pay a heavy price; a penalty of five thousand pounds for not marrying.

Keen observer and, at times, a victim of the power brokers at Elizabeth's Court, Edward never misses an opportunity to channel his ideas and feelings into literary form. He considers the theme of marriage: To marry or not to marry he considers as elements for a Comedy which he hopes to write and stage.

***

The timing and themes of *Venus and Adonis* and *Lucrece* could not be better. Edward's use of "William Shakespeare" he feels is the perfect marriage of author and Pen-name. With the publication of *Venus and Adonis*, more readers are drawn to his work. His poems are among the best-selling publications. And although *Lucrece* takes a while longer to become popular, publisher John Harrison, has the good fortune of having two best-sellers. This brand new publishing experience prompts him to reconsider and appreciate the overall composition of the title page of *Venus and Adonis*. Edward agrees with Harrison. And amidst the success of his poems, he leaves nothing unchecked. He thinks that the name William Shakespeare, not only looks good on the page, it has a special ring to it: The sounds of the spoken surnames: de Vere and Shakespeare are not that far apart! He remembers Harvey's Address in which he'd been mentioned as the man who "Shakes-spears." He confides and confirms to himself that it is a name worthy of the poems; and therefore worth promoting. When they had met, Harrison agreed, "Why not?" he'd said. He knew he was on to a good thing for already these two publications have made his publishing business a handsome profit. But there is more money to be made, he thinks. For Edward, writing these "best-seller" poems exacts its own price: not just in the amount of money it makes, but also in terms of hard work, testing yet again, his soulful ability, as a writer. He'd laboured for countless hours experimenting with words; a reflection of his fondness for punning in the forms of rhymes and metering, as he hones draft poems to fruition. Overall, the lines he writes, demands serious attention; and he is honest about the effort that goes into his poems and plays when he refers to the "pain to pen a book." So writing does not come easy for him; and now, for better or worse, increasingly his writings under the guise of "William Shakespeare" is becoming better known.

Harrison wastes no time in keeping the London Bookstalls well stocked: He reprints *Venus and Adonis* and *Lucrece*, time and again. Edward is delighted. And now, as William Shakespeare's popularity spreads, other writers enter the space opened up by the lucrative marketing phenomenon that the poems have created. Following Edward's lead, one writer, Thomas Nashe, writes a sexually demeaning version of *Venus and Adonis* in which he mimics Edward by dedicating the manuscript to "Lord S" – The Earl of Southampton. Edward wonders often enough, if Nashe is his enemy or friend? Whichever it is, at this time, in the ongoing literary war, this is how unpredictable and spiteful these authors are and could be.

Yet, another writer, Thomas Heywood, enters the literary fray. He too, homes in on *Venus and Adonis,* the poem of the day! But its attractiveness does not stop there. It catches the imagination of a few other writers like Richard Barnefield, John Dickenson, Michael Drayton and William Harbert. Not far below the surface, the sexual undertones of *Venus and Adonis* and *Lucrece* spreads across the nation. Received as erotic poems, they are a literary phenomenon. And people are curious, excited and intrigued by the printed name "WILLIAM SHAKESPEARE" that are linked to the poems. From here on, increasingly it becomes part of the history of English literature.

*

While Edward is pleased with the success of his poems, he is no less intrigued and excited by the rising interest that his Pen-name is creating. William Shakespeare is a mouthful to pronounce, but readers, it seems, do not mind. They like it! As Harrison profits, and other publishers take their chances, the poems' success is a beacon of hope for all writers. Edward takes great pride knowing now that he has, to some degree, fulfilled his boyhood ambition of long ago, of becoming a writer. Then, he was the writer to be! Now, he is! So the long, tortuous process of *becoming* William Shakespeare has come to fruition. "Labour," "fruits" and "fruition" are words, metaphors that he uses. Sitting at ease in his Study, he breathes deeply, exhales slowly, and considers his present position: "Whatever my earlier doubts and reservations," now with utter conviction, he says to himself: "*I am William Shakespeare*!"

*

Given the success he enjoys, he is confronted with a problem which is this: his officially recognised Pen-name William Shakespeare, as author of *Venus and Adonis* and *Lucrece* is beginning to become identified with the "Upstart Crow," Will Shakspere, who continues to tamper with his Anonymous plays. "Surely not," he says to himself. He is aghast. He realises now the difficulty of keeping "Shakespeare" as a separate, distinct name in relation to "Shakspere." So what he had thought of as a clever disguise, is now threatened. How great is the threat? he wonders. "Have I outwitted myself as author of my own writings? And if so, what could I do to stop the "Upstart Crow."

The continuing success of his epic poems proves the saleability of his labour with his pen. With an eye always on making some money, while he realises the importance of marketing the production of his plays, he finds that at least two of his dramas, one of them being *The Taming of the Shrew,* have been published. His worry continues for neither this, nor any of his anonymously published plays have been approved of, or, in any way overseen by himself. Put simply, they were stolen. He is alarmed that his writings are slowly, but surely, slipping out of his grasp. Then, he learns that another play – an inferior work - is registered and ready for printing. Soon copies of it appears in bookstalls under the initials "W.S." William Shakespeare? He is not amused. So not only are his works being usurped, even his Pen name is used and being usurped. Matters are getting out of control, he thinks, and overall, as pressure upon him builds, it becomes too much. He feels he must stem the flow. He thinks of writing to Burghley to complain about maltreatment in what he terms "My Office."

In other words, he means his official status as a Writer! Only the Queen and Burghley knows about this role that he plays for the State. Nonetheless, whatever the precise nature of his "Office," or job, he points to the widespread abuse of the Shakespeare name, which is linked to the "Shakespeare brand." So, in an official sense, this is indeed what Edward de Vere has become: A brand! And now, he turns to Burghley.

"My very good Lord," he writes:

"If it please you to remember that about six months or thereabout past, I was a suitor to Your Lordship for your favour because as I found sundry abuse whereby both Her Majesty and myself were in mine office greatly hindered...Yet, by reason at that time, mine attorney had departed the town, I could not then send him to attend upon your Lordship, according to your appointment. But I hope that the same disposition still remaineth towards the justness of a cause, and that Your Lordship to whom my estate is so well known and how much it standeth me on, not to neglect as heretofore such occasions as to amend the same may arise from mine office, I most heartily desire Your Lordship that it will please you to give ear to the state of my cause; and at your best leisure, admit either mine attorney or other of my counsel in law to inform Your Lordship that the same being perfectly laid open to Your Lordship, I may enjoy the favour from you which I most earnestly desire. In which doing, I shall think of myself singularly beholding in this, as I have been in other respects.

Your Lordship's ever to command,
EDWARD OXENFORD."

After sending the letter, Edward feels that his worry is fully justified. As he waits to hear from Burghley, he thinks about the effect of his plays and poems which makes readers across the land sit up, read and ponder the profound meanings behind the words and metered lines he'd written. But, in observing the conventions of the Class to which he belongs, he'd adopted a necessary, precautionary self-disguise that alarms him as being a double-bind: His wilful obscuring of himself. This is the awful predicament which he faces, as control over his writings continue to weaken.

While reading Edward's letter, Burghley stops here and there, largely to adjust to Edward's writing style. His own style is long winded and lacking artistic merit; so very different from Edward de Vere's. It mirrors his way of thinking. In linguistic structure, vocabulary and form of expression, Burghley thinks and admits, as he reads, that his own ability is inferior to Edward's. Soon, he reaches the point in the letter where Edward says that he had been abused. So out of desperation, Edward had made the best case for help that is now urgent and absolutely necessary to stem the trend of losing his dignity and the ownership of his hard-won acclaimed writings. But how could he persuade the seventy-three year old Burghley to make this happen when he is neither a lover of the theatre nor in favour of his "lewd friends." Edward was conscious of this, and his problematic relations with the powerful old man, while he was composing his letter. He felt he simply had no choice, but to turn to Burghley. Why? Because with the exception of the Queen, there is no higher authority to whom he could have turned to for meaningful official protection of his steadily accumulating body of manuscripts: of songs, plays and poems into which he'd poured his Soul.

But, as Edward knows, there is another reason why Edward has written so pleadingly to Burghley: As a man of the theatre, he feels the need to become more involved with England's foremost theatrical Company, the Lord Chamberlain's Men. He feels that the Master-puppeteer Burghley could, and should, do some string-pulling to stop the pirating: the theft of his plays. He sees his letter as his last hope. He waits. But abuse of his uncopyrighted literary masterpieces, continues. This does not surprise him; for so popular has his work as "William Shakespeare" become that many in the publishing industry takes every chance to exploit his literary disguise.

But while he deals with publishers and people in the theatre, his attention is now drawn again to relations with his wife and Southampton. He'd written about this matter in his work *Willobie and Avisa*, published by John Windet. Among those who'd read this true work of a "chaste and constant wife," is John Lyly, who knows the real identity of "Willobie" and "Avisa:" namely Edward and Elizabeth Trentham. "My Dear Lord," Lyly writes in a "Private and Confidential" letter to Edward, "I have seen a copy of your latest pirated work. Unlike the vast majority of readers, I enjoyed reading about people and places that I know so well. Be assured that the disguise of yourself and your wife are, of course, in safe keeping with me. I hope, and look forward to seeing you soon. Perhaps, on your next visit to the theatres in Shoreditch."

***

For those few who know who Willobie and Avisa are, if Willobie is to be believed, at the same time that Edward was trying to interest Southampton in his daughter, Southampton was paying much attention to "Avisa," Edward's wife! "H.W. falls in love with Avisa," Willobie explains, "he pines for her; his desire is strong and endures." Soon, H.W. speaks to his friend, W.S. who had experienced the same desire for Avisa, but now he has recovered from his love infection. So, the question arises: Is he, Edward, no longer married to an ideal woman? He says that as "William Shakespeare" (W.S.) he had experience of the same kind of feeling: The same kind of passion for Avisa when he'd married her. But strangely, he suggests that "W.S" has recovered from being smitten with love for Avisa; and that he, W.S, is "becoming just as fond of 'H.W'" as he was of his wife! What a strange *menage a trois*. So here, again, Edward refers to a same-sex relationship of which he had been charged by his enemies.

As the narrator of *Willobie and Avisa*, Edward admits to feeling jealous about H.W's attentions to his dear wife."But only for a while," he says. Then, strangely, Willobie has Southampton admitting to harbouring lustful feelings for his wife. Referring to himself as that old man of the stage, Edward portrays himself as being more mature.

Has he changed so much as to have gotten over his jealous tendencies? Perhaps. As he deals with the situation now, it seems that the master of "mistaken identities," mixed-up emotions and intentions, is able to relax a bit and have fun. He indulges in this ludicrous situation in which he presents himself as "Willobie," who plays the role of egging Southampton on, but he does so secure in the belief that his wife will not cheat on him. What trust and confidence he shows both in his Countess of Oxford and Southampton!

So, in *Willobie His Avisa,* comedy comes with some awkwardness and shame. Though the Pen-name "William Shakespeare" offers some cover, there are a few like Thomas Nashe who, while calling Edward "Gentle Master William," knows that Willobie is another *nom de plume*, offering further evidence that he knows Edward de Vere's hidden persona as "W.S." And, as if Windet had known enough to publish with confidence the solidity of Edward's and Elizabeth's marriage in *Willobie and Avisa*, the characters H.W and W.S. touches on the special, delicate matter of the art of Courtship, which is all the more interesting because ultimately, Avisa has to come to a decision about her wooer's attentions.

*

But what the printer Windet knows is just part of a threesome love affair. And though Edward is now seemingly a happily married man, the fair youth's involvement could still pose problems for Edward and his wife. Incredibly, Edward's affection for Southampton does not lessen even though the intended marriage of his daughter to the young Earl did not happen. But, Edward's maturity is now more clearly evident. In the three-some that now develops, Edward's innermost thoughts and feelings shows that his former jealous rages against his first wife Anne, are now under wraps. He is restrained; and a semblance of balance is struck between affection, admiration and trust: Admiration for Southampton, and trust in his chaste wife, his "Avisa."

So being the old man of the theatre, Edward's utter trust and confidence in Elizabeth Trentham overrides all of Southampton's youthful attentions. Given his ever changing persona and positions, Edward confides his deep feelings as never before to ink on paper. He writes poetry. Patiently, carefully, he composes three beautifully expressed Sonnets. In Sonnet Forty, he writes:

"Take all my loves, my love. yea, take them all.
What hast thou then, more than thou hadst before?
No love, my love, that thou mayest true love call;
All mine was thine, before thou hadst this more:
Then, if for my love, thou my love receivest,
I cannot blame thee for my love thou usest;
But yet be blam'd, if thou thyself deceivest
By wilful taste of what thy self refusest.
I do forgive thy robb'ry, gentle thief,
Although thou steal thee all my poverty;
And yet love knows it is greater grief
To bear love's wrong, than hate's known injury.
Lascivious grace, in whom all ill well shows,
Kill me with spites, yet we must not be foes."

And in Sonnet Forty One:

"Those pretty wrongs that liberty commits.
When I am sometime absent from thy heart,
Thy beauty and thy years full well befits;
For still temptation follows where thou art.
Gentle thou art, and therefore to be won;
Beauteous thou art, therefore to be assailed;
And when a woman woos, what woman's son
Will sourly leave her till we have prevailed?
Ay me, but yet thou might'st my seal forebear,
And chide thy beauty and thy straying youth,
Who lead thee in their riot even there
Where thou art forced to break a twofold truth:
Hers, by thy beauty tempting her to thee,
Thine by thy beauty being false to me."

The last of the three, is the exquisite Sonnet number Forty Two:

"That thou hast her, it is not all my grief,
And yet it may be said I loved her dearly;
That she hath thee is of my wailing chief,
A loss in love that touches me more nearly.
Loving offenders, thus I will excuse ye.
Thou dost love her, because thou know'st I love her,
And for my sake even so doth she abuse me,
Suff'ring my friend for my sake to approve her.
If I lose thee, my loss is my love's gain,
And losing her, my friend hath found that loss;
Both find each other, and I lose both twain,
And both for my sake lay on me this cross;
But here's the joy; my friend and I are one;
Sweet flatt'ry! then she loves but me alone."

For Edward, the relationship between himself, Southampton and his wife has changed him immeasurably. But knowing the value of experience, of loves past (the Queen and Anne Cecil) and present, in the Sonnets he lays bare his very Soul. And so, at least for now, he has achieved a degree of emotional stability.

***

The growing popularity of the "William Shakespeare" Pen-name does not surprise Edward. Secretly, he is very pleased for the protective cover it affords him and he expects Shakespeare's popular appeal to increase. He notes that since he'd published the Ovidian poetic reminiscence about Queen Elizabeth as the possessor of great political power and sexual attractiveness, he'd produced new writings that includes the rise of the Cecil family. On these works, the feedback he gets from Secretary Lyly, and others, is good. His readership warms to his mixing and melding of love, sex, scandal and power in his tales as dramatized on stage, and, as set down in his poems. These are what readers and theatre-goers want, he thinks.

"My Lord," Windet tells him, "The book-sellers' shelves are regularly topped-up." But, Edward is nagged, not only by talk of his plays being performed in London, but also by the similarity of his Pen-name with the name of the actor-theatre manager Shakspere, who so blatantly flaunts himself as an author. William Shakspere and "William Shakespeare" are familiar sounding names. But, they do not represent the same man! In his mind, he confronts the issue, time and again, but he knows he must continue to write; to live the life he has chosen. It is what he'd vowed to do. It is tough, but he reassures himself "I must keep the secret, and feel as secure as I can in my authorial identity."

By now, his affection for Southampton could not be clearer. Already he begins to feel it is a fateful, unequal relationship.

Perhaps there is no greater commitment to show how much he cares for Southampton than to desire his inclusion in the de Vere-Cecil family circle; and of personal feelings expressed in Sonnets which he, in part, addresses to Southampton. But none of this out-pouring brings forth either a sufficient, or an equal, response from the object of his affectionate attentions. Instead, Southampton looks elsewhere; to someone else. He sides with his hero, the Earl of Essex, and his faction! He breaks free from Edward and the cloying tentacles of the Cecils. But even through all the marriage negotiations, one question was overlooked: How much did Edward's daughter Elizabeth really care about Southampton? Did she really see him as a husband? And, looking back, Edward asks himself: "How does she feel about that difficult period of match-making?" These are questions that preoccupy him.

Meanwhile, at Court, not one to be disobeyed, Burghley's response to Southampton had been swift and severe. After Southampton's rebuff, Burghley turns to Elizabeth and says: "Never mind Lizzie, I've found for you a better suitor." Having disciplined Southampton, Burghley expects Elizabeth to be submissive, like Anne Cecil had always been, and to be grateful when he brings "good news" to her:

"There are other eligible bachelors, handsome young men, who are fine prospects," he says. From the high chair on which he sits, he looks down at Elizabeth. "The man you are about to meet today is on his way here." Elizabeth's expression of surprise, needs no words. "He is the Earl of Bedford," Burghley adds.

After the Earl arrives, he and Elizabeth meet in a room adjoining the Cecil House Library. But soon, the Earl bids farewell to Burghley and leaves. "The Earl really is a very fine man," Burghley says to Elizabeth. He pauses, unsure what next he should say about the Earl's disappointingly brief visit.

Elizabeth keeps her silence. But Burghley speaks:

"Elizabeth, tomorrow another visitor, the Earl of Northumberland will come to Court. He is, as he says in his letter, most interested in coming here. He is a fine and very interesting man. I have high hopes that your meeting with him will go well."

These words are an unusual show of optimism from her dour-looking grandfather. For now, at just nineteen years old, there is nothing Elizabeth could do, but wait.

The next day, a carriage and servants arrive at Cecil House. Burghley shows unusual interest: He is at the door to greet the Earl of Northumberland. Once more, Elizabeth is summoned. When she appears, Burghley says, "My Lord Northumberland, this is my grand-daughter Elizabeth." Northumberland's fat serious face is partially transformed by a pleasant smile. Burghley feels his own facial muscles relax. And surprise, surprise, Edward is there to show his face too.

"My Lord Northumberland, this is My Lord Oxford," Burghley says to Northumberland. "He is Elizabeth's father." Both Earls shake hands. It is a rare, but positive showing by Edward who stands side by side with Burghley. For once, at least, Edward thinks and acts responsibly as a father. He ensures that he is seen. After the introductory exchange of pleasantries, Burghley conducts the Earl of Northumberland and Elizabeth into a private room.

Edward's immediate impression of Northumberland is favourable. The Earl seems to be a good man; and the official meeting between himself and Elizabeth seems to have gone well. So far, so good. But alas, no amount of support, moral or otherwise, could persuade Elizabeth to accept Northumberland. Burghley is incensed. He is no less interested to know of Elizabeth's feelings about Northumberland than is Edward who asks: "What is your decision?" Though not wanting to either disappoint or hurt her father, she gets to the point:

"My Lord, I cannot marry this man, the Earl of Northumberland," she says.

"Why?" Burghley asks impatiently.

"For a simple reason," she says. "I love another man." Edward is speechless. He says nothing for a while. Then he smiles, something he rarely does. This is the daughter whom he'd for so long disowned. But now he is not just beside, but also fully behind her. He sees in her now: a stubborn will. She stands up for herself! This is something of himself writ large, he thinks. He is now smiling inside too as he comes to terms with the fact that Elizabeth's sights are set elsewhere: "I have met a man named William Stanley," Elizabeth says. "We are deeply attracted to each other. We have fallen in love." But who is William Stanley?

He is thirty-four years old: A Courtier and poet who is the younger brother of the theatrical patron, Ferdinando Stanley, the Fifth Earl of Derby, Lord Strange. The family's pedigree is of the highest order. The Stanley brothers' lineage links them to King Henry VIII. This Royal connection is music to Burghley's ears: As the opportunist social climber, he's elated. He is all for marrying upwards! But even with this high-class heritage, William is both landless and untitled. Then, suddenly, tragedy strikes. William's older brother Ferdinando dies. This leaves a vacancy for the Earldom of Derby. The Stanley family has to delay announcing the heir to the Earldom for several months until Ferdinando's pregnant widow gives birth. The circumstances are unusual. But the reasoning as to the outcome of the pregnancy is clear: If the Countess delivers a boy, he would be able to claim the right of Succession and become the next Earl of Derby. But if the child is a girl, William Stanley would become the next Earl of Derby. For many weeks everyone is on tenter-hooks. Then, as suddenly as

Ferdinando had died, the speculation ends when the Countess gives birth to a daughter. So, pending her marriage to William Stanley, the engaged Elizabeth de Vere becomes the Countess of Derby in-waiting.

It is a wintry Wedding Day. The chroniclers are present to witness the event. One of them records that William, Earl of Derby marries the Earl of Oxford's daughter. For his part, on this occasion, Edward observes Elizabeth's marriage. He acknowledges her as a proud father, while invited guests are Royally treated to a feast. But, this is no ordinary marriage: It is as close to being a Royal wedding as possible: Queen Elizabeth attends; and the Court of Greenwich is alive with merriment. So much so, that the Queen, good dancer that she is, takes to the floor and dazzles her Spanish Guests with some fancy footwork. As part of Elizabeth's wedding celebrations, Edward is delighted to have his play *A Midsummer Night's Dream* performed.

So, once again, his much-loved story is used to honour and celebrate another married couple. But this time, it is even more special and satisfying for Edward because it is staged for his own daughter. And since that performance, he is struck by how personal the play is to him: In terms of its theme and timeliness, notably by how events peculiar to the William Stanley and Elizabeth de Vere marriage are reflected in the story. So certain aspects of the play touches Edward. In particular, and in satirical form, his obsession with one of his daughter's potential bridegrooms, while she remains fixated upon the man she is determined to marry. This is exactly what has happened with Elizabeth, Southampton and now Stanley.

Following the wedding, Edward feels a renewed sense of the power of his pen; his ability to transform life into art. He considers how closely the four characters of the play HERMIA, DEMETRIUS and LYSANDER relate to Elizabeth, the Earl of Southampton, the Earl of Derby and himself as EGUS, HERMIA'S father. In spite of EGUS'S liking of DEMETRIUS (a reflection of Edward's affections for Southampton) the story ends happily with HERMIA and LYSANDER being committed to each other, as Elizabeth and Derby are. And so, through his art, once more, Edward mirrors combinations pertaining to real life. The play opens with the following characters and dialogue:

> "DEMETRIUS (as The Earl of Southampton): Relent,
> sweet Hermia; and Lysander yield
> Thy crazed title to my certain right
> LYSANDER (as Derby): You have her father's love.
> DEMETRIUS: Let me have Hermia. Do you marry him.
> EGUES (as Edward): Scornful Lysander! True he hath
> my love;
> And what is mine love shall render him;
> And she is mine, and all my right of her
> I do estate unto Demetrius.
> LYSANDER: I am my lord, as well derived as he,
> As well possess'd; My love is more than his,
> My fortunes every way as fairly ranked
> If not with vantage, as Demetrius."

So, having been landless and untitled before his brother's death, William Stanley is now the inheritor of the Earl of Derby's estate. While the Comedy *A Midsummer Night's Dream* ends with HERMIA and LYSANDER being married, a reflection of the real life unity of Elizabeth and William Stanley, Southampton, referred to in the Sonnets, had yet to meet his match. Overall after the performance of the play, Edward is overwhelmed. His emotions have been turned upside down. For having denied Elizabeth's paternity for so long, now he is as proud of her as a father can ever be.

Later, while composing an early draft of another play, *The Tempest*, Elizabeth's marriage comes to Edward's mind. He acknowledges Derby's brother Ferdinando and names a character in *The Tempest*, FERDINAND. And interestingly, he casts himself as PROSPERO who is, at first, reluctant to give FERDINAND consent to marry his daughter MIRANDA. But FERDINAND perseveres and eventually wins PROSPERO'S consent to wed his daughter. PROSPERO says:

> "If I have too austerely punish'd you.
> Your compensation makes amends, for I
> Have given you here a third of mine own life,
> Or that for which I live?...all thy vexations
> Were but my trials if thy love and thou
> Hast strangely stood the test."

***

As time moves swiftly on, Edward acknowledges another milestone: He is forty five years old. Of the sea of troubles he'd faced so far, two things loom large. First, taking all things into account, his financial position is still in a parlous state; secondly, his overall health is in decline. He suffers from aches and severe leg pains. Rising from a seated position is a struggle, never mind walking.

"The drag of your foot is a lot worse today," Countess Oxford says to Edward as he makes his way to the study. "At least, that's how it looks."

"The pain is worse in the morning," Edward admits readily. "But, glad to say, it improves a little in the course of the day." He grimaces, then he adds: "But not by much..." After a pause, he says: "I like it here: It feels like being in the countryside. It is a good retirement retreat. It is peaceful." Touching his leg, he adds: "But I must say, since we moved here, the pain has got worse."

It is midsummer. Edward enjoys the golden days, strolls in the grounds and garden. But, even the glorious weather cannot banish thoughts of his weak financial position. Added to his physical infirmity, in relative terms, he feels unhappy; cheated of his full inheritance. So need makes him uncomfortable; as indebtedness knocks at his door. Being poor, he thinks, is certainly not part of his inheritance! All his life, he was brought up to believe that being poor is the lot of other people: He means the masses: those living in hovels, huts, ayslums and insecure houses dotted about in hamlets, villages and the overcrowded slums. He feels, with his Countess's love and companionship, he could yet make money, not just to become solvent, but to make a small fortune. He has always believed in making money. Now, he attempts to get his pot of gold.

He thinks, mining tin could be profitable; a good business investment. Of all his great personal qualities, his venturesomeness stands out: He is not averse to risk-taking. Fired up by speculation; he is impatient, ready to go! He writes enthusiastic, hopeful letters, petitioning for a Royal Patent on tin mining. He is one of the few Courtiers who, in spite of the drop in tin production, believes in its profitable potential. Convinced of success, he persists; and soon his correspondence adds up: His rising pile of letters on mining becomes an invaluable accumulation from his pen. In such matters, two heads are perhaps better than one! He has the benefit of his business-minded wife.

He seeks her views on the figures involved in his business projections. In this way, he learns more about her. But, as good as things are in their relationship, he is protective of his role as a writer. He does not, in any way, surrender this aspect of his life to Elizabeth. Thus, he draws between them an unwritten, imaginary demarcation line. But, as a writer, tried and tested habits are hard to give up. Ever the literary stylist, in his tin-mining letters, Edward excels: Even when considering the bare facts of business-speak and managerial matters, he still uses certain imagery and phrases. Perusing a few of his legalistic tin petition-letters, Countess Elizabeth is struck by the intermingling of certain words and rhetorical phrases."My Lord," she says, "I enjoy reading your letters very much. Not just as business Petitions. But, for the way that you write them. What are these expressions?" She reads aloud: "slings and arrows of outrageous fortune;" "full of sound and fury" and "abstract and brief chronicles of time."

"My dear Elizabeth," Edward says, "they are called Hendiadys. They are expressions of a complex idea using two words connected with *and*: for example, goblets and gold instead of golden goblets. Hendiadys are part and parcel of my literary tool kit. I use them often in my plays."

"My Lord, I know you do." The Countess is duly impressed by how much better those otherwise dry business letters are to read. It reflects and confirms Edward's unique, judicious and rhetorical ability. Alas, all his best efforts to secure the Royal Patent, yields nothing. His Petition is passed over. Instead, the Queen chooses other Courtiers as "Supervisors" in the Stannaries. One of them is Sir Walter Raleigh. Edward is not amused. He feels abused. He is deeply disappointed that the Queen has rejected him. But, he thinks, "I need to move forward. I need to rise." This has often been his resolve in the past; his fall back position. But this time, it is different. Now, he knows he is no longer as strong as he used to be: age and injury makes him prone to moodiness. He feels he must guard against lapsing into melancholy moods. That would be much too easy. But rising up from disappointments, he thinks, is easier said than done, for in truth, a large part of his creeping depression is because his health is broken. Once again he writes to Burghley. And interestingly, the tone now is different. He apologises for his inability to keep up with him; a man who is thirty years older! "When Your Lordship shall have best time and leisure… I will attend Your Lordship as well as a lame man may at your house."

Three days later, he writes to one of Burghley's servants. "I am unable to visit you." He explains why: "Because I am not fit to do so." Edward's leg pain gets worse. Though he cannot walk and move around freely, he spares his Countess from repeated or excessive moanings. Nonetheless he needs a safety valve: He wields his pen to open up; to complain of ill-health, infirmity and lameness, arising from the violent act of a man who had used a sword against him. In Sonnet Thirty Seven he writes:

"As a decrepit father takes delight
To see his active child do deeds of youth,
So I, made lame by fortune's dearest spite
…am not lame, poor, nor despised,
Whilst that this shadow doth such substance give…"

And in Sonnet Eighty Nine, he says:

"Speak of my lameness, and I straight will halt,
Against thy reasons, make no defence."

Up till now, pride keeps him from admitting his pain too freely. But now he tells Burghley that his health is still "not so good. The doctors are bloodletting to fight the maladies that plague me." To lessen his pain, he plans, he says, to go to the city of Bath, where he hopes the curative properties of the mineral waters would help to ease his pain. So, to take the waters in Bath, he braves the journey and recalls the experience in his last two Sonnets. In Sonnet One Hundred and Fifty Three, he speaks of love, and the healing waters of Bath:

"In a cold valley-fountain of that ground,
Which borrowed from this holy fire of love,
A dateless lively heat still to endure,
And grew a seething bath, which men yet prove
Against strange maladies a sovereign cure;...
I sick, withal, the help of bath desired,
And thither hied, a sad distempered guest..."

Then, to lighten his mood, with thoughts stoked by "love's fire," in the last of his Sonnets, number One Hundred and Fifty Four, he writes:

"The little love-god lying once asleep,
Laid by his side his heart-inflaming brand.
Whilst many nymphs, that vowed chaste life to keep,
Came tripping by; but in her maiden hand
The fairest votary took up that fire
Which many legions of true hearts had warmed;
And so the general of hot desire
Was, sleeping, by a virgin hand disarmed.
This brand she quenched in a cool well by,
Which from love's fire took heat perpetual,
Growing a bath and healthful remedy
For men diseased; but I, my mistress' thrall,
Came there for cure, and this by that I prove:
Love's fire heats water, water cools not love. "

So Edward seeks ways and means of lessening his pain, both physical and mental. With these private expressions, he could hardly hide how he feels. Not surprisingly, now, there are whispers among some Courtiers of his illness. There is more than a hint of interest in what is being said. And soon, the gossipers amplify the whispers and the rumour that Edward's health has been bad, spreads. They say, he is struggling to survive his illness. What is his ailment? This is not specified. But the rumours come at a critical period of transition in England as Robert Cecil prepares to take over the reins of power from his aged father, Lord Burghley.

Rowland Whyte, a secret agent writes to his boss Robert Cecil: "Some say my Lord of Oxford *is dead!*" Robert is sceptical, as he and his group always are about most things to do with Edward de Vere. But now, Robert thinks, there is no smoke without fire. He reserves judgement as to how sick Edward really is. But amidst the gossip, rumours and fears, speculation is rife: George Chapman, a writer, no friend or fan of Edward's, writes a poetic critique in which he mentions an unnamed poet and playwright whose loose "feathers" adorn another man. That nameless poet and playwright is Edward. Chapman refers often to "Shakespeare's Sonnets" and other literary works, suggesting Edward is the *real writer*: The man behind the mask.

At this time, too, the poet Thomas Edwardes publishes, his own tribute to *Venus and Adonis* by William Shakespeare. In it he cites the masked poet, a Nobleman, who is much different from the men who had confronted each other on the streets of Blackfriars. But that is not the truth. Now, the pain Edward feels with every movement of his leg vividly reminds him of the vicious clash of swords as his Servant-supporters bravely fought against attacks from Sir Thomas Knyvet and his men.

This fight between two factions (arising from a defence of family honour on the Knyvets' part) comes about, because of love: The love affair between Anne Vavasour and Edward, which draws attention to its strong resemblance to the warring families in his play *Romeo and Juliet.*

So, for Edward, unlike the crowds who flock to the theatres to see the play, this is not mere entertainment, but a story grounded in reality. In effect, before, during and since he'd written *Romeo and Juliet* he'd been having nightmares; bad days!

*

Sitting in his Study, Edward feels awkward as he considers the rumour and gossip of his decline and "death." He feels a sharp twinge of pain as he vividly recalls his near-death sword fight. Unlike before, now he thinks that more than once during the street-fighting melee, he could have died. His blood had flowed freely down his leg and onto the cobble stones. Looking back, he is glad to have had the years of life since then. "I am lame, not dead!" he thinks, as if he is doing so for the first time. But, living is no joke; and mindful of Gray's warnings as well as the ever-growing London gossip, he is forced to take more seriously the Upstart Crow's encroachments; his brazen claims to the authorship of certain plays. While the similarity of the name Shakspere to his Pen-name William Shakespeare helps to protect his identity, the substitution of one for the other is not so outlandish. Rather, it is incredibly easy to mistake one for the other. The irony staggers him. What has he done? he questions himself. Is his disguise effective? Yes. So far, so good, he thinks. But, at what cost? This, he accepts, is the one and only question that remains. And now, all the more, because no other playwright comes close to his extraordinary ability of portraying "mistaken identities" for his Comedies and highly praised Tragedies. "Unfortunately," he says, to himself, "the situation I face is not fiction."

And so the concern and worry continue: He thinks more and more that the closeness of the names, makes it unlikely that people will see Shakespeare and Shakspere as the two very different people they are: One, a great writer; the other is plainly not so. But setting aside this threat of an Imposter-Usurper of his plays, as Gray had warned him about a country Clown without naming him as Shakspere (who uses his plays for his own self-promotion) the London gossipers persist in what they do best: gossip!

Winter approaches. The hours of daylight are shorter; and, as the nights draw in, dark thoughts enter Edward's mind and threaten, at times, to overshadow the wintry days. One morning after a leisurely breakfast with Elizabeth, he shuffles into his study later than usual, and sits at his large, low oak desk upon which are ink, quills and sheets of blank paper. With his special key, he unlocks the bottom drawer of the desk which is crammed with manuscripts: plays and poems, as well as loose pages of notes and notebooks. He lifts the larger of two bundles and places it on the desk. Then, he retrieves the other bundle. Altogether, they amount to quite a pile: In truth, it is a unique body of work. No other writer of his time, he thinks, has written this much. Even his critics and anthologists think highly of him. He is the "best for Comedy," one respected author-compiler rates him.

At a glance, he sees the stack of papers, as the physical evidence of his imagined compositions; creative thoughts over decades. He thinks of the various versions of each play: The drafts and rewritings, the alchemical transformation, the metamorphosis from idea to words, characters, storyline, production and performance; in effect, the process that translates thought into the magic of theatre founded upon a combination of intellect, artistry and collaboration. He thinks especially of the unnerving moments of the First-Night performances of plays that have been staged at Court and in public theatres. And once more, he considers his real identity, as well as his artistic-literary concealment. He is known as Edward de Vere, the Earl of Oxford, but only a few people in his inner circle know him as "William Shakespeare." This is, for better or worse, his dilemma. His elevated social status means he is largely isolated; separated from the rest of the ordinary people, largely the theatre-goers. He is not prone to chit-chat or to joining the flow of idle gossipers at Court. He tends therefore to keep his own Counsel; at times, he talks to himself, especially while he is composing his plays. No wonder soliloquies loom large. He finds writing soliloquies beneficial: a form of therapy, all the more so because he spends a great deal of time alone. Such Self-interrogations helps his overall well-being.

The plays before him are impressive; the evidence of countless days and nights of compositional mindfulness. He thinks of his strange literary journey: From "Anonymous" to "William Shakespeare." But of his various Pen-name disguises, none has been as popular as William Shakespeare is! It has caught the public imagination! He runs his fingers over the top and sides of the manuscripts before replacing them back into the drawer. He turns the key in the lock, and sits quietly for a while. It is not yet mid-day. But, he feels he's earned a break.

*

Later that day, he receives news that his brother-in-law, Robert Cecil, is officially promoted. He is now in the post for which his father had groomed him: the Secretary of State. This move invests more power in the Cecil faction. All who seek redress must submit to the new Supremo. In this capacity, Robert receives two letters from Edward. In the first, Edward mentions a "little desk" which he carries around on visits to the country. But of greater concern to him now, is what he hears about the alleged behaviour of his recently-wed daughter Elizabeth. What about it? he wonders.

He is surprised and displeased to hear that Elizabeth is behaving in a manner that is unworthy of a noble-born woman. Granted that she is just twenty years old and is trying to adjust to wife -hood, in his second letter to Robert Cecil, Edward writes:

"I most earnestly desire that you as Elizabeth's Uncle is the person nearest to her, apart from myself, will help her with good advice. Her youth; how she behaves and the place where she resides following her marriage, are matters much to the honor of both of our families. Above all, I hope for your true and faithful advice to Elizabeth, as her Uncle."

Edward's concern is palpable.

*

Just after he'd met his son-in-law William Stanley, the Earl of Derby, he'd learned of his interest in music and playwriting. This, Edward thinks, looks good for both himself and Derby in future relations. So before and after the marriage of William and Elizabeth, Edward and Derby had mutual respect; and growing shared interests. Now, after his marriage, Derby lives at Cannon Row in London: a residence which Edward has visited and where he had been a Guest. From this address, ever conscious of not having provided for his daughters, Edward writes again to Robert Cecil. This time, he seeks a formal agreement that would guarantee his daughter Elizabeth as much as one thousand pounds a year from her wealthy husband.

As good relations continue between father and daughter,

Edward treasures the moments they spend together because happy family ties had been such a rare thing in his life. He attends to Elizabeth as much as he could; and he shows much interest in reading and commenting on Derby's work as a Court poet and playwright. Throughout the time with his Group of Writers at Fisher's Folly, he wrote drafts of plays, which he often showed to his Secretaries. Now, knowing that Derby is a lover of the theatre and playwriting, a tantalising possibility opens up. Derby sees and reads copies of Edward's scripts. Certainly Edward remembers showing Derby draft copies of both *The Tempest* and *A Midsummer Night's Dream* around the time of Derby's marriage.

***

The induction of Royal Knights of the Garter is a major event at Court. It is a matter of which Edward had been aware for many years. Since his own candidacy for the honour had, so far, not been successful, from the age of twenty one, he'd been present at most of the Knighthood ceremonies. It is often a galling experience. But, did he look upon those who had become Knights with envy? The question is timely; and the answer is yes! He is now forty-seven years old; and this year he may well have one last chance. As a Courtier, he knows better than most, all the elements associated with the Order of the Garter.

His knowledge is such that he'd long thought of writing a story; a play, about the Order. The timing is perfect, for it is now April, when new Knights are about to be elected. One of them is Count Frederick Mompelgard of Wittenburg. The play Edward drafts is *The Merry Wives of Windsor*. In it, one of the newly elected Knights is the German Count Frederick. Edward learns that a few years before the English

Court had granted a Knighthood to the Count, it is said that he'd been making a nuisance of himself. But having given in to the Count's request, Queen Elizabeth is also up to her old tricks. She behaves like the wily politician that she is. She remembers a legal provision that would allow her to deal with the Count. She takes advantage of a particular Rule which says that a Garter inductee does not have to be informed of all proceedings. And so on the Ceremonial St George's Day when all the Knights to be inducted gathers before the Queen, Mompelgard is absent. Why? Because no Invitation was sent to him. Ever on the look out for the odd and the dramatic potential of real life events, Edward creates a scenario in his play *The Merry Wives of Windsor*, in which the host of the Garter Inn speaks with the character BARDOLPH about "a certain nameless unnamed German Duke:"

"BARDOLPH: Sir, the German desires to have three of your horses. The Duke himself will be tomorrow at Court and they are going to meet him.

HOST: What duke should that be comes so secretly? I hear not of him in the Court. Let me speak with the gentleman. They speak English?"

***

Though lameness checks Edward's stride, it has become a daily reminder of his mortality. He thinks of time and timing; and with urgency, he continues to indulge his habit of revising and rewriting his plays. Now he attends to *The Merchant of Venice* that is to be performed. He recalls the play's first Court performance, notably, the Queen's unforgettable delight that night. For this latest production, he adds a sub-plot to the play.

This arises from certain recent events and developments which, he thinks, the audience could, and would, relate to. What strikes him especially is the law of the land and its workings. It is a theme aimed at the highly-educated Courtiers: particularly professionals and students of law.

In *The Merchant of Venice*, historical events are integral. The play's underlying message is that as the law stands, in a Contract dispute, the disputants must work within the Common Law Court and the Chancery - Equity - Courts. While the Common Law Courts does things by the book, so to speak, the Equity Courts take a more liberal approach: They answer appeals to higher principles that relates to Mercy and Justice.

Having been a student of law at Gray's Inn, and as a Defendant in the Brincknell murder case, in which he had "allegedly" killed a man and was not convicted, the verdict being *se defendendo*, now he adds a new twist to his play that relates to his wife Elizabeth Trentham and the legal charge of the Gurlyn Case. In this Case, Elizabeth was implicated in relation to Edward's indebtedness: namely an outstanding bond: money Edward owes to the Plaintiff in the lawsuit, a man named Thomas Gurlyn. Edward had hoped the State would have made good this back-payment for soldiers' wages some twelve years before in the Lowlands war, but Gurlyn's loan, was never paid. In exasperation Gurlyn petitions Edward's wife Elizabeth, who is not a debtor in this case. She is caught up in the dispute simply because she now manages and controls Edward de Vere's finances.

Edward is vexed. He feels humiliated because he thinks his days of indebtedness were behind him. But, oh no! Now this! Another legal matter; a quagmire which he must get out of. Elizabeth Trentham had rescued him from impending financial debt before. So understandably, at first, he tries to hide this second embarrassment from his business-minded, kind wife who is ready to present herself as his defender before the law. The gravity of the case demands due consideration. After Edward and Elizabeth discuss the whys, wherefores and the legal technicalities, Edward says:

"My Dear Elizabeth, tomorrow I will appeal to my brother-in-law Robert." He means Robert Cecil. "As you know, after Lord Burghley, he is the most powerful Government official in England. And, I still regard him as a brother-in-law."

At heart, especially after Edward's wayward early years, Robert nurses an intense dislike for the way his family had been portrayed on stage by Edward. Overall, he thinks that himself, Anne and his father have been treated with no respect and wrongly. But regardless of what Robert feels about him, Edward's aim now is for Justice. Knowing as much as he does about English Law and its workings, he addresses his brother-in-law: "Good Sir Robert Cecil," he writes, "whereas my wife Countess Elizabeth hath showed me a supplication exhibited to the lands of the privy Council against her, I have longed both to yield thanks to you for your Courtesy to her and myself in making her acquainted therewith – and also to advertise how lewdly therein the man Gurlyn behaves himself."

Writing to Robert is a source of embarrassment for Edward. He regrets the legal maze that Elizabeth is drawn into because of him. "I do not doubt therefore," he adds in his letter, "but I hope you will let him, Gurlyn, have his just deserts according to his presumption."

Edward is hurt that Gurlyn's complaint is not aimed directly at himself for his own under-handed misdeeds; his knaveries. He expresses alarm that a case "so gross and palpable" should be brought against his wife, who is entirely innocent of the cause. At this moment, he stops writing. He laments how, by association, Elizabeth is entrapped; and has become legally embroiled. This thought does not go away. It lingers as he composes the last sentence of his letter in which he desires Robert Cecil to conceive how thankful he is of "this honourable dealing with my wife and friendly care to me, I will the less set forth in words what I the more desire in deeds to show, as I face the opposition."

And so, Edward and Elizabeth hopes and prepares for the chance to present their case. If the venue is going to be a Common Law Court, Edward thinks Gurlyn stands a very good chance of winning. During the hearings, the legal niceties of this Common Law Court, as Edward understands it, are such that he finds any prediction of the final verdict on his case difficult to call. Then comes Judgement day.

Edward and Elizabeth wins the case against Gurlyn. As if he'd been holding his breath for weeks, Edward breathes a deep sigh of relief! He feels a great indebtedness to Elizabeth for so valiantly championing his cause. But, this victorious outcome is not the end of the link between Edward, Elizabeth, Gurlyn and debt. Edward is so pleased with the verdict that as they leave the Courthouse, he says to Elizabeth: "Thanks for getting me out of jail!" But, more than these words, he thinks of a way of repaying her. Even while the case was being heard, inequities in the legal process and system had touched him enough for him to use certain Scenarios in his plays to get across essential messages, both historical and contemporary.

*

A while later, as he revises and adds to different play-scripts, his "retirement" arouses deep reflection of times past: He thinks of his travels in Italy: his connection with Venice, his life now with wife Elizabeth who is attentive and helpful; and surprisingly, the freshness of the Gurlyn Case overwhelms him.

He goes over in his mind, one of the many stories that he'd set in Italy. He is back at his desk where, given the fundamental problems behind Gurlyn's defence, he sets down a new draft of *The Merchant of Venice*. As he reads the script now, he stops here and there, to make changes. He underlines certain words and phrases; and on the margins, he writes notes to himself: One, in particular, is about ANTONIO'S loan from SHYLOCK, a transaction based upon ANTONIO'S expectation of receiving some money from abroad.

But when that money fails to arrive, ANTONIO is unable to pay his debt to SHYLOCK. Both characters confront each other in a Venetian Court of Law at which point Edward infuses their Trial Scene with legal talk. Why? Because the case of SHYLOCK versus ANTONIO loosely parallels the real life Gurlyn's Case; and it does more: It addresses the bigger issue that the Case raises: the question of JUSTICE versus MERCY as well as Common Law verdicts versus Chancery edicts. As Edward knows, among ordinary English people, Law versus Equity is the foremost judicial question. He sees and experiences the process up close in the Gurlyn Case. He firmly believes that the unresolved dispute between the opposing approaches of dispensing Justice leads to wrongful convictions and causes widespread distress to innocent people.

By now, Edward has become well-acquainted with the Judicial system and understands the Law better than perhaps any other contemporary playwright. So now after he re-reads the new copy of his play, he thinks about the verdict of the Gurlyn Case: his supplicant letter to Robert Cecil and the story of *The Merchant of Venice*. He notes that they all point to the same conclusion: That strict adherence to the letter of the law Verdicts has a corrupting influence. Therefore, Equity must prevail. He is passionate about this! But now as he creates and recreates the character PORTIA, he thinks of her *interpretation* of the law which marks a shift, in legal thinking: Through her, he considers representations from the Common Law as well as the Chancery Courts and shows how pleased he is with PORTIA'S original stance: Her strange argument that a too strict interpretation of the law must be subservient to the highest form of Justice which is the "quality that is mightiest in the mightiest!" He thinks about the seriousness of the impasse: The ongoing deadlock in English Courts and the pressing need for change. He thinks again about the Gurlyn Case and relates it to PORTIA'S summing up. He re-reads his words for pace and dramatic effect, while picturing the Courtroom scene. He is particularly drawn to the speech that PORTIA makes at this point in the play. He thinks what PORTIA says should, in essence, be a fervent appeal; one that is as powerful as he could present it to liberate the persecuted from the yoke of Common Law strictures. Then, in the spirit of justice and his abiding faith in the meaning and rhythmic power of words, his poetic mood propels him to read once more, the words which PORTIA speaks:

"The quality of mercy is not strained;
It droppeth as the gentle rain from heaven
Upon the place beneath. It is twice blest;
It blesseth him that gives, and him that takes.
'Tis mightiest in the mightiest; it becomes
The throned monarch better than his crown."

After this eloquent plea, Edward makes a few final additions to the play script. Later that day, as the shades of evening falls, while having tea, he says to Elizabeth:

"With my knowledge and understanding of the law, and your business brilliance, I have not only made some changes to the staging of *The Merchant of Venice,* I also dedicate to you the lines of the passage about the quality of mercy which PORTIA speaks."

He hands Elizabeth a copy of the play. She reads; and, for a moment, she considers the title. She'd never read from a play-script before. Then, for several minutes, she turns the pages in silence as she is drawn deep into the story.

Meanwhile, Edward thinks there is no one else who could fit the persona of PORTIA quite like Elizabeth Trentham. The speech he alludes to fits her. But then again, extraordinary playwright that he is, his fondness for double identities, composites, combinations of character traits of different real life people (at times, the Queen herself) are intertwined in his plays. Complexity of character creation is among Edward's supreme gifts. He is a man with an unusual depth of human understanding; and the nobility of PORTIA arguing the case for Mercy, is Edward's heartfelt tribute to his wife, who had twice rescued him from shameful debts.

Debts and indebtedness are much in his thoughts while he sits next to Elizabeth. She stops reading and places the script of *The Merchant of Venice* beside her. She is visibly overcome by what she'd read. And so with worsening lameness and the somewhat reduced prospects of further embarrassing debt and Court appearances, Edward had portrayed PORTIA as his legal Defender.

***

Soon after her marriage, Edward's daughter, now Elizabeth Stanley, Countess of Derby, becomes embroiled in the rumour that she and the Earl of Essex, one of Edward's rivals, are having a love affair. Her alleged unfaithfulness is a hammer blow to Edward, who feels distanced from Essex, in large part, because of his close relationship to Southampton.

While Essex's star is rising; and before he and Southampton had set out to plunder Spanish ships on the high seas, it was said that Derby's wife Elizabeth had slept with Essex. Derby is very upset. Thereafter, he and his Countess leaves London to live in the north of England. Robert Cecil, curious to know how things develop there ensures that one of his Agents becomes part of the Derby household. A short while later, as Derby's jealousy increases, the Cecil Spy takes note and reports on the marital discord.

On this delicate matter of Elizabeth's marriage, certain questions arise in Edward's mind: Did she commit adultery? Are the rumours true? Who knows? No answers are forthcoming. But those spreading such talk has to be careful because the young girl has the powerful support and protection of Robert, Lord Burghley and the rest of the Cecil household. Of one thing, Cecil's Agent, is absolutely clear. He tells Robert that "All of Derby's servants have got together and went to see their employer. With utter honesty, they say to Derby: 'We serve you well as we did your father. If you hate your wife Elizabeth, and do not stop your jealous rages and bitterness towards her Ladyship, and so doing dishonour yourself, we would dislike you. We would bring her Ladyship away from you and return her to her family.'" The Agent adds: "The servants are united. "They express strong feelings of love for the Countess. They say that she 'wanteth friends who are wise and experienced. They assure the Earl of Derby of their loyalty to him and his humorous house.' But still, Derby is in a state of jealous turmoil."

Soon after the Agent had written his report, Elizabeth receives more than just her house Servants' support: The Earl of Cumberland, Derby's Uncle, visits the Derby's home, and takes the Countess's side in the dispute. Derby is not amused. And so, private marital disharmony provokes a closing of ranks on behalf of Elizabeth. It is a decisive show of political power, too. Faced with the strong opposition to his behaviour, at last, Derby responds favourably to his Countess. "If anyone can say," he declares, "that I know my wife to be dishonest of her body, or that I can justly prove it by myself or anyone else, I challenge him to combat of life." How different is this statement from his well-observed jealous behaviour. And, for good measure, he adds: "If anyone suppose any speeches of mine to have proceeded out of that doubt, he doth me wrong." He could not be plainer. What an extraordinary turn around.

Together again, as one, Derby and his Countess Elizabeth is assured of the full support of her relieved father Edward, Lord Burghley and Robert Cecil, among others.

*

As Edward witnesses Robert Cecil taking control and assuming more of his father's political power, Southampton moves further away from the Cecils. He's had enough of Cecil House, where he grew up. And having rejected Edward's daughter as a marriage partner, he turns his amorous attention to a woman named Elizabeth Vernon, a Royal Maid of Honour. Edward knows that Vernon is the Earl of Essex's Cousin. But what he does not know, is that two years earlier, Southampton had been secretly courting Vernon. His disappointment over the failed attempt at marriage between Southampton and Elizabeth has echoes in his play *A Midsummer Night's Dream*. As before, when it was performed for the Heneage-Mary Browne Wriothesley wedding, the story is timely, because Edward continuously revises plot and characterisation as he incorporates contemporary events in new versions which his audiences recognise and welcome. He is canny for he knows the element of current affairs is a winner: Theatre-goers warm to events and themes that concern them. For Courtiers too, there is much of interest in dramas like *A Midsummer Night's Dream*. In it Edward had portrayed himself, Southampton and his daughter as EGUS, DEMETRIUS and HERMIA, respectively. Thus the parallels of the play and real life are clear.

So in his literary compositions, Edward de Vere's art follows life itself. His affection for, and infatuation with, Southampton, the once longed-for son-in-law which was not to be, is still, it seems, strong. But his disappointment deepens as Southampton gets even closer to the Earl of Essex, who is Commander of a Mission to the Azores. Essex's goal is to intercept and destroy Spanish ships. This is a big operation; which Edward thinks is over-ambitious. In this, he is proven right.

Essex's Azores Mission falls short: A lot of money and time was wasted; and it enraged the Spaniards. But, to Edward's surprise, Essex's botched adventure does not bring him to his senses. Instead, he shifts attention from his failed Mission by uprating Southampton's modest contribution. Essex then does something quite extraordinary: While he is on the high seas, he ceremoniously places himself in the Monarch's role. He bestows a Knighthood upon Southampton. The Queen is angry with Essex for audaciously assuming the power to so act on behalf of the Crown.

What is hidden, more often than not, comes to light: Essex, the Naval Commander, now fancies himself as a poet. But Edward, the Queen thinks, is the grandest and best of her writers; a poet of unrivalled grandiloquence. Against such excellence, Essex has a long way to go. He lacks the divine spark; that rare thing, the ability or capacity which Elizabeth believes opens a window from which a true poet could view aspects of human life, like truth and the human condition.

"For his part, Edward smiles at the thought of Essex in

his roles as Commander and poet. To him, Essex is one who writes poetically for political reasons. His sole aim is to win the attention of the Queen and Courtiers primarily for self-promotion. He is so smitten by the ambition to *write successfully* that on his return from the Azores, he composes Sonnets focused on the high seas adventures and Southampton. Edward does not ignore Essex's literary efforts. On the contrary, in a few of his Sonnets, he sees Essex as his rival for the attention of Southampton. Thus, they compete as Poets. But, it is Edward's dedication, his highly-valued affection for Southampton that clearly shines through. In Sonnet Seventy-Eight, Edward writes:

"So oft have I invoked thee for my Muse,
And found such fair assistance in my verse,
As every alien pen hath got my use,
And under thee their poesy disperse.
Thine eyes, that taught the dumb on high to sing,
And heavy ignorance aloft to fly,
Have added feathers to the learned's wing,
And given grace a double majesty.
Yet be most proud of that which I compile,
Whose influence is thine, and born of thee:
In others' works thou dost but mend the style,
And arts with thy sweet graces graced be;
But thou art all my art, and dost advance,
As high as learning, my rude ignorance."

Then, in Sonnet Seventy-Nine, he refers to Essex as a competitor for Southampton's friendship.

"Whilst I alone did call upon thy aid

My verse alone had all thy gentle grace,
But now my gracious numbers are decayed,
And my sick Muse doth give another place.
I grant, sweet love, thy lovely argument
Deserves the travail of a worthier pen;
Yet what of thee thy poet doth invent
He robs thee of, and pays it thee again;
He lends thee virtue, and he stole that word
From thy behaviour; beauty doth he give,
And found it in thy cheek; he can afford
No praise to thee, but what in thee doth live:
Then thank him not for that which he doth say,
Since what he owes thee, thou thyself dost pay."

Again, in Sonnet Eighty, he addresses Southampton:

"O how I faint when I of you do write,
Knowing a better spirit doth use your name,
And in praise thereof spends all his might,
To make me tongue-tied speaking of your fame.
But, since your worth, wide as the ocean is,
The humble as the proudest sail doth bear,
My saucy bark, inferior far to his,
On your broad main doth wilfully appear.
Your shallowest help will hold me up afloat,
Whilst he upon your soundless deep doth ride;
Or, being wracked, I am a worthless boat,
He a tall building, and goodly pride.
Then, if he thrive, and be cast away,
The worst was this: My love was my decay."

Edward's feelings for Southampton has not lessened. He is angry with the wooer Essex who, it was said, had boldly, drawn his daughter Elizabeth away from her husband the Earl of Derby. Edward was deeply upset by the talk that Essex had had an affair with Elizabeth. Having invested so much good feeling and energy into many literary characters and beautifully crafted poetic lines, now Edward is determined to stop Essex from widening the gap between himself and Southampton. Given the hard work that goes into penning a play, he feels the effort of writing more Sonnets is worth every thought in his brain and movement of his quill, as he'd already expressed in Sonnet Seventy Nine.

So, in essence, and in plain prose, Edward says to Southampton that he should not be beholden to Essex for the attention and praise he'd received for the Azores venture. Edward knows that Southampton is no lover of poetry: It seems, he couldn't care less. But Edward is hopeful, even though Southampton's friendship with Essex and his group gets stronger amidst growing factional strife. Essex, for his part, responds to protect his supporters from any attacks. He hires an Intelligence Agent, a man called Anthony Bacon. Edward knows the Bacon name.

"Is this Anthony related to Francis Bacon?" Edward asks John Lyly.

"Yes, My Lord," Lyly says. "He is."

Listening to what Lyly says, justifies Edward's next move. He is more Security-conscious than ever before. But also knowing the unrivalled power of his pen, he wastes no time. In Sonnet Eighty Six he writes about Essex, his rival for Southampton's friendship.

"Was it the proud full sail of his great verse,
Bound for the prize of all-to-precious you
That did my ripe thoughts in my brain in-hearse,
Making their tomb the womb wherein they grew?

Was it his spirit, by spirits thought to write
Above mortal pitch, that struck me dead?
No neither he nor his compeers by night,
Giving him aid, my verse astonished.
He, nor that affable familiar ghost,
Which nightly gulls him with intelligence,
As victors, of my silence cannot boast;
I was not sick of any fear from thence.
But when your countenance filled up his line,
Then lacked I matter, that enfeebled mine."

***

It is the Christmas Season of Revels, masques and plays. But for all the merriment it brings, the season of goodwill does not lessen rivalries: Statecraft and politics evolves as tension grows between the Cecil and Essex Factions. In the hope of escaping Courtly in-fighting, Southampton plans to get away, after the Queen grants him an overseas travel licence. Edward knows of this; and confides his feelings in private to Sonnet Eighty-Seven:

"Farewell, thou art too dear for my possessing." Then he adds:

"And like enough thou knowst thy estimate;
The charter of thy worth gives thee releasing;
My bonds in thee are all determinate.
For how do I hold thee but by thy granting,
And for that riches where is my deserving?
The cause of this fair gift in me is wanting,
And so my patent back gain is swerving.
Thyself thou gav'st, thy own worth then not knowing,
Or me, to whom thou gav'st it, else mistaking;
So thy great gift upon misprision growing

Comes home again, on better judgement making.
Thus have I had thee  as a dream doth flatter,
In sleep a king, but waking no such matter,"

Gradually, since his marriage, Edward had been spending less time at Court. He is forty seven years old; and familiarity had made the place somewhat predictable. The "Riotous Inn" holds no charm or special attraction for him. He is glad to have moved away from the noise and hubbub of central London. He hears a cock crowing. It is morning: He rises from bed and after taking a few steps, he is alarmed how bad his lameness has become. The occasional pain in his leg is now more or less continuous and more severe. He walks out of the bedroom, but, unlike the day before, he drags his foot. From here on, he could only walk with a slight drag of his left leg. But, as always, duty comes first. When the Queen summons Parliament to sit in Session in the autumn, Edward de Vere, as the Earl of Oxford, is there promptly. He listens, and speaks when the time is right, during proceedings. He looks around him; and suddenly he becomes acutely conscious of time slipping away. He has real doubts as to how many more times he'd be able to be present in the Chamber as a Member of Parliament.

***

1597: HACKNEY: KING'S PLACE. Marriage, Edward thinks, is serving him well. Since their wedding, he and Countess Elizabeth had lived in relative seclusion in Stoke Newington. But now they are packing up their belongings. They are getting ready to move out and on. Edward thinks his residence in the suburbs was a good thing. He hopes this next move will be even better. The House that he and his Countess had bought is just a short distance to the south. It is called

King's Place which is in the Parish of Hackney. Not far away, is the beautiful, well-tended grounds of the Church of St. Augustine. Immediately to the north of the Church, across Mare Street, is a lush green field of apple and lime trees as well as flowering plants; an area that is known as Clapton Square. On the south-east and western sides of the Church grounds are gravestones, marking burials. This area of Hackney has a pastoral feel, Edward thought when he'd last visited the house. It is, if anything, more peaceful and quiet than his abode in Stoke Newington. He was looking forward to moving in and being in new surroundings.

At last the day comes when all the prospecting, planning and packing at Stoke Newington, stops. Edward and Elizabeth get into their carriage; and with all their possessions they travel to the large, imposing new house, located in Lower Clapton. Having arrived, he stares up at the front of the building which he calls the Big House. "This is my new home in King's Place," he says to himself. He thinks it is appropriate for himself and his Countess. As he and Elizabeth enters the house they feel a new-found excitement, as they get through the preliminaries of settling-in.

As days pass, they grow to enjoy being in the quiet, leafy eerily quiet village. On their first Sunday there, they attend a service of worship in the Church of St Augustine. Though Elizabeth had been thinking of other house options, walking out of the Church after the Service and seeing the pleasant flower beds of the spacious grounds Elizabeth and Edward agrees that by moving south they had made the right choice.

Ensconced in his new home, Edward reminds himself that his full Inheritance as the Earl of Oxford has yet to be received. Being in debt and receiving demands from creditors have, more or less, dogged his life so far. From here on, he is determined to avoid any more legal cases against him and the property at King's Place which, he is careful to place in the joint ownership of his Countess.

As Edward warms to the Big House, he thinks of how different it is from his other properties; even spectacularly so. He feels good; more at home here. The rooms are mostly large and grander than in the house at Stoke Newington. From the Gallery, he gets a good view of the grounds and the dense covering of the varying greenness encircling the house.

Soon he must decide which of the rooms in the Big House will become his favourite: His Great Study! The creative space where he will spend more time than anywhere else. After just a few weeks, he feels the Big House is neither like Fisher's Folly, nor like Castle Hedingham. He feels a sense of solitude as if he is deep in the countryside; and, as he learns more about King's Place and the Big House, he reflects on the day of the move, when standing in the front yard, he oversaw the servants off-loading the carts and coaches containing his and the Countess's belongings and taking them to their respective places in the House. He was pleasantly surprised by the amount of material he had accumulated since he'd moved to Stoke Newington. While he was admiring the building from outside, he recalls someone saying:

"My Lord, the House was originally constructed for William Worsley." The voice belonged to the Stoke Newington-based Estate Agent. His name is Carstairs.

"Who is William Worsley?" Edward asks.

"He was a Curate of St Paul's Chapel," Carstairs says. "But that is far back in the last century. Let us go inside."

As they enter the house, Edward asks:

"How long did he live here?"

"For a good number of years," Carstairs says. "How many exactly, I cannot say. But, from a description in the Estate Agents advertisement, it seems that Worsley had *enjoyed* living in the house. He was here long enough to stamp his personality on it. As you see, from the interior decorations he has diligently adorned the house with art and arte-facts: paintings and such like that reflects his personal taste."

Holding a sheet of paper before him, Carstairs adds: "It says here, the House contains a painting of Worsley himself kneeling before St Peter. And, a wall is decorated with emblems of the Tudor Rose." He pauses; stares up at craftsmanship of the high ceiling, then he moves closer to a nearby wall with a painted image on it. "And yes," he says, "King Henry the Eight's Principal Minister, Thomas Cromwell, had been an occupant here at King's Place. And, I dare say, Henry himself would have visited him at some time or other!"

Following this conversation with Carstairs, as time passes and Edward gets more of a feel for the House, he learns that Lord Hunsdon was an occupant. He appreciates the decorations featuring the Hunsdon family's Arms, emblems and engravings, especially in the Gallery from the which the King's Place gardens and lawns can be viewed. And like a magnet, Edward is drawn to a particular room.

One day Edward says to Countess Elizabeth, "My dear, you asked which of the rooms I'd like to be my Study. Come with me."

They walk along a corridor towards a room where Edward stops. He opens the door. "Here it is," he says. "*This* will be my Great Study!" The Countess enters the room. She stands beside him. Together, they re-examine the space in which they had been in more than once before. After a while, they walk out of the room, hand in hand.

Since then, each day Edward sits for long periods at the large oak desk in his Great Study. He writes and continues to revise plays to be read and performed by the Lord Chamberlain's Men. The process is familiar, but each story is different. Conception is one thing, but execution is quite another. He thinks translating ideas into works of literary art calls for mental nimbleness of which he is never short. Since, he takes occasional breaks from work during which he explores a different part of the House. On one such break and exploration, his imagination takes flight: He learns more about the previous occupant of the House who had left his mark in the form of heraldic animals and birds, horses, bulls, swans and stags; as well as effigies, carefully placed, here and there. He understands the symbolism and reality of these feudal emblems for he too is a traditionalist: The historical playwright *par excellence* of his era! Curious and ambitious a man that he is, he is determined to leave his own mark; his own emblematic stamp on the House. So as time passes, he adorns the great Parlour with a military banner; a hanging of the heraldic Oxford blue and yellow colours of the de Vere family. And soon, on the wall facing his desk in the Great Study, he places a much-treasured painting. It is an allegorical art work of himself titled: "A Story of the Rich Man and Death." He sees the picture every day as he enters and inhabits his Great Study. The story the painting tells is of himself as a rich young Nobleman, aged twenty five. He is holding a skull and a Prayer book. Also featured is a verse about Time. The Prayer book and the skull reminds him of the words: "Alas, poor Yorick!" And being older, Time matters; a sober reminder of his mortality. Each day as he shuffles into his Great Study, he sees the portrait of his younger self: "Ah! The sweet bird of youth," he says to himself, wistfully, as he considers the long and bumpy road that has brought him at this time; to this place.

*

When Edward first saw the building, he was pleased. Now months later, living and working each day, he feels even more relaxed and at ease in his Big House. It is a place unlike any other. King's Place itself is much less noisy than the environs of Fisher's Folly – that hot-bed of discussions and lively debates; and the fact that many rooms are conducive to study, contemplation and writing, makes his Great Study more special. Before he'd left central London for the suburbs, he was a single man; a bachelor about town whose freedom had allowed him to enjoy, as and when possible, the company of his Secretaries, a few writers and various persons in the theatre scene. Now, the peacefulness of the Big House lulls him to reflect: He thinks of those feverish days of doubt and unhappiness about his marriage to Anne Cecil and his past jealous rages that no longer upset him, as much, for now he is in a very different relationship and environment: His King's Place and its connections with King Henry and Thomas Cromwell sits well with him. Knowing Henry's daughter as intimately as he does, he wonders about that Royal visit to King's Place; and he thinks, he deserves to be happy with his wife Countess Elizabeth. But his new surroundings means adapting to changed circumstances, which, in turn, makes him self-conscious about ageing and his health.

For most of his life, there was never any shortage of people around him. Now, his visitors are few; and though he and his wife sometimes visit the St George's pub, he is still coming to terms with the quieter life in Hackney: No longer does he have the regular company of Lyly and Munday. Their excited and exciting intellectual talks are now a pleasant memory. But he is thankful that though lame, his quick-silver brain ticks with brisk regularity, like a metronome; and that his boundless imagination, ever-ready to take flight, is being put to work.

With few visitors, the long silences of his days, amplify conversations he'd had with fellow-writers. Sitting in his Great Study, he thinks of Thomas Nashe who had recently joined forces with playwright Ben Jonson in writing a satirical work titled *The Isle of Dogs*. Given the political divide, the play is contentious and therefore not well received by some. It is "a lewd plaie," one Critic says, "containinge very seditious and slanderous matter." For his Scribal role, Jonson was imprisoned; and Nashe goes into hiding. As Edward knows, for writers who are outside the ranks of Nobility, making a living in the showy theatre world is tough; unpredictable and precarious. Hard times and desperation are never far away.

***

From King's Place, Edward keeps up his correspondence with his Secretaries. But circumstances have changed and their relationships are not as they were before. John Lyly, a man of conservative bearing and outlook, had been one of his most trusted confidantes, and, to some extent, he still is. As Edward knows, Lyly is a courageous man who tries his best at what he does. But, his "best" it seems is not always good enough for others. After repeated applications, he was never accepted for the post of Master of the Revels. But, like Edward, he too had moved on: He married, had a child and lives not far from Aldersgate. The responsibilities of marriage and having a family keeps Lyly, more or less, still in Service as Edward's Secretary.

*

Anthony Munday, Edward's other Secretary fares no less well than Lyly at this time. He is relatively poor; and Edward knows this. Being much older than Munday, Edward has a brotherly attitude towards him. He likes Munday's energy, ability and desire to write. But being a trustworthy colleague, the question now arises: Why, in the last few months, did Munday publish two English translated works using the Pen-name "Lazarus

Piot?"

The year before Edward had moved to Hackney, he'd used the Pen-name "Lazarous Piot" which echoes the Bible story of a lame and sick man named Lazarus. These ailments reflect Edward's state of health at this time, which is not the best. But the Pen-name "Lazarus Piot" has much to do with him and Munday, his researcher, who is also a writer and Translator in his own right. As Edward's employee, Munday's excellent work on Chivalric romances have been influential, as are, other works like the translation of *The Orator* in which a Jew demands, as a form of payment, a pound of flesh from a Christian borrower. These works are primary sources for early drafts of Edward's plays *The Tempest* and *The Merchant of Venice.* The latter though is already well known. So Edward thinks of how closely he'd worked with Munday, at times, showing and discussing aspects of plays with him. In this sense, some kind of collaboration is clear, notably, on a play in the making: *Sir Thomas More*. From this co-operation Edward has, in turn, to some degree, benefitted from the research and translations of his Secretary. So the question arises: Who is "Lazarus Piot"? It is a Pen-name that symbolises, perhaps a joint effort between Edward and Munday.

So Lyly and Munday pursue different lives now. And with both men living and working in the city centre and Edward in Hackney, there is some distance between them. They see less of Edward. And in a real sense, they have all moved on!

*

"I have not an able body," Edward writes in a letter to Robert Cecil. A rush of emotion takes him by surprise. He tries to calm himself: After a while, he thinks of his wife and the Big House in which they have settled. Then for the first time since he'd left Stoke Newington, he mulls over and fully appreciates where he is: "This house is unlike any other that I have known," he says to himself as he takes a closer look at the living room. "King's Place is *home*!"

***

It is late December. The wintry days before Christmas gets shorter. Edward thinks of the big changes and the year that is coming to an end. It is past mid-afternoon as he rises from his chair in the Great Study. He feels the now predictable sharp pain and stiffness in his legs. Slowly, he shuffles to the window. He looks out at the flower garden as slanting rays of light begins to fade. Gusts of wind sweep and swirl around, pressing hard against the flowering plants and the almost bare branches of trees. It is a wild scene. He thinks of nature: of its violence, of the falling and fallen leaves; and of the cycle of life. He recalls the conversation he'd had earlier in the day with Nicholas Hill, the philosopher, who now more regularly acts as his Secretary. He finds Hill to be an outstanding ranconteur: They have had many absorbing conversations. They share many ideas. They had discussed Hill's "Atomics;" a topic that had been of interest to Edward for years, aspects of which he'd used in his plays *Romeo and Juliet* and *As You Like It*. He is fascinated by Hill's idea of the measure of smallness. Philosophy, an integral part of Edward's way of thinking and composing, is much on his mind in relation to the merits and the potential longevity of his works.

"My Lord," Hill says, "you are without doubt our most productive playwright. What would you say is the value of your work?"

Just then, the thought of the "pain to pen a book" comes to mind. "All that I have written," he says, "arises from experience and observation. My aim in the plays (and, in my poems) is to be true to myself as I create characters and tell stories that dramatizes people's hopes and fears, both in my Tragedies and Comedies. People have dreams; and then, there is "reality:" By blending life and art, or vice-versa, in dramas, I hope to mirror the human condition. Theatre-goers, the audiences I address, recognise themselves in my plays. At least, I hope so. It is why they come to the theatre. It is why, I think, the plays are so popular."

"My Lord, I must confess," Hill says, "I am just one of those theatre-goers. I must say, after seeing one of your plays last year, I wanted to see more…" His voice trails off. Then, he says: "But since then, I can say that I have seen more."

Edward is delighted to hear of Hill's interest in, and response to, his work! Hill is the leading spokesman, arguing strongly in favour of atomic philosophy. For this, he had been lambasted by critics. But Hill is no shrinking violet; no push-over. He's a leader who holds his ground. Edward likes Hill, in large part, because he has something to say. And, he says it in an unbridled way; with gusto and learning. In a word, as a Thinker, Hill is unorthodox. And significantly, his views are timely, Edward thinks, as he remembers certain ideas related to Atomics that he'd used in *Romeo and Juliet* and *As You Like It.* He is mindful of another of his plays *The Merchant of Venice* in which he artistically infuses Hill's atomics with deep thoughtfulness as he considers the profound questions of human life, the Soul and Immortality. He puts these words in LORENZO'S mouth:

"Look how the floor of heaven
Is thick inlaid with patterns of bright gold.
There's not the smallest orb which thou behold'st
But in his motion, like an angel sings,
Still choiring to the young-eyed cherubims;
Such harmony is in immortal souls,

But whilst this muddy vesture of decay
Doth grossly close it in, we cannot hear it."

Small or large, all things matter, Edward thinks. They have their place. In truth, they gain value from other things. They have value: They are essential to life and living. Dealing with difference, the driver of evolution, combining the big picture with the detail, in a coherent tale, Edward thinks, is the *raison d'etre* of his task as a playwright.

"Having seen *Romeo and Juliet* and *As You Like It,"* he recalls Hill's words, "I am both humbled and honoured by the ingenious way that you have used Atomics. It makes me proud to be the promoter of such ideas."

The meeting with Hill leaves him in a good frame of mind: In writing mood! He dares to reconsider Hill's view that no other playwright of the day could write and present stories like *Romeo and Juliet* and *As You Like It* to such dramatic effect and, with such profound philosophical meaning, as he does. High praise indeed, he thinks, which he accepts, because of Hill's level-headedness.

After Hill had left the House, Edward re-runs other aspects of their conversation: In particular, Hill's blunt question about the value of his literary work. Before he could give the matter further consideration, other thoughts intervene: Foremost, is a reminder of his mortality. "I have not an able body," he had written in his letter to Robert Cecil. He recoils from these words now. But he can no longer ignore the direction of time's winged arrow for more than once since his move to Hackney, a strong feeling that gets stronger is this: That he and his Countess would spend the rest of their lives in the Big House.

*

At King's Place, he appreciates a new-found sense of marital contentment; a far cry from his wild and wilful accusations of infidelity and the upsets that he'd caused in his first marriage to Anne Cecil. The pastoral environment and warmth of a home life in Hackney calms his nerves: He likes more and more, the spaciousness of the rooms of the house, even though most of his days are spent in his Study. One can't have everything, he says self mockingly for he thinks, once again there is much more of his Inheritance that he could and should have had. But money can't buy time; or good health. He laments being unable to move around easily; never mind briskly. His injured leg is now so bad that once more, he complains to himself: "I have not an able body!" As he reflects upon these six words, a darker thought descends and threatens to overshadow his recent contentment with married life. That "thought" strengthens the feeling that it is in this Big House in King's Place where he, if not his Countess, would end his days. But that thought comes naturally, as a matter of course, and not because he is depressed.

*

While pleasant thoughts play on his mind, as ever, he hopes for better times. But soon the mood changes. Lord Burghley, whose presence and actions had overshadowed Edward from the age of twelve, is now very ill. The all-powerful Chief Treasurer is seventy seven years old. Years of pain from joint inflammation prevents him from conducting his crucial State duties. Pain in his bones is another ailment that troubles him. He tries hard to keep his composure, but being frail, helplessness prevails as his tenure of high office, his grasp on power, weakens, then slips dramatically, as he is forced to become bed-bound. But even in this state, his sense of duty to the Queen (to whom, through his devious dealings he owes everything) and Protestant England, persists: Now, and for months earlier, he talks about a truce with Spain in the Lowlands conflict; a position which the Earl of Essex is opposed to. Edward, like everyone else at Court, is aware that Burghley's time on earth is short. But while the great man's strength drains away, as Edward knows, he does not forget grudges or forgive his enemies. He is devious, but also pious. On one occasion before the Privy Committee, he targeted Essex. Holding a book of Scripture, he draws the Earl's attention to Psalm Fifty five, Verse twenty three: "The bloody and deceitful men," he reads, "shall not live out half their days."

For those Privy Councillors who know but pretends not to know, Essex is Burghley's enemy. He is a man who must be closely watched. Why? Because the defence of the Realm is paramount. It is what the old man cares about. Now, the Queen who had never known anyone quite like Burghley, is told that his health is much worse."He is nearing the end, fast," Robert Cecil informs Her Majesty. Without further ado, she hastens to be at Burghley's bedside. She remembers her long association, the closeness and trust between herself and Burghley. Overwhelmed by the impending loss of her foremost Statesman, Her Majesty makes a surprising gesture: She feeds the dying Burghley herself. Sadness is etched on her aging face as she looks pitifully at Burghley. "How much hope is there?" she asks the doctor.

"Very little, Your Majesty," the doctor says in a gentle tone that does not detract from the finality of what is imminent. When the news of death reaches the Queen, for a while, she looks composed. Then, suddenly she becomes tearful and inconsolable. A man had died. But he was no ordinary man. He was the main pillar in her Government. Her body shakes, almost to a point of losing her calm, dignified regal composure. Her feelings are new; unique. She has lost a dear Friend and a faithful Servant; the man she had so fondly and for so long called her "Sir Spirit." Where once there was always a man, now there is a void; a vacancy. Burghley was there since her Coronation. Now, she is brought low: Her bereavement begins. Apart from her father King Henry VIII, no other death has affected her as much as Burghley's. He was her rock; her friend  confidante and devoted Minister.

*

August 1598: King's Place, Hackney, London: It is mid-morning on a hot Summer's day as a messenger hurries to the Big House in King's Place. Edward is at work in his Study. A knock on the door interrupts his train of thought. "Come in!" he says. Countess Elizabeth enters. She hands a sealed document to Edward. He opens it and reads the formal announcement of Burghley's death. He feels duty-bound to tell his Countess the sad, but expected news. Respectfully, she says, "I am very sorry, My Lord." She leaves the Study.

For a while, Edward sits in reflective mood. He thinks of the long period of subservience in his relations with the man who was first his protector, then his father-in-law; a relationship characterised by envy and jealousy on Burghley's part, which roused growing frustration and bitterness from Edward. "Mostly," he thinks now, and, looking back, he says to himself, "we were at odds with each other. Nothing between us, was either straightforward or entirely pleasant. Certainly none of the letters I'd written to him was easy. As a Nobleman, I was always hopeful of receiving my full, rightful Inheritance. But whenever I'd asked for financial help, I hated the sense of submission I felt. It was like begging! So, from youth to manhood, our coming together was complex, intertwined and, alas emotional."

To his credit, Edward tries to strike a balance between what was good and what was bad about Burghley. He faces up to the one thing that was constant in their relations: Money. Or the lack of it, on Edward's part. "No other man has influenced my life so comprehensively," he mutters: "In particular, the context of my life was dependent upon Burghley's rise to political dominance: an elevation mirrored by his growing gains of titles and properties. It is a murky story. But I would admit that, to some extent, Burghley's spectacular rise is justified by the high praise he'd received from some quarters. To have achieved what he had in this Elizabethan England is remarkable, unrivalled and magnificent. No doubt about it. But, for me, being under his devious scrutiny and surveillance had meant no escape from entrapment each and every day. This is how it was. But that shadowing of me has not gone away. It continues under Robert Cecil. So it must, the Queen dictates. But, to be fair, there is another side to Burghley, to which I owe very much: It pertains to Cecil House."

***

With thoughts of Burghley in mind, Edward's Study feels stuffy. He shifts in his chair, and adjusts to a more comfortable position. But, he still feels an undeniable uneasiness about Burghley's overall attitude and behaviour. He knows that before his father, Earl John, had died, he'd spoken to Burghley, as a friend. He'd suggested that in the event of his death, his son Edward, should come under Burghley's care and guardianship. "This much," Edward says to himself, "I always knew since my father's passing. So, for better or worse, the die was cast; my destiny was in the hands of Burghley." This clarity of thought, darkens Edward's mood. He glances at the painting on the opposite wall, then, his gaze moves toward the large window. Beyond, high in the sky, dark-grey clouds are gathering. He thinks of his escapades: of the countries he'd visited; of people he'd met. He feels a mild dizziness as a jumble of thoughts crowd in. But soon his head clears. "Here I am in Hackney, my body aches; I am lame and despised by many," he says to himself. But he is in no mood to blame Burghley. He thinks of what Burghley had provided for his Wards of Court at Cecil House. He accepts, gratefully, and with no hesitation, that Burghley's private Library was for him, one of the finest collections of books, manuscripts and maps in Elizabethan England. It is the special place where he'd spent countless hours of extensive research relating to the rarest Classical material to be found anywhere in the world. And, it was Burghley who had hired the best Tutors to instruct him.

These learned men had largely shaped and developed his way of thinking and his character. "A writer to be," he'd said with boyish eagerness to tutor Laurence Nowell; and later, to Uncle Arthur Golding."Had I not come to Cecil House," he asks himself, "where would I be today?" This thought draws his attention once more to his beloved father. Amidst all the treachery that had surrounded him then, and now, he thinks, positively: "Yes, Burghley had kept his word to Earl John to look after his son. And what an odd pairing they were," Edward says to himself, "England's grand Spymaster and his warrior-like, but distinctly artistic, drama-loving father, the Sixteenth Earl of Oxford, one of the last representatives of the extraordinary and glorious 'fighting de Veres.'"

But though Edward has portrayed Burghley as a man to be wary of (having cast him as POLONIUS in *Hamlet*) as time passes, he depicts his father-in-law more favourably. In an early draft of another of his plays *The Tempest*, he had portrayed himself as PROSPERO and Burghley as GONZALO. He is extraordinarily good at rounding-off his characters, and passionate, but not a sentimental man and writer. He is clearly capable of being kind to adversaries. So Edward, as PROSPERO in *The Tempest* speaks well of the old and infirm Burghley as GONZALO; the man who had opened a literary window - the extraordinary Cecil House Library, through which, he has gained new perspectives, new horizons. Unlike money, which he spends extravagantly, at times carelessly, he was granted the most precious gift for any writer to be: The freedom to develop his mind; and, to use the quill to form meaningful symbols, black letters on white paper: Thus he gains the greatest respect for the written word; the essential art of writing which is at the core of human Civilisation. Without this invention, human progress would not have gotten off the ground! And enabling this process, Edward thinks, is the special privilege of the Nobility of having to hand an assortment of printed works: the great texts of Classical and modern history and literature. Mindful of this wonderful resource of precious books, Edward gives due respect to Burghley, as PROSPERO, in *The Tempest*:

> "PROSPERO: By Providence divine…
> A noble Neapolitan, GONZALO.
> Out of his charity…
> Who being then appointed Master…
> Knowing I loved my books, he furnished me
> From mine own library with volumes that
> I prize above my dukedom."

Looking back, Edward knows how priceless the Cecil House Library has been (and is). Hence, his life cannot be divorced from Burghley's. So while Burghley could be calculating and cold there was this other side to him, as well: While he lay sick in bed, he'd written to his son, Robert: "Serve God by serving the Queen, for all other Service is indeed bondage to the Devil." For Robert, the loss of his father could not be greater. All along, step by step, Burghley had been teaching him: discussing and grooming him, from youth to manhood, to take over the heavy responsibilities from him. The duties that Robert must perform, arises from assuming the highest, most powerful office in England. It is second only to the Monarch. Having earlier lost his wife, and now his father, compounds his bereavement. The days that follow are tough and sad. But, against his losses is the gain of great power and influence as the Secretary of State in England. There is not much time for grief; or grieving. "How would I cope with the high office I hold?" Robert asks himself. He wonders if his father's profound religious beliefs (which he does not share) would leave traces in the way he conducts himself. He knows the national spotlight, the eyes of friends and foes alike, are upon him. "Yes, I am now the Master Spy, but I am spied upon too," he thinks. He smiles at the irony of it. But, his gaze is firmly fixed on his high office. He knows the seriousness of his father's bequest to him: "I am now, and in deed, the new Elizabethan puppeteer!" he says to himself. "From now on, I will pull the strings."

"If this changing of the guards has consequences for the people of England, it is particularly so for me," Edward says to himself. He keeps a beady eye on the State administration and events at Court. Very soon, he learns what the difference is between Robert and his father; especially in exercising power. Robert had borne witness to the distress of his sister Anne during her tumultuous marriage to Edward. And over the years, like his father, he'd taken a dim view of Edward's aristocratic background, his privileges and his "lewd" theatrical friends. On this matter, Burghley had, by example, taught his son well. But that is not all. Robert himself had had the misfortune of an accident early in life; a fall when he was a child. The injury he suffered had left him in a physically deformed state. Added to his impairment, are embarrassing portrayals by characters in Edward's plays relating to Anne, her father and himself that had rankled with Robert for years. Being sensitive and secretive compounds Robert's anger and bitterness. Now he feels he has the last laugh: As the Queen's Chief Minister, he is in a position to act with little or no constraints, to correct the wrongs, as he sees them. They include those committed by Edward. And, like Burghley, he too, understands that his family has come up in the world from the lower ranks. But humility, or lack of ambition, are not part of his character. And so, not contented, he hopes to be elevated even higher. Strikingly, unlike his father, Robert Cecil, is not a devout religious believer; neither does he adhere to strict moral or ethical standards. On some matters, already before his rise to power, Edward sees Robert for what he really is: someone who is more of an eye-for-an-eye type of man; an Administrator on the brink of redressing certain wrongs done to his nearest and dearest. Now that his father and sister are gone, in these vengeful times, it is for him to take revenge, and thus from on high, administer retribution to his enemies.

*

Such reflections as Edward had had so far that morning in his Study, does not lessen his uneasiness. He looks at the official letter on his desk announcing Burghley's death. He considers the thoughts and feelings that the sad news has generated among the people in England; and has no regrets about not having done more revision on the play he was working on when the Countess had come into his Study. But, as he resumes work on the play-script, one of the questions that worries him is: What sort of regime would Robert Cecil now command?

So in the wake of Burghley's death, the seemingly never-ending apprenticeship of Robert Cecil is over. With Robert's succession to power, Edward turns to look again at a play he'd drafted some years earlier. He thinks of *Richard III,* in which he'd cast Robert as a deformed King who wallows in the power he wields.

Like his father, Robert is no great lover of the theatre, or of writers. As a playwright, Edward is not sure what Robert really thinks of him. But because he stands out among his contemporaries, famous for combining personality traits of real people (especially at Court) and melding them into distinctive characters in his plays, Edward wonders, perhaps foolishly if he is, or could be, a target of Robert's surveillance network?

Whatever Robert Cecil may or may not think about a resemblance between himself and the title character in *Richard III*, its publication now, would reach a wide audience. And surely he will know, Edward thinks, about the publication which is being sold in bookshops though not approved by him. Interestingly, the Title Page carries the author's name: William Shakespeare. Does Robert know of Edward as "William Shakespeare?" Maybe he does. Maybe not. Why is this important? Because Burghley's passing marks the changing of the guards: the instalment of a new Official Gate-keeper in Government. This is hugely significant in these times.

Overall, Robert Cecil is now in charge of what is kept, and what isn't, in the highly valued national archives and records. Crucially, it is he who decides for posterity, what should survive and what should be destroyed. Since the name William Shakespeare was first printed under the poems *Venus and Adonis* and *Lucrece*, Edward de Vere has *continued to use that Pen-name*. Now, more than ever, he needs the protective cover it affords of never revealing himself. So if he'd not authorised the printing of the play *Richard III*, who gave the printer permission to use the name "William Shakespeare?"

Since its appearance six years before, Edward's disguise in the public domain as "William Shakespeare" has become a brand! He is conscious of this branding when he writes Sonnet One Hundred and Eleven:

"O for my sake do you with fortune chide,
The guilty goddess of my successful deeds,
That did not better for my life provide
Than public means, which public manners breeds;
Thence comes it that *my name receives a brand,*
And almost thence my nature is subdued
To what it works in, like the dyer's hand;
Pity me then, and wish I were renewed,
Whilst like a willing patient I will drink
Potions of eisell 'gainst my strong infection;
No bitterness that I will better think,
Nor double penance to correct correction.
Pity me then, dear friend, and I assure ye,
Even that your pity is enough to cure me."

Edward pens these words with barely disguised restraint. With these anguished words, he feels his heart is ready to burst; and a deep reservoir of pent up emotion will pour forth. This Sonnet is the watershed moment when Edward secretly accepts his official "or not to be" brand name! But his Sonnets are not for the reading public. They record his private thoughts and feelings and as the "brand" name William Shakespeare becomes entrenched, he knows that his noble name Edward de Vere is now totally subsumed by his disguise "William

Shakespeare." And all the more so because of the similarity of the names: Shakespeare and Shakspere. Adding to Edward's worry over the continued usurpation of his plays, is the reality that as the "Shakespeare" brand takes hold, and becomes popular, though not officially sanctioned by the Stationer's Company, publishers take their chances: One of them is Cuthbert Burby.

Earlier, Burby was linked to another publication passed by State officials; a book titled *Palladis Tamia.* Edward gets hold of a copy which he peruses. In it, the author, Frances Meres, identifies Edward de Vere as an English playwright and praises him as the "best" for Comedy. But soon, Edward uncovers an interesting thing about Meres compilation of English writers. Mere's thinks that Edward de Vere and Shakespeare are two separate people!

Pen-names and author's attribution are not uncommon; and reading this, Edward smiles secretly at what he hears from critics and others who attempt to unmask him. His disguise as William Shakespeare has succeeded. Regardless of a deep, private sickening feeling of knowing the Truth about his hard-earned work in the face of provocations, he remains true to himself: "To thine own self be true" he'd written in his play *Romeo and Juliet*; words he'd taken from of all people, Burghley, who had penned them in a letter to his son.

He presses on, devotedly writing Sonnets, personal musings that releases pent-up feelings. Therein, he shows that the relationship to "William" (the first part of his Pen-name) is a complex one. Increasingly so because he cannot reveal who he is. This is cloak and dagger Elizabethan England; a dark and shadowy world teeming with Spies and Counter-spies. And so, the metamorphosis from Edward to Will reaches an interesting juncture, which provokes memories of his Uncle

Arthur Golding introducing him to Latin translations and earlier discussions on Ovid's *Metamorphoses.*

Little did he know then, between the ages of ten and twelve, that one day, his life would metamorphose in the way that it has until now. After all the material things that he has gained in life, now he sits alone in his Study nursing an increasingly painful leg. But this is not the only pain he feels. Like a shadow, the sense of loss comes again: It creeps over him. "Of all the Pen-names I have used," he says to himself, "I have willed 'Will' to come into being." And he has. He fully accepts that the evolution from Edward to Will is largely his own creation: And all things considered, he has no choice now. "William Shakespeare" is no longer a Pen-name he could control! The "Brand" has taken over. As if he'd been living in a dream from which he now awakes, he is appalled by what is now the hard reality. "Cloak-and-dagger," he thinks. Nothing about all this is straightforward: It is shot through with both shock, horror and some irresistible attraction, too. Cloak and dagger, indeed. But the stakes, his life's work, could not be higher, he thinks. He is disturbed by how wretched he feels. And, as he'd always done in life, in good times, as well as in bad times, he reaches for his pen, dips it in ink and does the most natural thing he could do: He writes.

But as always, since he'd come to Cecil House, thoughts of the Queen whom he'd angered so many times, is ever-present. He feels as if he'd been condemned as a writer. He thinks of the one thousand pounds a year Grant and Her Majesty. She has forbidden him from straying beyond certain bounds: Now he confronts the hard fact that he is a politically accommodating playwright whose Courtly dramatic episodes could never ever be claimed as his own authorship. "O the pain of this," he says in anguish to himself, "Only through the anonymity of a common 'Will' can I publish my work." *Common*? Common with whom? Gallingly for him, it is with Shakspere? Though befogged by disappointment, with Her Majesty in mind, he thinks clearly enough to compose two not very praiseful Sonnets. In Sonnet One Hundred and Thirty Five, he writes:

"Who ever hath her wish, thou hast thy Will,
And Will to boot, and Will in overplus;
More than enough am I, that vex thee still,
To thy sweet will making addition thus.
Wilt thou, whose Will is large and spacious,
Not once vouchsafe to hide my will in thine?
Shall will in others seem right gracious,
And in my will no fair acceptance shine?
The sea, all water, yet receives rain still,
And in abundance addeth to;
So thou, being rich in Will, add to thy Will
One Will of mine to make thy large Will more:
Let no unkind, nor fair beseechers kill;
Think all but one, and me in that one Will."

Then again in Sonnet One Hundred and Thirty Six:

If thy soul check thee that I come so near,
Swear to thy blind soul that I was thy Will,
And will, thy soul knows, is admitted there;
Thus far for love, my love-suit sweet fulfil.
Will will fulfil the treasure of thy love,
Ay, fill it full with wills, and my will one;
In things of great receipt with ease we prove
Among a number one is reckoned none.
Then in the number, let me pass untold,

Though in thy stores account I one must be.
For nothing hold me, so it please thee hold
That nothing, me, a something sweet to thee.
Make but my name thy love, and love that still;
And then thou lov'st me, for my name is Will."

Ever-conscious of how he came to adopt, and be stuck with the pen name "Shakespeare," to which he added William, he remembers Gabriel Harvey's stirring words before the Queen at Audley End: "Thine eyes flash fire, thy will shakes spears." Out of "will" and "shake spears" comes the brand name. And so, the *metamorphosis* from Edward to Will has come to pass. And continues...

***

# XII

## "Every word doth almost tell my name"

*"Be great in act as you have been in thought"*

After Southampton pays his fine to Burghley for not marrying his granddaughter Elizabeth, as her father, Edward does not let his disappointment get in the way of his complex feelings and relations with the wayward Southampton.

It is Spring: Southampton, foot-loose and free of Court constraints, crosses the English Channel. In Paris, he leads a bohemian lifestyle. But soon, his simmering secret romantic liaison in London is no longer hidden. Elizabeth Vernon, Cousin of the Earl of Essex, is with child. A few weeks later, as Vernon's pregnancy shows, Southampton gets the latest news of his Mistress's condition. Though he is not surprised, he is anxious. He interrupts his French holiday and, potentially, his care-free days. Quietly, he re-enters England in the hot month of August, amidst a pall of gloom as people mourn the death of Lord Burghley, who had for so long been a dependable fixture, but is now a giant English oak, felled. Southampton remembers how heavily he was penalised by the dead man; and, on that account, no love on his part, is lost. Now he does the decent thing: He marries Ms Vernon. But, soon after, he heads back to his life of leisure in Paris. Not everyone turns a blind eye. His stealthy movements in and out of England are known to the spymasters. And now that Burghley is no longer his problem, he feels he's escaped him, once and for all. But, he could not be more wrong for soon after he returns to Paris, Robert Cecil is on to him. Cecil tells Southampton that the Queen knows of his secret marriage; and demands that he should return to England, at once. This is easier said than done. Why? Because Southampton loves, with a passion, games of chance; and the gambling debts he has run-up keeps him in Paris. So, for a while yet, he delays returning to England, as requested.

*

Meanwhile Edward learns more about the Big House and finds contentment in it. He is happy with his wife and new Countess; a relationship that has many pluses. But his feelings are not confined to marriage. They continue to flow through his pen towards Southampton in the Sonnets that are close to being a secret notebook or diary. Among other things, he responds to a "sex scandal" about his "beloved youth." In Sonnet Eighty-Nine he writes that "thou did'st forsake me for some fault." And in Sonnet Ninety-Two, he expresses regret: "But do thy worst to steal thyself away." This relates to Southampton's short stay in England in August before going back to Paris. Then, he adds the following lines:

"For term of life thou art assured mine,
And life no longer than thy love will stay,
For it depends upon that love of thine.
Then need I not to fear the worst of wrongs,
When in the least of them my life hath end;
I see a better state to me belongs
Than that which on thy humour doth depend.
Thou canst not vex me with inconstant mind,
Since that my life on thy revolt doth lie.

What a happy title do I find,
Happy to have thy love happy to die!
But what's so blessed fair that fears no blot?
Thou mayest be false, and yet I know it not."

And in Sonnet Ninety-Five, he writes about the "beauty of thy budding name" – a reference to Southampton's youthful life. In full, the Sonnet reads:

"How sweet and lovely dost thou make the shame
Which like canker in the fragrant rose
Doth spot the beauty of thy budding name:
O in what sweets dost thou thy sins enclose!
That tongue that tells the story of thy days,
Making lascivious comments on thy sport.
Cannot dispraise, but in a kind of praise,
Naming thy name, blessed an ill report.
O what a mansion have those vices got,
Which for their habitation chose out thee,
Where beauty's veil doth cover every blot,
And all things turns to fair that eyes can see!
Take heed, dear heart, of this large privilege.
The hardest knife ill used doth lose its edge."

After Southampton's gambling and care-free days in Paris, on his return to England, he is arrested and imprisoned. When Edward hears of this, once more, he records how he feels in Sonnet Ninety-Seven:

"How like a winter hath my absence been,
From thee, the pleasure of the fleeting year!
What freezings have I felt, what dark days seen,
What old December's bareness everywhere!

And yet this time removed was summer's time,
The teeming autumn big with rich increase,
Bearing the wanton burden of the prime,
Like widowed wombs after their lords' decease:
Yet this abundant issue seemed to me
But hope of orphans, and unfathered fruit;
For summer and his pleasures wait on thee,
And thou away, the very birds are mute;
Or if they sing, 'tis with so dull a cheer
That leaves look pale, dreading the winter's near."

After these lines dedicated to Southampton, Edward confides his obsessive thoughts in another Sonnet with Spring-like optimism.

"From you have I been absent in the spring,
When proud-pied April, dressed in all his trim,
Hath put a spirit of youth in everything,
That heavy Saturn laughed and leaped with him.
Yet nor the lays of birds, nor the sweet smell
Of different flowers in odour and in hue,
Could make me any summer's story tell,
Or from their proud lap pluck them where they grew;
Nor did I wonder at the lily's white,
Nor praise the deep vermilion in the roses,
They were but sweet, but figures of delight,
Drawn after you, you pattern of all those.
Yet seemed it winter still, and you away,
As with your shadow I with these did play."

But in spite of such poetic expressions, Edward's feeling for his Countess Elizabeth is secure. She need not feel left out, or abandoned, because of the seemingly obsessive affections he'd expressed for Southampton in the Sonnets. But being grounded in a good stable marriage, it could not be clearer to him, how lamentably one-sided his feelings for, and relations with, Southampton really is.

So after the hot and scandalous summer, with autumn, the harvest has come: A bountiful time, Edward thinks, when Southampton becomes a parent. So now he has a child, which Edward had urged upon him when talks of marriage to his daughter Elizabeth were still ongoing. Pleased with Southampton's fatherhood; Edward hopes he would now settle down. But while he hopes for the best for Southampton, he is sharply reminded of his own youthful passions and rash actions. He knows stability in marriage is hard to achieve. Life's ups and downs have to be dealt with.

Soon after his child is born, Southampton joins the Earl of Essex who is to lead English troops in a military campaign in Ireland. Southampton is expected to be Essex's deputy, serving as General of the Horse; a highly-ranked, distinguished position. How interesting, Edward thinks, that Southampton's military appointment should come at a time when he harbours a well-kept secret: His long-held sympathy for aggrieved people who insists on being free: In this case, rebellious Irishmen. He is mindful of his feelings for the under-dog, which he'd expressed in these words in his play *Richard II*: "That England that is wont to conquer others, Hath made a shameful conquest of itself." But Conquest is an integral part of a growing English Empire. And he is a first-hand witness to England's budding overseas expansion. So when he rewrites his earlier play *Henry VI, part 2*, he includes Irish patriots for Patriotism is central to his heritage and belief.

He stands looking out from the window of his Great Study. His thoughts deflect attention from the stiffness and pain in his leg which is followed by a creeping, mild numbness. The weather is unsettled, blustery winds disturb everything under the slate-grey sky as curtain-like shades of evening descends. A depressing sight, he thinks, as he shuffles back to his desk, where he considers the work he'd done that morning: Revision of what he'd written the day before. But, of the thoughts he'd had earlier, foremost is the pending Irish Campaign. It is no idle matter: He is worried. Not only for the general safety of all the English soldiers in the battlefield, but more particulary for Southampton, who is at the forefront of the Campaign. He is in the firing line; in mortal danger. Edward's worry for Southampton gets worse because, once again, he is with Essex. The combined effect of all this stretches Edward's feelings almost to breaking point. He turns inwards. He tries to think the matter through; to make sense of it; and like almost everything else that has happened to him, he imputes it into his art.

A few weeks later, the Lord Chamberlain's Men performs his play *Henry V* at the newly constructed *Globe Theatre* on the South Bank of the River Thames. One of Edward's greatest gifts, and a key to his success in the theatre, is his understanding of audiences: Their interest in the plays because of his unique abilty of bringing together historical and current affairs, thus translating everyday life into the art of staged story telling. The topicality of the play, he knows, will attract greater interest and thus larger audiences. This understanding of a range of human concern and interest is at the heart of his work; a major component of his presentations. So after he'd written a first draft of *The Famous Victories of Henry V*, he shows how skilful he is at propaganda; and how, he feels about the Earl of Essex's Campaign in Ireland. He does his best to put aside his anti-Essex feelings and be hopeful that Southampton will return to England safe and well. So, in the new version of the play, he wears his heart on his sleeves, so to speak. "Where now the general of our gracious empires," he writes:

> "As in good time he may, from Ireland coming,
> Bringing rebellion broached on his sword,
> How many would the peaceful city quit
> To welcome him!"

"To welcome him!" After writing this line, Edward rests his quill. He leans back on his chair and sighs. Conscious of thinking too far ahead, he checks himself. There is a long way for the Campaign to go, never mind "welcoming" Southampton back from Ireland so soon. For a moment, his spirits are raised as he remembers how the people of London had flocked to the streets to give their brave countrymen full-throated support and encouragement. Of the troops who'd been assigned to fight abroad, he considers the fact that this Campaign had the largest number of soldiers that the Queen has ever sent abroad. Having expressed how he feels in the Sonnets, he is no less brave and inventive than he'd been in his poems and plays. Now, he dares to express his frank thoughts about Essex in his play *Coriolanus.* He portrays Essex as the Roman General Caius CORIOLANUS; a character through whom his dislike of Essex is plain.

The play exposes the human weakness of the General and Edward uses Plutarch's history to relate the story. In victory against a foreign rebellion, CORIOLANUS reveals his arrogance: Edward is unsparing and exact in drawing historical parallels between the play and the Irish Campaign led by Essex. Essex's tiresome boastfulness of unlimited privileges and high positions, puts distance between himself and the impoverished masses. CORIOLANUS sees the people as "dissentious rogues." You "make yourself scabs" by expressing "your opinions." MENENIUS, the friend of CORIOLANUS sets the tone early in the play:

> "MENENIUS: There was a time when all the body's
> members
> Rebelled against the belly, thus accused it:...
> The Senators of Rome are this good belly,
> And you the mutinous members: For examine
> Their counsels and their cares, digest things rightly
> Touching the weal o'th'common, you shall find
> No public benefit which you receive
> But it proceeds or comes from them to you,
> And no way from yourselves. What do you think,
> You, the great toe of this assembly?"

In this telling of the story, Edward is faithful to Plutarch. MENENIUS'S fable of the belly is instructive, but it means nothing to CORIOLANUS, who was never short of food. He blames the victims. He assumes that they will have no problem if only they could do the right thing! But the lies that CORIOLANUS feeds them are transparent and patently grievous. The fact that the Nobleman Edward could empathize and sympathize with the starving common folk is an aspect of his own evolution as a human being; and, as a writer, in CORIOLANUS, he is on his way to finding and expressing a more mature voice. He becomes more of a Humanist. And, from here on, like his problematic marriage to Anne Cecil which inspired so many characters in his writings, now his feelings for Southampton and Essex in relation to Elizabethan politics, inspires Edward to go further into his work: creating, revising and honing his plays, old and new, into extraordinary literary art!

***

By now Edward's second daughter, Bridget is a much sought after bride. Husbands-to-be come to Cecil House, and they depart. Among them was William Herbert, the son of Mary Sidney Herbert, Countess of Pembroke. As the name suggests, Mary is the sister of Philip Sidney, one of Edward's former rivals. After the Courtship and marriage of his first daughter, Elizabeth, what does Edward think about the prospects of a marriage match between Bridget and William Herbert? Of Herbert, he thinks that he is well brought up, fair conditioned and "hath many good parts to him." This sounds promising, but, as Edward knows, impressions of someone is no guarantee that a marriage match will be successful. He is right: Bridget and Herbert do not marry. And, like her elder sister, she turns her attention elsewhere; to a man named Francis Norris, who aspires to become a politician.

Coming so soon after the death of Lord Burghley, the marriage between Bridget and Norris is a relatively sombre affair. But whatever her disappointments, Bridget remains hopeful: She is happy to be married to Norris. But soon, she learns that Norris has to go overseas. She feels cruelly robbed of his presence at home. Thus, she is more or less wedded to an absentee-husband, much like her father Edward had been in relations with her mother Anne!

While Norris is away, Edward's thoughts are never far from the Campaign in Ireland. As news come through, it seems that Essex's leadership is becoming a costly disaster. Though Queen Elizabeth has reservations, she does not halt the Essex Mission. She makes it clear to Essex that she is displeased: She reproaches him for something she'd not known about: His promotion of Southampton to the position of General of the Horse. She informs Essex that Southampton should not be so promoted. But far from showing any concern for the Queen's orders, Essex does the very thing she warns against.

So promoting Southampton was a big mistake! But, a well calculated one, it seems, for while the Queen is no longer young and attractive, her commanding aristocratic power is no less than it had ever been. She acts swiftly. She demands the demotion of Southampton. At this point, relations between her and her Commander in Ireland are, to say the least, far from good. They quickly hit a new low.

Through the Summer and into the autumn of this Irish Campaign, instead of attacking the Rebels, Essex meets his "enemy" in secret. And most surprisingly, he agrees to a ceasefire with the Earl of Tyrone. This allows Tyrone to maintain his rebel strongholds. But how trustworthy is Tyrone? Suspicions are raised among high officials in England. Could it be that this truce is allowing Tyrone to bide his time until back-up forces from Catholic Spain could reach Catholic Ireland?

The Queen is upset and angry. And when she is told of Essex's understanding or Agreement with Tyrone, she reminds Essex that he has, once more exceeded his role. His Agreement is demeaning and meaningless; at best, it is a fragile peace.

Meanwhile, in England, Edward is as thoughtful as ever on the eve of his Fiftieth birth year. Though still mobile, the visible wear and tear mirrors his inner weariness. Nonetheless he still thinks a great deal about Southampton's safety. He follows closely the Irish Campaign: Essex's behaviour is quite unusual and puzzling; out of the ordinary, he thinks. He fears Essex's self-aggrandizement; the reflection of a Commander's hubris, and hence his insubordination!

He remembers Essex's celebrity status, his Courtly stardom as the Hero of Cadiz, two years before. But now, after he'd embarrassed himself in the failed Azores Mission, his disobedience of the Queen's orders puts him in a bad place. And, to make matters more interesting, one man with his ear close to the ground, the Elizabethan gossip, William

Reynolds, reports that in the sexually charged environment of War, Southampton had begun to dote upon a man named Pierce Edmonds. Reynolds, who had served under Essex and Southampton in Ireland, speaks of Southampton's close friendship with Edmonds; their exchange of gifts, their hugging and so on. All this gossip, as well as the real facts, are grist for Edward's artistic mill.

In a revised draft of *Troilus and Cressida*, Edward presents a scenario that parallels the Southampton-Edmond situation in Ireland. Having already written about a close same-sex relationship between OTHELLO and IAGO, in his play *Othello,* now, in *Troilus and Cressida* Edward addresses charges against ACHILLES and PETROCLUS made by THERSITES:

> "THERSITES: (To PATROCLUS) Thou art thought to be ACHILLES'S male varlet.
> PATROCLUS: Male varlet, you rogue? What's that?
> THERSITES: Why, his masculine whore. Now the rotten diseases of the South (venereal diseases) take and take again such preposterous discoveries!
> PATROCLUS: Why, thou damnable box of envy, thou? What mean'st thou to curse thus?
> THERSITES: Do I curse thee?
> PATROCLUS: Why, no, you ruinous butt, you whoreson indistinguishable cur, no.
> THERSITES: No? Why art thou then exasperate? Thou idle immaterial skein of sleeve silk, thou green sarsenet flap for a sore eye, thou tassel of a prodigal's purse, thou! Ah, how the world is pestered with such waterflies! Diminutives of nature."

Edward knows that other writers of his time have compared

Essex with Achilles. With such a reputation, it is easy to see how self-inflation could enter Essex's mind and affect his behaviour. In his portrayal of improper conduct between Officers, Edward casts himself as ULYSSES, and Southampton as PETROCLUS. Later, through his dialogue with ACHILLES, indirectly he warns Southampton of the fickleness of Courtly favour. In the interplay between ACHILLES and ULYSSES, he writes:

"ACHILLES: What, am I poor of late?
'Tis certain, greatness, once fall'n out with fortune,
Must fall out with men too. What the declines is
He shall as soon read in the eyes of others.
As feel in his own fall…
What, are my deeds forgot?
ULYSSES: Time hath, my lord,
A wallet at his back, wherein he puts
Alms for oblivion, a great siz'd monster
Of ingratitudes.
Those scraps are good deeds past,
Which are devour'd
As fast as they are made,
Forgot as soon
As done…
For beauty, wit,
High birth, vigour of bone, desert in service
Love, friendship, charity, one subjects all
To envious and calculating Time.
One, touch of nature makes the whole world kin."

And Edward uses another play to deal with deeply problematic personal matters: In this case, his relations with

Southampton and Essex.

***

The year Fifteen ninety eight is a most significant juncture in the story of Edward de Vere as "William Shakespeare." It was the first time that one of Edward's *plays*, appears in print under the Pen-name William Shakespeare. Around the same time, the play *Love's Labour's Lost*, appears for the first time, newly corrected and augmented by "W. Shakspere" the only time that the printed author's name is so spelled! By now, after the rumours, Edward comes to know that Shakspere plays the part of Manager-Producer with the Lord Chamberlain's Men, the Company that was producing most of Edward's anonymous plays. So Shakspere had worked his way (and continues to so do) through the ranks to hold the position that John Lyly had held for his employer Edward for more than a decade. But Shakspere's position now is more financial than literary. Nonetheless, Edward is alarmed and disgusted by what he hears about the usurpers of his plays. He shudders to think of the potential loss of his Anonymous works and is uncomfortable with his Pen name William Shakespeare being so close to Will Shakspere.

Now his attention is drawn to the appearance of an Anonymous play titled *Histrio-Mastrix,* an imitation of his *Troilus and Cressida*. How interesting, he thinks, that his play should be so treated. And how timely too, for though he is careful about his disguise in *Troilus and Cressida*, he'd used the phrase: *"Shakes a furious spear."* Is he furious about any misuse of his Pen-name William Shakespeare? Yes. And he reflects that a few fellow-writers and people in the theatre know about him as William Shakespeare. The man Shakspere, certainly knows the fact from fiction. Edward sees a copy of

*Histrio-Matrix* in which the character POVERTY scorns a scoffing fool, "an artless idiot." who usurps his throne. Who is this "artless idiot?" The poet and playwright, Ben Jonson, thinks Will Shakspere is stealing from Edward. Shakspere is a thief. But he is also a businessman in the theatre world, who is making money; and he is good at doing so. He is better off wheeling and dealing than if he was just a jobbing actor. But though Edward is upset, he is also intrigued by the bold self-promotion of the uncultured man. For a while, he nurses his wounds. But soon he is jolted out of his seeming complacency when others enter the debate on the play-stealing business. He learns how strongly Jonson feels about the stealer of literary works. In a piece titled the "Poet Ape," Jonson shows a manuscript copy to Edward. It reads:

"Poor poet-ape that would be thought our chief
Whose works are even the frippery of wit.
*From brokage is become so bold a thief*
As we the robbed, leave rage and pity it.
*At first*, he made *low shifts*, pick and glean,
Buy the reversion of old plays. Now grown
To a little wealth and credit in the scene,
He takes up all, makes each man's wit his own.
And told of this, he slights it. 'Tut, such crimes
The sluggish, gaping auditor devours;
He *marks not whose 'twas first and afterwards*
May judge it to be his as well as ours.'
Fool, as if half eyes will not know a fleece
From locks of wool are *shreds* from the *whole piece*."

In more prosy words, Jonson is saying that the man pretending to be the best English writer, Will Shakspere, is really a "Poet Ape;" an imposter whose extraordinary claim deflects attention and complicates the authorship of Edward's works. Anonymous plays, are fair game for men like the feather-plucking Shakspere, who has some money which attracts publishers. Such an advantage for the ambitious countryman, raises the question: Was Shakspere butchering and passing on Edward's plays to other authors for partial re-writing and eventually for production. All this adds to the confusion (and confusing situation) which Edward is trying to come to terms with: In essence, promotion of the lie and legend that "William Shakespeare" is not one man, but an amalgam: more than one author! This suits Will Shakspere. As the "Poet Ape" who began his career as a bit-part actor, then with a nose for business as a broker of plays, and, as a "playwright," he now has the grand ambition of climbing the Elizabethan social ladder. Class is paramount, especially the status of *Gentleman*. Nonetheless, making the journey from Country youth to Country Gentleman is his goal.

Shakspere works closely with the Lord Chamberlain's Men, the leading Troupe of actors, at this time. So, after some success in his business dealings, he takes every chance he gets to mingle with the leading actors and theatre professionals. As he gains in confidence and contacts, he becomes more emboldened. He becomes an undisguised play thief. Jonson knows how Anonymous plays are misused; and he confides in a player at the newly-built *Globe Theatre*: "Practice makes perfect." Saying this, he thinks of Shakspere who continues to thrive while his under-handedness is raised to another stage. He claims more plays to be his own as more people know who he is in the London theatre scene, mostly on the adminstrative side. This familiarity nudges him further into thinking of himself as the playwright William Shakespeare. Shakespeare-Shakspere: The names are twinned forever, he thinks. But, he asks himself: "Should Shakspere be pitied, or not, for his foolishness?"

Maybe. But knowing the Court and its intrigues, he wonders if Shakespere is aided and abetted by others: his rivals and enemies. He is thankful that his plays are eagerly anticipated by the public; and that his brand name "William Shakespeare" is high and rising. "A brand" it is as he'd confided in his Sonnet. There is nothing he could do about this branding. But, he is hopeful that sooner or later, knowledgeable theatre-goers will come to know who the real author of all that they see, hear and feel is. He keeps hope alive. It is his mainstay now, perhaps more than ever. But after he reads Jonson's Poet Ape words, his worry returns. The hard reality of what Will Shakspere, the Actor-manager, is doing coincides with the rising popularity of the *Globe Theatre.* Crowds flock to see the latest productions, one of which is *Hamlet.* The sense of history is strong in him. He feels he is at a crossroads in his tumultuous playwrighting career. Uppermost in his mind now are the original words that he'd written down: *"To be or not to be; Ay, there's the point…"*

In a pirated draft he'd seen, clearly, another hand has tampered with the original wording. Could this be an example of Shakspere's unfortunate practice of passing on plays to friends and other dramatists to tweak parts, add words and lines, here and there, and rewrite certain passages and scenes? The assertion that other writers have contributed to Edward's plays, increasingly takes hold, thus further obscuring the real author. The confusion deepens in the popular mind. Is it Shakspere or Shakespeare? Take your pick. The names could not be closer in terms of the sound and spelling! And so, Shakspere, given his links with the actors Company, the Lord Chamberlain's Men, acts more and more like a conductor: After all, he has, more or less a free-hand, as the Impressario of the moment; the conduit through which a few of Edward's plays gets into production. "Good for Shakspere," Edward says to himself. "But very upsetting for me." He feels there is nothing he could do to change the trend. He feels an unspeakable turmoil deep in his guts which spreads through his entire body. "Why?" he asks himself. Then, loud and clear, the answer comes in his own barely whispered, anguished words: "Because, all things considered, in this year Fifteen ninety-eight, the branded die, my Pen name William Shakespeare is irrevocably cast. It is official: The matter is out of my hands."

***

As weeks and months pass, Shakspere's thievery continues. While Edward monitors things from the side-lines, Jonson becomes more incensed. He is moved, once more, to write, not in Verse or Sonnet, but in a play titled *Every Man Out of His Humour*. In it, he tells the story of a clownish character named SOGLIARDO, who represents the real Will Shakspere. Jonson's portrayal of this character hits the mark. He represents Shakspere's upwardly mobile social aspirations, accurately: seeing him as a man who will stop at nothing to achieve the status of a "Gentleman." He is, if need be, ready and willing to *buy* the title. Jonson, in his play for the Lord Chamberlain's Men, publishes a cast list which does not include any actor by the name of Will Shakspere.

This is perhaps not difficult to understand, because of the close alignment of Shakspere and the character SOGLIARDO; a man so honoured to carry a Gentleman's name that he readily pays for it. Certainly at this time, Shakspere is here, there and, it seems, everywhere. He mingles with theatre connections, including a few Gentlemen of the highest rank. As he makes more money, he moves closer to his goal of buying himself into higher social standing. This ambition mirrors Shakspere's way of thinking, exactly. He feels he must justify leaving the Stratford countryside; and nothing could better reflect this than becoming a *country Gentleman*! To this grand end, just three years before, he'd submitted an application to the London College of Arms to *buy* his father John, a Coat of Arms. While his submission is being evaluated, Shakspere's excitement grows, day by day. Eventually, a Heraldic Crest and Motto are granted to the Shakspere family. So at last, Shakspere gains what he'd craved: The status of Gentleman. And not surprisingly, this rise to prominence is played out in the following Scene from *Every Man Out of His Humour*; a three-some dialogue between the characters SOGLIARDO, CARLO and PUNTARVOLO, who are in reality portrayals of Shakspere, Jonson and Edward, respectively.

"By this parchment gentlemen," SOGLIARDO says:
"I have been so toiled among the heralds yonder, you will not believe! They do speak in the strangest language and give a man the hardest terms for his money that ever you knew.

CARLO: But have you arms, have you arms?

SOGLIADO: I'faith, I can thank them. I can write myself gentlemen now. Here's my patent, it cost me thirty pound, by this breath.

PUNTARVOLO: A very fair coat, well charged and full of armoury.

SOGLIARDO: Nay, it has as much variety of colours in it as you have seen a coat have. How like you the crest, sir?

PUNTARVOLO: I understand it not well, what is it?

SOGLIARDO: Marry, sir, it is your Boar without a head, rampant. A boar without a head, that's very rare!"

To these words CARLO responds: "Ay, and rampant too! troth, I commend the herald's wit, decyphered him well: a swine without a head, without brain, wit, anything indeed, ramping to gentility…" PUNTARVOLO follows by saying: "Let the word be, 'Not without mustard: Your Crest is very rare, sir.' " SOGLIARDO then tells PUNTARVOLO that the recently granted Crest has "Your boar without a head;" a direct reference to Edward de Vere's ancient and legendary family crest.

So Jonson's pen is good and true. Usurpation of Edward's work is the central theme: His ancient ancestral crest as a Boar "without a head." And so three literary examples of this time: The "Poet Ape," "SOGLIARDO" and the "Artless Idiot," reflects Edward's dilemma. They reveal the hard truth about Will Shakspere and Edward as William Shakespeare, just when the brand name "William Shakespeare" appears more frequently in bookshops and theatres. By now, some people in the know are confused; none the wiser, as to who is who? Maybe this matters not. But perhaps that is the intention. Amidst this particular controversy in theatrical circles, as Edward approaches his fiftieth birthday, his anger and general unhappiness with Shakspere's insidious actions, are stretched to breaking point. Shakspere's pronounced bullishness in claiming plays that are not his, is heightened. Edward thinks of Shakspere as a grasping social climber, a "wannabe;" akin to a title-buyer who becomes a "Gentleman." But more seriously, Edward thinks Shakspere is dangerous. Very much so. Why? Because, he thinks, that Shakspere the manager, play-broker-actor is becoming even more ambitious. By now, Shakspere had accumulated a good sum of money; and in these hard, unpredictable times, he is able to sway publishers and needy theatre people to exploit the saleable "William Shakespeare" brand.

***

Edward's curiosity, sensitivity to, and interest in, Elizabethan politics never flags: Being a street-wise Nobleman, he hears the rumblings at Court and elsewhere in the land, as the feudal hierarchy is threatened with social Revolution. He is especially alarmed by how unstable and precarious the situation has become. Queen Elizabeth is older now, but she still thinks of herself as the "Virgin Queen." Be that as it may as everyone knows, she lacks an heir. "Who would succeed her to the Throne?" Edward asks himself. As the prospects of a new Ruler of England looms, he confides strictly to himself, what he thinks is best, for in these times it is High Treason to talk too loudly, never mind too openly, about Succession. He sees Elizabeth as a shadow of herself. May her heart beat for longer, but its lessening rapidity makes him think more and more about the future of England. Religion and politics are at the root of everything, and he wonders about the leaders who would decide the direction in which the nation should go. Lately, he'd been listening to talk about books, plays and writers; and how religious fanatics and Puritans have come to the fore. Among them, are writers of Verse, but not of the Edward -"William Shakespeare" kind. For the very few who know him, the cover of his Pen-name offers enough anonymity for him *not* to be recognised as one and the same man "William Shakespeare."

For zealots like the Puritans and extremists, a poet like Edward is out of bounds. They see his epic poem *Venus and Adonis,* as a work of sexual deviancy. They rail against it; all the more, as two different editions of it are published and sold out within twelve months. The ideas therein, the Puritans think, have infected the minds of those who read the poem. This must stop. Why? Because such literature fuels decadent life-styles, the self-appointed Moralists argue. A man named Joseph Hall denounces a writer who calls himself "Labeo." With suspicion thick in the air, Edward feels the need to adopt another layer of disguise. Hence he uses the Pen-name "Labeo."

"For shame," Hall says, "write better Labeo, or write nothing." Among contemporary writers is Thomas Bastard. After he critiques Shakespeare, Bastard is curious about the identity of the sinful "Labeo," whose writings are widely appreciated. This observation of Edward as Shakespeare, and Labeo's double identity is interesting and significant. Hall and Bastard are further aggravated by "Shakespeare's" most recent published work: *The Passionate Pilgrim*. They are aghast: They say the sexual content of the book makes it un-Christian and therefore unacceptable. But *The Passionate Pilgrim* is no ordinary run-of-the-mill publication; and rightly, Edward is unhappy with the publisher William Jaggard. Why? Because the material he prints under the Shakespeare name is *not* unauthorized. This is another indication of a publisher who assumes that he knows Edward and "William Shakespeare" are one and the same man, and exploits the Shakespeare name without Edward's permission. Surely, Edward thinks, "I should have had the chance to see and verify my work. It is an under-handed thing for Jaggard to have done." It is a complex situation; and Jaggard acts knowing well how securely Edward's tongue and hands are tied: He cannot declare who he is.

So he is embarrassed; and once again, he stops to reconsider who at this juncture, are friends and who are his enemies. He feels salt is rubbed into his wounds by Jaggard when he realises that most of *The Passionate Pilgrim's* poems are attributed to "W. Shakespeare." But this is not true: They are written by other authors. So who is the instigator of this latest published work? Does the Poet-ape, Will Shakspere have anything to do with it? Of one thing Edward is certain: His enemies are proving their worth!

As each day brings new knowledge, he considers how far publishers and writers have already gone and, are going, in targeting him. The political and social environment is unsettled; and unsettling. He notes the part high-minded leaders are playing; men like the Archbishop of Canterbury and the Bishop of London, who seem to have had enough. Their piety, he thinks, beggars belief. Unsurprisingly, he is alarmed by the turn of events as the two top Churchmen, secure in their self-styled, God-given authority, hands down, Moses-like, an Edict banning books and other writings by certain authors. They name works by John Davies, Joseph Hall, Gabriel Harvey and Thomas Nashe, among others. Such writings are recalled from publishers and bookshops.

"Burn them all!" the Registrar's voice rises outside the Stationers' Hall.

The order is loud and clear; almost a shout. For a while, Edward had had no news and thinks that his work has escaped the fire, as well as censorship. But later, he learns that copies of his best selling *Willobie His Avisa* have been recalled from the London bookshops and unceremoniously set ablaze! "Burning books?" he asks himself philosophically. What next?

So none of the authors named escapes the Bishops' Edict. Thomas Nashe finds himself a victim when the very Archbishop who had once been his Patron, now decrees, with no regrets, that "All books by Nashe and Harvey must be removed from wherever they are to be found. None of their writings must be printed hereafter." "*None of their writings must be printed hereafter.*" These eight words sound unreal to Nashe. He is not a man of means. And right now, he is down on his luck. Being an ill-fated author, he despairs as he watches the fire's fierce flames rising from precious books piled up in the yard of Stationers' Hall in London. As if his skin has been seared, Nashe is sad to see his hard-won life's works being reduced as part of a grey mound of ashes. He stands, stares in disbelief at the smouldering ground and shivers slightly, even on this hot summer's day. He feels disconsolate; his pride close to being utterly broken. Slowly he moves away from the fire. After a few yards, he stops. He looks back to where the pristine pile of books had been. He lifts his gaze from the ground to the familiar facade of the building that had given legitimation to all his youthful strivings and literary ambitions before they became printed Verses and published books. It is the emblematic staging post on his journey to authorial popularity and fame as Thomas Nashe, a man of literary merit. Those were proud and hopeful days: Now, it seems, the bonfire of books has destroyed his legacy; sealed his fate. Grim-faced, he walks away from Stationers Hall feeling more wretched than he'd ever felt.

***

Soon after the Bishop's Ban, Lyly visits Edward in Hackney. Edward still hopes his works have escaped the fire, even though he'd heard the rumours.

"I am told that at least one of my works did not escape the fire," he says to Lyly. "John, this is a very dark day for us. All writers are targets. I am told that *Willobie and Avisa* was not spared. It was quickly removed from every bookstand in the city's bookshops…"

"My Lord," Lyly intervenes, "I am very sorry…" He pauses. "Very sorry indeed to say that *Venus and Adonis* and *Lucrece* have also been among your writings that have been destroyed."

Both men, devoted scholars, scribes and book-lovers, look at each other sympathetically. No longer could they ignore the threats they face. Lyly had not seen Edward so upset.

"This is a sad time, John. Very sad. Not just for us as writers: It is sad for England," Edward says. "And, I dare say for civilised life! For humanity!"

Lyly's visit is short. As he leaves, Edward feels the aftermath of the Bishops' Ban, like a slap in the face. Unsure of what is to come, his concern grows. He wonders how other authors and publishers who abuse his original verses, poems and plays, would survive the Puritan purges.These are very dangerous times. From here on, he feels he cannot be too careful. The Puritans' message; their warning has been served: It is a message from hell; writ large in fire! How would he and his writings fare in the future? Literature, he thinks, is in the laps of the Gods. It is a thought that leads him to question how men, no less Puritans, use their pens and power in the name of God to deny others, their fellow-men, free expression. His poems, so dear to him, the first writings to appear with the name WILLIAM SHAKESPEARE, have been destroyed. Overwhelmed by that casual brutality, he remembers Lyly's woe-begone expression as he uttered his last words before Lyly had departed: "This is a sad time John; very sad for England…for civilised life! For humanity!"

***

After the book-burning, Edward seeks every scrap of information he could get about the Irish Campaign. From informed sources at Court, he receives the news that Essex and Southampton had taken a big, and unexpected decision because Essex is unhappy about the Queen's messages counteracting what he was doing in Ireland. He feels so strongly that he and Southampton ignores the Queen's Orders and leave the battlefield. They return to England. To add to their insubordination, they left an inexperienced officer in charge of the English soldiers in Ireland.

Halting, so suddenly, an ongoing Military Campaign, is behaviour that is tantamount to Essex declaring he is a law unto himself. He is no respecter of persons, not even the

Queen. This, in part is why Edward dislikes Essex. Having abandoned his post in Ireland, he seeks to justify his action: He feels he has earned the chance to speak in person to Her Majesty. Such confidence, bordering on arrogance, reminds Edward of himself committing a similar act of military insubordination when, during the Spanish Armada Campaign, he had abandoned his post at Tilbury.

Being back on English soil, Essex travels in haste to the Royal Nonsuch Palace. It is not far into the morning when he arrives; and unannounced, he makes his way directly to see the Queen. Riding roughshod over custom and practice, he insists on entering, of all places, the inner precincts, close to the Royal Bed Chamber, at a time when the Queen is not fully ready for public appearance. As she moves around, preoccupied by thoughts of the day's proceedings, her Lady-in-Waiting comes to her: "Your Majesty," she says. "The Earl of Essex is waiting to see you."

"What is he doing here?" she asks crossly. "He should be with his Troops in Ireland!" Her eyelids, heavy with residual sleep, open wide. A while later, Essex appears. She is astonished to see him. He in turn, is shocked to see the Queen in that, more or less, unprepared state. She is far from excited to see him. Though shaken, she diplomatically hides her feelings well. She regains composure; and wonders what could be so urgent to bring this disobedient man here! She listens stony-faced to what Essex has to say. But all too soon for Essex, the meeting is over; and Elizabeth bids him goodbye.

That meeting marks a major historical moment: It marks the beginning of Queen Elizabeth distancing herself from Essex. He walks away, troubled, but in a different way now from how he'd felt before he'd seen the Queen. By the time he reaches the Palace's entrance, the Queen had already made up her mind: "Essex must never again be allowed into my presence," she says to herself. But, that is not all. She orders that Essex should be detained in York House, pending his appearance before Members of the Star Chamber. When the Chamber met, they ruled that his large number of servants should be dismissed. This drastic action denies Essex of the most basic of a Nobleman's requirements. It dents his pride and high-minded sense of Nobility. And for him personally, certain questions arise: How does the Queen's action really affect him? Was he chastened? After hearing the news, Edward thinks "Only time will tell." For now, he is not holding his breath in the hope that there would be any change in Essex's irritating, brash haughtiness; his offensive, arrogant behaviour.

At Court, as across the Country, Edward sees a great new opportunity for the Cecil Faction to move ahead of their rivals, if only they could finish-off Essex for good. This is brutal thinking, Edward admits. But, it is not unusual. Meanwhile, his interest and concern for Southampton does not lessen. He fears that Southampton would be tainted even more now by his friendship and ever-closer alliance with Essex.

*

As he moves on, overall, he is greatly relieved about one thing: That Southampton is back safely in London. But the journey to, and experience in, Ireland, still lingers. He sees Southampton as crest-fallen; a man short on motivation, but seemingly long on spending time with the Earl of Rutland. The two Earls pass their time in London, mainly attending afternoon performances of plays. It is autumn; and playing at the *Globe Theatre* is *Julius Caesar*, the drama he had written some years before. Murder and politics are a potentially explosive combination which draws him towards the political force of gravity: To men's desire of gaining power over others. But, as he knows, there is in every political life, a rise and fall; a theme which he'd explored in another play that he'd written earlier: *Coriolanus.* Now, as he updates the play, he follows Essex's ambitious movements. He attends to character development; and bearing in mind CORIOLANUS'S background, he spotlights the Roman General's arrogance: His high-handed attitude towards people and government officials, which leads to his downfall and banishment. Edward respects the Feudal order into which he was born and bred, but he shows that unchecked privileges and power could be abused. In real life, this is exactly the relationship that he had had with Burghley in relation to his finances and inherited estates.

So, as he writes a new version of *Coriolanus,* he thinks of Essex's fall after returning from Ireland. He reaffirms his respect for Courtly behaviour, as an ideal. It is sacrosanct. Thus he uses Essex, the real life parallel of CORIOLANUS, and, by so doing he symbolises the ideal Courtier as championed by Castiglione in *The Courtier*. But while Essex has all the privileges of a princely Courtier, Edward feels he must pay the penalty for treating the people he depends upon badly. In *Coriolanus,* he reflects upon Essex's rise and decline, as well as aspects of his own life: From stardom to exile from Elizabeth's Court. In this complex combination of elements, he uses experience brilliantly to tell this story.

After he completes re-writing *Coriolanus,* he reviews another of his earlier plays, *Timon of Athens,* which mirrors himself, as a Nobleman, who falls from grace and favour. The play's theme is put simply when the character APEMANTUS tells TIMON that "The middle of humanity thou never knewest, but the extremity of both ends. When thou wast in thy guilt and thy perfume, they mocked thee for too much curiosity; in thy rags thou know'st none, but art despised for the contrary."

So TIMON reflects his own journey from glory to exile.

Thus *Timon of Athens* tells the story of Edward de Vere's fall. It is an amalgam of his many-sidedness; his complex personality. At the beginning of the play TIMON appears as a man of means, who supports worthy causes. Poets and artists receives his generous patronage; and in this, he enacts the ideals of Nobility. But unlike CORIOLANUS, TIMON is a man of the people. And, like another good man, ANTONIO in *The Merchant of Venice*, being generous does not mean he cannot be both careful and careless. As trouble looms, TIMON listens to FLAVIUS who says:

"...in the ebb of your estate
And your great flow of debt. My lov'd Lord
Though you hear now too late, yet now's a time
The greatest of your having lacks a half
To pay your present debts
TIMON: Let all my lands be sold!
FLAVIUS: 'Tis all engag'd, some forfeited and gone,
And what remains will hardly stop the mouth
Of present dues. The future comes apace...
How goes our reck'ning?"

Edward considers the characteristics he'd given to TIMON who at the end of the story is very unhappy about his banishment from Athens. He sees nothing good in anyone or anything. Writing this drama, Edward thinks and rethinks many things. Eventually, he selects episodes of his own life that would suit the main character. So unsurprisingly, TIMON'S experience mirrors Edward's: In particular, his doubts of being the father of his wife Anne's first child, Elizabeth. In the play, he puts these words in TIMON'S mouth:

"Spare not the babe

Whose dimpled smiles from fools exhaust their mercy.
Think it a bastard, whom the oracle
Hath doubtfully pronounced the throat shall cut,
And mince it sans remorse.
Swear against objects.
Put armour on thine ears and on thine eyes
Whose proof nor yells of mothers, maids, nor babes,
Nor sight of priests in holy vestments bleeding,
Shall pierce a jot.
There's gold to pay thy soldiers.
Make large confusion, and, thy fury spent,
Confounded be thyself. Speak not. Be gone."

So, through his art, Edward encapsulates an essential contradiction in his life which he weaves dramatically into *Timon of Athens.*

***

# XIII

**'I will attend my husband...let me have him home with me'**

HACKNEY: KING'S PLACE, DECEMBER 1599:

Retirement in King's Place with all its merits, does not lessen Edward's sense of shame. If anything, it deepens it. But being a hopeful, courageous man, it also makes him even more thoughtful: He runs through some of the highs and lows, reminding himself of his abiding belief in the power of his pen. On this matter, his attention never flags: He is a faithful servant to the essential needs of himself as a Thinker. He has always been receptive to ideas, translating the abstract into form; always writing and rewriting, improving upon dramas, often making them current.

Now, the December days get dark earlier and are much colder. On the first day of his working week, he wakes up early as usual, gets dressed and has breakfast. Slowly, he makes his way to the place he calls his Great Study, where he settles into the chair at his desk. The short walk from the dining room, alerts him to how weary he feels. But, looking around in the Study, he feels even more pleased now with the Big House than he was when he'd first moved in. Before him is a copy of *As You Like It.* Of late, he'd been giving much thought to this play which he is rewriting for a new production. After making his final corrections and additions, he remembers and anticipates his appointment for later that day. His expected Special Visitor is someone who will be a participant in one of his plays. That person is an Actor and Comedian named Robert Armin; a respected member of the Lord Chamberlain's Men.

The lines he writes in poetry and plays contain sounds that form a certain kind of music underscored by the rhythmic patterns of rhyming words. He *hears* what he writes! So speaking the lines in the required timing he chooses is the key. Of the many actors that he's worked with, few have impressed him as much as Robert Armin. Apart from Armin's professional brilliance, Edward is drawn to his intellectual interests too! Armin is an avid reader, who has written a Joke book. Now, he goes further: He writes a more serious piece titled an "Introductory Epistle" in which he makes a somewhat indiscreet statement about spending some time during the Festive Season with an unspecified Nobleman, whose name he does not mention. In this "Epistle" Armin is more conscious than usual of what he writes. Which raises the question: Is this Diary-like entry meant for posterity? Yes! Such is the high esteem in which he holds the man he calls "The Master;" the man whose name he withholds. So, ahead of his visit, he writes:

"On Christmas Day, which is a Tuesday, I will take my journey in an easterly direction. I will travel from central London to meet with the Right Honourable good My Lord, my Master whom I serve in Hackney." Who could this person be? Only two Noblemen had houses in Hackney in 1599. They are Edward de Vere and Lord Zouche. Zouche is away in Denmark. So the only Honourable Lord whom Armin is now on his way to meet in Hackney is Edward de Vere, the Seventeenth Earl of Oxford.

A few months before, Edward had mentioned to Armin the possibility of giving him the chance to play the part of an important character in *As You Like It*. Edward and Armin had then agreed to meet again just before Christmas to discuss and finalise details of the character and the play before production.

For Edward, *As You Like It* is a special play; and meeting Armin he feels will afford him special moments to clarify and enable him to insert a few new thoughts and finishing touches to the play about a distinguished family for whom he has great respect. Going forward, once more, he is reminded of the play's backstory; one, that in essence, features the inheritance of the executed Duke of Norfolk, portrayed as SIR ROWLAND DE BOYS? Two decades before Edward had attended the wedding of Norfolk's youngest son, William. And it is at this time of Armin's impending visit to King's Place that a long-standing agreement which allows William to have his full inheritance, looks likely. But, this is not why Edward has invited Armin to Hackney. There is the matter of the whole body of his literary work: His essential authorship in relation to his identity, too!

On the day that Armin arrives at the Big House, he is greeted at the door by Edward's Man-Servant, Quested. Armin is then ushered into the living room. While he waits, he thinks he'd not seen Edward for almost a year: On that last occasion, he was on stage at *The Curtain Theatre* in Shoreditch. Edward was struck then by Armin's rich deep voice as he paints colours both vivid and subtle, while speaking the words he'd written. Since then, Armin has gained an enviable reputation as being one of Edward's greatest Clowns; an actor who reminds him of another "Clown," the wonderful Will Somers, whom he'd first seen as a boy in Castle Hedingham. So, as a performer, either of Comedy or Tragedy, Armin is Edward's choice.

As he waits in his Great Study for Armin, Edward looks around the spacious room in which sounds echo; voices carry loud and clear. He thinks about the play in hand as very Special; and the actor he is about to meet as being no less so. He sits still with eyes closed in meditational mode. He thinks of his adventurousness as a writer of plays; not just in terms of plot and character, but in his playful usage and introduction of new words, new compositions and in his overall use and extension of the English language. For a while, an eerie silence intervenes, but it is rudely interrupted by a knock. He rises, shuffles to the door and opens it.

"My Lord," Quested says, "Mister Armin is here." Armin appears, smiling.

"Ah, Armin," Edward says. "Come in!" Armin walks into the Great Study, looks around, and sees the painting, Edward's portrait as a younger man on the wall opposite Edward's desk. On the next wall, there are a large number of books neatly placed on shelves. The ambience of the room touches Armin: He feels the spirit of Christmas in the air. For a moment, Edward too is reminded of Christmases past; of old times at Fisher's Folly. Armin and Edward shake hands, and, for a while, they exchange greetings and memories. Armin sits on a chair facing Edward who is at his usual place behind his desk. Edward turns the title page of a play Script before him. Then he speaks about *As You Like It*.

"When we last spoke," he says, "my re-working of the script was still in progress. Now, it is done. It is the finished play. And I am ready to have it performed…" He pauses. Then he says "I think the time is right for a clear message to go out for all to hear. The play-loving public should go to the theatre and see this play." Having said this, an anguished expression fleetingly appears on his face. Armin notices it.

"In the play," Edward continues, "the character *you* will play is, of course, TOUCHSTONE. It is a major role, not just for its comic element. Importantly, the character will utter words; lines of a truth that is being undermined, even now, as I speak."

Edward turns over several pages until he finds a page near the end of a crucial change that he'd made to an earlier draft.

"Here, have a look," he says as he hands the script to Armin. While Armin reads, Edward says: "As you see, I have used a trio of characters to deal with the man Will Shakspere, who steals my dramas. For the play you are reading, my Muse is the character AUDREY."

Armin reads; and fine actor that he is, he is sensitive to the rhythm and sounds of the words which he also listens too! He is intrigued by what Edward has said so far. He feels an undercurrent of what is to come. Edward does not disappoint him.

After years of rumour, now, given the real dangers of usurpation and obliteration of his authorship, Edward feels he has had enough. He decides, once and for all, to act: He takes a positive stand against the "Shakespeare Imposter." Using his specially sharpened, lethal quill, he delivers a literary attack upon Will Shakspere of Stratford. Armin, famous for his quick-wit, is totally absorbed as he reads more of Edward's lines and their stark meaning. His dancing eyes lock on to the words of each Scene, on each page, as his concentration takes him to another place: To the performing stage. He too, had heard about the man who is masquerading as his Master "William Shakespeare;" and he too has his doubts as to whether this man is a playwright. But, the last thing he'd expected to read are the unsettling, revealing words before him. He is deeply moved by the lines Edward has written for it is he (Armin), in the part of TOUCHSTONE (Edward de Vere), who will speak in Scene 1, when he confronts an ordinary young boy named WILLIAM. In this Scene Edward displays his best Comedic skill. He excels in it."TOUCHSTONE," he writes,"is intent on marrying AUDREY, but so too is WILLIAM. Two potential husbands create a problematic situation. And interestingly, Edward sets the play in the "forest of Arden" near his wider family's lands and houses at Bilton and Billesley, not far from Stratford-upon-Avon. For their marriage, TOUCHSTONE and AUDREY engages a Priest named SIR OLIVER MARTEXT. Here, Edward points to the Martin Marprelate pamphleteering menace and acknowledges the Government's success in doing away with Marprelatism.

Before the entry of the WILLIAM character in the play, Edward composes a marriage Scene in Act V for TOUCHSTONE and AUDREY. TOUCHSTONE says to AUDREY: "We shall find a time AUDREY, patience gentle AUDREY." AUDREY responds: "Faith the priest was good enough, for all the old gentleman's saying." The dialogue continues with TOUCHSTONE saying: "A most wicked SIR OLIVER, AUDREY, a most vile MARTEXT. But, AUDREY, there is a youth here in the forest lays claim to you." AUDREY says: "Ay, I know who 'tis; he hath no interest in me in the world. Here comes the man you mean."

Edward writes:

"Enter WILLIAM

TOUCHSTONE: It is meat and drink to me to see a clown.

By my troth, we that have good wits have much to answer for;

we shall be flouting.

We cannot hold

WILLIAM: Good ev'n, AUDREY.

AUDREY: Good ev'n WILLIAM

WILLIAM (To TOUCHSTONE): And good ev'n to you, sir.

TOUCHSTONE: Good ev'n gentle friend.

Cover thy head, cover thy head; nay, prithee be cover'd.

How old are you, friend?

WILLIAM: Five and twenty sir.

TOUCHSTONE: A ripe age. Is thy name WILLIAM?

WILLIAM: WILLIAM, sir.
TOUCHSTONE: A fair name. Wast born i'th forest here?
WILLIAM: Ay, sir, I thank God .
TOUCHSTONE: 'Thank God' – a good answer. Art rich ?
WILLIAM: Faith, sir, so-so.
TOUCHSTONE: 'So so' is good, very good, very excellent good. And yet it is not, it is but so-so. Art thou wise?
WILLIAM: Ay, sir, I have a pretty wit.
TOUCHSTONE: Why thou say'st well. I do now remember a saying, 'The fool doth think he is wise, but the wise man knows himself to be a fool.' "

Edward's use of the word "gentle" to describe WILLIAM, does not mean he is a kind person It refers to status, to a social class next to Yeoman. At this time, it becomes well known that Will Shakspere, the "Upstart Crow," had bought himself a Coat of Arms! Just as Ben Jonson's character SOGLIARDO is charmed by the name Gentleman that he will buy it, so too is Will Shakspere, who sees himself as a Gentleman of whom Edward writes in *As You Like It:*

"TOUCHSTONE. You do love this maid ?
WILLIAM: I do, sir.
TOUCHSTONE: Give me your hand. Art thou learned?
WILLIAM: No, sir.
TOUCHSTONE: Then learn this of me: To have is to have.
For it is a figure of rhetoric that drink, being poured out of a cup into a glass, by filling one doth empty the other. For all your writers do consent that ipse is he. Now, you are not ipse, for I am he."

"*For I am he,*" Edward asserts himself here, forcefully. At this point in his reading, Armin pauses. He glances at Edward.

"You and I understand," Edward says, "from our reading of Plato's Symposium, the rhetoric of transferring knowledge from one person to another."

"I do, My Lord," Armin says. "And, I understand…" He glances at the open script and adds: "I understand TOUCHSTONE'S part perfectly!" After this brief pause in his reading, and given the confusion of identities, Armin continues, then he pauses at a major dramatic point in the play, where WILLIAM is surprised by TOUCHSTONE'S sharp tone. TOUCHSTONE charges that WILLIAM is just pretending to be him. To this, WILLIAM responds: "Which he, sir?" TOUCHSTONE says: "He, sir that must marry this woman. Therefore you clown, abandon... the society of this female - or, clown, thou perishest; or, to thy better understanding, diest. Or, to wit, I will kill thee, make thee away, translate thy life into death, thy liberty into bondage. I will deal in poison with thee, or in bastinado, or in steel; I will bandy with thee in faction. I will o'errun thee with policy. I will kill thee a hundred and fifty ways. Therefore tremble and depart!

AUDREY: Do, good WILLIAM.

WILIAM: God rest you, merry sir."

At this stage WILLIAM exits from the Scene.

Robert Armin lifts his gaze momentarily from the play-script. He is amazed by Edward's self-revelation, in spite of being masked as TOUCHSTONE. Edward had been observing Armin's face while he was reading. He noted how much Armin seems to have gotten into the spirit of the part and reflects upon Armin's commanding stage presence; on his timing and articulation, and now, as he reads a few lines aloud. Then, he stops at the end of the Scene.

"How do you find it?" Edward asks.

"My Lord," Armin says, "I feel privileged. Very much so. And…" He pauses. "I am very happy to play the part. Thank you, sir! " He hands the script back to Edward. What a Christmas present, he thinks.

As Armin bids Edward farewell and leaves the Big House and King's Place, he could still hear the echo of his own voice while he was reading TOUCHSTONE'S words: "*Then learn this of me. To have is to have. For it is a figure of rhetoric: The drink being poured out of a cup into a glass by filling one doth empty the other. For all your writers do consent that ipse is he. Now, you are not ipse, for I am he.*" He is mightily pleased to be offered this revelatory part. And so, for both the playwright and the actor, as interpreters of truth in art, their understanding of the double-identities of characters in the play soon to be performed, is a rare and wonderful Christmas gift.

***

The tension between Edward and Shakspere does not lessen. Instead, it grows as the realities of national life becomes contentious and unstable. Factions continue to rail against each other. Overseeing it all, the Queen surveys the scene, and acts: She places Essex under house arrest, pending possible charges for his actions (and in actions) in Ireland. At his side, is his loyal friend and supporter Southampton. "Armed rebellion. Nothing less," Essex thinks, is an option; a practical way of bringing about timely reforms. It is change that would move the country forward. But, it is a dangerous, even foolhardy strategy, Edward thinks. The situation becomes so tense that Southampton goes back to Ireland, where he hopes for a relatively calmer environment, even in the midst of hostilities there.

A few weeks later, Southampton leaves Ireland and enlists in the Protestant Army fighting in the Lowlands. Meanwhile, Essex faces serious questioning for his earlier treacherous behaviour of making a deal with the Irish rebel leader, the Earl of Tryone. Far from rising, Essex's star is in decline: Well established families, who were his friends, withdraw their support. Among them is the Somerset family. Edward Somerset, Earl of Worcester, who, having come to Essex's aid on his return from the Irish battleground, now turns away. He becomes an ally of the Cecil family. And just before midsummer's day in 1600, Worcester's son, Henry, marries Anne Russell, a cousin of Robert Cecil.

***

While Elizabeth Trentham, Countess Oxford attends to her daily business as well as the property at King's Place, Edward is mired in his own problems: His finances still bedevils him. Time is fast running out: He feels the need to get back more of his Inheritance. "The time is now or never," he says to himself. "I have no choice but to get in touch with Robert Cecil and make a request for the Governorship of the Isle of Jersey." Such an administrative post would be a marked changed for Edward, who, in essence, is a man of an artistic sensibility.

In his letter, he says to Robert that so far, he'd had many unfulfilled promises from the Queen. But if she does not appoint him to a post soon, the only place he'd be able to enjoy his "benefits and good turns" would be in his grave. For days after the letter was sent, he speculates: "Overall, I am very hopeful," he says to himself. Then, Cecil's reply comes. Alas, his request is ignored by both the Queen and Robert Cecil. The disappointment is like a kick in the stomach. He is deeply hurt; and feels threatened by melancholy feelings. But though physical weakness reminds him of his mortality, he is hopeful of one day receiving his due. He thinks of being free of debt. He does not want to become dependent or a burdensome liability to his wife. So, believing he could get his hands on more of his Inheritance, he hatches new plans. He looks Westward: He applies for the Presidency of Wales. But again, his request is denied. With these rejections, a pattern of his general outlook emerges: His love for life keeps him alert. He thinks of other one-time Court favourites, who were refused special privileges in terms of gaining high offices and big incomes. His rival Essex is one, who having had a monopoly on sweet wines, is refused contractual renewal. But though he is still very close to the Queen and in spite of all the pomp and ceremony of being her Lord Great Chamberlain of England, altogether, it is not enough for there is no guarantee of Special Royal favours! It is no surprise, therefore, that he harps on this theme when he writes in Sonnet One Hundred and Twenty Five about "compound sweet":

> "Were't ought to me I bore the canopy,
> With my extern the outward honouring,
> Or laid great bases for eternity,
> Which proves more short than waste or ruining?
> Have I not seen dwellers on form and favour
> Lose all, the more, by paying too much rent,
> For compound sweet, forgoing simple savour,
> Pitiful thrivers, in their gazing spent?..."

*

At Elizabeth's Court, the lesson is perhaps clearer now than before: You take the rough with the smooth; and the sweetest of sweetness can leave a rancorous bitterness. On his journey, Edward reaches a major historical milestone: It is the year

Sixteen Hundred; and his Secretary, Anthony Munday, writes a Poem in which he seems to dissociate Edward de Vere from "Shakespeare." Why? Did Munday, a close confidante not know of Edward as the man "William Shakespeare?" Or, did Munday know and take this position out of loyalty to protect his former Boss's "secret" disguise? Whichever is the truth, Munday's separation of Edward as the Earl of Oxford from "William Shakespeare" deflects attention from Edward's rightful authorship. Given that Munday is a highly competent and competitive author, perhaps writers' envy and, the green-eyed monster jealousy, had come into play; rearing its ugly head all the more as Edward's Shakespeare works rises in popularity and maintains its best-seller status.

So even now, at the start of the new century, confusion over his literary works is being sown, largely – understandably - for self-interest by authors and those in power, who take political sides in Elizabeth's England. Enemies and friends: Who are they? Edward wonders. For him, the Munday publication is yet another reminder that, as an author, on top of his disguise, he is also forcefully being constrained from all angles: Notably, and significantly, by many in the publishing industry; as well as those in powerful positions. His frustration grows; and bitter feelings come to the fore, as in Sonnet Sixty Six:

"Tired with all these, for restful deals I cry:
As to behold desert a beggar born
And needy nothing trimmed in jollity,
And purest faith unhappily forsworn,
And gilded honour shamefully misplaced,
And maiden virtue rudely strumpeted,
And right perfection wrongfully disgraced,
And strength by limping sway disabled,
And art made tongue-tied by authority,

And folly, doctor-like, controlling skill,
And simple truth miscalled simplicity,
And captive good attending captain ill:
Tired with all these, from these would I be gone…"

So, with his art made "*tongue-tied by authority,*" namely by Queen Elizabeth and those in Government "who simple truth miscalled simplicity," from hereon, the artful voice either as himself, or increasingly now as "William Shakespeare," comes under stricter surveillance; and is denied. This official stamp of approval takes a new turn: The spotlight of Edward's literary works; his decades-long, hard-won, soulful authorship, steadily shifts away from him and follows Will Shakspere.

***

Meanwhile, stung by the Queen's disenchantment with him, Essex does not spare her from his own feelings. He dares to think of her as being past it; an ageing woman, deformed in mind and body, as he describes her. Since he'd returned from the Irish Campaign, his unpredictable behaviour has been closely watched. The Queen's last sight of him; and his meeting with her, was not a pleasant experience for either of them. Since then he had become erratic; and, of late, he seems to be losing his mind, too! One person who is allowed to visit him is Sir John Harrington. His mission is not merely to observe, but to spy on Essex, especially on his behaviour, and report back. To his alarm, Harrington carefully notes that Essex "Shifteth from sorrow and repentance to rage and rebellion so suddenly which proveth him devoid of good reason or right mind. He utters strange words which makes me hasten away from his presence." A disturbed mind? Alas, this is what the Queen already thinks of Essex.

Harrington's departure from Essex's presence further discredits the bad decisions that Essex and Southampton had taken in Ireland. Now in England, Essex calls for a new order; a revolution! On what basis is this declaration to be made: In the eyes of the Court and the people, he is remembered as a heroic leader of a few years before, and thus he could do no wrong. But the support he had then, has dwindled. Nonetheless, the idea and quest for glory prevails in Essex's impulsive mind. He thinks there is optimism and hope enough to make his vision reality. He could not think otherwise, for by nature, he is a man who believes he is untouchable. Edward's character CORIOLANUS, bears striking resemblance to Essex. The hope Essex harbours is a way of rousing more people to support him. He thinks of a book, *The Life and Reign of Henry V*, published a few months earlier by a man named John Hayward. It is a controversial work, but Essex is not put-off. On the contrary, it is exactly the thing he thinks he needs. Why? Because of the book's message and its relevance now.

Hayward is a friend and ally of the Essex and Southampton faction, and his book tells the story of the fall of King Richard II. He treads a dangerous path: In one of his writings, he sees similarities between the bad Government of King Richard II's Court and the wrong-doings of Queen Elizabeth's regime. History and the deposition of Monarch's of England are a contentious and explosive mix, especially now as the heirless Queen Elizabeth is surrounded by rival factions anticipating change in a future, post-Succession England. There are secret talks, meetings and much speculation.

The gist of Hayward's play is that like King Richard, who had been forced to leave his throne, Queen Elizabeth should not be protected from such an abdication. She is aware of the intent of Hayward's book, as nothing less than the call to revolt! At the heart of this are the ambitious Essex and

Southampton, who sees and seizes the chance to exploit the historical parallels. They hire the Lord Chamberlain's Men to perform Edward's history play *Richard II*. And interestingly, the play, more or less, reflects a Self-portrait of Edward.

As the Essex-Southampton revolutionary plan comes close to enactment, early in the first year of the new century, *Richard II* is performed at the *Globe Theatre*. Of central importance in the play is the Scene in which Richard is relieved of his Kingship. For theatre-goers and members of the general public, with Queen Elizabeth in mind, the dethronement Scene in Edward's play is both symbolic and real. It hits the mark. Essex is ecstatic; and Southampton is ever-supportive. The staging is timely and crucial, they feel. But their boldness is attended by dangers. For Queen Elizabeth, the fervent lover and benefactor of masques and plays, the stark message of the play is not lost. It stays in her mind: "I am Richard," she later says to a learned man: "Know ye not that?" Everyone at Court, or those who had seen the play, knows that. And surely, on the face of it, Edward's play could also be seen as inciting trouble. He is ill-at-ease, for he knows about the real risk of the Lord Chamberlain's Men staging the play at this time. Like Hayward, he feels that he too, could be hunted down and tried for Treason. But lo, and behold, none of the Queen's officials knocks on his door with the intention of arresting him as the author of *Richard II*. This outcome reflects a very fine line; and a close escape for Edward who asks himself the question: "Was Essex's intention to stage the play, apart from self-publicity towards achieving his revolutionary ambition, at least in part, designed to implicate me?" Maybe. Or, maybe not. He is unsure. But, whatever his worry over such an implication, already the Queen's Ministers know of his rivalry with, and distance from, Essex.

So Edward is mightily relieved to be seen as posing no

threat to the Crown. But, the aftermath of the *Richard II* performance is cause, on Edward's part, for more reflection: He thinks and feels his loyalty to Queen and country is even greater now: It is sacrosanct. "Above all," he says to himself, "as it had been for my de Vere family for centuries, loyalty to England is my bounden, sacred allegiance."

***

Hackney, Sunday evening 8 February, 1601: Edward is at home having an after-breakfast chat with his wife.

"I have eaten more today," he says, "than I've done for quite some time."

"So I have noticed, My Lord," Countess Elizabeth says. "Let us hope tomorrow you will have another good breakfast. You need to gain the weight you have been losing."

Weight loss had been a silent worry for a few weeks. Now his Countess speaks about it. This makes him nervous, but he smiles and says: "Let's hope so!" Just then, a Messenger arrives with a sealed envelope. Quested receives the Document; and immediately hands it to Edward who is sitting beside Elizabeth in the Living Room. Edward opens the envelope. As he reads what is written, the expression on his faces changes from being calm to one of concern. It is disturbing news. The over-hanging threat that he and many Nobles fears is now grounded; translated into action. Essex and Southampton have taken matters into their own hands. They have incited, and now leads a band of supporters of the Essex faction to join them in open rebellion. Essex leads them to Essex House, where they assemble and plan the next steps to be taken. But already, Robert Cecil is ahead of them: His Spies and Informers had forewarned Essex House employees with whom they work; and contact is made with law enforcement officials: the Lord Chief Justice, the Lord Keeper and other Councillors.

At Essex House, Essex tells his supporters that there have been plots to kill him. Southampton is outspoken too: He talks about an earlier attack upon him. In response to their complaints, officials insist that they should channel their grievances through the Government. But the disappointed rebellious leaders and the crowd hasten towards the Sheriff's residence shouting "For the Queen! For the Queen!" Not being able to speak to the Sheriff, Essex and his supporters make their way back to Essex House, but Robert Cecil's men had, once again, been ahead of them. Earlier on their way to Essex House, the Bishop of London had warned Essex that he and his followers should go no further. But Essex, as Ring-leader of the rebels, then, as now, ignores the warning and attacks the advancing members of the Cecil faction. The struggle that ensues is not entirely violent and short. At its end, four men die; and many are wounded.

Edward is surprised by this latest audacious move by Essex. He knows, more than anyone else, the harsh realities of street fighting which, for him was a personal matter. But this revolt is of wider significance; and he fears for the rebellious perpetrators. Essex and Southampton are unrepentant. They request a private meeting with the Queen. But this is rejected by Lord Grey de Wilton.

"Your actions are outrageous. An affront to the Queen," Wilton says. "Your demands are most unreasonable. I advise you to surrender!"

Later that Sunday night, Essex, Southampton and their rebel supporters agree to a truce. But after they surrender their weapons, what next? Edward asks himself before he puts the question to his Countess. "What do you think?" He knows the move that Essex and Southampton had made is grave. Consequences will follow. They will be tried. Edward fears the outcome.

A few days later, he is visited by another Messenger. The message he receives is that he is selected to be one of the Lords who will preside as a Juror on the jury which will deliver judgement on his favoured young friend, Southampton! At once, this news of Jury Service stirs powerful memories.

Soon he joins twenty five peers; his fellow-Jurors who assemble in Westminster Hall for the Trial of Essex and Southampton. The purpose, though not the venue, reminds Edward of the Trial of Mary, Queen of Scots. Now, the matter is more personal. The scene is set: He and the other officials sit and wait. Then the two prisoners are led into the Hall; and proceedings begins. The case for the Prosecution is led by Sir Francis Bacon, formerly a supporter of the Essex faction. And, in support of the Prosecution, two witnesses are called: One of them is Sir Walter Raleigh. As he takes the Oath: To tell nothing but the truth, Essex's behaviour becomes derisive. He's in a mocking mood. In his testimony, he wastes no time on niceties: His aim is direct; and more than a little surprising. He charges that none other than Robert Cecil, the Chief Minister himself, is a secret sympathiser of the Catholic Infanta Isabella Clara of Spain! Cecil, not expecting this attack upon himself, acts decisively: He walks towards the Lord High Steward. A hush falls in the Court Room. Cecil falls to his knees. He pleads to be allowed to address this "malicious fiction" against him. He turns, and faces Essex and Southampton.

"My Lords," he says, "tell the honourable peers, the name or names of those to whom I have, as you have charged me, advocated as a Spanish Successor to the throne of England." Essex and Southampton are silent: No name is given.

As the Trial continues, and more questions are asked, it turns out that as incriminating evidence against Cecil, it was a book that he, Cecil, had been reading which, it was argued, makes the case for Infanta Isabella's accession to the English throne. At this juncture, Cecil fixes his gaze upon Essex.

"Your malice," he says, "whereby you seek to push me to hate all men is contrary to my intention. I act from no other cause than my desire for peace, and for the good of all the people of my country."

This is a very rare moment; a spectacle of dramatic confrontation between the two rival leaders of the foremost factions vying for political power in Queen Elizabeth's England. What does Edward, a distinguished Lord and fellow Jurors make of what they'd seen and heard? They begin their deliberations and in just half an hour they deliver a Guilty verdict for High Treason. Essex and Southampton are condemned to death. A strange hush, then a murmur runs through the Court: The mood changes. An eerie silence descends upon the cavernous room, as Essex speaks:

"I am ready to die," he says. His voice is loud, clear, unrepentant. "But, I ask you to spare the life of my fellow-prisoner, the Earl of Southampton." Listening to this plea, Edward is moved. After he'd sat through the Court sessions, he thinks, how extraordinary this whole scene is, in which he is, once again, both a Judge and Juror. For his part, he has deliberated and condemned the beloved Southampton! Thereafter he is in turmoil: In a sad state; and with no one whom he could turn to on this matter, he confides to himself his innermost thoughts. Like a soliloquy for one of his plays, he lays bare his feelings poetically. He uses the medium of Sonnets: In Sonnet Thirty, he writes of summoning up "remembrance of things past;" of "precious friends," of "death's dateless night," of weeping afresh, and he ends thus:

"The sad account of fore-bemoaned moan,
Which I new pay, as if not paid before;
But if the while I think on thee, dear friend,

All losses are restored, and sorrows end."

Forgiveness now is the watershed.

***

But though the Trial is over and sentence passed, Edward's troubled mind leads him to plumb deeper depths in himself. It marks a period of intense soul-searching that leads to many Sonnets flowing from his pen. In Sonnet Thirty Five, he writes:

"No more be grieved at that which thou has done;
Roses have thorns, and silver fountains mud;
Clouds and eclipses stain both moon and sun,
And loathsome canker lives in sweetest bud.
All men make faults, and even I, in this,
Authorizing thy trespass with compare,
Myself corrupting, salving thy amiss,
Excusing these sins more than these sins are:
For to thy sensual fault I bring in sense;
Thy adverse party is thy advocate,
And 'gainst myself a lawful plea commence:
Such civil war is in my love and hate
That I an accessory needs must be
To that sweet thief which sourly robs from me."

"*All men have faults.*" The words reverberate in his brain as he writes Sonnet Forty Six:

"...To find this title is empanelled
A quest of thoughts, all tenants to the heart,
And by their verdict is determined
The clear eyes' moiety, and the dear heart's part:

As thus, mine eyes' due is thy outward part,
And my heart's right, thy inward love of heart."

*The eyes* and *heart*: Edward considers the words he'd set down; the inner and the outward parts of men. Nothing is at it seems! Such is his conflict within as he'd experienced being both witness and a Judge at Southampton's Trial.

*

Now, as Essex waits for the date of his Execution, Edward thinks about his rival's predicament. He asks himself: "Was Essex's action to lead a rebellion in London to change things, just a mere loss of temper, or, the manifestation of a much deeper malaise within himself?" Then, as he gets on with other things, the dreaded announcement of Essex's date with death comes.

And so, on the morning of Ash Wednesday, 1601, before eight o'clock, Essex's legs carry him for the last time. He walks to the Executioner's block where he rests his throbbing head. The Executioner stands over him, his axe raised in readiness. Then, one swift blow aimed at Essex's neck does not separate his head from his body. The generous flow of warm blood is instantly chilled in the wintry air. More blows follow to complete the Executioner's job. Of the two condemned prisoners, one is gone; one more to go.

As Southampton awaits his fate in the Tower of London, little does he know the depth of Edward's feeling for his welfare. Before, during and since the Trial, Edward's friendship and emotions have been tested to the limit, especially for his part of passing judgement as a Juror. Far from being a six-foot tall, beefy Englishman, he is of average height and of slight build. But, as always, his elegant (some say, exotic) dress-sense is in concert with the creative man that he is. His artistic sensibilities, so beautifully expressed in poetry and plays is underscored by a passionate reservoir of feeling that forms the core of his being. Southampton's penance in the Tower takes its toll on Edward, all the more so now that his infirmities grow. Sick with worry, his health hits a new low: The maladies that threaten his body are compounded by his depth of humanitarian feeling for Southampton. "My Life… Sinks down to death, oppressed with melancholy" he writes.

Meanwhile, as Southampton waits to know his fate, Petitions from his wife and his mother are sent to Robert Cecil. They request that Southampton's life be spared: They plead for clemency. Circumstances have in deed changed dramatically. For having removed Essex who was seen as a great threat, the Cecil faction, protectors of the Queen and her Realm, have no potent rival. Though the heightened tensions have lessened since Essex's Execution, the Southampton Petitions continue to reach Cecil. Precious time pass; and as Southampton spends each day wondering what his fate would be, Edward's hand is not idle. He composes more Sonnets, including number Ninety-Four which, in part, reads:

"…The summer's flower is to the summer sweet,
Though to itself it only live and die,
But if that flower with base infection meet,
The basest weed outbraves his dignity:
For sweetest things turn sourest by their deeds;
Lilies that fester smell far worse than weeds."

A beautifully written, poetic plea. But the question is this: Did he send such a Sonnet to Sir Robert Cecil? The answer is: He did not. Why? Simply because the Sonnets mirror deeply personal thoughts. He remembers his part in the Trial and the sense of inevitability about the Judgement passed upon the accused. Now Southampton bides his time in jail as family pressure for his release continues. Then, at last, news reach Edward: Southampton's life is spared! But, his sentence is commuted to life imprisonment. This is bad enough, but Edward is greatly relieved of dark visions of the Executioner's axe. He is deeply touched that Mercy, that precious, humane quality, has prevailed.

*

Sir Robert Cecil had read the Petitions and acted. Edward thinks his mitigating words to the Queen had been helpful in avoiding the death penalty for Southampton. But the Queen, who knows Southampton well, has her own personal reasons (one being that he was one of her former Royal Wards) for agreeing with the outcome. But Cecil, the Commoner, who rose to become Secretary of State, also has the power of sparing the life of the prisoner. Cecil's intercessions were forceful. How forceful is guesswork, Edward thinks. But one thing is abundantly clear: Cecil knows now that the High and Mighty Earl of Southampton is now much diminished in reputation and properties. He is now a man without a titled name: He is plain Henry Wriothesley. And thus, he has made the opposite journey from Nobleman downward, getting close to the status of Commoner which is a good thing, Cecil thinks. For his part, Edward also turns his thoughts to capturing Southampton's shocking fall. He thinks of doing so now in the form of a Sonnet which he begins to compose.

***

Weeks after Southampton's death sentence was lifted and thus removed from Edward's mind, his full attention is again directed at his self-willed literary fate; and on nagging thoughts about the end of life. The recent outbreaks and ever-present danger of Plague in London are sobering reminders of his mortality. On death and dying, he continues to commit his most private thoughts to the written word, which for him, is the most essential and sacred art form for channelling human expression. "*In the beginning was the word.*" He remembers The Book of John in the *Holy Bible* and has reached a point where he feels the need to bare his soul. The words do not come easily; but he perseveres. After sometime, a few heart-felt Sonnets take shape: They strikingly evoke a dark, sombre, philosophical tone; an expression of his accumulated mature musings; an older voice, so to speak, that now dictates and colours everything. In Sonnet Seventy he writes:

"That thou art blamed shall not be thy defect,
For slander's mark was ever yet the fair;
Thy ornament of beauty is suspect,
A crow that flies in heaven's sweetest air.
So thou be good, slander doth but approve
Thy worth the greater, being wooed of time;
For canker vice the sweetest buds doth love,
And thou presents'st a pure unstained prime.
Thou hast passed by the ambush of young days,..."

With Southampton's narrow escape from execution, Edward meditates on death and writing as expressed in a few Sonnets. In Sonnet Seventy-One he writes:

"No longer mourn for me when I am dead
Than thou shall hear the surly sullen bell
Give warning to the world that I am fled
From this vile world, with vilest worms do dwell:

Nay, if you read this line, remember not
The hand that writ it, for I love you so…
O if (I say) you look upon this verse,
When I, perhaps, compounded am with clay,
Do not so much as my poor name rehearse,
But let your love even with my life decay;
Lest the wise world should look into your moan,
And mock you with me after I am gone. "

He then shifts attention to the aftermath of his passing in Sonnet Seventy-Two:

"…After my death, forget me quite,
For you in me can nothing prove;
Unless you would devise some virtuous lie
To do more for me than mine own desert,
And hang more praise upon deceased I
Than niggard truth would willingly impart;…
My name is buried where my body is,
And live no more to shame nor me, nor you:
For I am shamed by that (literary work) which I bring
forth,
And so should you, to love things nothing worth."

Eventually his feelings overflows as he considers the onrush of time and the end of his life. "But be contented when that fell arrest, Without all bail shall carry me away;" he muses in Sonnet Seventy Four:

"…My life hath in this line some interest,
Which for memorial still with thee shall stay.
When thou reviewest this, thou dost review
The very part was consecrate to thee;

The earth can have but earth, which is his due,
My spirit is thine, the better part of me;
So then thou hast but lost the dregs of life,
The prey of worms, my body being dead,
The coward conquest of a wretch's knife,
Too base to be remembered:
The worth of that, is that which it contains,
And that is this, and this is with thee remains."

Edward is spent of emotion and energy after writing these Sonnets. His thoughts are tinged with melancholy as the word gets around that "William Shakespeare" is unwell. As the rumour spreads, apart from those closest to him, a few people narrow down "Shakespeare's" identity. While he himself admits that he is certainly not enjoying robust health, seclusion in his Hackney abode does not protect him from prying eyes and Inquisitors, one of whom has a name for him: "the Bard."

Charles Fitzgeffrey, a man of the cloth and a poet, addresses "To the Bard" a question about his health as an author for an older generation, "Let the Sonnets never be handed over... O Bard. Be silent." Of the Reverend, Edward asks himself questions: "Is Fitzgeffrey a Puritan zealot who because of the letters' or Sonnets' allusions to sexual love, see such acts as sinful? And why the warning to be silent?" On the other hand, there are others, like Lyly, who read Fitzgeffrey's words and ask: "Is he one of Edward's enemies, who is using his pious garb and learning as his own disguise to attack Edward?" In a sense, like Virgil's poetry, Edward's Sonnets are certainly shockingly unconventional and explosive. They are a clear shift away from the norm. They are not intended for publication.

But, if they are so private, how did Fitzgeffrey see a few of "these letters," meaning the Sonnets? These scripts and other writings are hidden away, Edward has a key for his desk's bottom drawer in which he keeps them. Altogether, they form part of his own private Diary-collection. And so far, he thinks that almost everything he'd written has either been published or performed. That the name (or brand) "William Shakespeare" now adds tantalisingly to who he is; and all that he writes, prompts the questions: Would the Sonnets ever be published? Who knows? Secrecy is necessary at this time for Edward has absolutely no plans to make his innermost feelings public: In other words, "A Fable of the world!" a phrase that he'd once used in relation to another private and personal matter. But whatever potential publishers and his enemies think, the beautiful, lyrical lines of the Sonnets are plain; and yet cryptic, not easy to decipher the person (or persons) upon whom Edward's adoration and attention is centred. Even those closest to him had as yet not seen these compositions which raises many questions: Is there just one real love object alluded to in his Sonnets? Or is it an amalgam of loves relating to his much loved Queen, Southampton and Anne Cecil? Or all three, at various times? Whatever Fitzgeffrey does or does not know, the timing of his address to "the Bard" and Edward's writing of the Sonnets, are timely. They mark the final, dramatic phase of Edward's extraordinary collection of workas Edward de Vere - "William Shakespeare."

***

Time takes its toll. Edward finds it harder to get through each day with growing pain. He is far from feeling well. He's sick; definitely not on the mend, but getting worse. Life is precarious. For the first time, it seems, everything is in the balance. In the wake of Essex's death, new rival factions confront each other for power; and things move fast.

While the Queen is in overall Command, in charge of the Government is the Cecil faction. As days pass, all eyes are turned towards the Queen from whom it is hoped an announcement will be made about her Successor. But so far, rising expectation comes to nothing. What remains certain though is the spectre of death, which, especially after he'd penned the latest Sonnets, is never far from his mind. Southampton's life is spared. But what a near miss it was! he thinks. He gasps at the thought and the worry it had caused. The pain in his leg is worse now. He winces and considers his steadily weakening body. Creeping melancholy persists; it comes and goes, not like black spots, but more insidiously like sinister shadows. His attention shifts. Alas, he thinks, the Queen is showing her age; and, whether or not she can come to grips with this fact, she too, is nearing the end of her journey! How well he'd come to know her over the years: He remembers himself and her in younger days when she was an alluring, vibrant Venus, who epitomised a combination of love and the exercise of Queenly power as being the Ruler. But what of their lives now?

Of himself, he is quite pleased to have written and, to be still writing, exquisite poems and enthralling plays. But, he has also shamelessly wasted much time, he thinks. Elizabeth, on the other hand, rules Supreme. For all he knows, he thinks, she will live and Rule for many years yet. Already, her reign is longer than any other English Monarch. But she is heirless. This reality crosses his mind often: What will be her legacy? She is proud about the myth of the "Virgin Queen" that she'd created; and now she dares to consider the image of a "phoenix rising" in the wake of her passing. Such emblematic thoughts in conjunction with her Succession, preoccupies her. So, as her beauty fades, the nagging question remains: What will her legacy be? Edward had known her for thirty nine years; and, as "William Shakespeare" his pen is never still for long. Now, he writes a poem in which he mourns the pending loss, not just of her beauty, but of Truth, too! "Truth?" It is a word most familiar to him; one that he has lived with all his life. On his de Vere family Motto are the words "Nothing truer than truth." And in a poem *The Turtle and the Phoenix,* as William Shakespeare, he juxtaposes the approaching end of his beloved Queen with his own death: He writes:

"Truth may seem, but cannot be;
Beauty brag, but 'tis not she;
Truth and beauty buried be.
To this urn, let those repair
That are either true or fair:
For these dead birds sigh a prayer."

So at this juncture, their long, and far from easy relationship that has intimately affected every aspect of his life has been intricately, brilliantly interwoven into his writings: His plays, poems and Sonnets are a complex mix of multifaceted love, affection and philosophical musings. Now, in Sonnet Seventy Six, he expresses more of his deepest feelings:

"Why is my verse so barren of new pride,
So far from variation or quick change?
Why with the time do I not glance aside
To new-found methods and to compounds strange?
Why write, I still all one, ever the same,
And keep invention in a noted weed,
That every word doth almost tell my name,
Showing their birth and where they did proceed?
O, know sweet love, I always write of you,
And you and love are still my argument:
So all my best is spending old words new,

Spending again what is always spent;
For as the sun is daily new, and old,
So is my love still telling what is told."

Remembrance of times and things past, bitter-sweetly enriches his present. And placed in the middle of the Sonnet is a heavy hint as to who he really is: "*That every word doth almost tell my name.*"

***

Lame and feeling unwell, for a while, he sits still in his Study at the start of a new day. He then reads the corrected lines of a few of his Sonnets. He is pleasantly surprised at how well words and thought flow as he skims over the familiar handwriting: The fine joined-up letters, that become words and lines that lean slightly to the right on the page. Each Sonnet, as he'd intended, stands on its own. He thinks of the thousands of lines he'd written, much of it in safe keeping, hidden away in bottom drawers. He regrets that so many of his plays have been, and are, pirated, butchered; parts restructured and rewritten by other hands. His plays are out there! But few among his literary circle know of him as the author. He never once doubted the power of his pen. His imagination, his hand, his creations: His verses, poems, allegorical comedies, histories and tragedies are his grand, profound, public statements. His mark, his imprint, his brand as Edward de Vere-William Shakespeare of which he clearly states in his Sonnet: "Why write, I still one, ever the same,...That every word doth almost tell my name." At times, especially now, all the concern he's had thus far about the usurpation of his work transmutes into more philosophical thoughts. "I must worry less," he says to himself. In this frame of mind, he lifts his quill, dips it in ink and writes soliloquy-wise another Sonnet:

"Or I shall live, your epitaph to make;
Or you survive, when I in earth am rotten;
From hence your memory death cannot take,
Although in me each part will be forgotten.
Your name from hence, immortal life shall have,
Though I, once gone, to all the world must die;
The earth can yield me but a common grave,
When you entombed in men's eyes shall lie.
Your monument shall be my gentle verse,
Which eyes not yet created shall o'er read,
And tongues to be your being shall rehearse,
When all the breathers of this world are dead.
You still shall live, such virtue hath my pen,
Where breath most breathless, even in the mouths of men"

These touching words reveal his feeling that his writings will live on as actors breathe and recreate the joys and sorrows that reflect the essence of the human predicament and condition. And importantly, he thinks that things yet unknown, will one day become known as the work of his pen!

***

Within the writing community, a new younger group of writers are doing well, but none comes close to the excellent quality of Edward's plays, poems and sonnets. Ensconced in his King's Place retreat, though he is less mobile, his creative impulse stirs afresh. England now, is certainly not what it once was, he thinks. Politically, and in other ways, the times are changing seemingly quicker by the day. The unknown beckons; and this too has some attraction and excitement. He feels a rare uplifting glow about being older: The desire and ambition of applying his maturer voice to composing new plays grow; and for a while, his thoughts wander to the threats his work faces. But, soon his thoughts are centred upon new plays: "What should I write next?" he asks himself. He responds to the question, by spending the next few hours considering various story lines, staged scenarios and making copious notes. Then, as he begins to structure and write, he feels the hand of Father Time upon his shoulder. The touch is not light. It rests heavily. His frail health deepens the sense of urgency he feels. The task he sets himself now is immense, but not unrealistic. As ever, he maintains a nimbleness of mind and good spirits. He feels the tales he wants to tell are within his grasp; that his body of work so far has been, not just for money-making, but above all, a labour of love! There is no question of love's labour lost in his mind. How well he knows the organic connection between "pain" and penning a book!

In his sights now are the plays *King Lear* and *Hamlet*. As he settles down to work, he remembers being drawn to reading the *Holy Bible*, that special copy which he'd bought as a teenager: his treasured Geneva Bible, which had been his companion to this day. Amidst the myriad thoughts of his ageing view of a darkening world, he needs light, more often than not. He turns to the "Good Book" often. And interestingly, as a student of, and believer in Christianity, in his Bible he makes a few underlinings. The passages he marks are from the books of *Revelations, Hebrews, Psalm 38* and *Micah.*

From *Revelations:* "Then I heard a voice from heaven saying unto me write. Blessed are the dead which hereafter die in the Lord. Even so sayeth the Spirit. For they rest from their labours; and their works follow them." So marking this passage containing the word "write" juxtaposed with the words "Blessed are the dead," raises the question: Does he feel he'd been ordained to write? A writer to be! he'd said loud and clear while he was still a boy, many years before he'd bought his Geneva Bible. If writing was to be his calling, from the moment of his four-word declaration: "A writer to be," he never had any doubt. And though he is not evangelical, from his holy book, he'd learned well about sin, love, darkness, light and righteousness.

In *Hebrew* and *Psalm 38,* he marked the following: "For God is not (so) unrighteous that he should forget your worth and labour of love..." And, "As the hope of the daylight causes us not to be offended with the darkness of the night, so aught we patiently to trust that God will clear our cause and restore us to our right."

Finally, from *Micah,* he underlined "I will bear the wrath of the Lord because I have sinned against him, until he plead my cause and execute judgement for me. Then will he bring me forth unto the light, and I shall see his righteousness."

He is not a fanatical believer or Church-goer, but when he looks up at the constellations in the night sky, the stars and vastness of the firmament brings him close to a Spiritual experience. So now, while shame, exile, anxieties, continuous labour (the "pain to pen a book") are all part of him and through it all he has had an abiding belief in something ineffable; something far larger than himself. He remembers his talks with Dr John Dee about Astronomy, Astrology and Magic; and, given all the uncertainties he'd faced, he hopes that one day righteousness will prevail and he will be named as the rightful author of his literary works. In other words: He recognises himself, even if nobody else does, as the ever-busy author bee who creates the honey for another to enjoy!

***

From Spiritual musings, Edward attends to his familiar,

insistent need for material gain. Early in the first year of the Seventeenth century, he makes a bid for the Presidency of Wales. He thinks it is a post that would suit him; that it would fit nicely because of a family connection to it. Henry Herbert, Earl of Pembroke, the last President had just died. He is the father of William, who, at the time, Edward had hoped would marry his second daughter, Bridget. But setting aside that potential family link, realistically, Edward thinks the Presidency is worth a try. While making his application, he remembers another, earlier diplomatic prospect, the Governorship of Jersey. In that quest, he was not successful; an outcome that now raises at least two questions: Why was this the case? And how much of an Administrator is he? The day-to-day political-diplomatic skills of an Administrator is a far cry from being a great artist! The demands, the mind-sets for both types of work are different. But Edward thinks a melding of the two would work effectively, and to his advantage.

In his application to Robert Cecil, he shows more than a little special pleading, on the grounds of family connections. "None is nearer or more allied to you than myself," he writes, "since of your sister, my late wife, only you have received nieces." Alas, serving the Welsh people at the Presidential Palace is not to be one of Edward's achievements. Cecil informs him, in no uncertain terms, that the job is not one that could be granted to him. Edward absorbs the disappointment well enough; but it does little for his fragile health, which is not just a niggle that would soon pass, or go away, but as a cold, hard insistent, reality! He considers how at Christmas he could barely make the journey from Hackney to Court to offer good tidings to Robert Cecil. In turn, Cecil had been aware of Edward's physical condition, his absences from Court and the knowledge that he, Edward, is a "hater of ceremonies." These are matters that have conspired against Edward getting the Presidency of

Wales; a job that is essentially ceremonial! Cecil sees Edward as a square peg in a round hole: That is his dilemma!

But, remarkably quickly, thoughts of disappointment; of what might have been, recedes. And soon his fertile mind transports him to a different realm. His creative thoughts are realigned to their rightful place as he lines up, so to speak, another play; a draft of which had already been sketched out and awaiting further composition. He titles it: *Measure For Measure*. It is set at the time when he was in his mid-Twenties and in exotic Italy. As the story evolves, there is a familiarity to the place and elements of the drama. It is both "abstract" as well as being based on experience. Though *Measure for Measure* echoes much of a comic play by Italian playwright Giraldi Cinthio titled *Epitia,* which Edward had read on his travels in Italy, it is not just a reworking of the original story. It is more compelling than that: It relates to Edward's own life. So far, in the matter of the usurpation of the authorship of his plays by Shakspere, at times, Edward had worried himself, to distraction. But now, through intense self-application, he infuses much-needed anger and attention into his wannabe imposter-characters. So, to a large extent, in *Measure for Measure,* he frees himself from the characters COSTARD and WILLIAM in his plays; and WILL, in the Sonnets. In essence, *Measure for Measure* deals in a comic way with the main character, the DUKE, the historical parallel of Edward, who is in a situation of which he has no control. A higher authority takes charge; and the DUKE is reduced to being an inarticulate playwright. Few things could be worse for a man as articulate and well-spoken as Edward. He feels odd. He pauses; and rests his pen. After a while, he resumes writing; and as events past and present, historical and topical, comes to mind in quick succession, he weaves in the rest of the story, ensuring that tension does not lessen.

As it turns out, *Measure for Measure* is a marvellous

Comedy that generates laughter and tears. In telling his story, which features his Anne Cecil marriage predicament, Edward plants clues about himself in the play. Truth-telling is a theme that runs through the drama. And words that he would later communicate to Cecil comes now into play in a Scene between ISABELLA and the DUKE:

> "ISABELLA: It is not truer he is ANGELO
> Than this is all as true as it is strange.
> Nay, it is ten times true. For truth is truth.
> To th' end of reckoning.
> DUKE: Away with her! Poor soul
> She speaks this in the infirmity of sense."

***

Edward's bravery and courage, as well as his maturer artistry is poured into the tale he tells as *Measure for Measure.* But ever-ready to manipulate art and life, he continues to be the essential, supreme artist, continuously pushing the boundaries of invention. He follows no set pattern or method. He is not a slave to any playwriting formula or strictures. He turns the language on its head. He makes the comic tragic, and the tragic comic. Coming to terms with his self- disguise as "William Shakespeare," and thus his potential self-obliteration, the passing of time does nothing to relieve him of worry about the authorship of his works. But such thoughts are not negative: They boost and inspire an audacious new resolve and determination in him to review and record, the connection between his experience and literary art; especially now that he is the pre-eminent playwright of his time.

***

# XIV

## 'All the world's a stage'

### ART AND LIFE

Edward thinks long and hard about his beloved, Feudal Conservative England. He'd gone through this routine countless times. He knows perhaps more intimately than any other man, how dangerous a place the country has become for a playwright like him. And to prove it, he'd suffered "the slings and arrows of outrageous fortune," to use his own words! Almost everything he writes and presents on the stage poses risk. In his heart of hearts, he is a risk-taker; a daring and courageous man. He is unafraid of taking the chance of a new experience. But scope alone is not enough, he has depth. The characters in his plays are not abstractions. Though lightly masked, they are recognisable: real flesh and blood people at Court and elsewhere. They are a testament to his skilful blending of Art and Life. He is aware that by necessarily extending conventional boundaries to reveal truths, he is seen as a threat by Conservative-minded government officials who, in a word, see him as radical. For better or worse, he uses the past and present to herald the future: To introduce and incorporate changes in the use of language and the way Englishmen see, think and do things. More and more, he writes for the experimental theatre. Therefore, he needs some latitude to say what he thinks; and to write what seems right. These things are only possible because, for some time, he had

had his own theatrical Troupe of actors. They were called the Earl of Oxford's Men; and they were popular. But Edward's weakness at managing money; and, thus his Troupe, led to problems.

Lyly and Munday, who were then his Secretaries, had ably assisted with the administration and production of the Troupe's plays. But after Essex had died, the Earl of Worcester, was appointed as Master of he Horse. Thereafter, competition was keen; and Worcester throws his hat into the theatrical ring. He takes over Edward's Company and uses the Boar's Head Inn in London as the home of his Troupe. But the "Boar's Head" is the image on the Head of Edward de Vere's family Crest. How dare Worcester do this? Alas, Edward recognises that the answer to the question he poses is this: The theatrical trend in terms of the plays written and performed is dull; far removed from the experimental theatre that he is now interested in. On this matter, he is not at one with Worcester; a social climber, who is willing just to please the Establishment. Thus Worcester's Troupe veers away from performing plays by Edward, who is now seen as a writer much too concerned with the hard realities of life and death. But why shouldn't he be, especially at this stage in his life?

So Worcester knows what the Establishment expects, and predictably his Troupe performs plays that are different from Edward's. As Worcester gives preference to his kind of plays, Edward's anonymity becomes doubly problematic. He worries that his existing plays and, very importantly, the accumulation of accompanying crucial Notes, Notebooks and Diaries are in various places. He feels a great urgency to bring them together. This collection of documents are the blueprints containing ideas and sketches that are the genesis; the raw material from which his plays were composed. Now, more than ever, he thinks, the time is right to assemble and store them in one room. As part of the process, most significantly, he feels the documents need to be re-read and written in narrative-form to show the *fundamental relationship* between his Art and Life. So the gradual drift away from performing his plays by Worcester's Company, sounds a serious warning to Edward.

And so, as he'd done some years earlier, with his "Italian" play-scripts, now he has another, but different pile of papers on his desk: a mixture of unsorted notes, Notebooks and Diaries stretching back to his Twenties. Without further ado, he unties the first bundle of papers nearest to him. His sole aim is to write, as clear an account as possible to show the correlation and connection between his life and literary work.

He collates the papers in some general chronological order. Then, he begins to write a coherent narrative from the scribblings and Notes. His plays, he thinks, should mirror his life; and vice-versa. He hopes the composition of this new "Secret Notebook" will reflect the creative process within the wider context of his experience, to date. For a while, as he holds the first few pages, he thinks about childhood days; about the strange relationship with his mother, Margery. Mothering, the closeness, or lack of it, between himself and Margery is there in his plays: she being aloof, detached, almost a cold figure. He reads now what he'd noted about his mothering and parenting experience in *The Merchant of Venice* through the characters LAUNCELOT and Old GOBBO:

"LAUNCELOT: Let's have no more fooling about it, but give me your blessing, I am Launcelot. Your boy that was, your son that is, your child that shall be.

OLD GOBBO: I cannot think you are my son.

LAUNCELOT: I know not what I shall think of that, but I am Launcelot, the Jew's man, and I am sure Mercury your wife is my mother. "

How close is "Mercury" to Margery, the name of is mother! Edward remembers his boyhood at Castle Hedingham and the actor Will Somers's friendliness; his playfulness, when he came to perform. He also had this comic performer in mind while composing *Hamlet.* "Alas, poor Yorick," he wrote, "I knew him  Horatio, a fellow of infinite jest, of most excellent fancy. He hath borne me on his back, a thousand times."

For his history plays, Edward had made copious notes, much of it from Holinshed's Chronicles and other sources. What he does with the knowledge he gains, is interesting: He changes things around, sometimes quite liberally: He rewrites English history in a propagandistic way. He glorifies the House of Tudor and Elizabethan England. Most of all, he enlarges upon some of the earlier Earls of Oxford's achievements, and overlooks certain less laudable aspects of theirs and his own life. In particular, the Third Earl, Robert de Vere, was one who had forced King John to sign the Magna Carta. But when the Earl took an anti-King position, it was a step too far; and the King laid siege to Castle Hedingham.

So though Edward's history plays presents the de Veres only in a positive light, he recognises the value of propaganda which could be quite compelling and powerful. He remembers Ankerwicke, the manor near the River Thames in Windsor, that had formed the backdrop of *The Merry Wives of Windsor* and realises how much Textbooks recommended by his tutor Thomas Smith, like *De Republica Anglorum* on government and politics, had influenced him, in terms of his interest in, and understanding of, history and playwriting, notably in the plays *Measure for Measure* and *Julius Caesar.*

Another vivid memory which he'd noted, is the Queen's double-standards when she'd stayed at Ipswich, where she was horrified to see women and children lodging at the Colleges and the Cathedral. Nonetheless, as a woman, she'd stayed in the University rooms on her visits, thus contradicting herself. "Do as I say, but not as I do," she seems to be saying. Edward refers to this regal approach in his play *Love's Labour's Lost.*

Going through more of the documents, he comes across notes he'd made on Burghley's spy network: In particular, the extent to which the Spy master would go to ensure England's safety and well-being. He spared no one; not even his own son, Thomas, who was the target of surveillance while he was in Paris. Edward incorporates this in *Hamlet* in which he portrays Burghley as POLONIUS, and his son as LAERTES, who is being spied upon! Further, Edward writes, before he'd reached his teens, that he was betrothed to Mary Hastings, who would have been his wife when he'd come of age. These he remembers as early years, when he was infatuated with Mary. But events, sadly Earl John's death, intervened to stop this arrangement. Through one character LONGUEVILLE, who reads from a Sonnet, Edward deals with this "vapour vow" in *Love's Labour's Lost,* which is through "no fault of mine."

Though he was then too young to be a player in high politics, now his thoughts are turned to the prospects should the Queen die, thus affording a good chance of Robert Dudley, the Earl of Leicester, becoming more powerful. Such a scenario, just eight weeks after his father's passing, would justifiably be a cause for much concern. "That it should come to this!" he reflects in *Hamlet,* in the guise of the PRINCE OF DENMARK who muses in his soliloquy: "But two months dead, nay, not so much, not two." In other notes on *Hamlet,* he reads of the links that he'd made between two sources: The Beowulf Saga and "Amleth," the original Hamlet myth. Arising from the same Scandinavian material, he'd scribbled: "Both sources to be used: Beowulf and Amleth."

*

Of the people he knew, he'd memorialized his Tutor Laurence Nowell. Notably in *Romeo and Juliet,* he combines aspects of the teacher's life with that of FRIAR LAURENCE'S in the play; the character who knows how to make potions: tinctures and tonics. Then, there is a reference to Robert Cecil, who features in the play *Richard III.*

Moving on, Edward reconsiders and writes of the taint of being called a "Bastard" in relation to the Inheritance of his father's estates. He deals with this in a play in which "bastard" and "legitimate" appears. In *King Lear,* the bastard EDMUND does his damndest to rob his legitimate half-brother EDGAR from becoming the Earl of Gloucester. "Why bastard?" asks EDMUND who says:

"When my dimensions are as well compact
My mind as generous, and my shape as true.
As honest madam's issue?...
As to th' legitimate. Fine word 'legitimate'
Well, my legitimate, of this letter speed
And my invention thrive, Edmund the base
Shall top the legitimate.
I grow, I prosper,
Now Gods, stand up for Bastards!"

The loss of Good Name, then (at the time of the play's composition) as now, makes Edward uneasy. On the legal matter of the illegitimacy charge in relation to his Inheritance claims, he was successfully represented by Arthur Golding, his Uncle, on his mother's side. Golding, the Translator of Ovid's *Metamorphoses*, one of Edward's earliest teachers, is remembered in *Titus Andronicus* when a copy of Ovid's work is brought on stage by a boy who says:

"'Tis Ovid's Metamorphoses. My mother gave it me." If true, it is the one recorded redeeming feature of his mother, Margery. This boyhood sight of, and introduction to, *Metamorphoses* helped in his education and had led to his remarkable early poetic understanding and proficiency in translations in the Latin and English languages

*

Turning the pages of one of his Notebooks, he continues his "Art and Life" narrative. The theme of women fraternizing with scholars again finds its way in a play: This time in *Love's Labour's Lost* which relates specifically to Royal hypocrisy and the presence of women at Cambridge University. But Queen Elizabeth is no ordinary woman. Edward also recalls his presentation of women in *The Two Noble Kinsmen* in which he'd written that "maidenheads are near akin;" and on the matter of rightful heirs being cheated of their inheritance, while he was studying at Gray's Inn, he'd made copious notes, some of which relates to ancestral lands being grabbed by the Earl of Leicester. So once more, as he thinks of his father's death, he goes further. He uses the Hales Versus Petit Case to critique the English Legal system for snatching his rightful property. Through the GRAVE-DIGGERS' in *Hamlet*, Edward re-runs certain issues raised by the real life Hales Versus Petit Case, as they mull over OPHELIA'S death:

"FIRST CLOWN: Is she to be buried in Christian burial that wilfully seeks her own salvation?

SECOND CLOWN: I tell thee she is and therefore make

her grave straight. The Coroner hath sat on her and finds it Christian burial.

FIRST CLOWN: How can that be, unless she drowned herself in her own defence?

SECOND CLOWN: Why 'tis found so.

FIRST CLOWN: It must be se offendendo; it cannot be else. For here lies the point: if I drown myself wittingly, it argues an act; and an act hath three branches: it is to act, to do, and to perform: argal, she drowned herself wittingly.

SECOND CLOWN: Nay, but hear you, goddamn Delver.

FIRST CLOWN: Give me leave: Here lies the water - good. Here stands the man - good. If the man go to this water and drown himself, it is, will he, nill he, he goes. Mark you that? But if the water come to him, and drown him, he drowns not himself; argal, he that is not guilty of his own death shortens not his own life.

SECOND CLOWN: But this is law?

FIRST CLOWN: Ay, marry, is't; coroner's quest law."

Among his "Gray's Inn Notes," he finds references to his brash act when he was seventeen years old. He remembers the cook Thomas Brincknell, collapsing and dying from a thrust of his sword. He was not convicted. Instead, he was defended by Burghley and his legal team. But, the murder has been seared in his memory; and he uses it, as part of the due process of law, in his art. In *Hamlet's* FIRST CLOWN-SECOND CLOWN dialogue, from the Notes he'd made, Edward conflates both OPHELIA'S drowning and the Brincknell legal outcomes!

*

Before he was seen as a possible husband for Anne Cecil, Philip Sidney, was the man she was linked to. While marriage talks were ongoing, he remembers this time in *The Merry Wives of Windsor.* In the play, he substitutes the characters ANNE PAGE, for Anne Cecil; SLENDER, for Sidney and SLENDER'S Uncle, for the Earl of Leicester. And so, *The Merry Wives of Windsor,* play out in comic detail, the lives of real people as art follows life!

At Gray's Inn, Edward's youthful interest in plays and playwriting, grew. Habitually, he took notes each day; and, at every event he attended. Apart from his student's work, he kept a "Diary." These were heady days when he'd seen a few Comedies such as George Gascoigne's *The Supposes*, which he remembered when he came to write *The Taming of the Shrew.* He recalls, too, the rented room in Windsor and the local story about a man who'd hanged himself on a big oak tree. In *The Merry Wives of Windsor*, both the hired room and the Ghost of the hanged man, appear. Later, Edward's long journey on horseback from London to join the Earl of Sussex and his soldiers in the North of England, features in Scenes of plays he'd titled Henry: The Fourth, The Sixth and Eighth And, by the time he'd reached twenty-one, he was strongly against rebellion, which he saw as a "sin against God and man." Such feelings, he immortalizes in *Henry IV.* In Part Two, MORTON says:

> "For that same word rebellion did divide
> The action of their bodies from their Souls; …
> But now the Archbishop turns our rebellion into a religious cause."

In this reflective "Secret" narrative, he now writes about his Courtship with Anne Cecil from notes upon which he'd based

*The Merry Wives of Windsor* and *All's Well That Ends Well.* In these two dramas, he'd cast himself as the Groom to be, who is of a higher social class as FENTON is in the first story; and BERTRAM is in the second. In *All's Well That Ends Well,* BERTRAM objects to marrying HELENA, who is beneath his rank! Edward's marriage to Anne, as it turned out, was far from happy. Anne bore the brunt of it. And interestingly, their married life was conducted against a backdrop of national and international affairs. All through Anne's miserable years, English French relations were quite good; even "convivial," as Edward had noted.

In *Hamlet*, he portrays Burghley as POLONIUS, Anne Cecil as OPHELIA, and himself, as the PRINCE OF DENMARK. As a playwright, his inventiveness knows no bounds. Alas, the same freedom could not be effected elsewhere. But, as an English Nobleman and citizen, he is hopeful of an alliance between England and France. This is a theme that runs through *Twelfth Night.* He pauses momentarily, and reflects on how, through artful reason, he'd created Scenarios: Ingenious, entrancing plot lines and memorable, believable characters. Thus art mirrors life! He remembers too, what a traumatic experience the beheading of his relative, the Duke of Norfolk was for him. And, thereafter, how much closer he was drawn to the Duke's three sons. The troubled lives of these boys in marriage, their Inheritance and Courtly lives, feature prominently in *As You Like It.* Personally, soon after he'd reached the age of twenty one, he'd become impatient about his own Inheritance. When he went to see Burghley about it, he was told not to worry: "All will be well, in due course." But that is not how things had been evolving. As he knows now, his anxieties persisted; and are expressed in *Hamlet* by Prince FORTINBRAS: "I have some rights of memory in this Kingdom, which now to claim my vantage doth unite me." Edward does not allow Burghley to escape his poisonous, lethal, pen. Thus Burghley's devious delaying tactics on Edward's Inheritance earns him the stage characterisation of POLONIUS.

As Edward reads more Notes and writes, he remembers the tension and rivalry that had existed between Queen Elizabeth and Mary, Queen of Scots. The story was told of Elizabeth sending a Messenger to meet Mary. On the Messenger's return, Elizabeth enquired if Mary "is too high, for I myself am neither too high nor too low." This memory finds its way into Edward's play *Antony and Cleopatra* in which CLEOPATRA demands to know what OCTAVIA, her rival, looks like:

"CLEOPATRA: Is she as tall as me ?
MESSENGER: She is not Madam
CLEOPATRA: Dids't hear her speak: Is she shrill tongued or low?
MESSENGER: Madam, I heard her speak:
She is low-voiced…
CLEOPATRA: That's not so good…What Majesty is in her gait? Remember, if e'er thou look'dst on Majesty."

He writes now that while he moved through the Royal Court, light-heartedly, jestingly, he portrayed himself in *Twelfth Night* as FESTE, who was Queen Elizabeth's "allowed fool." His ability to step out of himself and, in all seriousness, see himself as a character, is quite extraordinary. Also in *Twelfth Night* is Philip Sidney. He appears as SIR ANDREW AGUECHEEK. And so, time and again, historic originals - real people - become characters in his plays. Furthermore, in large part, BENEDICK in *Much Ado About Nothing* and HAMLET in *Hamlet* are based upon himself. In terms of character, characterisation and life's events, the parallels between Edward and HAMLET are spot on: most revealing!

Like HAMLET, Edward was shocked by his mother's hasty and dishonourable marriage to Charles Tyrell so soon after his father's death. And arising from the practice of Courtship and, especially from that phase of it which regards women as the epitome, the inspiration of Courtship and the mainstay of Courtliness, he believes that beauty and goodness are one! He sees the endowment of physical strength, courage and Courtliness, as well as skill in Fencing, as integral to being a Courtier, a Prince and, in part, HAMLET. But becoming a "sweet Prince" does not mean he is not capable of violent acts.

Following the ideal as presented by Castiglione, he'd adopted the appropriate dress-style. He is partial to wearing black clothing. He appreciates and considers other Courtier attributes like becoming a musician or aspiring to become a Painter. Why? Because a Painter sees the physical world with an appreciation for Line, Form and Mass, without which, Castiglione says, man cannot be great! He adds that anyone who esteemeth not the art of painting is far from all reason. But, by this reasoning, Edward comes across a seeming contradiction; a kind of recklessness and nonchalance which is Castiglione's measure of Gentility. Reading this, Edward recognises the recklessness in himself. The nature of Man concentrates his mind as he now considers certain ideas that he has woven into his plays *Hamlet* and *Much Ado About Nothing*. Elements, or traits, like recklessness and nonchalance, features in *Hamlet* in which the celebration of the "Masterpiece Man" is placed in the context of Nature: "The most excellent canopy of air." He considers these words as he'd written them down in note-form, before including them in the play: "Think now of the shape of man." He reflects now on his own actions as a Courtier that have been marked by a certain recklessness and nonchalance, the character traits that fit HAMLET'S profile perfectly. But more than that, another character, BENEDICK in *Much Ado*

*About Nothing,* mirrors himself.

***

The next document he appraises is an edited version of Thomas Twyne's Dedication to him in his translated book *A Breviary of Britain.* Twyne expressed the hope that the young Earl Edward would "become th' chieftest stay of this your commonwealth and country." These words, interestingly, find expression through KING CLAUDIUS who in *Hamlet,* Act I, Scene 2 says: "Our chieftest Courtier, cousin and son." So now, he recalls those essential, influential ideas contained in *The Courtier.* Already his writing style is vocally expressive, direct; and his repeated use of certain words in different places, or contexts, as in Sonnets Forty-Eight and Sixty-Five in which the thought and phrasing are almost the same. Now, he is reminded of having used the words: "chests" "trifles" "freed chest" "jewels" and "comfort" which links the Thomas Bedingfield Prefatory letter and the Sonnets. In Sonnet Ninety-Four, he writes: "The summer's flower is to the summer sweet. Though to itself it only live and die." These words are familiar: a re-wording of a line from him about the scent of Roses: "What doth avail the rose unless another took pleasure in the smell." Overall, these examples are akin to, and are echoes of, Castiglione's *The Courtier,* as well as the usurped Virgil poem about "honey" and "bees."

From the pile of papers on his desk, he now considers what he'd scribbled while composing *Much Ado About Nothing.* In this play too, he uses material from *The Courtier* for BENEDICK, who is Edward himself. In Act V, Scene 2 he'd written: "If a man do not erect in this age his own tomb ere he dies, he shall live no longer in monument than the bell rings and the widow weeps." Compare these words with those in the Bedingfield Letter: "By erecting ...tombs...make we them live as it were again through their monument...But with me behold it happeneth far better: for in your lifetime I shall erect you such a Monument." So, Edward had used the words "erect," "tomb" and "monument" in both passages. He recognises this borrowing from himself, as a lifelong habit!

Now he scans a few pages of jottings that he'd made for one of his first history plays: *The Famous Histories of Henry V.* With hindsight, he is not entirely pleased with the play: "I have taken many liberties," he admits to himself. "It is more a mish-mash of historical events than an accurate story. But that, in large part, is what I'd intended! It is absolutely essential to the art of story-telling and the stage."

Since that first foray into historical drama, he thinks of how much he has matured as a playwright. As he reads more notes that he'd taken for his play *Hamlet,* he realises how much of the ideas in the book *Cardanus Comfort* by Gerolamo Cardanus he'd used in the play. He reconsiders what he'd written about the "To be or not to be," speech: "Recklessness and nonchalance indeed! Death, sleep, dream, travel to strange places; inspiration from the consolations of gambling scholars." He pauses his reading, rises from his chair and retrieves a copy of *Cadanus Comfort* from the bookshelf. He re-reads sections of it and meditates upon dream and travel to foreign lands.

Moving on, he considers a matter of much importance: Soon after he'd married Anne Cecil, he'd given away one of his family's estates to a musician named William Byrd. This act of generosity makes him smile at the irony of doing so. He was not a man with ready cash to hand; at least, not yet. He recalls that after marriage, he'd begun to have money troubles; a clear warning that he would have to be more careful with the money he has and the property he owns. Later, when he wrote *All's Well That Ends Well,* he makes light of his gift to Byrd, the musician. "I know a man," the CLOWN says, "that sold a goodly manor for a song."

In the period when he was especially close to Queen Elizabeth, his insider Court knowledge served him well. In *Troilus and Cressida*, the satirical character PANDARUS, boldly sets up a romantic meeting between the leading characters, who represent the Queen and himself. Looking back "How daring was this?" he asks himself. And continuing his writing, he reflects upon how, at that youthful time, he was blissfully unaware of what was to come!

Money aside, he removes a few sheets of paper and uncovers a small notebook. It relates to the "Manuscript" that Countess Lennox had loaned to him: It is titled "Macbeth." From the moment he'd seen the Manuscript, he'd thought of it as precious research material. Nothing less than gold! Having that Document helped him enormously to create a compelling portrait of the harsh, unforgiving Lady Macbeth. He'd not returned the Manuscript, as he'd hoped to. "Why?" he questions himself. Because Countess Lennox, upon whom he'd based Lady Macbeth, had said he could keep the Manuscript! It was a generous offer that the real-life "Lady Macbeth" had made to him. But, instead of consulting the original copy of the Manuscript that he was given, it is the pages of notes, arising therefrom, which he scans now: He considers the sketches, the scenes, conversations, set pieces and the numerous bits of paper on which are jottings which add colour and flavour that intensifies the dramatic turning points. By the end of the first draft, he was right in thinking that there is nothing quite like this Scottish tragedy. But where does it come from?

Frustratingly, a dozen years later, this ancient tale of Scottish regicide had topical currency for he was party to the condemnation and execution of the Scottish Monarch, Mary, Queen of Scots. And so he rethinks how he'd accumulated the material for his memorably tragic play, *Macbeth.*

Next, he considers "Paracelsis Medicine" and healing which found expression in *All's Well That Ends Well.* And once more, his wife Anne, comes into play. This time, she is portrayed as the character HELENA. Through her, he projects his views on Paracelsis teaching. His interest in medicines, chemical distillations, also known as "simples" which leads him to better understand the use of it, not only in *All's Well That Ends Well*, but also in *Romeo and Juliet* and *The Merry Wives of Windsor.*

Of the many thoughts and ideas that had filled his head while composing his stories, he remembers that few have been as mind sharpening as the "knife," the "Merchant" and the "pound of flesh." On his visit to Italy, he'd recorded a great deal of what he'd seen of Renaissance drama and theatre. He was especially struck by certain characters and performances; notably, by Pantalone of the Commedia dell' arte. No wonder, he now sees the strong resemblance of the Pantalone plot-lines with characters and situations in *The Merchant of Venice.* But this is just one more of his indebtedness to the Commedia dell'arte.

"Ah! Venice!" he sighs wistfully, as he uncovers a larger, well thumbed, dog-eared, notebook titled: "ITALIAN JOURNAL" in which he'd written regularly on his travels. Though memory serves him well, nonetheless, he is glad he'd taken these notes. Reading the "Journal" he re-acquaints himself with sketches and important details of the journey he'd made in *The Two Gentlemen of Verona*: From the "tides" and ship-wreck causing Spring surges of the Adige River to "St Gregory's Well" just outside the gates to the north-west of Milan.

Overlaying all that he'd seen and heard in Italy was his undivided attention and deep appreciation of literature, art, culture and bustling business. He was drawn to the central area of Venice, in particular, to the Piazza and the Rialto. It is around this area, where SHYLOCK'S Servant GOBBO becomes known in *The Merchant of Venice*. But this is not the only play which he had set in Venice. Another, was *Othello*, which mirrors Venetian contemporary affairs; military commanders and campaigns at sea, as well as on the island of Cyprus. Now, his attention shifts. He writes about composing *The Winter's Tale*: "Scenes for the play to be set along the coast of Bohemia," he noted. "There are few safe places for docking as we travel in and around Ragusa." On another page, he refers to *Twelfth Night* in which OLIVIA speaks of SIR TOBY BELCH, who is only "fit for the mountains and the barbarous caves where manners ne'er were preached." The inclusion of manners and morals are not surprising because they are integral to his experience: his Noble upbringing.

In addition to *The Winter's Tale*, he also mentions the Oracle in *Timon of Athens*. He'd used this ancient, legendary oracular test to allay nagging doubts about his wife's fidelity, and thus his first daughter's paternity. Looking back, he's surprised how far he'd taken his wife Anne's "guilt" of unfaithfulness. So, in both plays, almost in an act of self-flagellation, he seeks and satirises the Delphic Oracle's final verdict as to whether or not his wife's child is his!

Later on, he'd set another play *Much Ado About Nothing* in Italy.The location is Messina on the island of Sicily, where a scheming bastard brother of King Philip II of Spain, DON JOHN enters the action. Wars are being fought and DON JOHN arrives in Messina, following a successful Mission that he and Italian Nobles had completed. At this point the Notes he is reading ends. The next document is a summary of his play *As You Like It*. He reads what he'd written on the margins: "Courtier JACQUES is a man who sells his own lands to see other men's." Having sold many of his own estates to travel this is a clear reference to himself!

His notes "On Art" are more detailed: They relate to the artists Titian and Julio Romano. He was especially struck by Titian's painting of Ovid's *Metamorphoses.* He revisits a clear distinction: That while the Classical scribes of the fable *Venus and Adonis* presents the couple's relationship as mutually passionate, in Titian's version - his large impressive painting - ADONIS seems less interested than VENUS. This is how Edward had portrayed the couple in his epic poem *Venus and Adonis.* In sum, his words are a poetic evocation of Titian's painting.

The artist Romano, on the other hand, is mentioned in the play *The Winter's Tale* in relation to a "painted statue" of the ill-treated wife HERMIONE which is compared to a statuary by that other Italian Master artist, Julio Romano. Romano, Edward had noted, was not just a Painter; he was also a Sculptor. The seminal connection that he makes with Romano is this: He was only a day's journey from the city of Mantua, where his hero Castiglione had lived and worked. Castiglione was buried in the Church of Santa Maria dell Grazie, about five miles outside of the city of Mantua's walls. In the Church were statues of local leaders and distinguished people; one of them is Castiglione's tomb, which also contains his wife, Ippolita. The designer and Sculptor of Castiglione's tomb is Julio Romano himself. Ippolita had died before Castiglione; and the tomb records his sadness. In *The Winter's Tale*, comparison between HERMIONE'S statue and reference to the sculpture by Romano is Edward's clear recall of having seen Castiglione's tomb.

While he was in Mantua, he had learned much about the history of the Gonzaga Dynasty: He'd read that one member of the Gonzaga family had been accused of murdering the Duke of Urbina. How? By *pouring poison in his ear*, Edward tells the *same story* in *Hamlet*: "His name's GONZAGO," HAMLET says, "The story is extant and writ in choice Italian: you shall see anon how the murderer gets the love of Gonzago's wife."

In Italy, Edward had noted that Ottonello Discalzio is a famous Law Professor at the University of Padua. Quite a name, Edward muses, as he considers his use of Discalzio as his inspiration for *The Merchant of Venice's* Padua University Professor of Law, BELLARIO, who is consulted to settle the case of SHYLOCK versus ANTONIO.

Edward smiles at the accuracy of all that he'd written down so far on his narrative on art and life. He uncovers a note on *The Merchant of Venice*. In it, he mentions the trip PORTIA makes from Padua to Venice, which she calls "The tranect, the common ferry." As Edward knows, the River Brenta connects the University town to the Venetian lagoon. He also remembers how analogically he'd used "circumstance, situation and character" to tell those stories that he'd invented in *Measure for Measure*, as well as in the first three Acts of *The Winter's Tale*. Another reference to *Measure for Measure* is of the Burghley-like character described as "short of composition" in the "matter of financing husband and daughter." And, as ANGELO (an Edward-like portrayal) the Earl in the play says, his wife's

"reputation was disvalued
In levity; since which time of five years
I never spake with her, saw her, nor heard from her."

On the different, but delicate subject of her love for him, he writes: "To be continued…"

In his draft of *The Tempest*, Edward has PROSPERO telling his daughter "Thy mother was a piece of virtue, she said thou was't my daughter." After all these years, even though he thought he'd dealt fully and finally in various plays with the matter of his wife's unfaithfulness, now again, in *The Tempest* there is doubt about MIRANDA'S paternity!

Now, he reads notes on *Othello* and writes about his turning a blind eye to IAGO'S dishonesty. He thinks of his model for IAGO: The man named Roland Yorke, a roguish person whose ambition is to become a Lieutenant in the Armed Forces. Yorke is violent and untrustworthy. And in two plays *Othello* and *Cymbeline,* Edward invents distrustful characters: namely, IAGO in *Othello,* and IACHIMO in *Cymbeline*, who drive their bosses, OTHELLO and POSTHUMOUS into jealous rages against their wrongly accused wives! Looking back, Edward believes the Earl of Leicester was behind Yorke's devious machinations.

To his credit, Edward had claimed that, at various times, Burghley had left him without money; and, that he, Burghley, had shown one of his letters to the Queen, with the aim of setting her against him. He relates this matter in his art. Besmirching his "Good name," is the charge he lays against Burghley, in words spoken by IAGO in *Othello*:

"IAGO: Good name in man and woman, dear my Lord,
Is the immediate jewel of their souls,
Who steals my purse, steals trash, 'tis something, nothing;
'Twas mine, 'tis his and has been slave to thousands,
But he that filches from me my good name
Robs me of that which not enriches him,
And makes me poor indeed."

While he sets the record straight, Edward de Vere is acutely aware of being the supreme autobiographical artist of his time! Often his lowest experiences have provided profound insights and inspiration. As his random jottings and notetaking have so far revealed, the fourteen months or so of his adventurous travels in Italy have been character defining. He recalls now how deeply upset he was on his return to London after the birth of his first child; a matter which haunted him so much that he continues to ask questions: "Was Yorke the instigator of his marriage crisis? Did Yorke whisper lies into his ears for some reason? And if so, what was that reason? To gain favours, perhaps? How believable were Yorke's lies?" These questions does not help as he knows so distressingly well. His mind had been so infected by the matter of Anne's supposed infidelity that he never fully recovered from it. Indeed marital discord and separation from his wife had lead to a plea from the Queen that he should be reunited in marriage.

But, the estrangement had continued; and had affected others. Having aroused the Queen's displeasure, she had distanced herself from him. Although he'd felt low, profound thoughts of life and death had tended to overtake him. Years later, when he'd come to write *Hamlet*, he'd noted: "HAMLET warns POLONIUS, saying: 'Good my Lord, will you see the players well bestow'd? Do you hear, let them be well us'd for they are abstract and brief chronicles of time. After your death you were better have a bad epitaph than their ill report while you live.'"

Amongst the bundle of papers he finds a few of his early Verses, one of which had matured to become *A Lover's Complaint*. This snapshot of his younger questionings and quests, are rough sketches and outlines; early compositions of characters in the making like OTHELLO, HAMLET, ROMEO and BERTRAM. In one of his notes appended at the end of a draft of *Hamlet,* he'd written: "So this, more or less, is my progress in playwriting." And now, from memory, he recalls important words about appearance and reality that he'd given the following characters to say:

HAMLET: "I am not as I seem to be."
OTHELLO: "Smiles to shade my bitter spite."
BERTRAM: Cruel hap…that forceth me to love my foe."
ROMEO: "So long to fight with sweet sore? And find no secret salve therefore."

All the accumulated slights and hints comes through in these characters' voices.

Reviewing notes on *The Two Gentlemen of Verona*, he is reminded of regular self-examination: deep consideration of two sides of himself. To explore these aspects, he'd created two Grooms, as characters; and the love interest in the story is, in part, based on his former wife, Anne. The love-triangle between the two Gentlemen and the woman (PROTEUS, VALENTINE and SILVIA) mirrors aspects of the Commedia dell' arte dramas. For a while, he pauses to consider how self-conscious he was when he was composing *The Two Gentlemen of Verona*.

Then riffling further through the papers, he is transported back to England and to a matter close to his heart: Inheritance that pertains to members of his extended family. On the Inheritance of the Duke of Norfolk's three sons who had married three sisters, he is reminded of how he'd composed *As you Like It*.

Moving on to another family reference, as the notes before him show, he'd recorded details of the marriage of his sister Mary to Peregrine Bertie. In particular, how stubborn they both were as people and lovers; and how they got through tempestuous wooing before getting married. In *The Taming of the Shrew*, he'd cast Peregrine as PETRUCHIO and Mary as KATHERINE. At the time of the play's composition, a Comet had appeared in the sky; and Edward gives PETRUCHIO these words to speak:

"Where is my lovely bride...?
Gentiles methinks you frown,
And wherefore gaze this goodly company
As if they saw some wondrous monument,
Some comet or unusual prodigy."

The parallels between Mary and Peregrine, KATHERINE and PETRUCHIO in *The Taming of the Shrew,* are clear. Like Edward, Mary was known for her lively temper and bold speech. As PETRUCHIO says to KATHERINE, so might Peregrine have said to his bride: "I am as they do consume the thing that feeds their fury."

Edward's notes, at this stage, continue: "Mary and Peregrine's relationship (or aspects of it) can be portrayed to powerful comic effect in my next play: *Twelfth Night,* in which the characters SIR TOBY BELCH and his companion MARIA can be seen, like PETRUCHIO and his less volatile KATHERINE some years after they were married. The similarities between MARIA, a Lady-in-Waiting corresponds to Mary de Vere's role as a Lady-in-Waiting to Queen Elizabeth." Furthermore, as the stories evolve, both KATHERINE in *The Taming of the Shrew* and MARIA in *Twelfth Night* become faithful and true-bred wives.

Another example of Edward's art and life is the draft of his play *The Tempest.* In it, he shows his interest in people of foreign lands: Like the native Indians whom Frobisher had brought to England following his failed Expedition to find the Northwest Passage. In the play, the character TRINCULO thinks about the behaviour of Englishmen who were inclined to avoid giving a penny to a disabled beggar, but will spend a goodly sum to see the corpses of native Indians! This refers, as Edward is now reminded by his notes, to the bodies of the dead Indians that were on Exhibition in London. Though macabre, it was an exotic sight which crowds flocked to see. This attitude towards otherness is summarized in Edward's words:

"That England that was won't to conquer others
Hath made a shameful conquest of itself."

Edward is acutely aware of the new class of power-hungry, profiteering business men, merchant adventurers and pirates, who were looking beyond England. He remembers, with great regret, the investment of three thousand pounds that he'd lost. It's a big sum; a failed financial venture so disappointing that he imputes it in his literary art. In *The Merchant of Venice*, he'd created the character ANTONIO, who takes a loan of three thousand ducats from money-lender SHYLOCK. At the time when Edward had invested his money, Michael Lok, was heading the Company concerned with financing the Frobisher Expedition. Edward, the inventive artist, had noted the resemblance in the names: Lok and SHYLOCK. And cleverley, he used "SHY" as part of the characters name when he was not shy at all!

Though he'd suffered a heavy loss of money in the failed Expedition, he has remained hopeful. He is not deterred from making further investments. Investing is risky, he knows. But did he see investment as a form of gambling? Yes. He accepts that he was addicted; and acknowledges this trait in *Hamlet* who says that the PRINCE OF DENMARK was "but mad north-north-west."

In this review of documents, Edward now comes across the name of one of his female characters: HELEN, who appears in both *Troilus and Cressida* and *All's Well That Ends Well.* She is a dramatic portrayal of none other than his first wife, Anne.

So, he reflects that while he uses his early experience to create BERTRAM in *All's Well That Ends Well* and HAMLET in *Hamlet,* Anne Cecil also appears in his other dramas: *Titus Andronicus, The Winter's Tale, Cymbeline* and *Othello.* He thinks of the challenges, as well as the great, meaningful satisfaction that he's gained, and feels now, from translating life into art; the *raison d'etre* of his life: A writer to be! He smiles at the thought and recalls, with some pride, how he'd dealt with his insane, jealous rages on the matter of Anne's unfaithfulness. Having cast himself as FORD in *The Merry Wives of Windsor*, now he puts the matter in perspective like this: When PAGE says: "Good Master FORD, be contented. You wrong yourself too much," FORD responds:

"True Master PAGE.
Up, gentlemen! You shall see sport anon. Follow me gentlemen.
EVANS: This is fiery fantastical humours and jealousies.
CAIUS: By Gar; 'tis no the fashion in France, it is not jealous in France;
PAGE: Nay, follow him, gentlemen. See the issue of his search…
EVANS: If there be anybody in the house, and in the chambers, and in the Coffers, and the passes, heaven forgive my sins on the day of judgement.
CAIUS: Be Gar, Nor I too. There is no bodies?
PAGE: Fie, fie, Master FORD. Are you not ashamed?
What spirit, what devil suggests this imagination?
I would not ha' your distemper in this kind for the wealth of Windsor Castle.
FORD: 'Tis my fault Master Page. I suffer for it.
EVANS: You suffer for a pad conscience. Your wife is as honest a 'omans as I will desires among five thousand,

and five hundred too.
CAIUS: By Gar, I see 'tis an honest woman."

After reading this section of dialogue, Edward finally accepts that his accusation of Anne's infidelity was wrong! Now he comes to a noted reference on his Tennis Court row with his younger contemporary, Philip Sidney, whom he'd cast in *Twelfth Night* as SIR ANDREW AGUECHEEK. In one Scene, AGUECHEEK says to SIR TOBY BELCH: "I am a fellow o' th strangest mind ith' world: I delight in masques and revels sometimes altogether." And later, instead of the duel they were expected to engage in, Edward wielded his pen, sword-like, against Sidney. Given that his hallmark as a playwright is to combine various elements: shifting time, mood and settings, he'd used the Tennis Court quarrel in the play *Henry V*; and when in *Hamlet* he casts Burghley as POLONIUS, the Tennis Court quarrel is referenced as: "There was he gaming, there o'ertook insrouse. There falling out at tennis."

When he'd lived at Fisher's Folly, the nearby Bedlam, or Insane Asylum, was a place of particular interest, as his memory-jogging Notes and Notebooks now show. The chattering and screaming of the mentally deranged was never far from his thoughts: Elements of the distracted mind form part of his compositions of the personalities of characters like OPHELIA and KING LEAR. How many "Tom o' Bedlams" are there in London? he wonders. He thinks too, about life in the round. The human condition in all its stark manifestations compels him to write: To allow him to explore the whys and wherefores as he'd done so far. Not surprisingly, he portrays the miscarriage of a child on the stage, too. This is part of his play *Much Ado About Nothing,* in particular, the relationship between BENEDICK and BEATRICE. In this connection, he thinks of the pregnant Anne Vavasour, who had miscarried;

and remembers the great relief he'd felt on receiving the news. But, he could never forget the uproar the news had caused. He still feels some tension about that time of turmoil, of shame, in his life. In the play, he felt he could not exclude the situation in which BEATRICE had conceived a still born child!

His thoughts of *Much Ado About Nothing* now also takes him back to a no less contentious period in his life when the slanderous charges of Arundel and Howard were levelled against him. In response to the accusations, he uses his play as best he could. One of his interesting characters is Constable DOGBERRY, through whom he does his best to highlight the Arundell Libels, satirically. Arundell says that Edward is a multiple perjuror and, as such, he deserves to be in hell! For his part, DOGBERRY puts it thus: "Why, this is flat perjury, to call a prince's brother 'villain'…O villain, thou wilt be condemned into everlasting redemption for this." But, it seems, Edward the risk-taker, the adventurer, never learns. He cringes now at the thought: That soon after Vavasour's miscarriage, she was pregnant once again by him. Though his embarrassment was great, this time, there was no miscarriage; and, he could not disown the child. There is no escape. He felt exasperated and wretched. In his predicament, he asks himself: "What should I do?" Uppermost in his mind was fleeing from England. But thinking like this, at once, he remembers what Sir Thomas More had said about those who flee, and those who show traitorious, rebellious, behaviour. He is mindful that during his time in the Tower of London, he'd thought about More's own incarceration there and how the dramatic surroundings had set creative thoughts in train. The story of More haunted him. And soon, the idea of a play had come to him; a story about which he'd spoken to Munday. Before him now is a sketch of the play that had preoccupied him in "idle cell." Most of the other notes on the play he'd given to

Munday who, having fleshed out the story had passed on a copy to Edward. He reads with great interest, an excerpt which begins with More's question: "Who will obey a traitor?" and continues:

"Or how can well that proclamation sound
When there is no additional but a rebel
To qualify, a rebel?...
Wither would you go?
What country by the nature of your error,
Should give you harbour? Go you to France or Flanders,
To any German province, to Spain or Portugal,
Nay, any where that not adheres to England,
Why, you must needs be strangers
Would you be pleased to find a nation of such barbarous temper…
Submit you to these noble gentlemen,
Entreat their mediation to the King,
Give up yourself to form, obey the magistrate,
And there's no doubt but mercy may be found
If you so seek it.
To persist in it is present death."

Edward considers these words ,even now, with remorse. He pauses his narrative briefly. Looking around, his gaze falls on the painting on the wall of himself as a young man standing beside a human skull. How quickly time passes, he thinks, as he resumes writing. He is conscious that the first mention of debilitating lameness appears in his private letters; and, in a few Sonnets. In Sonnet Thirty-Seven, he reads these words:

"Thus I made lame by fortune's dearest spite.

Take all my comfort of my worth and truth…"

Immediately, vivid images of the stab that caused his injury, come to him. He thinks of the clash of swords; the hateful violence that gave rise to the drama of *Romeo and Juliet*. He remembers his part in the brawls: the Blackfriars street-fights and the lines he'd written for the PRINCE OF VERONA to speak:

"PRINCE: Three civil brawls bred of an airy word
By thee, old Capulet, and Montague,
Have thrice disturb'd the quiet of our streets
And made Verona's ancient citizens
Cast by their grave-beseeming ornaments
To wield old partisans, in hands as old,
Cankered with peace to part your cankered hate.
If ever you disturb our streets again
Your lives shall pay the forfeit of the peace."

This transfer of locations and identities in his art makes him pause again. He thinks of his lameness: How incredibly lucky he was to escape death. And, quite rightly, he'd used it in his story of the star-crossed young lovers, which is one of his most disturbing, but favourite plays.

Having written several pages on his Art and Life narrative, now he turns to notes he'd taken for his play *Much Ado About Nothing* into which, once more, he'd channelled his marital problem through the characters CLAUDIO and HERO. He acknowledges that HERO is decent and pure, whereas CLAUDIO is at fault. In this play, his innate authorial stubbornness comes through. He does not give in easily to anything; and while, at times, he'd been guilty of wrong-doing, he always acts on the understanding that he is right. So now, as if for the first time, he re-acquaints himself with this stubbornness which he fully accepts, is part of who he is.

Looking back, he sees that while *Much Ado About Nothing* works well as a romantic Comedy, it did him no favours socially and politically. Portraying Anne Vavasour as BEATRICE, as he'd learned, did not absolve him from blame for having such an extra marital affair. Nonetheless, he profoundly believes that the power of the art of his pen would redeem him from any, or all, his perceived misdemeanours. With this in mind, he reflects the lives of real people on the dramatic stage. His casting of characters includes himself in relation to other people like Burghley, who had kept him under constant surveillance. Their relationship was a vexed one; and unsurprisingly in *Hamlet*, he portrays himself as the DANISH PRINCE and Burghley as POLONIUS. This juxtaposition confirms that while thinking and writing the play, increasingly, he saw himself and HAMLET as one. This through his art, he felt he could get his own back. He was fed up of being shadowed; and now from the pile on his desk, he retrieves, and reads one of his Sonnets in which he repeats words he'd used in a letter to Burghley, as well as a few from the Book of Exodus: "I am that I am" reflects his stubborn, God-given right and claim to be himself. These four words of being himself are contained in the Sonnet's full text:

"'Tis better to be vile esteemed,
When not to be receives reproach of being;
And the just pleasure lost, which is so deemed
Not by our feeling, but by others' seeing;
For why should others' false adulterate eyes
Give salvation to my sportive blood?
Or on my frailties why are frailer spies,
Which their will count bad what I think good

> No, *I am that I am*, and they that level
> At my abuses reckon up their own:
> By their rank thoughts my deeds must not be shown
> All men are bad and in their badness reign."

Thus Edward's "*I am that I am*" and "*All men are bad*" justifies where he stands.

Other documents on his desk reveal more of his thinking on his dramas: In *Hamlet*, his pride in social status is evident as frustration boils over, and his nobleman's rank-pulling is mirrored in his "Get thee to the Nunnery" speech to OPHELIA. "Virtue shall not so inoculate our old stock, but we shall relish of it," HAMLET says. But though Class differences between the Nobility and Commoners were clear, in real life, Anne Cecil had always been dictated to by her father and brother; and as lovers, both Edward and Anne were closely watched, as were HAMLET and OPHELIA under the control of POLONIUS! Thus the devious Burghley had relied on Spies as Edward had confirmed in what he'd written in *Hamlet*: That the triangular relationship between himself, Anne and Burghley corresponds to HAMLET, OPHELIA and POLONIUS.

*

Edward remembers well the heady years of the Lowlands conflict and his nationalist, patriotic pride: His desire to serve at the highest level had been intense. To convince the Queen, he had written plays to prove his commitment.

While he was, at this time, maturing into HAMLET, nonetheless, there was also a brave, courageous, warrior-like ULYSSES side to him, reflecting the staid feudal system, founded upon a God-given order. Now, he lifts a loose sheet of paper on which he'd hurriedly written a note about English troops under Commander Norris who was leaving for the battlefront during the Lowlands Campaign. This military build-up is mirrored in *Hamlet*, as a Palace Guard asks:

"Why is there such daily cast of canon
And foreign mart for implements of war?
Why such impress of shipwrights, whose sore task
Does not divide the Sunday from the week:
What might be toward that this sweaty haste
Doth make the night joint-labourer with the day..."

Linked to these scribblings are some notes on the impending threat of invasion by the Spanish Armada. He'd written that just before the Armada attack, he had joined Sir Francis Drake and other Commanders of the Naval fleet on the south coast of England. And much later, when he came to compose a first draft of *The Tempest,* he drew upon his experience of those worrying, but exciting, days. The notes he'd written prompts vivid images of that time. In the days leading up to the battle, he remembers the English Fleet's patrolling exercises near Plymouth; and tellingly, memorably, he'd recorded what he'd experienced and heard aboard ship. Amidst gale-force tempests, on windswept decks, he'd listened as the Boatswain spoke certain nautical words and phrases, which he used in his draft of *The Tempest*:

"Fall to it yarely or we run ourselves aground."
"Tend to th' Master's whistle."
"Lay her a–hold, a-hold."
And: "Lay her off!"

But that Summer month of June, as the English Fleet weathered the storm in and around Plymouth, Edward had received urgent news from London: His wife, Anne, had died. At once, his worry about the imminent Spanish attack had receded. For a while, it was replaced by shock and overwhelming sadness. The circumstances of being by the sea and hearing sad news were not dissimilar from the Scene he'd written for HAMLET and OPHELIA. Anne's death dramatized the loss of a loved one, his wife that was much greater than he could have imagined. Now, he reads the lines that he'd written for his play:

> "HAMLET: I lov'd OPHELIA. Forty thousand brothers
> Could not, with all their quantity of love,
> Make up my sum. What will thou do for her...?
> HAMLET (To LAERTES): 'Swoons, show me what thou'lt do.
> ...Woo't weep, woo't fight, woo't fast, woo't tear thyself?
> Woo't drink up easel, eat a crocodile?
> I'll do it."

Wretchedness had taken hold of him. Perusing an old dog-eared Diary, he recognises the progression of his work as he adopted a maritime persona. As he scans the notes he'd made for his play *Antony and Cleopatra*, he reflects upon an excerpt of dialogue between CLEOPATRA and ANTONY, during which CLEOPATRA asks ANTONY about his marriage. He responds:

> "Let's not unfound the time with conference harsh.
> There's not a minute of our lives should stretch
> Without some pleasure now."

After reading these lines, Edward realises the shift he'd made from his life as HAMLET to blending his experience with tales of olden times. With hindsight, in *Antony and Cleopatra*, he sees the strides he'd made more clearly, when, on hearing of OPHELIA'S (Anne's) passing, he wrote the following exchange between the MESSENGER and ANTONY:

"THIRD MESSENGER: FULVIA thy wife is dead.
ANTONY: Where died she?
THIRD MESSENGER: In Sicyon.
ANTONY: There's a great spirit gone!
Thus did I desire it:
What our contempts doth often hurl from us,
We wish it ours again. The present pleasure,
By revolution low'ring does become
The opposite of itself: She's good being gone,
The hand would pluck her back that shov'd her on."

These lines confirm, his evolved, post-Anne Cecil voice. He next looks at four pages of writing under the headings: "FISHER'S FOLLY: DISCUSSIONS WITH LYLY AND MUNDAY." Beneath these pages is a bulky manuscript containing poems and verses. It is titled: "The Commonplace Book." Apart from one poem, most of the hand-writing of the manuscript of the "Book" belongs to Anne Cornwallis, the daughter of William Cornwallis, the man who had bought Fisher's Folly from Edward. Living in that property and knowing of its literary legacy, young Anne aspired to become a writer of verses and poetry. Cornwallis had talked to Edward about his daughter's love of literature and writing. On two pages, there are nine Stanzas of a particular poem attributed to an "Anonymous" hand. Edward recognises the poem as his: The first six lines are:

"When that thine eyes hath chose the dame,
And stalled the deer that thou would strike,

Let reason rule things worthy blame,
As well as fancy, partial like,
Ask counsel by some other head
Neither unwise nor yet unwed..."

As Edward knows, these lines, and other poems and verses, comes from an anthology titled *The Passionate Pilgrim* by W. Shakespeare. That brand name again, he thinks.

Moving on through the pile of papers, he opens a large brown envelope. In it there are two pages of Sonnets he'd composed at the time of Southampton's imprisonment in the Tower of London while he was awaiting execution. On life and death, he'd committed his private thoughts to the following lines:

"...My life...sinks down to death, oppressed with
melancholy, Until life's composition be recurred
By those swift messengers returned from thee
Who even but now come back again assured
Of thy fair health, recounting it to me.
This told, I joy, but then no longer glad,
I send them back again and straight grow sad."

Southampton's life is in the balance: The circumstances are utterly dire. Just over two weeks after Essex's beheading, his accomplices Gelly Merrick and Henry Cuffe had met their grisly ends at Tyburn. The scene was horrific; barbaric. They were hanged; and while still alive, their bodies were dissected; quartered. For his part, Sir Charles Danvers, after a spell in the Tower of London, is spared the suffering of Merrick and Cuffe. His life, like Essex's, ends with one deadly blow from the Executioner's axe. As a Juror, though it was not Edward's motivation to have found Danvers guilty, nonetheless his death would have an unforeseen benefit for Edward.

After Essex's death, as precious time pass, and Southampton was in the Tower still waiting to know the dreaded date of his Execution, Edward's hand was not idle. He'd committed his thoughts to paper in a few more Sonnets. In Sonnet Ninety Four, he'd written:

"They that have the power to hurt, and will do none,
That do not do the thing they most do show,
Who, moving others, are themselves as stone,
Unmoved, cold, and to temptation, slow:
They rightly do inherit heaven's graces,
And husband nature's riches from expense;
They are the lords and owners of their faces,
Others, but Stewards of their excellence..."

Having been immersed in dark thoughts of the Executioner's approach when Edward had heard the news that mercy had been granted; that Southampton's death sentence was commuted to life imprisonment, his relief was incalculable. He felt the need for expression and reached for his pen. In Sonnet Sixty Eight, he mused:

"Before the golden tresses of the dead,
The right of sepulchres, were shorn away.
To live a second life on second head;
Ere beauty's dead fleece made another gay.
In him those holy antique hours are seen,
Without all ornament, itself and true,
Making no summer, of another's green,
Robbing no old to dress his beauty now;

And him as for a map doth nature store
To show false art what beauty was of yore."

He thinks of the power and status of a Commoner like Burghley and his son Robert Cecil who rose up through the ranks; and now, of Southampton who has made the opposite journey. It is a dangerously chastening experience. Robbed of his titles, Southampton is now plain Henry Wriothesley. No one is more empathetic and sympathetic of Southampton's status than Edward, who captures his dear youthful friend's shocking fall in another Sonnet:

"Those parts of thee that the world's eye doth view
Want nothing that the thought of hearts can mend;
All tongues, the voice of souls, give thee that due,
Utt'ring bare truth, even so as foes commend:
But those same tongues that give thee so thine own
In other accents do this praise confound,
By seeing further than the eye hath shown;
They look into the beauty of thy mind,
And that in guess they measure by thy deeds;
Then churls their thoughts (although their eyes were kind)
To thy fair flower add the rank smell of weeds.
But thy odour matcheth not thy show,
The soil is this that thou dost common grow."

For a while, he meditates on this Sonnet and dark times, before moving on. From the now much reduced pile, he delves into another bundle of spell-binding pages titled: "ON MAGIC AND MY PLAYS."

Some years earlier, Edward had met the learned Dr John Dee a few times. They had had many discussions on

Astronomy, Astrology and Magic. During these meetings, Edward had taken copious notes amounting to several pages that are before him now, as he proceeds with writing this narrative on "Art and Life." He was at the time of his meetings with Dr Dee (and now) particularly interested in Magic. All the more so, because as a playwright, he is sensitive to what matters to his audiences: Current affairs and popular beliefs. The influence of Magic on social life in England is all around him: And not surprisingly, Ghosts, Fairies, Spirits, Conjurers, Witches, Soothsayers, Apparitions and Supernatural beings are integral aspects of his *Dramatis Personae* in his Comedies and Tragedies.

So far, Magic has featured in at least eleven of his plays. In a draft of one of his most recent offerings *The Tempest,* ARIEL and Spirits who, commanded by PROSPERO, a Practitioner of Magic, raises fierce tempests which wrecks the ships of Rulers like the King and the Duke of Milan. Another character, the deformed, rugged, uncultured CALIBAN, "a freckled whelp, hag-born," is the son of a Witch. The magical power of PROSPERO seems boundless. He also has, at his command, Goblins and Nymphs whom he summons to take revenge, as well as Spirits in the form of hounds:

"Go, charge my goblins that they grind their joints
With dry convolutions; shorten up their sinews
With aged cramps."

Later in the play, dressed in his wizard's robes, PROSPERO draws his Magic Circle and declares:

"Graves, at my command,
Have waked their sleepers, oped, and let 'em forth
By my so potent art."

The characters ALONSO, ANTONIO and SEBASTIAN enter the Magic Circle and are "charmed."

In *The Comedy of Errors*, PINCH combines the profession of Schoolmaster and Conjurer in Ephesus, which, as ANTIPHOLUS OF SYRACUSE says has the reputation of being a centre for practitioners of magical arts:

"They say this town is full of cozenage;
As nimble jugglers that deceive the eye,
Dark-working sorcerers that change the mind,
Soul-killing witches that deform the body,
Disguised cheaters, prating mountebanks,
And many such-like liberties of sin."

ANTIPHOLUS'S wife calls upon PINCH to exorcise the troublesome demon that has taken possession of her husband. She says:

"Good Doctor Pinch, you are a Conjurer,
Establish him in his true sense again,
And I will please you what you will demand."

PINCH goes to ANTIPHOLUS and says: "Give me your hand, and let me feel your pulse." To this, ANTIPHOLUS replies: "There is my hand, let me feel your ear." PINCH then gives his Conjuration:

"I charge thee, Satan, housed within this man,
To yield possession to my holy prayers,
And to thy state of darkness hie thee straight;
I conjure thee by all the Saints in heaven."

Thereafter, unflatteringly, ANTIPHOLUS says to PINCH:

"They brought one Pinch, a hungry lean faced villain,
A mere anatomy, a mountebank,
A threadbare juggler, and a fortune-teller,
A needy, hollow-eyed, sharp-looking wretch,
A living-dead man. This pernicious slave,
Forsooth, took on him as a conjurer,
And, gazing in mine eyes, feeling my pulse,
And with no face, as 'twere, out-facing me,
Cries out, I was possessed."

*

Edward then considers what he'd written about Magic in *A Midsummer Night's Dream*. In this play, a fairyland is ruled by King OBERON and his Queen TITANIA. The character, a FAIRY, is portrayed as a "knavish sprite called Robin Goodfellow," who

"frights the maidens of the villag'ry;
Skim milk, and sometimes labour in the quern,
And bootless make the breathless housewife churn,
And sometime make the drink to bear no barm -
Mislead night-wanderers, laughing at their harm?"

In short, he is a troublesome hobgoblin.

Thereafter, the touching of TITANIA'S eyes with a magic herb to change her back into a Fairy shows how much Edward knows of the herb – a little plant called "Eye Bright."

Now Edward turns to his most complete description of a Magical Conjuration in Part Two of his play *King Henry VI*. This occurs when BOLINGBROKE raises the Spirit of the Duke of Gloucester's garden. As Magician and Conjurer, BOLINGBROKE enters accompanied by MARGARET JOURDAIN, a Witch, together with Hume and Southwell who are Priests. Then, after Hume leaves to inform the DUCHESS, BOLINGBROKE addresses the Witch as the Séance starts, thus: "Mother Jourdain, be you prostrate and grovel on earth; John Southwell, read you; and let us to our work."

At this juncture, the DUCHESS enters, followed by Hume. The DUCHESS says:

> "Well said my Masters, and welcome all. To this gear the sooner the better."

BOLINGBROKE responds:

> "Patience, good Lady; wizards know their times:
> Deep night, dark night, the silent of the night,
> The time of the night when Troy was set on fire;
> The time when screech-owls cry, and ban-dogs howl,
> And spirits walk and ghosts break up their graves,
> That time best fits the work we have in hand.
> Madam, sit you and fear not: whom we raise,
> We will make fast within a hollow'd verge."

Now the requisite Ceremonies are performed. After making the Magic Circle, BOLINGBROKE reads the Conjuration; and, accompanied by loud thunder and flashes of lightning, the Spirit speaks:

> "SPIRIT: Adsum
> MARGARET JOURDAIN: Asmath,
> By the eternal God, whose name and power

Thou tremblest at, answer that I shall ask;
For till thou speak, thou shalt not pass from hence.
SPIRIT: Ask what thou wilt.
That I had said and done!"

After BOLINGBROKE raises the question, and the Spirit responds, he gives the order to leave:

"Descend to darkness and the burning lake!
False fiend, avoid!"

At this point, Edward stops writing: He reflects upon his intimate knowledge of Conjuration and Magical Ceremonial. Not only had he met Dr Dee, and had the benefit of his learning, he had read widely too, notably, the works of a few leading lights on the dark arts, practitioners of Magic like Edward Kelly and Simon Forman. Because such works on the rites and Ceremonials of Magic were not widely available, Dr Dee had given Edward access to a few private manuscripts. Thereafter, his knowledge grew; and his detailed understanding comes into play in the following exchange between SMITH and CADE:

"SMITH: Has a book in her pocket with red letters in't
CADE: Nay, then he is a Conjurer."

The colour red is most interesting because manuscripts on Magical Ceremonial are written in inks of red and black. Another aspect of the ritual, he recalls, is that the Conjurer is accompanied by a Reader who has a book of the Ceremonies and spoke in relation to the conjuration and prayers. Notably his use of history and current affairs in this play is abundantly clear: It is the time of the Trial of the Duchess of Gloucester,

Margery Jourdain, Southwell, Hume and Bolingbroke for Sorcery and Witchcraft, for which Jourdain was condemned to be burnt as a Witch; and the men to be hanged. The play mirrors historical facts of a real life drama, namely, the case against the Duchess was of compassing the death of the King, with Marie Gardimain and Bolingbroke through the use of the dark arts. Edward uses the real life Marie Gardimain as his model for Margaret Jourdain. Eventually, Gardimain was burnt at the stake, Bolingbroke was hanged and the Duchess was condemned to life imprisonment.

Ghosts also appear in *Richard III*. In *Julius Caesar*, the SOOTHSAYER warns: "Good sir beware the ides of March;" and, in *Antony and Cleopatra*, Edward introduces a SOOTHSAYER, who apart from Fortune-telling says to CHARMIAN: "Is't you, sir, that know things?" to which the SOOTHSAYER responds:

"In nature's infinite book of secrecy
A little I can read.
ALEXAS: Show him your hand...,
CHARMIAN: Good sir, give me good fortune.
SOOTHSAYER: I make not, but forsee."

Later in the play, ANTONY brings a Soothsayer from Egypt and takes him to Caesar's house.

"ANTONY: Say to me,
Whose fortunes shall rise higher, Caesar's or mine?
SOOTHSAYER: Caesar's. Therefore, O Antony stay not by his side.
Thy demon, that thy spirit which keeps thee, is
Noble, courageous, high, unmatchable,
Where Caesar's is not; but near him thy angel
Becomes afeard as being o'erpower'd. Therefore

Make space enough between you."

*

Edward is reminded now of another Soothsayer that he'd used in *Cymbeline*, who tells LUCIUS of his vision:

"SOOTHSAYER: Last night the very gods showed
me a vision -
I fast and pray'd for their intelligence -
thus I saw Jove's bird, the Roman eagle, winged.
From the spongy south to this part of the west,
There vanished in the sunbeams; which portends,
Unless my sins abuse my divination,
Success to th' Roman host."

As the story evolves, the imprisoned POSTHUMOUS has a vision in which his father SICILIUS LEONATUS, his wife and two young brothers appear. They encircle him; and call on the aid of JUPITER who arrives from on high amidst lightning and thunder, sitting on an eagle. He throws a thunderbolt and, as the Ghosts fall to their knees, he says to them:

"No more, you petty spirits of region low,
Offend our hearing. Hush! How dare you ghosts
Accuse the Thunderer, whose bolt you know,
Sky-planted, batters all rebelling coasts?"

When POSTHUMOUS wakes, he finds a book. And, at the end of the play, the SOOTHSAYER explains the parable with the promise of peace and prosperity in the country.

In his draft of *Macbeth,* Edward had introduced Witches in two Acts. They appear before MACBETH and BANQUO. In his description of them, BANQUO says:

"What are these
So wither'd and so wild in their attire,
That look not like th' inhabitants o'th' earth,
And yet are on't? Live you, or are you aught
That man may question? You seem to understand me
By each at once her choppy finger laying
Upon her skinny lips. You should be women,
And yet your beards forbid me to interpret
That you are so."

Soon, they disappear; and BANQUO adds:

"Were such things here as we do speak about,
Or have we eaten on the insane root,
That takes the reason prisoner."

The "insane root"? What is it? Edward smiles as he reviews his understanding of the thing. It is a plant to which superstitions are attached. The root of this plant is said to possess strong narcotic properties that bring on hallucinations. Such effects justify its description as the "insane root." The shape of the root, he'd noted, bears resemblance to the human form; and was used by Witches to do harm to their enemies. When HECATE speaks to the Witches, a clear allusion is made to an ancient tradition of the magical effect of mist around the Moon:

"Upon the corner of the moon
There hangs a vap'rous drop profound.

I'll catch it ere it comes to ground,
And that, distilled by magic sleights
Shall raise such artificial sprites."

Edward is mindful of the focus of his interpretation of the ingredients that the Witches use in making their hell-broth; their use of mysterious things, as part of their practice. As they engage in incantation while they mill around a boiling cauldron, they chant:

"Round about the cauldron go;
In the poison'd entrails throw.
Toad, that under cold stone,
Days and nights, hast thirty-one
Swelter'd venom sleeping got,
Boil thou first I the charmed pot.
Double; double, toil and trouble;
Fire burn and cauldron bubble."

In this way, the Witches measure time. By repetition of Verses, the Witches felt they could regulate the time of boiling with some accuracy. Historically, apothecaries had used the Moon as a method of calculating the time that some processes took; and the word Menstruum, as Edward knows, is still in use.

In his allusion to the "Root of hemlock, digg'd i' the dark," Edward refers to another ancient custom of gathering herbs at night in the belief that their properties after dark were more potent than in daytime. But not everyone either understood this, or believed in Ghosts. So by making reference to Ghosts and Spirits in *Hamlet,* Edward, once again, uses Magic to explain the failure of HAMLET to recognise the Ghost of his father:

"HAMLET: Be thou a spirit of health or goblin damn'd,
Bring with thee airs of heaven or blasts from hell,
Be thy intents wicked, or charitable,
Thou com'st in such questionable shape."

In reply, the GHOST says:

"I am thy father's spirit,
Doom'd for a certain term to walk the night,
And for the day confin'd to fast in fires,
Till the foul crimes done in my days or nature,
Are burnt and purged away."

With these few lines, Edward ends this section of writing on "MAGIC AND MY PLAYS" for his narrative.

*

Finally, from the now reduced pile of Documents, Edward reads a last page of scribble he'd made while he was composing *The Winter's Tale*. He refers to "perfumed gloves," that famous pair which he'd brought back from Italy as a gift for Queen Elizabeth. In Act IV, Scene 4 of the play, AUTOLYCUS sings of "gloves as sweet as Damask roses." The gloves are symbolic of the close relations and love between Edward and the Queen who greatly appreciated those gloves. And, for quite some time, especially when Edward was much in favour, she'd proudly worn the gloves in public! Such a personal gift had deep meaning. It was emblematic of past intimacies. But now, that long-standing secret bond of love in its many guises between himself and Queen Elizabeth is no less powerful and symbolic than is his favourite flower: The Tudor Rose of England. On this note, he ends this narrative.

He pushes his chair back and surveys the fresh pile of pages he'd written. He feels empowered that he'd given coherent form to disparate sources from which he'd made organic connections between art and life while composing his poems and plays. After a while, he moves closer to his desk, dips his quill in ink and on a blank page in bold letters, he writes the title: "ART AND LIFE: MY SECRET NOTEBOOK. "

Why "Secret?" Because like all his other writings as Edward de Vere, this manuscript is for his eyes only, and like so many of his "Anonymous" works, it is meant to be nowhere else, but locked away in the bottom drawers of his desk.

***

# XV

## "What a piece of work is a man!... What is this quintessence of dust?"

### FINAL ACTS

Edward is fifty-two years old. While Worcester's Troupe of Players and the Lord Chamberlain's Men thrive, Edward feels he should be doing much better in the theatrical presentation of his plays. And on his depleted finances, he is still hopeful of recouping his full Inheritance. Earlier, he'd petitioned Robert Cecil for the vacant Wiltshire estate of Sir Charles Danvers and now he is no less determined than he'd been on previous occasions when he'd petitioned for this property. He claims that the Queen had promised to give him the estate, but, as yet, the promise is unfulfilled. His frustration boils over: "I find by this waste of time," he writes, "that lands will not be carried without deeds." Official documentation, he thinks, is the only sensible way forward for he adds, "my suit is, as it was the first day."

Alas, his Danvers petition is rejected. It is one more blow for him to bear. Overall, he tempers his exuberance for risky business speculations, and for now, apart from a legal matter about tax indebtedness, he is relatively free of being in dire need. On the plus side, his marriage has achieved a degree of companionship; a togetherness that is comfortable, as well as being socially acceptable. So much so, that by Christmas, he and Countess Elizabeth are able to present a New Year's gift to the Queen who, in turn, gives them theirs. As supreme controller of all Courtly relationships, the Queen seems to have come to terms with Edward's dealings with women. Her own relationship with him has been anything but straightforward. Often, it was tempestuous, with bitter words exchanged; and punishment in the form of imprisonment and exile. Now, he is back in the fold. That, he thinks, is good for him; not just because he's older, perhaps wiser and has mellowed a bit, but because he is by nature not a man who is incapable of forgiveness. Though he feels deeply about his work and people, his heart and head are unusually well-balanced. Compassion and hope underscore his character.

*

Months later, in February 1603, the aging Queen Elizabeth looks much weaker than of late. Alas, the self-styled "Virgin Queen" is dying. Her cherished Coronation ring is in its rightful place, where it has always been since she became Monarch over four decades earlier. Symbols matter hugely to her: Apart from her Crown, this ring is deeply meaningful. Having never married, when the ring is removed because it had been so embedded into her finger, the separation has a profound effect upon her. She had had a long and sacred bond with her country. And with each year of her reign, she'd gained in Might and Confidence. Hitherto, everything had been rosy for the Tudor Rose, herself. But now, it seems, something precious is slipping away from her. Her grasp on power is no longer secure. In her weakening state, she suffers a great loss when her very close, dear friend, Catherine Carey, Countess of Nottingham dies. Catherine's long-standing presence and friendship has always been reassuring; most comforting for Elizabeth. Now, her sudden absence dramatizes Elizabeth's own approaching death.

Each day, as she lies in queenly repose on her stately bed, woeful thoughts come and go. They are interspersed with the more familiar, but no less troubling thoughts of Succession to the Throne of England when she is gone. Though no one at Court openly talks about it, she knows it is on their minds, too! Alas, the fact that all good things must end, is a reality which she tries to think of sagely. But the pending loss of her Supreme power is too much to bear: She struggles to keep her wits about her. Lying in bed, suddenly, she sits bolt upright as a surge of energy, contrary to her earlier supine state, courses through her body. She has been doing this sitting-up every time she thinks not only of having lost her ring, but also of losing her Crown! As such thoughts takes a firmer hold, she is, at times, overwhelmed, especially in these last few days.

*

At every turn, Edward hears the Royal Court gossip and rumours. Among members of the warring factions vying for political power, news of the dying Queen does not arouse either much genuine sympathy or empathy. "Why should it?" Edward asks himself. The rivals are not sentimental, but power hungry, practical men. They will stop at nothing to achieve their ends. There is much gloom in these wintry, uncertain days; and to lighten the mood, Edward hosts a Dinner Party at his home in King's Place, Hackney. During the evening, the subject of Succession to the Throne is raised by one of the invited Guests: The Earl of Lincoln. The atmosphere is convivial; and, with drinks in hand, Edward and Lincoln move away from the main group of Guests. They go to the Gallery and talk about the future of England, albeit in low voices, well into the night. Among the questions they discuss is: "What should the Nobility do about any transfer of power?"

"We must take a stand," Edward says. "A stand of one sort or another is necessary. We cannot, indeed, we must not, stand aside and let whoever it might be just walk in! It is not the way we do things in England."

"Quite so, My Dear Lord Edward," Lincoln says. "I would not, of course, call a name or names, but we both know who the front runners are."

"My Dear Lincoln, I know of one, at least," Edward says. "And, he is not an Englishman." Edward and Lincoln look at each other knowingly.

"My Dear Lord, I know who you mean," says Lincoln. He is encouraged by Edward's silence; even excited by what his host says about a non-Englishman as a Contender. Boldly, he puts forward his own version; his "Plan," as he calls it, of Succession. Edward knows of Lincoln's proneness to hot-headedness; and thinks what he says about his "Plan" is more than a little dangerous. Edward recalls that at the time when he was getting married to Anne Cecil, the Duke of Norfolk was tried and sentenced to death for Treason, because he, Norfolk, was plotting against Queen Elizabeth. More to the point, he was hoping to marry the Catholic Mary, Queen of Scots, and depose Queen Elizabeth. So what Lincoln says is not so far-fetched, as to think that the wine he is drinking has gone to his head.

In the meantime, not far away from Hackney are Robert Cecil's Spies. According to one Informer, during the after dinner conversation between Edward and Lincoln, Edward had expressed opposition to a Scotsman becoming King of England. But, the Informer reports: "I do not fear Lord Edward Oxford as a danger to the country because he is so weak in body and friends that he is unlikely to raise any great opposition."

The day after the Dinner Party, Edward feels it was good

to clear the air, and he has no doubt that the gathering had achieved its purpose: "As Noblemen," he says to himself, "it gives Lincoln and myself a chance to express feelings that are strong and real, especially now: a precipitous and historic moment in England's history."

***

A few weeks later, more news of the ailing Queen reaches Edward. There is little doubt in the Queen's doctor's mind that her days are numbered. Her weakened, wasted body is close to shutting down: She is unable to eat. She takes no medication; and refuses to lie in bed. On this last refusal, she says, she sees things when she is in bed. What "things?" She does not say. Cushions are put on the floor, where she sleeps. It is shocking thus far, how badly illness has damaged her body and mind. But she has nothing to say on the question of her Succession. Why? Because for months before, she'd been in correspondence with King James VI of Scotland. Unbeknownst to many Nobles and Courtiers, she had seriously begun to consider James, a fellow-Monarch, as a potential Successor. But now, after a few days of hoarseness, she loses her voice. It is another terrible blow. As her time on earth gets nearer to the end, many people wonder: Having lost her voice, did she, or did she not, name a Successor, at least in her letters? Time's winged arrow speeds on. As days pass, her once strong, authoritarian feelings about Succession is markedly reduced. It wanes. Her breathing is laboured as she emits wheezy, scratchy sounds.

Sometime before three o'clock in the morning of 24 March 1603, Queen Elizabeth dies. From her bed-chamber, muted sobs becomes loud wails, signalling that her struggle for breath, for life, has ended. The dreadful noises, a dirgelike murmur, from the Queen's Ladies-in-Waiting reaches the ear of Sir Robert Carey. He hastens to Westminster to receive the Official order for travel to Scotland to inform King James of the Queen's death; and thus his new official assignment in England. Events are fast-moving. As Carey heads for Scotland on horse-back, Edward's response as a Nobleman, is to wait and see.

*

And so, the earlier Court gossip of the Queen's illness is now overtaken by the big news: The Queen is dead! Tributes pour forth. The English hierarchy jostle to be seen and heard as Queen Elizabeth is immortalised in poems and books that appear in the London bookshops. England enters a period of deep mourning. These are historic moments. They mark the end of the Elizabethan era of Governance. While writers express themselves, where is Edward de Vere? He is around and acutely conscious of his pact with the dead Queen: That he would keep silent about his identity as "William Shakespeare." Having had money troubles all his life, he is most mindful now about the one thousand pounds he receives each year for his silence. On this matter, he has, so far, not wavered. But now, the Queen's death has created great expectations; a new beginning, and therefore a leap into the unknown. England is, in the interim, on the brink of installing the reign of a new Ruler. Many Courtiers already know who Elizabeth's Successor is. But, the majority of Commoners across the land ("my people," as Elizabeth used to say on her Royal Progresses) are still not sure who the contenders are; and, if they did perhaps they may not have cared too much.

These are interesting times, Edward thinks. In the aftermath of the Queen's death, leaders of all shades of political and religious persuasions, as well as members of the general public, consider the hard reality of accepting a Scottish King as England's new Monarch. So Carey's courageous marathon horse-back journey to and from Scotland, results in King James VI of Scotland being renamed King James I of England, Scotland and Wales. His enthronement has a unifying effect: It brings together three separate countries as a United Kingdom. And so, after months and years of speculation and foreboding, a remarkable thing had happened with the stroke of a pen, instead of shots being fired!

Such a peaceful transition is largely due to Robert Cecil. The political astuteness that saw him move from the role of Under Study to his father to becoming the new Master Spy and political- religious manipulator, is no mean achievement. This, at least, must be granted, Edward thinks. Before Elizabeth had died, she was entirely in Cecil's hands, so to speak. Now, as the in-coming King enters England, for a while, a least, he too is dependent upon Cecil. Such great power in Robert's hands hits Edward hard. He could hardly believe it. But King James is no fool.

He knows he will be unable to satisfy all those bullish Englishmen who aspire to high office, particularly to fill key positions in his Government. Now from his exalted perch as Ruler, King James of England has a new perspective on past deeds. He has not forgotten his predecessor's execution of his mother Mary, Queen of Scots. It was cold-blooded murder! And, at the time, he felt he could do nothing about it. But now, he has the power to do, more or less, as he pleases. Some things need to be put right, one of which is to honour his mother's memory. But, he thinks, that is for later; not right now. Thoughts and acts of retribution as he envisages them are in keeping with the way political power is used at this critical time of transition in England's history.

But, Edward, the history-oriented playwright thinks, if an

eye for an eye, and a tooth for a tooth, is to be part of the guiding principle behind the King's decisions he may be generous, too. One of James's first acts is to order that Henry Wriothesley be released from jail; and that his entitlements be restored. Though this order by the King is not welcomed by everyone at Court, Edward is overjoyed! To honour Southampton's release, he does something quite special and moving: He uses his pen in an extraordinary way: Starting from the day of Southampton's release from the Tower of London until Queen Elizabeth's burial, a period of just under three weeks, he writes intensely: He composes a series of Sonnets averaging at least one each day. His feelings are in turmoil, having been stretched from both ends of the emotional spectrum: In Southampton's case: From execution to a reprieve, and now the death of the Queen. With no one in whom he could confide, the Sonnets provide some release for pent-up emotions. He pours his heart out; more private and personal than writing these sonnets, he could not get.

"So what is the truth about Southampton, Queen Elizabeth and myself?" He considers how they are related? For one thing, and significantly so, the Queen's death marks the end of the House of Tudor. And, he, feels he can claim an historical marker too: His unrivalled pedigree of an ancestry that goes back to William the Conqueror. Nonetheless as the third person in this triangular relationship, who, in truth, is Southampton? To the question, Edward alone knows the answer. But in two Sonnets at least, feelings for his beloved Queen, seeps through: First, in Sonnet One Hundred and Seven, he writes:

"Not mine own fears, nor the prophetic soul
Of the wide world, dreaming of things to come,
Can the lease of my true love control,
Supposed as forfeit to a confined doom.

The mortal moon hath her eclipse endured,
And the sad augurs mock their own presage;
Uncertainties now crown themselves assured,
And peace proclaims olives of endless age.
Now with the drops of this most balmy time
My love looks fresh, and death to me subscribes,
Since 'spite of him I'll live in this poor rhyme,
While he insults o'er dull and speechless tribes;
And thou in this shalt find thy monument,
When tyrants' quests and tombs of brass are spent."

Then, in Sonnet One Hundred and Nine, he unburdens himself of emotional build-up thus:

"O never say that I was false of heart,
Though absence seemed my flame to qualify;
As easy I might from myself depart
As from my soul which in thy breast doth lie:
This is my home of love; if I have ranged,
Like him that travels I return again,
Just to the time, not with the time exchanged,
So that myself bring water for my stain;
Never believe, though in my nature reigned
All frailties that besiege all kinds of blood,
That it could so preposterously be stained,
To leave for nothing all thy sum of good:
For nothing this wide universe I call,
Save thou, my rose; in it thou art my all."

Is "*Save thou, my rose; in it art my all,*" a direct reference to the Queen, his Tudor Rose?

While the Queen's death and Southampton's release play

on his mind, so too are such other profound matters like the grievous loss of any claim he could make to his own writings and death. He writes in Sonnet One Hundred and Eleven:

"O, for my sake with Fortune chide,
The guilty goddess of my harmful deeds,
That did not better for my life provide
Than public means, which public manners breeds;
Thence comes it that my name receives a brand,
And almost thence my nature is subdued
To what it works in, like the dyer's hand;
Pity me, then, and wish I were renewed,
Whilst like a willing patient I will drink
Potions of eisell 'gainst my strong infection;
No bitterness that I will bitter think,
Nor double penance to correct correction.
Pity me then, dear friend, and I assure ye,
Even that your pity is enough to cure me."

Later, he muses in Sonnet One Hundred and Fifteen:

"Those lines that I before have writ to lie,
Even those that said I could not love you dearer;
Yet then my judgement knew no reason why
My most full flame should afterwards burn clearer.
But reckoning time, whose millioned accidents
Creep in 'twixt vows, and change decrees of kings,
Tan sacred beauty, blunt the sharp'st intents,
Divert strong minds to th' course of alt'ring things;
Alas, why, fearing of time's tyranny,
Might I not then say, 'Now I love you best,'
When I was certain o'er uncertainty,

Crowning the present, doubting the rest?
Love is a babe; then I might not say so,
To give full growth to that which still doth grow?"

"Time's tyranny" coupled with remembrance of things past are inescapable. Edward's worsening health is ever-present: It becomes more and more troublesome. Thoughts of the Grim Reaper makes him melancholy, while preparations for Elizabeth's State Funeral are being made. Later, in the Funeral procession, as a last act, he plays his part as a Royal Canopy Bearer. And once more, his private thoughts find literary expression: In Sonnet One Hundred and Twenty-Five, he speaks his mind:

"Were't aught to me I bore the canopy
With my extern the outward honouring,
Or laid great bases for eternity,
Which proves more short than waste or ruining?
Have I not seen dwellers on form and favour
Lose all, and more, by paying too much rent,
From compound sweet forgoing simple savour,
Pitiful thrivers, in their gazing spent?
No, let me be obsequious in thy heart,
And take thou my oblation, poor but free,
Which is not mixed with seconds, knows no art,
But mutual render, only me for thee.
Hence, thou suborned informer, a true soul
When most impeached, stands least in thy control."

***

The Queen's magnificent generosity of a Grant was not, Edward reminds himself, a one-off payment for a job he'd done for her.

It will, as stipulated, to continue, year on year; and being older and infirm, he is glad to receive the money which he now fears would be stopped. Why? Because King James I may take a different view of such a regular, yearly payment. That is a real possibility. But while he enjoys the money, surely he cannot have things his own way, especially now that a new political reality has dawned.

Elizabeth's Grant symbolised complexity; and a large part of it was the price that he'd paid to keep his silence as an author. Silence! Silence! Silence! Each annual payment reminds him of this pact that he'd signed with the Queen; the woman who had been his enabler, as well as the one to discipline him. But now she is dead; on the eve of her funeral, in plain prose, he expresses his thoughts to Sir Robert Cecil:

"I cannot but find a great grief in myself," he writes, "to remember the mistress which we have lost – under whom both you and myself from our greenest years have been in a manner brought up. And although it hath pleased God, after an earthly kingdom, to take her up into a more permanent and heavenly state wherein I do not doubt but she is crowned with glory…yet, the long time which we spent in her service, we cannot look for so much left of our days as to bestow upon another…" He pauses. Then he considers his use of the word "We" in association with Robert Cecil, the man who does not like him very much. For a moment, he thinks of the harsh reality between them.

"In this common shipwreck," he continues, "mine is above all the rest – who least regarded, though often comforted of all her followers, she hath left to try my fortune among the alterations of time and chance: either without sail whereby to take advantage of any prosperous gale; or without anchor to ride till the storm is past."

Edward's mood-inducing remembrance of things past,

persists. His historical sense and understanding gives perspective and clarity as he thinks now of his life's highs and lows, which he likens to gales, stormy seas and shipwrecks. Why such metaphors? Because he is composing a brand new play. And, in the process, past and present events, and future speculations, cohere. He remembers his Italian travels, those "greenest of years" when, spell-bound in Italy, in the place called Genoa, he'd met Prospero Fattinanti.

It was a meeting of two Lords: One of Milan, the other, of Oxford. Edward remembers their talk: The threats of a Civil War in Milan; how much he was ready for action and the offer of a Dukedom of Milan, which Queen Elizabeth had forbidden him from accepting. But that was a long time ago, when he'd journeyed to and fro in Italy. Now, aged fifty three, he is firmly anchored at his beloved desk in the now familiar Great Study in Hackney, where he is repossessed by the ideas of Castiglione. He had stuck with the essential Castiglionian ideal of princely behaviour. But, the winds of change are getting up, and he is acutely aware that like Feudalism, the Courtierly ideal and behaviour are passing away; just as he too, is fading. But instead of melancholia, thoughts of death and dying triggers inventiveness. Inveterate scribbler that he is, he consults his "Italian Notes." He remembers Anthony Munday's translations of stories about a Magician, a Prince and others on an island where conflicts are resolved, and lovers meet. But, well before this moment, following his Italian visit, he'd already written a rough draft of *The Tempest*. Then, one of his characters, Burghley, was still very much alive. Now, he retrieves that draft from the bundle of "Italian plays," and takes another look at it. With Burghley and the Queen dead, he tweaks the play. Having cast Burghley as GONZALO, his own daughter Elizabeth, as MIRANDA, and her husband, the Earl of Derby as FERDINAND, in Act I, Scene 2,

PROSPERO says:

"By Providence divine
Some food we had, and some fresh water, that
A noble Neapolitan GONZALO
Out of his charity – who after being then appointed
Master of this design …
Knowing I loved my books, he furnished me
From mine own library with volumes that
I prize above my dukedom."

In this latest version of *The Tempest,* following the Sonnets, Edward expresses his thought on the quelled rebellion led by Essex, Southampton and others. The character he casts as the leader is CALIBAN, whom he presents as not quite human: A caricature; a grotesque being. PROSPERO'S perceived magic - and magical powers - is CALIBAN'S target. He needs some magic, but he fails in his attempts to get any. CALIBAN (a portrayal of Essex) and his rebels, are imprisoned. Early in the play, PROSPERO says to ARIEL:

"Let them be hunted soundly. At this hour
Lies at my mercy all mine enemies,
Shortly shall all my labours end, and thou
Shalt have the air at freedom. For a little,
Follow, and do me service."

So, in *The Tempest,* Edward casts himself as a Magician and Creator; a true artist. But though art is not life; and vice-versa, he knows, they are intertwined; profoundly inseparable. But Essex's execution is not quite the end that Edward creates for CALIBAN. Time: Remembrance of things past. Edward is the word-wizard; the sorcerer of *The Tempest* which brings dead men: Kings and Noblemen to life as he does in his historical dramas. But, if the past is about the present, he could not be more self-aware now.

Like PROSPERO, he knows the time for his extraordinary powers of creating original art, is getting shorter. This realisation of life and art, hits him hard as he re-reads the lines he'd written:

PROSPERO: "Go release them Ariel.
My charms I'll break, their sense I'll restore,
And they shall be themselves...
With (Jove's) own bolt; the strong-based promontory
Have I made shake, and by the spurs plucked up
The pine of cedar; graves at my command
Have waked their sleepers, oped and let 'em forth
By my so potent art. But this rough magic
I here abjure,...And when I have required
Some heavenly music...
To work mine end upon their senses that
This airy charm is for, I'll break my staff,
Bury it certain fathoms in the earth,
And deeper than did ever plummet sound
I'll drown my book."

"*I'll drown my book.*" Is this his final act of self-obliteration as a writer? He agonises as he thinks of being silent in the straight-jacketed anonymity he had been in. He is the tongue-tied poet! But he feels some consolation trusting in the value; the wisdom and power of his words. And through PROSPERO'S last words, he is not looking just at life's end. He dares to look beyond: To the after-life of silence; to the achingly sad realisation of forever being an anonymous author.

He writes:

"Now my charms are all o'erthrown,  
And what strength I have's mine own,  
Which is most faint.  
Now, 'tis true  
I must be here confused by you.  
In this bare Island by your spell."

He goes on to say:

"But release me from my bands  
With the help of your good hands  
Gentle breath of yours my sails  
Must fill, or else my project fails,  
Which was to please. Now I want  
Spirits to enforce, art to enchant,  
And my ending is despair.  
Unless I be relieved by prayer,  
Which pierces so, that it assaults  
Mercy itself, and frees all faults.  
As you from crimes would pardoned be,  
Let your indulgence set me free."

***

Far from being indulgent, at this time, he questions: "What about the matter of my Inheritance?" Ever the risk-taker, a relentless trier, Edward perseveres. But time, he thinks, is running out. Once more, he writes to Cecil, pressing for the return of the properties of Waltham Forest and Havering House. He draws attention to the long-standing family ownership of these estates stretching back to the iconic invader, William the Conqueror. He says to Cecil, he'd earlier written to the Queen for help, but restoring that property is easier said than done. The Queen is good at making promises, but she is not so ready, "to perform her word as I was too ready to believe it."

After he'd penned the letter to Cecil, he rests his quill. He breathes deeply and exhales slowly. Feeling slightly irritated, he tries to calm himself as he thinks of the paper-work he'd done over the years: largely formal pleas for public appointments and financial assistance. Too many, he thinks; and, so far, he has little or nothing to show for it. He feels there is a limit; a boundary which he would not cross.

"I am not a beggar," he says to Cecil. "Everything that I've asked of officials had been done with dignity and respect. My honour, and that of my family, is paramount."

Before he sends the letter to Cecil, once more, he considers his failures. He feels more positive that there is a change at the top: A new King! He is my best hope, Edward thinks. After sending the letter, he tries to relax amidst nagging doubts as to how Cecil would receive it. Cecil duly reads the letter. Then he reads it once again. He thinks long and hard about Edward's request.

Weeks later, King James orders that the estates requested by Edward be returned to him. Justice is done: Thanks to the King whom he was so reluctant to endorse. This good news lifts his mood: It marks the end of decades of uncertainty, hoping and waiting for his Inheritance. A few days later, he is back in favour, attending to important matters at Court: The King's Coronation Dinner, and the Coronation Service.

Soon after the Coronation, Edward follows his hunch about King James. Although he does not rush to sign the Nobles Declaration for James as Successor of Elizabeth, so far, the indications have been good. Eight days after the Coronation

Dinner, his deepest anxieties, it seems, are allayed as King James extends his annual Grant of one thousand pounds! Thus the King behaves in kingly fashion: He is benevolent. But what lay behind this generosity? Edward speculates. Only time will tell, he thinks.

After the continuation of Edward's Grant is confirmed, the King goes on his Inaugural Royal Progress. He covers a wide area of the south and west of England. William Pembroke, the Earl of Pembroke is in the King's entourage; and when the Progress stops at Salisbury, he receives a letter. It is from his mother the Dowager Countess of Pembroke, who is a friend of Edward's. She is known as a lover of literature; and in the letter to her son, she says that *As You like It* is being rehearsed for performance at Wilton House. "While rehearsals continue, Shakespeare is present," she wrote.

"My Lord. Edward," Pembroke says,"My mother tells me that the play *As You Like It* is being performed by the King's Men Company."

Edward is intrigued to hear this. He knows that as a Theatre manager, Will Shakspere, is now working for the King's Men Company (previously known as the Lord Chamberlain's Men) which is performing in the Provinces because the London Theatres are shut by plague. The mention of the man "Shakespeare" being at Wilton House is, for Edward, quite unpleasant, like salt being poured into an open wound. At once, his worry is renewed about the confusion arising from the closeness of his Pen-name "Shakespeare" with Shakspere. So, for Edward, a matter that has been for some time of much concern, having found its way in the Dowager's letter, becomes even more serious. Though King James's enjoyment of *As You Like It* is not dependent upon his knowledge of who the true author is, relations between the two men, are good. But, for all James's generous gestures and the developing good relations,

Edward's financial position is, in reality, still, it seems, not as good as he'd like it to be.

The restoration of his ownership of properties does not immediately translate into hard cash, which had been the ongoing problem between him and Burghley upon whom he was dependent for ready money. So, in this sense, he feels relatively poor; and his worry is not helped by his worsening physical disability: His lameness is more debilitating; his limp is more pronounced. Physically, he is smaller. In these reduced circumstances, Susan, his youngest unmarried daughter, has just turned sixteen; a sweet age which draws her to the Match-makers in the marriage market. For her part, Susan is ready to see suitable suitors. But, the question is: How do they see her?

Already, she'd written to her Uncle Robert Cecil to borrow money for a visit to see Queen Anne. Money, money, money! The word has gotten round to eligible bachelors that Edward is not a rich man, who could offer a goodly dowry to a potential husband. His financial position means Susan's chances of matrimony is less good. Some months earlier, in celebration of Elizabeth de Vere's wedding, the poet John Davies had written a Masque for women of high-standing, one of whom was Susan de Vere. Davies, a former supporter of Essex, knows of Edward's dire financial predicament and the words that Susan was given to read during her appearance in the Masque were: "Nothing's your lot. That's more than can be told."

The word 'Nothing,' in the context of marriage, is provocative. On hearing the words given to Susan, Edward is incensed. He blushes with shame. He is glad that Elizabeth and Bridget are both married, but Davies's words then, as now, is almost more than he could bear. When he returns to reviewing and rewriting drafts of his play *King Lear,* he has Susan in mind while composing the character CORDELIA. He writes:

"LEAR: Although our last and least...what can you say to draw a third more opulent than your sisters? Speak.
CORDELIA: Nothing. Nothing, my lord.
LEAR: Nothing?
CORDELIA: Nothing.
LEAR: Nothing will come of nothing. Speak again.
CORDELIA: Unhappy that I am, I cannot heave
My heart into my mouth. I love your Majesty
According to my bond, no more, nor less.
LEAR: How, how Cordelia? Mend your speech a little
Less you mar your fortunes.
CORDELIA: Good my lord, You begot me, bred me, loved me...I shall never marry like my sisters.
LEAR: But goes thy heart with this?
CORDELIA: Ay, my good lord.
LEAR: So young and so untender?
CORDELIA: So young, my lord and true.
LEAR: Let it be so. Thy truth then be thy dower."

Truth!

As Edward reflects on this dialogue between LEAR and CORDELIA, he thinks of the word *truth* in relation to his illustrious de Vere family's motto: "Nothing Truer than Truth."

After all the journeys he'd made both physically and mentally, he comes to terms now with his mature self. In the play, considering the matter of usurpation, he gives the character EDGAR these words to speak:

"Men must endure
Their going hence, even as their coming hither
Ripeness is all."

And so now Edward's identity: The experience that has brought him thus far, haunts him: The "pain to pen a book;" anonymity, loss of name and his enduring sense of Nobility's dignity, are thoughts that fill his mind.

***

A new year begins. It is 1604. It is bitterly cold. Among high officials there is talk about a grand project which, it is hoped, will have immense value: What is it? he wonders. The plan is to compose from existing Scriptural texts, a book, namely, the King James version of the Holy Bible. As work on this grand book idea gets off the ground, after further revision and a few corrections, Edward eventually completes *The Tempest* and *King Lear,* in which he embeds essential messages. And, significantly, he returns to a play he'd already written: His cherished *Hamlet.* "Is this the leading contender to being my favourite play?" he asks himself. "Maybe. Maybe not." He admits to having a few "favourites," and *Hamlet,* is at the top. It is the play within a play; and a whole lot more! It is the play now in hand. Each day, his attention is fixed on the story. He attends to the script as if, of all his possessions, it is the dearest thing in the world! It is very special: The only play that he carries around with him: At least twice he'd taken it away from his Great Study for perusal in the Living Room. It is the play that haunts him as he reads and indulges in his reviewing habit, tweaking it here and there. He listens to the music: the timing of the dialogue; the vocal expressiveness and rhythm of the soliloquies. He is as interested, as ever, in the characters: How well they understand the story; and how well they deliver their lines. He thinks of the particular abilities of a few actors; some better than others. As he reads his work critically, he listens to the lilting sounds of the verbal music, ever on the look-out for a discordant note in the overall orchestration of the characters' voices. He is specially interested now in the meanings of this play in which philosophical questions arises from the statement: "What a piece of work is man!....What is this quintessence of dust?"

***

In the weeks since the Coronation of King James I, after he'd completed *The Tempest* and *King Lear*, Edward feels a second wind of playwriting energy and ambition. For the most part, this has to do with taking another look, which he does not mind doing, at works that he'd already done. This means revising! His voice, he feels, is more assured now as he re-engages with *Hamlet*. Overall, he thinks that he'd not, for any prolonged period, served his Queen and Country as a military stalwart in the theatres of war as his glorious de Vere ancestors had done for so long. But he is proud that his choice of weapon in dealing with the inherent highs and lows of life's struggles, is his pen! Light as a feather, but far mightier than the sword, he thinks. Since he'd declared his ambition: "A writer to be," now he feels utterly justified in the choice he'd made. He has no doubt about the profound value of the Comedies and Tragedies he has written.

He is pleased with the revisions he'd done to all his plays. Beside him is a copy of the story of the Danish Prince which he is once again, revising. After two hours of close reading, with thoughts of being an anonymous author and encroaching death, he considers his well-chosen words: "What a piece of work is man!" Then, he flicks the pages to the final Scene of *Hamlet*. In the last moments before HAMLET dies, he sees FORTINBRAS as the new King James, and himself as HAMLET. His doubts about James's Succession are no longer present: Both King and Nobleman are now respectful of each other. He uses his high rank and privilege of addressing the King person to person. In his first letter to James, he thanks him, especially for granting his full Inheritance with the return of the family's Havering and Waltham estates.

After the letter is sent, his health lapses. It is a dramatic turn to his well being. He tries desperately, but cannot make it to the warmth and familiarity of his beloved Great Study. He is bitterly disappointed. But, he thinks, it is just another one of those temporary set-backs that he'd been experiencing of late. "It will go away in a day; in two days, at most," he says to himself.

The next day he breathes with difficulty. He stops work, rises from his chair and goes to the window. He looks out at the wintry scene. He hopes that soon he'd be able to go outside and, as best he could, walk again and enjoy the aromas of the colourful flowers. The dew-wet roses were in bloom the last time he was out. Red roses, in particular, always lift his spirit that so far today has been low.

He cannot be supine: He needs to pick himself up for as a Noble Member of Parliament, he has official duties to perform. Retirement is not an immediate step for him, he thinks. With the new Monarch making his presence felt, he is called forth. From Hackney, he travels to Westminster to join others who escort the King through London. So doing, he remembers the first time he'd seen London: It was on the day of his arrival at the head of an impressive Procession, as a twelve year old, from Castle Hedingham. No one else in England or Scotland could claim a pedigree such as his. But memory and feelings are not reflected in his outward bearing. For now, he unflinchingly comes to terms with his mature self: "Ripeness is all," he thinks, as he tries to keep up; and, as the distinguished Earl of Oxford, do his bounden duty. As he marches, holding aloft a Canopy over the King; something he'd done often for Queen

Elizabeth, he thinks: The Queen is dead. Long Live the King!

Two days later, he sits in his Hackney Study, mulling over the grand Processional occasion with King James; a brand new experience, which leaves him still feeling exhausted. His dutiful exertions, the pain and stiffness in his leg is now more severe, and lasts longer. He thinks of the inner man; as well as the public persona: How at odds they are. Meanwhile, King James calls together his first Session in Parliament. Edward and fellow Lords are summoned to Whitehall. Alas, Edward fails to attend. Why? Because of a combination of reasons: One that figures prominently, is money. It beggars belief, but even now he is indebted. It is another long overdue payment, this time to a "Joiner;" a man who had worked on two of his properties: Fisher's Folly and a house in East London. This late claim stirs a deep sense of shame in Edward. He holds his head between his hands: Shame! Shame! Shame! Under Queen Elizabeth, he'd survived unprecedented imprisonment and exile. Now, in spite of good relations, he asks himself: "How would I fare under King James? How forgiving would he be? Time will tell. But, how much time do I really have?"

***

While Robert Cecil sits in his office attending to the matters of Government, he already knows about Edward's bad health: That his inability to move around had prevented him from attending to his official State duties at Westminster. But now, new rumours abound:

"I hear that the Earl of Oxford is gravely ill," Falconbridge, one of Cecil's senior administrators says. "The rumour has it that the Earl has contracted the deadly Plague."

Cecil is taken aback. "Is this true?" he asks himself. He is inclined to believe what Falconbridge says and feels he must be ready for the worst that can happen.

Plague in London is not a new phenomenon: It comes and goes with devastating effect. To avoid infection, Noblemen and their families, especially in the warmer months, tended to leave London. Now, in May, as summer looms, and Edward's health declines, Cecil thinks very seriously what action he should take. He considers his options: His main concern is not just to remove Edward from his King's Place home, but also to allocate a secret place for him outside England. He knows only too well of Edward's back-story of exile from the Court for misdemeanours, and realises that this is now a matter of life and death: "I will not be sending Edward to one more period of exile," he says to himself. "I will be banishing him to the place of his death. Such a Scenario, would be not the final act in one of his tragic plays, but the hard reality of the present situation." Thus, Cecil thinks of moving the allegedly plague-ridden Edward away from Hackney to the Isle of Man! The more he thinks of this move, the more it appeals to him. It is not too distant from London; just outside the bounds of mainland England. At this moment, Cecil sees Edward as a man at his mercy: A diminished, almost leprous figure. To remove the exalted Earl of Oxford from his beloved England would be the ultimate revenge. "Such a consideration is all well and good," Cecil says and checks himself, "but it needs more thought; more planning." For now, as the rumours of Edward's worsening health spreads, Cecil waits. He knows time is of the essence.

***

Soon after Edward settles his latest debt, the persistent fever and sweating that had overtaken him since the winter, lays him low. It is the start of the week: Monday morning. He feels ill. He finds it painful to walk. "How would I get to my Study," he wonders.

"You must rest more, My Lord," Countess Elizabeth says.

Four days later, after Edward had had a sleepless night, the Countess says: "I've been observing you, My Lord. Over the last few days your health has not improved."

"You are right," Edward says with a painful grimace.

He struggles valiantly as he tries to move around. His body feels leaden. At his Countess's insistence, for the first time since he'd come to the Big House, he decides to stay in bed and rest. "But, only for a day or so," he stressed. For the rest of the following week, he'd been in bed. Here, he reads and writes; and is attended to by his Countess who brings to him all that he needs. Fever and chills attack his body, time and again. As days pass, medicines and potions are to hand on the bedside table.

He coughs: "My Lord, I'll get you some water," the Countess says. She leaves the room. When she returns, her worry grows as Edward slips in and out of consciousness. She is alarmed that in less than a week, his medium-sized body has shrunk. His face is gaunt. His breathing is laboured. His body shakes; then a bout of fever overtakes him. Another day passes with no improvement: He deteriorates fast: His body is frail, skeletal-looking. By now, the Plague has been raging in some parts of London. He feels suicidal; but is conscious enough to feel undignified. Beside his bed is the play-script of *Hamlet* which, in various places, he'd marked and had underlined certain passages.

Over many years, from drafts to the final version of the play, he was immersed in thoughts of madness, suicide, sleep, dream and death. He is familiar with the words: "I am dead, HORATIO." In this play which mirrors so much of himself and death uppermost in his mind, is the loss of his claim to the authorship of *Hamlet* and other writings. In the last six lines of the final passage of the play, he'd written "I am dead" twice! Death stalks him as he remembers HAMLET'S plea to HORATIO to restore his "cause." Now, in his pitiful, reduced state, he is incapable of reciting any of *Hamlet's* soliloquies, but he mumbles: This catches the Countess's attention: She moves closer to him. She listens, but, except for a few words, she could hardly make out what he'd been saying. He mumbles again; and she recognises a few words: "What a piece of work is man!" A prolonged, hoarse cough breaks up what he'd been saying. Then, he adds: "What is this quintessence of dust? Dust. Dust..." The words trail-off; they fade to a whisper. After a while, he turns his head towards the bedside table. On it is a copy of the script of *Hamlet.* For a while, he stares at the script with a puzzled expression. Suddenly, in a strong voice, and with utter clarity, which takes the Countess by surprise, he recalls familiar words: Those that he'd written for HAMLET to speak:

"I am dead, HORATIO…
Thou livest. Report me and my cause aright…
Things standing thus unknown, shall I leave behind me!..."

A long pause follows. Then, he says:

"in this harsh world,
draw thy breath in pain
To tell my story."

The last three words: "tell my story!" ring out like the resonant bell of the Church of St Augustine. In his delirium, this direct appeal seems to echo and re-echo in the room. The

Countess waits in expectation. But no more sound or words pass Edward's lips. There is only silence. Edward de Vere dies. But the name: William Shakespeare lives. The date is 24 June 1604. The brain and hand that had moved the pen to write immortal words of unsurpassed beauty about the human condition; indeed the human predicament: "To be or not to be?" was no more.

Countess Elizabeth sits on the bed. She weeps. Her life of togetherness and happiness with Edward is gone forever. The Man-Servant, Quested, bent with age, hears her cries as he too, feels the loss. Edward de Vere was fifty-four years old.

Twelve days later, from the Big House, which he'd predicted would be his last home, his body is taken a short distance south of King's Place to the Church of St Augustine at Hackney, where he was buried in the Church.

Edward's former Secretaries, Lyly and Munday, had come to Hackney to pay their respects to their literary Master. Before they part company, Lyly says:

"When I last saw Lord Edward just a few months ago, I'd promised to come back to Hackney to see him. Alas, I had no idea how ill he really was. He hid his pain well. I certainly didn't think he would die so soon."

"Though he was a man of unrivalled status and privilege," Munday says, "he was never lazy or lacking in enterprise, as we both know!"

"His broad understanding as a Scholar, his refreshing, inventive use of words all fed into his extraordinary ability, in particular, his brilliance as a playwright which grew and grew," says Lyly, who knew him perhaps better than anyone else. "We had our differences, but they were minor compared to the great privilege and honour of having been in his Service. Almost at once, I was stunned by what an industrious, prodigious writer Lord Edward was. While writing my Euphues novels, he was most encouraging and helpful. 'Be playful. Be inventive with the words you use. Push the boundaries of language,' he used to say. I have learned so much from him. More than from any other writer."

"On the matter of learning from him," Munday says, "I could not agree more. I was, at first, taken aback by the scope and depth of his knowledge. But, as time passed, he continued to surprise me. And yes you are right, his all round ability and grasp of things was unrivalled. His self-awareness was outstanding. 'All men have faults,' he'd written."

"One abiding quality about Lord Edward which I think stands out like a beacon," Lyly says, "is hope. His attitude always was: The show must go on! No matter how trying the circumstances, he always hoped for the best outcome."

"I absolutely agree," Munday says.

"Now, like the great writers of Antiquity, of whom he knew so much," Lyly says, "he belongs to the Ages. May he rest in Eternal and Glorious peace."

***

Later, in his Eulogy, a relative, Percival Golding, says of Edward: "He had spoken what all men's voices confirm: That he was a man who, in mind and body, was absolutely accomplished with honourable endowments." Golding dare not go any further towards publicly acknowledging that Edward de Vere was William Shakespeare.

A writer to be! That Edward de Vere had become: And further, a writer like no other. "You write best about what you know." He knew the *truth* about what he was writing. In *Hamlet,* he implored HORATIO "To tell his story." It has since been shrouded in mystery; an ever-deafening silence. But now at last, that story has come to life in vivid detail.

It is a story of truth and being human.

It is a story of hope.

It is a story to pass on...

***

# EPILOGUE

## Hackney: St John-at-Hackney Church grounds, June 2020.

The Story-Teller sits on a bench along the path between the lawn and flower beds. A few yards behind him is the iron rail fence that borders the grounds. He is facing South; and just a few yards directly opposite is the imposing front Entrance of the Church of St John-at-Hackney. When he'd lived in Hackney, he had neither been in the Church grounds nor had he looked at the Church so knowingly, as he does now, over thirty years later.

The Story-Teller observes with pleasure the colourful blooms across the pathway: mostly daffodils and tulips. But rising above them is a lone, large red rose. Just ahead of him is the looming stone tower, a remnant of the Medieval St Augustine Church. Hackney in Tudor times comes to mind. From all the knowledge that he'd garnered, he thinks of Queen Elizabeth as Edward's Tudor Rose, the "Virgin Queen;" and he reflects upon a few tantalisingly awkward questions that he'd posed while researching and writing his novel. One concerns Edward's special relationship with the Queen: Why did she give him that one thousand pounds a year Grant for the rest of his life? Another puzzling, deeply troubling question for the Story-Teller relates to his reading of the Sonnets: Why, he wondered, had Edward written so cryptically, and in such a complex way, about relations between himself, the Queen and Henry Wriothesley, the Earl of Southampton? The themes of love and loss binds them, it seems, in a few Sonnets and other writings. He finds this intriguing. "Was there a blood relationship between the three of them?" he dares to ask himself.

And now he thinks about another matter to do with the Sonnets. It is about the timing of three things: The potential scandal and shame that would have affected three noble families - The Burghleys, the Oxfords and the Southamptons, as a result of the close relationship between Edward and Southampton; the appearance for the first time in print of the name WILLIAM SHAKESPEARE; and the matter of Will Shakspere having come into enough money to buy a large property in Stratford-upon-Avon. "Given the similarity of the names" the Story-Teller says to himself, "was Shakspere paid to accept an agreement whereby he would keep his silence about not being the true author of the works of William Shakespeare, the brand name?" The Story-Teller answers himself positively: "Yes!"

He casts his mind back to those very different days when sex, status, religion and power kept Royal and Noble families together. At once he comes to grips with those unstable, unsentimental times; an understanding which deepens respect for his Hero Edward, who, in spite of his covert, difficult life and struggles had managed to maintain a passionate desire and determination to write. Significantly it was a work ethic that encompassed a human and humane perspective. Mulling over these thoughts, the Story-Teller remembers another timely piece of information about the Churchyard graves. He'd read that Edward's wife, Countess Elizabeth Trentham - de Vere had requested in her Will that her body should be buried here in Hackney.

"Please ensure," she'd instructed the Executor of her Will, "that I am placed as near unto the body of my said late dear and Noble Lord and husband as may be." She then makes another request: "And, be sure that there be in the said Hackney Church erected for us a Tomb fitting our degree."

Now as the Story-Teller looks at the gravestones, he wonders where exactly was the last resting place of Edward de Vere - William Shakespeare. Wherever that may be, the knowledge that Edward de Vere had lived in Hackney and worshipped in the original St Augustine Church that had stood here, astonishes him. He reflects, once more, upon his regular walks along Kenninghall Road, Brooke Road and Hackney Downs Park (the area known in the Sixteenth century as King's Place) where Edward had spent his last days. How odd; how ironic the Story-Teller thinks, that he is now able to link these places with his writing about William Shakespeare. Was it mere coincidence? No. As a Story-Teller, a perspective on times past is fundamental, he thinks.

Beside him is his *finished manuscript.* Now he has a full title for it: *OR NOT TO BE: The True Story of William Shakespeare.* In all, it has been more than a decade in the making. The "pain to pen a book," he recalls Edward's words. He remembers too, Professor Nidmar Nora's statement: "You write best about what you know." He gently touches the manuscript as if he could hardly believe he'd at last completed the herculean task that he'd set for himself. He'd been through countless difficulties; and had some very dark days. He understands the "pain." He puts the manuscript on his lap. It is bulky; its contents substantial: a richly textured story. More than that, it is, in many ways, a pioneering novel about the true identity of William Shakespeare. It is *not* just another book. Above all, the Story-Teller thinks the book has *personality!* Early in his research, he had read what one famous English Shakespearean actor had said: "We know so little about the Bard!" This public declaration had added to his excitement and commitment to complete the novel. On top of that "declaration," he had to contend with the fact that he was going against the grain. The Establishment loomed large! But given that so many things were yet unknown, he persevered: The more he delved into the story about the man, the personality of Edward de Vere - William Shakespeare, the more an essential *truth* emerged to reveal a centuries-old wrongly-placed belief. At every turn of his learning experience, he realised the truth, as Edward de Vere had done: confirmation that "you write best about what you know." Edward knew the people about whom he wrote. His detailed, intimate knowledge of Kings, Queens, Noblemen, Generals and all levels of the people in society, had qualified him to write so assuredly his brilliant, sublime Comedies and Tragedies. As he himself had written in a letter to Burghley: "For truth is truth, though never so old, and time cannot make that false which once was true." Uncovering the *truth*, the Story-Teller confirms his own belief that what he's written is testament to the fact that through the art of the novel; in effect, through story-telling, the *truth* is the stronger for having recognised the *lie.*

"A Writer to be!" So began the story Dear Reader, that the Story-Teller have so far told; a story in which the writer Edward de Vere becomes William Shakespeare.

As a warm gust of wind lifts the top end of the manuscript's Title Page, the Story-Teller places a hand on it. He looks up: The sun shines brightly. It is a clear, beautiful day. His gaze falls upon the Church where Edward de Vere had worshipped. It is an impressive, monumental facade; even inviting, he thinks. He is not religious, but at this moment thoughts of life, death and resurrection preoccupy him. He remembers, and smiles, as he thinks of Edward's abiding belief that the clues he'd inserted in his plays would one day come to light: "*Every word doth almost tell my name,*" he'd written. His resilience was remarkable:

He had subjected himself to punishing writing schedules to achieve his goals, but though his forebears enjoyed the Glory of the Sword he was never recognised for the Mighty Glory of his pen! For him, it was *not to be*! But, his self-belief since boyhood: From his "maverick Boy Poet" phase into manhood and maturity, cannot be doubted. With few people around him, and often no one in whom in he could confide, he tended to talk to himself. Was this a sign of madness? Alone in his Study, he talked (sometimes silently) as he wrote dialogues that came from deep within: Soliloquies that are poetic, profound and dramatically moving. Such compositions arises mostly when life pressed him hardest; when he was sharply reminded of "The pain to pen a book!" Like other writers, he struggled. He was not a mirage-like mythical figure. He was flesh and blood; a fundamentally flawed man who worked hard at honing his talent while he aspired to be good and thus avoid Shame and the loss of Good Name.

As he'd lived, loved and worried, in his art he dramatically, lyrically and beautifully captured the lowest and noblest qualities. At best, his characters evoke the indomitable human spirit; the essence of being human and humane. In a word, he was an optimist. "Hope springs eternal in the human breast," he'd written. Centuries have passed since he died, and life in England has been transformed. But his plays and poems have continued to touch the people of Britain and lovers of drama, poetry an literature around the world. Now, as the Story-Teller looks at the Church and the grave stones, he is mindful of John Lyly's words after Edward's Funeral Service: "*He belongs to the Ages.*"

Moments later, the Story-Teller rises from the bench. He looks up at the high, cloudless sky; then at the lime trees to his right. He carefully lifts up the manuscript, holds it close to his chest, considers once more the title *OR NOT TO BE: The*

*True Story of William Shakespeare* and feels its weight. Then, for a while, he looks around him one last time. Memories of Hackney flood in after his long absence. And as he leaves the Churchyard, he is struck by the one great idea that had governed and guided Edward de Vere – William Shakespeare's life*: The timelessness of Truth.* He knows the great value of truth, the *raison d'etre* of art: There is mythical truth and there is factual truth. But what about a combination or collage of the two to bring into being Artful Reason, from which a *new reality* is created: Art! To suspend belief unreasonably, he thinks, defeats the purpose of Art which is, in essence, to reveal truth.

When the Story-Teller arrives home, on the last page of the manuscript of his novel, as Edward de Vere had done in various places of his Geneva Bible, he underlines the following words:

*OR NOT TO BE* is a timely novel.

It is a story of truth and humanity.

It is a story of hope.

It is a story to pass on…

***

# ACKNOWLEDGEMENTS

Over many decades of research before and since the historic audio recording of my Interview with Sam Wanamaker at Shakespeare's Globe Theatre about *Othello*, Paul Robeson and Shakespearean acting, the British Library's unrivalled collections have served me well. Crucially, I was able to read and study a range of material, including letters, manuscripts and books: histories, autobiographies, biographies and academic texts, ranging over many disciplines. Taken together, they have been invaluable. Without access to such a wealth of documents, the requisite knowledge demanded to write this unique literary-historical novel would not have been possible. Prior to and throughout the many years of research for this book, my regular seat number 60 in the Rare Books Reading Room has been my regular place of thought and relentless work.

I am thankful to the members of staff at the British Library. My thanks also to Paul Rowe, Fabrizio Fenu, Elizabeth Mor and Renee Euchner.

'A Masterpiece' – *Amazon Books*

"…through the written word and simultaneously the attempt to get a hold on the language, the Griot encounters the sublime…it is rare to meet with a literary work where the plot and the style are a message in themselves…where the search creates a melody that is read poetically between and beyond the words…"

Dr Ariella Atzmon
*The Hebrew University of Jerualem*

'The characters are so well co-ordinated that it is like an orchestra using all its players to perform a piece of great music'. –
*The Sunday Guardian*

'…Today, I want to notice *Turning Pages* by Ron Ramdin, the Trinidadian/British writer. Its sub-title is *The Extraordinary Autobiography of Ron Ramdin,* and extraordinary it is, because of the author's remarkable achievements…'
(Professor Bridget Brereton, Emeritus Professor of History, University of West Indies).

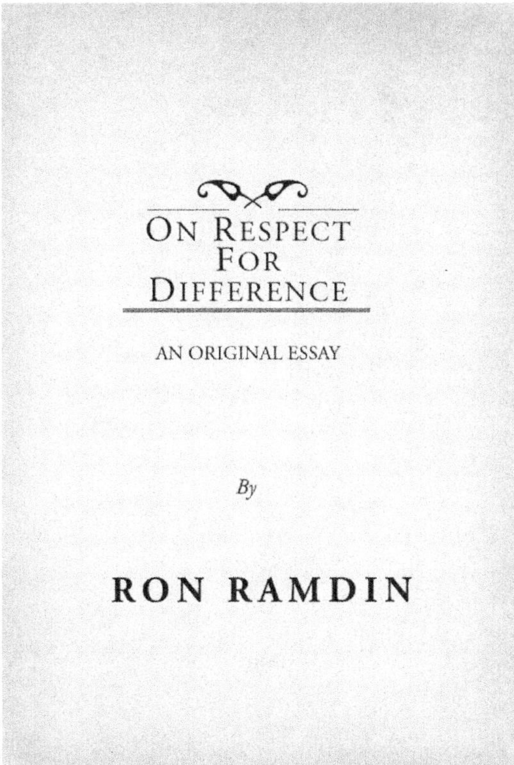


In this original Essay on human relations in the modern world, focusing on the evolutionary nature of his ideas and contradictions at the heart of the human condition, Ron Ramdin reveals a profound truth.

A Memorable Book Launch:
On the Bronze Book Sculpture in the British Library, the institution which has been Ron Ramdin's Spiritual-Intellectual home.

PHOTOGRAPH by Stefano Cagnoni.

Printed in Great Britain
by Amazon

82155306R00434